17. ALL cynicism masks a failure to cope
49. first impression of Greece

FICTION BY JOHN FOWLES

101 Geckos live seldom used rooms
101 It was much too obsessive to be erotic

The Collector
"There is not a page in this first novel which does not
prove that its author is a master storyteller."
—*New York Times Book Review*

The Magus
"Thoroughly enjoyable. . . . What makes the book so
unabandonable is its ability to surprise, and never
twice in the same way." —*National Review*

The French Lieutenant's Woman
"A miracle of sorts . . . an absorbingly dramatic love story
and a virtuoso stylistic performance." —*New Republic*

The Ebony Tower
"Magical, shocking, mysterious wise . . . Fowles's stories
never fail to move the reader on the deepest levels."
—*Los Angeles Times*

Daniel Martin
"A masterpiece of symbolically charged realism. . . .
Fowles is the only writer in English who has the power,
range, knowledge, and wisdom of a Tolstoy or James."
—*Saturday Review*

Mantissa
"Splendid. . . . Fowles can spin a web which is so light,
and yet so strong." —*Washington Post Book World*

A Maggot
"Wonderful . . . a daring, mesmerizing mystery story that
is an enormous pleasure to read." —*Chicago Tribune*

Books by John Fowles

THE COLLECTOR

THE ARISTOS

THE MAGUS

THE FRENCH LIEUTENANT'S WOMAN

POEMS

THE EBONY TOWER

SHIPWRECK

DANIEL MARTIN

ISLANDS

THE TREE

THE ENIGMA OF STONEHENGE

MANTISSA

A SHORT HISTORY OF LYME REGIS

A MAGGOT

LYME REGIS CAMERA

WORMHOLES

John Fowles

The **MAGUS**
a revised version

With a Foreword by the Author

LITTLE, BROWN AND COMPANY

New York   Boston

Back Bay Books / Little, Brown and Company
Time Warner Book Group
1271 Avenue of the Americas, New York, NY 10020
Visit our Web site at www.twbookmark.com

Original version of *The Magus* published in hardcover by Little, Brown
and Company, 1966
Revised version of *The Magus* published in hardcover by Little, Brown
and Company, 1978
First Back Bay paperback edition, January 2001

Grateful acknowledgment is made to the following for permission to quote copyrighted
material:

To Faber and Faber Ltd. and Harcourt, Brace & World, Inc., for lines from "Little Gidding" from FOUR QUARTETS by T. S. Eliot.

To New Directions for lines from "The Needle" from PERSONAE by Ezra Pound.
Copyright 1926 by Ezra Pound. Reprinted by permission of New Directions Pub-
lishing Corporation. And for lines from "Canto XLVII" from CANTOS by Ezra
Pound. Copyright 1937 by Ezra Pound. Reprinted by permission of New Directions
Publishing Corporation.

LIBRARY OF CONGRESS CATALOGING-IN-PUBLICATION DATA
Fowles, John.
    The magus.
    I. Title.
    PZ4.F788Mag   1978 [PR6056.085]   823'.9'14   77-17343
    ISBN 0-316-29092-0 (hc) / 0-316-29619-8 (pb)

                    10 9 8 7 6 5

                        Q-FF

Foreword

Though this is not, in any major thematic or narrative sense, a fresh version of *The Magus*, it is rather more than a stylistic revision. A number of scenes have been largely rewritten, and one or two new ones invented. I have taken this somewhat unusual course not least because – if letters are any test – the book has aroused more interest than anything else I have written. I have long learnt to accept that the fiction that professionally always pleased me least (a dissatisfaction strongly endorsed by many of its original reviewers) persists in attracting a majority of my readers most.

The story appeared in 1965, after two other books, but in every way except that of mere publishing date, it is a first novel. I began writing it in the early 1950s, and both narrative and mood went through countless transformations. In its original form there was a clear supernatural element – an attempt at something along the lines of Henry James's masterpiece, *The Turn of the Screw*. But I had no coherent idea at all of where I was going, in life as in the book. A more objective side of me did not then believe I should ever become a publishable writer; a subjective one could not abandon the myth it was trying, clumsily and laboriously, to bring into the world; and my strongest memory is of constantly having to abandon drafts because of an inability to describe what I wanted. Both technique and that bizarre face of the imagination that seems to be more like a failure to remember the already existent than what it really is – a failure to evoke the non-existent – kept me miserably aground. Yet when the success of *The Collector* in 1963 gave me some literary confidence, it was this endlessly tortured and recast cripple that demanded precedence over various other novels I had attempted in the 1950s ... and at least two of which were, I suspect, more presentable and might have done my name, at least in my own country, more good.

In 1964 I went to work and collated and rewrote all the previous drafts. But *The Magus* remained essentially where a tyro taught himself to write novels – beneath its narrative, a notebook of an exploration, often erring and misconceived, into an unknown land.

Even in its final published form it was a far more haphazard and naïvely instinctive work than the more intellectual reader can easily imagine; the hardest blows I had to bear from critics were those which condemned the book as a coldly calculated exercise in fantasy, a cerebral game. But then one of the (incurable) faults of the book was the attempt to conceal the real state of endless flux in which it was written.

Besides the obvious influence of Jung, whose theories deeply interested me at the time, three other novels were of importance in the writing. The model I was most conscious of was Alain-Fournier's *Le Grand Meaulnes*, indeed so conscious that in the course of revision I suppressed a number of too overt references. The parallels may not be very striking to the literal-minded analyst, but *The Magus* would have been a profoundly different book if it were not for its French forebear. The capacity of *Le Grand Meaulnes* (for some of us, at any rate) to provide an experience beyond the literary was precisely what I wanted to instil in my own story. Another failure in *The Magus*, which again I can't now remedy, was my inability to see that this is a characteristic longing of adolescence. At least the adolescence of Henri Fournier's protagonist is open and specific.

The second influence may seem surprising, but it was undoubtedly that of a book which haunted my childhood imagination, Richard Jefferies' *Bevis*. I believe novelists are formed, whether they know it or not, very young indeed; and *Bevis* shares a quality with *Le Grand Meaulnes*, that of projecting a very different world from the one that is – or was to the middle-class suburban child I had outwardly to be. I cite it as a reminder that the deep pattern, and mood, of such books remains long after one has graduated from them in more obvious ways.

The third book that lies behind *The Magus* I did not recognize at the time, and can list now thanks to the percipience of a student at Reading University, who wrote to me one day, years after publication, and pointed out the numerous parallels with *Great Expectations*. What she was not to know is that it is the one novel of Dickens for which I have always had an undivided admiration and love (and for which I forgive him so much else I dislike in his work); that during the earlier writing of my own novel I was even teaching it, with great enjoyment, as a set book; and that I long toyed with the notion

6

of making Conchis a woman – an idea whose faint ghost, Miss Havisham's, remains in the figure of Mrs de Seitas. One small new passage in this revised text is in homage to that unseen influence.

Two other more considerable changes need a brief word. The erotic element is stronger in two scenes. I regard that as merely the correction of a past failure of nerve. The other change is in the ending. Though its general intent has never seemed to me as obscure as some readers have evidently found it – perhaps because they have not given due weight to the two lines from the *Pervigilium Veneris* that close the book – I accept that I might have declared a preferred after-math less ambiguously ... and now have done so.

No writer will happily disclose the deeper biographical influences of his work, which are seldom those of outward date and occupation, and I am no exception. But my island of Phraxos (the 'fenced' island) was the real Greek island of Spetsai, where I taught in 1951 and 1952 at a private boarding-school – not, in those days, very like the one in the book. If I had attempted a true portrait of it, I should have been committed to a comic novel.*

The well-known Greek millionaire who has now taken over a part of Spetsai is in no way connected with my fictional one; the arrival of Mr Niarchos came much later. Nor was the then owner of the villa of 'Bourani', some of whose outward appearance and whose superb site I did appropriate, in the least the model for my character, though I understand that this is now by way of becoming another local legend. I met the gentleman – a friend of the elder Venizelos – only twice, and very briefly. It was his house that I remembered.

It is probably impossible today – I speak from hearsay, never having returned there – to imagine Spetsai as I have pictured it just after the war. Life there was lonely in the extreme, though there were always two English masters at the school, not the one of the book. I was fortunate in my chance-brought colleague, and now old friend, Denys Sharrocks. He was exceptionally well-read, and far wiser in the ways of the Greeks than myself. He first took me to the villa. He had recently decided to kill a literary ambition of his own.

*Another, and curious, novel about the school exists: Kenneth Matthews, *Aleko* (Peter Davies, 1934). The French writer Michel Déon has also published the autobiographical *Le Balcon de Spetsaï* (Gallimard, 1961).

'Bourani', he declared wrily, was where he had on a previous visit written the last poem of his life. In some peculiar way this fused a spark in my imagination; the strangely isolated villa, its magnificent setting, the death of a friend's illusion; and as we approached the villa on its cape that first time, there came a very bizarre sound indeed for a classical landscape ... not the august Pleyel harpsichord of my book, but something much more absurdly reminiscent of a Welsh chapel. I hope the harmonium is still there. It also gave birth to something.

Foreign faces on the island – even Greek ones – were then great rarities. I remember a boy rushing up to Denys and myself one day to announce that another Englishman had landed from the Athens steamer – and how we set off, like two Dr Livingstones, to greet this unheard-of arrival on our desert island. On another occasion it was Henry Miller's Colossus of Maroussi, Katsimbalis, whom we hastened to pay our respects to. There was still a touching atmosphere of a one village about Greece then.

Away from its inhabited corner Spetsai was truly haunted, though by subtler – and more beautiful – ghosts than those I have created. Its pine-forest silences were uncanny, unlike those I have experienced anywhere else; like an eternally blank page waiting for a note or a word. They gave the most curious sense of timelessness and of incipient myth. In no place was it less likely that something would happen; yet somehow happening lay always poised. The *genius loci* was very similar indeed to that of Mallarmé's finest poems of the unseen flight, of words defeated before the inexpressible. I am hard put to convey the importance of this experience for me as a writer. It imbued and marked me far more profoundly than any of my more social and physical memories of the place. I already knew I was a permanent exile from many aspects of English society, but a novelist has to enter deeper exiles still.

In most outward ways this experience was depressive, as many young would-be writers and painters who have gone to Greece for inspiration have discovered. We used to have a nickname for the sense of inadequacy and accidie it induced – the 'Aegean Blues'. One has to be a very complete artist to create good work among the purest and most balanced landscapes on this planet, and especially when one knows that their only conceivable human match was met in a time beyond re-entry. The Greece of the islands is Circe still; no place for the artist-voyager to linger long, if he cares for his soul.

No correlative whatever of my fiction, beyond the above, took place on Spetsai during my stay. What ground the events of the book have in reality came after I had returned to England. I had escaped Circe, but the withdrawal symptoms were severe. I had not then realized that loss is essential for the novelist, immensely fertile for his books, however painful to his private being. This unresolved sense of a lack, a missed opportunity, led me to graft certain dilemmas of a private situation in England on the memory of the island and its solitudes, which became increasingly for me the lost Eden, the *domaine sans nom* of Alain-Fournier – even Bevis's farm, perhaps. Gradually my protagonist, Nicholas, took on, if not the true representative face of a modern Everyman, at least that of a partial Everyman of my own class and background. There is a private pun in the family name I gave him. As a child I could not pronounce *th* except as *f*, and Urfe really stands for Earth – a coining that long preceded the convenient connection with Honoré d'Urfé and *L'Astrée*.

The foregoing will, I hope, excuse me from saying what the story 'means'. Novels, even much more lucidly conceived and controlled ones than this, are not like crossword puzzles, with one unique set of correct answers behind the clues – an analogy ('Dear Mr Fowles, Please explain the real significance of ... ') I sometimes despair of ever extirpating from the contemporary student mind. If *The Magus* has any 'real significance', it is no more than that of the Rorschach test in psychology. Its meaning is whatever reaction it provokes in the reader, and so far as I am concerned there is no given 'right' reaction.

I should add that in revising the text I have not attempted to answer the many justified criticisms of excess, over-complexity, artificiality and the rest that the book received from the more sternly adult reviewers on its first appearance. I now know the generation whose mind it most attracts, and that it must always substantially remain a novel of adolescence written by a retarded adolescent. My only plea is that all artists have to range the full extent of their own lives freely. The rest of the world can censor and bury their private past. We cannot, and so have to remain partly green till the day we die ... callow-green in the hope of becoming fertile-green. It is a constant complaint in that most revealing of all modern novels about novelists, Thomas Hardy's agonized last fiction, *The Well-Beloved*: how the much younger self still rules the supposedly 'mature' and middle-aged artist. One may reject the tyranny, as Hardy himself did; but the cost is the end of one's ability to write novels. *The Magus* was also (though quite unconsciously) an out-of-hand celebration of acceptance of the yoke.

If there was some central scheme beneath the (more Irish than Greek) stew of intuitions about the nature of human existence – and of fiction – it lies perhaps in the alternative title, whose rejection I still sometimes regret: *The Godgame*. I did intend Conchis to exhibit a series of masks representing human notions of God, from the supernatural to the jargon-ridden scientific; that is, a series of human illusions about something that does not exist in fact, absolute knowledge and absolute power. The destruction of such illusions seems to me still an eminently humanist aim; and I wish there were some super-Conchis who could put the Arabs and the Israelis, or the Ulster Catholics and Protestants, through the same heuristic mill as Nicholas.

I do not defend Conchis's decision at the execution, but I defend the reality of the dilemma. God and freedom are totally antipathetic concepts; and men believe in their imaginary gods most often because they are afraid to believe in the other thing. I am old enough to realize now that they do so sometimes with good reason. But I stick by the general principle, and that is what I meant to be at the heart of my story: that true freedom lies between each two, never in one alone, and therefore it can never be absolute freedom. All freedom, even the most relative, may be a fiction; but mine, and still today, prefers the other hypothesis.

1976

JOHN FOWLES

The Magus

I

Un débauché de profession est rarement un homme pitoyable.
De Sade, *Les Infortunes de la Vertu*

I

I was born in 1927, the only child of middle-class parents, both English, and themselves born in the grotesquely elongated shadow, which they never rose sufficiently above history to leave, of that monstrous dwarf Queen Victoria. I was sent to a public school, I wasted two years doing my national service, I went to Oxford; and there I began to discover I was not the person I wanted to be.

I had long before made the discovery that I lacked the parents and ancestors I needed. My father was, through being the right age at the right time rather than through any great professional talent, a brigadier; and my mother was the very model of a would-be major-general's wife. That is, she never argued with him and always behaved as if he were listening in the next room, even when he was thousands of miles away. I saw very little of my father during the war, and in his long absences I used to build up a more or less immaculate conception of him, which he generally – a bad but appropriate pun – shattered within the first forty-eight hours of his leave.

Like all men not really up to their job, he was a stickler for externals and petty quotidian things; and in lieu of an intellect he had accumulated an armoury of capitalized key-words like Discipline and Tradition and Responsibility. If I ever dared – I seldom did – to argue with him, he would produce one of these totem words and cosh me with it, as no doubt in similar circumstances he quelled his subalterns. If one still refused to lie down and die, he lost, or loosed, his temper. His temper was like a red dog, and he always had it close to hand.

The wishful tradition is that our family came over from France after the Revocation of the Edict of Nantes – noble Huguenots remotely allied to Honoré d'Urfé, author of the seventeenth-century best-seller *L'Astrée*. Certainly – if one excludes another equally unsubstantiated link with Tom Durfey, Charles II's scribbling friend – no other of my ancestors showed any artistic leanings whatever: generation after generation of captains, clergymen, sailors, squire-lings, with only a uniform lack of distinction and a marked penchant for gambling, and losing, to characterize them. My grandfather had four sons, two of whom died in the First World War; the third took an unsavoury way of paying off his atavism (gambling debts) and disappeared to America. He was never referred to as still existing by my father, a youngest brother who had all the characteristics that eldest sons are supposed to possess; and I have not the least idea whether he is still alive, or even whether I have unknown cousins on the other side of the Atlantic.

During my last years at school I realized that what was really wrong with my parents was that they had nothing but a blanket contempt for the sort of life I wanted to lead. I was 'good' at English, I had poems printed pseudonymously in the school magazine, I thought D. H. Lawrence the greatest human being of the century; my parents certainly never read Lawrence, and had probably never heard of him except in connection with *Lady Chatterley's Lover*. There were things, a certain emotional gentleness in my mother, an occasional euphoric jolliness in my father, I could have borne more of; but always I liked in them the things they didn't want to be liked for. By the time I was eighteen and Hitler was dead they had become mere providers, for whom I had to exhibit a token gratitude, but could muster very little else.

I led two lives. At school I got a small reputation as a wartime aesthete and cynic. But I had to join the regiment – Tradition and Sacrifice pressganged me into that. I insisted, and luckily the head-master of my school backed me, that I wanted to go to university afterwards. I went on leading a double life in the Army, queasily playing at being Brigadier 'Blazer' Urfe's son in public, and ner-vously reading *Penguin New Writing* and poetry pamphlets in pri-vate. As soon as I could, I got myself demobilized.

I went to Oxford in 1948. In my second year at Magdalen, soon after a long vacation during which I hardly saw my parents, my father had to fly out to India. He took my mother with him. Their plane crashed, a high-octane pyre, in a thunderstorm some forty miles east of Karachi. After the first shock I felt an almost immediate sense of relief, of freedom. My only other close relation, my mother's brother, farmed in Rhodesia, so I now had no family to trammel what I regarded as my real self. I may have been weak in filial charity, but I was strong on the discipline in vogue.

At least, along with a group of fellow odd men out at Magdalen, I thought I was so. We formed a small club called Les Hommes Révoltés, drank very dry sherry, and (as a protest against those shabby duffel-coated last years of the 'forties) wore dark-grey suits and black ties for our meetings. There we argued about being and nothingness and called a certain kind of inconsequential behaviour 'existentialist'. Less enlightened people would have called it capricious or just plain selfish; but we didn't understand that the heroes, or anti-heroes, of the French existentialist novels we read were not supposed to be realistic. We tried to imitate them, mistaking metaphorical descriptions of complex modes of feeling for straightforward prescriptions of behaviour. We duly felt the right anguishes. Most of us, true to the eternal dandyism of Oxford, simply wanted to look different. In our club, we did.

I acquired expensive habits and affected manners. I got a third-class degree and a first-class illusion: that I was a poet. But nothing could have been less poetic than my seeing-through-all boredom with life in general and with making a living in particular. I was too green to know that all cynicism masks a failure to cope – an impotence, in short; and that to despise all effort is the greatest effort of all. But I did absorb a small dose of one permanently useful thing, Oxford's greatest gift to civilized life: Socratic honesty. It showed me, very intermittently, that it is not enough to revolt against one's past. One day I was outrageously bitter among some friends about the Army; back in my own rooms later it suddenly struck me that just because I said with impunity things that would have apoplexed my dead father, I was still no less under his influence. The truth was I was not a cynic by nature; only by revolt. I had got away from what I hated, but I hadn't found where I loved, and so I pretended that there was nowhere to love.

Handsomely equipped to fail, I went out into the world. My father hadn't kept Financial Prudence among his armoury of essential words; he ran a ridiculously large account at Ladbroke's and his mess bills always reached staggering proportions, because he liked to be popular and in place of charm had to dispense alcohol. What remained of his money when the lawyers and the tax men had had their share yielded not nearly enough for me to live on. But every kind of job I looked at – the Foreign Service, the Civil, the Colonial, the banks, commerce, advertising – was transpierceable at a glance. I went to several interviews. Since I didn't feel obliged to show the eager enthusiasm our world expects from the young executive, I was successful at none.

In the end, like countless Oxford men before me, I answered an advertisement in *The Times Educational Supplement*. I went to the place, a minor public school in East Anglia; was cursorily scrutinized, then offered the post. I learnt later that there were only two other applicants, both Redbrick, and term was beginning in three weeks.

The mass-produced middle-class boys I had to teach were bad enough; the claustrophobic little town was a nightmare; but the really intolerable thing was the common-room. It became almost a relief to go into class. Boredom, the numbing annual predictability of life, hung over the staff like a cloud. And it was real boredom, not my modish ennui. From it flowed cant, hypocrisy, and the impotent rage of the old who know they have failed and the young who suspect they will fail. The senior masters stood like gallows sermons; with some of them one had a sort of vertigo, a glimpse of the bottomless pit of human futility … or so I began to feel during my second term.

I could not spend my life crossing such a Sahara; and the more I felt it the more I felt also that the smug, petrified school was a toy model of the entire country and that to quit the one and not the other would be ridiculous. There was also a girl I was tired of.

My resignation, I would see the school year out, was accepted with resignation. The headmaster briskly supposed from my vague references to a personal restlessness that I wanted to go to America or the Dominions.

'I haven't decided yet, headmaster.'

'I think we might have made a good teacher of you, Urfe. And you might have made something of us, you know. But it's too late now.'

'I'm afraid so.'

'I don't know if I approve of all this wandering off abroad. My advise is, don't go. However … *vous l'avez voulu, Georges Danton. Vous l'avez voulu.*'

The misquotation was typical.

It poured with rain the day I left. But I was filled with excitement, a strange exuberant sense of taking wing. I didn't know where I was going, but I knew what I needed. I needed a new land, a new race, a new language; and, although I couldn't have put it into words then, I needed a new mystery.

2

I heard that the British Council were recruiting staff, so in early August I went along to Davies Street and was interviewed by an eager lady with a culture-stricken mind and a Roedean voice and vocabulary. It was frightfully important, she told me, as if in confidence, that 'we' were represented abroad by the right type; but it was an awful bore, all the posts had to be advertised and the candidates chosen by interview, and anyway they were having to cut down on overseas personnel – actually. She came to the point: the only jobs available meant teaching English in foreign schools – or did that sound too ghastly?

I said it did.

In the last week of August, half as a joke, I advertised: the traditional insertion. I had a number of replies to my curt offer to go anywhere and do anything. Apart from the pamphlets reminding me that I was God's, there were three charming letters from fundless and alert swindlers. And there was one that mentioned unusual and remunerative work in Tangiers – could I speak Italian? – but my answer went unanswered.

September loomed: I began to feel desperate. I saw myself cornered, driven back in despair to the dreaded *Educational Supplement* and those endless pale-grey lists of endless pale-grey jobs. So one morning I returned to Davies Street.

I asked if they had any teaching jobs in the Mediterranean area, and the woman with the frightful intensifiers went off to fetch a file. I sat under a puce and tomato Matthew Smith in the waiting-room and began to see myself in Madrid, in Rome, or Marseilles, or Barcelona ... even Lisbon. It would be different abroad; there would be no common-room, and I should write poetry. She returned. All the good things had gone, she was terribly afraid. But there were these.

She handed me a sheet about a school in Milan. I shook my head. She approved.

'Well actually then there's only this. We've just advertised it.' She handed me a clipping.

THE LORD BYRON SCHOOL, PHRAXOS

The Lord Byron School, Phraxos, Greece, requires in early October an assistant master to teach English. Candidates must be single and must have a degree in English. A knowledge of Modern Greek is not essential. The salary is worth about £600 per annum, and is fully convertible. Two-year contract, renewable. Fares paid at the beginning and end of contract.

There was an information sheet that long-windedly amplified the advertisement. Phraxos was an island in the Aegean about eighty miles from Athens. The Lord Byron was 'one of the most famous boarding schools in Greece, run on English public-school lines' – whence the name. It appeared to have every facility a school should have. One had to give a maximum of five lessons a day.

'The school's terribly well spoken of. And the island's simply heavenly.'

'You've been there?'

She was about thirty, a born spinster, with a lack of sexuality so total that her smart clothes and too heavy make-up made her pathetic; like an unsuccessful geisha. She hadn't been there, but everybody said so. I re-read the advertisement.

'Why've they left it so late?'

'Well, we understand they did appoint another man. Not through us. But there's been some awful mess-up.' I looked again at the information sheet. 'We haven't actually recruited for them before. We're only doing it out of courtesy now, as a matter of fact.' She gave me a patient smile; her front teeth were much too big. I asked, in my best Oxford voice, if I might take her out to lunch.

When I got home, I filled in the form she had brought to the restaurant, and went straight out and posted it. That same evening, by a curious neatness of fate, I met Alison.

3

I suppose I'd had, by the standards of that pre-permissive time, a good deal of sex for my age. Girls, or a certain kind of girl, liked me; I had a car – not so common among undergraduates in those days – and I had some money. I wasn't ugly; and even more important, I had my loneliness, which, as every cad knows, is a deadly weapon with women. My 'technique' was to make a show of unpredictability, cynicism, and indifference. Then, like a conjurer with his white rabbit, I produced the solitary heart.

I didn't collect conquests, but by the time I left Oxford I was a dozen girls away from virginity. I found my sexual success and the apparently ephemeral nature of love equally pleasing. It was like being good at golf, but despising the game. One was covered all round, both when one played and when one didn't. I contrived most of my affaires in the vacations, away from Oxford, since the new term meant that I could conveniently leave the scene of the crime. There were sometimes a few tedious weeks of letters, but I soon put the solitary heart away, 'assumed responsibility with my total being' and showed the Chesterfieldian mask instead. I became almost as neat at ending liaisons as at starting them.

This sounds, and was, calculating, but it was caused less by a true coldness than by my narcissistic belief in the importance of the life-style. I mistook the feeling of relief that dropping a girl always brought for a love of freedom. Perhaps the one thing in my favour was that I lied very little; I was always careful to make sure that the current victim knew, before she took her clothes off, the difference between coupling and marrying.

But then, in East Anglia, things became complicated. I started to take the daughter of one of the older masters out. She was pretty in a stock English way, as province-hating as myself, and she seemed rather passionate, but I belatedly realized she was passionate for a purpose: I was to marry her. I began to be sick of the way a mere bodily need threatened to distort my life. There were even one or two evenings when I felt myself near surrendering to Janet, a fundamentally silly girl I knew I didn't love and would never love. Our parting scene, an infinitely sour all-night of nagging and weeping in the car beside the July sea, haunted me. Fortunately I knew, and she knew I knew, that she was not pregnant. I came to London with the firm determination to stay away from women for a while.

The Russell Square flat below the one I had rented had been empty through most of August, but then one Sunday I heard movements, doors slammed, and there was music. I passed a couple of uninterest-ing-looking girls on the stairs on the Monday; heard them talking, all their short *a*'s flattened into short *e*'s, as I went on down. They were Australians. Then came the evening of the day I had lunch with Miss Spencer-Haigh; a Friday.

About six, there was a knock on the door, and the stockier of the two girls I had seen was standing there.

'Oh hi. I'm Margaret. From below.' I took her outstretched hand. 'Gled to know you. Look, we're heving ourselves a bottle pardy. Like to come along?'

'Oh. Well actually ...'

'It'll be noisy up here.'

It was the usual thing: an invitation to kill complaint. I hesitated, then shrugged.

'All right. Thanks.'

'Well thet's good. Eight?' She began to go downstairs, but she called back. 'You hev a girl-friend you'd like to bring?'

'Not just now.'

'We'll fix you up. Hi.'

And she was gone. I wished then that I hadn't accepted.

So I went down when I could hear that a lot of people had already arrived. The ugly girls – they always arrive first – would, I hoped, have been disposed of. The door was open. I went in through a little hall and stood in the doorway of the living-room, holding my bottle of Algerian burgundy ready to present. I tried to discover in the crowded room one of the two girls I had seen before. Loud Australian voices; a man in a kilt, and several West Indians. It didn't look my sort of party, and I was within five seconds of slipping back out. Then someone arrived and stood in the hall behind me.

It was a girl of about my own age, carrying a heavy suitcase, with a small rucksack on her shoulders. She was wearing a whitish mackintosh, creased and travel-weary, and she had the sort of tan that only weeks in hot sun can give. Her long hair was not quite blonde, but bleached almost to that colour. It looked odd, because the urchin cut was the fashion: girls like boys, not girls like girls; and there was something German, Danish, about her – waif-like, yet perversely or immorally so. She kept back from the open doorway, beckoned me. Her smile was very thin, very insincere, and very curt.

'Could you find Maggie and ask her to come out?'

'Margaret?'

She nodded. I forced my way through the packed room and eventually caught sight of Margaret in the kitchen.

'Hi there! You made it.'

'Someone wants to see you outside. A girl with a suitcase.'

'Oh no!' She turned to a woman behind her. I sensed trouble. She hesitated, then put down the quart beer-bottle she was opening. I followed her plump shoulders back through the crowd.

'Alison! You said next week.'

'I spent all my money.' The waif gave the older girl an oddly split look, half guilty and half wary. 'Is Pete back?'

'No.' The voice dropped, half warning. 'But Charlie and Bill are.'

'Oh *merde*.' She looked outraged. 'I *must* have a bath.'

'Charlie's filled it to cool the beer. It's stecked to the brim.'

The girl with the tan sagged. I broke in.

'Use mine. Upstairs.'

'Yes? Alison, this is … '

'Nicholas.'

'Would you mind? I've just come from Paris.' I noticed she had two voices; one almost Australian, one almost English.

'Of course. I'll take you up.'

'I must go and get some gear first.' As soon as she went into the room there was a shout.

'Hey Allie! Where you been, girl?'

Two or three of the Australian men gathered round her. She kissed them all briefly. In a minute Margaret, one of those fat girls who mother thin girls, pushed them away. Alison reappeared with the clothes she wanted, and we went up.

'Oh Jesus,' she said. 'Australians.'

'Where've you been?'

'All over. France. Spain.'

We went into the flat.

'I'll just clean the spiders out of the bath. Have a drink. Over there.'

When I came back, she was standing with a glass of Scotch in her hand. She smiled again, but it was an effort; shut off almost at once. I helped her remove her mackintosh. She was wearing a French perfume so dark it was almost carbolic, and her primrose shirt was dirty.

'You live downstairs?'

'Uhuh. Share.'

She raised her glass in silent toast. She had candid grey eyes, the only innocent things in a corrupt face, as if circumstances, not nature, had forced her to be hard. To fend for herself, yet to seem to need defending. And her voice, only very slightly Australian, yet not English, veered between harshness, faint nasal rancidity, and a strange salty directness. She was bizarre, a kind of human oxymoron.

'Are you alone? At the party?'

'Yes.'

'Would you keep with me this evening?'

'Of course.'

'Come back in about twenty minutes?'

'I'll wait.'

'I'd rather you came back.'

We exchanged wary smiles. I went back to the party.

Margaret came up. I think she'd been waiting. 'I've a nice English girl enxious to meet you, Nicholas.'

'I'm afraid your friend's jumped the gun.'

She stared at me, then round, then motioned me back into the hall. 'Listen, this is a liddle difficult to expline, but ... Alison, she's engaged to my brother. Some of his friends are here tonight.'

'So?'

'She's been very mixed up.'

'I still don't understand.'

'Just that I don't want a rough-house. We hed one once before.' I looked blank. 'People grow jealous on other people's behalf?'

'I shan't start anything.'

Someone called her from inside. She tried to feel sure of me, but failed, and apparently decided she couldn't do anything about it. 'Fair deal. But you hev the message?'

'Absolutely.'

She gave me a veteran's look, then a nod, not a very happy one, and went away. I waited for about twenty minutes, near the door, and then I slipped out and went back up to my own flat. I rang the bell. There was a long pause, then there was a voice behind the door.

'Who is it?'

'Twenty minutes.'

The door opened. She had her hair up, and a towel wrapped round her; very brown shoulders, very brown legs. She went quickly back into the bathroom. Draining water gurgled. I shouted through the door.

'I've been warned off you.'

'Maggie?'

'She says she doesn't want a rough-house.'

'Fucking cow. She's my potential sister-in-law.'

'I know.'

'Studying sociology. London University.' There was a pause. 'Isn't it crazy? You go away and you think people will have changed and they're just the same.'

'What does that mean?'

'Wait a minute.'

I waited several. But then the door opened and she came out into the living-room. She was wearing a very simple white dress, and her hair was down again. She had no make-up, and looked ten times prettier.

She gave me a little bitten-in grin. 'I pass?'

'The belle of the ball.' Her look was so direct I found it disconcerting. 'We go down?'

'Just one finger?'

I filled her glass again, and with more than one finger. Watching the whisky fall, she said, 'I don't know why I'm frightened. Why am I frightened?'

'What of?'

'I don't know. Maggie. The boys. The dear old diggers.'

'This rough-house?'

'Oh God. It was *so* stupid. There was a nice Israeli boy, we were just kissing. It was a party. That was all. But Charlie told Pete, and they just picked a quarrel, and … oh God. You know. He-men.'

Downstairs I lost her for a time. A group formed round her. I went and got a drink and passed it over someone's shoulder; talk about Cannes, about Collioure and Valencia. Jazz had started in the back room and I went to the doorway to watch. Outside the window, past the dark dancers, were dusk trees, a pale amber sky. I had a sharp sense of alienation from everyone around me. A girl with spectacles, myopic eyes in an insipidly soft face, one of those soulful-intellectual creatures born to be preyed on and exploited by phonies, smiled coyly from the other side of the room. She was standing alone and I guessed that she was the 'nice English girl' Margaret had picked for me. Her lipstick was too red; and she was as familiar as a species of bird. I turned away from her as from a cliff edge, and went and sat on the floor by a bookshelf. There I pretended to read a paperback.

Alison knelt beside me. 'I'm sloshed. That whisky. Hey, have some of this.' It was gin. She sat sideways, I shook my head. I thought of that white-faced English girl with the red smudged mouth. At least this girl was alive; crude, but alive.

'I'm glad you returned tonight.'

She sipped her gin and gave me a small sizing look.

I tried again. 'Ever read this?'

'Let's cut corners. To hell with literature. You're clever and I'm beautiful. Now let's talk about who we really are.'

The grey eyes teased; or dared.

'Pete?'

'He's a pilot.' She mentioned a famous airline. 'We shack together. Off and on. That's all.'

'Ah.'

'He's doing a conversion course. In the States.' She stared at the floor, for a moment a different girl, more serious. 'Engaged is Maggie talk. We're not like that.' She half flicked a glance at me. 'Free people.'

It wasn't clear whether she was talking about her fiancé or for my benefit; or whether freedom was her pose or her truth.

'What do you do?'

'Things. Reception mostly.'

'Hotels?'

'Anything.' She wrinkled her nose. 'I've applied for a new job. Air hostess. That's why I went off polishing French and Spanish these last weeks.'

'Can I take you out tomorrow?'

A heavy Australian in his thirties came and leant against a door-jamb opposite. 'Oh Charlie,' she cried across the room, 'he's just lent me his bath. It's nothing.'

Charlie nodded his head slowly, then pointed an admonitory stubby finger. He pushed himself vertical and went unsteadily away.

'Charming.'

She turned over her hand and looked at the palm.

'Did you spend two and a half years in a Jap prisoner-of-war camp?'

'No. Why?'

'Charlie did.'

'Poor Charlie.'

There was a silence.

'Australians are boors, and Englishmen are prigs.'

'If you – '

'I make fun of him because he's in love with me and he likes it. But no one else makes fun of him. If I'm around.'

There was another silence.

'Sorry.'

'That's okay.'

'About tomorrow.'

'No. About you.'

Gradually, though I was offended at having been taught a lesson in the art of not condescending, she made me talk about myself. She did it by asking blunt questions, and by brushing aside empty answers. I began to talk about being a brigadier's son, about loneliness, and for once mostly not to glamourize myself but simply to explain. I discovered two things about Alison: that behind her bluntness she was an expert coaxer, a handler of men, a sexual diplomat, and that her attraction lay as much in her candour as in her having a pretty body, an interesting face, and knowing it. She had a very un-English ability to flash out some truth, some seriousness, some quick surge of interest. I fell silent. I knew she was watching me. After a moment I looked at her. She had a shy, thoughtful expression; a new self.

'Alison, I like you.'

'I think I like you. You've got quite a nice mouth. For a prig.'

'You're the first Australian girl I've ever met.'

'Poor Pom.'

All the lights except one dim one had long ago been put out, and there were the usual surrendered couples on all available furniture and floor-space. The party had paired off. Maggie seemed to have disappeared, and Charlie lay fast asleep on the bedroom floor. We danced. We began close, and became closer. I kissed her hair, and then her neck, and she pressed my hand, and moved a little closer still.

'Shall we go upstairs?'

'You go first. I'll come in a minute.' She slipped away, and I went up to my flat. Ten minutes passed, and then she was in the doorway, a faintly apprehensive smile on her face. She stood there in her white dress, small, innocent-corrupt, coarse-fine, an expert novice.

She came in, I shut the door, and we were kissing at once, for a minute, two minutes, pressed back against the door in the darkness. There were steps outside, and a sharp double rap. Alison put her hand over my mouth. Another double rap; and then another. Hesitation, heart-beats. The footsteps went away.

'Come on,' she said. 'Come on, come on.'

4

It was late the next morning when I woke. She was still asleep, with her naked brown back turned away from me. I went and made some coffee and took it into the bedroom. She was awake then, staring at me over the top of the bedclothes. It was a long expressionless look that rejected my smile and ended abruptly in her turning and pulling the bedclothes over her head. I sat beside her and tried rather amateurishly to discover what was wrong, but she kept the sheet pulled tight over her head; so I gave up patting and making noises and went back to my coffee. After a while she sat up and asked for a cigarette. And then if I would lend her a shirt. She wouldn't look me in the eyes. She pulled on the shirt, went to the bathroom, and brushed me aside with a shake of her hair when she came and got back into bed again. I sat at the foot of the bed and watched her drink her coffee.

'What's up?'

'Do you know how many men I've slept with the last two months?'

'Fifty?'

She didn't smile.

'If I'd slept with fifty I'd just be an honest professional.'

'Have some more coffee.'

'Half an hour after I first saw you last night I thought, if I was really vicious I'd get into bed with him.'

'Thank you very much.'

'I could tell about you from the way you talked.'

'Tell what?'

'You're the *affaire de peau* type.'

'That's ridiculous.'

A silence.

'I was sloshed,' she said. 'So tired.' She gave me a long look, then shook her head and shut her eyes. 'I'm sorry. You're nice. You're terribly nice in bed. Only now what?'

'I'm not used to this.'

'I am.'

'It's not a crime. You're just proving you can't marry this chap.'

'I'm twenty-three. How old are you?'

'Twenty-five.'

'Don't you begin to feel things about yourself you know are you? Are going to be you for ever? That's what I feel. I'm going to be a stupid Australian slut for ever.'

'Come on.'

'I tell you what Pete's doing right now. You know, he writes and tells me. "I took a piece out last Friday and we had a wuzzamaroo."'

'What's that mean?'

'It means "and you sleep with anyone you like, too".' She stared out of the window. 'We lived together, all this spring. You know, we get on, we're like brother and sister when we're out of bed.' She gave me a slanting look through the cigarette smoke. 'You don't know what it's like waking up with a man you didn't even know this time yesterday. It's losing something. Not just what all girls lose.'

'Or gaining something.'

'God, what can we gain. Tell me.'

'Experience. Pleasure.'

'Did I tell you I love your mouth?'

'Several times.'

She stubbed the cigarette out and sat back.

'Do you know why I tried to cry just now? Because I'm going to marry him. As soon as he comes back, I'm going to marry him. He's all I deserve.' She sat leaning back against the wall, with the too-large shirt on, a small female boy with a hurt face, staring at me, staring at the bedcover, in our silence.

'It's just a phase. You're unhappy.'

'I'm unhappy when I stop and think. When I wake up and see what I am.'

'Thousands of girls do it.'

'I'm not thousands of girls. I'm me.' She slipped the shirt over her head, then retreated under the bedclothes. 'What's your real name? Your surname?'

'Urfe. U, R, F, E.'

'Mine's Kelly. Was your dad really a brigadier?'

'Yes. Just.'

She gave a timid mock salute, then reached out a brown arm. I moved beside her.

'Don't you think I'm a tramp?'

Perhaps then, as I was looking at her, so close, I had my choice. I could have said what I was thinking: Yes, you are a tramp, and even worse, you exploit your tramp-hood, and I wish I'd taken your sister-in-law-to-be's advice. Perhaps if I had been farther away from her, on the other side of the room, in any situation where I could have avoided her eyes, I could have been decisively brutal. But those grey, searching, always candid eyes, by their begging me not to lie, made me lie.

'I like you. Really **very** much.'

30

'Come back to bed and hold me. Nothing else. Just hold me.'

I got into bed and held her. Then for the first time in my life I made love to a woman in tears.

She was in tears more than once, that first Saturday. She went down to see Maggie about five and came back with red eyes. Maggie had told her to get out. Half an hour later Ann, the other girl in the flat, one of those unfortunate females whose faces fall absolutely flat from nostrils to chin, came up. Maggie had gone out and wanted Alison to remove all her things. So we went down and brought them up. I had a talk with Ann. In her quiet, rather prim way she showed more sympathy for Alison than I was expecting; Maggie was evidently and aggressively blind to her brother's faults.

For days, afraid of Maggie, who for some reason stood in her mind as a hated but still potent monolith of solid Australian virtue on the blasted moor of English decadence, Alison did not go out except at night. I went and bought food, and we talked and slept and made love and danced and cooked meals at all hours, *sous les toits*, as remote from ordinary time as we were from the dull London world outside the windows.

Alison was always feminine; she never, like so many English girls, betrayed her gender. She wasn't beautiful, she very often wasn't even pretty. But she had a fashionably thin boyish figure, she had a contemporary dress sense, she had a conscious way of walking, and her sum was extraordinarily more than her parts. I would sit in the car and watch her walking down the street towards me, pause, cross the road; and she looked wonderful. But then when she was close, beside me, there so often seemed to be something rather shallow, something spoilt-child, in her appearance. Even close to her, I was always being wrong-footed. She would be ugly one moment, and then some movement, expression, angle of her face, made ugliness impossible.

When she went out she used to wear a lot of eye-shadow, which married with the sulky way she sometimes held her mouth to give her a characteristic bruised look; a look that subtly made one want to bruise her more. Men were always aware of her, in the street, in restaurants, in pubs; and she knew it. I used to watch them sliding their eyes at her as she passed. She was one of those rare, even among already pretty, women that are born with a natural aura of sexuality: always in their lives it will be the relationships with men, it will be how men react, that matters. And even the tamest sense it.

There was a simpler Alison, when the mascara was off. She had not been typical of herself, those first twelve hours; but still always a little unpredictable, ambiguous. One never knew when the more sophisti-cated, bruised-hard persona would reappear. She would give herself violently; then yawn at the wrongest moment. She would spend all one day clearing up the flat, cooking, ironing, then pass the next three or four bohemianly on the floor in front of the fire, reading *Lear*, women's magazines, a detective story, Hemingway – not all at the same time, but bits of all in the same afternoon. She liked doing things, and only then finding a reason for doing them.

One day she came back with an expensive fountain pen.

'For *monsieur*.'

'But you shouldn't.'

'It's okay. I stole it.'

'Stole it!'

'I steal everything. Didn't you realize?'

'Everything!'

'I never steal from small shops. Only the big stores. They ask for it. Don't look so shocked.'

'I'm not.' But I was. I stood holding the pen gingerly. She grinned.

'It's just a hobby.'

'Six months in Holloway wouldn't be so funny.'

She had poured herself a whisky. '*Santé*. I hate big stores. And not just capitalists. Pommy capitalists. Two birds with one steal. Oh, come on, sport, smile.' She put the pen in my pocket. 'There. Now you're a cassowary after the crime.'

'I need a Scotch.'

Holding the bottle, I remembered she had 'bought' that as well. I looked at her. She nodded.

She stood beside me as I poured. 'Nicholas, you know why you take *things* too seriously? Because you take yourself too seriously.'

She gave me an odd little smile, half tender, half mocking, and went away to peel potatoes. And I knew that in some obscure way I had offended her; and myself.

One night I heard her say a name in her sleep.

'Who's Michel?' I asked the next morning.

'Someone I want to forget.'

But she talked about everything else; about her English-born mother, genteel but dominating; about her father, a station-master who had died of cancer four years before.

'That's why I've got this crazy between voice. It's Mum and Dad living out their battles again every time I open my mouth. I suppose it's why I hate Australia and I love Australia and I couldn't ever be happy there and yet I'm always feeling homesick. Does that make sense?'

She was always asking me if she made sense.

'I went to see the old family in Wales. Mum's brother. Jesus. Enough to make the wallabies weep.'

But she found me very English, very fascinating. Partly it was because I was 'cultured', a word she often used. Pete had always 'honked' at her if she went to galleries or concerts. She mimicked him: 'What's wrong with the boozer, girl?'

One day she said, 'You don't know how nice Pete is. Besides being a bastard. I always know what he wants, I always know what he thinks, and what he means when he says anything. And you, I don't know anything. I offend you and I don't know why. I please you and I don't know why. It's because you're English. You couldn't ever understand that.'

She had finished high school in Australia, and had even had a year doing languages at Sydney University. But then she had met Pete, and it 'got complicated'. She'd had an abortion and come to England.

'Did he make you have the abortion?'

She was sitting on my knees.

'He never knew.'

'Never knew!'

'It could have been someone else's. I wasn't sure.'

'You poor kid.'

'I knew if it was Pete's he wouldn't want it. And if it wasn't his he wouldn't have it. So.'

'Weren't you – '

'I didn't want a baby. It would have got in the way.' But she added more gently, 'Yes, I was.'

'And still?'

A silence, a small shrug.

'Sometimes.'

I couldn't see her face. We sat in silence, close and warm, both aware that we were close and aware that we were embarrassed by the implications of this talk about children. In our age it is not sex that raises its ugly head, but love.

One evening we went to see Carné's old film *Quai des Brumes*. She was crying when we came out and she began to cry again when we were in bed. She sensed my disapproval.

'You're not me. You can't feel like I feel.'

'I can feel.'

'No, you can't. You just choose not to feel or something, and everything's fine.'

'It's not fine. It's just not so bad.'

'That film made me feel what I feel about everything. There isn't any meaning. You try and try to be happy and then something chance happens and it's all gone. It's because we don't believe in a life after death.'

'Not don't. Can't.'

'Every time you go out and I'm not with you I think you may die. I think about dying every day. Every time I have you, I think this is one in the eye for death. You know, you've got a lot of money and the shops are going to shut in an hour. It's sick, but you've got to spend. Does that make sense?'

'Of course. The bomb.'

She lay smoking.

'It's not the bomb. It's us.'

She didn't fall for the solitary heart; she had a nose for emotional blackmail. She thought it must be nice to be totally alone in the world, to have no family ties. When I was going on one day in the car about not having any close friends – using my favourite metaphor: the cage of glass between me and the rest of the world – she just laughed. 'You like it,' she said. 'You say you're isolated, boyo, but you really think you're different.' She broke my hurt silence by saying, too late, 'You are different.'

'And isolated.'

She shrugged. 'Marry someone. Marry me.'

She said it as if she had suggested I try an aspirin for a headache. I kept my eyes on the road.

'You're going to marry Pete.'

'And you wouldn't marry me because I'm a whore and a colonial.'

'I wish you wouldn't use that word.'

'And because you wish I wouldn't use that word.'

Always we edged away from the brink of the future. We talked about *a* future, about living in a cottage, where I should write, about buying a jeep and crossing Australia. 'When we're in Alice Springs … ' became a sort of joke – in never-never land.

One day drifted and melted into another. I knew the affaire was like no other I had been through. Apart from anything else it was so much happier physically. Out of bed I felt I was teaching her, anglicizing her accent, polishing off her roughnesses, her provincialisms; in bed she did the teaching. We knew this reciprocity without being able, perhaps because we were both single children, to analyse it. We both had something to give and to gain … and at the same time a physical common ground, the same appetites, the same tastes, the same freedom from inhibition. She was teaching me other things, besides the art of love; but that is how I thought of it at the time.

I remember one day when we were standing in one of the rooms at the Tate. Alison was leaning slightly against me, holding my hand, looking in her childish sweet-sucking way at a Renoir. I suddenly had a feeling that we were one body, one person, even there; that if she had disappeared it would have been as if I had lost half of myself. A terrible deathlike feeling, which anyone less cerebral and self-absorbed than I was then would have realized was simply love. I thought it was desire. I drove her straight home and tore her clothes off.

Another day, in Jermyn Street, we ran into Billy Whyte, an Old Etonian I had known quite well at Magdalen; he'd been one of the Hommes Révoltés. He was pleasant enough, not in the least snobbish – but he carried with him, perhaps in spite of himself, an unsloughable air of high caste, of constant contact with the nicest best people, of impeccable upper-class taste in facial expression, clothes, vocabulary. We went off to an oyster bar; he'd just heard the first Colchesters of the season were in. Alison said very little, but I was embarrassed by her, by her accent, by the difference between her and one or two debs who were sitting near us. She left us for a moment when Billy poured the last of the Muscadet.

'Nice girl, dear boy.'
'Oh ... ' I shrugged. 'You know.'
'Attractive.'
'Cheaper than central heating.'
'I'm sure.'
But I knew what he was thinking.

Alison was very silent after we left him. We were driving up to Hampstead to see a film. I glanced at her sullen face.

'What's wrong?'
'Sometimes you sound so mean, you upper-class Poms.'
'I'm not upper-class. I'm middle-class.'
'Upper, middle – God, who cares.'
I drove some way before she spoke again.
'You treated me as if I didn't really belong to you.'
'Don't be silly.'
'As if I'm a bloody abo.'
'Rubbish.'
'In case my pants fell down or something.'
'It's so difficult to explain.'
'Not to me, sport. Not to me.'

One day she said, 'I've got to go for my interview tomorrow.'
'Do you want to go?'
'Do you want me to go?'
'It doesn't mean anything. You haven't got to make up your mind.'

36

'It'll do me good if I get accepted. Just to know I'm accepted.'

She changed the subject; and I could have refused to change the subject. But I didn't.

Then, the very next day, I too had a letter about an interview. Alison's took place – she thought she had done well. Three days later she received a letter saying that she had been accepted for training, to start in ten days' time.

I had my own examination from a board of urbane officials. She met me outside and we went for an awkward meal, like two strangers, in an Italian restaurant. She had a grey, tired face, and her cheeks looked baggy. I asked her what she'd been doing while I was away.

'Writing a letter.'

'To them?'

'Yes.'

'Saying?'

'What do you think I said?'

'You accepted.'

There was a difficult pause. I knew what she wanted me to say, but I couldn't say it. I felt as a sleepwalker must feel when he wakes up at the end of the roof parapet. I wasn't ready for marriage, for settling down. I wasn't psychologically close enough to her; something I couldn't define, obscure, monstrous, lay between us, and this obscure monstrous thing emanated from her, not from me.

'Some of their flights go via Athens. If you're in Greece we can meet. Maybe you'll be in London. Anyway.'

We began to plan how we would live if I didn't get the job in Greece.

But I did. A letter came, saying my name had been selected to be forwarded to the school board in Athens. This was 'virtually a formality'. I should be expected in Greece at the beginning of October.

I showed Alison the letter as soon as I had climbed the stairs back to the flat, and watched her read it. I was looking for regret, but I couldn't see it. She kissed me.

'I told you.'

'I know.'

'Let's celebrate. Let's go out into the country'.

I let her carry me away. She wouldn't take it seriously, and I was too much of a coward to stop and think why I was secretly hurt by her refusing to take it seriously. So we went out into the country, and when we came back we went to see a film and later went dancing in Soho; and still she wouldn't take it seriously. But then, late, after love, we couldn't sleep, and we had to take it seriously.

'Alison, what am I going to do tomorrow?'

'You're going to accept.'

'Do you want me to accept?'

'Not all over again.'

We were lying on our backs, and I could see her eyes were open. Somewhere down below little leaves in front of a lamp-post cast nervous shadows across our ceiling.

'If I say what I feel about you, will you ... '

'I know what you feel.'

And it was there: an accusing silence.

I reached out and touched her bare stomach. She pushed my hand away, but held it. 'You feel, I feel, what's the good. It's what *we* feel. What you feel is what I feel. I'm a woman.'

I was frightened; and calculated my answer.

'Would you marry me if I asked you?'

'You can't say it like that.'

'I'd marry you tomorrow if I thought you really needed me. Or wanted me.'

'Oh Nicko, Nicko.' Rain lashed on the window-panes. She beat my hand on the bed between us. There was a long silence.

'I've just got to get out of this country.'

She didn't answer; more silence, and then she spoke.

'Pete's coming back to London next week.'

'What will he do?'

'Don't worry. He knows.'

'How do you know he knows?'

'I wrote to him.'

'Has he answered?'

She breathed out. 'No strings.'

'Do you want to go back to him?'

She turned on her elbow and made me turn my head, so that our faces were very close together.

'Ask me to marry you.'

'Will you marry me?'

'No.' She turned away.

'Why did you do that?'

'To get it over. I'm going to be an air hostess, and you're going to Greece. You're free.'

'And you're free.'

'If it makes you happier – I'm free.'

The rain came in sudden great swathes across the tree-tops and hit the windows and the roof; like spring rain, out of season. The bedroom air seemed full of unspoken words, unformulated guilts, a vicious silence, like the moments before a bridge collapses. We lay side by side, untouching, effigies on a bed turned tomb; sickeningly afraid to say what we really thought. In the end she spoke, in a voice that tried to be normal, but sounded harsh.

'I don't want to hurt you and the more I … want you, the more I shall. And I don't want you to hurt me and the more you don't want me the more you will.' She got out of bed for a moment. When she came back she said, 'We've decided?'

'I suppose.'

We said no more. Soon, too soon, I thought, she went to sleep.

In the morning she was determinedly gay. I telephoned the Council. I went to receive Miss Spencer-Haigh's congratulations and briefings, and took her out for a second and – I prayed – last lunch.

5

What Alison was not to know – since I hardly realized it myself – was that I had been deceiving her with another woman during the latter part of September. The woman was Greece. Even if I had failed the board I should have gone there. I never studied Greek at school, and my knowledge of modern Greece began and ended with Byron's death at Missolonghi. Yet it needed only the seed of the idea of Greece, that morning in the British Council. It was as if someone had hit on a brilliant solution when all seemed lost. Greece – why hadn't I thought of it before? It sounded so good: '*I'm going to Greece.*' I knew no one – this was long before the new Medes, the tourists, invaded – who had been there. I got hold of all the books I could find on the country. It astounded me how little I knew about it. I read and read; and I was like a medieval king, I had fallen in love with the picture long before I saw the reality.

It seemed almost a secondary thing, by the time I left, that I wanted to escape from England. I thought of Alison only in terms of my going to Greece. When I loved her, I thought of being there with her; when I didn't, then I was there without her. She had no chance.

I received a cable from the school board confirming my appointment, and then by post a contract to sign and a courteous letter in atrocious English from my new headmaster. Miss Spencer-Haigh produced the name and address in Northumberland of a man who had been at the school the year before. He hadn't been appointed by the British Council, so she could tell me nothing about him. I wrote a letter, but that was unanswered. Ten days remained before I was due to go.

Things became very difficult with Alison. I had to give up the flat in Russell Square and we spent three frustrating days looking for somewhere for her to live. Eventually we found a large studio-room off Baker Street. The move, packing things, upset us both. I didn't have to go until October 2nd, but Alison had already started work, and the need to get up early, to introduce order into our life, was too much for us. We had two dreadful rows. The first one she started, and stoked, and built up to a white-hot outpouring of contempt for men, and me in particular. I was a snob, a prig, a twopenny-halfpenny Don Juan – and so on. The next day – she had been icily mute at breakfast – when I went in the evening to meet her, she was not there. I waited an hour, then I went home. She wasn't there, either. I telephoned: no air-hostess trainees had been kept late. I waited, getting angrier and angrier, until eleven o'clock, and then she came in. She went to the bathroom, took her coat off, put on the milk she always had before bed, and said not a word.

'Where the hell have you been?'

'I'm not going to answer any questions.'

She stood over the stove in the kitchen recess. She had insisted on a cheap room. I loathed the cooking-sleeping-everything in one room; the shared bathroom; the having to hiss and whisper.

'I know where you've been.'

'I'm not interested.'

'You've been with Pete.'

'All right. I've been with Pete.' She gave me a furious dark look. 'So?'

'You could have waited till Thursday.'

'Why should I?'

Then I lost my temper. I dragged up everything I could remember that might hurt her. She didn't say anything, but undressed and got into bed, and lay with her face turned to the wall. She began to cry. In the silence I kept remembering, with intense relief, that I should soon be free of all this. It was not that I believed my own accusations; but I still hated her for having made me make them. In the end I sat beside her and watched the tears trickle out of her swollen eyes.

'I waited hours for you.'

'I went to the cinema. I haven't seen Pete.'

'Why lie about it?'

'Because you can't trust me. As if I'd do that.'

'This is such a lousy way to end.'

'I could have killed myself tonight. If I'd had the courage, I'd have thrown myself under the train. I stood there and thought of doing it.'

'I'll get you a whisky.' I came back with it and gave it to her.

'I wish to God you'd live with someone. Isn't there another air hostess who'd –'

'I'm never going to live with another woman again.'

'Are you going back to Pete?'

She gave me an angry look.

'Are you trying to tell me I shouldn't?'

'No.'

She sank back and stared at the wall. For the first time she gave a faint smile. The whisky was beginning to work. 'It's like those Hogarth pictures. Love *à la mode*. Five weeks later.'

'Are we friends again?'

'We can't ever be friends again.'

'If it hadn't been you, I'd have walked out this evening.'

'If it hadn't been you I wouldn't have come back.'

She held out her glass for more whisky. I kissed her wrist, and went to fetch the bottle.

'You know what I thought today?' She said it across the room.

'No.'

'If I killed myself, you'd be pleased. You'd be able to go round saying, she killed herself because of me. I think that would always keep me from suicide. Not letting some lousy shit like you get the credit.'

'That's not fair.'

'Then I thought I could do it if I wrote a note first explaining why I did it.' She eyed me, still unmollified. 'Look in my handbag. The shorthand pad.' I got it out. 'Look at the back.'

There were two pages scrawled in her big handwriting.

'When did you write this?'

'Read it.'

I don't want to live any more. I spend most of my life not wanting to live. The only place I am happy is here where we're being taught, and I have to think of something else, or reading books, or in the cinema. Or in bed. I'm only happy when I forget to exist. When just my eyes or my ears or my skin exist. I can't remember having been happy for two or three years. Since the abortion. All I can remember is forcing myself sometimes to look happy so if I catch sight of my face in the mirror I might kid myself for a moment I really am happy.

There were two more sentences heavily crossed out. I looked up into her grey eyes.

'You can't mean this.'

'I wrote it today in coffee-time. If I'd known how to quietly kill myself in the canteen I'd have done it.'

'It's ... well, hysterical.'

'I *am* hysterical.' It was almost a shout.

'And histrionic. You wrote it for me to see.'

There was a long pause. She kept her eyes shut.

'Not just for you to *see*.'

And then she cried again, but this time in my arms. I tried to reason with her. I made promises: I would postpone the journey to Greece, I would turn down the job – a hundred things that I didn't mean and she knew I didn't mean, but finally took as a placebo.

In the morning I persuaded her to ring up and say that she wasn't well, and we spent the day out in the country.

The next morning, my last but two, came a postcard with a Northumberland postmark. It was from Mitford, the man who had been on Phraxos, to say that he would be in London for a few days, if I wanted to meet him.

I rang him up on the Wednesday at the Army and Navy Club and asked him out for a drink. He was two or three years older than myself, tanned, with blue staring eyes in a narrow head. He had a dark young-officer moustache which he kept on touching, and he wore a dark-blue blazer, with a regimental tie. He reeked mufti; and almost at once we started a guerilla war of prestige and anti-prestige. He had been parachuted into Greece during the German occupation, and he was very glib with his Xans and his Paddys and the Christian names of all the other well-known *condottieri* of the time. He had tried hard to acquire the triune personality of the philhellene in fashion – gentleman, scholar, thug – but he spoke with a second-hand accent and the clipped, sparse prep-schoolisms of a Viscount Montgomery. He was dogmatic, unbrooking, lost off the battlefield. I managed to keep my end up, over pink gins: I told him my war had consisted of two years' ardent longing for demobilization. It was absurd. I wanted information from him, not antipathy; so in the end I confessed I was a regular army officer's son, and asked him what the island looked like.

He nodded at the food-stand on the bar in the pub where we'd met. 'There's the island.' He pointed with his cigarette. 'That's what the locals call it.' He said some word in Greek. 'The Pasty. Shape, old boy. Central ridge. Here's your school and your village in this corner. All the rest of this north side and the entire south side deserted. That's the lie of the land.'

'The school?'

'Best in Greece, actually.'

'Discipline?' He stiffened his hand *karate*-fashion.

'Teaching problems?'

'Usual stuff.' He preened his moustache in the mirror behind the bar; mentioned the names of two or three books.

I asked him about life outside the school.

'Isn't any. Island's quite pretty, if you like that sort of thing. Birds and the bees, all that caper.'

'And the village?'

He smiled grimly. 'Old boy, your Greek village isn't like an English one. Absolute bloody dump socially. Masters' wives. Half a dozen officials. Odd pater and mater on a visit.' He raised his neck, as if his shirt collar was too tight. It was a tic; made him feel authoritative. 'A few villas. But they're all boarded up for ten months of the year.'

'You're not exactly selling the place to me.'

'It's remote. Let's face it, bloody remote. And you'd find the people in the villas pretty damn dull, anyway. There's one that you might say isn't, but I don't suppose you'll meet him.'

'Oh?'

'Actually, we had a row and I told him pretty effing quick what I thought of him.'

'What was it all about?'

'Bastard collaborated during the war. That was really at the root of it.' He exhaled smoke. 'No – you'll have to put up with the other beaks if you want chat.'

'They speak English?'

'Most of 'em speak Frog. There's the Greek chap who teaches English with you. Cocky little bastard. Gave him a black eye one day.'

'You've really prepared the ground for me.'

He laughed. 'Got to keep 'em down, you know.' He felt his mask had slipped a little. 'Your peasant, especially your Cretan peasant, salt of the earth. Wonderful chaps. Believe me. I know.'

I asked him why he'd left.

'Writing a book actually. Wartime experiences and all that. See my publisher.'

There was something forlorn about him; I could imagine him briskly dashing about like a destructive Boy Scout, blowing up bridges and wearing picturesque off-beat uniforms; but he had to live in this dull new welfare world, like a stranded archosaur. He went hurriedly on.

'You'll piss blood for England. Be worse for you, with no Greek. And you'll drink. Everyone does. Have to.' He talked about *retsina* and *aretsinato, raki* and *ouzo* – and then about women. 'The girls in Athens are strictly O.O.B. Unless you want the pox.'

'No talent on the island?'

'Nix, old boy. Women are about the ugliest in the Aegean. And anyway – village honour. Makes that caper highly dangerous. Shouldn't advise it. Discovered that somewhere else once.' He gave me a curt grin, with the appropriate hooded look in his eyes.

I drove him back towards his club. It was a bronchial mid-afternoon, already darkening, the people, the traffic, everything fish-grey. I asked him why he hadn't stayed in the Army.

'Too damn orthodox, old boy. Specially in peacetime.'

I guessed that he had been rejected for a permanent commission; there was something obscurely wild and unstable about him, under the mess mannerisms.

We came to where he wanted to be dropped off.

'Think I'll do?'

His look was doubtful. 'Treat 'em tough. It's the only way. Never let 'em get you down. They did the chap before me, you know. Never met him, but apparently he went bonkers. Couldn't control the boys.'

He got out of the car.

'Well, all the best, old man.' He grinned. 'And listen.' He had his hand on the door-handle. 'Beware of the waiting-room.'

He closed the door at once, as if he had rehearsed that moment. I opened it quickly and leant out to call after him. 'The *what*?'

He turned, but only to give a sharp wave. The Trafalgar Square crowd swallowed him up. I couldn't get the smile on his face out of my mind. It secreted an omission; something he'd saved up, a mysterious last word. Waiting-room, waiting-room, waiting-room; it went round in my head all that evening.

6

I picked up Alison and we went to the garage that was going to sell the car for me. I'd offered it to her some time before, but she had refused.

'If I had it I'd always think of you.'

'Then have it.'

'I don't want to think of you. And I couldn't stand anyone else sitting where you are.'

'Will you take whatever I get for it? It won't be much.'

'My wages?'

'Don't be silly.'

'I don't want anything.'

But I knew she wanted a scooter. I could leave a cheque with 'Towards a scooter' on a card, and I thought she would take that, when I had gone.

It was curious how quiet that last evening was; as if I had already left, and we were two ghosts talking to each other. We arranged what we should do in the morning. She didn't want to come and see me off – I was going by train – at Victoria; we would have breakfast as usual, she would go, it was cleanest and simplest that way. We arranged our future. As soon as she could she would try to get herself to Athens. If that was impossible, I might fly back to England at Christmas. We might meet halfway somewhere – Rome, Switzerland.

'Alice Springs,' she said.

In the night we lay awake, knowing each other awake, yet afraid to talk. I felt her hand feel out for mine. We lay for a while without talking. Then she spoke.

'If I said I'd wait?' I was silent. 'I think I could wait. That's what I mean.'

'I know.'

'You're always saying "I know". But it doesn't answer anything.'

'I know.' She pinched my hand. 'Suppose I say, yes, wait, in a year's time I shall know. All the time you'll be waiting, waiting.'

'I wouldn't mind.'

'But it's mad. It's like putting a girl in a convent till you're ready to marry her. And then deciding you don't want to marry her. We have to be free. We haven't got a choice.'

'Don't get upset. Please don't get upset.'

'We've got to see how things go.'

There was a silence.

'I was thinking of coming back here tomorrow night. That's all.'

'I'll write. Every day.'

'Yes.'

'It's a sort of test, really. We'll see how much we miss each other.'

'I know what it's like when people go away. It's agony for a week, then painful for a week, then you begin to forget, and then it seems as if it never happened, it happened to someone else, and you start shrugging. You say, dingo, it's life, that's the way things are. Stupid things like that. As if you haven't really lost something for ever.'

'I shan't forget. I shan't ever forget.'

'You will. And I will.'

'We've got to go on living. However sad it is.'

After a long time she said, 'I don't think you know what sadness is.'

We overslept in the morning. I had deliberately set the alarm late, to make a rush, not to leave time for tears. Alison ate her breakfast standing up. We talked about absurd things; cutting the milk order, where a library ticket I had lost might be. And then she put down her coffee-cup and we were standing at the door. I saw her face, as if it was still not too late, all a bad dream, her grey eyes searching mine, her small puffy cheeks. There were tears forming in her eyes, and she opened her mouth to say something. But then she leant forward, desperately, clumsily, kissed me so swiftly that I hardly felt her mouth; and was gone. Her camel-hair coat disappeared down the stairs. She didn't look back. I went to the window, and saw her walking fast across the street, the pale coat, the straw-coloured hair almost the same colour as the coat, a movement of her hand to her handbag, her blowing her nose; not once did she look back. She broke into a run. I opened the window and leant out and watched until she disappeared round the corner at the end of the street into

Marylebone Road. And not even then, at the very end, did she look back.

I turned to the room, washed up the breakfast things, made the bed; then I sat at the table and wrote out a cheque for fifty pounds, and a little note.

Alison darling, please believe that if it was to be anyone, it would have been you; that I've really been far sadder than I could show, if we were not both to go mad. Please wear the ear-rings. Please take this money and buy a scooter and go where we used to go – or do what you want with it. Please look after yourself. Oh God, if only I was worth waiting for ...

NICHOLAS

It was supposed to sound spontaneous, but I had been composing it on and off for days. I put the cheque and the note in an envelope, and set it on the mantelpiece with the little box containing the pair of jet ear-rings we had seen in a closed antique-shop one day. Then I shaved and went out to get a taxi.

The thing I felt most clearly, when the first corner was turned, was that I had escaped; and hardly less clearly, but much more odiously, that she loved me more than I loved her, and that consequently I had in some indefinable way won. So on top of the excitement of the voyage into the unknown, the taking wing again, I had an agreeable feeling of emotional triumph. A dry feeling; but I liked things dry. I went towards Victoria as a hungry man goes towards a good dinner after a couple of glasses of Mananzilla. I began to hum, and it was not a brave attempt to hide my grief, but a revoltingly unclouded desire to celebrate my release.

7

Four days later I was standing on Hymettus, looking down over the great complex of Athens-Piraeus, cities and suburbs, houses split like a million dice over the Attic plain. South stretched the pure blue late-summer sea, pale pumice-coloured islands, and beyond them the serene mountains of the Peloponnesus stood away over the horizon in a magnificent arrested flow of land and water. Serene, superb, majestic: I tried for adjectives less used, but anything else seemed underweight. I could see for eighty miles, and all pure, all noble, luminous, immense, all as it always had been.

It was like a journey into space. I was standing on Mars, knee-deep in thyme, under a sky that seemed never to have known dust or cloud. I looked down at my pale London hands. Even they seemed changed, nauseatingly alien, things I should long ago have disowned.

When that ultimate Mediterranean light fell on the world around me, I could see it was supremely beautiful; but when it touched me, I felt it was hostile. It seemed to corrode, not cleanse. It was like being at the beginning of an interrogation under arc-lights; already I could see the table with straps through the open doorway, already my old self began to know that it wouldn't be able to hold out. It was partly the terror, the stripping-to-essentials, of love; because I fell totally and for ever in love with the Greek landscape from the moment I arrived. But with the love came a contradictory, almost irritating, feeling of impotence and inferiority, as if Greece were a woman so sensually provocative that I must fall physically and desperately in love with her, and at the same time so calmly aristocratic that I should never be able to approach her.

None of the books I had read explained this sinister-fascinating, this Circe-like quality of Greece; the quality that makes it unique. In England we live in a very muted, calm, domesticated relationship with what remains of our natural landscape and its soft northern light; in Greece landscape and light are so beautiful, so all-present, so intense, so wild, that the relationship is immediately love-hatred, one of passion. It took me many months to understand this, and many years to accept it.

Later that day I was standing at the window of a room in the hotel to which the bored young man who received me at the British Council had directed me. I had just written a letter to Alison, but already she seemed far away, not in distance, not in time, but in some dimension for which there is no name. Reality, perhaps. I looked down over Constitution Square, the central meeting-place of Athens, over knots of strolling people, white shirts, dark glasses, bare brown arms. A sibilant murmur rose from the crowds sitting at the café tables. It was as hot as a hot English July day, and the sky was still perfectly clear. By craning out and looking east I could see Hymettus, where I had stood that morning, its sunset-facing slope an intense soft violet-pink, like a cyclamen. In the other direction, over the clutter of roofs, lay the massive black silhouette of the Acropolis. It was too exactly as imagined to be true. But I felt as gladly and expectantly disorientated, as happily and alertly alone, as Alice in Wonderland.

Phraxos lay eight dazzling hours in a small steamer south of Athens, about six miles off the mainland of the Peloponnesus and in the centre of a landscape as memorable as itself: to the north and west, a great fixed arm of mountains, in whose crook the island stood; to the east a distant gently-peaked archipelago; to the south the soft blue desert of the Aegean stretching away to Crete. Phraxos was beautiful. There was no other adjective; it was not just pretty, picturesque, charming – it was simply and effortlessly beautiful. It took my breath away when I first saw it, floating under Venus like a majestic black whale in an amethyst evening sea, and it still takes my breath away when I shut my eyes now and remember it. Its beauty was rare even in the Aegean, because its hills were covered with pine trees, Mediterranean pines as light as greenfinch feathers. Nine-tenths of the island was un-inhabited and uncultivated: nothing but pines, coves, silence, sea. Herded into one corner, the north-west, lay a spectacular agglomeration of snow-white houses round a couple of small harbours.

But there were two eyesores, visible long before we landed. One was an obese Greek-Edwardian hotel near the larger of the two harbours, as at home on Phraxos as a hansom cab in a Doric temple. The other, equally at odds with the landscape, stood on the outskirts of the village and dwarfed the cottages around it: a dauntingly long building several storeys high and reminiscent, in spite of its ornate Corinthian façade, of a factory – a likeness more than just visually apt, as I was to discover.

But the Lord Byron School, the Hotel Philadelphia, and the village apart, the body of the island, all thirty square miles of it, was virgin. There were some silvery olive-orchards and a few patches of terrace cultivation on the steep slopes of the north coast, but the rest was primeval pine-forest. There were no antiquities. The ancient Greeks never much liked the taste of cistern-water.

This lack of open water meant also that there were no wild animals and few birds on the island. Its distinguishing characteristic, away from the village, was silence. Out on the hills one might pass a goatherd and his winter flock (in summer there was no grazing) of bronze-belled goats, or a bowed peasant-woman carrying a huge faggot, or a resin-gatherer; but one very rarely did. It was the world before the machine, almost before man, and what small events happened – the passage of a shrike, the discovery of a new path, a glimpse of a distant caïque far below – took on an unaccountable significance, as if they were isolated, framed, magnified by solitude. It was the least eerie, the most un-Nordic solitude in the world. Fear had never touched the island. If it was haunted, it was by nymphs, not monsters.

I was forced to go frequently for walks to escape the claustrophobic ambience of the Lord Byron School. To begin with there was something pleasantly absurd about teaching in a boarding school (run on supposedly Eton–Harrow lines) only a look north from where Clytemnestra killed Agamemnon. Certainly the masters, victims of a country with only two universities, were academically of a far higher standard than Mitford had suggested, and in themselves the boys were no better and no worse than boys the world over. But they were ruthlessly pragmatic about English. They cared nothing for literature, and everything for science. If I tried to read the school eponym's poetry with them, they yawned; if I taught the English names for the parts of a car, I had trouble getting them out of the class at lesson's end; and often they would bring me American scientific textbooks full of terms that were just as much Greek to me as the expectant faces waiting for a simple paraphrase.

Both boys and masters loathed the island, and regarded it as a sort of self-imposed penal settlement where one came to work, work, work. I had imagined something far sleepier than an English school, and instead it was far tougher. The crowning irony was that this obsessive industry, this mole-like blindness to their natural environment, was what was considered to be so typically English about the system. Perhaps to Greeks, made blasé by living among the most beautiful landscapes in the world, there was nothing discordant in being cooped up in such a termitary; but it drove me mad with irritation.

One or two of the masters spoke some English, and several French, but I found little in common with them. The only one I could tolerate was Demetriades, the other teacher of English, and that was solely because he spoke and understood the language so much more fluently than anyone else. With him I could rise out of Basic.

He took me round the village *kapheneia* and tavernas, and I got a taste for Greek food and Greek folk music. But there was always something mournful about the place in daylight. There were so many villas boarded up; there were so few people in the alley-streets; one had always to go to the same two better-class tavernas for a meal, and one met the same old faces, a stale Levantine provincial society that belonged more to the world of the Ottoman Empire, Balzac in a fez, than to the 1950s. I had to agree with Mitford: it was desperately dull. I tried one or two of the fishermen's wine-shops. They were jollier, but I felt they felt I was slumming; and my Greek never rose to the island dialect they spoke.

I made inquiries about the man Mitford had had a row with, but no one seemed to have heard of either him or it; or, for that matter, of the 'waiting-room'. Mitford had evidently spent a lot of time in the village, and made himself unpopular with other masters besides Demetriades. There was also a heavy aftermath of anglophobia, aggravated by the political situation at that time, to be endured.

Soon I took to the hills. None of the other masters ever stirred an inch farther than they needed to, and the boys were not allowed beyond the *chevaux de frise* of the high-walled school grounds except on Sundays, and then only for the half-mile along the coast road to the village. The hills were always intoxicatingly clean and light and remote. With no company but my own boredom, I began for the first time in my life to look at nature, and to regret that I knew its language as little as I knew Greek. I became aware of stones, birds, flowers, land, in a new way, and the walking, the swimming, the magnificent climate, the absence of all traffic, ground or air – for there wasn't a single car on the island, there being no roads outside the village, and aeroplanes passed over not once a month – these things made me feel healthier than I had ever felt before. I began to get some sort of harmony between body and mind; or so it seemed. It was an illusion.

There had been a letter from Alison waiting for me when I arrived at the school. It was very brief. She must have written it at work the day I left London.

> I love you, you can't understand what that means because you've never loved anyone yourself. It's what I've been trying to make you see this last week. All I want to say is that one day, when you do fall in love, remember today. Remember I kissed you and walked out of the room. Remember I walked all the way down the street and never once looked back. I knew you were watching. Remember I did all this and I love you. If you forget everything else about me, please remember this. I walked down that street and I never looked back and I love you. I love you. I love you so much that I shall hate you for ever for today.

Another letter came from her the next day. It contained nothing but my cheque torn in two and a scribble on the back of one half: 'No thanks.' And two days later there was a third letter, full of enthusiasm for some film she had been to see, almost a chatty letter. But at the end she wrote: 'Forget the first letter I sent you. I was so upset. It's all over now. I won't be old-fashioned again.'

Of course I wrote back, if not every day, two or three times a week; long letters full of self-excuse and self-justification, until one day she wrote,

> Please don't go on so about you and me. Tell me about things, about the island, the school. I know what you are. So be what you are. When you write about things I can think I'm with you, seeing them with you. And don't be offended. Forgiving's forgetting.

Imperceptibly information took the place of emotion in our letters. She wrote to me about her work, a girl she had become friendly with, about minor domestic things, films, books. I wrote about the school and the island, as she asked. One day there was a photograph of her in her uniform. She'd had her hair cut short and it was tucked back under her fore-and-aft cap. She was smiling, but the uniform and the smile combined gave her an insincere, professional look; she had become, the photo sharply warned me, someone not the someone I liked to remember; the private, the uniquely my, Alison. And then the letters became once-weekly. The physical ache I had felt for her during the first month seemed to disappear; there were still times when I knew I wanted her very much, and would have given anything to have her in bed beside me. But they were moments of sexual frustration, not regretted love. One day I thought: if I wasn't on this island I should be dropping this girl. The writing of the letters had become as often as not more of a chore than a pleasure, and I didn't hurry back to my room after dinner to write them – I scribbled them off hurriedly in class and got a boy to run down to the gate at the last minute to give them to the school postman.

At half-term I went with Demetriades to Athens. He wanted to take me to his favourite brothel, in a suburb. He assured me the girls were clean. I hesitated, then – isn't it a poet's, to say nothing of a cynic's, moral duty to be immoral? – I went. When we came out, it was raining, and the shadowing wet leaves on the lower branches of a eucalyptus, caught under a light in the entrance, made me remember our bedroom in Russell Square. But Alison and London were gone, dead, exorcized; I had cut them away from my life. I decided I would write a letter to Alison that night, to say that I didn't want to hear from her again. I was too drunk by the time we got back to the hotel, and I don't know what I would have said. Perhaps that I had proved beyond doubt that I was not worth waiting for; perhaps that she bored me; perhaps that I was lonelier than ever – and wanted to stay that way. As it was, I sent her a postcard telling her nothing; and on the last day I went back to the brothel alone. But the Lebanese nymphet I coveted was taken, and I didn't fancy the others.

December came, and we were still writing letters. I knew she was hiding things from me. Her life, as she described it, was too simple and manless to be true. When the final letter came, I was not surprised. What I hadn't expected was how bitter I should feel, and how betrayed. It was less a sexual jealousy of the man than an envy of Alison; moments of tenderness and togetherness, moments when the otherness of the other disappeared, flooded back through my mind for days afterwards, like sequences from some cheap romantic film that I certainly didn't want to remember, but did; and there was the read and re-read letter; and that such things could be ended so, by two hundred stale, worn words.

Dear Nicholas,

I can't go on any more. I'm so sorry if this hurts you. Please believe that I'm sorry, please don't be angry with me for knowing you will be hurt. I can hear you saying, I'm not hurt.

I got so terribly lonely and depressed. I haven't told you how much, I can't tell you how much. Those first days I kept up such a brave front at work, and then at home I collapsed.

I'm sleeping with Pete again when he's in London. It started two weeks ago. Please *please* believe me that I wouldn't be if I thought ... you know. I know you know. I don't feel about him as I used to do, and I don't begin to feel about him as I felt about you, you *can't* be jealous.

It's just he's so uncomplicated, he stops me thinking, he stops me being lonely, I've sunk back into all the old Australians-in-London thing again. We may marry. I don't know.

It's terrible. I still want to write to you, and you to me. I keep on remembering.

Goodbye.

ALISON

You will be different for me. Always. That very first letter I wrote the day you left. If you could only understand.

I wrote a letter in reply to say that I had been expecting her letter, that she was perfectly free. But I tore it up. If anything might hurt her, silence would; and I wanted to hurt her.

8

I was hopelessly unhappy in those last few days before the Christmas holidays. I began to loathe the school irrationally: the way it worked and the way it was planted, blind and prisonlike, in the heart of the divine landscape. When Alison's letters stopped, I was also increasingly isolated in a more conventional way. The outer world, England, London, became absurdly and sometimes terrifyingly unreal. The two or three Oxford friends I had kept up a spasmodic correspondence with sank beneath the horizon. I used to hear the B.B.C. Overseas Service from time to time, but the news broadcasts seemed to come from the moon, and concerned situations and a society I no longer belonged to, while the rare newspapers from England that I saw became more and more like their own 'One hundred years ago today' features. The whole island seemed to feel this exile from contemporary reality. The harbour quays were always crowded for hours before the daily boat from Athens appeared on the northeastern horizon; even though people knew that it would stop for only five minutes, that probably not five passengers would get off, or five get on, they had to watch. It was as if we were all convicts still hoping faintly for a reprieve.

Yet the island was so beautiful. Near Christmas the weather became wild and cold. Enormous seas of pounding Antwerp blue roared on the shingle of the school beaches. The mountains on the mainland took snow, and magnificent white shoulders out of Hokusai stood west and north across the angry water. The hills became even barer, even more silent. I often started off on a walk out of sheer boredom, but there were always new solitudes, new places. Yet in the end this unflawed natural world became intimidating. I seemed to have no place in it, I could not use it and I was not made for it. I was a townsman; and I was rootless. I rejected my own age, yet could not sink back into an older. So I ended like Sciron, a mid-air man.

The Christmas holidays came. I went off to travel round the Peloponnesus. I had to be alone, to give myself a snatch of life away from the school. If Alison had been free, I would have flown back to England to meet her. I had thoughts of resigning; but then that seemed a retreat, another failure, and I told myself that things would be better once spring began. So I had Christmas alone in Sparta and I saw the New Year in alone in Pyrgos. I had a day in Athens before I caught the boat back to Phraxos, and visited the brothel again.

I thought very little about Alison, but I felt about her; that is, I tried to erase her, and failed. I had days when I thought I could stay celibate for the rest of my life – monastic days; and days when I ached for a conversable girl. The island women were of Albanian stock, dour and sallow-faced, and about as seducible as a Free Church congregation. Much more tempting were some of the boys, possessors of an olive grace and a sharp individuality that made them very different from their stereotyped English private-school equivalents – those uniformed pink ants out of the Arnold mould. I had Gide-like moments, but they were not reciprocated, because nowhere is pederasty more abominated than in bourgeois Greece; there at least Arnold would have felt thoroughly at home. Besides, I wasn't queer; I simply understood (nailing a lie in my own education) how being queer might have its consolations. It was not only the solitude – it was Greece. It made conventional English notions of what was moral and immoral ridiculous; whether or not I did the socially unforgivable seemed in itself merely a matter of appetite, like smoking or not smoking a new brand of cigarette – as trivial as that, from a moral point of view. Goodness and beauty may be separable in the north, but not in Greece. Between skin and skin there is only light.

And there was my poetry. I had begun to write poems about the island, about Greece, that seemed to me philosophically profound and technically exciting. I dreamt more and more of literary success. I spent hours staring at the wall of my room, imagining reviews, letters written to me by celebrated fellow-poets, fame and praise and still more fame. I did not at that time know Emily Dickinson's great definition, her 'Publication is not the business of poets'; being a poet is all, being known as a poet is nothing. The onanistic literary picture of myself I caressed up out of reality began to dominate my life. The school became a convenient scapegoat – how could one compose flawless verse if one was surrounded by futile routine?

But then, one bleak March Sunday, the scales dropped from my eyes. I read the Greek poems and saw them for what they were: undergraduate pieces, without rhythm, without structure, their banalities of perception clumsily concealed under an impasto of lush rhetoric. In horror I turned to other poems I had written – at Oxford, in East Anglia. They were no better; even worse. The truth rushed down on me like a burying avalanche. I was not a poet.

I felt no consolation in this knowledge, but only a red anger that evolution could allow such sensitivity and such inadequacy to co-exist in the same mind. In one ego, my ego, screaming like a hare caught in a gin. Taking all the poems I had ever written, page by slow page, I tore each one into tiny fragments, till my fingers ached.

Then I went for a walk in the hills, even though it was very cold and began to pour with rain. The whole world had finally declared itself against me. Here was something I could not shrug off, an ab-solute condemnation. One aspect of even my worse experiences had always been that they were fuel, ore; finally utilizable, not all waste and suffering. Poetry had always seemed something I could turn to in need – an emergency exit, a lifebuoy, as well as a justification. Now I was in the sea, and the lifebuoy had sunk, like lead. It was an effort not to cry tears of self-pity. My face set into a stiff mask, like that of an acroterion. I walked for hours and I was in hell.

One kind of person is engaged in society without realizing it; an-other kind engages in society by controlling it. The one is a gear, a cog, and the other an engineer, a driver. But a person who has opted out has only his ability to express his disengagement between his existence and nothingness. Not *cogito*, but *scribo, pingo, ergo sum*. For days after I felt myself filled with nothingness; with something more than the old physical and social loneliness – a metaphysical sense of being marooned. It was something almost tangible, like cancer or tuberculosis.

Then one day, not a week later, it was tangible: I woke up one morning and found I had two sores. I had been half expecting them. In late February I had gone to Athens, and paid another visit to the house in Kephissia. I knew I had taken a risk. At the time it hadn't seemed to matter.

For a day I was too shocked to act. There were two doctors in the village: one active, who had the school in his practice, and one, a taciturn old Rumanian, who though semi-retired still took a few patients. The school doctor was in and out of the common-room continually. I couldn't go to him. So I went to see Dr Patarescu.

He looked at the sores, and then at me, and shrugged.

'*Félicitations,*' he said.

'*C'est …* '

'*On va voir ça à Athènes. Je vous donnerai une adresse. C'est bien à Athènes que vous l'avez attrapé, oui?*' I nodded. '*Les poules là-bas. Infectes. Seulement les fous qui s'y laissent prendre.*'

He had an old yellow face and pince-nez; a malicious smile. My questions amused him. The chances were I could be cured; I was not contagious but I must have no sex, he could have treated me if he had had the right drug, benzathine penicillin, but he could not get it. He had heard one could get it at a certain private clinic in Athens, but I would have to pay through the nose; it would be eight weeks before we could be sure it had worked. He answered all my questions drily; all he could offer was the ancient arsenic and bismuth treatment, and I must in any case have a laboratory test first. He had long ago been drained of all sympathy for humanity, and he watched me with tortoise eyes as I put down the fee.

I stood in his doorway, still foolishly trying for his sympathy.

'*Je suis maudit.*'

He shrugged, and showed me out, totally indifferent, a sere notifier of what is.

It was too horrible. There was still a week to the end of term, and I thought of leaving at once and going back to England. Yet I couldn't bear the idea of London, and there was a sort of anonymity in Greece, if not on the island. I didn't really trust Dr Patarescu; one or two of the older masters were his cronies and I knew they often saw him for whist. I searched every smile, every word spoken to me, for a reference to what had happened; and I thought that the very next day I saw in various eyes a certain dry amusement. One morning during break the headmaster said, 'Cheer up, *kyrios* Urfe, or we shall say the beauties of Greece have made you sad.' I thought this was a direct reference; and the smiles that greeted the remark seemed to me to be more than it merited. Within three days of seeing the doctor I decided that everyone knew about my disease, even the boys. Every time they whispered I heard the word 'syphilis'.

Suddenly, in that same terrible week, the Greek spring was with us. In only two days, it seemed, the earth was covered with anemones, orchids, asphodels, wild gladioli; for once there were birds everywhere, on migration. Undulating lines of storks croaked overhead, the sky was blue, pure, the boys sang, and even the sternest masters smiled. The world around me took wing, and I was stuck to the ground; a Catullus without talent forced to inhabit a land that was Lesbia without mercy. I had hideous nights, in one of which I wrote a long letter to Alison, trying to explain what had happened to me, how I remembered what she had said in her letter in the canteen, how now I could believe her; how I loathed myself. Even then I managed to sound resentful, for my leaving her began to seem like the last and the worst of my bad gambles. I might have married her; at least I should have had a companion in the desert.

I did not post the letter, but again and again, night after night, I thought of suicide. It seemed to me that death had marked my family down, right back to those two uncles I had never known, one killed at Ypres and the other at Passchendaele; then my parents. All violent, pointless deaths, lost gambles. I was worse off than even Alison was; she hated life, I hated myself. I had created nothing, I belonged to nothingness, to the *néant*, and it seemed to me that my own death was the only thing left that I could create; and still, even then, I thought it might accuse everyone who had ever known me. It would validate all my cynicism, it would prove all my solitary selfishness; it would stand, and be remembered, as a final dark victory.

The day before term ended I felt the balance tip. I knew what to do. The gatekeeper at the school had an old twelve-bore, which he had once offered to lend me if I wanted to go shooting in the hills. I went and asked to borrow it. He was delighted and loaded my pocket with cartridges; the pine-forests were full of passage quail.

I walked up a gulley behind the school, climbed to a small saddle, and went into the trees. I was soon in shadow. To the north, across the water, the golden mainland still lay in the sun. The air was very light, warm, the sky of an intense luminous blue. A long way away, above me, I could hear the bells of a flock of goats being brought back to the village for the night. I walked for some time. It was like looking for a place to relieve oneself in; I had to be sure I couldn't be observed. At last I found a rocky hollow.

I put a cartridge in the gun, and sat on the ground, against the stem of a pine tree. All around me grape hyacinths pushed through the pine-needles. I reversed the gun and looked down the barrel, into the black O of my non-existence. I calculated the angle at which I should have to hold my head. I held the barrel against my right eye, turned my head so that the shot would mash like black lightning through the brain and blast the back wall of my scull off. I reached for the trigger – this was all testing, rehearsing – and found it difficult. In straining forward, I thought I might have to twist my head at the last moment and botch the job, so I searched and found a dead branch that would fit between the guard and the trigger. I took the cartridge out and slipped the stick in, and then sat with the gun between my knees, the soles of my shoes on the stick, the right barrel an inch from my eye. There was a click as the hammer fell. It was simple. I reloaded the cartridge.

From the hills behind came the solitary voice of a girl. She must have been bringing down the goats, and she was singing wildly, at the limit of her uninhibited voice; without any recognizable melody, in Turkish-Muslim intervals. It sounded disembodied, of place, not person. I remembered having heard a similar voice, perhaps this same girl's, singing one day on the hill behind the school. It had drifted down into the classroom, and the boys had begun to giggle. But now it seemed intensely mysterious, welling out of a solitude and suffering that made mine trivial and absurd. I sat with the gun across my knees, unable to move while the sound floated down through the evening air. I don't know how long she sang, but the sky darkened, the sea paled to a nacreous grey. Over the mountains there were pinkish bars of high cloud in the still strong light from the set sun. All the land and the sea held light, as if light was warmth, and did not fade as soon as the source was removed. But the voice dwindled towards the village; then died into silence.

I raised the gun again until the barrel was pointing at me. The stick projected, waiting for my feet to jerk down. The air was very silent. Many miles away I heard the siren of the Athens boat, approaching the island. But it was like something outside a vacuum. Death was now.

I did nothing. I waited. The afterglow, the palest yellow, then a luminous pale-green, then a limpid stained-glass blue, held in the sky over the sea of mountains to the west. I waited, I waited, I heard the siren closer, I waited for the will, the black moment, to come to raise my feet and kick down; and I could not. All the time I felt I was being watched, that I was not alone, that I was putting on an act for the benefit of someone, that this action could be done only if it was spontaneous, pure – and moral. Because more and more it crept through my mind with the chill spring night that I was trying to commit not a moral action, but a fundamentally aesthetic one; to do something that would end my life sensationally, significantly, consistently. It was a Mercutio death I was looking for, not a real one. A death to be remembered, not the true death of a true suicide, the death obliterate.

And the voice; the light; the sky.

It began to grow dark, the siren of the receding Athens boat moaned, and I still sat smoking, with the gun by my side. I re-evaluated myself. I saw that I was from now on, for ever, contemptible. I had been, and remained, intensely depressed, but I had also been, and always would be, intensely false; in existentialist terms, inauthentic. I knew I would never kill myself, I knew I would always want to go on living with myself, however hollow I became, however diseased.

I raised the gun and fired it blindly into the sky. The crash shook me. There was an echo, some falling twigs. Then the heavy well of silence.

'Did you kill anything?' asked the old man at the gate.

'One shot,' I said. 'I missed.'

9

Years later I saw the *gabbia* at Piacenza: a harsh black canary-cage strung high up the side of the towering campanile, in which prisoners were once left to starve to death and rot in full view of the town below. And looking up at it I remembered that winter in Greece, that *gabbia* I had constructed for myself out of light, solitude, and self-delusions. To write poetry and to commit suicide, apparently so contradictory, had really been the same, attempts at escape. And my feelings, at the end of that wretched term, were those of a man who knows he is in a cage, exposed to the jeers of all his old ambitions until he dies.

But I went to Athens, to the address the village doctor gave me. I was given a Kahn test and Dr Patarescu's diagnosis was confirmed. The ten days' treatment was very expensive; most of the drugs had been smuggled into Greece, or stolen, and I was at the receiving end of a Third Man network. The smooth young American-trained doctor told me not to worry; the prognosis was excellent. At the end of the Easter holidays, when I returned to the island, I found a card from Alison. It was a garishly coloured thing with a kangaroo on it balloon-saying 'Thought I'd forgot?' My twenty-sixth birthday had taken place while I was in Athens. The post-mark was Amsterdam. There was no message. It was simply signed 'Alison'. I threw it into the waste-paper basket. But that evening, I took it out again.

To get through the anxious wait for the secondary stage not to develop, I began quietly to rape the island. I swam and swam, I walked and walked, I went out every day. The weather rapidly became hot, and during the heat of the afternoon the school slept. Then I used to take off into the pine-forest. I always went over the central crest to the south side of the island if I could, away from the village and the school. There, was absolute solitude: three hidden cottages at one small bay, a few tiny chapels lost among the green downward of pines and deserted except on their saints' days, and one almost invisible villa, which was in any case empty. The rest was sublimely peaceful, as potential as a clean canvas, a site for myths. It was as if the island was split into dark and light; so that the teaching timetable, which made it difficult to go far except at week-ends or by getting up very early (school began at half past seven), became as irksome as a short tether.

I did not think about the future. In spite of what the doctor at the clinic had said I felt certain that the cure would fail. The pattern of destiny seemed clear: down and down, and down.

But then the mysteries began.

2

Irrités de ce premier crime, les monstres ne s'en tinrent pas là ; ils l'étendirent ensuite nue, à plat ventre sur une grande table, ils allumèrent des cierges, ils placèrent l'image de notre sauveur à sa tête et osèrent consommer sur les reins de cette malheureuse le plus redoutable de nos mystères.

De Sade, *Les Infortunes de la Vertu*

10

It was a Sunday in late May, blue as a bird's wing. I climbed up the goat-paths to the island's ridge-back, from where the green froth of the pine-tops rolled two miles down to the coast. The sea stretched like a silk carpet across to the shadowy wall of mountains on the mainland to the west, a wall that reverberated away south, fifty or sixty miles to the horizon, under the vast bell of the empyrean. It was an azure world, stupendously pure, and as always when I stood on the central ridge of the island and saw it before me, I forgot most of my troubles. I walked along the central ridge, westwards, between the two vast views north and south. Lizards flashed up the pine-trunks like living emerald necklaces. There was thyme and rosemary, and other herbs; bushes with flowers like dandelions dipped in sky, a wild, lambent blue.

After a while I came to a place where the ridge fell away south in a small near-precipitous bluff. I always used to sit on the brink there, to smoke a cigarette and survey the immense expanse of sea and mountains. Almost as soon as I sat down, that Sunday, I saw that something in the view had changed. Below me, halfway along the south coast of the island, there was the bay with the three small cottages. From this bay the coast ran on westwards in a series of low headlands and hidden coves. Immediately to the west of the bay with the cottages the ground rose steeply into a little cliff that ran inland some hundreds of yards, a crumbled and creviced reddish wall; as if it was some fortification for the solitary villa that lay on the headland beyond. All I knew of this house was that it belonged to a presumably well-to-do Athenian, who used it only in high summer. Because of an intervening rise in the pine-forest, one could see no more than the flat roof of the place from the central ridge.

But now a thin wisp of pale smoke curled up from the roof. It was no longer deserted. My first feeling was one of resentment, a Crusoe-like resentment, since the solitude of the south side of the island must now be spoilt and I had come to feel possessive about it. It was my secret province and no one else – I permitted the poor fishermen in the three cottages – no one else risen beyond peasant-hood had any right to it. For all that I was curious, and I chose a path that I knew led down to a cove the other side of Bourani, the name of the headland the villa stood on.

The sea and a strip of bleached stones finally shone through the pines. I came to the edge of them. It was a large open cove, a stretch of shingle, the sea as clear as glass, walled by two headlands. On the left and steeper, the eastward one, Bourani, lay the villa hidden in the trees, which grew more thickly there than anywhere else on the island. It was a beach I had been to before two or three times, and it gave, like many of the island beaches, the lovely illusion that one was the very first man that had ever stood on it, that had ever had eyes, that had ever existed, the very first man. There was no sign of any-one from the villa. I installed myself at the more open westward end of the beach, I swam, I ate my lunch of bread, olives and *zouzoukakia*, fragrant cold meatballs, and I saw no one.

Some time in the early afternoon I walked down the burning shingle to the villa end of the cove. There was a minute whitewashed chapel set back among the trees. Through a crack in the door I saw an overturned chair, an empty candle-stand, and a row of naively painted ikons on a small screen. A tarnished paper-gilt cross was pinned on the door. On the back of it someone had scrawled *Agios Demetrios* – Saint James. I went back to the beach. It ended in a fall of rocks which mounted rather forbiddingly into dense scrub and trees. For the first time I noticed some barbed wire, twenty or thirty feet from the foot of this slope; the fence turned up into the trees, isolating the headland. An old woman could have got through the rusty strands without difficulty, but it was the first barbed wire I had seen on the island, and I didn't like it. It insulted the solitude.

I was staring up at the hot, heavy slope of trees, when I had the sensation that I was not alone. I was being looked at. I searched the trees in front of me. There was nothing. I walked a little nearer the rocks above which the wire fence ran through the scrub.

A shock. Something gleamed behind the first rock. It was a blue rubber footfin. Just beyond it, partially in the thin clear shadow of another rock, was the other fin, and a towel. I looked round again, then moved the towel with my foot. A book had been left beneath. I recognized it at once by the cover design: one of the commonest paperback anthologies of modern English verse, which I had myself in my room back at the school. It was so unexpected that I remained staring stupidly down with the idea that it was in fact my own copy, stolen.

It was not mine. The owner had not written his or her name inside, but there were several little slips of plain white paper, neatly cut. The first one I turned to marked a page where four lines had been underscored in red ink; from 'Little Gidding'.

> We shall not cease from exploration
> And the end of all our exploring
> Will be to arrive where we started
> And know the place for the first time.

The last three lines had an additional mark vertically beside them. I looked up to the dense bank of trees again before I turned to the next little slip of paper. That, and all the other slips, were at pages where there were images or references concerning islands or the sea. There must have been about a dozen of them. Later, that night, I rediscovered a few passages in my own copy.

> Each in his little bed conceived of islands ...
> Where love was innocent, being far from cities.

Those two lines from Auden had been marked, and the two intervening ones not. There were several, also discontinuous, from Ezra Pound.

> Come, or the stellar tide will slip away.
> Eastward avoid the hour of its decline,
> Now! for the needle trembles in my soul! ...
> Mock not the flood of stars, the thing's to be.

And this:

> Who even dead, yet hath his mind entire!
> This sound came in the dark
> First must thou go the road
> > to hell
> And to the bower of Ceres' daughter Proserpine,
> Through overhanging dark, to see Tiresias,

Eyeless that was, a shade, that is in hell
So full of knowing that the beefy men know less than he,
Ere thou come to thy road's end.
     Knowledge the shade of a shade,
Yet must thou sail after knowledge
Knowing less than drugged beasts.

The sun-wind, the breeze that blows almost every summer day in the Aegean, sent little waves curling like lazy whips along the shingle. Nothing appeared, everything waited. For the second time that day I felt like Robinson Crusoe.

I put the book back beneath the towel and faced the hill in a rather self-conscious way, convinced by now that I was indeed being watched; then bent down and picked up the towel and the book and put them on top of the rock with the fins, where they would be easier to find if someone came looking for them. Not out of kindness, but to justify my curiosity to the hidden eyes. The towel had a trace of feminine perfume on it; suntan oil.

I went back to where my own clothes were and watched out of the corner of my eye along the beach. After a time I withdrew to the shade of the pine trees behind the beach. The white spot on the rock gleamed in the sun. I lay back and went to sleep. It can't have been for long. But when I woke up and looked down the beach, the things had gone. The girl, for I'd decided it was a girl, had done her retrieving unseen. I dressed and walked down to the place.

The normal path back to the school was from the middle of the bay. At this end I could see another small path that led up away from the beach where the wire turned. It was steep, and the undergrowth inside the fence was too dense to see through. Small pink heads of wild gladioli flopped out of the shadows, and some warbler in the thickest of the bushes reeled out a resonant, stuttering song. It must have been singing only a few feet from me, with a sobbing intensity, like a nightingale, but much more brokenly. A warning or a luring bird? I couldn't decide, though it was difficult not to think of it as meaningful. It scolded, fluted, screeched, jug-jugged, entranced.

Suddenly a bell sounded, from some way beyond the undergrowth. The bird stopped singing, and I climbed on. The bell sounded again, three times. It was evidently calling people to some meal, English tea, or perhaps a child was playing with it. After a while the ground levelled out on the back of the headland, and the trees thinned a little, though the undergrowth kept on as thickly as ever.

Then there was a gate, chained and painted. But the paint was peeling, the chain rusty, and a well-worn way had been forced through the wire by the right-hand gatepost. A wide, grassy track led along the headland, seawards and slightly downhill. It curved between the trees and revealed nothing of the house. I listened for a minute, but there was no sound of voices. Down the hill the bird began to sing again.

Then I saw it. I went through the gap. It was two or three trees in, barely legible, roughly nailed high up the trunk of a pine, in the sort of position one sees *Trespassers will be prosecuted* notices in England. But this notice said, in dull red letters on a white background, SALLE D'ATTENTE. It looked as if years ago it had been taken from some French railway station; some ancient student joke. Enamel had come off and cancerous patches of rusty metal showed through. At one end were three or four of what looked like old bullet holes. It was Mitford's warning: Beware of the waiting-room.

I stood on the grassy track, in two minds whether to go on to the house, caught between curiosity and fear of being snubbed. I guessed immediately that this was the villa of the collaborationist he had quarrelled with; but I had pictured a shifty, rat-faced Greek Laval rather than someone cultured enough to read, or have guests who could read, Eliot and Auden in the original. I stood so long that I became impatient with my indecision, and forced myself to turn away. I went back through the gap and followed the track up towards the central ridge. It soon petered out into a goat-path, but one that had been recently used, because there were overturned stones that showed earth-red among the sun-bleached greys. When I reached the central ridge, I looked back. From that particular point the house was invisible, but I knew where it lay. The sea and the mountains floated in the steady evening sunshine. It was all peace, elements and void, golden air and mute blue distances, like a Claude; and as I wound down the steep schoolward paths, the northern side of the island seemed oppressed and banal in comparison.

I I

The next morning after breakfast I crossed over to Demetriades's table. He had been in the village the previous evening and I hadn't bothered to wait up until he returned. Demetriades was small, very plump, frog-faced, a Corfiot, with a pathological dislike of sunshine and the rural. He grumbled incessantly about the 'disgusting' provincial life we had to lead on the island. In Athens he lived by night, indulging in his two hobbies, whoring and eating. He spent all his money on these two pursuits and on his clothes, and he ought to have looked sallow and oily and corrupt, but he was always pink and immaculate. His hero in history was Casanova. He lacked the Boswellian charm, to say nothing of the genius, of the Italian, but he was in his alternately gay and lugubrious way better company than Mitford had suggested. And at least he was not a hypocrite. He had the charm of all people who believe implicitly in themselves, that of integration.

I took him out into the garden. His nickname was Méli, or honey. He had a childlike passion for sweet things.

'Méli, what do you know about the man over at Bourani?'

'You've met him?'

'No.'

'*Aï*!' He shouted petulantly at a boy who was carving a word on an almond tree. The Casanova persona was confined strictly to his private life; in class he was a martinet.

'You don't know his name?'

'Conchis.' He pronounced the *ch* hard.

'Mitford said he had a row with him. A quarrel with him.'

'He was telling lies. He was always telling lies.'

'Maybe. But he must have met him.'

'*Po po.*' *Po po* is Greek for 'Tell that to the marines.' 'That man never sees anyone. Never. Ask the other professors.'

'But why?'

'Ech ... ' He shrugged. 'Many old stories. I don't know them.'

'Come on.'

'It is not interesting.'

We walked down a cobbled path. Méli disliked silence, and in a moment he began to tell me what he knew about Conchis.

'He worked for the Germans in the war. He never comes to the village. The villagers would kill him with stones. So would I, if I saw him.'

I grinned. 'Why?'

'Because he is rich and he lives on a desert island like this when he could be in Paris ... ' He waved his pink right hand in rapid small circles, a favourite gesture. It was his own deepest ambition – an apartment overlooking the Seine, containing a room with no windows and various other peculiar features.

'Does he speak English?'

'I suppose. But why are you so interested?'

'I'm not. I just saw the house.'

The bell for second school rang through the orchards and paths against the high white walls of the grounds. On the way back to class I invited Méli to have dinner with me in the village the next day.

The leading *estiatoras* of the village, a great walrus of a man called Sarantopoulos, knew more about Conchis. He came and had a glass of wine with us while we ate the meal he'd cooked. It was true that Conchis was a recluse and never came to the village, but that he had been a collaborationist was a lie. He had been made mayor by the Germans during the Occupation, and had in fact done his best for the villagers. If he was not popular now, it was because he ordered most of his provisions from Athens. He launched out on a long story. The island dialect was difficult, even for other Greeks, and I couldn't understand a word. He leant earnestly across the table. Demetriades looked bored and nodded complacently in the pauses.

'What's he say, Méli?'

'Nothing. A war story. Nothing at all.'

Sarantopoulos suddenly looked past us. He said something to Demetriades, and rose. I turned. In the door stood a tall, mournful-looking islander. He went to a table in the far corner, the islanders' corner, of the long bare room. I saw Sarantopoulos put his hand on

73

the man's shoulder. The man stared at us doubtfully, then gave in and allowed himself to be led to our table.

'He is the *agogiati* of Mr Conchis.'

'The how much?'

'He has a donkey. He takes the mail and the food to Bourani.'

'What's his name?' His name was Hermes. I had become far too used to hearing not conspicuously brilliant boys called Socrates and Aristotle, and to addressing the ill-favoured old woman who did my room out as Aphrodite, to smile. The donkey-driver sat down and rather grudgingly accepted a small tumbler of retsina. He fingered his *koumbologi*, his amber patience-beads. He had a bad eye, fixed, with a sinister pallor. From him Méli, who was much more interested in eating his lobster, extracted a little information.

What did Mr Conchis do? He lived alone – yes, alone – with a housekeeper, and he cultivated his garden, quite literally, it seemed. He read. He had many books. He had a piano. He spoke many languages. The *agogiati* did not know which – all, he thought. Where did he go in winter? Sometimes he went to Athens, and to other countries. Which? The man did not know. He knew nothing about Mitford visiting Bourani. No one ever visited.

'Ask him if he thinks I might visit Mr Conchis.'

No; it was impossible.

Our curiosity was perfectly natural, in Greece – it was his reserve that was strange. He might have been picked for his sullenness. He stood up to go.

'Are you sure he hasn't got a harem of pretty girls hidden there?' said Méli. The *agogiati* raised his blue chin and eyebrows in a silent no, then turned contemptuously away.

'What a villager!' Having muttered the worst insult in the Greek language at his back Méli touched my wrist moistly. 'My dear fellow, did I ever tell you about the way two men and two ladies I once met on Mykonos made love?'

'Yes. But never mind.'

I felt oddly disappointed. And it was not only because it was the third time I had heard precisely how that acrobatic quartet achieved congress.

Back at the school I picked up, during the rest of the week, a little more. Only two of the masters had been there before the war. They had both met Conchis once or twice then, but not since the school had re-started in 1949. One said he was a retired musician. The other had found him a very cynical man, an atheist. But they both agreed that Conchis was a man who cherished his privacy. In the war the Germans had forced him to live in the village. They had one day captured some *andarte* – resistance fighters – from the mainland and ordered him to execute them. He had refused and had been put before a firing-squad with a number of the villagers. But by a miracle he had not been killed outright, and was saved. This was evidently the story Sarantopoulos had told us. In the opinion of many of the villagers, and naturally of all those who'd had relatives massacred in the German reprisal, he should have done what they ordered. But that was all past. If he had been wrong, it was to the honour of Greece. However, he had never set foot in the village again.

Then I discovered something small, but anomalous. I asked several people besides Demetriades, who had been at the school only a year, whether Leverrier, Mitford's predecessor, or Mitford himself had ever spoken about meeting Conchis. The answer was always no – understandably enough, it seemed, in Leverrier's case, because he was very reserved, 'too serious' as one master put it, tapping his head. It so happened that the last person I asked, over coffee in his room, was the biology master. Karazoglou said in his aromatic broken French that he was sure Leverrier had never been there, as he would have told him. He'd known Leverrier rather better than the other masters; they had shared a common interest in botany. He rummaged about in a chest of drawers, and then produced a box of sheets of paper with dried flowers that Leverrier had collected and mounted. There were lengthy notes in an admirably clear handwriting and a highly technical vocabulary, and here and there professional-looking sketches in Indian ink and water-colour. As I sorted uninterestedly through the box I dropped one of the pages of dried flowers, to which was attached a sheet of paper with additional notes. This sheet slipped from the clip that was holding it. On the back was the beginning of a letter, which had been crossed out, but was still legible. It was dated June 6th, 1951, two years before. *Dear Mr*

Conchis, I am much afraid that since the extraordinary ... and then it stopped.

I didn't say anything to Karazoglou, who had noticed nothing; but I then and there decided to visit Mr Conchis.

I cannot say why I suddenly became so curious about him. Partly it was for lack of anything else to be curious about, the usual island obsession with trivialities; partly it was that one cryptic phrase from Mitford and the discovery about Leverrier; partly, perhaps mostly, a peculiar feeling that I had a sort of right to visit. My two predecessors had both met this unmeetable man; and not wanted to talk about it. In some way it was now my turn.

I did one other thing that week: I wrote a letter to Alison. I sent it inside an envelope addressed to Ann in the flat below in Russell Square, asking her to post it on to wherever Alison was living. I said almost nothing in the letter; only that I'd thought about her once or twice, that I had discovered what 'the waiting-room' meant; and that she was to write back only if she really wanted to, I'd quite understand if she didn't.

I knew that on the island one was driven back into the past. There was so much space, so much silence, so few meetings that one too easily saw out of the present, and then the past seemed ten times closer than it was. It was likely that Alison hadn't given me a thought for weeks, and that she had had half a dozen more affaires. So I posted the letter rather as one throws a message in a bottle into the sea; not quite as a joke, perhaps, but almost.

12

The absence of the usually unfailing sun-wind made the next Saturday oppressively hot. The cicadas had begun. They racketed in a ragged chorus, never quite finding a common beat, rasping one's nerves, but finally so familiar that when one day they stopped in a rare shower of rain, the silence was like an explosion. They completely changed the character of the pine-forest. Now it was live and multitudinous, an audible, invisible hive of energy, with all its pure solitude gone, for besides the *tzitzikia* the air throbbed, whined, hummed with carmine-winged grasshoppers, locusts, huge hornets, bees, midges, bots, and ten thousand other anonymous insects. In some places there were nagging clouds of black flies, so that I climbed through the trees like a new Orestes, cursing and slapping.

I came to the ridge again. The sea was a pearly turquoise, the far mountains ash-blue in the windless heat. I could see the shimmering green crown of pine trees around Bourani. It was about noon when I came through the trees out on to the shingle of the beach with the chapel. It was deserted. I searched among the rocks, but there was nothing, and I didn't feel watched. I had a swim, then lunch, black bread and ochra and fried squid. A long way south a plump caique thudded past towing a line of six little lamp-boats, like a mallard with ducklings. Its bow-wave made a dark miraging ripple on the creamy blue surface of the sea, and that was all that remained of civilization when the boats had disappeared behind the western headland. There was the infinitesimal lap of the transparent blue water on the stones, the waiting trees, the myriad dynamos of the insects, and the enormous landscape of silence. I dozed under the thin shade of a pine, in the agelessness, the absolute dissociation of wild Greece.

The sun moved, came on me, and made me erotic. I thought of Alison, of sex things we had done together. I wished she was beside me, naked. We would have made love against the pine-needles, then swum, then made love again. I was filled with a dry sadness, a mixture of remembering and knowing; remembering what was and what might have been and knowing it was all past; at the same time knowing, or beginning to know, that other things were happily past – at least some of my illusions about myself, and then the syphilis, for there were no signs that it was going to come back. I felt physically very well. What was going to become of my life I didn't know; but lying there that day by the sea it didn't seem to matter much. To be was enough. I felt myself in suspension, waiting without fear for some impulse to drive me on. I turned on my stomach and made love to the memory of Alison, like an animal, without guilt or shame, a mere machine for sensation spreadeagled on the earth. Then I ran across the burning stones into the sea.

I climbed the path by the wire and the undergrowth, passed beside the peeling gate, stood once more before the mysterious sign. The grassy track ran level, curved and dipped a little, emerged from the trees. The house, dazzlingly white where the afternoon sun touched it, stood with its shadowed back to me. It had been built on the seaward side of a small cottage that had evidently existed before it. It was square, with a flat roof and a colonnade of slender arches running round the south and east sides. Above the colonnade was a terrace. I could see the open french windows of a first-floor room giving access to it. To the east and back of the house there were lines of swordplants and small clumps of bushes with vivid scarlet and yellow flowers. In front, southwards and seawards, there was a stretch of gravel and then the ground fell away abruptly down to the sea. At both corners of the gravel stood palm trees, in neat white-washed rings of stones. The pines had been thinned to clear the view.

The house abashed me. It was too reminiscent of the Côte d'Azur, too un-Greek. It stood, white and opulent, like Swiss snow, and made me feel sticky-palmed and uncouth.

I walked up a small flight of steps to the red-tiled side colonnade. There was a closed door with an iron knocker cast in the shape of a dolphin. The windows beside it were heavily shuttered. I knocked on the door; the knocks barked sharply over stone floors. But no one came. The house and I waited silently in a sea of insect sound. I went along the colonnade to the corner of the southern front of the house. There the colonnade was wider and the slender arches more open; standing in the deep shade, I looked out over the tree-tops and the sea to the languishing ash-lilac mountains ... a *déjà vu* feeling of having stood in the same place, before that particular proportion of the arches, that particular contrast of shade and burning landscape outside – I couldn't say.

There were two old cane chairs in the middle of the colonnade, and a table covered with a blue-and-white folkweave cloth, on which were two cups and saucers and two large plates covered in muslin. By the wall stood a rattan couch with cushions; and hanging from a bracket by the open french windows was a small brightly polished bell with a faded maroon tassel hanging from the clapper.

I noticed the twoness of the tea-table, and stood by the corner, embarrassed, aware of a trite English desire to sneak away. Then, without warning, a figure appeared in the doorway.

It was Conchis.

13

Before anything else, I knew I was expected. He saw me without surprise, with a small smile, almost a grimace, on his face.

He was nearly completely bald, brown as old leather, short and spare, a man whose age was impossible to tell: perhaps sixty, perhaps seventy; dressed in a navy-blue shirt, knee-length shorts, and a pair of salt-stained gym shoes. The most striking thing about him was the intensity of his eyes; very dark brown, staring, with a simian penetration emphasized by the remarkably clear whites; eyes that seemed not quite human.

He raised his left hand briefly in a kind of silent salutation, then strode to the corner of the colonnade, leaving me with my formed words unspoken, and called back to the cottage.

'Maria!'

I heard a faint wail of answer.

'My name is ... ' I began, as he turned.

But he raised his left hand again, this time to silence me; took my arm and led me to the edge of the colonnade. He had an authority, an abrupt decisiveness, that caught me off balance. He surveyed the landscape, then me. The sweet saffron-like smell of some flowers that grew below, at the edge of the gravel, wafted up into the shade.

'I chose well?'

His English sounded perfect.

'Wonderfully. But you must let me –'

Once again his arm, brown and corded, swept silencingly towards the sea and the mountains and the south, as if I might not have properly appreciated it. I looked sideways at him. He was obviously a man who rarely smiled. There was something mask-like, emotion-purged, about his face. Deep furrows ran from beside his nose to the corners of his mouth; they suggested experience, command, impatience with fools. He was slightly mad, no doubt harmlessly so, but mad. I had an idea that he thought I was someone else. He kept his ape-like eyes on me. The silence and the stare were alarming, and faintly comic, as if he was trying to hypnotize a bird.

Suddenly he gave a curious little rapid shake of the head; quizzical, rhetorical, not expecting an answer. Then he changed, as if what had happened between us till then was a joke, a charade, that had been rehearsed and gone according to plan, but could now be ended. And I was completely off balance again. He wasn't mad after all. He even smiled, and the ape-eyes became almost squirrel-eyes.

He turned back to the table. 'Let us have tea.'

'I only came for a glass of water. This is ... '

'You came here to meet me. Please. Life is short.'

I sat down. The second place was mine. An old woman appeared, in black, a black grey with age, her face as lined as an Indian squaw's. She was incongruously carrying a tray with an elegant silver teapot, a kettle, a bowl of sugar, a saucer with sliced lemon.

'This is my housekeeper, Maria.'

He spoke to her in very precise Greek, and I heard my own name and the name of the school. The old woman bobbed at me, her eyes on the ground, unsmiling, and then unloaded her tray. Conchis plucked the muslin away from one of the plates with the quick aplomb of a conjurer. I saw cucumber sandwiches. He poured the tea, and indicated the lemon.

'How do you know who I am, Mr Conchis?'

'Anglicize my name. I prefer the "ch" soft.' He sipped his tea. 'If you question Hermes, Zeus will know.'

'I'm afraid my colleague was tactless.'

'You no doubt found out all about me.'

'I found out very little. But that makes this even kinder of you.'

He looked out to sea. 'There is a poem of the T'ang dynasty.' He sounded the precious glottal stop. '"Here at the frontier, there are falling leaves. Although my neighbours are all barbarians, and you, you are a thousand miles away, there are always two cups on my table."'

I smiled. 'Always?'

'I saw you last Sunday.'

'They were your things down there?'

He bowed his head. 'And I also saw you this afternoon.'

'I hope I haven't kept you from your beach.'

'Not at all. My private beach is down there.' He pointed over the gravel. 'But I always like a beach to myself. And I presume the same of you. Now. Eat the sandwiches.'

He poured me more tea. It had huge torn leaves and a tarry China fragrance. On the other plate were *kourabièdes*, conical butter-cakes rolled in icing sugar. I'd forgotten what a delicious meal tea could be; and sitting there I felt invaded by the envy of the man who lives in an institution, and has to put up with institution meals and institution everything else, for the rich private life of the established. I remembered having tea with one of my tutors, an old bachelor don at Magdalen; and the same envy for his rooms, his books, his calm, precise, ticking peace.

I bit into my first *kourabiè*, and gave an appreciative nod.

'You are not the first English person to have admired Maria's cooking.'

'Mitford?' His eyes fixed me sharply again. 'I met him in London.'

He poured more tea. 'How did you like Captain Mitford?'

'Not my type.'

'He spoke of me?'

'Not at all. That is … ' His eyes were intent. 'He just said you'd had a … disagreement?'

'Captain Mitford made me ashamed to have English blood.'

Till then I had felt I was beginning to get his measure; first of all, his English, though excellent, was somehow not contemporary, more that of someone who hadn't been in England for many years; and then his whole appearance was foreign. He had a bizarre family resemblance to Picasso; saurian as well as simian, decades of living in the sun, the quintessential Mediterranean man, who had discarded everything that lay between him and his vitality. A monkey-glander, essence of queen bees; and intense by choice and exercise as much as by nature. He was plainly not a dandy about clothes; but there are other sorts of narcissism.

'I didn't realize you were English.'

'I spent the first nineteen years of my life in England. Now I have Greek nationality and my mother's name. My mother was Greek.'

'You go back to England?'

'Rarely.' He jumped swiftly on. 'Do you like my house? I designed and built it myself.'

I looked round. 'I envy you.'

'And I envy you. You have the one thing that matters. You have all your discoveries before you.'

His face was without the offensively avuncular smile that usually accompanies such trite statements; and something intent about the look he gave me made it clear he did not mean it tritely.

'Well. Now I will leave you for a few minutes. Then we shall have a look round.' I had risen with him, but he gestured me down again. 'Finish the cakes. Maria will be honoured. Please.'

He walked into the sunlight at the edge of the colonnade, stretched his arms and fingers, and with another gesture to me to help myself passed back inside the room. From where I was sitting I could see one end of a cretonne-covered sofa, a table with a bowl of milky flowers on it. The wall behind was covered by book-shelves, from the ceiling to the floor. I stole another *kourabiè*. The sun was beginning to float down on the mountains, and the sea glittered lazily at the foot of their ashy, opaque shadows. Then there was an unannounced shock of antique sound, a rapid arpeggio, far too real to come from a radio or record. I stopped eating, wondering what new surprise I was being presented with.

There was a moment's silence, perhaps to leave me guessing. Then came the quiet plangent sound of a harpsichord. I hesitated, then decided that two could play the independence game. He played quickly, and then tranquilly; once or twice he stopped and retook a phrase. The old woman came and silently cleared away, without once looking at me, even when I pointed at the few cakes left and praised them in my stilted Greek; the hermit master evidently liked silent servants. The music came clearly out of the room, and flowed round me and out through the colonnade into the light. He broke off, repeated a passage, and then stopped as abruptly as he had begun. A door closed, there was a silence. Five minutes passed, then ten. The sun crept towards me over the red tiles.

I felt I ought to have gone in earlier; that now I had put him in a huff. But he appeared in the doorway, speaking.

'I have not driven you away.'

'Not at all. It was Bach?'

'Telemann.'

'You play very well.'

'Once, I *could* play. Never mind. Come.' His jerkiness was pathological; not only as if he wanted to get rid of me, but of time itself.

I stood up. 'I hope I shall hear you play again.' He made a little bow, refusing the invitation to invite. 'One gets so starved of music here.'

'Only of music?' He went on before I could answer. 'Come now. Prospero will show you his domaine.'

As we went down the steps to the gravel I said, 'Prospero had a daughter.'

'Prospero had many things.' He turned a dry look on me. 'And not all young and beautiful, Mr Urfe.'

I smiled tactfully, thinking he must be referring to memories of the war, and left a little silence.

'You live alone here?'

'What some would call alone. What others would not.'

It was said with a kind of grim contempt, and he stared ahead as he spoke. Whether to mystify me once more or because there was no more to be said to a stranger, I couldn't tell.

He walked rapidly on, incessantly pointing things out. He showed me round his little vegetable-garden terrace; his cucumbers, his almonds, his long-leaved loquats, his pistachios. From the far edge of the terrace I could see down to where I had been lying only an hour or two before.

'Moutsa.'

'I haven't heard it called that before.'

'Albanian.' He tapped his nose. 'Snout. Because of the cliff over there.'

'Not very poetic for such a lovely beach.'

'The Albanians were pirates, not poets. Their word for this cape was Bourani. Two hundred years ago it was their slang word for gourd. Also for skull.' He moved away. 'Death and water.'

As I walked behind him, I said, 'I wondered about the sign by the gate. *Salle d'attente.*'

'The German soldiers put it there. They requisitioned Bourani during the war.'

'But why that?'

'I think they had been stationed in France. They found it dull being garrisoned here.' He turned and saw me smile. 'Precisely. One must be grateful for the smallest grain of humour from the Germans. I should not like the responsibility of destroying such a rare plant.'

'You know Germany?'

'It is not possible to know Germany. Only to endure it.'

'Bach? Isn't he reasonably endurable?'

He stopped. 'I do not judge countries by their geniuses. I judge them by their racial characteristics. The ancient Greeks could laugh at themselves. The Romans could not. That is why France is a civilized society and Spain is not. That is why I forgive the Jews and the Anglo-Saxons their countless vices. And why I should thank God, if I believed in God, that I have no German blood.'

We had come to an arbour of bourgainvillaea and morning glory at the end of the kitchen-garden terrace, set back and obliquely. He gestured me in. In the shadows, in front of an outcrop of rock, stood a pedestal. On it was a bronze manikin with a grotesquely enormous erect phallus. Its hands were flung up as well, as if to frighten children; and on its face it had a manic-satyric grin. It was only eighteen inches or so high, yet it emitted a distinct primitive terror.

'You know what it is?' He was standing close behind me.

'Pan?'

'A Priapus. In classical times every garden and orchard had one. To frighten away thieves and bring fertility. It should be made of pearwood.'

'Where did you find it?'

'I had it made. Come.' He said 'Come' as Greeks prod their donkeys; as if, it later struck me, I was a potential employee who had to be shown briefly round the works.

We went back towards the house. A narrow path zigzagged steeply down from in front of the colonnade to the shore. There was a small cove there, not fifty yards across at its cliffed mouth. He had built a miniature jetty, and a small green and rose-pink boat, an open island boat with an engine fitted, was tied up alongside. At one end of the beach I could see a small cave; drums of kerosene. And there was a little pump-house, with a pipe running back up the cliff.

'Would you like to swim?'

We were standing on the jetty.

'I left my trunks at the house.'

'A costume is not necessary.' His eyes were those of a chess-player who has made a good move. I remembered a joke of Demetriades' about English bottoms; and the Priapus. Perhaps this was the explanation: Conchis was simply an old queer.

'I don't think I will.'

'As you please.'

We moved back to the strip of shingle and sat on a large baulk of timber that had been dragged up away from the water.

I lit a cigarette and looked at him; tried to determine him. I was in something not unlike a mild state of shock. It was not only the fact that this man who spoke English so fluently, who was seemingly cultured, cosmopolitan, had come to 'my' desert island, had sprung almost overnight from the barren earth, like some weird plant. It was not even that he conformed so little to what I had imagined. But I knew that there must really be some mystery about the previous year, some deliberate and inexplicable suppression on Mitford's part. Second meanings hung in the air; ambiguities, unexpectednesses.

'How did you first come here, Mr Conchis?'

'Will you forgive me if I ask you not to ask me questions?'

'Of course.'

'Good.'

And that was that. I bit my lip. If anyone else had been there I should have had to laugh.

Shadows began to fall across the water from the pines on the bluff to our right, and there was peace, absolute peace over the world; the insects stilled and the water like a mirror. He sat in silence with his hands on his knees, apparently engaged in deep-breathing exercises. Not only his age but everything about him was difficult to tell. Outwardly he seemed to have very little interest in me, yet he watched me; even when he was looking away, he watched me; and he waited. Right from the beginning I had this: he was indifferent to me, yet he watched and he waited. So we sat there in the silence as if we knew each other well and had no need merely to talk; and as a matter of fact it seemed in a way to suit the stillness of the day. It was an unnatural, but not an embarrassing, silence.

Suddenly he moved. His eyes had flicked up to the top of the small cliff to our left. I looked round. There was nothing. I glanced back at him.

'Something there?'

'A bird.'

Silence.

I watched his profiled face. Was he mad? Was he making fun of me? I tried to make conversation again.

'I gather you've met both my predecessors.' His head turned on me with a snake-like swiftness, accusingly, but he said nothing. I prompted. 'Leverrier?'

'Who told you this?'

For some reason he was terrified about what we might have said of him behind his back. I explained about the sheet of notepaper, and he relaxed a little.

'He was not happy here. On Phraxos.'

'So Mitford told me.'

'Mitford?' Again the accusing stare.

'I suppose he heard gossip at the school.'

He searched my eyes, then nodded, but not very convincedly. I smiled at him, and he gave me the trace of a wary smile back. We were playing obscure psychological chess again. I apparently had the advantage, but I didn't know why.

From the invisible house above came the sound of the bell. It rang twice; then after a moment, three times; then twice again. It clearly had a meaning, and it gave a voice to the peculiar state of tension that seemed to pervade both the place and its owner, and which clashed so oddly with the enormous peace of the landscape. Conchis stood at once.

'I must go. And you have a long walk.'

Halfway up the cliff, where the steep path broadened, there was a small cast-iron seat. Conchis, who had set a quickish pace, sat down gratefully on it. He was breathing hard; so was I. He patted his heart. I put on a look of concern, but he shrugged.

'When you grow old. The annunciation in reverse.' He grimaced. 'Not to be.'

We sat in silence and got our breaths back. I watched the yellowing sky through the delicate fenestrations in the pines. The sky in the west was hazy. A few evening wisps of cloud were curled high, tranced over the stillness of the world.

Then once more out of the blue he said quietly, 'Are you elect?'

'Elect?'

'Do you feel chosen by anything?'

'Chosen?'

'John Leverrier felt chosen by God.'

'I don't believe in God. And I certainly don't feel chosen.'

'I think you may be.'

I smiled dubiously. 'Thank you.'

'It is not a compliment. Hazard makes you elect. You cannot elect yourself.'

'And what chooses me?'

'Chance wears many faces.'

But then he stood, although his hand rested momentarily on my shoulder, as if to reassure me; to say it did not matter. We climbed the rest of the hill. At last we were on the gravel by the side colonnade. He stopped.

'So.'

'Thank you very much indeed.' I tried to get him to return my smile, to confess that he had been pulling my leg; but his brooding face was drained of humour.

'I make two requests of you. One is that you tell no one over there that you have met me. This is because of certain events that happened during the war.'

'I've heard about that.'

'What have you heard?'

'The story.'

'There are two versions of the story. But never mind now. For them I am a recluse. No one ever sees me. You understand?'

'Of course. I shan't tell anyone.'

I knew what the next request would be: not to visit him again.

'My second request is that you come here next week-end. And stay Saturday and Sunday nights. That is, if you do not mind the walking back early on Monday morning.'

'Thank you. Thank you very much. I'd love to.'

'I think we have many things to discover.'

' "We shall not cease from exploration"?'

'You read that in the book on the beach?'

'Didn't you leave it for me to read?'

'How should I have known you were coming?'

'I had a feeling someone was watching me.'

His dark-brown eyes burnt into mine; he took a long moment to reply. The faintest ghost of a smile.

'Do you feel you are being watched now?'

And once again his eyes flicked past my shoulders, as if he could see something inside the trees. I looked round. The pines were empty. I looked back at him; a joke? He was still smiling, a small dry smile.

'Am I?'

'I merely wondered, Mr Urfe.' He held out his hand. 'If for some reason you cannot come, leave a message at Sarantopoulos's for Hermes. It will get here the next day.'

Looking as wary as he had begun to make me, I took his hand. He retained it beyond courtesy. There was a stronger pressure in his grip, a quizzical searching in his eyes.

'Remember. Hazard.'

'If you say.'

'Go now.'

I had to smile. It was too absurd – the invitation, then this curt dismissal, as if I had exhausted his patience. But he would concede nothing, and in the end I gave him a dry little bow and thanked him for the tea. All I received was a dry little bow in return. I could only make my exit.

After fifty yards I looked back. He was still standing there, master of his domaine. I waved and he raised both his arms in an outlandish hieratic gesture, one foot slightly advanced, as if in some kind of primitive blessing. When I looked back again, just before the trees hid the house, he had disappeared.

Whatever else he was he was not like anyone else I had ever met. Something more than mere loneliness, mere senile fantasies and quirks, burnt in his striking eyes, in that abrupt, probing then dropping conversation, in those sudden oblique looks at nothing. But I certainly didn't think, as I went into the trees, that I should have the apparent answer within another hundred yards.

14

Long before I came up to the gate out of Bouranı, I saw something whitish lying in the gap. At first I thought it was a handkerchief, but when I stooped to pick it up I saw it was a cream-coloured glove; and of all gloves, an elbow-length woman's glove. Inside the wrist was a yellowish label with the words *Mireille, gantière* embroidered on it in blue silk. The label, like the glove, seemed unreasonably old, something from the bottom of a long-stored trunk. I smelt it, and there it was, that same scent as on the towel the week before – musky, old-fashioned, like sandalwood. When Conchis had said that he'd been down on Moutsa the week before, it had been this one fact, the sweet womanish perfume, that had puzzled me.

Now I began to understand why he might not want unexpected visits, or gossip. Why he should want to risk his secret with me, per-haps, next week, let me know it, I couldn't imagine; what the lady was doing out in Ascot gloves, I couldn't imagine; and who she was, I couldn't imagine. She might be a mistress, but she might equally well be a daughter, a wife, a sister – perhaps someone weak-minded, perhaps someone elderly. It flashed through my mind that it was someone who was allowed out in the grounds of Bourani and down at Moutsa only on pain of keeping herself concealed. She would have seen me the week before; and this time, have heard my arrival and tried to catch a glimpse of me – that explained the old man's quick looks past me, and perhaps some of his nervous strangeness. He knew she was 'out'; it explained the second place at the tea-table, and the mysterious bell.

I turned round, half-expecting to hear a giggle, a rather inane giggle; and then as I looked at the thick shadowy scrub near the gate, and remembered the grim reference to Prospero, a more sinister explanation came to me. Not weak-mindedness, but some terrible disfigurement. '*Not all young and beautiful, Mr Urfe.*' I felt, for the first time on the island, a small cold shiver of solitary-place fear.

The sun was low and night comes with near-tropical speed in

Greece. I didn't want to have to negotiate the steep north-side paths in darkness. So I hung the glove neatly over the centre of the top bar of the gate and went on quickly. Half an hour later the charming hypothesis occurred to me that Conchis was a transvestite. After a while I began, for the first time in months, to sing.

I told no one, not even Méli, about my visit to Conchis, but I spent many hours conjecturing about the mysterious third person in the house. I decided that a weak-minded wife was the most likely answer; it would explain the seclusion, the taciturn servants.

I tried to make up my mind about Conchis too. I was far from sure that he was not just a homosexual; that would explain Mitford's inadequate warning, though not very flatteringly to me. The old man's nervous intensity, that jerking from one place to another, one subject to another, his jaunty walk, the gnomic answers and mystifications, the weird flinging-up of his arms when I left – all his mannerisms suggested, were calculated to suggest, that he wanted to seem younger and more vital than he was.

There remained the peculiar business of the poetry book, which he must have had ready to puzzle me. I had been swimming a long time that first Sunday, far out in the bay, and he could easily have slipped the things on to the Bourani end of the beach while I was in the water. But it seemed an oddly devious means of introduction. Then what did my being 'elect' mean – our having 'many things to discover'? In itself it could mean nothing; in regard to him it could mean only that he was mad. And 'Some would say I lived alone': I remembered the scarcely concealed contempt with which he had said that.

I found a large-scale map of the island in the school library. The boundaries of the Bourani estate were marked. I saw it was bigger, especially to the east, than I had realized: six or seven hectares, some fifteen acres. Again and again I thought of it, perched on its lonely promontory, during the weary hours of plodding through Eckersley's purgatorial *English Course*. I enjoyed conversation classes, I enjoyed doing more advanced work with what was known as the Philologic Sixth, a small group of eighteen-year-old duds who were doing languages only because they were hopeless at science, but the endless business of 'drilling' the beginners bored me into stone. *'What am I doing? I am raising my arm. What is he doing? He is raising his arm. What are they doing? They are raising their arms. Have they raised their arms? They have raised their arms.'*

It was like being a champion at tennis, and condemned to play with rabbits, as well as having always to get their wretched balls out of the net for them. I would look out of the window at the blue sky and the cypresses and the sea, and pray for the day's end, when I could retire to the masters' wing, lie back on my bed and sip an ouzo. Bourani seemed greenly remote from all that; so far, and yet so near; its small mysteries, which grew smaller as the week passed, no more than an added tang, or hazard, in its other promise of civilized pleasure.

15

This time he was waiting for me at the table. I dumped my duffel bag by the wall and he called for Maria to bring the tea. He was much less eccentric, perhaps because he had transparently determined to pump me. We talked about the school, about Oxford, my family, about teaching English to foreigners, about why I had come to Greece. Though he kept asking questions, I still felt that he had no real interest in what I was saying. What interested him was something else, some syndrome I exhibited, some category I filled. I was not interesting in myself, but only as an example. I tried once or twice to reverse our roles, but he again made it clear that he did not want to talk about himself. I said nothing about the glove.

Only once did he seem really surprised. He had asked me about my unusual name.

'French. My ancestors were Huguenots.'

'Ah.'

'There's a writer called Honoré d'Urfé –'

He gave me a swift look. 'He is an ancestor of yours?'

'It's just a family tradition. No one's ever traced it. As far as I know.' Poor old d'Urfé; I had used him before to suggest that centuries of high culture lay in my blood. Conchis's smile was

91

genuinely warm, almost radiant, and I smiled back. 'That makes a difference?'

'It is amusing.'

'It's probably all rubbish.'

'No no, I believe it. And have you read *L'Astrée*?'

'For my pains. Terrible bore.'

'*Oui, un peu fade. Mais pas tout à fait sans charmes.*' Impeccable accent; he could not stop smiling. 'So you speak French.'

'Not very well.'

'I have a direct link with *le grand siècle* at my table.'

'Hardly direct.'

But I didn't mind his thinking it, his sudden flattering benignity. He stood up.

'Now. In your honour. Today I will play Rameau.'

He led the way into the room, which ran the whole width of the house. Books lined three walls. At one end there was a green-glazed tile stove under a mantelpiece on which stood two bronzes, both modern. Above them was a life-size reproduction of a Modigliani, a fine portrait of a sombre woman in black against a glaucous green background.

He sat me in an armchair, sorted through some scores, found the one he wanted; began to play; short, chirrupy little pieces, then some elaborately ornamented courantes and passacaglias. I didn't much like them, but I realized he played with some mastery. He might be pretentious in other ways, but he was not posing at the keyboard. He stopped abruptly, in midpiece, as if a light had fused; pretension began again.

'*Voilà.*'

'Very charming.' I determined to stamp out the French 'flu before it spread. 'I've been admiring that.' I nodded at the reproduction.

'Yes?' We went and stood in front of it. 'My mother.'

For a moment I thought he was joking.

'Your mother?'

'In name. In reality, it is his mother. It was always his mother.' I looked at the woman's eyes; they hadn't the usual fish-like pallor of Modigliani eyes. They stared, they watched, they were simian. I also looked at the painted surface. I belatedly realized I was not looking at a reproduction.

'Good lord. It must be worth a fortune.'

'No doubt.' He spoke without looking at me. 'You must not think that because I live simply here I am poor. I am very rich.' He said it as if 'very rich' was a nationality; as perhaps it is. I stared at the picture again. 'It cost me ... nothing. And that was charity. I should like to say that I recognized his genius. But I did not. No one did. Not even the clever Mr Zborowski.'

'You knew him?'

'Modigliani? I met him. Many times. I knew Max Jacob, who was a friend of his. That was in the last phase of his life. He was quite famous by then. One of the sights of Montparnasse.'

I stole a look at Conchis as he gazed up at the picture; he had, by no other logic than that of cultural snobbery, gained a whole new dimension of respectability for me, and I began to feel much less sure of his eccentricity and his phoniness, of my own superiority in the matter of what life was really about.

'You must wish you'd bought more from him.'

'I did.'

'You still own them?'

'Of course. Only a bankrupt would sell beautiful paintings. They are in my other houses.' I stored away that plural; one day I would mimic it to someone.

'Where are your ... other houses?'

'Do you like this?' He touched the bronze of a young man beneath the Modigliani. 'This is a maquette by Rodin. My other houses. Well. In France. In the Lebanon. In America. I have business interests all over the world.' He turned to the other characteristically skeletal bronze. 'And this is by Giacometti.'

'I'm staggered. Here on Phraxos.'

'Why not?'

'Thieves?'

'If you have many valuable paintings, as I have – I will show you two more upstairs later – you make a decision. You treat them as what they are – squares of painted canvas. Or you treat them as you would treat gold ingots. You put bars on your windows, you lie awake at night worrying. There.' He indicated the bronzes. 'If you want, steal them. I shall tell the police, but you may get away with them. The only thing you will not do is make me worry.'

'They're safe from me.'

'And on Greek islands, no thieves. But I do not like everyone to know they are here.'

'Of course.'

'This picture is interesting. It was omitted from the only *catalogue raisonné* of his work I have seen. You see also it is not signed. However – it would not be difficult to authenticate. I will show you. Take the corner.'

He moved the Rodin to one side and we lifted the frame down. He tilted it for me to see. On the back were the first few lines of a sketch for another painting, then scrawled across the lower half of the untreated canvas were some illegible words with numbers beside them, added up at the bottom, by the stretcher.

'Debts. That one there. "Toto." Toto was the Algerian he bought his hashish from.' He pointed. ' "Zbo." Zborowski.'

I stared down at those careless, drunken scrawls; felt the immediacy of the man; and the terrible but necessary alienation of genius from ordinariness. A man who would touch you for ten francs, and go home and paint what would one day be worth ten million. Conchis watched me.

'This is the side the museums never show.'

'Poor devil.'

'He would say the same of us. With much more reason.'

I helped him put the frame back.

Then he made me look at the windows. They were rather small and narrow, arched, each one with a centre pillar and a capital of carved marble.

'These come from Monemvasia. I found them built into a cottage. So I bought the cottage.'

'Like an American.'

He did not smile. 'They are Venetian. Of the fifteenth century.' He turned to the bookshelves and pulled down an art book. 'Here.' I looked over his shoulder and saw Fra Angelico's famous 'Annunciation'; and at once knew why the colonnade outside had seemed so familiar. There was even the same white-edged floor of red tiles.

'Now what else can I show you? My harpsichord is very rare. It is one of the original Pleyels. Not in fashion. But very beautiful.' He stroked its shining black top, as if it were a cat. There was a music-stand on the far side, by the wall. It seemed an unnecessary thing to have with a harpsichord.

'You play some other instrument, Mr Conchis?'

He looked at it, shook his head. 'No. It has sentimental value.' But he sounded quite unsentimental.

'Good. Well. Now I must leave you to your own devices for a while. I have some correspondence to deal with.' He gestured. 'You will find newspapers and magazines over there. Or books – take what you want. You will excuse me? Your room is upstairs … if you wish?'

'No, this is fine. Thank you.'

He went; and I stared again at the Modigliani, caressed the Rodin, surveyed the room. I felt rather like a man who has knocked on a cottage door and found himself in a palace; vaguely foolish. I took a pile of the French and American magazines that lay on a table in the corner and went out under the colonnade. After a while I did something else I hadn't done for several months: I began to rough out a poem.

> From this skull-rock strange golden roots throw
> Ikons and incidents; the man in the mask
> Manipulates. I am the fool that falls
> And never learns to wait and watch,
> Icarus eternally damned, the dupe of time …

He suggested we look over the rest of the house.

A door led into a bare, ugly hall. There was a dining-room, which he said he never used, on the north side of the house, and another room which resembled nothing so much as a second-hand bookshop; a chaos of books – shelves of books, stacks of books, piles of magazines and newspapers, and one large and evidently newly arrived parcel that lay unopened on a desk by the window.

He turned to me with a pair of calipers in his hand.

'I am interested in anthropology. May I measure your skull?' He took my permission for granted, and I bent my head. As he gently pinched it, he said, 'You like books?'

He seemed to have forgotten, but perhaps he hadn't, that I had read English at Oxford.

'Of course.'

'What do you read?' He wrote down my measurements in a little notebook.

'Oh … novels mainly. Poetry. And criticism.'

'I have not a single novel here.'

'No?'

'The novel is no longer an art form.'

I grinned.

'Why do you smile?'

'It was a sort of joke when I was at Oxford. If you didn't know what to say at a party, you used to ask a question like that.'

'Like what?'

'"Do you think the novel is exhausted as an art form?" No serious answer was expected.'

'I see. It was not serious.'

'Not at all.' I looked at the notebook. 'Are my measurements interesting?'

'No.' He dismissed that. 'Well – I am serious. The novel is dead. As dead as alchemy.' He cut out with his hands, with the calipers, dismissing that as well. 'I realized that one day before the war. Do you know what I did? I burnt every novel I possessed. Dickens. Cervantes. Dostoievsky. Flaubert. All the great and all the small. I even burnt something I wrote myself when I was too young to know better. I burnt them out there. It took me all day. The sky took their smoke, the earth their ashes. It was a fumigation. I have been happier and healthier ever since.' I remembered my own small destroying; and thought, grand gestures are splendid – if you can afford them. He picked up a book and slapped the dust off it. 'Why should I struggle through hundreds of pages of fabrication to reach half a dozen very little truths?'

'For fun?'

'Fun!' He pounced on the word. 'Words are for truth. For facts. Not fiction.'

'I see.'

'For this.' A life of Franklin Roosevelt. 'This.' A French paperback on astrophysics. 'This. Look at this.' It was an old pamphlet – *An Alarme for Sinners, Containing the Last Words of the Murderer Robert Foulkes, 1679*. 'There, take that and read it over the week-end. See if it is not more real than all the historical novels ever written.'

His bedroom extended almost the seaward width of the house, like the music-room below. At one end was a bed – a double bed, I noticed – and a huge wardrobe; at the other, a closed door led through into what must have been a very small room, a dressing-room perhaps. Near that door stood a strange-looking table, the top of which he lifted. It was (I had to be told) a clavichord. The centre of the room was fitted out as a kind of sitting-room and study. There was another tiled stove, and a desk littered with the papers he must have been working on, and two armchairs upholstered in pale brown to match a chaise-longue. In a far corner, a triangular cabinet full of pale-blue and green Isnik ware. Flooded with evening light, it was altogether a more homely room than the one downstairs, and by contrast pleasantly free of books.

But its tone was really set by its two paintings: both nudes, girls in sunlit interiors, pinks, reds, greens, honeys, ambers; all light, warmth, glowing like yellow fires with life, humanity, domesticity, sexuality, Mediterraneity.

'You know him?' I shook my head. 'Bonnard. He painted them both five or six years before he died.' I stood in front of them. He said, behind me, 'These, I paid for.'

'They were worth it.'

'Sunlight. A naked girl. A chair. A towel, a bidet. A tiled floor. A little dog. And he gives the whole of existence a reason.'

I stared at the one on the left, not the one he had inventoried. It showed a girl by a sunlit window with her back turned, apparently drying her loins and watching herself in the mirror at the same time. I was remembering Alison, Alison wandering about the flat naked, singing, like a child. It was an unforgettable painting; it set a dense golden halo of light round the most trivial of moments, so that the moment, and all such moments, could never be completely trivial again.

Conchis moved out on to the terrace, and I followed him. By the westward of the two french doors stood a small Moorish ivory-inlaid table. It carried a bowl of flowers set, as if votively, before a photograph.

It was a large picture in an old-fashioned silver frame. A girl in an Edwardian dress stood by a vase of roses on an improbable Corinthian pedestal, while painted foliage drooped sentimentally across the background. It was one of those old photographs whose dark chocolate shadows are balanced by the creamy richness of the light surfaces; of a period when women had bosoms, not breasts. The young girl in the picture had a massed pile of light hair, and a sharp waist, and that plump-softness of skin and slightly heavy Gibson-girl handsomeness of feature that the age so much admired.

Conchis saw me giving it a lingering glance. 'She was once my fiancée.'

I looked again. The photographer's name was stamped floridly in gold across the bottom corner – a London address.

'You never married her?'

'She died.'

'She looks English.'

'Yes.' He paused, surveying her. The girl seemed absurdly historical, standing by the pompous vase in front of the faded, painted grove. 'Yes, she was English.'

I looked at him. 'What was your English name, Mr Conchis?'

He smiled one of his rare smiles; like a monkey's paw flashing out of a cage. 'I have forgotten.'

'You never married at all?'

He remained staring down at the the photograph, then slowly shook his head.

'Come.'

A table stood in the south-east corner of the parapeted L-shaped terrace. It was already laid with a cloth, presumably for dinner. We looked over the trees at the superb view, the vast dome of light over land and sea. The mountains of the Peloponnesus had turned a violet-blue, and Venus hung in the pale-green sky like a white lamp, with the steady soft brilliance of gaslight. The photo stood in the doorway, placed rather in the way children put dolls in a window to let them look out.

He sat against the parapet with his back to the view.

'And you? You are engaged?' In my turn I shook my head. 'You must find life here very lonely.'

'I was warned.'

'A good-looking young man of your age.'

'Well, there was a girl, but ... '

'But?'

'I can't explain.'

'Is she English?'

I thought of the Bonnard; that was the reality; such moments; not what one could tell. I smiled at him.

'May I ask you what you asked me last week? No questions?'

'Of course.'

We sat in silence then, that same peculiar silence he had imposed on the beach the Saturday before. At last he turned to the sea and spoke again.

'Greece is like a mirror. It makes you suffer. Then you learn.'

'To live alone?'

'To live. With what you are. A Swiss came to end his days here – many years ago now – in an isolated ruined cottage at the far end of the island. Over there, under Aquila. A man of my age now. He had spent all his life assembling watches and reading about Greece. He had even taught himself classical Greek. He repaired the cottage himself, cleared the cisterns, made some terraces. His passion became – you cannot guess – goats. He kept one, then two. Then a small flock of them. They slept in the same room as he did. Always exquisite. Always combed and brushed, since he was Swiss. He used to call here sometimes in spring and we would have the utmost difficulty in keeping his seraglio out of the house. He learnt to make excellent cheeses – they fetched good prices in Athens. But he was alone. No one ever wrote to him. Visited him. Totally alone. And I believe the happiest man I have ever met.'

'What happened to him?'

'He died in 1937. A stroke. They did not discover him till a fort-night later. By then all his goats were dead too. It was winter, so you see the door was fastened.'

His eyes on mine, Conchis grimaced, as if he found death a joker. His skin clung very close to his skull. Only the eyes lived. I had the strange impression that he wanted me to believe *he* was death; that at any moment the leathery old skin and the eyes would fall, and I should find myself the guest of a skeleton.

Later we went back indoors. There were three other rooms on the north side of the first floor. One room he showed me only a glimpse of, a lumber-room. I saw crates piled high, and some furniture with dust-covers on. Then there was a bathroom, and beside the bath-room, a small bedroom. The bed was made, and I saw my duffel bag lying on it. I had fully expected one locked room, the woman-of-the-glove's room. Then I thought that she lived in the cottage – Maria looked after her, perhaps; or perhaps this room that was to be mine for the week-end was normally hers.

He handed me the seventeenth-century pamphlet, which I had left on a table on the landing.

'I usually have an aperitif downstairs in about half an hour. I will see you then?'

'Of course.'

'I must tell you something.'

'Yes.'

'You have heard some disagreeable things about me?'

'I only know one story about you and that seems very much to your credit.'

'The execution?'

'I told you last week.'

'I have a feeling that you have heard something else. From Captain Mitford?'

'Absolutely nothing. I assure you.'

He was standing in the doorway, giving me his intensest look. He seemed to gather strength; to decide that the mystery must be cleared up; then spoke.

'I am psychic.'

The house seemed full of silence; and suddenly everything that had happened earlier led to this.

'I'm afraid I'm not psychic. At all.'

We seemed drowned in dusk; two men staring at each other. I could hear a clock ticking in his room.

'That is unimportant. In half an hour?'

'Why did you tell me that?'

He turned to a small table by the door, struck a match to light the oil-lamp, and then carefully adjusted it, making me wait for an answer. At last he straightened and smiled.

'Because I am psychic.'

He went down the passage and across the landing into his own room. His door shut, then silence welled back.

16

The bed was a cheap iron one. Besides a second table, a carpet, and an armchair, there was only an old, locked *cassone*, of a kind to be found in every cottage on the island. It was the least likely million-aire's spare-room imaginable. The walls were bare except for a photograph of a number of village men standing in front of a house – the house. I could make out a younger Conchis in the centre, wearing a straw hat and shorts, and there was one woman, a peasant-woman, though not Maria, because she was Maria's age in the photo and it was plainly twenty or thirty years old. I held up the lamp and turned the picture round to see if there was anything written on the back. But the only thing there was a fragile gecko, which clung splay-footed to the wall and watched me with cloudy eyes. Geckoes like seldom-used rooms.

On the table by the head of the bed there was a flat shell to serve as an ashtray, and three books: a collection of ghost stories, an old Bible and a large thin volume entitled *The Beauties of Nature*. The ghost stories purported to be true, 'authenticated by at least two reliable witnesses'. The list of contents – 'Borley Rectory', 'The Isle of Man Polecat', 'No. 18 Dennington Road', 'The Man with the Limp' – reminded me of being ill at boarding school. I opened *The Beauties of Nature*. The nature was all female, and the beauty all pectoral. There were long shots of breasts, shots of breasts of every material from every angle, and against all sorts of background, closer and closer, until the final picture was of nothing but breast, with one dark and much larger-than-natural nipple staring from the centre of the glossy page. It was much too obsessive to be erotic.

I picked up the lamp and went into the bathroom. It was well fitted out, with a formidable medicine chest. I looked for some sign of a woman's occupation, and found none. There was running water, but it was cold and salt; for men only.

I went back to my room and lay on the bed. The sky in the open window was a pale night-blue and one or two first faint northerly stars blinked over the trees. Outside, the crickets chirped monotonously, with a Webern-like inconsistency yet precision of rhythm. I heard small noises from the cottage below my window, and I could smell cooking. In the house was a great stillness.

I was increasingly baffled by Conchis. At times he was so dogmatic that I wanted to laugh, to behave in the traditionally xenophobic, continentals-despising way of my race; at times, rather against my will, he impressed me – not only as a rich man with some enviable works of art in his house. And now he frightened me. It was the kind of illogical fear of the supernatural that in others made me sneer; but all along I had felt that I was invited not out of hospitality, but for some other reason. He wanted to use me in some way. I now discounted homosexuality; he had had his chances and ignored them. Besides, the Bonnards, the fiancée, the book of breasts, all discounted it.

Something much more bizarre was afoot. *'Are you elect?'* ... *'I am psychic'* ... it all pointed to spiritualism, to table-tapping. Perhaps the lady of the glove was a medium of some kind. Certainly Conchis hadn't got the petty-bourgeois gentility and the woolly vocabulary I associated with *séance*-holders; but he was equally certainly not a normal man.

I lit a cigarette, and after a while I smiled. In that small bare room, it seemed not to matter, even if I was a shade scared. The truth was that I was full of a sort of green stir. Conchis was no more than the chance agent, the event that had come at the right time; just as in the old days I might, after a celibate term at Oxford, have met a girl and begun an affaire with her, I had begun something exciting with him. It seemed linked in a way with my wanting to see Alison again. I wanted to live again.

The house was as quiet as death, as the inside of a skull; but the year was 1953, I was an atheist and an absolute non-believer in spiritualism, ghosts and all that mumbo-jumbo. I lay there waiting for the half-hour to pass; and the silence of the house was still, that day, much more a silence of peace than one of fear.

17

When I went downstairs, the music-room was lamplit but empty. There was a tray on the table in front of the stove with a bottle of ouzo, a jug of water, glasses, and a bowl of fat blue-black Amphissa olives. I poured out some ouzo and added enough water to make it go milkily opaque. Then, glass in hand, I began a tour of the bookshelves. The books were methodically arranged. There were two entire sections of medical works, mostly in French, including many – they hardly seemed to go with spiritualism – on psychiatry, and another two of scientific books of all kinds; several shelves of philosophical works, and also a fair number of botanical and ornithological books, mostly in English and German; but the great majority of the rest were autobiographies and biographies. There must have been thousands of them. They appeared to have been collected without any method: Wordsworth, Mae West, Saint-Simon, geniuses, criminals, saints, nonentities. The collection had the eclectic impersonality of a public library.

Behind the harpsichord and under the window there was a low glass cabinet which contained two or three classical pieces. There was a rhyton in the form of a human head, a black-figure kylix on one side, a small red-figure amphora on the other. On top of the cabinet were also three objects: a photo, an eighteenth-century clock, and a white-enamelled snuff-box. I went behind the music-stool to look at the Greek pottery. The painting on the flat inner bowl of the kylix gave me a shock. It involved two satyrs and a woman and was very obscene indeed. Nor were the paintings on the amphora of a kind any museum would dare put on display.

Then I looked closer at the clock. It was mounted in ormolu with an enamelled face. In the middle was a rosy little naked cupid; the shaft of the one short hand came through his loins, and the rounded tip at its end made it very clear what it was meant to be. There were no hours marked round the dial, and the whole of the right-hand half was blacked out, with the one word *Sleep* in white upon it. On the white enamel of the other half were written in neat black script the following faded but still legible words: at six, *Encounter*; at eight, *Enchantment*; at ten, *Erection*; at twelve, *Ecstasy*. The cupid smiled; the clock was not going and his manhood hung permanently askew at eight. I opened the innocent white snuff-box. Beneath the lid was enacted, in Boucheresque eighteenth-century terms, exactly the same scene as some ancient Greek had painted in the kylix two thousand years before.

It was between these two *objets* that Conchis had chosen, whether with perversion, with humour, or with simple bad taste, I couldn't decide, to place another photo of the Edwardian girl, his dead fiancée.

She looked out of the oval silver frame with alert, smiling eyes. Her splendidly white skin and fine neck were shown off by a square *décolletage*, messy swathes of lace tied over her bosom by what seemed a white shoe-lace. By one armpit was a floppy black bow. She looked very young, as if she was wearing her first evening dress; and in this photo she looked less heavy-featured; rather piquant, a touch of mischief, almost a shy delectation in being queen of a cabinet of *curiosa*.

A door closed upstairs, and I turned away. The eyes of the Modigliani seemed to glare at me severely, so I sneaked out under the colonnade, where a minute later Conchis joined me. He had changed into a pair of pale trousers and a dark cotton coat. He stood silhouetted in the soft light that flowed out of the room and silently toasted me. The mountains were just visible, dusky and black, like waves of charcoal, the sky beyond still not quite drained of afterglow. But overhead – I was standing on the steps down to the gravel – the stars were out. They sparkled less fierily than they do in England; tranquilly, as if they were immersed in limpid oil.

'Thank you for the bedside books.'

'If you see anything more interesting on the shelves, take it. Please.'

There was a strange call from the dark trees to the east of the house. I had heard it in the evenings at the school, and at first thought it made by some moronic village boy. It was very high-pitched, repeated at regular intervals: Kew. Kew. Kew. Like a melancholy transmigrated bus-conductor.

'There is my friend,' said Conchis. For an absurd and alarming moment I thought he must mean the woman of the glove. I saw her flitting through the island trees in her Ascot gloves, for ever searching for Kew. The call came again, eery and stupid, from the night behind us. Conchis counted five slowly, and the call came as he raised his hand. Then five again, and again it came.

'What is it?'

'*Otus scops*. The scops owl. It is very small. Not twenty centimetres. Like this.'

'I saw you had some books on birds.'

'Ornithology interests me.'

'And you have studied medicine.'

'I studied medicine. Many years ago.'

'And never practised?'

'Only on myself.'

Far out to sea to the west I saw the bright lights of the Athens boat. On Saturday nights it went on south down to Kythera. But instead of relating Bourani to the ordinary world, the distant ship seemed only to emphasize its hiddenness, its secrecy. I took the plunge.

'What did you mean by saying that you were psychic?'

'What did you think I meant?'

'Spiritualism?'

'Infantilism.'

'That's what I think.'

'Of course.'

I could just make out his face in the light from the doorway. He could see more of mine, because I had swung round during that last exchange.

'You haven't really answered my question.'

'Your first reaction is the characteristic one of your contrasuggestible century: to disbelieve, to disprove. I see this very clearly underneath your politeness. You are like a porcupine. When that animal has its spines erect, it cannot eat. If you do not eat, you will starve. And your prickles will die with the rest of your body.'

I swilled the last of the ouzo round in my glass. 'Isn't it your century too?'

' I have lived a great deal in other centuries.'

'You mean in literature?'

'In reality.'

The owl called again, at monotonously regular intervals. I stared out into the darkness of the pines.

'Reincarnation?'

'Is rubbish.'

'Then … ' I shrugged.

'I cannot escape my human life-span. So there is only one way I could have lived in other centuries.'

I was silent. 'I give up.'

'Not give up. Look up. What do you see?'

'Stars. Space.'

'And what else? That you know are there. Though they are not visible.'

'Other worlds?'

I turned to look at him. He sat, a black shadow. I felt a small chill run down my spine. He took the thought out of my mind.

'I am mad?'

'Mistaken.'

'No. Neither mad nor mistaken.'

'You … travel to other worlds?'

'Yes. I travel to other worlds.'

I put the glass down and pulled out a cigarette; lit it before speaking.

'In the flesh?'

'If you can tell me where the flesh ends and the mind begins, I will answer that.'

'You um … you have some evidence of this?'

'Ample evidence.' He allowed a moment to pass. 'For those with the intelligence to see it.'

'This is what you meant by election and being psychic?'

'In part.'

I was silent, thinking that I must make up my mind what course of action to take. I sensed an inherent hostility, which rose from beyond anything that had passed between us; the subconscious resistance of water to oil. A course of polite scepticism seemed best.

'You do this … travelling by, I don't know, something like telepathy?'

But before he could answer there was a soft slap of footsteps round the colonnade. Maria stood and bobbed.

'*Sas efcharistoume*, Maria. Dinner is served,' said Conchis.

We stood and went into the music-room. As we put our glasses on the tray he said, 'There are things that words cannot explain.'

I looked down. 'At Oxford we were taught to assume that if words can't explain, nothing else is likely to.'

'Very well.' He smiled. 'May I call you Nicholas now?'

'Of course. Please.'

He poured a drop of ouzo into our glasses. We raised and clinked them.

'*Eis 'ygeia sas, Nicholas.*'

'*Sygeia.*'

But I had a strong suspicion even then that he was drinking to something other than my health.

The table in the corner of the terrace glittered, an unexpectedly formal island of glass and silver in the darkness. It was lit by one tall lamp with a dark shade; the light flowed downwards, concentrated on the white cloth, and was then reflected up, lighting our faces strangely, Caravaggio fashion, against the surrounding darkness.

The meal was excellent. We ate small fish cooked in wine, a delicious chicken, herb-flavoured cheese and a honey-and-curd flan, made, according to Conchis, from a medieval Turkish recipe. The wine we drank had a trace of resin, as if the vineyard had merely been beside a pine-forest, and was nothing like the harsh turpentine-tasting rotgut I sometimes drank in the village. We ate largely in silence. He evidently preferred this. If we talked, it was of the food. He ate slowly, and very little, but I left nothing to take away.

When we had finished, Maria brought Turkish coffee in a brass pot and took the lamp, which was beginning to attract too many insects. She replaced it by a single candle. The flame rose untrembling in the still air; now and again a persistent insect would fly round, in, round and away. I lit my cigarette, and sat like Conchis, half-turned towards the sea and the south. He did not want to talk, and I was content to wait.

Suddenly there were footsteps below on the gravel. They were going away from the house towards the sea. At first I took them for Maria's, though it seemed strange that she should be going down to the beach at that time. But a second later I knew that they could not, or could no more plausibly than the glove, be hers.

They were light, rapid, quiet steps, as if the person was trying to make as little noise as possible. They might even have belonged to a child. I was sitting away from the parapet, and could see nothing below. I glanced at Conchis. He was staring out into the darkness as if the sound was perfectly normal. I shifted unobtrusively, to crane a look over the parapet. But the steps had passed away into silence. With alarming speed a large moth dashed at the candle, repeatedly and frantically, as if attached to it by elastic cord. Conchis leant forward and snuffed the flame.

'You do not mind sitting in darkness?'

'Not at all.'

It occurred to me that it might after all have really been a child, from one of the cottages at the bay to the east; someone who had come to help Maria.

'I should tell you how I came here.'

'It must have been a marvellous site to find.'

'Of course. But I am not talking of architecture.' He paused, seemingly at a loss to say what he did mean. 'I came to Phraxos looking for a house to rent. A house for a summer. I did not like the village. I do not like coasts that face north. On my last day I had a boatman take me round the island. For pleasure. By chance he landed me for a swim at Moutsa down there. By chance he said there was an old cottage up here. By chance I came up. The cottage was crumbled walls, a litter of stones choken with thorn-ivy. It was very hot. About four o'clock on the afternoon of April the eighteenth, 1928.'

He paused again, as if the memory of that year had stopped him; and to prepare me for a new facet of himself, a new shift.

'There were many more trees then. One could not see the sea. I stood in the little clearing round the ruined walls. I had immediately the sensation that I was expected. Something had been waiting there all my life. I stood there, and I knew who waited, who expected. It was myself. I was here and this house was here, you and I and this evening were here, and they had always been here, like reflections of my own coming. It was like a dream. I had been walking towards a closed door, and by a sudden magic its impenetrable wood became glass, through which I saw myself coming from the other direction, the future. I speak in analogies. You understand?'

I nodded, cautious, not concerned with understanding; because underlying everything he did I had come to detect an air of stage-management, of the planned and rehearsed. He did not tell me of his coming to Bourani as a man tells something that chances to occur to him; but far more as a dramatist tells an anecdote where the play requires. He went on.

'I knew at once that I must live here. I could not go beyond. It was only here that my past would merge into my future. So I stayed. I am here tonight. And you are here tonight.'

In the darkness he was looking sideways at me. I said nothing for a moment; there had seemed to be some special emphasis on the last sentence.

'Is this also what you meant by being psychic?'

'It is what I mean by hazard. There comes a time in each life like a point of fulcrum. At that time you must accept yourself. It is not any more what you will become. It is what you are and always will be. You are too young to know this. You are still becoming. Not being.'

'Perhaps.'

'Not perhaps. For certain.'

'What happens if one doesn't recognize the ... point of fulcrum?' But I was thinking, I have had it already – the silence in the trees, the siren of the Athens boat, the black mouth of the shotgun barrel.

'You will be like the many. Only the few recognize this moment. And act on it.'

'The elect?'

'The elect. The chosen by hazard.' I heard his chair creak. 'Look over there. The lamp-fishermen.' Away at the far feet of the mountains there was a thin dust of ruby lights in the deepest shadows. I didn't know whether he meant simply, look; or that the lamps were in some way symbolic of the elect.

'You're very tantalizing sometimes, Mr Conchis.'

'I am prepared to be less so.'

'I wish you would be.'

He was silent again.

'Suppose that what I tell you should mean more to your life than the mere listening?'

'I hope it would.'

Another pause.

'I do not want politeness. Politeness always conceals a refusal to face other kinds of reality. I am going to say something about you that may shock you. I know something about you that you do not know yourself.' He paused, again as if to let me prepare myself. 'You too are psychic, Nicholas. You are sure you are not. I know that.'

'Well, I'm not. Really.' I waited, then said, 'But I'd certainly like to know what makes you think I am.'

'I have been shown.'

'When?'

'I prefer not to say.'

'But you must. I don't even know what you really mean by the word. If you merely mean some sort of intuitive intelligence, then I hope I am psychic. But I thought you meant something else.'

Again silence, as if he wanted me to hear the sharpness in my own voice. 'You are treating this as if I have accused you of some crime. Of some weakness.'

'I'm sorry. But I've never had a psychical experience in my life.' I added, naively, 'Anyway, I'm an atheist.'

His voice was gentle and dry. 'If a person is intelligent, then of course he is either an agnostic or an atheist. Just as he is a physical coward. They are automatic definitions of high intelligence. But I am not talking about God. I am talking about science.' I said nothing. His voice became much drier. 'Very well. I accept that you believe that you are ... *not* psychic.'

'You can't refuse to tell me what you promised now.'

'I wished only to warn you.'

'You have.'

'Excuse me for one minute.'

He disappeared into his bedroom. I got up and went to the corner of the parapet, from where I could see in three directions. All round the house lay the silent pine trees, dim in the starlight. Absolute peace. High and very far to the north I could just hear an aeroplane, only the third or fourth I had heard at night since coming to the island. I thought of an Alison on it, moving down a gangway with a trolley of drinks. Like the ship the faint drone accentuated, rather than diminished, the remoteness of Bourani. I had an acute sense of the absence of Alison, of the probably permanent loss of her; I could imagine her beside me, her hand in mine; and she was human warmth, normality, standard to go by. I had always seen myself as potentially a sort of protector of her; and for the first time, that evening at Bourani, I saw that perhaps she had been, or could have been, a protector of me.

A few seconds later Conchis returned. He went to the parapet, and breathed deeply. The sky and the sea and the stars, half the universe, stretched out before us. I could still just hear the aeroplane. I lit a cigarette, as Alison, at such a moment, would have lit a cigarette.

18

'I think we should be more comfortable in the lounging-chairs.'

I helped him pull the two long wicker chairs from the far end of the terrace. Then we both put our feet up and sat back. And at once I could smell it on the tied-on head-cushion – that same elusive, old-fashioned perfume of the towel, of the glove. I was sure it did not belong to Conchis or old Maria. I should have smelt it by then. There was a woman, and she often used this chair.

'It will take me a long time to define what I mean. It will take me the story of my life.'

'I've spent the last seven months among people who can speak only the most rudimentary English.'

'My French is better than my English now. But no matter. *Comprendre, c'est tout.*'

' "Only connect." '

'Who said that?'

'An English novelist.'

'He should not have said it. Fiction is the worst form of connection.'

I smiled in the darkness. There was silence. The stars gave signals. He began.

'I told you my father was English. But his business, importing tobacco and currants, lay mainly in the Levant. One of his competitors was a Greek living in London. In 1892 this Greek had tragic news. His eldest brother and his wife had been killed in an earthquake over the mountains there on the other side of the Peloponnesus. Three children survived. The two youngest, two boys, were sent out to South America, to a third brother. And the eldest child, a girl of seventeen, was brought to London to keep house for her uncle, my father's competitor. He had long been a widower. She had the prettiness that is characteristic of Greek women who have some Italian blood. My father met her. He was much older, but quite good-looking, I suppose, and he spoke some demotic Greek. There were business interests which could be profitably merged. In short, they married ... and I exist.

'The first thing I remember clearly is my mother's singing. She always sang, whether she was happy or sad. She could sing classical music quite well, and play the piano, but it was the Greek folk-tunes I remember best. Those she always sang when she was sad. I remember her telling me – much later in life – of that standing on a distant hillside and seeing the ochre dust float slowly up into the azure sky. When the news about her parents came, she was filled with a black hatred of Greece. She wanted to leave it then, never to return. Like so many Greeks. And like so many Greeks she never accepted her exile. That is the cost of being born in the most beautiful and the most cruel country in the world.

'My mother sang – and music was the most important thing in my life, from as far back as I can remember. I was something of a child prodigy. I gave my first concert at the age of nine, and people were very kind. But I was a bad pupil at all the other subjects at school. I was not stupid, but I was very lazy. I knew only one obligation: to play the piano well. Duty largely consists of pretending that the trivial is critical, and I was never accomplished at that.

'I was fortunate, I had a very remarkable music-teacher – Charles-Victor Bruneau. He had many of the traditional faults of his kind. Vain of his methods and vain of his pupils. A sarcastic agony if one was not talented, and a painstaking angel if one was. But he was a very learned man musicologically. In those days that meant he was *rarissima avis*. Most executants then wanted only to express themselves. And so they developed accomplishments like enormous velocity and great skill at expressive rubato. No one today plays like that. Or could play like it, even if they wanted to. The Rosenthals and Godowskis are gone for ever. But Bruneau was far in advance of his time and there are still many Haydn and Mozart sonatas I can hear only as he played them.

'However, his most remarkable acquirement – I speak of before 1914 – was the then almost unknown one of being as good a harpsichordist as a pianist. I first came under him at a period in his life when he was abandoning the piano. The harpsichord requires a very different finger technique from the piano. It is not easy to change. He dreamed of a school of harpsichord players trained as early as possible as pure harpsichordists. And not, as he used to say, *des pianistes en costume de bal masqué*.

'When I was fifteen, I had what we could call today a nervous breakdown. Bruneau had been driving me too hard. I never had the least interest in games. I was a day-boy, I had permission to concentrate on music. I never made any real friends at school. Perhaps because I was taken for a Jew. But the doctor said that when I recovered I would have to practise less and go out more often. I made a face. My father came back one day with an expensive book on birds. I could hardly tell the commonest birds apart, had never thought of doing so. But my father's was an inspired guess. Lying in bed, looking at the stiff poses in the pictures, I began to want to see the living reality – and the only reality to begin with for me was the singing that I heard through my sickroom window. I came to birds through sound. Suddenly even the chirping of sparrows seemed mysterious. And the singing of birds I had heard a thousand times, thrushes, blackbirds in our London garden, I heard as if I had never heard them before. Later in my life – *ça sera pour un autre jour* – birds led me into a very unusual experience.

'You see the child I was. Lazy, lonely, yes, very lonely. What is that word? A cissy. Talented in music, and in nothing else. And I was an only child, spoilt by my parents. As I entered my fourth lustre, it became evident that I was not going to fulfil my early promise. Bruneau saw it first, and then I did. Though we tacitly agreed not to tell my parents, it was difficult for me to accept.

113

Sixteen is a bad age at which to know one will never be a genius. But by then I was in love.

'I first saw Lily when she was fourteen, and I was a year older, soon after my breakdown. We lived in St John's Wood. In one of those small white mansions for successful merchants. You know them? A semi-circular drive. A portico. At the back was a long garden, at the end of it a little orchard, some six or seven overgrown apple and pear trees. Unkempt, but very green. I had a private "house" under a lime tree. One day – June, a noble blue day, burning, clear, as they are here in Greece – I was reading a life of Chopin. I remember that exactly. You know at my age you recall the first twenty years far better than the second – or the third. I was reading and no doubt seeing myself as Chopin, and I had my new book on birds beside me. It is 1910.

'Suddenly I hear a noise on the other side of the brick wall which separates the garden of the next house from ours. This house is empty, so I am surprised. And then ... a head appears. Cautiously. Like a mouse. It is the head of a young girl. I am half hidden in my bower, I am the last thing she sees, so I have time to examine her. Her head is in sunshine, a mass of pale blonde hair that falls behind her and out of sight. The sun is to the south, so that it is caught in her hair, in a cloud of light. I see her shadowed face, her dark eyes, and her small half-opened inquisitive mouth. She is grave, timid, yet determined to be daring. She sees me. She stares at me for a moment in her shocked haze of light. She seems more erect, like a bird. I stand up in the entrance of my bower, still in shadow. We do not speak or smile. All the unspoken mysteries of puberty tremble in the air. I do not know why I cannot speak ... and then a voice called her name.

'The spell was broken. And all my past was broken, too. There is a line from Seferis – "The broken pomegranate is full of stars"? It was like that. She disappeared, I sat down again, but to read was impossible. I went to the wall near the house, and heard a man's voice and silver female voices that faded through a door.

'I was in a morbid state. But that first meeting, that mysterious ... how shall I say, message from her light, from her light to my shadow, haunted me for weeks.

'Her parents moved into the house next door. I met Lily face to face. And there was some bridge between us. It was not all my imagination, this something came from her as well as from me – a joint umbilical cord, something we dared not speak of, of course, yet which we both knew was there.

'She was not unlike me in many ordinary ways. She too had few friends in London. And the final touch to this fairy story was that she too was musical. Not very strikingly gifted, but musical. Her father was a peculiar man, Irish, with private means, and with a passion for music. He played the flute very well. Of course he had to meet Bruneau, who sometimes came to our house, and through Bruneau he met Dolmetsch, who interested him in the recorder. Another forgotten instrument in those days. I remember Lily playing her first solo on a flat-sounding descant recorder made by Dolmetsch and bought for her by her father.

'Our two families grew very close. I accompanied Lily, we sometimes played duets, sometimes her father would join us, sometimes the two mothers would sing. We discovered a whole new continent of music. The Fitzwilliam Virginal Book, Arbeau, Frescobaldi, Froberger – in those years people suddenly realized that there had been music before 1700.'

He paused. I wanted to light a cigarette, but more than that I wanted not to distract him; his reaching back. So I held the cigarette between my fingers, and waited.

'She had, yes, I suppose a Botticelli beauty, long fair hair, grey-violet eyes. But that makes her sound too pale, too Pre-Raphaelite. She had something that is gone from the world, from the female world. A sweetness without sentimentality, a limpidity without naivety. She was so easy to hurt, to tease. And when she teased, it was like a caress. I make her sound too colourless to you. Of course, in those days, what we young men looked for was not so much the body as the soul. Lily was a very pretty girl. But it was her soul that was *sans pareil*.

'No obstacles except those of propriety were ever put between us. I said just now that we were alike in interests and tastes. But we were opposites in temperament. Lily was always so very self-controlled, patient, helping. I was temperamental. Moody. And very selfish. I never saw her hurt anyone or anything. But if I wanted something I wanted it at once. Lily used to disgust me with myself. I used to think of my Greek blood as dark blood. Almost Negro blood.

'And then too I soon began to love her physically. Whereas she loved me, or treated me, as a brother. Of course we knew we were going to marry, we promised ourselves to each other when she was only sixteen. But I was hardly ever allowed to kiss her. You cannot imagine this. To be so close to a girl and yet so rarely be able to caress her. My desires were very innocent. I had all the usual notions of the time about the need for chastity. But I was not completely English.

'There was *o Pappous* – my grandfather – really my mother's uncle. He had become a naturalized Englishman, but he never carried his anglophilia to the point of being puritan, or even respectable. He was not, I think, a very wicked old man. What I knew of him corrupted me far less than the false ideas I conceived. I always spoke with him in Greek, and as you perhaps realize, Greek is a naturally sensual and uneuphemistic language. I surreptitiously read certain books I found on his shelves. I saw *La Vie Parisienne*. I came one day on a folder full of tinted engravings. And so I began to have erotic daydreams. The demure Lily in her straw hat, a hat I could describe to you now, still, as well as if I had it here in front of me, the crown swathed in a pale tulle the colour of a summer haze … in a long-sleeved, high-necked, pink-and-white striped blouse … a dark-blue hobble skirt, beside whom I walked across Regent's Park in the spring of 1914. The entranced girl I stood behind in the gallery at Covent Garden in June, nearly fainting in the heat – such a summer, that year – to hear Chaliapin in *Prince Igor* … Lily – she became in my mind at night the abandoned young prostitute. I thought I was very abnormal to have created this second Lily from the real one. I was bitterly ashamed again of my Greek blood. Yet possessed by it. I blamed everything on that, and my mother suffered, poor woman. My father's family had already humiliated her enough, without her own son joining in.

'I was ashamed then. I am proud now to have Greek and Italian and English blood and even some Celtic blood. One of my father's grandmothers was a Scotswoman. I am European. That is all that matters to me. But in 1914 I wanted to be purely English so as to be able to offer myself untainted to Lily.

'You know, of course, that something far more monstrous than my adolescent Arabian Nights was being imagined in the young mind of twentieth-century Europe. I was just eighteen. The war began. They were unreal, the first days. So much peace and plenty, for so long a time. In the collective unconscious, perhaps everyone wanted a change, a purge. A holocaust. But it appeared to us unpolitical citizens a matter of pride, of purely military pride. Something which the Regular Army and His Majesty's invincible Navy would settle. There was no conscription, no feeling in my world, of necessity to volunteer. It never crossed my mind that I might one day have to fight. Moltke, Bülow, Foch, Haig, French – the names meant nothing. But then came the sombre *coup d'archet* of Mons and Le Cateau. That was totally new. The efficiency of the Germans, the horror stories about the Prussian Guards, the Belgian outrages, the black shock of the casualty lists. Kitchener. The Million Army. And then in September the battle of the Marne – that was no longer cricket. Eight hundred thousand – imagine them drawn up down there on the sea – eight hundred thousand candles all blown out in one gigantic breath.

'December came. The "flappers" and the "nuts" had disappeared. My father told me one evening that neither he nor my mother would think the worse of me if I did not go. I had started at the Royal College of Music, and the atmosphere there was at first hostile to volunteering. The war had nothing to do with art or artists. I remember my parents and Lily's discussing the war. They agreed it was inhuman. But my father's conversation with me became strained. He became a special constable, a member of the local emergency committee. Then the son of his head clerk was killed in action. He told us that one silent dinner-time, and left my mother and me alone immediately afterwards. Nothing was said, but everything was plain. One day soon afterwards, Lily and I stood and watched a contingent of troops marching through the streets. It was wet after rain, the pavements were shining. They were going to France, and someone beside us said they were volunteers. I watched their singing faces in the yellow of the gas-lamps. The cheering people around us. The smell of wet serge. They were drunk, marchers and watchers, exalted out of themselves, their faces set in the rictus of certainty. Medieval in their certainty. I had not then heard the famous phrase. But this was *le consentement frémissant à la guerre*.

'They are mad, I said to Lily. She did not seem to hear me. But when they had gone she turned and said, If I was going to die to-morrow I should be mad. It stunned me. We went home in silence. And all the way she hummed, I now – but could not then – believe without malice, a song of the day.'

He paused, then half sung it:

> '"We shall miss you, we shall kiss you,
> But we think you ought to go."

'I felt like a small boy beside her. Once again I blamed my miserable Greek blood. It had made me a coward as well as a lecher. I see, when I look back, that indeed it had. Because I was less a true coward, a calculating coward, than someone so innocent, or so Greek, that he could not see what the war had to do with him. Social responsibility has never been a Greek characteristic.

'When we reached our houses, Lily kissed my cheek and ran in. I understood. She could not apologize, but she could still pity. I spent a night and a day and a second night in agony. The next day I saw Lily and told her I was going to volunteer. All the blood left her cheeks. Then she burst into tears and threw herself into my arms. So did my mother when I told her. But hers was a purer grief.

'I was passed fit, accepted. I was a hero. Lily's father presented me with an old pistol he had. My father opened champagne. And then when I got to my room, and sat on my bed with the pistol in my hands, I cried. Not from fear – for the sheer nobility of what I was doing. I had never felt public-spirited before. And I also thought that I had conquered that Greek half of me. I was fully English at last.

'I was pushed into the 13th London Rifles – Princess Louise's Kensington Regiment. There I became two people – one who watched and one who tried to forget that the other watched. We were trained less to kill than to be killed. Taught to advance at two-pace intervals – against guns that fired two hundred and fifty bullets a minute. The Germans and the French did the same. No doubt we should have objected if we had ever seriously thought about action. But the current myth at that time maintained that the volunteers were to be used only for guard and communication duties. The regulars and the reservists were the fighting troops. Besides, every week we were told that because of its enormous cost the war could not last another month.'

I heard him move in his chair. In the silence that followed I waited for him to continue. But he said nothing. The stars shimmered in their dustless, glittering clouds; the terrace was like a stage beneath them.

'A glass of brandy?'

'I hope you're not going to stop.'

'Let us have some brandy.'

He stood up and lit the candle. Then he disappeared.

I lay in my chair and stared up at the stars. 1914 and 1953 were aeons apart; 1914 was on a planet circling one of those furthest faintest stars. The vast stretch, the pace of time.

Then they came again, those footsteps. This time, they approached. It was the same rapid walk. But it was much too warm for rapid walking. Someone wanted to reach the house urgently, and without being seen. I got quickly to the parapet.

I was just in time to glimpse a pale shape at the far end of the house move up the steps and under the colonnade. I could not see well, my eyes had been dazzled, after the darkness, by the candle. But it was not Maria; a whiteness, a flowing whiteness, a long coat or a dressing-gown – I had only a second's sight, but I knew it was a woman and I knew it was not an old woman. I suspected, too, that I had been meant to see her. Because if one wanted to get into the house unheard, one wouldn't cross the gravel, but approach the house from the rear, or the far side.

There was a sound from the bedroom and Conchis appeared in the lamplit doorway, carrying a tray with a bottle and two glasses. I waited till he had set it by the candle.

'You know someone has just come in downstairs.'

He betrayed not the least surprise. He uncorked the bottle and carefully poured the brandy. 'A man or a woman?'

'A woman.'

'Ah.' He handed me my brandy. 'This is made at the monastery of Arkadion in Crete.' He snuffed the candle and went back to his chair. I remained standing.

'You did say you lived alone.'

'I said that I liked to give the islanders the impression that I lived alone.'

The dryness in his voice made me feel that I was being very naive. The woman was simply his mistress, whom for some reason he did not want me to meet; or who perhaps did not want to meet me. I went and sat down on the lounging-chair.

'I'm being tactless. Forgive me.'

'Not tactless. Perhaps a little lacking in imagination.'

'I thought perhaps I was meant to notice what obviously I'm not meant to notice.'

'Noticing is not a matter of choice, Nicholas. But explaining is.'

'Of course.'

'Patience.'

'I'm sorry.'

'Do you like the brandy?'

'Very much.'

'It always reminds me of Armagnac. Now. Shall I continue?'

As he began to speak again I smelt the night air, I felt the hard concrete under my feet, I touched a piece of chalk in my pocket. But a strong feeling persisted, when I swung my feet off the ground and lay back, that something was trying to slip between me and reality.

19

'I found myself in France a little more than six weeks after I enlisted. I had no aptitude with the rifle. I could not even bayonet an effigy of Kaiser Bill convincingly. But I was considered "sharp" and they also discovered that I could run quite fast. So I was selected as company runner, which meant that I was also a kind of servant, I forget the word ... '

'Batman.'

'That is it. My training company commander was a Regular Army officer of thirty or so. His name was Captain Montague. He had broken his leg some time before and so had been unfit for active service till then. A kind of phosphorescent pale elegance about his face. A delicate, gallant moustache. He was one of the most supremely stupid men I have ever met. He taught me a great deal.

'Before our training was finished, he received an urgent posting to France. That same day he told me, as if he were giving me a magnificent present, that he thought he could pull strings and have me posted with him. Only a man as blank as he would have failed to see the hollowness of my enthusiasm. But unfortunately he had grown fond of me.

'He had a brain capable of only one idea at a time. With him it was the *offensive à outrance* – the headlong attack. Foch's great contribution to the human race. "The force of the shock is the mass," he used to say – "the force of the mass is the impulsion and the force of the impulsion is the morale. High morale, high impulsion, high shock – victory!" Thump on the table – "Victory!" He made us all learn it by heart. At bayonet-drill. Vic-tor-ee! Poor fool.

'I spent a last two days with my parents and Lily. She and I swore undying love. The idea of heroic sacrifice had contaminated her, as it had contaminated my father. My mother said nothing, except an old Greek proverb: A dead man cannot be brave. I remembered that later.

'We went straight to the front. One of the company commanders there had died of pneumonia, and it was his place Montague had to take. This is early in 1915. It sleeted and rained incessantly. We spent long hours in stationary trains in railway-sidings, in grey towns under greyer skies. One knew the troops who had been in action. The ones who sang their way to death, the new recruits, were the dupes of the romance of war. But the others were dupes of the reality of war, of the ultimate *Totentanz*. Like those sad old men and women who haunt every casino, they knew the wheel must always win in the end. But they could not force themselves to leave.

'We spent a few days on manoeuvres. And then one day Montague addressed the company. We were going into battle, a new sort of battle, one in which victory was certain. One that was going to bring us to Berlin in a month. The night of the next day we entrained. The train stopped somewhere in the middle of a flat plain and we marched eastwards. Dykes and willows in the darkness. Endless drizzle. It crept down the columns that the place we were to attack was a village called Neuve Chapelle. And that the Germans were to receive something revolutionary. A giant gun. A mass attack by the new aeroplanes.

'After a while we turned into a field, thick with mud, and were marched up to some farm-buildings. Two hours' rest before taking up position for the attack. No one can have slept. It was very cold, and fires were forbidden. My real self began to appear, I began to be afraid. But I told myself that if I was ever to be truly frightened, I should have known it before then. This is what I had willed to execute. That is how war corrupts us. It plays on our pride in our own free will.

'Before dawn we filed slowly forward, many stops, to the assault positions. I overheard Montague talking with a staff officer. The entire First Army, Haig's, was engaged, with the Second in support. And there seemed to me a safety, a kind of warmth in such numbers. But then we entered the trenches. The terrible trenches, with their stench of the urinal. And then the first shells fell near us. I was so innocent that in spite of our so-called training, of all the propaganda, I had never really been able to believe that someone might want to kill me. We were told to halt and stand against the walls. The shells hissed, whined, crashed. Then silence. Then a splatter of falling clods. And shivering, I awoke from my long sleep.

'I think the first thing I saw was the isolation of each. It is not the state of war that isolates. It is well known, it brings people together. But the battlefield – that is something different. Because that is when the real enemy, death, appears. I no longer saw any warmth in numbers. I saw only Thanatos in them, my death. Just as much in my own comrades, in Montague, as in the invisible Germans.

'The madness of it, Nicholas. Standing in holes in the ground, thousands of men, English, Scots, Indians, French, Germans, one March morning – and what for? If there is a hell, then it is that. Not flames, not pitchforks. But a place without the possibility of reason, like Neuve Chapelle that day.

'A reluctant light began to spread over the eastern sky. The drizzle stopped. A trill of song from somewhere outside the trench. I recognized a hedge-sparrow, the last voice from the other world. We moved forward again some way and into the assault trenches – the Rifle Brigade was to form the second wave of the attack. The German trenches were less than two hundred yards ahead, with our front trench only a hundred yards from theirs. Montague looked at his watch. He raised his hand. There was complete silence. His hand fell. For some ten seconds nothing happened. Then, far behind us, there was a gigantic drum-roll, a thousand tympani. A pause. And then the whole world ahead exploded. Everyone ducked. A shaking of earth, sky, mind, all. You cannot imagine what the first few minutes of that bombardment were like. It was the first massive artillery barrage of the war, the heaviest ever delivered.

'A runner came from the front trenches, down the communicating trench. His face and uniform were streaked with red. Montague asked if he was hit. He said everyone in the front trenches was splashed with blood from the German trenches. They were so close. If only they could have stopped to think how close ...

'After half an hour the barrage was moving over the village. Montague, at the periscope, cried "They're up!" And then – "The Boches are done for!" He leapt on to the parapet, and waved to all of us around him to look over the edge of the trench. A hundred yards ahead a long line of men trotted slowly across the scarred earth towards some shattered trees and broken walls. A few isolated shots. A man fell. Then stood up and ran on. He had simply tripped. The men about me began to shout as the line reached the first houses and a cheer came back. A red light soared up, and then we in our turn advanced. It was difficult to walk. And as we went forward, fear was driven out by horror. Not a shot was fired at us. But the ground became increasingly hideous. Nameless things, pink, white, red, mud-bespattered, still with rags of grey or khaki. We crossed our own front trench and traversed the no-man's-land. When we came to the German trenches there was nothing to see. Everything had been either buried or blown out of them. There we halted for a moment, lying down in the craters, almost in peace. To the north the firing was very intense. The Cameronians had been caught on the wire. In twenty minutes they lost every officer except one. And four-fifths of their men were killed.

'Figures appeared between the wrecked cottages ahead, their hands high. Some of them being held up by friends. They were the first prisoners. Many of them were yellow with lyddite. Yellow men out of the white curtain of light. One walked straight towards me, lurching, with his head tilted, as if in a dream, and fell straight into a deep crater. A moment later he reappeared, crawling up over the edge, then slowly standing. Lurching forward again. Other prisoners came weeping. One vomited blood in front of us, and collapsed.

'Then we were running towards the village. We came into what must have once been a street. Desolation. Rubble, fragments of plastered wall, broken rafters, the yellow splashes of lyddite everywhere. The drizzle that had started again gleaming on the stones. On the skin of corpses. Many Germans had been caught in the houses. In ten minutes I saw a summary of the whole butcher's shop of war. The blood, the gaping holes, the bone sticking out of flesh, the stench of burst intestines – I am telling you this only because the effect on me, a boy who had never seen even a peacefully dead body before that day, was one I should never have predicted. It was not nausea and terror. I saw several men being sick. But I was not. It was an intense new conviction. Nothing could justify this. It was a thousand times better that England should be a Prussian colony. One reads that such scenes give the green soldier nothing but a mad lust to kill in his turn. But I had exactly the contrary feeling. I had a mad lust not to be killed.'

He stood up.

'I have a test for you.'

'A test?'

He went into his bedroom, returned almost at once with the oil-lamp that had been on the table when we had dinner. In the white pool of light he put what he had brought. I saw a dice, a shaker, a saucer, and a pill-box. I looked up at him on the other side of the table, at his severe eyes on mine.

'I am going to explain to you why we went to war. Why mankind always goes to war. It is not social or political. It is not countries that go to war, but men. It is like salt. Once one has been to war, one has salt for the rest of one's life. Do you understand?'

'Of course.'

'So in my perfect republic it would be simple. There would be a test for all young people at the age of twenty-one. They would go to a hospital where they would throw a dice. One of the six numbers would mean death. If they threw that they would be painlessly killed. No mess. No bestial cruelty. No destruction of innocent onlookers. But one clinical throw of the dice.'

'Certainly an improvement on war.'

'You think so?'

'Obviously.'

'You are sure?'

'If it was possible.'

'You said you never saw action in the last war?'

'No.'

He took the pill-box, and shook out, of all things, six large molars; yellowish, two or three with old stoppings.

'These were issued to spies on both sides during the last war, for use if they were interrogated.' He placed one of the teeth on the saucer, then with a small downward jab of the shaker crushed it; it was brittle, like a liqueur chocolate. But the odour of the colourless liquid was of bitter almonds, acrid and terrifying. He hastily removed the saucer at arm's length to the far corner of the terrace; then returned.

'Suicide pills?'

'Precisely. Hydrocyanic acid.' He picked up the dice, and showed me six sides.

I smiled. 'You want me to throw?'

'I offer you an entire war in one second.'

'Supposing I don't want it?'

'Think. In a minute from now you could be saying, I risked death. I threw for life, and I won life. It is a very wonderful feeling. To have survived.'

'Wouldn't a corpse be rather embarrassing for you?' I was still smiling, but it was wearing thin.

'Not at all. I could easily prove it was suicide.' He stared at me, and his eyes went through me like a trident through a fish. With ninety-nine persons out of a hundred, I would have known it was a bluff; but he was different, and a nervousness had hold of me before I could resist it.

'Russian roulette.'

'Less fallible. These pills work within a few seconds.'

'I don't want to play.'

'Then you are a coward, my friend.' He leant back and watched me.

'I thought you believed brave men were fools.'

'Because they persist in rolling the dice again and again. But a young man who will not risk his life even once is both a fool and a coward.'

'Did you try this on my predecessors?'

'John Leverrier was neither a fool nor a coward. Even Mitford was not the second.'

And he had me. It was absurd, but I would not let my bluff be called. I reached for the shaker.

'Wait.' He leant forward, and put his hand on my wrist; then placed a tooth by my side. 'I am not playing at make-believe. You must swear to me that if the number is six you will take the pill.' His face was totally serious. I felt myself wanting to swallow.

'I swear.'

'By all that is most sacred to you.'

I hesitated, shrugged, then said, 'By all that is most sacred to me.'

He held out the dice and I put it in the shaker. I shook it loosely and quickly and threw the dice. It ran over the cloth, hit the brass base of the lamp, rebounded, wavered, fell.

It was a six.

Conchis was absolutely motionless, watching me. I knew at once that I was never, never going to pick up the pill. I could not look at him. Perhaps fifteen seconds passed. Then I smiled, looked at him and shook my head.

He reached out again, his eyes still on me, took the tooth beside me, put it in his mouth and bit it and swallowed the liquid. I went red. Still watching me, he reached out and put the dice in the shaker, and threw it. It was a six. Then again. And again it was a six. He spat out the empty shell of the tooth.

'What you have just decided is precisely what I decided that morning forty years ago at Neuve Chapelle. You have behaved exactly as any intelligent human being should behave. I congratulate you.'

'But what you said? The perfect republic?'

'All perfect republics are perfect nonsense. The craving to risk death is our last great perversion. We come from night, we go into night. Why live in night?'

'But the dice was loaded.'

'Patriotism, propaganda, professional honour, *esprit de corps* – what are all those things? Cogged dice. There is just one small difference, Nicholas. On the other table these are real.' He put the remaining teeth back in the box. 'Not just ratafia in coloured plastic.'

'And the other two – how did they react?'

He smiled. 'Another means society employs to control hazard – to prevent a freedom of choice in its slaves – is to tell them that the past was nobler than the present. John Leverrier was a Catholic. And wiser than you. He refused even to be tempted.'

'And Mitford?'

'I do not waste time teaching the blind.'

His eyes lingered a dry moment on mine, as if to make sure I took the implicit compliment; and then, as if to limit it, he turned out the lamp. I was left in more than the literal darkness. What last thin pretence had remained that I was merely a guest lay discarded. He had evidently been through all this before. The horrors of Neuve Chapelle had been convincing enough as he described them, yet they turned artificial with this knowledge of repetition. Their living reality became a matter of technique, of realism gained through rehearsal. It was like being earnestly persuaded an object was new by a seller who simultaneously and deliberately revealed it must be second-hand: an affront to all probability. I was not to believe in appearances ... but why, why, why?

Meanwhile he had started weaving his web again; and once more I flew to meet it.

20

'The middle six hours of that day we passed in waiting. The Germans hardly shelled us at all. They had been bombarded to their knees. The obvious thing would have been to attack at once. But it takes a very brilliant general, a Napoleon, to see the obvious.

'About three o'clock the Gurkhas came alongside us and we were told an attack on the Aubers Ridge was to be launched. We were to be the first line. Just before half past three we fixed bayonets. I was beside Captain Montague, as usual. I think he knew only one thing about himself. That he was fearless, and ready to swallow the acid. He kept looking along the lines of men beside him. He scorned the use of a periscope, and stood and poked his head over the parapet. The Germans still seemed stunned.

'We began to walk forward. Montague and the sergeant-major

called incessantly, keeping us in line. We had to cross a cratered ploughed field to a hedge of poplars, and then across another small field lay our objective, a bridge. I suppose we had gone about half the distance we had to cover, and then we broke into a trot and some of the men began to shout. The Germans seemed to stop firing altogether. Montague called triumphantly. "On, lads! Victoree!"

'They were the last words he ever spoke. It was a trap. Five or six machine guns scythed us like grass. Montague spun round and fell at my feet. He lay on his back, staring up at me, one eye gone. I collapsed beside him. The air was nothing but bullets. I pressed my face right into the mud, I was urinating, certain that at any moment I should be killed. Someone came beside me. It was the sergeant-major. Some of the men were firing back, but blindly. In despair. The sergeant-major, I do not know why, began dragging Montague's corpse backwards. Feebly, I tried to help. We slipped down into a small crater. The back of Montague's head had been blown away, but his face still wore an idiot's grin, as if he were laughing in his sleep, mouth wide open. A face I have never forgotten. The last smile of a stage of evolution.

'The firing stopped. Then, like a flock of frightened sheep, everyone who survived began to run back towards the village. I as well. I had lost even the will to be a coward. Many were shot in the back as they ran, and I was one of the few who reached the trench we had started from unhurt – alive, even. We were no sooner there than the shelling began. Our own shells. Owing to the bad weather conditions, the artillery were shooting blind. Or perhaps still according to some plan established days before. Such irony is not a by-product of war. But typical of it.

'A wounded lieutenant was now in command. He crouched beside me, with a great gash across his cheek. His eyes burned dully. He was no longer a nice upright young Englishman, but a neolithic beast. Cornered, uncomprehending, in a sullen rage. Perhaps we all looked like that. The longer one survived the more unreal it was.

'More troops came up with us, and a colonel appeared. Aubers Ridge must be captured. We had to have the bridge by nightfall. But I had meanwhile had time to think.

'I saw that this cataclysm must be an expiation for some barbarous crime of civilization, some terrible human lie. What the lie was, I had too little knowledge of history or science to know then. I know now it was our believing that we were fulfilling some end, serving some plan – that all would come out well in the end, because there was some great plan over all. Instead of the reality. There is no plan. All is hazard. And the only thing that will preserve us is ourselves.'

He was silent; I could just make out his face, his staring to sea, as if Neuve Chapelle was out there, grey mud and hell, visible.

'We attacked again. I should have liked simply to disobey orders and stay in the trench. But of course cowards were treated as deserters, and shot. So I clambered up with the rest when the order came. A sergeant shouted at us to run. Exactly the same thing happened as earlier that afternoon. There was a little firing from the Germans, just enough to bait the trap. But I knew that there were half a dozen eyes watching down their machine-guns. My one hope was that they would be truly German. That is, methodical, and not open fire until the same point as before.

'We came to within fifty yards of that point. Two or three bullets ricocheted close by. I clasped my heart, dropped my rifle, staggered. Just in front of me I had seen a large shell-crater, an old one. I stumbled, fell and rolled over the edge of it. I heard the cry "Keep on!" I lay with my feet in a pool of water, and waited. A few seconds later there was the violent unleashing of death I had expected. Someone leapt in the other side of the shell-hole. He must have been a Catholic, because he was gabbling Ave's. Then there was another scuffle and I heard him go in a falling of bits of mud. I drew my feet out of the water. But I did not open my eyes until the firing had stopped.

'I was not alone in that shell-hole. Half in, half out of the water opposite me was a greyish mass. A German corpse, long dead, half eaten by rats. Its stomach gaped, and it lay like a woman with a still-born child beside it. And it smelt … it smelt as you can imagine.

'I stayed in that crater all night. I accustomed myself to the mephitic stench. It grew cold, and I thought I had a fever. But I made up my mind not to move until the battle was over. I was without shame. I even hoped the Germans would overrun our positions and so allow me to give myself up as a prisoner.

'Fever. But what I thought was fever was the fire of existence, the passion to exist. I know that now. A *delirium vivens*. I do not mean to defend myself. All deliria are more or less anti-social, and I speak clinically, not philosophically. But I possessed that night an almost total recall of physical sensations. And these recalls, of even the simplest and least sublime things, a glass of water, the smell of frying bacon, seemed to me to surpass or at least equal the memories of the greatest art, the noblest music, even my tenderest moments with Lily. I experienced the very opposite of what the German and French metaphysicians of our century have assured us is the truth: that all that is other is hostile to the individual. To me all that is other seemed exquisite. Even that corpse, even the squealing rats. To be able to experience, never mind that it was cold and hunger and nausea, was a miracle. Try to imagine that one day you discover you have a sixth, a till then unimagined new sense – something not comprehended in feeling, seeing, the conventional five. But a far profounder sense, the source from which all others spring. The word "being" no longer passive and descriptive, but active ... almost imperative.

'Before the night was ended I knew that I had had what religious people would call a conversion. A light in heaven indeed shone on me, for there were constant star-shells. But I had no sense of God. Only of having leapt a lifetime in one night.'

He was silent for a moment. I wished there was someone beside me, an Alison, some friend, who could savour and share the living darkness, the stars, the terrace, the voice. But they would have had to pass through all those last months with me. The passion to exist: I forgave myself my failure to die.

'I am trying to describe to you what happened to me, what I was. Not what I should have been. Not the rights and wrongs of conscientious objection. I beg you to remember that.

'Before dawn there was another German bombardment. They attacked at first light, their generals having made exactly the same mistake as ours the day before. They suffered even heavier casualties. They got past my crater and to the trenches we had attacked from, but they were driven back again almost at once. All I knew of this was the noise. And the foot of a German soldier. He used my shoulder for a support while he was firing.

'Night fell again. There was war to the south, but our sector was quiet. The battle was over. Our casualties were some thirteen thousand killed. Thirteen thousand minds, memories, loves, sensations, worlds, universes – because the human mind is more a universe than the universe itself – and all for a few hundred yards of useless mud.

'At midnight I crawled back to the village on my stomach. I was afraid I might be shot by a startled sentry. But the place was manned by corpses, and I was in the middle of a desert of the dead. I found my way down a communication trench. There, too, only silence and corpses. Then a little further on I heard English voices ahead, and called out. It was a party of stretcher-bearers, passing round for a final ascertaining that only the dead remained. I said I had been knocked out by a shell-blast.

'They did not doubt my story. Stranger things had happened. From them I learnt where what was left of my battalion were. I had no plan, nothing but the instinct of a child to return to its home. But as the Spanish say, a drowning man soon learns to swim. I knew I must be officially dead. That if I ran away, at least no one would be running after me. By dawn I was ten miles behind the lines. I had a little money and French had always been the lingua franca of my home. I found peasants who sheltered and fed me that next day. The next night I marched again, over the fields, always westwards, across the Artois towards Boulogne.

'A week later, travelling always like this, like the émigrés in the 1790s, I arrived there. It was full of soldiers and of military police, and I was near despair. Of course it was impossible to board a returning troopship without papers. I thought of presenting myself at the docks and saying that my pocket had been picked ... but I lacked the impudence to carry it off. Then one day fate was kind to me. She gave me an opportunity to pick pockets myself. I met a soldier from the Rifle Brigade who was very drunk, and I made him drunker. I caught the leave ship while he, poor man, was still snoring in a room above an *estaminet* near the station.

'And then my real troubles began. But I have talked enough.'

21

There was silence. The crickets chirped. Some night-bird, high over-head, croaked primevally in the stars.

'What happened when you got home?'

'It is late.'

'But – '

'Tomorrow.'

He lit the lamp again. As he straightened up from adjusting the wick, he stared at me.

'You are not ashamed to be the guest of a traitor to his country?'

'I don't think you were a traitor to the human race.'

We moved towards his bedroom windows.

'The human race is unimportant. It is the self that must not be betrayed.'

'I suppose one could say that Hitler didn't betray his self.'

He turned.

'You are right. He did not. But millions of Germans did betray their selves. That was the tragedy. Not that one man had the courage to be evil. But that millions had not the courage to be good.'

He led the way through to my room, and lit the lamp there for me.

'Good night, Nicholas.'

'Good night. And ... '

But his hand was up, silencing me and what he must have guessed were to be my thanks. Then he was gone.

When I came back from the bathroom, I looked at my watch. It was a quarter to one. I undressed and turned out the lamp, then stood a moment by the open window. There was a vague smell of drains in the still air, of a cesspool somewhere. I got into bed, and lay thinking about Conchis.

Or losing him, since all my thoughts ended in paradox. If in one way he seemed much more human, more normally fallible, than before, that was tainted by what seemed like a lack of virginity in the telling. Calculating frankness is very different from the spontaneous variety; there was some fatal extra dimension in his objectivity, which was much more that of a novelist before a character than of even the oldest, most changed man before his own real past self. It was finally much more like biography than the autobiography it purported to be; patently more concealed lesson than true confession. It was not that I was so self-blind that I saw nothing to be learnt. But how could he presume this on so little knowledge of me? Why should he care?

And then there were the footsteps, a whole tangle of unrelated ikons and incidents, the photo on the *curiosa* cabinet, oblique looks, Alison, the little girl called Lily with her head in sunlight ...

I was about to go to sleep.

At first hallucinatorily faint, impossible to pinpoint, it began. I thought it must be coming through the walls from a gramophone in Conchis's bedroom. I sat up, put my ear to the wall, listened. And then I leapt out of bed and went to the window. It was creeping down from outside, from somewhere far to the north, well up in the hills a mile or more away. There was no light, no obvious sound except the crickets in the garden. Only, so barely perceptible that it fringed the imagined, this faintest drone of men, a lot of men, singing. I thought: fishermen. But why should they be in the hills? Then shepherds – but shepherds are solitaries.

It grew a little clearer, as if on a gust of wind – but there was no wind; swelling, then fading away. I thought for an incredible moment that I caught something familiar in the sound – but it couldn't be. And it sank away, almost to complete silence.

Then – unimaginable the strangeness of it, the shock of it – the sound swelled again and I knew beyond doubt what was being sung up there. It was 'Tipperary'. Whether it was the distance, whether the record, because it must have been a record, had been deliberately slowed – there seemed to be some tonal distortion as well – I couldn't tell, but the song came with a dreamlike slowness and dimness, almost as if it was being sung out of the stars and had had to cross all that night and space to reach me.

I went to the door of my room and opened it. I had some idea that the record-player must be in Conchis's room. Somehow he had had the sound relayed to a speaker, or speakers, in the hills – perhaps that was what was in the little room, relaying equipment, a generator. But there was absolute silence in the house. I closed the door and leant back against it. The voices and the song washed dimly down out of the night, through the pine-forest, over the house and out to sea. Suddenly the humour, the absurd, tender, touching poetry of the whole thing, made me smile. It must be some elaborate joke of Conchis's, mounted for my exclusive benefit; and as a subtle test of my own humour, tact and intelligence. There was no need to rush about trying to discover how it was done. I should find that out in the morning. Meanwhile, I was to enjoy it. I went back to the window.

The voices had become very dim, barely audible; but something else had grown penetratingly strong. It was the cesspool smell I had noticed earlier. Now it was an atrocious stench that infested the windless air, a nauseating compound of decomposing flesh and excrement, so revolting that I had to hold my nose and breathe through my mouth.

Below my room there was a narrow passage between the cottage and the house. I craned down, because the source of the smell seemed so close. It was clear to me that the smell was connected with the singing. I remembered that corpse in the shell-hole. But I could see nothing anomalous, no movement.

The sound faded, went completely. After a few minutes, the smell too was fainter. I stood another ten or fifteen minutes, straining eyes and ears for the faintest stir. But there was none. And there was no sound inside the house. No creeping up the stairs, no doors gently closed, nothing. The crickets chirped, the stars pulsed, the experience was wiped clean. I sniffed at the window. The foul odour still lingered, but under the normal antiseptic smell of the pines and the sea, not over it.

Soon it was as if I had imagined everything. I lay awake for at least another hour. Nothing more happened; and no hypothesis made sense.

I had entered the domaine.

22

Someone was knocking at the door. Through the shadowy air of the open window, the burning sky. A fly crawled across the wall above the bed. I looked at my watch. It was half past ten. I went to the door, and heard the slap of Maria's slippers going downstairs.

In the glaring light, the racket of cicadas, the events of the night seemed in some way fictional; as if I must have been slightly drugged. But I felt perfectly clear-headed. I dressed and shaved and went down to breakfast under the colonnade. The taciturn Maria appeared with coffee.

'*O kyrios?*' I asked.

'*Ephage. Eine epano.*' Has eaten; is upstairs. Like the villagers, with foreigners she made no attempt to speak more comprehensibly, but uttered her usual fast slur of vowel-sounds.

I had my breakfast and carried the tray back along the side colonnade and down the steps to the open door of her cottage. The front room was fitted out as a kitchen. With its old calendars, its lurid cardboard ikons, its bunches of herbs and shallots and its blue-painted meat-safe hanging from the ceiling, it was like any other cottage living-kitchen on Phraxos. Only the utensils were rather more ambitious, and the stove larger. I went in and put the tray on the table.

Maria appeared out of the back room; I glimpsed a large brass bed, more ikons, photographs. A shadow of a smile creased her mouth; but it was circumstantial, not genuine. It would have been difficult enough in English to ask questions without appearing to be prying; in my Greek it was impossible. I hesitated a moment, then saw her face, as blank as the door behind her, and gave up.

I went through the passage between house and cottage to the vegetable garden. On the western side of the house a shuttered window corresponded to the door at the end of Conchis's bedroom. It appeared as if there was something more than a cupboard there. Then I looked up at the north-facing back of the house, at my own room. It was easy to hide behind the rear wall of the cottage, but the ground was hard and bare; showed nothing. I strolled on into the arbour. The little Priapus threw up his arms at me, jeering his pagan smile at my English face.

No entry.

Ten minutes later I was down on the private beach. The water, blue and green glass, was for a moment cold, then deliciously cool; I swam out between the steep rocks to the open sea. After a hundred yards or so I could see behind me the whole cliffed extent of the headland, and the house. I could even see Conchis, who was sitting where we had sat on the terrace the night before, apparently reading. After a while he stood up, and I waved. He raised both his arms in his peculiar hieratic way, a way in which I knew now that there was something deliberately, not fortuitously, symbolic. The dark figure on the raised white terrace; legate of the sun facing the sun; the most ancient royal power. He appeared, wished to appear, to survey, to bless, to command; *dominus* and domaine. And once again I thought of Prospero; even if he had not said it first, I should have thought of it then. I dived, but the salt stung my eyes and I surfaced. Conchis had turned away – to talk with Ariel, who put records on; or with Caliban, who carried a bucket of rotting entrails; or perhaps with … but I turned on my back. It was ridiculous to build so much on the sound of quick footsteps, the merest glimpse of a glimpse of a white shape.

When I got back to the beach ten minutes later he was sitting on the baulk. As I came out of the water he stood and said, 'We will take the boat and go to Petrocaravi.' Petrocaravi, the 'ship of stone', was a deserted islet half a mile off the western tip of Phraxos. He was dressed in swimming-shorts and a garish red-and-white water-polo player's cap, and in his hand he had the blue rubber flippers and a pair of underwater masks and schnorkels. I followed his brown old back over the hot stones.

'Petrocaravi is very interesting underwater. You will see.'

'I find Bourani very interesting above water.' I had come up beside him. 'I heard voices in the night.'

'Voices?' But he showed no surprise.

'The record. I've never had an experience quite like it. An extraordinary idea.' He didn't answer, but stepped down into the boat and opened the engine housing. I untied the painter from its iron ring in the concrete, then squatted on the jetty and watched him fiddle inside the hatch. 'I suppose you have speakers in the trees.'

'I heard nothing.'

I teased the painter through my hand, and grinned. 'But you know I heard something.'

He looked up at me. 'Because you tell me so.'

'You're not saying, how extraordinary, voices, what voices. That would be the normal reaction, wouldn't it?' He gestured curtly to me to get aboard. I stepped down and sat on the thwart opposite to him. 'I only wanted to thank you for organizing a unique experience for me.'

'I organized nothing.'

'I find it hard to believe that.'

We remained staring at each other. The red-and-white skull-cap above the monkey eyes gave him the air of a performing chimpanzee. And there stood the sun, the sea, the boat, so many unambiguous things, around us. I still smiled; but he wouldn't smile back. It was as if I had committed a *faux pas* by referring to the singing. He stooped to fit the starting-handle.

'Here, let me do that.' I took the handle. 'The last thing I want to do is to offend you. I won't mention it again.'

I bent to turn the handle. Suddenly his hand was on my shoulder. 'I am not offended, Nicholas. I do not ask you to believe. All I ask you is to pretend to believe. It will be easier.'

It was strange. By that one gesture and a small shift in expression and tone of voice, he resolved the tension between us. I knew on the one hand that he was playing some kind of trick on me; a trick like the one with the loaded dice. On the other, I felt that he had after all taken a sort of liking for me. I thought, as I heaved at the engine, if this is the price, I'll seem his fool; but not be his fool.

We headed out of the cove. It was difficult to talk with the engine going, and I stared down through fifty or sixty feet of water to patches of pale rock starred black with sea-urchins. On Conchis's left side were two puckered scars. They were both back and front, obviously bullet wounds; and there was another old wound high on his right arm. I guessed that they came from the execution during the second war. Sitting there steering he looked ascetic, Ghandi-like; but as we approached Petrocaravi, he stood up, the tiller expertly

137

against his dark thigh. Years of sunlight had tanned him to the same mahogany brown as the island fishermen.

The rocks were gigantic boulders of conglomerate, monstrous in their barren strangeness, much larger now we were close to them than I had ever realized from the island. We anchored about fifty yards away. He handed me a mask and schnorkel. At that time they were unobtainable in Greece, and I had never used them before.

I followed the slow, pausing thresh of his feet over a petrified landscape of immense blocks of stone, among which drifted and hovered shoals of fish. There were flat fish, silvered, aldermanic; slim, darting fish; palindromic fish that peered foully out of crevices; minute poised fish of electric blue, fluttering red-and-black fish, slinking azure-and-green fish. He showed me an underwater grotto, a light-shafted nave of pale-blue shadows, where the large wrasse floated as if in a trance. On the far side of the islet the rocks plunged precipitously away into a mesmeric blind indigo. Conchis raised his head above the surface.

'I am going back to fetch the boat. Stay here.'

I swam on. A shoal of several hundred golden-grey fish followed me. I turned, they turned. I swam on, they followed, truly Greek in their obsessive curiosity. Then I lay over a great slab of rock which warmed the water almost to bath-heat. The shadow of the boat fell across it. Conchis led me a little way to a deep fissure between two boulders, and there suspended a piece of white cloth on the end of a line. I hung like a bird in the water overhead, watching for the octopus he was trying to entice. Soon a sinuous tentacle slipped out and groped the bait, then other swift tentacles, and he began skilfully to coax the octopus up. I had tried this myself and knew it was not nearly as simple as the village boys made it seem. The octopus came reluctantly but inevitably, slow-whirling, flesh of drowned sailors, its suckered arms stretching, reaching, searching. Conchis suddenly gaffed it into the boat, slashed its sac with a knife, turned it inside out in a moment. I levered myself aboard.

'I have caught a thousand in this place. Tonight another will move into that same hole. And let himself be caught as easily.'

'Poor thing.'

'You notice reality is not necessary. Even the octopus prefers the ideal.' A piece of old white sheeting, from which he had torn his 'bait', lay beside him. I remembered it was Sunday morning; the time for sermons and parables. He looked up from the puddle of sepia.

'Well, how do you like the world below?'

'Fantastic. Like a dream.'

'Like humanity. But in the vocabulary of millions of years ago.' He threw the octopus under the thwart. 'Do you think that has a life after death?'

I looked down at the viscid mess and up to meet his dry smile. The red-and-white skull-cap had tilted slightly. Now he looked like Picasso imitating Ghandi imitating a buccaneer. He let in the clutch lever and we moved forward. I thought of the Marne, of Neuve Chapelle; and shook my head. He nodded, and raised the white sheeting. His even teeth gleamed falsely, vividly in the intense sunlight. Stupidity is lethal, he implied; and look at me, I have survived.

23

We had lunch, a simple Greek meal of goat's-milk cheese and green pepper salad with eggs, under the colonnade. The cicadas rasped in the surrounding pines, the heat hammered down outside the cool arches. I had, on the way back, made one more effort to penetrate the situation; by trying, too casually, to get him to talk about Leverrier. He had hesitated, then glanced at me with a gravity that did not quite hide the smile behind it.

'Is this how they teach you at Oxford now? One reads last chapters first?'

And I had had to smile and look down. If his answer had not quenched my curiosity at all, it had at least jumped another pretence, and moved us on. In some obscure way, one I was to become very familiar with, it flattered me: I was too intelligent not to be already grasping the rules of the game we played. It was no good my knowing that old men have conned young ones like that ever since time began. I still fell for it, as one still falls for the oldest literary devices in the right hands and contexts.

All though the lunch we talked of the undersea world. For him it was like a gigantic acrostic, an alchemist's shop where each object had a mysterious value, an inner history that had to be deduced, unravelled, guessed at. He made natural history sound and feel like something central and poetic; not an activity for Scoutmasters and a butt for *Punch* jokes.

The meal ended, and he stood up. He was going upstairs for his siesta. We would meet again at tea.

'What will you do?'

I opened the old copy of *Time* magazine I had beside me. Tucked carefully inside lay his seventeenth-century pamphlet.

'You have not read it yet?' He seemed surprised.

'I intend to now.'

'Good. It is rare.'

He raised his hand and went in. I crossed the gravel and started idly off through the trees to the east. The ground rose slightly, then dipped; after a hundred yards or so a shallow outcrop of rocks hid the house. Before me lay a deep gulley choked with oleanders and thorny scrub, which descended precipitously down to the private beach. I sat back against a pine-stem and became lost in the pamphlet. It contained the posthumous confessions and letters and prayers of a Robert Foulkes, vicar of Stanton Lacy in Shropshire. Although a scholar, and married with two sons, in 1677 he had got a young girl with child, and then murdered the child; for which he was condemned to death.

He wrote the fine muscular pre-Dryden English of the mid-seventeenth century. He had 'mounted to the top of impiety', even though he had known that 'the minister is the people's Looking-glass'. 'Crush the cockatrice,' he groaned, from his death-cell. 'I am dead in law' – but of the girl he denied that he had 'attempted to vitiate her at Nine years old'; for 'upon the word of a dying man, both her Eyes did see, and her Hands did act in all that was done'.

The pamphlet was some forty pages long, and it took me half an hour to read. I skipped the prayers, but it was as Conchis had said, more real than any historical novel – more moving, more evocative, more human. I lay back and stared up through the intricate branches into the sky. It seemed strange, to have that old pamphlet by me, that tiny piece of a long-past England that had found its way to this Greek island, these pine trees, this pagan earth. I closed my eyes and watched

the sheets of warm colour that came as I relax[e]
tension of the lids. Then I slept.

When I woke, I looked at my watch without rais[ing]
Half an hour had passed. After a few minutes more of doz[ing]

He was there, standing in the dark ink-green shadow [of a]
dense carob tree seventy or eighty yards away on the other side [of the]
gulley, at the same level as myself. I got to my feet, not know[ing]
whether to call out, to applaud, to be frightened, to laugh, too
astounded to do anything but stand and stare. The man was costumed
completely in black, in a high-crowned hat, a cloak, a kind of skirted
dress, black stockings. He had long hair, a square collar of white lace
at the neck, and two white bands. Black shoes with pewter buckles.
He stood there in the shadows, posed, a Rembrandt, disturbingly
authentic and yet enormously out of place – a heavy, solemn man
with a reddish face. Robert Foulkes.

I looked round, half expecting to see Conchis somewhere behind
me. But there was no one. I looked back at the figure, which had not
moved, which continued to stare at me from the shade through the
sunlight over the gulley. And then another figure appeared from
behind the carob. It was a white-faced young girl of fourteen or so,
in a long dark-brown dress. I could make out a sort of close-fitting
purple cap on the back of her head. Her hair was long. She came
beside him, and she also stared at me. She was much shorter than he
was, barely to his ribs. We must have stood, the three of us, staring at
each other for nearly half a minute. Then I raised my arm, with a
smile on my face. There was no response. I moved ten yards or so
forward, out into the sunlight, as far as I could, to the edge of the
gulley.

'Good day,' I called in Greek. 'What are you doing?' And then
again: '*Ti kanete?*'

But they made not the least reply. They stood and stared at me –
the man with a vague anger, it seemed, the girl expressionlessly. A
flaw of the sun-wind blew a brown banner, some part of the back of
her dress, out sideways.

I thought, it's Henry James. The old man's discovered that the
screw could take another turn. And then, his breathtaking impudence.
I remembered the conversation about the novel. '*Words are for facts.
Not fiction.*'

141

rds the house; Conchis must declare
here was myself, with an increasingly
d there were the two in their green
closer to the man, who put his hand
ner near shoulder. They seemed to be
g. Words were no use. I had to get
ulley. It was uncrossable for at least a
e appeared to slope more easily to its
nation, I started up the hill. I looked
nt pair under the tree. They turned
on their side of the small ravine hid
them from view. I broke into a run.

The gulley was finally negotiable, though it was a tough scramble up the far side through some disagreeably sharp-thorned smilax. Once through that I was able to run again. The carob came into sight below. There was nothing there. In a few seconds – it had been perhaps a minute in all since I had lost sight of them – I was standing under the tree, on an unrevealing carpet of shrivelled carats. I looked to where I had slept. The small grey and red-edged squares of the pamphlet and *Time* lay on the pale carpet of needles. I went well beyond the carob until I came to strands of wire running through the trees, at the edge of the inland bluff, the eastern limit of Bourani. The three cottages lay innocently below in their little orchard of olives. In a kind of panic I walked back to the carob and along the east side of the gulley to the top of the cliff that overlooked the private beach. There was more scrub there, but not enough for anyone to hide, unless they lay flat. And I could not imagine that choleric-looking man lying down flat, in hiding.

Then from the house I heard the bell. It rang three times. I looked at my watch – teatime. The bell rang again: quick, quick, slow, and I realized it was sounding the syllables of my name.

I ought, I suppose, to have felt frightened. But I wasn't. Apart from anything else I was too intrigued and too bewildered. Both the man and the whey-faced girl had looked remarkably English; and whatever nationality they really were, I knew they didn't live on the island. So I had to presume that they had been specially brought; had been standing by, hiding somewhere, waiting for me to read the Foulkes pamphlet. I had made it easy by falling asleep, and at the edge of the gulley. But that had been pure chance. And how could Conchis have such people standing by? And where had they disappeared to?

For a few moments I had let my mind plunge into darkness, into a world where the experience of all my life was disproved and ghosts existed. But there was something far too unalloyedly physical about all these supposedly 'psychic' experiences. Besides, 'apparitions' obviously carry least conviction in bright daylight. It was almost as if I was intended to see that they were not really supernatural; and there was Conchis's cryptic, doubt-sowing advice that it would be easier if I pretended to believe. Why easier? More sophisticated, more polite, perhaps; but 'easier' suggested that I had to pass through some ordeal.

I stood there in the trees, absolutely at a loss; and then smiled. I had somehow landed myself in the centre of an extraordinary old man's fantasies. That was clear. Why he should hold them, why he should so strangely realize them, and above all, why he should have chosen me to be his solitary audience of one, remained a total mystery. But I knew I had become involved in something too uniquely bizarre to miss, or to spoil, through lack of patience or humour.

I recrossed the gulley and picked up *Time* and the pamphlet. Then, as I looked back at the dark, inscrutable carob tree, I did feel a faint touch of fear. But it was a fear of the inexplicable, the unknown, not of the supernatural.

As I walked across the gravel to the colonnade, where I could see Conchis was already sitting, his back to me, I decided on a course of action – or rather, of reaction.

He turned. 'A good siesta?'

'Yes, thank you.'

'You have read the pamphlet?'

'You're right. It is more fascinating than any historical novel.' He kept a face impeccably proof to my ironic undertone. 'Thank you very much.' I put the pamphlet on the table.

Calmly, in my silence, he began to pour me tea.

He had already had his own and he went away to play the harpsichord for twenty minutes. As I listened to him, I thought. The incidents seemed designed to deceive all the senses. Last night's had covered smell and hearing; this afternoon's, and that glimpsed figure of yesterday, sight. Taste seemed irrelevant – but touch ... how on earth could he expect me even to pretend to believe that what I might touch was 'psychic'? And then what on earth – appropriately, on earth – had these tricks to do with 'travelling to other worlds'? Only one thing was clear; his anxiety about how much I might have heard from Mitford and Leverrier was now explained. He had practised his strange illusionisms on them, and sworn them to secrecy.

When he came out he took me off to water his vegetables. The water had to be drawn up out of one of a battery of long-necked cisterns behind the cottage, and when we had done that and fed the plants we sat on a seat by the Priapus arbour, with the unusual smell, in summer Greece, of verdant wet earth all around us. He did his deep-breathing exercises; evidently, like so much else in his life, ritual; then smiled at me and jumped back twenty-four hours.

'Now tell me about this girl.' It was a command, not a question; or a refusal to believe I could refuse again.

'There's nothing really to tell.'

'She turned you down.'

'No. Or not at the beginning. I turned her down.'

'And now you wish ... ?'

'It's all over. It's all too late.'

'You sound like Adonis. Have you been gored?'

There was a silence. I took the step; something that had nagged me ever since I had discovered he had studied medicine; and also to shock his mocking of my fatalism.

'As a matter of fact I have.' He looked sharply at me. 'By syphilis. I managed to get it early this year in Athens.' Still he observed me. 'It's all right. I think I'm cured.'

'Who diagnosed it?'

'The man in the village. Patarescu.'

'Tell me the symptoms.'

'The clinic in Athens confirmed his diagnosis.'

'No doubt.' His voice was dry; so dry that my mind leapt to what he hinted at. 'Now tell me the symptoms.'

In the end he got them out of me; in every detail.

'As I thought. You had soft sore.'

144

'Soft sore?'

'Chancroid. *Ulcus molle*. A very common disease in the Mediterranean. Unpleasant, but harmless. The best cure is frequent soap and water.'

'Then why the hell ... '

He rubbed his thumb and forefinger together in the ubiquitous Greek gesture for money, for money and corruption.

'You have paid?'

'Yes. For this special penicillin.'

'You can do nothing.'

'I can damn well sue the clinic.'

'You have no proof that you did not have syphilis.'

'You mean Patarescu – '

'I mean nothing. He acted with perfect medical correctness. A test is always advisable.' It was almost as if he were on their side. He shrugged gently: thus the world goes.

'He could have warned me.'

'Perhaps he considered it more important to warn you against venery than venality.'

'Christ.'

In me battled a flood of relief at being reprieved and anger at such vile deception. After a moment Conchis spoke again.

'Even if it had been syphilis – why could you not return to this girl you love?'

'Really – it's too complicated.'

'Then it is usual. Not unusual.'

Slowly, disconnectedly, prompted by him, I told him a bit about Alison; remembering his frankness the night before, produced some of my own. Once again I felt no real sympathy coming from him; simply his obsessive and inexplicable curiosity. I told him I had recently written a letter.

'And if she does not answer?'

I shrugged. 'She doesn't.'

'You think of her, you want to see her – you must write again.' I smiled then, briefly, at his energy. 'You are leaving it to hazard. We no more have to leave everything to hazard than we have to drown in the sea.' He shook my shoulder. 'Swim!'

'It's not the swimming. It's knowing in which direction.'

'Towards the girl. She sees through you, you say, she understands you. That is good.'

I was silent. A primrose-and-black butterfly, a swallowtail, hovered over the bougainvillaea round the Priapus arbour; found no honey, and glided away through the trees. I scuffed the gravel. 'I suppose I don't know what love is, really. If it isn't all sex. And I don't even really care a damn any more, anyway.'

'My dear young man, you are a disaster. So defeated. So pessimistic.'

'I was rather ambitious once. I ought to have been blind as well. Then perhaps I wouldn't feel defeated.' I looked at him. 'It's not all me. It's in the age. In all my generation. We all feel the same.'

'In the greatest age of enlightenment in the history of this earth? When we have destroyed more darkness in this last fifty years than in the last five million?'

'As at Neuve Chapelle? Hiroshima?'

'But you and I! We live, we are this wonderful age. *We* are not destroyed. We did not even destroy.'

'No man is an island.'

'Pah. Rubbish. Every one of us is an island. If it were not so we should go mad at once. Between these islands are ships, aeroplanes, telephones, wireless – what you will. But they remain islands. Islands that can sink or disappear for ever. You are an island that has not sunk. You cannot be such a pessimist. It is not possible.'

'It seems possible.'

'Come with me.' He stood up, as if time was vital. 'Come. I will show you the innermost secret of life. Come.' He walked quickly round to the colonnade. I followed him upstairs. There he pushed me out on to the terrace.

'Go and sit at the table. With your back to the sun.'

In a minute he appeared, carrying something heavy draped in a white towel. He put it carefully on the centre of the table. Then he paused, made sure I was looking, before gravely he removed the cloth. It was a stone head, whether of a man or a woman it was difficult to say. The nose had been broken short. The hair was done in a fillet, with two sidepieces. But the power of the fragment was in the face. It was set in a triumphant smile, a smile that would have been smug if it had not been so full of the purest metaphysical good humour. The eyes were faintly oriental, long, and as I saw, for Conchis put a hand over the mouth, also smiling. The mouth was beautifully modelled, timelessly intelligent and timelessly amused.

'That is the truth. Not the hammer and sickle. Not the stars and stripes. Not the cross. Not the sun. Not gold. Not *yin* and *yang*. But the smile.'

'It's Cycladic, isn't it?'

'Never mind what it is. Look at it. Look into its eyes.'

He was right. The little sunlit thing had some numen; or not so much a divinity, as a having known divinity, in it; of being ultimately certain. But as I looked, I began to feel something else.

'There's something implacable in that smile.'

'Implacable?' He came behind my chair and looked down over my head. 'It is the truth. Truth is implacable. But the nature and meaning of this truth is not.'

'Tell me where it came from.'

'From Didyma in Asia Minor.'

'How old is it?'

'The sixth or seventh century before Christ.'

'I wonder if it would have that smile if it knew of Belsen.'

'Because they died, we know we still live. Because a star explodes and a thousand worlds like ours die, we know this world is. That is the smile: that what might not be, is.' Then he said, 'When I die, I shall have this by my bedside. It is the last human face I want to see.'

The little head watched our watching; bland, certain, and almost maliciously inscrutable. It flashed on me that it was also the smile that Conchis sometimes wore; as if he sat before the head and practised it. At the same time I realized exactly what I disliked about it. It was above all the smile of dramatic irony, of those who have privileged information. I looked back up at Conchis's face; and knew I was right.

24

A starry darkness over the house, the forest, the sea; the dinner cleared away, the lamp extinguished. I lay back in the long chair. He let the night silently envelop and possess us, let time fall away; then began to draw me back down the decades.

'April, 1915. I returned without trouble to England. I did not know what I should become. Except that I had in some way to justify myself. At nineteen one is not content simply to do things. They have to be justified as well. My mother fainted when she saw me. For the first and last time in my life I saw my father in tears. Until that moment of confrontation I had determined that I would tell the truth. That I could not deceive them. Yet before them ... perhaps it was pure cowardice, it is not for me to say. But there are some truths too cruel, before the faces one has to announce them to, to be told. So I said that I had been lucky in a draw for leave, and that now Montague was dead I was to rejoin my original battalion. I grew possessed by madness to deceive. Not economically, but with the utmost luxury. I invented a new battle of Neuve Chapelle, as if the original had not been bad enough. I even told them I had been recommended for a commission.

'At first fortune was on my side. Two days after I returned, official notification came that I was missing, believed killed in action. Such mistakes occurred frequently enough for my parents to suspect nothing. The letter was joyously torn up.

'And Lily. Perhaps what had passed had made her see more clearly her real feelings for me. Whatever it was, I could no longer complain that she treated me more like a brother than a lover. You know, Nicholas, that whatever miseries the Great War brought it destroyed a great deal that was unhealthy between the sexes. For the first time for a century woman discovered that men wanted something more human from them than a nun-like chastity, a *bien pensant* idealism. I do not mean that Lily suddenly lost all reserve. Or gave herself to me. But she gave as much to me as she could. The time I spent alone with her ... those hours allowed me to gather strength to go on with my deception. At the same time as they made it more terrible. Again and again I was possessed by a desire to tell her all, and before justice caught up with me. Every time I returned home I expected to find the police waiting. My father outraged. And worst of all, Lily's eyes on mine. But when I was with her I refused to talk about the war. She misinterpreted my nervousness. It touched her deeply and brought out all her gentleness. Her warmth. I sucked on her love like a leech. A very sensual leech. She had become a very beautiful young woman.

'One day we went for a walk in woods to the north of London – near Barnet, I think, I no longer recall the name, except that they were in those days very pretty and lonely woods for a place so near London.

'We lay on the ground and kissed. Perhaps you smile. That we only lay on the ground and kissed. You young people can lend your bodies now, play with them, give them as we could not. But remember that you have paid a price: that of a world rich in mystery and delicate emotion. It is not only species of animal that die out, but whole species of feeling. And if you are wise you will never pity the past for what it did not know, but pity yourself for what it did.

'That afternoon Lily said she wanted to marry me. To marry by special licence, and if necessary without her parents' permission, so that before I went away again we should have become one in body as we were in – dare I say spirit? – at any rate, in mind. I longed to sleep with her, I longed to be joined to her. But always my dreadful secret lay between us, like the sword between Tristan and Isolde. So I had to assume, among the flowers, the innocent birds and trees, an even falser nobility. How could I refuse her except by saying my death was so probable that I could not allow such a sacrifice? She argued. She cried. She took my faltering, my tortured refusals for something far finer than they really were. At the end of the afternoon, before we left the wood, and with a solemnity and sincerity, a complete dedication of herself that I cannot describe to you because such unconditional promising is another extinct mystery ... she said, "Whatever happens I shall never marry anyone but you."'

He stopped speaking for a moment, like a man walking who comes to a brink; perhaps it was an artful pause, but it made the stars, the night, seem to wait, as if story, narration, history, lay imbricated in the nature of things; and the cosmos was for the story, not the story for the cosmos.

'My fortnight's supposed leave drew to an end. I had no plan, or rather a hundred plans, which is worse than having none at all. There were moments when I considered returning to France. But then I saw ghastly yellow figures staggering like drunkards out of the wall of smoke ... I saw the war and the world and why I was in it. I tried to be blind, but I could not.

'I put on my uniform and let my father and mother and Lily see me off at Victoria. They believed I had to report to a camp near Dover. The train was full of soldiers. I once again felt the great current of war, the European death-wish, rushing me along. When the train stopped at some town in Kent I got off. For two or three days I stayed there in a commercial travellers' hotel. I was hopeless. And purposeless. One could not escape the war. It was all one saw, all one heard. In the end I went back to London to the one person in England where I thought there might be refuge: to my grandfather's – my great-uncle in fact. I knew he was Greek, that he loved me because I was my mother's child, and that a Greek will put family above every other consideration. He listened to me. Then he stood up and came to me. I knew what he was going to do. He struck me hard, very hard, so hard that I still feel it, across the face. Then he said, "That is what I think."

'I knew very well that when he said that he meant "in spite of whatever help I shall give you". He was furious with me, he poured every insult in the Greek language over my head. But he hid me. Perhaps because I said that even if I returned I should now be shot for desertion. The next day he went to see my mother. I think that he may have given her the choice. Of doing her duty as a citizen or as a mother. She came to see me, with a lack of spoken reproach that was worse to me than o *Pappous*'s anger. I knew what she would suffer when my father heard the truth. She and o *Pappous* came to a decision. I would have to be smuggled out of England to our family in the Argentine. Fortunately o *Pappous* had both the money and the necessary friends in the shipping world. The arrangements were made. A date was fixed.

'I lived in his house for three weeks, unable to go out, in such an agony of self-disgust and fear that many times I wanted to give myself up. Above all it was the thought of Lily that tortured me. I had promised to write every day. And of course I could not. What other people thought of me, I did not care. But I was desperate to convince her that I was sane and the world was mad. It may have something to do with intelligence, but I am certain it has nothing to do with knowledge – I mean that there are people who have an instinctive yet perfect moral judgment, who can perform the most complex ethical calculations as Indian peasants can sometimes perform astounding mathematical feats in a matter of seconds. Lily was such a person. And I craved her approval.

'One evening I could stand it no longer. I slipped out of my hiding-place and went to St John's Wood. It was an evening when I knew Lily went to a weekly patriotic sewing and knitting circle in a near-by parish hall. I waited in the road I knew she must take. It was a warm May dusk. I was fortunate. She came alone. Suddenly I stepped out into her path from the gateway where I had been waiting. She went white with shock. She knew something terrible had happened, by my face, my civilian clothes. As soon as I saw her my love for her overwhelmed me – and what I had planned to say. I cannot remember now what I said. I can remember only walking beside her in the dusk towards Regent's Park, because we both wanted darkness and to be alone. She would not argue, she would not say anything, she would not look at me for a long time. We found ourselves by the gloomy canal that runs through the north of the park. On a seat. Then she began to cry. I was not allowed to comfort her. I had deceived her. That was the unforgivable. Not that I had deserted. But that I had deceived. For a time she stared away from me, down the black canal. Then she put her hand on mine and stopped me talking. Finally she put her arms round me, and still without words. And I felt myself all that was bad in Europe in the arms of all that was good.

'But there was so much misunderstanding between us. It is possible, even normal, to feel right in front of history and very wrong in front of those one loves. After a while Lily began to talk, and I realized that she understood nothing of what I had said about the war. That she saw herself not as I so much wanted, as my angel of forgiveness, but as my angel of salvation. She begged me to go back. She thought I would be spiritually dead until I did. Again and again she used the word "resurrected". And again and again, on my side, I wanted to know what would happen to us. And finally she said, this was her judgment, that the price of her love was that I should return to the front – not for her, but for myself. To find my true self again. And that the reality of her love was as it had been in the wood: she should never marry anyone else, whatever happened.

'In the end we were silent. You will have understood. Love is the mystery between two people, not the identity. We were at the opposite poles of humanity. Lily was humanity bound to duty, unable to choose, suffering, at the mercy of social ideals. Humanity both crucified and marching towards the cross. And I was free, I was Peter three times to renounce – determined to survive, whatever the cost. I still see her face. Her face staring, staring into the darkness, trying to gaze herself into another world. It was as if we were locked in a torture chamber. Still in love, yet chained to opposite walls, facing each other for eternity and for eternity unable to touch.

'Of course, as men always will, I tried to extract some hope from her. That she would wait for me, not judge me too quickly ... such things. But she stopped me with a look. A look I shall never forget, because it was almost one of hatred, and hatred in her face was like spite in the Virgin Mary's; it reversed the entire order of nature.

'I walked back beside her, in silence. I said goodbye to her under a street lamp. By a garden full of lilac trees. We did not touch. Not a single word. Two young faces, suddenly old, facing each other. The moment that endures when all the other noises, objects, all that dull street, have sunk into dust and oblivion. Two white faces. The scent of lilac. And bottomless darkness.'

He paused. There was no emotion in his voice; but I was thinking of Alison, of that last look she had given me.

'And that is all. Four days later I spent a very disagreeable twelve hours crouched in the bilges of a Greek cargo boat in Liverpool docks.'

There was a silence.

'And did you ever see her again?'

A bat squeaked over our heads.

'She died.'

I had to prompt him.

'Soon after?'

'In the early hours of February the nineteenth, 1916.' I tried to see the expression on his face, but it was too dark. 'There was a typhoid epidemic. She was working in a hospital.'

'Poor girl.'

'All past.'

'You make it seem present.' He inclined his head. 'The scent of lilac.'

'Old man's sentiment. Forgive me.'

He was staring into the night. The bat flitted so low that I saw its silhouette for a brief moment against the Milky Way.

'Is this why you never married?'

'The dead live.'

The blackness of the trees. I listened for footsteps, but none came. A suspension.

'How do they live?'

And yet again he let the silence come, as if the silence would answer my questions better than he could himself; but just when I had decided he would not answer, he spoke.

'By love.'

It was as if he said it not to me, but equally to everything around us; as if she stood listening, in the dark shadows by the doors; as if the telling of his past had reminded him of some great principle he was seeing freshly again. I found myself touched, and this time let the silence stay.

A minute later, he turned to me.

'I should like you to come next week. If your duties permit.'

'If you invite me nothing could keep me away.'

'Good. I am glad.' But his gladness now sounded merely polite. Peremptoriness had regained command. He stood. 'To bed. It is late.'

I followed him through to my room, where he bent to light the lamp.

'I do not want my life discussed over there.'

'Of course not.'

He straightened, faced me.

'So. I shall see you next Saturday?'

I smiled. 'You know you will. I shall never forget these last two days. Even though I don't know why I'm elect. Or elected.'

'Perhaps your ignorance is why.'

'As long as you know the election feels a great privilege.'

He searched my eyes, then did something strange: reached out, as he had in the boat, and touched my shoulder paternally. I had indeed, it seemed, passed some test.

'Good. Maria will have some breakfast for you. Till next week.'

And he was gone. I went to the bathroom, closed my door, turned the lamp out. But I didn't undress. I stood by the window and waited.

25

For at least twenty minutes there was no sound. Conchis went to the bathroom and back to his room. Then there was silence. It went on so long that finally I did undress and started to give in to the sleep I could feel coming on me. But the silence was broken. His door opened and closed, quietly, but not secretively, and I heard him going down the stairs. A minute, two minutes passed; then I sat up and swung out of bed.

It was music again, but from downstairs, the harpsichord. It echoed, percussive but dim, through the stone house. For a few moments I felt disappointment. It seemed merely that Conchis was sleepless, or sad, and playing to himself. But then there was a sound that sent me swiftly to the door. I cautiously opened it. The downstairs door must also have been open, because I could hear the clatter of the harpsichord mechanism. But the thing that sent a shiver up my back was the thin, haunted piping of a recorder. I knew it was not on a gramophone; someone was playing it. The music stopped and went on in a brisker six-eight rhythm. The recorder piped solemnly along, made a mistake, then another; though the player was evidently quite skilled, and executed professional-sounding trills and ornaments.

I went out naked on the landing and looked over the banisters. There was a faint radiance on the floor outside the music-room. I was probably meant to listen, not to go down; but this was too much. I pulled on a sweater and trousers and crept down the stairs in bare feet. The recorder stopped and I heard the rustle of paper being turned – the music-stand. The harpsichord began a long lute-stop passage, a new movement, as gentle as rain, the sounds stealing through the house, mysterious, remote-sounding harmonies. The recorder came in with an adagio-like slowness and gravity, momentarily wobbled off-key, then recovered. I tiptoed to the open door of the music-room, but there something held me back – an odd child-like feeling of misbehaving after bedtime. The door was wide open, but it opened towards the harpsichord, and the end of one of the bookshelves blocked the view through the crack.

The music came to a stop. A chair shifted, my heart raced, Conchis spoke a single indistinguishable word in a low voice. I flattened myself against the wall. There was a rustle. Someone was standing at the door of the music-room.

It was a slim girl of about my own height, in her early twenties. In one hand she held a recorder, in the other a small crimson flue-brush for it. She was wearing a wide-collared blue-and-white striped dress, that left her arms bare. There was a bracelet above one elbow, and the skirt came down, narrowing at the bottom, almost to her ankles. She had a ravishingly pretty face, but completely untanned, without any make-up, and her hair, her outline, the upright way she held herself, everything about her was of forty years before.

I knew I was supposed to be looking at Lily. It was unmistakably the same girl as in the photographs; especially that on the cabinet of *curiosa*. The Botticelli face; grey-violet eyes. The eyes especially were beautiful; very large, their ovals faintly twisted, a cool doe's eyes, almond eyes, giving a natural mystery to a face otherwise so regular that it risked perfection.

She saw me at once. I stood rooted to the stone floor. For a moment she seemed as surprised as I was. Then she looked swiftly, secretly with her large eyes back to where Conchis must have been sitting at the harpsichord, and then again at me. She raised the flue-brush to her lips, shook it, forbidding me to move, to say anything, and she smiled. It was like some genre picture – The Secret. The Admonition. But her smile was strange – as if she was sharing a secret with me, that this was an illusion it was for us two, not the old man, to foster. There was something about her mouth, calm and amused, that was at the same time enigmatic and debunking; pretending and admitting the pretence. She flashed another covert look back at Conchis, then leant forward and lightly pushed my arm with the tip of the brush, as if to say, Go away.

The whole business can't have taken more than five seconds. The door was closed, and I was standing in darkness and an eddy of sandal-wood. I think if it *had* been a ghost, if the girl had been transparent and headless, I might have been less astonished. She had so clearly implied that of course it was all a charade, but that Conchis must not know it was; that she was in fancy-dress for him, not for me.

I went swiftly down the hall to the front door, and eased its bolts open. Then I padded out on to the colonnade. I looked through one of the narrow arched windows and immediately saw Conchis. He had begun to play again. I moved to look for the girl. I was sure that no one could have had time to cross the gravel. But she was not there. I moved round behind his back, until I had seen into every part of the room. And she was not there. I thought she might be under the front part of the colonnade, and peered cautiously round the corner. It was empty. The music went on. I stood, undecided. She must have run through the opposite end of the colonnade and round the back of the house. Ducking under the windows and stealing past the open doors, I stared out across the vegetable terrace, then walked round it. I felt sure she must have escaped this way. But there was no sign of anybody, no sound. I waited out there for several minutes, and then Conchis stopped playing. Soon the lamp went out and he disappeared. I went back and sat in the darkness on one of the chairs under the colonnade. There was a deep silence. Only the crickets cheeped, like drops of water striking the bottom of a gigantic well. Conjectures flew through my head. The people I had seen, the sounds I had heard, and that vile smell, had been real, not supernatural; what was not real was the absence of any visible machinery – no secret rooms, nowhere to disappear – or of any motive. And this new dimension, this suggestion that the 'apparitions' were mounted for Conchis as well as myself, was the most baffling of all.

I sat in the darkness, half hoping that someone, I hoped 'Lily', would appear and explain. I felt once again like a child, like a child who walks into a room and is aware that everyone there knows something about him that he does not. I also felt deceived by

Conchis's sadness. '*The dead live by love*'; and they could evidently also live by impersonation.

But I waited most for whoever had acted Lily. I had to know the owner of that young, intelligent, amused, dazzlingly pretty North European face. I wanted to know what she was doing on Phraxos, where she came from, the reality behind all the mystery.

I waited nearly an hour, and nothing happened. No one came, I heard no sounds. In the end I crept back up to my room. But I had a poor night's sleep. When Maria knocked on the door at half past five I woke as if I had a hangover.

Yet I enjoyed the walk back to the school. I enjoyed the cool air, the delicate pink sky that turned primrose, then blue, the still-sleeping grey and incorporeal sea, the long slopes of silent pines. In a sense I re-entered reality as I walked. The events of the week-end seemed to recede, to become locked away, as if I had dreamt them; and yet as I walked there came the strangest feeling, compounded of the early hour, the absolute solitude, and what had happened, of having entered a myth; a knowledge of what it was like physically, moment by moment, to have been young and ancient, a Ulysses on his way to meet Circe, a Theseus on his journey to Crete, an Oedipus still searching for his destiny. I could not describe it. It was not in the least a literary feeling, but an intensely mysterious present and concrete feeling of excitement, of being in a situation where anything still might happen. As if the world had suddenly, during those last three days, been re-invented, and for me alone.

26

There was a letter. The Sunday boat had brought it.

Dear Nicholas,
    I thought you were dead. I'm on my own again. More or less. I've been trying to decide whether I want to see you again – the point is, I could. I come through Athens now. I mean I haven't decided whether you aren't such a pig that it's crazy to get involved with you again. I can't forget you, even when

I'm with much nicer boys than you'll ever be. Nicko, I'm a little bit drunk and I shall probably tear this up anyway.

Well, I may send a telegram if I can work a few days off at Athens. If I go on like this you won't want to meet me. You probably don't now as it is. When I got your letter I knew you'd just written it because you were bored out there. Isn't it awful I still have to get boozed to write to you. It's raining, I've got the fire on it's so bloody cold. It's dusk, it's grey it's so bloody miserable. The wallpaper's muave or is it mauve hell with green plums. You'd be sick all down it.

A.

Write care of Ann.

Her letter came at the wrongest time. It made me realize that I didn't want to share Bourani with anyone. After the first knowledge of the place, and still after the first meeting with Conchis, even as late as the Foulkes incident, I had wanted to talk about it – and to Alison. Now it seemed fortunate that I hadn't; just as it seemed, though still obscurely, fortunate that I hadn't lost my head in other ways when I wrote to her.

One doesn't fall in love in five seconds; but five seconds can set one dreaming of falling in love, especially in a community as un-relievedly masculine as that of the Lord Byron School. The more I thought of that midnight face, the more intelligent and charming it became; and it seemed too to have had a breeding, a fastidiousness, a delicacy, that attracted me as fatally as the local fishermen's lamps attracted fish on moonless nights. I reminded myself that if Conchis was rich enough to own Modiglianis and Bonnards, he was rich enough to pick the very best in mistresses. I had to presume some sort of sexual relationship between the girl and him – to do otherwise would have been naive; but for all that there had been something much more daughterly, affectionately protective, than sexual in her glance back at him.

I must have read Alison's letter a dozen times that Monday, trying to decide what to do about it. I knew it had to be answered, but I came to the conclusion that the longer I left it, the better. To stop its silent nagging I pushed it away in the bottom drawer of my desk; went to bed, thought about Bourani, drifted into various romantic-

158

sexual fantasies with that enigmatic figure; and failed entirely, in spite of my tiredness, to go to sleep. The crime of syphilis had made me ban sex from my mind for weeks; now I was found not guilty – half an hour with a textbook Conchis had given me to look at had convinced me his diagnosis was right – the libido rose strong. I began to think erotically of Alison again; of the dirty week-end pleasures of having her in some Athens hotel bedroom; of birds in the hand being worth more than birds in the bush; and with better motives, of her loneliness, her perpetual mixed-up loneliness. The one sentence that had pleased me in her unfastidious and not very delicate letter was the last of all – that simple 'Write care of Ann.' Which denied the gaucheness, the lingering resentment, in all the rest.

I got out of bed and sat in my pyjama trousers and wrote a letter, quite a long letter, which I tore up at the first re-reading. The second attempt was much shorter and hit off, I thought, the right balance between regretful practicality and yet sufficient affection and desire for her still to want to climb into bed if I got half a chance.

I said I was rather tied up at the school over most week-ends; though the half-term holiday was the week-end after next and I might just be in Athens then – but I couldn't be sure. But if I was, it would be fun to see her.

As soon as I could I got Méli on his own. I had decided that I had to have a partial confidant at the school. One did not have to attend school meals with the boys over the week-end if one was off duty; and the only master who might have noticed I had been away was Méli himself, but as it happened he'd been in Athens. We sat after lunch on Monday in his room; or rather he sat chubbily at his desk, living up to his nickname, spooning Hymettus honey out of a jar and telling me of the flesh and fleshpots he had bought himself in Athens; and I lay on his bed, only half listening.

'And you, Nicholas, you had a nice week-end?'

'I met Mr Conchis.'

'You ... no, you are joking.'

'You are not to tell the others.'

He raised his hands in protest. 'Of course, but how ... I can't believe it.'

I gave him a very expurgated version of the first visit, the week before, and made Conchis and Bourani as dull as possible.

'He sounds as stupid as I thought. No girls?'

'Not a sign. Not even little boys.'

'Nor even a goat?'

I threw a box of matches at him. Half by desipience, half by proclivity, he had come to live in a world where the only significant leisure activities were coupling and consuming. His batrachian lips pursed into a smile, and he dug again into the honey.

'He's asked me over next week again. As a matter of fact, Méli, I wondered, if I do two preps for you … would you do my noon to six on Sunday?' Sunday duty was easy work. It meant only that one had to stay inside the school and stroll through the grounds a couple of times.

'Well. Yes. I will see.' He sucked the spoon.

'And tell me what to tell the others, if they ask. I want them to think I'm going somewhere else.'

He thought a moment, waved the spoon, then said, 'Tell them you are going to Hydra.'

Hydra was a stop on the way to Athens, though one didn't have to catch the Athens boat to go there, as there were often caïques doing the run. It had an embryonic artistic colony of sorts; the kind of place I might plausibly choose to go to. 'Okay. And you won't tell anyone?'

He crossed himself. 'I am as silent as the … the what is it?'

'Where you ought to be, Méli. The bloody grave.'

I went to the village several times that week, to see if there were any strange faces about. There was no sign of the three people I was looking for, although there were a few strange faces: three or four wives with young children sent out to grass from Athens, and one or two old couples, dehydrated *rentiers*, who doddered in and out of the mournful lounges of the Hotel Philadelphia.

One evening I felt restless and walked down to the harbour. It was about eleven at night and the place, with its catalpas and its old black cannon of 1821, was almost deserted. After a Turkish coffee and a nip of brandy in a *kapheneion* I started to walk back. Some way past the hotel, still on the few hundred yards of concrete 'promenade', I saw a very tall elderly man standing and bending in the middle of the road, apparently looking for something. He looked up as I approached – he was really remarkably tall and strikingly well-dressed for Phraxos; evidently one of the summer visitors. He wore a pale fawn suit, a white gardenia in his button-hole, an old-fashioned white panama hat with a black band, and he had a small goatee beard. He was holding by its middle a cane with a meer-schaum handle, and he looked gravely distressed, as well as naturally grave.

I asked in Greek if he had lost anything.

'*Ah pardon ... est-ce que vous parlez français, monsieur?*'

I said, yes, I spoke some French.

It seemed he had just lost the ferrule of his stick. He had heard it drop off and roll away. I struck a few matches and searched round, and after a little while found the small brass end.

'*Ah, très bien. Mille mercis, monsieur.*'

He produced a pocket-book and I thought for a moment he was going to tip me. His face was as gloomy as an El Greco; insufferably bored, decades of boredom, and probably, I decided, insufferably boring. He didn't tip me, but placed the ferrule carefully inside the wallet, and then politely asked me who I was, and fulsomely, where I had learnt such excellent French. We exchanged a few sentences. He himself was here for only a day or two. He wasn't French, he said, but Belgian. He found Phraxos '*pittoresque, mais moins belle que Délos*'.

After a few moments more of this platitudinous chat we bowed and went our ways. He expressed a hope that we might meet again during the remaining two days of his stay and have a longer conversation. But I took very good care that we didn't.

At last Saturday came. I had done the two extra duties during the week to clear my Sunday, and was thoroughly exhausted with the school. As soon as the morning lessons were over and I had snatched a quick lunch I headed towards the village with my bag. Yes, I told the old man at the gate – a sure method of propagating the lie – I was off to Hydra for the week-end. As soon as I was out of sight of the school I cut up through the cottages and round the back of the school on to the path to Bourani. But I didn't go straight there.

I had speculated endlessly during the week about Conchis, and as futilely as endlessly. I thought I could discern two elements in his 'game' – one didactic, the other aesthetic. But whether his cunningly mounted fantasies hid ultimately a wisdom or a lunacy I could not decide. On the whole I suspected the latter. Mania made more sense than reason.

I had also wondered more and more during the week about the little group of cottages at Agia Varvara, the bay east of Bourani. It was a wide sweep of shingle with a huge row of *athanatos*, or agaves, whose bizarre twelve-foot candelabra of flowers stood facing the sea. I lay on a thyme-covered slope above the bay, having come quietly through the trees, and watched the cottages below for any sign of unusual life. But a woman in black was the only person I saw. Now I examined it, it seemed an unlikely place for Conchis's 'assistants' to live. It was so open, so easy to watch. After a while I wound my way down to the cottages. A child in a doorway saw me coming through the olives and called, and then the entire population of the tiny hamlet appeared – four women and half a dozen children, unmistakably islanders. With the usual peasant hospitality they offered me a little saucer of quince jam and a thimbleful of *raki* as well as the glass of cistern water I requested. Their men were all off fishing. I said I was going to see *o kyrios* Conchis, and their surprise seemed perfectly genuine. Did he ever visit them? Their heads all went back swiftly together, as if the idea was unheard of. I had to listen to the story of the execution again – at least, the oldest woman launched out into a welter of words among which I heard 'mayor' and 'Germans'; and the children raised their arms like guns.

Maria, then? They saw her, of course? But no, they never saw her. She is not a Phraxiot, one of them said.

Then the music, the songs in the night? They looked at one another. What songs? I was not too surprised. Very probably they went to bed and woke with the sun.

'And you,' asked the grandmother, 'are you a relation of his?' They evidently thought of him as a foreigner.

I said I was a friend. He has no friends here, said the old woman, and with a faint hostility in her voice she added, bad men bring bad luck. I said he had guests – a young girl with fair hair, a tall man, a younger girl so high. They had seen them? They had not. Only the grandmother had even been inside Bourani; and that was long before the war. Then they had their way and asked me the usual series of childish but charmingly eager questions about myself, about London, about England.

I got free in the end, after being presented with a sprig of basil, and walked inland along the bluff until I could climb on to the ridge that led to Bourani. For some time three of the barefoot children accompanied me along the seldom-used path. We topped a crest among the pines, and the distant flat roof of the house came into sight over the sea of trees ahead. The children stopped, as if the house was a sign that they should go no farther. I turned after a while and they were still wistfully standing there. I waved, but they made no gesture in return.

27

I went with him and sat in his music-room and listened to him play the D minor English suite. All through tea I had waited for some indication on his part that he knew I had seen the girl – as he must have known, for it was obvious that the nocturnal concert had been given to announce her presence. But I intended to follow the same course of action as I had over the earlier incident: to say nothing until he gave me an opening. Not the slightest chink had appeared in our conversation.

Conchis seemed to me, no expert, to play as if there was no barrier between him and the music; no need to 'interpret', to please an audience, to satisfy some inner vanity. He played as I suppose Bach himself would have played – I think at a rather slower tempo than most modern pianists and harpsichordists, though with no loss of rhythm or shape. I sat in the cool, shuttered room and watched the slightly bowed bald head behind the shining black harpsichord. I heard the driving onwardness of Bach, the endless progressions. It was the first time I had heard him play great music, and I was moved as I had been by the Bonnards; moved in a different way, but still moved. Once again his humanity rose uppermost. It came to me as I listened that I didn't want to be anywhere else in the world at that moment, that what I was feeling at that moment justified all I had been through, because all I had been through *was* my being there. Conchis had spoken of meeting his future, of feeling his life balanced on a fulcrum, when he first came to Bourani. I was experiencing what he meant; a new self-acceptance, a sense that I had to be this mind and this body, its vices and its virtues, and that I had no other chance or choice. It was an awareness of a new kind of potentiality, one very different from my old sense of the word, which had been based on the illusions of ambition. The mess of my life, the selfishnesses and false turnings and the treacheries, all these things *could* fall into place, they *could* become a source of construction rather than a source of chaos, and precisely because I had no other choice. It was certainly not a moment of new moral resolve, or anything like it. No doubt our accepting what we are must always inhibit our being what we ought to be; for all that, it felt like a step forward – and upward.

He had finished, was watching me.

'You make words seem shabby things.'

'Bach does.'

'And you.'

He grimaced, but I could see he was not unpleased, though he tried to hide it by marching me off to give his vegetables their evening watering.

An hour later I was in the little bedroom again. I saw that I had new books by my bedside. There was first a very thin volume in French, a bound pamphlet, anonymous and privately printed, Paris, 1932; it was entitled *De la communication intermondiale*. I guessed the author easily enough. Then there was a folio: *Wild Life in Scandinavia*. As with *The Beauties of Nature* of the week before, the 'wild life' turned out to be all female – various Nordic-looking women lying, standing, running, embracing among the fir-forests and fjords. There were lesbian nuances I didn't much like; perhaps because I was beginning to take against the facet in Conchis's polyhedral character that obviously enjoyed 'curious' objects and literature. Of course I was not – at least I told myself I was not – a puritan. I was too young to know that the having to tell myself gave the game away; and that to be uninhibited about one's own sexual activities is not the same as being unshockable. I was English; *ergo*, puritan. I went twice through the pictures; they clashed unpleasantly with the still-echoing Bach.

Finally there was another book in French – a sumptuously produced limited edition: *Le Masque Français au Dix-huitième Siècle*. This had a little white marker in. Remembering the anthology on the beach, I turned to the page, where there was a passage bracketed. It read:

> Aux visiteurs qui pénétraient dans l'enceinte des murs altiers de Saint-Martin s'offrait la vue délectable des bergers et bergères qui, sur les verts gazons et parmi les bosquets, dansaient et chantaient entourés de leurs blancs troupeaux. Ils ne portaient pas toujours les costumes de l'époque. Quelquefois ils étaient vêtus à la romaine ou à la grecque, et ainsi réalisait-on des odes de Théocrite, des bucoliques de Virgile. On parlait même d'évocations plus scandaleuses, de charmantes nymphes qui les nuits d'été fuyaient au clair de lune, poursuivies par d'étranges silhouettes, moitié homme, moitié chèvre ...*

At last it began to seem plain. All that happened at Bourani was in the nature of a private masque; and no doubt the passage was a hint to me that I should, both out of politeness and for my own pleasure, not poke my nose behind the scenes. I felt ashamed of the questions I had asked at Agia Varvara.

I washed and, in deference to the slight formality Conchis apparently liked in the evenings, changed into a white shirt and a summer suit. When I came out of my room to go downstairs the door of his bedroom was open. He called me in.

'We will have our ouzo up here this evening.'

He was sitting at his desk, reading a letter he had just written. I

*'Visitors who went behind the high walls of Saint-Martin had the pleasure of seeing, across the green lawns and among the groves, shepherds and shepherdesses who danced and sang, surrounded by their white flocks. They were not always dressed in eighteenth-century clothes. Sometimes they wore costumes in the Roman and Greek styles; and in this way the odes of Theocritus and the bucolics of Virgil were brought to life. It was even said that there were more scandalous scenes – charming nymphs who on summer nights fled in the moonlight from strange dark shapes, half man, half goat ... '

waited behind him a moment, looking at the Bonnards again while he addressed the envelope. The door of the little room at the end was ajar. I had a glimpse of clothes, of a press. It was simply a dressing-room. By the open doors, Lily's photograph stared at me from its table.

We went out on to the terrace. There were two tables there, one with the ouzo and glasses on, the other with the dinner things. I saw at once that there were three chairs at the dinner-table; and Conchis saw me see.

'We shall have a visitor after dinner.'

'From the village?' But I was smiling, and he was too when he shook his head. It was a magnificent evening, one of those limitless Greek spans of sky and world fluxed in declining light. The mountains were the grey of a Persian cat's fur, and the sky like a huge unfaceted primrose diamond. I remembered noticing, one similar sunset in the village, how every man outside every taverna had turned to face the west, as if they were in a cinema, with the eloquent all-saying sky their screen.

'I read the passage you marked in *Le Masque Français*.'

'It is only a metaphor. But it may help.'

He handed me an ouzo. We raised glasses.

Coffee was brought and poured, and the lamp moved to the table behind me, so that it shone on Conchis's face. We were both waiting.

'I hope I shan't have to forgo the rest of your adventures.'

He raised his head, in the Greek way, meaning no. He seemed a little tense, and looked past me at the bedroom door; and I was reminded of that first day. I turned, but there was no one there.

He spoke. 'You know who it will be?'

'I didn't know if I was meant to come in last week or not.'

'You are meant to do as you choose.'

'Except ask questions.'

'Except ask questions.' A thin smile. 'Did you read my little pamphlet?'

'Not yet.'

'Read it carefully.'

'Of course. I look forward to it.'

'Then tomorrow night perhaps we can perform an experiment.'

'On communicating with other worlds?' I didn't bother to keep scepticism out of my voice.

'Yes. Up there.' The star-heavy sky. 'Or across there.' I saw him look down, making the visual analogy, to the black line of mountains to the west.

I risked facetiousness. 'Up there – do they speak Greek or English?'

He didn't answer for nearly fifteen seconds; didn't smile.

'They speak emotions.'

'Not a very precise language.'

'On the contrary. The most precise. If one can learn it.' He turned to look at me. 'Precision of the kind you mean is important in science. It is unimportant in – '

But I never found out what it was unimportant in.

We both heard the footsteps, those same light footsteps I had heard before, on the gravel below, coming as if up from the sea. Conchis looked at me quickly.

'You must not ask questions. That is most important.'

I smiled. 'As you wish.'

'Treat her as you would treat an amnesiac.'

'I'm afraid I've never met an amnesiac.'

'She lives in the present. She does not remember her personal past – she has no past. If you question her about the past, you will only disturb her. She is very sensitive. She would not want to see you again.'

I wanted to say, I like your masque, I shan't spoil it. I said, 'If I don't understand why, I begin to understand how.'

He shook his head. 'You are beginning to understand why. Not how.'

His eyes lingered on me, burning the sentence in; then looked aside, at the doors. I turned.

I realized then that the lamp had been put behind me so that it would light her entrance; and it was an entrance to take the breath away.

She was dressed in what must have been the formal evening style of 1915: an indigo silk evening wrap over a slim ivory-coloured dress of some shot material that once more narrowed and ended just above her ankles. The hobble skirt trammelled her steps, yet charmingly; she swayed a little, seemed to both hesitate and float as she came towards us. Her hair was up, in a sort of Empire fashion. She was smiling and looking at Conchis, though she glanced with a cool interest at me as I stood. Conchis was already on his feet. She looked as stunningly elegant, as poised and assured – because even her slight nervousness seemed professional – as if she had just stepped out of a *cabine* at Dior. That was indeed my immediate thought: She's a professional model. And then, The old devil.

The old devil spoke, after first kissing her hand.

'Lily. May I present Mr Nicholas Urfe. Miss Montgomery.'

She held out her hand, which I took. A cool hand, no pressure. I had touched a ghost. Our eyes met, but hers gave nothing away. I said, 'Hallo.' But she replied only with a slight inclination, and then turned for Conchis to take off her wrap, which he placed over the back of his own chair.

She had bare shoulders and arms; a heavy gold and ebony bracelet; an enormously long necklace of what looked like sapphires, though I presumed they must be paste, or ultramarines. I guessed her to be about twenty-two or three. But there clung about her something that seemed much older, ten years older, a sort of coolness – not coldness or indifference, but a limpid aloofness; coolness in the way that one thinks of coolness on a hot summer's day.

She arranged herself in her chair, folded her hands, then smiled faintly at me.

'It is very warm this evening.'

Her voice was completely English. For some reason I had expected a foreign accent; but I could place this exactly. It was my own; product of boarding school, university, the accent of what a sociologist once called the Dominant Hundred Thousand.

I said, 'Isn't it?'

Conchis said, 'Mr Urfe is the young schoolmaster I mentioned.' His voice had a new tone in it: almost deference.

'Yes. We met last week. That is, we caught a glimpse of each other.' And once again she smiled faintly, but without collusion, at me before looking down.

I saw that gentleness Conchis had prepared me for. But it was a teasing gentleness, because her face, especially her mouth, could not conceal her intelligence. She had a way of looking slightly obliquely at me, as if she knew something I did not – not anything to do with the role she was playing, but about life in general; as if she too had been taking lessons from the stone head. I had expected, perhaps because the image she had presented me with the week before had been more domestic, someone less ambiguous and far less assured.

She opened a small peacock-blue fan she had been holding and began to fan herself. Her skin was very white. She obviously never sunbathed. And then there was a curious little embarrassed pause, as if none of us knew what to say. She broke it, rather like a hostess dutifully encouraging a shy dinner-guest.

'Teaching must be a very interesting profession.'

'Not for me. I find it rather dull.'

'All noble and honest things are dull. But someone has to do them.'

'Anyway, I forgive teaching. Since it's brought me here.' She slipped a look at Conchis, who bowed imperceptibly. He was playing a kind of Talleyrand role: the gallant old fox.

'Maurice has told me that you are not completely happy in your work.' She pronounced Maurice in the French way.

'I don't know if you know about the school, but – ' I paused to give her a chance to answer. She simply shook her head, with a small smile. 'I think they make the boys work too hard, you see, and I can't do anything about it. It's rather frustrating.'

'Could you not complain?' She gave me an earnest look; beautifully and convincingly earnest. I thought, she must be an actress. Not a model.

'You see … '

So it went on. We must have sat talking for nearly fifteen minutes, in this absurd stilted way. She questioned, I replied. Conchis said very little, leaving the conversation to us. I found myself formalizing my speech, as if I too was pretending to be in a drawing-room of forty years before. After all, it was a masque, and I wanted, or after a very short while began to want, to play my part. I found something a shade patronizing in her attitude, and I interpreted it as an attempt to upstage me; perhaps to test me, to see if I was worth playing against. I thought once or twice that I saw a glint of sardonic amusement in Conchis's eyes, but I couldn't be sure. In any case, I found her far too pretty, both in repose and in action (or acting), to care. I thought of myself as a connoisseur of girls' good looks; and I knew that this was one to judge all others by.

There was a pause, and Conchis spoke.

'Shall I tell you now what happened after I left England?'

'Not if it would bore ... Miss Montgomery.'

'No. Please. I like to listen to Maurice.'

He kept watching me, ignoring her.

'Lily always does exactly what I want.'

I glanced at her. 'You're very fortunate, then.'

He did not take his eyes off me. The furrows beside his nose caught shadow, deepening them.

'She is not the real Lily.'

This sudden dropping of the pretence took all the wind, as once again he knew it would, out of my sails.

'Well ... of course.' I shrugged and smiled. She was staring down at her fan.

'Neither is she anyone impersonating the real Lily.'

'Mr Conchis ... I don't know what you're trying to tell me.'

'Not to jump to conclusions.' He gave one of his rare wide smiles. 'Now. Where was I? But first I must warn you that this evening I give you not a narrative. But a character.'

I looked at Lily She seemed to me to be perceptibly hurt; and just as another wild idea was beginning to run through my mind, that she really was an amnesiac, some beautiful amnesiac he had, somehow, literally and metaphorically laid his hands on, she gave me what was beyond any doubt a contemporary look, a look out of role – a quick, questioning glance that flicked from me to Conchis's averted head and back again. At once I had the impression that we were two actors with the same doubts about the director.

28

'Buenos Ayres. I lived there for nearly four years, until the spring of 1919. I quarrelled with my uncle Anastasios, I gave English lessons, I taught the piano. And I felt perpetually in exile from Europe. My father was never to speak or write to me again, but after a while I began to hear from my mother.'

I glanced at Lily, but now, back in role, she was watching Conchis with a politely interested expression on her face. Lamplight became her, infinitely.

'Only one thing of importance happened to me in the Argentine. A friend took me one summer on a tour of the Andean provinces. I learnt about the exploited conditions under which the peons and gauchos had to live. I urgently felt the need to sacrifice myself for the underprivileged. Various things we saw decided me to become a doctor. But the reality of my new career was harsh. The medical faculty at Buenos Ayres would not accept me, and I had to work day and night for a year to learn enough science to be enrolled.

'But then the war ended. My father died soon after. Though he never forgave me, or my mother for having helped me, both into his world and out of it, he was sufficiently my father to let sleeping dogs lie. So far as I know my disappearance was never discovered by the authorities. My mother was left a sufficient income. The result of all this was that I returned to Europe and settled in Paris with her. We lived in a huge old flat facing the Panthéon, and I began to study medicine seriously. Among the medical students a group formed. We all regarded medicine as a religion, and we called ourselves the Society of Reason. We saw the doctors of the world uniting to form a scientific and ethical elite. We should be in every land and in every government, moral supermen who would eradicate all demagogy, all self-seeking politicians, reaction, chauvinism. We published a manifesto. We held a public meeting in a cinema at Neuilly. But the Communists got to hear of it. They called us Fascists and wrecked the cinema. We tried another meeting in another place. That was attended by a group who called themselves the Militia of Christian Youth – Catholic *ultras*. Their manners, if not their faces, were identical with those of the Communists. Which was what they termed us. So our grand scheme for utopianizing the world was settled in two scuffles. And heavy bills for damages. I was secretary of the Society of Reason. Nothing could have been less reasonable than my fellow-members when it came to paying their share of the bills. No doubt we deserved what we received. Any fool can invent a plan for a more reasonable world. In ten minutes. In five. But to expect people to live reasonably is like asking them to live on paregoric.' He turned to me. 'Would you like to read our manifesto, Nicholas?'

'Very much.'

'I will go and get it. And fetch the brandy.'

And so, so soon, I was alone with Lily. But before I could phrase the right remark, the question that would show her I saw no reason why in Conchis's absence she should maintain the pretending to believe, she stood up.

'Shall we walk up and down?'

I walked beside her. She was only an inch or two shorter than myself, and she walked slowly, slimly, a shade self-consciously, looking out to sea, avoiding my eyes, as if she now was shy. I looked round. Conchis was out of hearing.

'Have you been here long?'

'I have not been anywhere long.'

She gave me a quick look, softened by a little smile. We had gone round the other arm of the terrace, into the shadow cast by the corner of the bedroom wall.

'An excellent return of service, Miss Montgomery.'

'If you play tennis, I must play tennis back.'

'Must?'

'Maurice must have asked you not to question me.'

'Oh come on. In front of him, okay. I mean, good God, we're both English, aren't we?'

'That gives us the freedom to be rude to each other?'

'To get to know each other.'

'Perhaps we are not equally interested in ... getting to know each other.' She looked away into the night. I was nettled.

'You do this thing very charmingly. But what exactly is the game?'

'Please.' Her voice was faintly sharp. 'I really cannot stand this.' I guessed why she had brought me round into the shadow. I couldn't see much of her face.

'Stand what?'

She turned and looked at me and said, in a quiet but fiercely precise voice, 'Mr Urfe.'

I was put in my place.

She went and stood against the parapet at the far end of the terrace, looking towards the central ridge to the north. A breath of listless air from the sea washed behind us.

'Would you shawl me, please?'

'Would I?'

'My wrap.'

I hesitated, then went back for the indigo wrap. Conchis was still indoors. I returned and put it round her shoulders. Without warning she reached her hand sideways and took mine and pressed it, as if to give me courage; and perhaps to make me identify her with the original, gentle Lily. She remained staring out across the clearing to the trees.

'Why did you do that?'

'I did not mean to be unkind.'

I mimicked her formal tone. 'Can, may I, ask you … where you live here?'

She turned and leant against the edge of the parapet, so that we were facing opposite ways, and came to a decision.

'Over there.' She pointed with her fan.

'That's the sea. Or are you pointing at thin air?'

'I assure you I live over there.'

An idea struck me. 'On a yacht?'

'On land.'

'Curious. I've never seen your house.'

'I expect you have the wrong kind of sight.'

I could just make out that she had a little smile at the corner of her lips. We were standing very close, the perfume around us.

'I'm being teased.'

'Perhaps you are teasing yourself.'

'I hate being teased.'

She made a little mock inclination. She had a beautiful neck; the throat of a Nefertiti. The photo in Conchis's room made her look heavy-chinned, but she wasn't.

'Then I shall continue to tease you.'

There was silence. Conchis was away far too long for the excuse he had given. Her eyes sought mine, a shade uncertainly, but I kept silent, and she looked away. Very gently, as to a wild animal, I reached out my hand and made her turn her head. She let my fingers rest on the cool skin of her cheek; but something in her now steady look, a declaration of inaccessibility, made me take my hand away. Yet our eyes lingered, and hers conveyed both an indication and a warning: Subtlety may win me, but force never will.

She turned to face the sea again.

'Do you like Maurice?'

'This is only the third time I've met him.' She appeared to wait for me to go on. 'I'm very grateful for his asking me over here. Especially – '

She cut short the compliment. 'We all love him very much.'

'Who is we?'

'His other visitors and myself.' I could hear the inverted commas.

'"Visitor" seems an odd way of putting it.'

'Maurice does not like "ghost".'

I smiled. 'Or "actress"?'

Her face betrayed not the least preparedness to concede, to give up her role.

'We are all actors and actresses, Mr Urfe. You included.'

'Of course. On the stage of the world.'

She smiled and looked down. 'Be patient.'

'I couldn't imagine anyone I'd rather be more patient with. Or credulous about.'

She stared out over the sea. Her voice was suddenly lower, more sincere, out of role.

'Not for me. For Maurice.'

'And for Maurice.'

'You will understand.'

'Is that a promise?'

'A prediction.'

There was a sound from the table. She glanced back, then into my eyes. She had the face I had first seen in the music-room door: both amused and conspiratorial, and now appealing as well.

'Please pretend.'

'Okay. But only in his presence.'

She took my arm and we moved back towards him. He gave us both his little interrogatory headshake.

'Mr Urfe is very understanding.'

'I am glad.'

'All will be well.'

She smiled at me and sat down and remained thoughtfully for a while with her chin resting on her hand. Conchis had poured her a minute glass of *crème de menthe*, which she sipped. He pointed to an envelope he had put in my place.

'The manifesto. It took me a long time to find. Read it later. There is an anonymous criticism of great force at the end.'

29

'I still loved, at any rate practised, music. I had the big Pleyel harpsichord I use here in our Paris flat. One warm day in spring, it would have been in 1920, I was playing by chance with the windows open, when the bell rang. The maid came in to say that a gentleman had called and wished to speak to me. In fact, the gentleman was already behind the maid. He corrected her – he wanted to listen to me, not speak to me. He was such an extraordinary-looking man that I hardly noticed the extraordinariness of the intrusion. About sixty, extremely tall, faultlessly dressed, a gardenia in his buttonhole ... '

I looked sharply at Conchis. He had turned and, as he seemed to like to, was looking out to sea as he spoke. Lily swiftly, discreetly raised her finger to her lips.

'And also – at first sight – excessively morose. There was beneath the archducal dignity something deeply mournful about him. Like the actor Jouvet, but without his sarcasm. Later I was to discover that he was less miserable than he appeared. Almost without words he sat down in an armchair and listened to me play. And when I had finished, almost without words he picked up his hat and his amber-topped stick ... '

I grinned. Lily saw my grin, but looked down and refused to share it; as if to ban it.

' ... and presented me with his card and asked me to call on him the next week. The card told me that his name was Alphonse de Deukans. He was a count. I duly presented myself at his apartment. It was very large, furnished with the severest elegance. A man-servant showed me into a *salon*. De Deukans rose to greet me. At once he took me, with the minimum of words, through to another room. And there were five or six harpsichords, old ones, splendid ones, all museum pieces, both as musical instruments and as decorative objects. He invited me to try them all, and then he played himself. Not as well as I could then. But very passably. Later he offered me a collation and we sat on Boulard chairs, gravely swallowing *marennes* and drinking a Moselle that he told me came from his own vineyard. So began the most remarkable friendship of my life.

'I learnt very little about him for many months, although I saw him often. This was because he had never anything to say about himself or his past. And discouraged every kind of question. All that I could find out was that his family came from Belgium. That he was immensely rich. That he appeared, from choice, to have very few friends. No relations. And that he was, without being a homosexual, a misogynist. All his servants were men, and he never referred to women except with distaste.

'De Deukans's real life was lived not in Paris, but at his great château in eastern France. It was built by some peculating surintendant in the late seventeenth century, and set in a park far larger than this island. One saw the slate-blue turrets and white walls from many miles away. And I remember, on my first visit, some months after our first meeting, I was very intimidated. It was an October day, all the cornfields of the Champagne had long been cut. A bluish mist over everything, an autumn smoke. I arrived at Givray-le-Duc in the car that had been sent to fetch me, I was taken up a splendid staircase to my room, or rather my suite of rooms, and then I was invited to go out into the park to meet de Deukans. All his servants were like himself – silent, grave-looking men. There was never laughter around him. Or running feet. No noise, no excitement. But calm and order.

'I followed the servant throught a huge formal garden behind the château. Past box-hedges and statuary and over freshly raked gravel, and then down through an arboretum to a small lake. We came out at its edge and on a small point some hundred yards ahead I saw, over the still water and through the October leaves, an oriental tea-house. The servant bowed and left me to go on my way alone. The path led beside the lake, over a small stream. There was no wind. Mist, silence, a beautiful but rather melancholy calm.

'The tea-house was approached over grass, so de Deukans could not hear me coming. He was seated on a mat staring out over the lake. A willow-covered islet. Ornamental geese that floated on the water as in a silk painting. Though his head was European, his clothes were Japanese. I shall never forget that moment. How shall I say it – that *mise en paysage*.

'His whole park was arranged to provide him with such decors, such ambiances. There was a little classical temple, a rotunda. An English garden, a Moorish one. But I always think of him sitting there on his *tatami* in a loose kimono. Greyish-blue, the colour of the mist. It was unnatural, of course. But all dandyism and eccentricity is more or less unnatural in a world dominated by the desperate struggle for economic survival.

'Constantly, during that first visit, I was shocked, as a would-be socialist. And ravished, as an *homme sensuel*. Givray-le-Duc was nothing more nor less than a vast museum. There were countless galleries, of paintings, of porcelain, of *objets d'art* of all kinds. A famous library. A really unsurpassed collection of early keyboard instruments. Clavichords, spinets, virginals, lutes, guitars. One never knew what one would find. A room of Renaissance bronzes. A case of Breguets. A wall of magnificent Rouen and Nevers faïence. An armoury. A cabinet of Greek and Roman coins. I could inventory all night, for he had devoted all his life to this collecting of collections. The Boulles and Rieseners alone were enough to furnish six smaller châteaux. I suppose only the Hertford Collection could have rivalled it in modern times. Indeed when the Hertford was split up, de Deukans had bought many of the best pieces in the Sackville legacy. Seligmann's gave him first choice. He collected in order to collect, of course. Art had not then become a branch of the stock market.

'On a later visit he took me to a locked gallery. In it he kept his company of automata – puppets, some almost human in size, that seemed to have stepped, or whirred, out of a Hoffman story. A man who conducted an invisible orchestra. Two soldiers who fought a duel. A prima donna from whose mouth tinkled an aria from *La Serva Padrona*. A girl who curtsied to a man who bowed, and then danced a pallid and ghostly minuet with him. But the chief piece was Mirabelle, *la Maîtresse-Machine*. A naked woman, painted and silk-skinned, who when set in motion lay back in her faded four-poster bed, drew up her knees and then opened them together with her arms. As her human master lay on top of her, the arms closed and held him. But de Deukans cherished her most because she had a device that made it unlikely that she would ever cuckold her owner. Unless one moved a small lever at the back of her head, at a certain pressure her arms would clasp with vice-like strength. And then a stiletto on a strong spring struck upwards through the adulterer's groin. This repulsive thing had been made in Italy in the early nineteenth century. For the Sultan of Turkey. When de Deukans demonstrated her "fidelity" he turned and said, *"C'est ce qui en elle est le plus vraisemblable."* It is the most lifelike thing about her.'

I looked at Lily covertly. She was staring down at her hands.

'He kept Madame Mirabelle behind locked doors. But in his private chapel he kept an even more – to my mind – obscene object. It was encased in a magnificent early-medieval reliquary. It looked much like a withered sea-cucumber. De Deukans called it, without any wish to be humorous, the Holy Member. He knew, of course, that a merely cartilaginous object could not possibly survive so long. There are at least sixteen other Holy Members in Europe. Mostly from mummies, and all equally discredited. But for de Deukans it was simply a collectable, and the religious or indeed human blasphemy it represented had no significance for him. This is true of all collecting. It extinguishes the moral instinct. The object finally possesses the possessor.

'We never discussed religion or politics. He went to Mass. But only, I think, because the observance of ritual is a form of the cultivation of beauty. In some ways, perhaps because of the wealth that had always surrounded him, he was an extremely innocent man. Self-denial was incomprehensible to him, unless it formed part of some aesthetic regimen. I stood with him once and watched a line of peasants labouring a turnip-field. A Millet brought to life. And his only remark was, "It is beautiful that they are they and that we are we." For him even the most painful social confrontations and contrasts, which would have pricked the conscience of even the vulgarest *nouveau riche*, were stingless. Without significance except as vignettes, as interesting discords, as pleasurable because vivid examples of the algedonic polarity of existence.

'Altruistic behaviour – what he termed *"le diable en puritain"* – upset him deeply. For instance, since the age of eighteen I have refused to eat wild birds in any form at table. I would as soon eat human flesh as I would an ortolan, or a wild duck. This to de Deukans was distressing, like a false note in a music manuscript. He could not believe things had been written thus. And yet there I was, in black and white, refusing his *pâté d'alouettes* and his truffled woodcock.

'But not all his life was to do with the dead. He had an observatory on the roof of his château, and a well-equipped biological laboratory. He never walked out in the park without carrying a small *étui* of test-tubes. To catch spiders. I had known him over a year before I discovered that this was more than another eccentricity. That he was in fact one of the most learned amateur arachnologists of his day. There is even a species named after him: *Theridion deukansii*. He was delighted that I also knew something of ornithology. And he encouraged me to specialize in what he jokingly called ornithosemantics – the meaning of bird-sound.

'He was the most abnormal man I had ever met. And the politest. And the most distant. And certainly the most socially irresponsible. I was twenty-five – your age, Nicholas, which will perhaps tell you more than anything I can say how unable I was to judge him. It is, I think, the most difficult and irritating age of all. Both to be and to behold. One has the intelligence, one is in all ways treated as a grown man. But certain persons reduce one to adolescence, because only experience can understand and assimilate them. In fact de Deukans, by being as he was – certainly not by arguing – raised profound doubts in my philosophy. Doubts he was later to crystallize for me, as I will tell you, in five simple words.

'I saw the faults in his way of life and at the same time found myself enchanted. That is, unable to act rationally. I have forgotten to tell you that he had manuscript after manuscript of unpublished music of the seventeenth and eighteenth centuries. To sit at one of the magnificent old harpsichords in his musicarium – a long rococo gallery in faded gold and pomona green, always in sunlight, as tranquil as an orchard – such experiences, such happiness, always give rise to the same problem: of the nature of evil. Why should such complete pleasure be evil? Why did I believe that de Deukans was evil? You will say, "Because children were starving while you played in your sunlight." But are we never to have palaces, never to have refined tastes, complex pleasures, never to let the imagination fulfil itself? Even a Marxist world must have some destination, must develop into some higher state, which can only mean a higher pleasure and richer happiness for the human beings in it.

'And so I began to comprehend the selfishness of this solitary man. More and more I came to see that his blindness was a pose and yet his pose was an innocence. That he was a man from a perfect world lost in a very imperfect one. And determined, with a monomania as tragic, if not quite so ludicrous, as Don Quixote's, to maintain his perfection. But then one day – '

Conchis never finished his sentence. With an electrifying suddenness a horn clamoured out of the darkness to the east. I thought immediately of an English hunting-horn, but it was harsher, more archaic. Lily's previously wafting fan was frozen, her eyes on Conchis. He was staring out to sea, as if the sound had turned him to stone. As I watched, his eyes closed, almost as if he was silently praying. But prayer was totally foreign to his face.

The horn broke the tense night again. Three notes, the middle the highest. They echoed faintly from some steep hillside inland, the primitive timbre seeming to wake the landscape and the night, to summon from an evolutionary sleep.

I said to Lily, 'What is it?'

She held my eyes for a moment; with a strange hint of doubt, as if she half suspected me of knowing perfectly well what it was.

'Apollo.'

'Apollo!'

Again the horn was blown, but at a higher pitch, and closer, too close to the house now for me to see anything, because of the parapet, even if it had not been night. Conchis still sat with his oblivious face. Lily stood and held out a hand.

'Come.'

I let her lead me to where we had stood before, at the eastern end of the terrace. She stared down into the trees, and I glanced at her profile.

'Someone seems to be mixing metaphors.'

She couldn't quite press the smile out of her mouth. My hand was gently squeezed.

'Be good. Watch.'

The gravel, the clearing, the trees: I could see nothing unusual.

'I just wish I had a programme. That's all.'

'How very dull of you, Mr Urfe.'

'Nicholas. Please.'

But whatever answer she might have given to that was forestalled. From somewhere between the house and Maria's cottage there came a beam of light. It was not very strong, from a small electric torch. In it, some sixty yards away on the edge of the pines, a figure stood like a marble statue. With a new shock I realized that it was that of an absolutely naked man. He was just near enough for me to make out the black pubic hair, the pale scape of his penis; tall, well-built, well cast to be Apollo. His eyes seemed exaggeratedly large, as if they had been made up. On his head there was a glint of gold, a crown of leaves; laurel-leaves. He was facing us, immobile, with his yard-long horn, a narrow crescent with a flared end, held slightly out from his waist in his right hand. It struck me after a few seconds that his skin was an unnatural white, almost phosphorescent in the weak beam, as if his body as well as his face had been painted.

I looked back: Conchis still sat as before ... then at Lily, who watched the figure without expression, yet with a kind of intentness – as if she had seen this rehearsed, and was now curious to see the full performance – that silenced any desire in me to be facetious. The charade itself shocked me less than the revelation that I was not the only young male at Bourani. I knew that at once.

'Who is he?'

'My brother.'

'I thought you were meant to be an only child.'

The Apollo figure raised his horn sideways and blew a different note, sustained, yet more urgent, as if calling lost hounds.

Lily said slowly, without taking her eyes from him, 'That is in the other world.' And then, before I could challenge her further, she pointed to our left, beyond the cottage. A faint light shape came running out of the dark tunnel where the track to the house emerged from the trees. The torch-beam moved to her – it was a girl, and she too was naked, except for antique sandals that were laced up her calves; or perhaps not quite naked – either the pubic hair had been shaved or she wore some kind of *cache-sexe*. Her hair was bound back in a classical style, and as with the Apollo her body and face seemed unnaturally white. She was running too quickly for me to see her features. She threw a look back as she came towards us, she was being chased.

She ran towards the sea, between the Apollo and the two of us standing on the terrace. Then a third figure appeared behind her. Another man, running out of the trees and down the track. He was got up as a satyr, in some kind of puffed-out hairy tights, goat-haunches; and he had the traditional head, a beard, two stubby horns. His naked torso was dark, almost black. As he ran closer, gaining on the girl, I had my next shock. A huge phallus rose from his loins. It was nearly eighteen inches long, far too massive to be meant realistically, but it was effectively obscene. I suddenly remembered the painting in the bowl of the kylix in the room below us; and also remembered I was a long way from home. I felt unsure, out of my depth, a lot more innocent and unsophisticated at heart than I liked to pretend. I slid a quick look at the girl beside me. I thought I detected a faint smile, a kind of excitement at cruelty, even when being mimed, that I did not like; it was very remote from the Edwardian 'other world' whose clothes she still wore.

I looked back at the nymph, at her white back and dishevelled hair, her seemingly near-exhausted legs. She plunged into the trees going down towards the sea, and disappeared – and then, in a *coup de théâtre*, a much stronger beam shone out from directly beneath where we stood. Standing there, in the place where the first girl had just disappeared, a place where the ground rose a little before falling abruptly towards the beach, was yet another, the most striking figure of all, a woman in a long saffron chiton. It had a blood-red hem where it ended at the knees. On her feet were black buskins with silver greaves, which gave her a grim gladiatorial look, in strange contrast to the bare shoulders and arms. Again the skin was unnaturally white, the eyes elongated by black make-up, and the hair was also elongated backwards in a way that was classical yet sinister. Over her shoulders she had a silver quiver and in her left hand, a silver bow. Something in her stance, as well as the distorted face, was genuinely frightening.

She stood there for several moments, cold and outraged and ominously barring the way. Then she reached back with her free hand and with a venomous quickness pulled an arrow out of the quiver. But before she could fit it to the bow-string, the beam tracked back to the arrested satyr. He stood spectacularly terrified, his arms flung back and his head averted, the mock phallus – in the better light I could see it was jet black – still erect. It was a pose without realism, yet dramatic. The beam swept back to the goddess. She had her bow at full stretch, the arrow went. I saw it fly, but lost it in the darkness. A moment later the beam returned to the satyr. He was clutching the arrow – or an arrow – to his heart. He fell slowly to his knees, swayed a second, then slumped sideways among the stones and thyme-bushes. The stronger torch lingered on him, as if to impress the fact of his death; then it was extinguished. Beyond, in the weaker original beam, Apollo stood impassively, surveying, a pale marmoreal shadow, like some divine umpire, president of the arena. The goddess began to walk, a striding huntress walk, her silver bow held in one hand by her side, towards him. They stood facing us for a moment, then each raised a free hand, the palm bent back, in a kind of final tableau, a grave salutation. It was another effective gesture. It had a fleeting, but genuine, dignity, the farewell of immortals. But then the remaining light went out. I could still just distinguish the two pale shadows, turning away now with the rather mundane haste of actors eager to get off stage while the lights are down.

Lily moved, as if to distract me from this more pedestrian side of things.

'Excuse me one moment.'

She crossed towards where Conchis sat. I saw her bend over and whisper something. Then I looked back to the east. A dark shape moved towards the trees: the satyr. There was a tiny sound from the colonnade below, someone had accidentally bumped into a chair and made its legs scrape. Four other actors, two people doing the lighting ... the mechanics of the mounting of this and the other incidents began to seem quite as uncanny as truly supernatural happenings. I tried to imagine what connection there was between the elderly man on the road by the hotel, the 'pre-haunting', and this scene I had just witnessed. I thought I had grasped, during Conchis's telling, the point of the *caractère* of de Deukans. He had been talking of himself and me – the parallels were too close for it to mean anything else. '*And discouraged every kind of question*' ... '*how unable I was to judge him*' ... '*very few friends and no relations*' ... but where did that tie in with this latest episode?

Plainly it was an attempt at the sort of 'scandalous evocation' mentioned in *Le Masque Français*. At that level I could laugh at it,

183

and at any attempt to resurrect the psychic nonsense. But more and more I smelt some nasty drift in Conchis's divertimenti. That phallus, the nakedness, the naked girl ... I had an idea that sooner or later I was going to be asked to perform as well, that this was some initiation to a much darker adventure that I was prepared for, a society, a cult, I didn't know what, where Miranda was nothing and Caliban reigned. I also felt irrationally jealous of all these other people who had appeared from nowhere to poach in 'my' territory, who were in some way in conspiracy against me, who knew more. I could try to be content as a spectator, to let these increasingly weird incidents flow past me as one sits in a cinema and lets the film flow past. But even as I thought that, I knew it was a bad analogy. People don't build cinemas for an audience of one, unless they mean to use that one for a very special purpose.

At last Lily straightened from where she had stood bent beside Conchis, talking in a low voice to him. She came back towards me. There was a little sliver of knowingness in her eyes now: an unmistakable curiosity to see how I had reacted to this latest development. I smiled and made a little movement of the head: I was impressed, but not fooled ... and I was very careful to show her that I was not shocked, either. She smiled.

'I must go now, Mr Urfe.'

'Congratulate your friends on their performance.'

She pretended to be taken aback, and her eyelids fluttered as if she knew she was being teased.

'You surely did not suppose they were merely performing?'

I said gently, 'Come off it.'

But I received no answer. Her eyes had the tiniest trace of a smile, and then she very delicately bit her lips, before touching her skirt and dropping me the ghost of a curtsey.

'When shall I see you again?'

Her eyes flicked back towards Conchis, though her head did not move. Once again I was to believe we were in collusion together.

'That depends on when I am next woken from my immemorial sleep.'

'I hope it's very soon.'

She raised her fan to her lips, just as she had with the recorder brush, and pointed surreptitiously back to Conchis. I watched her disappear into the house, then I went and stood across the table from him. He seemed recovered from his trance. His eyes were even more intense than usual, like black phosphorus, almost leechlike; much more the eyes of a scientist checking the result of an experiment, the state of the guinea-pig, than of a host seeking approval from a guest after a spectacular entertainment. I knew he knew I was confused, even though I looked down at him from behind my chair with the same small sceptical smile I had tried on Lily. Somehow I also knew that he no longer expected me to believe what I was supposed to believe. I sat down, and still he stared, and I had to say something.

'I'd enjoy it all more if I knew what it meant.'

That pleased him. He sat back and smiled.

'My dear Nicholas, man has been saying what you have just said for the last ten thousand years. And the one common feature of all the gods he has said it to is that not one of them has ever returned an answer.'

'Gods don't exist to answer. You do.'

'I am not going to venture where even the gods are powerless. You must not think I know every answer. I do not.'

I stared at the now bland mask of his face, then said quietly, 'Why me?'

'Why anyone? Why anything?'

I pointed to the east, behind him. 'All that – just to give me a lesson in theology?'

He pointed up to the sky. 'I think we would both agree that any god who created all that just to give us a lesson in theology was gravely lacking in both humour and imagination.' He left a pause. 'You are perfectly free to return to your school if you wish. Perhaps it would be wiser.'

I smiled and shook my head. 'This time I take the tooth.'

'This time it may be real.'

'At least I'm beginning to realize that all your dice are loaded.'

'Then you cannot possibly win.' But he went on quickly, as if he had taken a step too far. 'I will tell you one thing. There is only one answer to your question, both in general terms and in those of your presence here. I gave it to you on your first visit. Why everything is,

185

including you, including me, and all the gods, is a matter of hazard. Nothing else. Pure hazard.'

I searched his eyes and at last found something in them that I could believe; and grasped dimly, somewhere, that my ignorance, my nature, my vices and virtues were somehow necessary in his masque. He stood and fetched the brandy bottle from beside the lamp on the other table. He poured me a glass, then a little in his own, and still standing, raised it to me.

'Let us both drink to knowing each other better, Nicholas.'

'I'll second that.' I drank, then gave him a cautious smile. 'You didn't finish your story.' Strangely, that seemed to set him back, as if he had forgotten – or presumed I would have no further interest in it. He hesitated, then he sat again.

'Very well. I was going … but no matter now.' He paused. 'Let us jump to the climax. To the moment when these gods that neither of us believes in lost patience with such hubris.'

He leant back, once more turned a little to the sea.

'Whenever I see a photograph of a teeming horde of Chinese peasants, or of some military procession, whenever I see a cheap newspaper crammed with advertisements for mass-produced rubbish. Or the rubbish itself that large stores sell. Whenever I see the horrors of the *pax Americana*, of civilizations condemned to century after century of mediocrity because of over-population and under-education, I see also de Deukans. Whenever I see lack of space and lack of grace, I think of him. One day, many millennia from now, there will perhaps be a world in which there are only such châteaux, or their equivalents, and such men and women. And instead of their having to grow, like mushrooms, from a putrescent compost of inequality and exploitation, they will come from an evolution as controlled and ordered as de Deukans's tiny world at Givray-le-Duc. Apollo will reign again. And Dionysus will return to the shadows from which he came.'

Was that it? I saw the Apollo scene in a different light. Conchis was evidently like certain modern poets: he tried to kill ten meanings with one symbol.

'One day one of his servants introduced a girl into the château. De Deukans heard a woman laughing, I do not know how … perhaps an open window, perhaps she was a little drunk. He sent to find out who had dared to bring a real mistress into his world. It was one of the chauffeurs. A man of the machine age. He was dismissed. Soon afterwards de Deukans went to Italy on a visit.

'One night at Givray-le-Duc the major-domo smelt smoke. He went to look. The whole of one wing and the centre portion of the château were on fire. In their master's absence most of the servants were away at their homes in the neighbouring villages. The few who were sleeping at the château started to carry buckets of water to the mass of flames. An attempt was made to telephone for the *pompiers*, but the line had been cut. When they finally arrived, it was too late. Every painting was shrivelled, every book ashes, every piece of porcelain twisted and smashed, every coin melted, every exquisite instrument, every piece of furniture, each automaton, even Mirabelle, charred to nothingness. All that was left were parts of the walls and the eternally irreparable.

'I was also abroad at the time. De Deukans was woken somewhere near dawn in his hotel in Florence and told. He went home at once. But they say he turned back before he got to the still smouldering remains. As soon as he was near enough to realize what the fire had done. Two days later he was found dead in his bedroom in Paris. He had taken an enormous quantity of drugs. His valet told me that he was found with a kind of sneer on his face. It had shocked the man.

'I returned to France a month after his funeral. My mother was in South America and I did not hear what had happened till my return. One day I was asked to go and see his lawyers. I thought he might have left me a harpsichord. So he had. Indeed, all his surviving harpsichords. And also ... but perhaps you have guessed.'

He paused, as if to let me guess, but I said nothing.

'By no means all his fortune, but what was, in those days, to a young man still dependent on his mother, a fortune. At first I could not believe it. I knew that he liked me, that he had come perhaps to look on me rather as an uncle, a nephew. But so much money. And so much hazard. Because I played one day with opened windows. Because a peasant-girl laughed too loud ... ' Conchis sat in silence for a moment or two.

'But I promised to tell you the words de Deukans also left me, with his money and his memory. No message. But one fragment of

Latin. I have never been able to trace its source. It sounds Greek. Ionian or Alexandrian. It was this. *"Utram bibis? Aquam an undam?"* Which are you drinking? The water or the wave?'

'He drank the wave?'

'We all drink both. But he meant the question should always be asked. It is not a precept. But a mirror.'

I thought; could not decide which I was drinking.

'What happened to the man who set fire to the house?'

'The law had its revenge.'

'And you went on living in Paris?'

'I still have his apartment. And the instruments he kept there are now in my own château in the Auvergne.'

'Did you discover where his money came from?'

'He had large estates in Belgium. Investments in France and Germany. But the great bulk of his money was in various enterprises in the Congo. Givray-le-Duc, like the Parthenon, was built on a heart of darkness.'

'Is Bourani built on it?'

'Would you leave at once if I said it was?'

'No.'

'Then you have no right to ask.'

He smiled: I was not to take him too seriously; and stood up, as if to kill any further argument. 'Take your envelope.'

He led the way through to my room, and lit my lamp, and wished me good night. But in his own door he turned and looked back towards me. For once his face showed a moment's doubt, a glimpse of a lasting uncertainty.

'The water or the wave?'

Then he went.

30

I waited. I went to the window. I sat on the bed. I lay on the bed. I went to the window again. In the end I began to read the two pamphlets. Both were in French, and the first had evidently once been pinned up; there were holes and rustmarks.

We, doctors and students of the faculties of medicine of the universities of France, declare that we believe:

1. Man can progress only by using his reason.
2. The first duty of science is to eradicate unreason, in whatever form, from public and international affairs.
3. Adherence to reason is more important than adherence to any other ethos whatever, whether it be of family, caste, country, race, or religion.
4. The only frontier of reason is the human frontier; all other frontiers are signs of unreason.
5. The world can never be better than the countries that constitute it, and the countries can never be better than the individuals that constitute them.
6. It is the duty of all who agree with these statements to join the Society for Reason.

Membership of the Society is obtained by signing the formula below.

1. I promise to give one-tenth of my annual income to the Society of Reason for the furtherance of its aims.
2. I promise to introduce reason at all times and places into my own life.
3. I shall never obey unreason, whatever the consequences; I shall never remain silent or inactive in front of it.
4. I recognize that the doctor is the spearhead of humanity. I shall do my utmost to understand my own physiology and psychology, and to control my life rationally according to those knowledges.
5. I solemnly acknowledge that my first duty is always to reason.

Brother and sister human beings, we appeal to you to join in the struggle against the forces of unreason that caused the blood-dementia of the last decade. Help to make our society powerful in the world against the conspiracies of the priests and the politicians. Our society will one day be the greatest in the history of the human race. Join it now. Be among the first who saw, who joined, who stood!

Across the last paragraph someone a long time before had scrawled the word *Merde*.

Both text and comment, in view of what had happened since 1920, seemed to me pathetic; like two little boys caught fighting at the time of an atomic explosion. We were equally tired, in mid-century, of cold sanity and hot blasphemy; of the over-cerebral and of the over-faecal; the way out lay somewhere else. Words had lost their power, either for good or for evil; still hung, like a mist, over the reality of action, distorting, misleading, castrating; but at least since Hitler and Hiroshima they were seen to be a mist, a flimsy superstructure.

I listened to the house and the night outside. Silence; and turned to the other, bound, pamphlet. Once again, the browning paper and the old-fashioned type showed it to be unmistakably a genuine pre-war relic.

ON COMMUNICATION WITH OTHER WORLDS

To arrive at even the nearest stars man would have to travel for millions of years at the speed of light. Even if we had the means to travel at the speed of light we could not go to, and return from, any other inhabited area of the universe in any one lifetime; nor can we communicate by other scientific means, such as some gigantic heliograph or by radio waves. We are for ever isolated, or so it appears, in our little bubble of time.

How futile all our excitement over aeroplanes! How stupid this fictional literature by writers like Verne and Wells about the peculiar beings that inhabit other planets!

But it is without doubt that there are other planets round other stars, that life obeys universal norms, and that in the cosmos there are beings who have evolved in the same way and with the same aspirations as ourselves. Are we then condemned never to communicate with them?

Only one method of communication is not dependent on time. Some deny that it exists. But there are many cases, reliably guaranteed by reputable and scientific witnesses, of thoughts being communicated at *precisely the moment* they were conceived. Among certain primitive cultures, such as the Lapp, this phenomenon is so frequent, so accepted, that it is used as a matter of everyday convenience, as we in France use the telegraph or telephone.

Not all powers have to be discovered; some have to be regained.

This is the only means we shall ever have of communicating with mankind in other worlds. *Sic itur ad astra.*

This potential simultaneity of awareness in conscious beings operates as the pantograph does. As the hand draws, the copy is made.

The writer of this pamphlet is not a spiritualist and is not interested in spiritualism. He has for some years been investigating telepathic and other phenomena on the fringe of normal medical science. His interests are purely scientific. He repeats that he does not believe in the 'supernatural'; in rosicrucianism, hermetism, or other such aberrations.

He maintains that already more advanced worlds than our own are trying to communicate with us; and that a whole category of noble and beneficial mental behaviour, which appears in our societies as good conscience, humane deeds, artistic inspiration, scientific genius, is really dictated by half-understood telepathic messages from other worlds. He believes that the Muses are not a poetic fiction; but a classical insight into scientific reality we moderns should do well to investigate.

He pleads for more public money and co-operation in research into telepathy and allied phenomena; above all he pleads for more scientists in this field.

Shortly he will publish direct proof of the feasibility of intercommunication between worlds. Watch the Parisian press for an announcement.

I had never had a telepathic experience in my life, and I thought it unlikely I should start with Conchis; and if benevolent gentlemen from other worlds were feeding good deeds and artistic genius into me, they had done it singularly badly – and not only for me, for most of the age I was born into. On the other hand, I began to understand why Conchis had told me I was psychic. It was a sort of softening-up process, in preparation for the no doubt even stranger scene that would take place in the masque that next night ... the 'experiment'.

The masque, the masque: it fascinated and irritated me, like an obscure poem – more than that, for it was not only obscure in itself, but doubly obscure in why it had even been written. During the evening a new theory had occurred to me: that Conchis was trying to recreate some lost world of his own and for some reason I was cast as the *jeune premier* in it, his younger self. I was intensely aware that our relationship, or my position, had changed again; as I had been shifted from guest to pupil, now I uneasily felt myself being manoeuvred into a butt. He clearly meant me not to be able to relate the conflicting sides of his personality. Things like the humanity in his playing of Bach, in certain aspects, however embroidered, of his autobiography, were undermined, nullified by his perversity and malice elsewhere. He must know it, therefore must want me to flounder; flounder indeed, since the 'curious' books and objects he put in my way, Lily herself, and now the myth-figures in the night with all their abnormal undertones had to be seen as a hook, and I couldn't pretend that it had not sunk home. But the more I thought about it, the more I suspected the authenticity of that Belgian count ... or at any rate, of Conchis's account of him. He was no more than a stalking-horse for Conchis himself. De Deukans had some sort of truth by analogy, perhaps; but far less than a literal one.

Meanwhile, the masque was letting me down. Silence still reigned. I looked at my watch. Nearly half an hour had passed. I could not sleep. After some hesitation, I crept downstairs and out through the music-room under the colonnade. I walked a little way into the trees in the direction the 'god' and 'goddess' had disappeared; then turned back and went down to the beach. The sea lapped slowly, dragging down a few small pebbles now and again, making them rattle drily, though there was no wind, no air. The cliffs and trees and the little boat lay drenched in starlight, in a million indecipherable thoughts from other worlds. The mysterious southern sea, luminous, waited; alive yet empty. I smoked a cigarette, and then climbed back to the fraught house and my bedroom.

3 I

I had my breakfast alone again. It was a day of wind, the sky as blue as ever, but the breeze tore boisterously off the sea, typhooning the fronds of the two palms that stood like sentinels in front of the house. Farther south, off Cape Matapan, the *meltemi*, the tough summer gale from the Ionian islands, was blowing.

I went down to the beach. The boat was not there. It confirmed my half-formed theory about the 'visitors' – that they were on a yacht in one of the many deserted coves round the west and south sides of the island, or anchored among the group of deserted islets some five miles to the east. I swam out of the cove to see if Conchis was visible on the terrace. But it was empty. I lay on my back and floated for a while, feeling the cool slop of the waves over my sun-warmed face, thinking of Lily.

Then I looked towards the beach.

She was standing on it, a brilliant figure on the salt-grey shingle, with the ochre of the cliff and the green plants behind her. I began to swim towards the shore, as fast as I could. She moved a few steps along the stones and then stopped and watched me. At last I stood up, dripping, panting, and looked at her. She was about ten yards away, in an exquisitely pretty First World War summer dress. It was striped mussel-blue, white and pink, and she carried a fringed sunshade of the same cloth. She wore the sea-wind like a jewel. It caught her dress, moulded it against her body. Every so often she had a little struggle with the sunshade. And all the time fingers of wind teased and skeined her long, silky-blonde hair around her neck or across her mouth.

She showed a little *moue*, half mocking herself, half mocking me as I stood knee-deep in the water. I don't know why silence descended on us, why we were locked for a strange few moments in a more serious look. It must have been transparently excited on my side. She looked so young, so timidly naughty. She gave an embarrassed yet mischievous smile, as if she should not have been there, had risked impropriety.

'Has Neptune cut your tongue off?'

'You look so ravishing. Like a Renoir.'

She moved a little farther away, and twirled her sunshade. I slipped into my beach-shoes and, towelling my back, caught up with her. She smiled with a sort of innocent sideways slyness; then sat down on a flat rock overshadowed by a solitary pine-tree, where the precipitous gulley ran down to the shingle. She closed her sunshade and pointed with it to a stone beside the rock, in the sun, where I was to sit. But I spread my towel on the rock and perched close beside her. The moist mouth, the down on the bare forearms, a scar above her left wrist, the loose hair: the grave young creature of the previous night had completely disappeared.

'You're the most deliciously pretty ghost I've ever seen.'

'Am I?'

I had meant it; and I had also meant to embarrass her. But she simply widened her smile.

'Who are the other girls?'

'Which other girls?'

'Come on. A joke's a joke.'

'Then pray do not spoil it.'

'At least you admit it is a joke?'

'I admit nothing.'

She was avoiding my eyes – and also biting her lips. I took a breath. She was so patently waiting to parry whatever next thrust I made. She shifted a pebble with the tip of her shoe. It was elegant, buttoned, of grey kid, over a white silk stocking with little open clocks, tiny petals of bare skin that ran up her ankles and disappeared under the hem of the dress some four inches higher. I had a feeling the foot was held out so that I should not miss this charming period detail. Her hair blew forward, clouding her face a little. I wanted to brush it back, or to shake her hard; I wasn't quite sure which. In the end I stared out to sea, a little on the same principle as Ulysses when he tied himself to the mast.

'You keep suggesting you're playing this pretend game to please the old man. If you want me to join in, I think you'd better explain why. Especially why I should believe that he doesn't know exactly what's going on.'

She hesitated, and for a moment I thought I had broken through.

'Give me your hand. I will read your fortune. You may sit a little nearer, but you must not wet my dress.'

I took another breath, but I gave her my hand. Perhaps this was at least to be some sort of indirect admission. She held the hand lightly by the wrist and traced the palmistry lines with a forefinger. I was able to see the shape of her breasts at the bottom of the opening in her dress; very pale skin, the seductive beginning of soft curves. She managed to suggest that this hackneyed sex-gambit was rather daring, mama-defying. The fingertip ran innocently yet suggestively over my palm. She began to read.

'You will have a long life. You will have three children. At forty years old you will nearly die. You are stronger in mind than in heart. Your mind betrays your heart. There are ... I see many treacheries in your life. Sometimes you betray your true self. Sometimes you betray those who love you.'

'Now will you answer my question?'

'The palm says what is. Never why it is.'

'Can I read yours?'

'I have not finished. You will never be rich. Beware of black dogs, strong drink and old women. You will make love to many girls, but you will love truly only one – her you will marry ... and be very happy.'

'In spite of nearly dying at forty.'

'Perhaps because you nearly die at forty. Here is where you nearly die. The happiness line is most strong after that.'

She let go of my hand, and folded her own primly on her lap.

'Now can I read yours?'

'Can is not may.'

She played coy a moment after this little lesson in correct English usage, but then suddenly held her hand out. I pretended to read it, did the same tracing of the lines; and tried to read it quite seriously in the manner of Sherlock Holmes. But even that great master at detecting in a second Irish maidservants from Brixton with a mania for boating and bullseyes would have been baffled. However, Lily's hands were smooth and unblemished; whatever else she was, she was not a maidservant from anywhere.

'You are taking a long time, Mr Urfe.'

'Nicholas.'

'You may call me Lily, Nicholas. But you may not sit for hours canoodling.'

'I see only one thing clearly.'

'And what is that?'

'A great deal more intelligence than you're showing at the moment.'

She snatched her hand away, and contemplated it with a sort of pout. But she wasn't the sort of girl who went in for pouting. A wisp of hair blew across her cheek; the wind kindled in her clothes a wantonness, a coquettishness, aiding her impersonation of someone younger than I knew she must be. I remembered what Conchis had said about the original Lily. The girl beside me was making a brave effort – or perhaps casting had preceded narrating. But all the acting skill in the world couldn't carry off this present role. She tilted the palm a little towards me again.

'And death?'

'You're forgetting your part. You're already dead.'

She folded her arms and stared out to sea.

'Perhaps I have no choice.'

This was a new tack. I thought I heard a faint note of regret, something obscurely mutinous; a note of the real year we were in, from behind her disguise. I searched her face.

'Meaning?'

'Everything we say, he hears. He knows.'

'You have to reveal it to him?' I sounded incredulous. She nodded, and I knew she was not unmasking at all. 'Don't tell me. Telepathy?'

'Telepathy and – ' she looked down.

'And?'

'I cannot say more.'

She picked up the sunshade and opened it, as if she were thinking of going away. It had little black tassels that hung from the ends of the ribs.

'Are you his mistress?' She flashed a look at me, and I had the impression that for once I had shocked her out of acting. I said, 'In view of last night's strip show.' Then, 'I just want to know where I am.'

She stood up and began to walk quickly away over the shingle towards the path that led up to the house. I ran after her and blocked her way. She stopped, her eyes down, then she looked up at me with a sharp blend of petulance and reproach. There was almost a passion in her voice.

'Why must you always know where you are? Have you never heard of imagination?'

'Nice shot. But it won't work.'

She stared coldly at my grin, then looked down again.

'Now I know why you cannot write good poetry.'

It was my turn to feel shocked. I had mentioned my failed literary aspirations to Conchis during that first week-end.

'What a pity I haven't lost an arm. Then you could all make fun of that as well.'

This provoked what I felt was a look out of her real self: quick, yet very direct, for a brief moment almost ... she turned a little to one side.

'I should not have said that. I apologize.'

'Thank you.'

'I am *not* his mistress.'

'Or anyone else's, I hope.'

She turned her back on me and faced the sea.

'That is a very impertinent remark.'

'But not half so impertinent as your expecting me to swallow all this nonsense.'

She was holding the sunshade so that it hid her face, but I craned round its edge; and once again her expression contradicted what she had just said. I saw far less a prim mouth than one trying not very successfully to conceal its amusement. Her eyes half slipped to meet mine, then she nodded towards the jetty.

'Shall we walk out there?'

'If that's what the script says.'

She turned to face me, and raised an admonitory finger. 'But since it is clear that we are incapable of speaking the same language, we shall just walk.'

I smiled and shrugged: a truce, if she must.

There was more wind on the jetty, and she kept on having trouble with her hair; delicious trouble. The ends of it floated up in the sunshine, silky wings of light. In the end I held her closed shade for her, and she tried to tame the mischievous skeins. Her mood had veered abruptly again. She kept on laughing, fine white teeth catching the sunlight, skipping, swaying back when a wave hit the jetty-end and sent up a little spray. Once or twice she caught my arm, but she seemed absorbed in this game with the wind and the sea ... a pretty, rather skittish schoolgirl in a gay striped dress.

I stole looks at the sunshade. It was newly made. I supposed a ghost from 1915 would have been carrying a new sunshade; but somehow it would have been more authentic, though less logical, if it had been old and faded.

Then the bell rang, from the house. It was that same ring I had heard the week-end before, in the rhythm of my own name. Lily stood still, and listened. Wind-distorted, the bell rang again.

'Nich-o-las.' She looked mock-grave. 'It tolls for thee.'

I looked up through the trees.

'I can't think why.'

'You must go.'

'Will you come with me?' She shook her head. 'Why not?'

'Because it did not toll for me.'

'I think we ought to show that we're friends again.'

She was standing close to me, holding her hair from blowing across her face. She gave me a severe look.

'Mr Urfe!' She said it exactly as she had the night before, the same chilly over-precise pronunciation. 'Are you asking me to commit osculation?'

And that was perfect; a mischievous girl of 1915 poking fun at a feeble Victorian joke; a lovely double remove; and she looked absurd and lovely as she did it. She closed her eyes and pushed her cheek forward, and I hardly had time to touch it with my lips before she had skipped back. I stood and watched her bent head.

'I'll be as quick as I can.'

I handed her back her sunshade with what I trusted was both a hopelessly attracted and a totally unduped look, then set off. Turning every so often, I climbed up the path. Twice she waved from the jetty. I came over the steep rise and started through the last of the thinned trees towards the house. I could see Maria standing by the music-room door, at the bell. But I hadn't taken two steps across the gravel before the world split in half. Or so it seemed.

A figure had appeared on the terrace, not fifty feet away, facing and above me. It was Lily. It couldn't be her, but it was her. The same hair blew about in the wind; the dress, the sunshade, the figure, the face, everything was the same. She was staring out to sea, over my head, totally ignoring me.

It was a wild, dislocating, disactualizing shock. Yet I knew within the first few seconds that although I was obviously meant to believe that this was the same girl as the one I had just left down on the beach, it was not. But it was so like her that it could be only one thing – a twin sister. There were two Lilies in the field. I had no time to think. Another figure appeared beside the Lily on the terrace.

It was a man, much too tall to be Conchis. At least, I presumed it was a man; perhaps 'Apollo', or 'Robert Foulkes' – or even 'de Deukans'. I couldn't see, because the figure was all in black, shrouded in the sun, and wearing the most sinister mask I had ever seen: the head of an enormous black jackal, with a long muzzle and high pointed ears. They stood there, the possessor and the possessed, looming death and the frail maiden. There was almost immediately, after the first visual shock, something vaguely grotesque about it; it had the overdone macabreness of a horror-magazine illustration. It certainly touched on some terrifying archetype, but it shocked common sense as well as the unconscious.

Again, I had no feeling of the supernatural, no belief that this was more than another nasty twist in the masque, a black inversion of the scene on the beach. That does not mean I was not frightened. I was, and very frightened; but my fear came from a knowledge that anything might happen. That there were no limits in this masque, no normal social laws or conventions.

I had stood frozen for perhaps ten seconds. Now Maria came towards me; and the two figures withdrew, as if to avoid any chance of her seeing them. Lily's *Doppelgänger* was pulled back imperiously by the black hand on her shoulder. At the very last moment she looked down at me, but her face was expressionless.

Beware of black dogs.

I began to run back towards the path. I flung a look over my shoulder. The figures on the terrace had disappeared. I came to the bend from which I could see down, from where, not half a minute before, I had last watched the Lily on the beach wave. The jetty was deserted; that end of the small cove was empty. I ran farther down, to the little flat space with the bench, from where I could see almost all the beach and most of the path up. I waited in vain for the mounting bright dress to appear. I thought, she must be hiding in the little cave, or among the rocks. Then, I must not react as they will expect. I turned and began to climb back towards the house.

Maria was still waiting for me at the edge of the colonnade. She had been joined by a man. I recognized Hermes, the taciturn donkey-driver. He could have been the man in black, he had the right height; but he looked unruffled, a mere bystander. I said quickly in Greek, '*Mia stigmi*,' one second, and walked indoors past them. Maria was holding out an envelope, but I took no notice. Once inside I raced up the stairs to Conchis's room. I knocked on the door. No sound. I knocked again. Then I tried the handle. It was locked.

I went back down, and paused in the music-room to light a cigarette; and to take a grip on myself.

'Where is Mr Conchis?'

'*Then eine mesa.*' He's not in. Maria raised the envelope again, but I still ignored it.

'Where's he gone?'

'*Ephyge me ti varca.*' Gone with the boat.

'Where?'

She didn't know. I took the envelope. It had *Nicholas* written on it. Two folded papers.

One was a note from Conchis.

Dear Nicholas, I am obliged to ask you to entertain yourself until this evening. Unexpected business requires my presence urgently in Nauplia.   M.C.

The other was a radiogram. There was no telephone or cable line to the island, but the Greek coastguard service ran a small radio station.

It had been sent from Athens the evening before. I assumed that it would explain why Conchis had had to go. But then I had the third shock in three minutes. I saw the name at the end. It read:

BACK NEXT FRIDAY STOP THREE DAYS FREE STOP AIRPORT SIX EVENING STOP PLEASE COME ALISON.

It had been sent on Saturday afternoon. I looked up at Maria and Hermes. Their eyes were blank, simply watching.

'When did you bring this?'

Hermes answered. '*Proi proi.*' Early that morning.

'Who gave it to you to bring?'

A professor. At Sarantopoulos's, the last evening.

'Why didn't you give it to me before?'

He shrugged and looked at Maria, and she shrugged. They seemed to imply that it had been given to Conchis. It was his fault. I read it again.

Hermes asked me if I wanted to send an answer; he was going back to the village. I said, no, no reply.

I stared at Hermes. His wall eye gave little hope. But I demanded, 'Have you seen the two young ladies this morning?'

He looked at Maria. She said, 'What young ladies?'

I looked at Hermes again. 'You?'

'*Ochi.*' His head went back.

I returned to the beach. All the time I had been watching the place where the path came up. Down there I went straight to the cave. No sign of Lily. A couple of minutes convinced me that she was not hiding anywhere on the beach. I looked up the little gulley. It might have been just possible to scramble up it and to get away to the east, but I found it difficult to believe. I climbed up some way to see if she was crouching behind a rock. But there was no one.

32

Sitting under the little pine, I stared out to sea and tried to gather my shaken wits. One twin came close to me, talked to me. She had a scar on her left wrist. The other did the *Doppelgänger* effects. I would never get close to her. I would see her on the terrace, in the starlight; but always at a distance. Twins – it was extraordinary, but I had begun to realize enough about Conchis to see that it was predictable. If one was very rich … why not the rarest? Why anything but the strangest and the rarest?

I concentrated on the Lily I knew, the scar-Lily. This morning, even last night, she had set out to make herself attractive to me; and if she really was Conchis's mistress, I couldn't imagine why he should allow it, and so obviously leave us alone together, unless he was much more profoundly perverted than I could bring myself seriously to suspect. She gave strongly the impression that she was playing with me – amusing herself as much as acting a role at Conchis's command. But all games, even the most literal, between a man and a woman are implicitly sexual; and here on the beach she had almost ingenuously set out to captivate me. It must have been on the old man's orders, yet behind the flirtatiousness, the mischief, I had glimpsed a different sort of amusement – and one not compatible with that of a mere actress for hire. Besides, her 'performance' had been much closer to inspired amateurishness than to the professional. Everything beneath the surface hinted at a girl from a world and background very like my own: a girl with both an inborn sense of decency and an inborn sense of English irony. In theatrical terms, the effect, despite the elaboration of the mounting, was much more of a family charade than of the wished-for total illusion of the true theatre; in her every glance and humour hung the suggestion that of course my leg was being pulled. Indeed, I knew already that this was what attracted me to her, beyond the physical. In a way the flirting had been over-kill. I had been set to chase from the moment I saw her ambiguous smile, the week before. In short, if it was her role in the charade to seduce me, I should be seduced. I couldn't do anything about it. I was both a sensualist and an adventurer; a failed poet, still seeking resurrection in events, if not in lines. I had to drink the wave, once offered.

Which led me to Alison. Her radiogram was like grit in the eye when one particularly wants to see clearly. I could guess what had happened. My letter of the Monday before would have arrived on Friday or Saturday in London, she would have been on a flight out of England that day, perhaps feeling fed up, half an hour to kill at Ellenikon – on impulse, a cable. But it came like an intrusion – of dispensable reality into pleasure, of now artificial duty into instinct. I couldn't leave the island, I couldn't waste three days in Athens. I read the wretched thing again. Conchis must have read it too – there was no envelope. Demetriades would have opened it when it was first delivered at the school.

So Conchis would know I was invited to Athens – and would guess that this was the girl I had spoken about, the girl I must 'swim towards'. Perhaps that was why he had had to go away. There might be arrangements to cancel for the next week-end. I had assumed that he would invite me again, give me the whole four days of half-term; that Alison would not take my lukewarm offer.

I came to a decision. A physical confrontation, even the proximity that Alison's coming to the island might represent, was unthinkable. Whatever happened, if I met her, it must be in Athens. If he invited me, I could easily make some excuse and not go. But if he didn't, then after all I would have Alison to fall back on. I won either way.

The bell rang again for me. It was lunch-time. I collected my things and, drunk with the sun, walked heavily up the path. But I was covertly trying to watch in every direction, preternaturally on the alert for events in the masque. As I walked through the wind-swept trees to the house, I expected some strange new sight to emerge, to see both twins together – I didn't know. I was wrong. There was nothing. My lunch was laid; one place. Maria did not appear. Under the muslin lay *taramasalata*, boiled eggs, and a plate of loquats.

By the end of the meal under the windy colonnade I had banned Alison from my mind and was ready for anything that Conchis might now offer. To make things easier, I went through the pine trees to where I had lain and read of Robert Foulkes the Sunday before. I took no book, but lay on my back and shut my eyes.

33

I was given no time to doze off. I had not been there five minutes before I heard a rustle and, simultaneously, smelt the sandalwood per-fume. I pretended to be asleep. The rustle came closer. I heard the tiny crepitation of pine-needles. Her feet were just behind my head. There was a louder rustle; she had sat down, and very close behind me. I thought she would drop a cone, tickle my nose. But in a very low voice she began to recite Shakespeare.

'Be not afeard; the isle is full of noises,
Sounds, and sweet airs, that give delight, and hurt not.
Sometimes a thousand twangling instruments
Will hum about mine ears; and sometimes voices
That, if I then had wak'd after long sleep,
Will make me sleep again: and then, in dreaming,
The clouds methought would open, and show riches
Ready to drop upon me; that, when I wak'd,
I cried to dream again.'

All the time I was silent, and kept my eyes closed. She teased the words, giving them double meanings. Her dry-sweet voice, the wind in the pines above. She ended, but I kept my eyes closed.

I murmured, 'Go on.'

'A spirit of his comes to torment you.'

I opened my eyes. A fiendish green-and-black face, with protuberant fire-red eyes, glared down at me. I twisted up. She was holding a Chinese carnival mask on a stick, in her left hand. I saw the scar. She had changed into a long-sleeved white blouse and a long grey skirt and her hair was tied back by a black velvet bow. I pushed the mask aside.

'You make a rotten Caliban.'

'Then perhaps you shall take the part.'

'I was rather hoping for Ferdinand.'

She half-raised the mask again and quizzed me over the top of it with a decided dryness. We were evidently still playing games, but in a different, rather franker key.

'Are you sure you have the skill for it?'

'What I lack in skill I'll try to make up for in feeling.'

A tiny mocking glint stayed in her eyes. 'Forbidden.'

'By Prospero?'

'Perhaps.'

'That's how it began in Shakespeare. By being forbidden.' She looked down. 'Although of course his Miranda was a lot more innocent.'

'And his Ferdinand.'

'Except I tell you the truth. And you tell me nothing but lies.'

204

Her eyes were still downcast, but she bit her lips. 'I have told you some truths.'

'Such as that black dog you so kindly warned me about?' I added quickly, 'And for God's sake don't ask me which black dog.'

She put her hands round her enskirted knees and leant back and stared into the trees behind me. She was wearing absurd black lace-up boots. The echo now was of some antiquated village schoolroom, or perhaps of Mrs Pankhurst, a first timid attempt at female emancipation. She left a long pause.

'Which black dog?'

'The one your twin sister was out with this morning.'

'I have no sister.'

'Balls.' I reclined back on an elbow, smiling at her. 'Where did you hide?'

'I went home.'

It was no good; she wouldn't lay down the other mask. I examined her guarded face and then reached for my cigarettes. She watched me strike the match and inhale a couple of times, then unexpectedly reached out her hand. I passed her the cigarette. She pecked out her lips at it in the characteristic way of first smokers; took a little puff, then a bigger one, which made her cough. She buried her head in her knees, holding the cigarette out for me to take back; coughed again. I looked at the nape of her neck, her slim shoulders; and remembered that naked nymph of the night before, who had also been slim, small-breasted, the same height.

I said, 'Where did you train?'

'Train?'

'Which drama school? RADA?' That received no answer. I tried another line of attack. 'You're trying – very successfully – to captivate me. Why?'

She made no attempt this time to be offended. One realized progress more by omissions than anything else; by pretences dropped. She raised her head, and sat back propped on one arm, slightly turned away. Then she picked up the mask and held it like a yashmak again.

'I am Astarte, mother of mystery.'

The piquant grey-violet eyes dilated, and I smiled, but thinly. I wanted her to know that she was getting very near the bottom of the locker in her improvisings.

'Sorry, I'm an atheist.'

She put down the mask.

'Then I shall have to teach you faith.'

'In mystification?'

'Among other things.'

I heard the sound of a boat-engine out at sea. She must have heard it as well, but her eyes revealed nothing.

'I wish I could meet you away from here.'

She looked up from the ground and through the trees to the south. There was suddenly a much more contemporary tone in her voice.

'Next week-end perhaps?'

I guessed at once that she had been told about Alison; but two could play at false ignorance.

'Why not?'

'Maurice would never allow it.'

'You're past the age of consent.'

'I understood you were to be in Athens.'

I left a pause. 'I don't find one aspect of your antics here quite so amusing as the others.'

Now she too lay on an elbow, with her back to me. When at last she spoke it was in a lower voice.

'Your sentiments are not altogether unshared.'

I felt a jab of excitement – this really was progress. I sat up, so that I could at least observe the side of her face. It was closed, reluctant, but it seemed to be acting no longer.

'Then you admit it is a game?'

'Part of it.'

'If you really feel the same, the remedy's simple – tell me what's going on. Why my private life has to be spied on like this.'

She shook her head. 'Not spied on. It was mentioned. That was all.'

'I'm not going to Athens. It's all over between us.' She said nothing. 'It's partly why I came here. To Greece. To get away from what was becoming messy.' I said, 'She's Australian. An air hostess.'

'And you no longer … ?'

'No longer what?'

'Love her?'

'It wasn't that kind of relationship.' Again she said nothing. She had picked up a cone, and was looking down at it, fiddling with it, as if she found all this embarrassing. But there seemed to be something truly shy about her now, not just to do with her role; and suspicious, as if she did not know whether to believe me. I said, 'I don't know what the old man's told you.'

'Only that she wishes to meet you again.'

'We're just friends now. We both knew it couldn't last. We write from time to time.' I added, 'You know what Australians are like.' She shook her head. 'They're terribly half-baked culturally. They don't really know who they are, where they belong. Part of her was very ... gauche. Anti-British. Another side ... I suppose I felt sorry for her, basically.'

'You ... lived together as man and wife?'

'If you must put it in that absurd way. For a few weeks.' She nodded gravely, as if in gratitude for this intimate information. 'And I'd very much like to know why you're so interested.'

All she did was to move her head sideways, in the way people do when they acknowledge that they can't really answer your question; but such simplicity seemed a more natural response than words. She did not know why she was interested. So I went on.

'I haven't been very happy on Phraxos. Not until I came here, as a matter of fact. I've been, well, pretty lonely. I know I don't love ... this other girl. It's just that she's been the only person. That's all.'

'Perhaps to her *you* seem the only person.'

I gave a little sniff of amusement. 'There are dozens of other men in her life. Honestly. At least three since I left England.' A runner ant zigzagged neurotically up the white back of her blouse and I reached and flicked it off. She must have felt me do it, but she did not turn. 'And I wish you'd stop play-acting. There must have been affaires like that in your own real life.'

'No.' Once more she shook her head.

'But you admit you have a real life. Pretending to be shocked is absurd.'

'I did not mean to pry.'

'You also know I've seen through your role. This is getting moronic.'

She was silent a moment, then she sat and faced me. She gave two

207

glances to either side, then one straight into my eyes; it was searching and uncertain, but at least it partly conceded what I had just said. Meanwhile the invisible boat had been coming closer. It was definitely heading for the cove.

I said, 'We're being watched?'

She made the ghost of a shrug. 'Everything is watched here.'

I looked round, but I could see nothing. I stared at her again. 'Maybe. But I'm not going to believe that everything is heard.'

She put her elbows on her knees, and cupped her chin in her hands, stared beyond me.

'It is like hide-and-seek, Nicholas. One has to be sure the seeker wants to play. One also has to stay in hiding. Or there is no game.'

'There's also no game when you won't concede you've been found. When you have.' I said, 'You are not Lily Montgomery. If she ever existed in the first place.'

She gave me a little look. 'She did exist.'

'But even the old man admits it wasn't you. And how are you so sure?'

'Because I exist myself.'

'You're her daughter now?'

'Yes.'

'Along with your twin sister.'

'I was an only child.'

It was too much. Before she could move, I had knelt up and forced her on her back, gripping her shoulders, so that she had to look me in the eyes. I saw a distinct tinge of fear in hers, and I worked on it.

'Now listen. All this is very amusing. But you've got a twin sister, and you know it. You do these disappearing tricks, and you have this fancy line in period dialogue and mythology and all the rest. But there are a couple of things you can't hide. You're intelligent. And you're as physically real as I am.' I gripped her shoulders harder through the thin blouse, and she winced. 'I don't know whether you're doing this because you love the old man. Because he pays you. Because it amuses you. I don't know where you and your sister and your other friends hang out. I don't really care, because I think the whole idea's fantastic, I like you, I like Maurice, in front of him I'm prepared to play along every bit as much as you want ... but don't let's take it all so bloody seriously. Play your charade. But for Christ's sake stop flogging a dead horse. Right?'

I remained staring down into her eyes, and I knew I had won. The fear had given way to a surrender.

She said, 'You're killing my back. There's a stone or something.'

Victory was confirmed; I noted those two verbal contractions.

'That's better.'

I knelt away, then stood and lit a cigarette. She sat up, straightened a little and rubbed her back, I saw there had indeed been a cone where I had pressed her to the ground; then she drew up her knees and buried her face in them. I stared down at her, thinking that I ought to have realized earlier that a little force would do the trick. She buried her face deeper in her knees, her arms enlacing her legs. There was a silence, the pose went on too long. I belatedly realized she was pretending to cry.

'That won't wash either.'

She took no notice for a few seconds, but then she raised her head and looked ruefully up at me. The tears were real, I could see them on her eyelashes. She looked away, as if she were being foolish, then brushed the eyes with the back of her wrist.

I squatted beside her; offered her my cigarette, which she took.

'Thanks.'

'I didn't mean to hurt you.'

She drew on the cigarette, normally, not as a tyro.

'I did try.'

'You're wonderful ... you've no idea how strange this experience has been. Beautifully strange. Only, you know, it's one's sense of reality. It's like gravity. One can resist it only so long.'

She gave me a shy, and oddly glum, little grimace. 'If you only realized how well I know exactly what you mean.'

I was shown a new vista: the possibility that she had been playing her part under some form of duress.

'I'm all ears.'

Once more she looked beyond me.

'What you said this morning ... there is a kind of script. I'm meant to take and show you something. Just a statue.'

'Fine. Lead me to it.' I stood up. She turned and screwed the end of the cigarette carefully into the ground, then gave me a distinctly submissive glance.

'Would you let me just … recover? Not bully me for five minutes?'

I looked at my watch. 'I'll even give you six. But not a second more.' She reached a hand and I helped her to her feet, but kept the hand. 'And I don't call wanting to know better someone I find quite extraordinarily attractive bullying.'

She lowered her eyes. 'She doesn't have to act being … rather less experienced than you.'

'That doesn't make her any less attractive.'

She said, 'It's not far. Just up the hill.'

We began to walk hand-in-hand up the slope. After a while I squeezed hers, and there was a small pressure back. It was more a promise of friendship than anything sexual, but I found her last remark about herself credible. It was partly her looks, since she had that exceptional delicacy of feature that often goes with a blend of timidity and fastidiousness about physical contact. I sensed, behind the outward daring, the duplicities of the past she had been playing, a delicious ghost of innocence, perhaps even of virginity; a ghost I felt peculiarly well equipped to exorcize, just as soon as time allowed. I had also a return of that headlong, fabulous and ancient sense of having entered a legendary maze; of being infinitely privileged. There was no one in the world I wanted to change places with, now that I had found my Ariadne, and held her by the hand. I knew already that all my past relationships with girls, my selfishnesses, caddishnesses, even that belittling dismissal of Alison to my past that I had just perpetrated, could now be justified. It was always to be this, and something in me had always known it.

34

She led me through the pines to a point higher than where I had forced my way over the gulley the week before. There was a path across, with some rough-hewn steps. On the other side, over a further little rise, we came on a small hollow, like a minute natural amphitheatre facing the sea. In the centre of its floor, on a pedestal of unshaped rock, stood the statue. I recognized it at once. It was a copy of the famous Poseidon fished out of the sea near Euboea at the beginning of the century. I had a postcard of it in my room. The superb man stood, his legs astride, his majestic forearm pointed south to the sea, as inscrutably royal, as mercilessly divine as any artefact in the history of humanity; a thing as modern as a Henry Moore and as old as the rock it stood on. Even then I was still surprised that Conchis had not shown it to me before; I knew a replica like that must have cost a small fortune; and to keep it so casually, so in a corner, unspoken of … again I was reminded of de Deukans – and of that great dramatic skill, the art of timing one's surprises.

We stood and looked at it. She smiled at my impressed face, then wandered on up to a wooden seat under the shade of an almond tree at the top of the slope behind the statue. One could see the distant sea over the trees, but the statue itself was invisible to anyone close to the shore. She sat naturally, without elegance, tacitly turning her clothes into a costume. It was a kind of undressing. I sat three feet away, and she must have known I was looking at her. The 'breathing-space' was over. But she avoided my eyes, and said nothing.

'Tell me your real name.'

'Don't you like Lily?'

'Splendid. For a Victorian barmaid.'

She smiled, but in a very token way. 'I don't like my real name much better.' Then she said, 'I was christened Julia, but it's been Julie ever since.'

'Julie what?'

'Holmes.' She murmured, 'But I've never lived in Baker Street.'

'And your sister?'

She hesitated. 'You seem very convinced about her.'

'Shouldn't I be?'

Again she hesitated, then came to a decision. 'We were summer born. My parents didn't show great imagination.' She shrugged, as if it was silly. 'Her name's June.'

'June and Julie.'

'You mustn't tell Maurice.'

'Have you known him long?'

She shook her head. 'But it seems long.'

'How long?'

She looked down. 'I feel a kind of traitor.'

'The last thing I'll do is sneak on you.'

And again she gave me that look, searching and uncertain, almost reproaching me for being so insistent; but she must have seen I was not going to be put off again. She leant forward a little, looking down at the ground.

'We were brought here under completely false pretences. A few weeks ago. In a way it's absurd that we haven't walked out.'

I hesitated, because my mind had leapt at once to Leverrier and Mitford. But I decided to save that card.

'You've never been here before?'

Her quick look of surprise seemed very genuine. 'Why … ?'

'I just wondered.'

'But why do you ask?'

'I thought this might have gone on last year.'

Her eyes searched mine, full of some suspicion.

'Have you heard … ?'

'No, no.' I smiled. 'Just guessing. Speculating. What were the false pretences?'

It was a little like goading a recalcitrant mule – a very charming mule, but one that seemed scared of every step it took forward. She stared at the ground, searching for words. 'I'm trying to say that in spite of everything we are here of our own free will. Even though we're not at all sure what's behind … everything that's happening, we do feel a sort of gratitude – a kind of trust, really.' She paused, and I opened my mouth, but she flashed me a glance of appeal. 'Please let me finish.' She put her hands to her cheeks for a moment. 'It's so difficult to explain. But we both feel we owe him a lot. And the point is, if I answer all the questions I fully understand you must be burning to ask, it … it would be like telling you the story of a mystery film just before you went to see it.'

'But surely you can tell me how you got into the film.'

'Not really. Because that's part of the plot.'

Once again I was losing her. A huge bronze maybug boomed round the upper branches of the almond. The statue below stood in the sun and eternally commanded the wind and the sea. I watched her face in the shadow, hanging a little, almost timid now.

'You're, I don't know, being paid to do this?'

She hesitated. 'Yes, but ... '

'But what?'

'It's not that. The money.'

'Just now, down there, you didn't seem at all sure you liked what he's making you do.'

'It's because we never know how much of what he tells us can be believed. You mustn't think we know everything where you know nothing. We've been told a lot more about what he's trying to do. But it may only be more lies.' She shrugged. 'If you like we're a few steps further into the maze. That doesn't mean we're any nearer the centre than you.'

I left a silence. 'You have acted at home?'

'Yes. Not really professionally.'

'At university?'

She had a wry smile. 'There's something else. There is a sense in which he perhaps can hear everything we say. I can't tell you how, but I think you'll understand by the end of today.' She quickly forestalled my scepticism. 'Nothing to do with telepathy. That's just a blind. A metaphor.'

'Then what?'

'If I tell you ... it would spoil it. I will tell you one thing. It's a unique experience. Quite out of this world. Literally out of this world.'

'You've had it?'

'Yes. It's one reason June and I have decided to trust him. It's not something that could be created by an evil mind.'

'I still don't understand how he can hear what we say.'

She contemplated the empty miles of sea. 'If I'm not explaining, it's also because I'm not sure that he won't hear because you tell him.'

'For God's sake, I've just said – I wouldn't dream of giving you away.'

She looked briefly at me, then out to sea again. Her voice dropped. 'We're not sure if you're what you say you are – what Maurice has told us you are.'

'But that's mad!'

'I'm only trying to explain that you aren't the only person who doesn't know what to believe. You could be hiding from us. In spite of appearances.'

'You only have to cross the island. The school's there. Ask anyone.' I said, 'And what about all the others here?'

'They're not English. And absolutely under Maurice's thumb. We hardly see them, anyway. They've only been here very briefly.'

'You mean I've been hired to fool you?'

'It is possible.'

'Jesus.' I looked at her, trying to force her to admit it was ridiculous; but she remained obstinately serious. 'Come on. Nobody could act that well.'

That did extract a faint smile. 'I have rather felt that.'

'Surely you can get away – I can take you round the school.'

'He's made it very clear that I mustn't do that.'

'It would only be paying him back in kind.'

'The irony is, I ... ' but she shook her head.

'Julie, you *can* trust me.'

She took a breath. 'The irony is that I'm not even sure that I'm not meant to break the rules. He is the most fantastic person. Hide-and-seek ... it's really much more like blind man's buff. Being spun so much that you lose all sense of direction. You begin to see double, triple meanings in everything he says and does.'

'Then break the rules. And see what happens.'

Again she hesitated, then gave me a rather more sincere smile. It seemed to suggest both that she wanted to trust me and that I must be patient with her.

'Would you like it if this whole thing was called off? Ended tomorrow?'

'No.'

'I think we're here very much on his sufferance. I tried once or twice to suggest that to you.'

'I got the message.'

'It's all so fragile. Like a spider's web. Intellectually. Theatrically, if you like. There are ways we could behave that might destroy it all at once.' She gave me another look. 'Seriously. I'm not playing games now.'

'Has he threatened to call it off?'

'He doesn't have to. If we didn't feel we were going through the most extraordinary experience of our lives ... I know he can seem absurd. Maddening. An old ham. But I think he's discovered a clue to something ... ' again she did not finish the sentence.

'Which I'm not allowed to know.'

'Something we might all kick ourselves for having spoilt.' She said, 'I'm only just beginning to glimpse what it may be about. It's not that I could tell you coherently, even if ... '

There was a silence.

'Well, he obviously has powers of persuasion. I presume that was your sister last night.'

'Were you shocked?'

'Only now I know who she was.'

She said softly, 'Even twin sisters don't always have the same views on things.' After a moment she said, 'I can guess what you must be thinking. But there hasn't been the slightest sign of ... we shouldn't still be here if there had been.' Then she added, 'June's always been less of a prude about that sort of thing than me. Actually she was nearly sent – '

She broke off at once, but it was too late. I saw her make a little gesture of prayer, as if to crave forgiveness for the slip. I grinned at the grim little expression that appeared on her face.

'I'd have known about you at Oxford. So why was she nearly sent down from the other place?'

'Oh God, I am a fool.' She gave me a look of dry entreaty. 'You mustn't tell him.'

'I promise.'

'It was nothing. She modelled in the nude once. For a joke. And it got out.'

'What did you read?'

She smiled gently. 'One day. Not yet.'

'But you were at Cambridge.' She gave a reluctant nod. 'Lucky Cambridge.'

There was a little silence. She spoke in a lower voice. 'He's so shrewd, Nicholas. If I tell you more than you're meant to know, he'll cotton on at once.'

'He surely can't expect me to go on swallowing the Lily thing.'

'No. He doesn't. You needn't pretend to.'

'So all this could be a part of the plot?'

215

'Yes. In a way it is.' She took a deep breath. 'Very soon your credulity is going to be stretched even further.'

'How soon?'

'If I know him, within an hour from now you won't know whether to believe a word of anything I've just been saying.'

'That was him in the boat?'

She nodded. 'He's probably watching us at the moment. Waiting for his cue.'

I looked cautiously past her through the trees towards the direction of the house; felt like turning and looking behind me. I could see nothing.

'How much longer have we got?'

'It's all right. It's partly up to me.'

She bent and picked a sprig of origan from a bush beside the bench and smelt it. I stared into the trees below us, still searching for a glint of colour, a movement ... trees, and a very elusive wood. She had of course neatly pre-empted the thousand questions I wanted to ask; but about her I was getting, if not many factual, at least some psychological and emotional answers ... I imagined a girl who had perhaps been a little bit of a blue-stocking, despite her looks; certainly more an intellectual than an animal creature, but with a repeated and teasing hint of something dormant there, waiting to be awakened; for whom acting at university must have provided some sort of release. I knew she was still acting in a way, but I felt it was defensive now, a way of hiding what she felt about me.

'It seems to me there's one part of the plot that does call for a little collaboration.' I added, 'Rehearsal discussion.'

'Which is that?'

'You and me.'

She smoothed her skirt over a crossed knee. 'You aren't the only one who's had a shock today. Two hours ago was the first time I heard about your Australian friend.'

'I told you the perfect truth down there. That's exactly how it is.'

'I'm sorry I sounded so inquisitive. It was just ... '

'Just what?'

'Suspicious. If you had meant to confuse me.'

'If I'm asked here, nothing will take me to Athens.' She said nothing. 'Is that the general plan?'

'As far as I know.' She shrugged. 'But it depends on Maurice.' My eyes were sought. 'We really are also flies in his web.' She smiled. 'I'll be honest. He was going to ask you. But we were warned at lunch that it may be called off.'

'I thought he was in Nauplia.'

'No. He's been on the island all day.'

She fingered her sprig of origan and I kept looking at her. 'But my original point. This first act has apparently required you to attract me. Anyway, that's been the effect. You may be another fly in the web, but you've also been doubling as the kind they tie on hooks.'

'It was a very artificial fly.'

'Sometimes they work the best.' Her eyes were down, she said nothing. 'You look as if I shouldn't have brought this up.'

'No, I ... you're quite right.'

'If it was a reluctant performance, I think you ought to tell me.'

'If I said yes, or no, to that, it wouldn't be the complete truth. Either way.'

'Then where do we go from here?'

'I think as if we'd met quite naturally. Somewhere else.'

'In which case?'

She hesitated, she was shredding the leaves from the little stem, preternaturally intent on that. 'I think I'd have looked forward to knowing you better.'

I thought of her performance on the beach that morning, but I knew what she meant: her real self was not one that could be rushed. I also knew that I must show her I had understood that. I leant forward, elbows on knees.

'That's all I wanted to know.'

She said slowly, 'Obviously. I am meant to be one reason you want to come back here.'

'It's working.'

She said diffidently, 'This has been something else that's worried me. Now it's come to this, I don't want to mislead you.'

She said no more, and I jumped to a wrong conclusion. 'There's someone else?'

'Just that I've made it very clear to Maurice that I'll play parts for him, I'll do what I did this morning, but beyond that ...'

'You're your own mistress.'

'Yes.'

'Has he suggested ... ?'

'Absolutely not. He's said all along that if there's something we don't want to do, we needn't.'

'I wish you'd just give me some clue about what's behind it all.'

'You must have made some guesses.'

'I feel I'm some sort of guinea-pig, God knows why. It's mad, I turned up here by pure chance, three weeks ago. Just for a glass of water.'

'I don't think it was pure chance. I mean, you may have come like that. But if you hadn't, he'd have found some way.' She said, 'We were told you were coming, before you did. When our own first supposed reason for coming here was blown sky-high.'

'He must have sold you something better than just playing games.'

'Yes.' She turned towards me, an arm along the back of the seat, with an apologetic grimace. 'Nicholas, I can't tell you more now. Apart from anything else, I must leave you. But yes, he did sell us something better. And guinea-pig ... that's not quite right. Something better than that, too. That's one reason we're still here. However it may seem at the moment.' She looked down at the sea between us. 'And one other thing. This last hour's been a tremendous relief to me. I'm so glad you forced it on us.' She murmured, 'We may have got Maurice very wrong. In which case we shall need a knight errant.'

'I'll get my lance sharpened.'

She gave me a long look, still with a hint of doubt in it, but which ended in a faint smile. Then she stood.

'We walk to the statue. Say goodbye. You return to the house.'

I kept sitting. 'Shall I see you later?'

'He's asked me to stand by. I'm not sure.'

'I feel like an over-carbonated soda-bottle. Bubbling with questions.'

'Be patient.' She reached out a hand to make me stand.

As we made our way down the slope, I said, 'Anyway, you did the forcing – pretending Lily Montgomery was your mother.' She grinned. 'Did she ever exist?'

'Your guess is as good as mine.' She slipped a look at me. 'If not better.'

'I'm glad of that.'

'You must have seen you're in the hands of someone who's very skilled at rearranging reality.'

We came beneath the statue.

I said, 'This thing tonight.'

'Don't be afraid. It's … in a way it's outside the game. Or perhaps at the heart of it.' She left a second, then she turned to face me. 'You must go now.'

I took her hands. 'I'd like to kiss you.'

She looked down, there was a faint return of the Lily persona about her.

'I'd rather you didn't.'

'Because you don't want me to?'

'We are being watched.'

'That's not what I asked.'

She said nothing, but neither were the hands taken away. I put my arms round her and drew her close. For a moment she held her face turned, then I was allowed to find her lips. They remained tightly closed, ungiving against mine except for one small tremor of response just before she pushed me away. By the standards of my past it was hardly a sexual embrace at all, but there was something oddly shocked and disturbed in her eyes for a moment or two, as if it had meant more to her than to me; as if something she had determined should not happen very nearly had. I smiled, to reassure her, a kiss like that was no crime, she could trust me; she stared, then her eyes dropped. It was disconcerting, all the rationality of the last half-hour seemed to lapse for no reason. I thought perhaps she was acting a part again, for the benefit of Conchis or whoever else was watching. But her eyes came up again, and I knew they were meant for me alone.

'If I ever find you were lying to me, I won't go on.'

She turned before I could answer, and began walking away, quickly, almost hurriedly. I watched her for a few moments, then turned to look back across the gulley. I was in two minds whether to follow her, she was going down between the pines towards the sea. In the end I lit a cigarette, gave the magnificent but enigmatic Poseidon one last glance, and started towards the house. Just before the gulley I looked back. There was one flash of white among the foliage, then she was gone. But I was not to be left alone. No sooner had I climbed the steps on the far side of the gulley than I saw Conchis.

He was standing some forty yards away, his back to me, and he appeared to be watching, through binoculars, some bird high in the trees beyond him. As I walked towards him, he lowered the glasses and turned, and made as if he had just seen me. It was not an impressive piece of acting; but then I hadn't realized that he was saving his talents for the scene to follow.

35

As I walked over the carpet of pine-needles to meet him – he was more formally dressed than usual by day, in dark blue trousers and an even darker blue polo-necked jumper – I decided to be very much on guard, which something about his quizzical look did nothing but confirm as wise. I felt pretty sure that his leading actress had not been lying to me, at least as regards her admiration for him and her belief that he was not an evil man. I had also detected a stronger residue of doubt, even of fear, than she had actually revealed to me. She had needed to convince herself as well as me. I had only to set eyes on the old man again to know that I retained more of the doubt than the rest.

'Hallo.'

'Good afternoon, Nicholas. I must apologize for my absence. There has been a small scare on Wall Street.' Wall Street seemed to be on the other side of the universe, not just of the world. I tried to look concerned.

'Oh?'

'I foolishly entered a financing consortium two years ago. Can you imagine Versailles with not one *Roi Soleil*, but five of them?'

'Financing what?'

'Many things.' He went on quickly. 'I had to go to Nauplia to telephone Geneva.'

'I hope you're not bankrupt.'

'Only a fool is ever bankrupt. And he is bankrupt from birth. You have been with Lily?'

'Yes.'

'Good.'

We began to walk back towards the house. I sized him up, and said, 'And I've met her twin sister.'

He touched the powerful glasses round his neck. 'I thought I heard a sub-alpine warbler. It is very late for them to be still on migration.' It was not exactly a snub, but a sort of conjuring trick: how to make the subject disappear.

'Or rather, *seen* her twin sister.'

He walked several steps on; I had an idea that he was thinking fast.

'Lily had no sister. Therefore no sister here.'

'I only meant to say that I've been very well entertained in your absence.'

He did not smile, but inclined his head. We said nothing more. I had the distinct feeling that he was a chess master caught between two moves; immensely rapid calculation of combinations. Once he even turned to say something, but changed his mind.

We reached the gravel.

'Did you like my Poseidon?'

'Wonderful. I was going to – '

He put his hand on my arm and stopped me, and looked down, almost as if he was at a loss for words.

'She may be amused. That is what she needs. But not upset. For reasons you of course now realize. I am sorry for all this little mystery we spread around you before.' He pressed my arm, and went on.

'You mean the ... amnesia?'

He stopped again; we had just come to the steps.

'Nothing else about her struck you?'

'Lots of things.'

'Nothing pathological?'

'No.'

He raised his eyebrows a fraction, as if I surprised him, but went up the steps; put his glasses on the old cane couch, and turned back to the tea-table. I stood by my chair, and gave him his own interrogative shake of the head.

'This obsessive need to assume disguises. To give herself false motivations. That did not strike you?'

I bit my lips, but his face, as he whisked the muslin covers away, was as straight as a poker.

'I thought that was rather required of her.'

'Required?' He seemed momentarily puzzled, then clear. 'Ah, you mean that schizophrenia produces these symptoms?'

'Schizophrenia?'

'Did you not mean that?' He gestured to me to sit. 'I am sorry. Perhaps you are not familiar with all this psychiatric jargon.'

'Yes I am. But – '

'Split personality.'

'I know what schizophrenia is. But you said she did everything ... because you wanted it.'

'Of course. As one says such things to a child. To encourage them to obey.'

'But she isn't a child.'

'I speak metaphorically. As of course I was speaking last night.'

'But she's very intelligent.'

He gave me a professional look. 'The correlation between high intelligence and schizophrenia is well known.'

I ate my sandwich, and then grinned at him.

'Every day I spend here I feel my legs get a little longer.'

He looked amazed, even a shade irritated. 'I am most certainly not pulling your leg at the moment. Far from it.'

'I think you are. But I don't mind.'

He pushed his chair away from the table and made a new gesture; pressing his hands to his temples, as if he had been guilty of some terrible mistake. It was right out of character; and I knew he was acting.

'I was so sure that you had understood by now.'

'I think I have.'

He gave me a piercing look I was meant to believe, and didn't.

'There are personal reasons I cannot go into now why I should – even if I did not love her as a daughter – feel the gravest responsibility for the unfortunate creature you have been with today.' He poured hot water into the silver teapot. 'She is one of the principal, *the* principal reason why I come to Bourani and its isolation. I thought you had realized that by now.'

'Of course I had ... in a way.'

'This is the one place where the poor child can roam a little and indulge her fantasies.'

'Are you trying to tell me that she's mad?'

'Mad is a meaningless non-medical word. She suffers from schizophrenia.'

'So she believes herself to be your long-dead fiancée?'

'I gave her that role. It was deliberately induced. It is quite harmless and she enjoys playing it. It is in some of her other roles that she is not so harmless.'

'Roles?'

'Wait.' He disappeared indoors and came back almost at once with a book. 'This is a standard textbook on psychiatry.' He searched for a moment. 'Allow me to read a passage. "One of the defining characteristics of schizophrenia is the formation of delusions which may be elaborate and systematic, or bizarre and incongruous."' He looked up at me. 'Lily falls into the first category.' He went on reading. '"They, these delusions, have in common the same tendency to relate always to the patient; they often incorporate elements of popular prejudice against certain groups of activities; and they take the general form of self-glorification or feelings of persecution. One patient may believe she is Cleopatra, and will expect all around her to conform to her belief, while another may believe that her own family have decided to murder her and will therefore make even their most innocent and sympathetic statements and actions conform to her fundamental delusion." And here. "There are frequently large areas of consciousness untouched by the delusion. In all that concerns them, the patient may seem, to an observer who knows the full truth, bewilderingly sensible and logical."'

He took a gold pencil from his pocket, marked the passages he had read and passed the open book over the table to me. I glanced at the book, then, still smiling, up at him.

'Her sister?'

'Another cake?'

'Thank you.' I put the book down. 'Mr Conchis – her sister?'

He smiled. 'Yes, of course, her sister.'

'And – '

'Yes, yes, and the others. Nicholas – here, she is queen. For a month or two we all conform to the needs of her unhappy life.'

And he had that, very rare in him, gentleness, solicitude, which only Lily seemed able to evoke. I realized that I had stopped smiling; I was beginning to lose my sense of total sureness that he was inventing a new stage of the masque. So I smiled again.

'And me?'

'Do children in England still play that game ... ' he put his hand over his eyes, at a loss for the word, 'cache-cache?'

I took a breath, remembering only too vividly the subject of our conversation's recent use of the same image; and thought, the cunning little bitch, the cunning old fox, they're throwing me backwards and forwards like a ball. That last strange look she had given me, all that talk of not betraying her, a dozen other things; I felt humiliated, and at the same time fascinated.

'Hide-and-seek? Of course.'

'The hider must have a seeker. That is the game. A seeker who is not too cruel. Not too observant.'

'I'd rather got the impression that I was the centre of attention.'

'I wish to involve you, my friend. I wish you to gain something from this. I cannot insult you by offering you money. But I hope there will be reward for you too.'

'I'm not complaining about my salary. But I would like to know a little more about my employer.'

'I think I told you that I had never practised medicine. That is not quite true, Nicholas. In the twenties I studied under Jung. I do not now count myself a Jungian. But my principal interest in life has remained psychiatry. Before the war I had a small practice in Paris. I specialized in schizophrenic cases.' He put his hands on the edge of the table. 'Do you wish to see evidence? I can show you papers I published in various journals.'

'I'd like to read them. But not now.'

He sat back. 'Very well. You must in no circumstances reveal what I am going to tell you.' His eyes bored gravely into mine. 'Lily's real name is Julie Holmes. Four or five years ago her case attracted a great deal of attention in psychiatric circles. It is one of the best documented. Even if it was not already highly unusual in itself, it was virtually unique in there being a twin sister of a perfectly normal psychological type who could provide what scientists call a control. The aetiology of schizophrenia has long caused fierce debate between the neuro-pathologists and psychiatrists proper – whether it is essentially a physical and genetically conditioned or a spiritual disorder. Julie and her sister clearly suggest the latter is the case. Whence the great interest they have aroused.'

'Are these documents available?'

'One day you shall read them. But at the moment it would only hamper your role here. It is vital that she believes you do not know who she really is. You cannot create that impression if you know all the clinical facts and background. Agreed?'

'I suppose so.'

'Julie was in danger of becoming, like many such striking cases, something of a monster in a psychiatric freak show. That is what I am now trying to guard against.'

I began to swing the other way – after all, she had warned me, I was to have my credulity put on the rack again. I could not believe that the girl I had just left suffered from some deep mental flaw. A liar, yes; but not a celebrated lunatic.

'May I ask how you come to take such an interest in her?'

'For the simplest and most non-medical of reasons. Her parents are very old friends. She is not only my patient, Nicholas. But my godchild.'

'I thought you'd lost all contact with England.'

'They do not live in England. Switzerland. Where she spends most of her year now. In a private clinic. I cannot alas give all my life to her.'

I could almost feel him willing me to believe. I looked down, then up at him with a small grin. 'Before you told me this, I was going to congratulate you on hiring such a skilled young actress.'

His stare at me was unexpectedly fierce, somehow put on the alert.

'She did not by any chance suggest that to you herself?'

'Of course not.'

But he didn't believe me; and of course, I realized at once, he didn't have to believe me. He bowed his head a moment, then stood and went to the edge of the colonnade and stared out. Then he gave me a smile back. It was almost one of concession.

'I see events have forestalled me. She has adopted a new role towards you. Yes?'

'She certainly didn't tell me about this.'

He remained scrutinizing me, and I stared blandly back. He struck his hands together in front of him, as if in self-reproach at his own stupidity. Then he returned to his chair and sat again.

'In a way you are right, Nicholas. I have most certainly not hired her, as you put it. But she *is* a skilled young actress. Let me warn you that some of the cleverest confidence tricksters in the history of crime have also been schizophrenics.' He leant forward on the table, clasping his elbows. 'You must not force her into corners. If you do, she will tell you lie upon lie – until your head swims with them. You are normal, for you that is bearable. But for her it may mean a grave relapse. Years of work undone.'

'Then shouldn't you have warned me before?'

For a second he continued staring at me, then he looked down.

'Yes. You are right. I should have warned you. I begin to see I have miscalculated badly.'

'Why?'

'Too much insistence on the truth can spoil our little – but I assure you clinically fruitful – amusements here.' He hesitated, then went on. 'It has long struck some of us that there is a paradox in the way we treat mental abnormalities of a paranoiac cast. We place our patients where they are constantly questioned, supervised, watched … all the rest. Of course it can be argued that it is for their good. But we really mean that it is for our good. Society's good. In fact, only too often unimaginative institutional treatment gives plausible substance to the basic delusions of persecution. What I am trying to create here is an ambience in which Julie can believe she has some command over circumstance. If you like, in which for once she is not the one being persecuted … the one who always knows least. We all try to contribute to give her this impression. I also allow her to think on occasion that I do not know quite what is going on, that she is leading me by the nose.'

His tone of voice managed to suggest that I was rather slow not to have guessed this for myself. I had the familiar feeling that came in conversation at Bourani, of not knowing quite what statements applied to – in this case, whether to the assumption that 'Lily' really was a schizophrenic or to the assumption that of course I knew that her 'schizophrenia' was simply a new hiding-place in the masque.

'I'm sorry.' He raised his hand, kind man; I was not to excuse myself. 'This is why you won't let her go outside Bourani?'

'Of course.'

'Couldn't she go out … ' I looked at the tip of my cigarette ' … under supervision?'

'She is, in law, certifiable. That is the personal responsibility I have undertaken. To ensure that she never enters an asylum.'

'But you let her wander around. She could easily escape.'

He raised his head in sharp contradiction. 'Never. Her nurse never leaves her.'

'Her nurse!'

'He is very discreet. It distresses her to have him always by her, especially here, so he keeps well in the background. One day you will see him.'

With his jackal-head on. It would not wash; but the extraordinary thing was that I more than half suspected that Conchis knew it would not wash. I hadn't played chess for years; but I remembered that the better you got, the more it became a game of false sacrifices. He was assaying not my powers of belief, but my powers of unbelief.

'This is why you keep her on the yacht?'

'Yacht?'

'I thought you kept her on a yacht.'

'That is her little secret. Allow her to keep it.'

'You bring her here every year?'

'Yes.'

I swallowed my knowledge that one of them must be lying; and my growing feeling that it was not the girl I must now think of as Julie.

I smiled. 'So this is why my two predecessors came here. And were so quiet about it.'

'John was an excellent … seeker. But Mitford was quite the reverse. You see, Nicholas, he was totally tricked by Julie. In one of her persecution phases. As usual I, who devote my summers to her, became the persecutor. And Mitford attempted one night – in the crudest and most harmful way – to, as he put it, rescue her. Of course her nurse stepped in. There was a most disagreeable *fracas*. It upset her deeply. If I sometimes seem irritable to you, it is because I am so anxious not to see any repetition of last year.' He raised his hand. 'I mean nothing personal. You are very intelligent, and you are a gentleman; they are both qualities that Mitford was without.'

I rubbed my nose. I thought of other awkward questions I could ask, and decided not to ask them. The constant harping on my intelligence made me as suspicious as a crow. There are three types of intelligent person: the first so intelligent that being called very intelligent must seem natural and obvious; the second sufficiently intelligent to see that he is being flattered, not described; the third so little intelligent that he will believe anything. I knew I belonged to the second kind. I could not *absolutely* disbelieve Conchis; all he said could – just – be true. I supposed there were still poor little rich psychotics kept out of institutions by their doting relations; but Conchis was the least doting person I had ever met. It didn't wash, it didn't wash. There were various things about Julie, looks, emotional *non sequiturs*, those sudden tears, that in retrospect seemed to confirm his story. They proved nothing; and perhaps this development had always been planned, and she had not wanted to spoil it completely ...

'Well,' he said, 'do you believe me?'

'Do I look as if I don't?'

'We are none of us what we look.'

'You shouldn't have offered me that suicide pill.'

'You think all my prussic acid is ratafia?'

'I didn't say that. I'm your guest, Mr Conchis. Naturally I take your word.'

For a moment, masks seemed to drop on both sides; I was looking at a face totally without humour and he, I suppose, was looking at one without generosity. A hostility was at last proclaimed; a clash of wills. We both smiled, and we both knew we smiled to hide a fundamental truth: that we could not trust each other one inch.

'I wish to say two final things, Nicholas. Whether you believe what I have said is comparatively unimportant. But you must believe one thing. Julie is susceptible and very dangerous – both things without realizing it herself. Like a fine blade, she can easily be hurt – but she can also hurt. We have all learnt, had to learn to remain completely detached emotionally from her. Because it is on our emotions that she will prey – if we give her the chance.'

I remained staring at the edge of the table-cloth, recalling that impression I had had of a timidity, a virginity; and realizing that the temperamental cause of that could equally well be clinical ... her seeming physical innocence, a lifelong and enforced ignorance of men in sexual situations. It was absurd. I could not absolutely disbelieve him.

'And the second thing?'

'Is embarrassing to me, but it must be said. One of the tragedies of Julie's situation is that she is a normally sexed young woman, yet with no normal outlet for her feelings. As a personable young male, you represent such an outlet – which is in itself of considerable benefit to her. Not to put too fine a point upon it, she needs someone to flirt with ... to exercize her physical charms on. I gather she has already achieved some success in that way.'

'You saw me kiss her just now. But as you didn't warn me – '

He cut me short with a raised hand. 'You are not to blame. If a pretty girl asks you to kiss her ... naturally. But now you know the facts, I must point out the very difficult, and delicate, role I am asking you to play. I should not want you to repel every advance she makes, every hint of physical intimacy, but you must accept that there are certain bounds that cannot be transgressed. I cannot allow that, for obvious medical reasons. If – I speak purely hypothetically – some situation should arise where you found temptation too strong, I should be obliged to intervene. She even managed to convince Mitford last year that she would be a normal young woman if he would only take her away and marry her ... not that she is scheming. When she says such things, she believes them. That is why her lies can be so convincing.'

I wanted to smile. Even if he was telling me the truth about the rest, I could not believe she would have had any sympathy for the idiotic Mitford. But there was something so obsessively severe and convinced of his own role in the old man's eyes that I lacked the nerve to mock him.

'I wish you'd told me all this before.'

'That I did not you must blame partly on yourself. I did not anticipate quite such a quick response from the patient.' He smiled, then leant back a little. 'There is one other consideration, Nicholas. I should most emphatically not have embarked on all this if I had not felt sure that you had no emotional attachment elsewhere. From what you said – '

'That's over. If you're talking about that radiogram ... I'm not going to meet her in Athens.'

He looked down, shook his head. 'Of course it is not my business. But what you said of the young lady – of your deeper feelings to-wards her – impressed me. I must say I think you would be foolish to turn down this offer of renewed friendship.'

'With respect ... it really isn't your business.'

'I should regret it very much if your decision were in any way coloured by what is happening here.'

'It isn't.'

'Nevertheless, I think it is better, now that you understand what is really involved, that you should reflect on whether you wish to continue your visits here. I should fully understand if you decided to have no more to do with us.' He stopped me speaking. 'In any case I wish to give my unfortunate godchild some respite. I have decided to take her away for ten days or so.' He consulted me as if I were some psychiatric colleague. 'Over-stimulation has a negative therapeutic value.'

I felt bitterly disappointed, and mentally damned Alison and her accursed radiogram. At the same time I was determined not to show it.

'I don't have to think about going on. I want to.'

He contemplated me, and finally nodded – the old devil, as if it were for him to accept *my* genuineness. 'All the same, I recommend further thought – and an enjoyable week-end with what sounds a charming young woman in Athens.' I drew a breath, and he went on quickly. 'I am a doctor, Nicholas. Permit me to be frank. Young men were not designed for the celibate life you lead here.'

'I've already paid to discover that.'

'As I recall. Then for all the more reason.'

'And the week-end after next?'

'We will see. Let us leave it like that.' He suddenly stood up and extended his hand, which I took. 'Good. Excellent. I am so glad the air is cleared between us.' He put his hands on his hips. 'Now. Do you feel like some hard work?'

'No. But take me to it.'

He led me round to one of the corners of the vegetable garden. Part of a wall supporting a terrace had collapsed and he wanted it built up again. He gave instructions. The dry earth had to be broken up with a pickaxe, the stones lifted back, arranged, packed with the earth, which had to be watered to bind the wall together again. As soon as I started work, he disappeared. The breeze was still blowing, though it was the time of day it normally dropped, and it was cooler than usual; but I was soon sweating like a pig. I guessed the real reason I had been turned labourer: I had to be kept busy, out of the way, while he found Julie and tried to discover exactly what had gone on between us ... or perhaps congratulated her on playing her new part so well.

After some forty minutes I gave myself a break to have a cigarette. Suddenly Conchis appeared on the terrace above where I sat with my already aching back against a pine-trunk. He looked sardonically down.

'Labour is man's crowning glory.'

'Not this man's.'

'I quote Marx.'

I raised my hands. The pickaxe handle had been rough.

'I quote blisters.'

'Never mind.'

He remained staring down at me, as if I pleased him, or as if something he had learnt of me since tea pleased him; as clowns sometimes please philosophers. I asked a question I had been saving up.

'I'm to believe nothing of her stories – am I to believe anything of yours about your past?'

I had thought it might offend him, but his smile deepened.

'Human truths are always complex.'

I smiled warily back. 'I'm not quite sure what the difference is between what you're doing here and the thing you hate so much – fiction.'

'I do not object to the principles of fiction. Simply that in print, in books, they remain mere principles.' He said, 'Let me pass on an axiom about our species, Nicholas: Never take another human being literally.' He added, 'Even when they are so ignorant that they do not know what "literally" means.'

'There's no danger of that. Here, anyway.'

He looked down, then straight at me. 'What I am employing is a very new psychiatric technique. It has been only very recently developed in America. They call it situation therapy.'

'I'd like to read those papers of yours.'

'Which reminds me. I looked for them just now. I seem to have mislaid them.'

It was shameless, he made it sound like a blandly deliberate lie; as if he wished me to stay in doubt.

'Too bad.'

He folded his arms. 'I have been thinking ... your friend. As you perhaps know, I own the house that Hermes lives in in the village. He uses only the ground floor. It occurred to me that you might like to bring her to Phraxos for a while. She is most welcome to the upper floor. It is primitive. But sufficiently furnished. And quite spacious.'

That really did take the wind out of my sails, though it seemed a colossal nerve rather than a kindness ... to have taken all this trouble to net me, and now to be offering every kind of escape. He must have been so sure that he had me, and for a moment I felt like taking the offer; not that I wanted Alison within a hundred miles of the island, but just to spite him.

'Then I couldn't help here any more.'

'Perhaps you could both help here.'

'She wouldn't give up her job. And I really don't want to be involved with her any more.' I added, 'But thanks all the same.'

'Well. The offer stands.'

He turned rather abruptly away then, as if this time I had offended him. I set to again, expending on the job my growing sense of frustration. Another forty minutes later the wall was back to something like its proper shape. I carried the tools to a shed behind the cottage, then went round to the front of the house. Conchis sat there under the colonnade, quietly reading a Greek newspaper.

'Is it done? Thank you.'

I made one last effort.

'Mr Conchis, you've got the whole thing with this other girl ludicrously wrong. It was just an affaire. It's past history now.'

'But she wishes to see you again?'

'Nine tenths out of curiosity. You know what women are like. And probably just because the man she now lives with is out of London for a few days.'

'Forgive me. I will interfere no further. You must do as you feel. Of course.'

I turned away, wishing I'd kept my mouth shut, when he said my name. I looked back at him from the open doors into the music room. He gave me a powerful yet paternal look.

'Go to Athens, my friend.' He glanced towards the trees to the east. *'Guai a chi la tocca.'*

I had very little Italian, but I knew what he meant. I went on up to my room, undressed; then to the bathroom and the salt-water shower. In an odd way I knew what he was really saying. She was not for me because she was not for me; not because she was a ghost, or a schizophrenic, or anything else in the masque. It was a sort of ultimate warning-off; but you can't warn off a man with gambling in his ancestry.

I lay naked on my bed after the shower, staring at the ceiling, trying to evoke Julie's face, the curve of her eyelashes, the feel of her hand, her mouth, that frustratingly brief pressure of her body as we kissed; and her sister's body seen the night before. I imagined Julie coming to me there, in the bedroom; or in the pine-forest, darkness, a wildness, a willing rape ... I became the satyr; but then, remembering what had happened to him, realizing now what lay behind that little bit of classical hocus-pocus, I opted for detumescence and dressing. I too was beginning to learn to wait.

36

I did not enjoy dinner. Once again he tripped me up, by handing me a book as soon as I appeared.

'My papers. They were on the wrong shelf.'

It wasn't a very thick book, and cheaply bound in green cloth, without indication of the contents. I opened it – the page sizes and types of print differed, they were obviously pieces taken *ad hoc* from various journals and bound up. The texts seemed to be in French throughout. I saw a date: 1936. One or two titles. *Early prognosis of mild schizophrenia. The influence of profession on syndromes of paranoia. A psychiatric experiment in the use of Stramonium.* I looked up.

'What's Stramonium?'

'*Datura.* The thorn-apple. It produces hallucinations.'

I put the book down. 'I look forward to reading it.'

In a way it turned out to be an unnecessary proof. By the time dinner was ended I was at least convinced that Conchis had far more than even a knowledgeable layman's familiarity with psychiatry; and also that he had known Jung. That did not necessarily mean, of course, that I had to believe him about Julie. I tried to bring her in, but he was adamant – the less I knew of her case, at this stage, the better … though he promised that by the end of the summer I should be given the full picture. All the time I wanted to challenge him, but I was frightened of the growing resentment I was beginning to store against him: that things might explode into the kind of confrontation where I could only lose everything – be firmly told never to return. Then I sensed that he was in any case prepared, more than ready to throw up further clouds of obfuscating sepia if I really pressed him. My only defence was, as best as I could, to answer enigma with enigma; and my consolation, an intuition that he avoided all further reference to Athens and Alison for something of the same reason – that he might exasperate me into awkward questions.

So the meal passed – on one level I listened to an impressively shrewd old doctor, on another I was a mouse before a cat. I was also on tenterhooks for Julie to appear; and curious to know what experience I was to have that evening. A lingering aftermath of the *meltemi* made the lamp between us tremble and glow and fade intermittently, and this seemed to increase the general restlessness. Only Conchis seemed calm and at ease.

After the table had been cleared he poured me a drink from a small carboy-shaped bottle. It was clear, the colour of straw.

'What's this?'

'*Raki*. From Chios. It is very strong. I want to intoxicate you a little.'

All through the dinner he had also been pressing me to drink more of the heavy *rosé* from Antikythera.

'To dull my critical faculties?'

'To make you receptive.'

'I read your pamphlet.'

'And thought it was nonsense.'

'Difficult to verify.'

'Verification is the only scientific criterion of reality. That does not mean that there may not be realities that are unverifiable.'

'Did you get any response from your pamphlet?'

'A great deal. From the wrong people. From the miserable vultures who prey on the human longing for the solution of final mysteries. The spiritualists, the clairvoyants, the cosmopaths, the summerlanders, the blue-islanders, the apportists – all that *galère*.' He looked grim. 'They responded.'

'But not other scientists?'

'No.'

I sipped the *raki*; it was like fire, almost pure alcohol.

'But you spoke about having proof.'

'I had proof. But it was not easily communicable. And I later decided that it was better that it was not communicable, except to a few.'

'Who you elect.'

'Whom I elect. This is because mystery has energy. It pours energy into whoever seeks an answer to it. If you disclose the solution to the mystery you are simply depriving the other seekers ... ' he emphasized the special meaning the word had for me ' ... of an important source of energy.'

'No scientific progress?'

'Of course scientific progress. The solution of the physical problems that face man – that is a matter of technology. But I am talking about the general psychological health of the species, man. He needs the existence of mysteries. Not their solution.'

I finished the *raki*. 'This is fantastic stuff.'

He smiled, as if my adjective might be more accurate than I meant; raised the bottle.

'One more glass. Then no more. *La dive bouteille* is also a poison.'

'And the experiment begins?'

'The experience begins. I should like you to take your glass and lie in one of the lounging-chairs. Just here.' He pointed behind him. I went and pulled the chair there. 'Lie down. There is no hurry. I want you to look at a certain star. Do you know Cygnus? The Swan? That cross-shaped constellation directly above?'

I realized that he was not going to take the other chaise-longue; and suddenly guessed.

'Is this ... hypnosis?'

'Yes, Nicholas. There is no need to be alarmed.'

Lily's warning: '*Tonight you will understand.*' I hesitated, then lay back.

'I'm not. But I don't think I'm very amenable. Someone tried it at Oxford.'

'We shall see. It is a harmony of wills. Not a contest. Just do as I suggest.' At least I did not have to stare into those naturally mesmeric eyes. I could not back down; but forewarned is forearmed. 'You see the Swan?'

'Yes.'

'And to the left a very bright star, one of a very obtuse triangle.'

'Yes.' I drained down the last of the *raki* in a gulp; almost choked, then felt it flush through my stomach.

'That is a star known as *alpha* Lyrae. In a minute I shall ask you to watch it closely.' The blue-white star glittered down out of the wind-cleared sky. I looked at Conchis, who was still sitting at the table, but had turned with his back to the sea to face me. I grinned in the darkness.

'I feel I'm on the couch.'

'Good. Now lie back. Contract, then relax your muscles a little. That is why I have given you the *raki*. It will help. Julie will not appear tonight. So clear your mind of her. Clear your mind of the other girl. Clear your mind of all your perplexities, all your longings. All your worries. I bring you no harm. Nothing but good.'

'Worries. That's not so easy.' He was silent. 'I'll try.'

'It will help if you look at that star. Do not shift your eyes from it. Lie back.'

I began to stare at the star; moved a little to make myself more comfortable. I felt the cloth of my coat with my hand. The walling had made me tired, I began to guess its real purpose, and it was good to lie back and stare up and wait. There was a long silence, several minutes. I shut my eyes for a while, then opened them. The star seemed to float in its own small sea of space, a minute white sun. I could feel the alcohol, but I was perfectly conscious of everything around me, far too conscious to be amenable.

I was perfectly conscious of the terrace, I was lying on the terrace of a house on an island in Greece, there was wind, I could even hear the faint sound of the waves on the shingle down at Moutsa. Conchis began to speak.

'Now I want you to watch the star, I want you to relax all your muscles. It is very important that you should relax all your muscles. Tense a little. Now relax. Tense ... relax. Now watch the star. The name of the star is *alpha* Lyrae.'

I thought, my God, he *is* trying to hypnotize me; and then, I must play by the rules, but I'll lie doggo and pretend I am hypnotized.

'Are you relaxing yes you are relaxing.' I noted the lack of punctuation. 'You are tired so you are relaxing. You are relaxing. You are relaxing. You are watching a star you are watching ... ' the repetition; I remembered that from before at Oxford. An insane Welshman from Jesus, after a party. But with him it had developed into a staring match.

'I say you are watching a star a star and you are watching a star. It is that gentle star, white star, gentle star ... '

He went on talking, but all the curtness, the abruptness of his ordinary manner had disappeared. It was as if the lulling sound of the sea, the feel of the wind, the texture of my coat, and his voice dropped out of my consciousness. There was a stage when I was myself looking at the star, still lying on the terrace; I mean aware of lying and watching the star, if not of anything else.

Then came a strange illusion; that I was not looking up, but down into space, as one looks down a well.

Then there was no clearly situated and environmented self; there was the star, not closer but with something of the isolation a telescope gives; not one of a pattern of stars, but itself, floating in the blue-black breath of space, in a kind of void. I remember very clearly this sense, this completely new strange perceiving of the star as a ball of white light both breeding and needing the void around it; of, in retrospect, a related sense that I was exactly the same, suspended in a dark void. I was watching the star and the star was watching me. We were poised, exactly equal weights, if one can think of awareness as a weight, held level in a balance. This seemed to endure and endure, I don't know how long, two entities equally suspended in a void, equally opposite, devoid of any meaning or feeling. There was no sensation of beauty, of morality, of divinity, of physical geometry; simply the sensation of the situation. As an animal might feel.

Then a rise of tension. I was expecting something. The waiting was a waiting for. I did not know if it would be audible or visible, which sense. But it was trying to come, and I was trying to discover its coming. There seemed to be no more star. Perhaps he had made me close my eyes. The void was all. I remember two words, Conchis must have spoken them: glisten, and listen. There was the glistening, listening void; darkness and expectation. Then there came a wind on my face, a perfectly physical sensation. I tried to face it, it was fresh and warm, but I suddenly realized, with an excited shock, not at anything but the physical strangemess of it, that it was blowing on me from all directions at the same time. I raised my hand, I could feel it. The dark wind, like draught from thousands of invisible fans, blowing in on me. And again this seemed to last for a long time.

At some point it began imperceptibly to change. The wind became light. I don't think there was any visual awareness of this, it was simply that I knew, without surprise, that the wind had become light (perhaps Conchis had told me the wind was light) and this light was intensely pleasing, a kind of mental sun-bathing after a long dark winter, an exquisitely agreeable sensation both of being aware of light and attracting it. Of having power to attract and power to receive this light.

From this stage I moved to one where it dawned on me that this was something intensely true and revealing; this being something that drew all this light upon it. I mean it seemed to reveal something deeply significant about being; I was aware of existing, and this being aware of existing became more significant than the light, just as the light had become more significant than the wind. I began to get a sense of progress, that I was transforming, as a fountain in a wind is transformed in shape; an eddy in the water. The wind and the light became mere secondaries, roads to the present state, this state without dimensions or sensations; awareness of pure being. Or perhaps that is a solipsism; it was simply a pure awareness.

That lasted; and then changed, like the other states. This state was being imposed on me from outside, I knew this, I knew that although it did not flow in on me like the wind and the light, it nevertheless flowed, though flowed was not the word. There was no word, it arrived, descended, penetrated from outside. It was not an immanent state, it was a conferred state, a presented state. I was a recipient. But once again there came this strange surprise that the emitters stood all around me. I was not receiving from any one direction, but from all directions; though once again, direction is too physical a word. I was having feelings that no language based on concrete physical objects, on actual feeling, can describe. I think I was aware of the metaphoricality of what I felt. I knew words were like chains, they held me back; and like walls with holes in them. Reality kept rushing through; and yet I could not get out to fully exist in it. This is interpreting what I struggled to remember feeling; the act of description taints the description.

I had the sense that this was the fundamental reality and that reality had a universal mouth to tell me so; no sense of divinity, of communion, of the brotherhood of man, of anything I had expected before I became suggestible. No pantheism, no humanism. But something much wider, cooler and more abstruse. That reality was endless inter-action. No good, no evil; no beauty, no ugliness. No sympathy, no antipathy. But simply interaction. The endless solitude of the one, its total enislement from all else, seemed the same thing as the total inter-relationship of the all. All opposites seemed one, because each was indispensable to each. The indifference and the indispensability of all seemed one. I suddenly knew, but in a new hitherto unexperienced sense of knowing, that all else exists.

Knowing, willing, being wise, being good, education, information, classification, knowledge of all kinds, sensibility, sexuality, these things seemed superficial. I had no desire to state or define or analyse this interaction, I simply wished to constitute it – not even 'wished to' – I constituted it. I was volitionless. There was no meaning. Only being.

But the fountain changed, the eddy whirled. It seemed at first to be a kind of reversion to the stage of the dark wind breathing in on me from every side, except that there was no wind, the wind had been only a metaphor, and now it was millions, trillions of such consciousnesses of being, countless nuclei of hope suspended in a vast solution of hazard, a pouring out not of photons, but nöons, consciousness-of-being particles. An enormous and vertiginous sense of the innumerability of the universe; an innumerability in which transience and unchangingness seemed integral, essential and uncontradictory. I felt like a germ that had landed, like the first penicillin microbe, not only in a culture where it was totally at home, totally nourished; but in a situation in which it was infinitely significant. A condition of acute physical and intellectual pleasure, a floating suspension, a being perfectly adjusted and *related*; a quintessential arrival. An intercognition.

At the same time a parabola, a fall, an ejaculation; but the transience, the passage, had become an integral part of the knowledge of the experience. The becoming and the being were one.

I think I saw the star again for a while, the star as it simply was, hanging in the sky above, but now in all its being-and-becoming. It was like walking through a door, going all round the world, and then walking through the same door but a different door.

Then darkness. I remember nothing.

Then light.

37

Someone had knocked on the door. I was staring at a wall. I was in bed, I was wearing pyjamas, my clothes were folded on the chair. It was daylight, very early, the first thin sunlight on the tops of the pines outside. I looked at my watch. Just before six o'clock.

I sat on the edge of the bed. I had a black plunge of shame, of humiliation; of having been naked in front of Conchis, of having been in his power; even worse, others could have seen. Julie. I saw myself lying there and all of them sitting and grinning while Conchis asked me questions and I gave naked answers. But Julie – he must also hypnotize her; this was why she could not lie.

Svengali and Trilby.

Then the mystical experience itself, still so vivid, as clear as a learnt lesson, as the details of a drive in new country, hit me. I saw how it had been done. There would have been some drug, some hallucinogene in the *raki* – perhaps the Stramonium of his paper. Then he had suggested these things, these stages of knowledge, he had induced them as I lay there helpless. I looked round for the green-bound volume of his medical papers. But it was not in the room. I was to be denied even that clue.

The richness of what I remembered; the potential embarrassment of what I could not; the good of it and the evil of it; these two things made me sit for minutes with my head in my hands, torn between resentment and gratitude.

I went and washed, stared at myself in the mirror, went down to the coffee the silent Maria had waiting for me. I knew Conchis would not appear. Maria would say nothing. Nothing was to be explained, everything was planned to keep me in suspense until I came again.

As I walked back to the school, I tried to assess the experience; why, though it was so beautiful, so intensely real, it seemed also so sinister. It was difficult in that early-morning light and landscape to believe that anything on earth was sinister, yet the feeling persisted with me and it was not only one of humiliation. It was one of new danger, of meddling in darker, stranger things that needed to be meddled with. It also made Julie's fear of Conchis much more convincing than his pseudo-medical pity for her; she might just be schizophrenic, but he was proven a hypnotist. But this was to assume that they were not working together to trick me; and then I began clawing, in a panic of memory, through all my meetings with Conchis, trying to see if he could ever have hypnotized me before, without my being aware of it ...

I remembered bitterly that only the afternoon before I had said to Julie that my sense of reality was like gravity. For a while I was like a man in space, whirling through madness. I remembered Conchis's trance-like state during the Apollo scene. Had he hypnotized me into imagining it all? Had he willed me to go to sleep when I did that afternoon, so conveniently placed for the Foulkes apparition? Had there ever been a man and a girl standing there? Now Julie even ... but I recalled the feel of her skin, of those ungiving lips. I got back to earth. But I was badly shaken.

It was not only the being hypnotized by Conchis that unanchored me; in a subtler but similar way I knew I had been equally hypnotized by the girl. I had always believed, and not only out of cynicism, that a man and a woman could tell in the first ten minutes whether they wanted to go to bed together; and that the time that passed after those first ten minutes represented a tax, which might be worth paying if the article promised to be really enjoyable, but which nine times out of ten became rapidly excessive. It wasn't only that I foresaw a very steep bill with Julie; she shook my whole theory. She had a certain exhalation of surrender about her, as if she was a door waiting to be pushed open; but it was the darkness beyond that held me. Perhaps it was partly a nostalgia for that extinct Lawrentian woman of the past, the woman inferior to man in everything but that one great power of female dark mystery and beauty; the brilliant, virile male and the dark, swooning female. The essences of the two sexes had become so confused in my androgynous twentieth-century mind that this reversion to a situation where a woman was a woman and I was obliged to be fully a man had all the fascination of an old house after a cramped, anonymous modern flat. I had been enchanted into wanting sex often enough before; but never into wanting love.

All that morning I sat in classes, teaching as if I was still hypnotized, in a dream of hypotheses. Now I saw Conchis as a sort of psychiatric novelist sans novel, creating with people, not words; now I saw him as a complicated but still very perverse old man; now as a Svengali; now as a genius among practical jokers. But whichever way I saw him I was fascinated, and Julie, as Lily with her hair blown sideways, with her tear-stained face, at that first moment, in the lamplight, cool ivory ... I didn't try to pretend that I was anything else than quite literally bewitched by Bourani. It was almost a force, like a magnet, drawing me out of the classroom windows, through the blue air to the central ridge, and down there where I so wanted to be. The rows of olive-skinned faces, bent black heads, the smell of chalk-dust, an old inkstain that rorschached my desk – they were like things in a mist, real yet unreal; obstacles in limbo.

After lunch Demetriades came into my room and wanted to know who Alison was; and began being obscene, dreadful stock Greek *facetiae* about tomatoes and cucumbers, when I refused to tell him anything. I shouted at him to fuck off; had to push him out by force. He was offended and spent the rest of that week avoiding me. I didn't mind. It kept him out of my way.

After my last lesson I couldn't resist it. I had to go back to Bourani. I didn't know what I was going to do, but I had to re-enter the domaine. As soon as I saw it, the hive of secrets lying in the last sunshine over the seething pine-tops, far below, I was profoundly relieved, as if it might not have been still there. The closer I got, the more nefarious I felt, and the more nefarious I became. I simply wanted to see them; to know they were there, waiting for me.

I approached at dusk from the east, slipped between the wire, and walked down cautiously past the statue of Poseidon, over the gulley, and through the trees to where I could see the house. Every window at the side was shuttered up. There was no smoke from Maria's cottage. I worked round to where I could see the front of the house. The french windows under the colonnade were shuttered. So were the ones that led from Conchis's bedroom on to the terrace. It was clear that no one was there. I walked back through the darkness, feeling depressed, and increasingly furious that Conchis could spirit his world away; deprive me of it, like a callous drug-ward doctor with some hooked addict.

The next day I wrote a letter to Mitford, telling him that I'd been to Bourani, met Conchis, and begging him to come clean on his own experience there. I sent it to the address in Northumberland.

I also saw Karazoglou again, and tried to coax more information out of him. He was obviously quite sure that Leverrier had never met Conchis. He told me what I already knew, that Leverrier had been 'religious'; he had used to go to Mass in Athens. And he said more or less the same as Conchis: '*Il avait toujours l'air un peu triste, il ne s'est jamais habitué à la vie ici.*' Yet Conchis had also said that he had made an excellent 'seeker'.

I got Leverrier's address in England out of the school bursar, but then decided not to write; I had it to hand if I needed it.

I also did a little research on Artemis. She *was* Apollo's sister in mythology; protectress of virgins and patroness of hunters. The saffron dress, the buskins and the silver bow (the crescent new moon) constituted her standard uniform in classical poetry. Though she seemed permanently trigger-happy where amorous young men were concerned I could find no mention of her being helped by her brother. She was 'an element in the ancient matriarchal cult of the Triple Moon-goddess, linked with Astarte in Syria and Isis in

Egypt'. Isis, I noted, was often accompanied by the jackal-headed Anubis, guardian of the underworld, who later became Cerberus.

On Tuesday and Wednesday prep duties kept me at the school. On Thursday I went over to Bourani again. Nothing had changed. It was as deserted as it had been on the Monday.

I walked round the house, tried the shutters, roamed the grounds, went down to the private beach, from which the boat was gone. Then I sat brooding for half an hour in the twilight under the colonnade. I felt both exploited and excluded, and as much angry with myself as with them. I was mad to have got involved in the whole business, and even madder both to want it to go on and be frightened of its going on. I had changed my mind once again in those intervening days. More and more I no longer knew about the schizophrenia; from faintly possible it began to grow probable. I could not imagine why else he should have halted the masque so abruptly. If it had been only an amusement ...

I suppose there was a large component of envy too – I thought of Conchis's foolishness, or arrogance, in leaving the Modigliani and the Bonnards like that, in a deserted house ... and from those Bonnards, my mind grasshoppered to Alison. There was that day a special midnight boat to take the boys and masters back to Athens for their half-term holiday. It meant sitting up all night dozing in an armchair in the scruffy first-class saloon, but it gave one the Friday in Athens. I'm not quite sure what it was – anger, spite, revenge? – that made me decide to take the boat. It was certainly not the thought of Alison, beyond a need of someone to talk to. Perhaps it was a last whiff of my old would-be existentialist self: founding freedom on caprice.

A minute later I was walking fast down the track to the gate. Even then, at the last moment I looked back and hoped, with one-thousandth of a hope, that someone might be beckoning me to return.

But no one was. So I embarked for my lack of a better.

38

Athens was dust and drought, ochre and drab. Even the palm trees looked exhausted. All the humanity in human beings had retreated behind dark skins and even darker glasses, and by two in the afternoon the streets were empty, abandoned to indolence and heat. I lay slumped on a bed in a Piraeus hotel, and dozed fitfully in the shuttered twilight. The city was doubly too much for me. After Bourani, the descent back into the age, the machinery, the stress, was completely disorientating.

The afternoon dragged out its listless hours. The closer I came to meeting Alison, the more muddle-motived I grew. I knew that if I was in Athens at all, it was out of a desire to play my own double game with Conchis. Twenty-four hours before, under the colonnade, Alison had seemed a pawn to be used – at least one counter-move I could make; but now, two hours before meeting ... sex with her was unthinkable. So too, so close, was to tell her what was happening at Bourani. I no longer knew why I had come. I felt strongly tempted to sneak away back to the island. I wanted neither to deceive Alison nor to reveal the truth.

Yet something kept me lying there, some remnant of interest in hearing what had become of her, some pity, some memory of past affection. I saw it as a kind of test, as well: of both my depth of feeling about Julie and my doubts. Alison could stand for past and present reality in the outer world, and I would put her secretly in the ring with my inner adventure. Also I had hit, during the long night on the boat, on a way of keeping the meeting safely antiseptic – something that would make her feel sorry for me *and* keep her at arm's length.

At five I got up, had a shower, and caught a taxi out to the airport. I sat on a bench opposite the long reception counter, then moved away; finding, to my irritation, that I was increasingly nervous. Several other air hostesses passed quickly – hard, trim, professionally pretty, the shallow unreality of characters from science fiction.

Six came, six-fifteen. I goaded myself to walk up to the counter.

There was a Greek girl there in the right uniform, with flashing white teeth and dark-brown eyes whose innuendoes seemed put on with the rest of her lavish make-up.

'I'm supposed to be meeting one of your girls. Alison Kelly.'

'Allie? Her flight's in. She'll be changing.' She picked up a telephone, dialled a number, gleamed her teeth at me. Her accent was impeccable; and American. 'Allie? Your date's here. If you don't come right away he's taking me instead.' She held out the receiver. 'She wants to speak to you.'

'Tell her I'll wait. Not to hurry.'

'He's shy.' Alison must have said something, because the girl smiled. She put the phone down.

'She'll be right over.'

'What did she say then?'

'She said you're not shy, it's just your technique.'

'Oh.'

She gave me what was meant to be a coolly audacious look between her long black eyelashes, then turned to deal with two women who had mercifully appeared at the other end of the counter. I escaped and went and stood near the entrance. When I had first lived on the island, Athens, the city life, had seemed like a normalizing influence, as desirable as it was still familiar. Now I realized that it began to frighten me, that I loathed it; the slick exchange at the desk, its blatant implications of contracepted excitement, the next stereotyped thrill. I came from another planet.

A minute or two later Alison appeared through the door. Her hair was short, too short, she was wearing a white dress, and immediately we were on the wrong foot, because I knew she had worn it to remind me of our first meeting. Her skin was paler than I remembered. She took off her dark glasses when she saw me and I could see she was tired, her most bruised. Pretty enough body, pretty enough clothes, a good walk, the same old wounded face and truth-seeking eyes. Alison might launch ten ships in me; but Julie launched a thousand. She came and stood and we gave each other a little smile.

'Hi.'

'Hallo, Alison.'

'Sorry. Late as usual.'

She spoke as if we had last met the week before. But it didn't work. The nine months stood like a sieve between us, through which words came, but none of the emotions.

'Shall we go?'

I took the airline bag she was carrying and led her out to a taxi. Inside we sat in opposite corners and looked at each other again. She smiled.

'I thought you wouldn't come.'

'I didn't know where to send my refusal.'

'I was cunning.'

She glanced out of the window, waved to a man in uniform. She seemed older to me, over-experienced by travel; needing to be learnt again, and I hadn't the energy.

'I've got you a room overlooking the port.'

'Fine.'

'They're so bloody stuffy in Greek hotels. You know.'

'*Toujours* the done thing.' She gave me a tweak of irony from her grey eyes, then covered up. 'It's fun. *Vive* the done thing.' I nearly made my prepared speech, but it annoyed me that she assumed I hadn't changed, was still slave to English convention; it even annoyed me that she felt she had to cover up. She held out her hand and I took it and we pressed fingers. Then she reached out and took off my dark glasses.

'You look devastatingly handsome now. Do you know that? You're so brown. Dried in the sun, sort of beginning to be ravaged. Jesus, when you're forty.'

I smiled, but I looked down and let go of her hand to get a cigarette. I knew what her flattery meant; the invitation extended.

'Alison, I'm in a sort of weird situation.'

It knocked all the false lightness out of her. She stared straight ahead.

'Another girl?'

'No.' She flashed a look at me. 'I've changed, I don't know how one begins to explain things.'

'But you wish to God I'd kept away.'

'No, I'm … glad you've come.' She glanced at me suspiciously again. 'Really.'

She was silent for a few moments. We moved out on to the coast road.

'I'm through with Pete.'

'You said.'

'I forgot.' But I knew she hadn't.

'And I've been through with everyone else since I've been through with him.' She kept staring out of the window. 'Sorry. I ought to have started with the small talk.'

'No. I mean ... you know.'

She slid another look at me; hurt and trying not to be hurt. She made an effort. 'I'm living with Ann again. Only since last week. Back in the old flat. Maggie's gone home.'

'I liked Ann.'

'Yes, she's nice.'

There was a long silence as we drove down past Phaleron. She stared out of the window and after a minute reached into her white handbag and took out her dark glasses. I knew why, I could see the lines of wet light round her eyes. I didn't touch her, take her hand, but I talked about the difference between the Piraeus and Athens, how the former was more picturesque, more Greek, and I thought she'd like it better. I had really chosen the Piraeus because of the small, but horrifying, possibility of running into Conchis and Julie. The thought of *her* cool, amused and probably contemptuous eyes if such a thing happened sent shivers down my spine. There was something about Alison's manner and appearance; if a man was with her, he went to bed with her. And as I talked, I wondered how we were going to survive the next three days.

I tipped the boy and he left the room. She went to the window and looked down across the broad white quay, the slow crowds of evening strollers, the busy port. I stood behind her. After a moment's swift calculation I put my arm round her and at once she leant against me.

'I hate cities. I hate aeroplanes. I want to live in a cottage in Ireland.'

'Why Ireland?'

'Somewhere I've never been.'

I could feel the warmth, the willingness to surrender, of her body. At any moment she would turn her face and I would have to kiss her.

'Alison, I ... don't quite know how to break the news.' I took my arm away, and stood closer to the window, so that she could not see my face. 'I caught a disease two or three months ago. Well ... syphilis.' I turned and she gave me a look – concern and shock and incredulity. 'I'm all right now, but ... you know, I can't possibly ... '

'You went to a ... ' I nodded. The incredulity became credulity. She looked down.

'You had your revenge.'

She came and put her arms round me. 'Oh Nicko, Nicko.'

I said over her head, 'I'm not meant to have oral or closer contact for at least another month. I didn't know what to do. I ought never to have written. This was never really on.'

She let go of me and went and sat on the bed. I saw I had got myself into a new corner; she now thought that this satisfactorily explained our awkwardness till then. She gave me a kind, gentle little smile.

'Tell me all about it.'

I walked round and round the room, telling her about Patarescu and the clinic, about the poetry, even about the venture at suicide, about everything except Bourani. After a while she lay back on the bed, smoking, and I was unexpectedly filled with a pleasure in duplicity; with that pleasure, I imagined, Conchis felt when he was with me. In the end I sat on the end of the bed. She lay staring up at the ceiling.

'Can I tell you about Pete now?'

'Of course.'

I half listened, playing my part, and suddenly began to enjoy being with her again; not particularly with Alison, but being in this hotel bedroom, hearing the murmur of the evening crowds below, the sound of sirens, the smell of the tired Aegean. I felt no attraction and no tenderness for her; no real interest in the break-up of her long relationship with the boor of an Australian pilot; simply the complex, ambiguous sadness of the darkening room. The light had drained out of the sky, it became rapid dusk. All the treacheries of modern love seemed beautiful, and I had my great secret, safe, locked away. It was Greece again, the Alexandrian Greece of Cavafy; there were only degrees of aesthetic pleasure; of beauty in decadence. Morality was a North European lie.

There was a long silence.

She said, 'Where are we, Nicko?'

'How do you mean?'

She was leaning on her elbow, staring at me, but I wouldn't look round at her.

'Now I know – of course ... ' she shrugged. 'But I didn't come to be your old chum.'

I put my head in my hands.

'Alison, I'm sick of women, sick of love, sick of sex, sick of everything. I don't know what I want. I should never have asked you to come.' She looked down, seeming tacitly to agree. 'The fact is ... well, I suppose I have a sort of nostalgia for a sister at the moment. If you say fuck that – I understand. I have no right not to understand.'

'All right.' She looked up again. 'Sister. But one day you'll be cured.'

'I don't know. I just don't know.' I sounded suitably distraught. 'Look – please go away, curse me, anything, but I'm a dead man at the moment.' I went to the window. 'It's all my fault. I can't ask you to spend three days with a dead man.'

'A dead man I once loved.'

A long silence crept between us. But then she briskly sat up and got off the bed; and went and switched on the light and combed her hair. She produced the jet ear-rings I had left that last day in London and put them on; then lipstick. I thought of Julie, of lips without lipstick; coolness, mystery, elegance. It seemed almost marvellous, to be so without desire; at last in my life, to be able to be so faithful.

By an unhappy irony the way to the restaurant I had chosen lay through the red-light area of the Piraeus. Bars, multilingual neon signs, photos of strippers and bellydancers, sailors in lounging groups, glimpses through bead curtains of Lautrec-like interiors, women in lines along the padded benches. The streets were thronged with pimps and tarts, barrow-boys selling pistachios and sunflower-pips, chestnut-sellers, pasty-sellers, lottery-ticket hawkers. Doormen invited us in, men slid up with wallets of watches, packets of Lucky Strike and Camel, shoddy souvenirs. And every ten yards someone whistled at Alison.

We walked in silence. I had a vision of 'Lily' walking through that street, and silencing everything, purifying everything; not provoking and adding to the vulgarity. Alison had a set face, and we started to walk quickly to get out of the place; but I thought I could see in her walk a touch of that old amoral sexuality, that quality she could not help offering and other men noticing.

When we got to Spiro's, she said, too brightly, 'Well, brother Nicholas, what are you going to do with me?'

'Do you want to call it off?'

She twisted her glass of ouzo.

'Do you?'

'I asked first.'

'No. Now you.'

'We could do something. Go somewhere you haven't seen.' To my relief she'd already told me that she had spent a day in Athens earlier that summer; had done the sights.

'I don't want to do a tourist thing. Think of something no one else ever does. Somewhere where we shall be alone.' She added quickly, 'Because of my job. I hate people.'·

'How's your walking?'

'I'd love to. Where?'

'Well, there's Parnassus. Apparently it's a very easy climb. Just a long walk. We could hire a car. Go on to Delphi afterwards.'

'Parnassus?' She frowned, unable to quite place it.

'Where the muses dash about. The mountain.'

'Oh, Nicholas!' A flash of her old self; the headlong willingness to go.

Our *barbounia* came and we started eating. She suddenly became over-vivacious, over-excited by the idea of climbing Parnassus, and she drank glass for glass of retsina with me; did everything that Julie would never have done; then called, in her characteristic way, her own bluff.

'I know I'm trying too hard. But you make me like that.'

'If –'

'Nicko.'

'Alison, if only you – '

'Nicko, listen. Last week I was in my old room in the flat. The first night. And I could hear footsteps. Upstairs. And I cried. Just as I cried in the taxi today. Just as I could cry now but I'm not going to.'

She smiled, a little twisted smile. 'I could even cry because we keep on using each other's names.'

'Shouldn't we?'

'We never did. We were so close we didn't have to. But what I'm trying to say is … all right. But please be kind to me. Don't always sit so in judgment on everything I say, everything I do.' She stared at me and forced me to look her in the eyes. 'I can't help being what I am.' I nodded, looked sorry and touched her hand to mollify her. The one thing I did not want was a row; emotion; this eternal reattachment to the past.

After a moment she bit her mouth and the small grins we exchanged then were the first honest looks since we had met.

I said good night to her outside her room. She kissed me on the cheek, and I pressed her shoulders as if, really, it was a far, far better thing that I did then than woman could easily imagine.

39

By half past eight we were on the road. We drove over the wide mountains to Thebes, where Alison bought herself some stronger shoes and a pair of jeans. The sun was shining, there was a wind, the road empty of traffic, and the old Pontiac I had hired the night before still had some guts in its engine. Everything interested Alison – the people, the country, the bits in my 1909 Baedeker about the places we passed. Her mixture of enthusiasm and ignorance, which I remembered so well from London, didn't really irritate me any more. It seemed part of her energy, her candour; her companionability. But I had, so to speak, to be irritated; so I seized on her buoyancy, her ability to bob up from the worst disappointment. I thought she ought to have been more subdued, and much sadder.

She asked me at one point whether I had discovered any more about the waiting-room; but, eyes on the road, I said no, it was just a villa. What Mitford had meant was a mystery; and then I slid the conversation off on to something else.

We drove fast down the wide green valley between Thebes and Livadia, with its cornfields and melon-patches. But near the latter place a large flock of sheep straggled across the road and I had to slow down to a stop. We got out to watch them. There was a boy of fourteen, in ragged clothes and grotesquely large army boots. He had his sister, a dark-eyed little girl of six or seven, with him. Alison produced some airline barley-sugar. But the little girl was shy and hid behind her brother's back. Alison squatted in her green sleeveless dress ten feet away, holding out the sweet, coaxing. The sheep-bells tinkled all around us, the girl stared at her, and I grew restless.

'How do I ask her to come and take it?'

I spoke to the little girl in Greek. She didn't understand, but her brother decided we were trustworthy and urged her forward.

'Why is she so frightened?'

'Just ignorance.'

'She's so sweet.'

Alison put a piece of barley-sugar in her own mouth and then held out another to the child, who pushed by her brother went slowly forwards. As she reached timidly for the barley-sugar Alison caught her hand and made her sit beside her; unwrapped the sweet. The brother came and knelt by them, trying to get the child to thank us. But she sat gravely sucking. Alison put her arm round her and stroked her cheeks.

'I shouldn't do that. She's probably got lice.'

'I know she's probably got lice.'

She didn't look up at me or stop caressing the child. But a second later the little girl winced. Alison bent back. 'Look at this, oh, look at this.' It was a small boil, scratched and inflamed, on the child's shoulder. 'Bring my bag.' I went and got it and watched her poke back the dress and rub cream on the sore place, and then without warning dab some on the child's nose. The little girl rubbed the spot of white cream with a dirty finger, and suddenly, like a crocus bursting out of winter earth, she looked up at Alison and smiled.

'Can't we give them some money?'

'No.'

'Why not?'

'They're not beggars. They'd refuse it anyway.'

She fished in her bag and produced a small note, and held it out to the boy and pointed to him and the girl. They were to share it. The boy hesitated, then took it.

'Please take a photo.'

I went impatiently to the car, got her camera, and took a photo. The boy insisted that we take his address; he wanted a copy, to remember.

We started back for the car with the little girl beside us. Now she seemed unable to stop smiling – that beaming smile all Greek peasant children have hidden behind their solemn shyness. Alison bent and kissed her, and as we drove off, turned and waved. And waved again. Out of the corner of my eye I saw her bright face turn to me, then take in my expression. She settled back.

'Sorry. I didn't realize we were in such a hurry.'

I shrugged; and didn't argue.

I knew exactly what she had been trying to tell me. Perhaps not all of it had been put on for me; but some of it had. We drove for a mile or two in silence. She said nothing until we got to Livadia. We had to talk then, because there was food to buy.

It should have cast a shadow over the day. But it didn't, perhaps because it was a beautiful day and the landscape we came into one of the greatest in the world; what we were doing began to loom, like the precipitous blue shadow of Parnassus itself, over what we were.

We wound up the high hills and glens and had a picnic lunch in a meadow dense with clover and broom and wild bees. Afterwards we passed the crossroad where Oedipus is reputed to have killed his father. We stopped and stood among the sere thistles by a drystone wall; an anonymous upland place, exorcized by solitude. All the way in the car up to Arachova, prompted by Alison, I talked about my own father, and perhaps for the first time in my life without bitterness or blame; rather in the way that Conchis talked about *his* life. And then as I glanced sideways at Alison, who was against the door, half-turned towards me, it came to me that she was the only person in the world that I could have been talking like that to; that without noticing it I had slipped back into something of our old relationship ... *too close to need each other's names*. I looked back to the road, but her eyes were still on me, and I had to speak.

'A penny for them.'

'How well you look.'

'You haven't been listening.'

'Yes, I have.'

'Staring at me. It makes me nervous.'

'Can't sisters look at their brothers?'

'Not incestuously.'

She sat back obediently against the seat, and craned up at the colossal grey cliffs we were winding under.

'Just a walk.'

'I know. I'm having second thoughts.'

'For me or for you?'

'Mainly for you.'

'We'll see who drops first.'

Arachova was a romantic shoulder of pink and terracotta houses, a mountain village perched high over the Delphi valley. I made an inquiry and was sent to a cottage near the church. An old woman came to the door; beyond her in the shadows stood a carpet-loom, a dark-red carpet half-finished on it. A few minutes' talk with her confirmed what the mountain had made obvious.

Alison looked at me. 'What's she say?'

'She says it's about six hours' walk. Hard walk.'

'But that's fine. It's what Baedeker says. One must be there at sundown.' I looked up at the huge grey mountainside. The old woman unhooked a key from behind the door. 'What's she saying?'

'There's some kind of hut up there.'

'Then what are we worrying about?'

'She says it will be damn cold.' But it was difficult to believe, in the blazing midday heat. Alison put her hands on her hips.

'You promised me an adventure. I want an adventure.'

I looked at the old woman and then back at Alison. She whisked her dark glasses off and gave me a hard, sideways, tough-woman's stare; and although it was half-joking I could see the hint of suspicion in her eyes. If she once began to guess that I was anxious not to spend the night in the same room with her, she would also begin to guess that my halo was made of plaster.

At that moment a man led a mule past and the old woman called to him. He was going to fetch wood down from near the refuge. Alison could ride on the packsaddle.

'Ask her if I can go in and change into my jeans.'

It was destined.

40

The long path zigzagged up a cliff-face, and leaving the lower world behind, we came over the top into the upper Parnassus. A vernally cool wind blew across two or three miles of meadowland. Beyond, sombre black firwoods and grey buttresses of rock climbed, arched and finally disappeared into fleecy white clouds. Alison dismounted and we walked over the turf beside the muleteer. He was about forty, with a fierce moustache under a broken nose and a fine air of independence about him. He told us about the shepherd life; a life of sun-hours, counting, milking, brittle stars and chilling winds, endless silences broken only by bells, alarms against wolves and eagles; a life unchanged in the last six thousand years. I translated for Alison. She warmed to him at once, establishing a half-sexual, half-philanthropic rapport across the language barrier.

He said he had worked in Athens for a time, but *then hyparchi esychia*, there was no silent peace there. Alison liked the word: *esychia*, *esychia*, she kept on repeating. He laughed and corrected her pronunciation; stopping and conducting her, as if she were an orchestra. Her eyes flicked defiantly at me, to see if she was behaving properly in my eyes. I kept a neutral face; but I liked the man, one of those fine rural Greeks who constitute the least servile and most likeable peasantry in Europe, and I couldn't help liking Alison for liking him back.

On the far side of the grassland we came to two *kalyvia*, rough stone huts, by a spring. Our muleteer was taking another path from then on. Alison fished impulsively in her red Greek shoulder-bag, and pressed on him two packets of airline cigarettes. '*Esychia*,' the muleteer said. He and Alison stood interminably shaking hands, while I took their photo.

'*Esychia, esychia*. Tell him I know what he means.'

'He knows you know. That's why he likes you.'

At last we set off through the firs.

'You think I'm just sentimental.'

'No, I don't. But one packet would have been enough.'

'No, it wouldn't. I felt two packets fond of him.'

Later she said, 'That beautiful word.'

'It's doomed.'

We climbed a little way. 'Listen.'

We stopped on the stony track and listened and there was nothing but silence, *esychia*, the breeze in the fir-branches. She took my hand and we walked on.

The path mounted interminably through the trees, through clearings alive with butterflies, over rocky stretches where we several times lost the path. As we came higher, it grew cooler, and the mountain ahead, a damp polar grey, disappeared completely into the cloud. We spoke very little because we seldom had breath to speak. But the solitude, the effort, the need I had continually to take her hand to help her when the path became, as it frequently did, a rough staircase rather than a path – all this broke some of the physical reserve between us; instituted a sort of sexless camaraderie that we both accepted as the form.

It was about six when we came to the refuge. It was tucked away above the tree-line in a goyal, a minute windowless building with a barrel-vaulted roof and a chimney. The door was of rusty iron, perforated with jagged bullet-holes from some battle with the Communist *andarte* during the Civil War: we saw four bunks, a pile of old red blankets, a stove, a lamp, a saw and an axe, even a pair of skis. But it looked as if no one had stayed there for years.

I said, 'I'm game to call it a day here.' But she didn't even answer; simply pulled on a jumper.

The clouds canopied us, it began to drizzle, and as we turned up over a crest, the wind cut like January in England. Then suddenly the clouds were all around us, a swirling mist that cut visibility down to thirty yards or less. I turned to look at Alison. Her nose had gone red and she looked very cold. But she pointed up the next boulder-strewn slope.

At the top of it we came to a col and miraculously, as if the mist and the cold had been a small test, the sky began to clear. The clouds thinned, were perfused by oblique sunlight, then burst open into great pools of serene blue. Soon we were walking in sunshine again. Before us lay a wide basin of green turf, ringed with peaks and festooned by streaks of snow still clinging to the screes and hollows of the steeper slopes. Everywhere there were flowers – harebells, gentians, deep magenta-red alpine geraniums, intense yellow asters, saxifrage. They burst out of every cranny in the rocks, they enamelled every stretch of turf. It was like stepping back a season. Alison ran on ahead, wildly, and turned, grinning, her arms held out, like a bird about to take wing; then ran on again, dark-blue and jeans-blue, in absurd childish swoops.

Lykeri, the highest peak, was too steep to be climbed quickly. We had to scramble up, using our hands, resting frequently. Near the top we came on beds of violets in bloom, huge purple flowers that had a delicate scent; and then at last, hand in hand, we struggled up the last few yards and stood on the little platform with its crowning cairn.

Alison said, 'Oh my God, oh my God.'

On the far side a huge chasm plunged down two thousand feet of shadowy air. The westering sun was still just above the horizon, but the clouds had vanished. The sky was a pale, absolutely dustless, absolutely pure, azure. There were no other mountains near to crowd the distances out. We seemed to stand immeasurably high, where land and substance drew up to a narrow zenith, remote from all towns, all society, all drought and defect. Purged.

Below, for a hundred miles in each direction, there were other mountains, valleys, plains, islands, seas; Attica, Boeotia, Argolis, Achaia, Locris, Aetolia, all the old heart of Greece. The setting sun richened, softened, refined all the colours. There were deep-blue eastern shadows and lilac western slopes; pale copper-green valleys, Tanagra-coloured earth; the distant sea dreaming, smoky, milky, calm as old blue glass. With a splendid classical simplicity someone had formed in small stones, just beyond the cairn, the letters $\Phi\Omega\Sigma$ – 'light'. It was exact. The peak reached up into a world both literally and metaphorically of light. It didn't touch the emotions; it was too vast, too inhuman, too serene; and it came to me like a shock, a delicious intellectual joy marrying and completing the physical one, that the reality of the place was as beautiful, as calm, as ideal, as so many poets had always dreamed it to be.

We took photographs of each other, of the view, and then sat down on the windward side of the cairn and smoked cigarettes, huddled together because of the cold. Alpine crows screeched overhead, torn in the wind; wind as cold as ice, as astringent as acid. There came back the memory of that mind-voyage Conchis had induced in me under hypnosis. They seemed almost parallel experiences; except that this had all the beauty of its immediacy, its un-inducedness, its being-now-ness.

I looked covertly at Alison; the tip of her nose was bright red. But I was thinking that after all she had guts; that if it hadn't been for her we wouldn't have been there, this world at our feet, this sense of triumph – this transcendent crystallization of all I felt for Greece.

'You must see things like this every day.'

'Never like this. Never even beginning to be like this.' Two or three minutes later she said, 'This is the first decent thing that's happened to me for months. Today. And this.' After a pause, she added, 'And you.'

'Don't say that. I'm just a mess. A defilement.'

'I still wouldn't want to be here with anyone else.' She stared out towards Euboea; bruised face, being dispassionate for once. She turned and looked at me. 'Would you?'

'I can't think of any other girl I've ever known who could walk this far.'

She thought it over, then looked at me again. 'What an evasive answer *that* was.'

'I'm glad we came. You're a trouper, Kelly.'

'And you're a bastard, Urfe.'

But I could see that she wasn't offended.

41

Almost at once tiredness, as we returned, attacked us. Alison discovered a blister on her left heel, where the new shoe had rubbed. We wasted ten minutes of the quick-dying light trying to improvise a bandage for it; and then, almost as abruptly as if a curtain had dropped, night was on us. With it came wind. The sky remained clear, the stars burned frantically, but somewhere we went down the wrong rocky slope and at the place I expected the refuge to be there was nothing. It was difficult to see footholds, increasingly difficult to think sensibly. We foolishly went on, coming into a vast volcanic bowl, a stark lunar landscape; snow-streaked cliffs, violent winds howling round the sides. Wolves became real, not an amusing reference in a casual conversation.

Alison must have been far more frightened, and probably far colder, than I was. At the centre of the bowl it became clear that it was impossible to get out except by going back, and we sat for a few minutes to rest in the lee of a huge boulder. I held her close against me for warmth's sake. She lay with her head buried in my sweater, in a completely unsexual embrace; and cradling her there, shivering in that extraordinary landscape, a million years and miles from the sweltering Athens night, I felt ... it meant nothing, it must mean nothing. I told myself I would have felt the same with anyone. But I looked out over the grim landscape, an accurate enough simile of my life, and remembered something the muleteer had said earlier: that wolves never hunt singly, but always in a pack. The lone wolf was a myth.

I forced Alison to her feet and we stumbled back the way we had come. Along a ridge to the west another col and slope led down towards the black distant sea of trees. Eventually we saw contoured against the sky a tor-shaped hill I had noticed on the way up. The refuge was just the other side of it. Alison no longer seemed to care; I kept hold of her hand and dragged her along by main force. Bullying her, begging her, anything to keep her moving. Twenty minutes later the squat dark cube of the refuge appeared in its little combe.

I looked at my watch. It had taken us an hour and a half to reach the peak; and over three hours to get back.

I groped my way in and sat Alison on a bunk. Then I struck a match, found the lamp and tried to light it; but it had no wick and no oil. I turned to the stove. That, thank God, had dry wood. I ripped up all the paper I could find: a Penguin novel of Alison's, the wrappings off the food we had bought; then lit it and prayed. There were back-puffs of papery, then resinous smoke, and the kindling caught. In a few minutes, the hut grew full of flickering red light and sepia shadows, and even more welcome heat. I picked up a pail. Alison raised her head.

'I'm going to get some water now.'

'Okay.' She smiled wanly.

'I should get under some blankets.' She nodded.

But when I came back from the stream five minutes later she was gingerly feeding logs through the upper door of the stove; bare-footed, on a red blanket she had spread over the floor between the bunks and the fire. On a lower bunk she had laid out what was to be our meal; bread, chocolate, sardines, *paximadia*, oranges; and she had even found an old saucepan.

'Kelly, I ordered you to bed.'

'I suddenly remembered I'm meant to be an air hostess. The life and soul of the crash.' She took the pail of water and began to wash the saucepan out. As she crouched, I could see the sore red spots on her heels. 'Do you wish we hadn't done it?'

'No.'

She looked back up at me. 'Just no?'

'I'm delighted we did it.'

Satisfied, she went back to the saucepan, filled it with water, began to crumble the chocolate. I sat on the edge of the bunk and took my own shoes and socks off. I wanted to be natural, and I couldn't; and she couldn't. The heat, the tiny room, the two of us, in all that cold desolation.

'Sorry I went all womany.'

There was a ghost of sarcasm in her voice, but I couldn't see her face. She had begun to stir the chocolate over the stove.

'Don't be silly.'

A squall of wind battered against the iron roof, and the door groaned half open.

She said, 'Saved from the storm.'

I looked at her from the door, after I had propped it to with one of the skis. She was stirring the melting chocolate with a twig, standing sideways to avoid the heat, watching me. She pulled a flushed face, and swivelled her eyes round the dirty walls. 'Romantic, isn't it?'

'As long as it keeps the wind out.' She smiled secretly at me and looked down at her saucepan. 'Why do you smile?'

'Because it is romantic.'

I sat down on the bunk again. She pulled off her jumper and shook her hair free. I invoked the image of Julie; but somehow it was a situation that Julie could never have got into. I tried to sound at ease.

'You look fine. In your element.'

'So I should. I spend most of my life slaving in a four-by-two galley.' She stood with one hand on her hip; a minute of silence; old domestic memories from Russell Square. 'What was that Sartre play we saw?'

'*Huis Clos.*'

'This is *Huis* even closer.'

'Why?'

She kept her back turned. 'Being tired always makes me feel sexy.' I breathed in. She said softly, 'One more risk.'

'Just because the first tests are negative, it doesn't mean –'

She lifted a black-brown dob from the saucepan. 'I think this delicious *consommé à la reine* is ready.'

She came and bent beside me with that peculiar downwards look and automatic smile of air hostesses.

'Something to drink before dinner, sir?'

She thrust the saucepan under my nose, mocking herself and my seriousness, and I grinned; but she didn't grin back, she gave me one of her gentlest smiles. I took the saucepan. She went to the bunks at the far end of the hut; began to unbutton her shirt.

'What are you doing?'

'Undressing.'

I looked away. A few seconds later she was standing by me with one of the blankets wrapped sarong fashion round her; then quietly sat on another folded blanket, on the floor, a careful two feet away from me. As she turned to reach for the food behind her, the blanket fell apart over her legs. She readjusted it when she turned back; but somewhere in the recesses of my mind that little Priapus threw up his hands, and that other member of his body, and leered wildly.

We ate. The *paximadia*, rusks fried in olive oil, were as uninteresting as always, the hot chocolate watery and the sardines inappropriate, but we were too hungry to care. Finally we sat – I had slipped on to the floor as well – satiated, backs against the edge of the bunk, adding more smoke to that from the stove. We were both silent, both

262

waiting. I felt like a boy with his first girl, at the moment when the thing has to stop, or to go on to the end. Frightened to make any move. Her bare shoulders were small, round, delicate. The end of the blanket she had tucked in under her armpit had become loose. I could see the top of her breasts.

The silence grew acutely embarrassing, at least to me; a sort of endurance test, to see which of us would have to break it first. Her hand lay on the blanket between us, for me to reach out and touch. I began to feel that she had exploited the whole situation, engineered everything to place me in this predicament: this silence in which it was only too clear that she was in command, not myself; only too clear that I wanted her – not Alison in particular, but the girl she was, any girl who might have been beside me at that moment. In the end I threw my cigarette into the stove and lay back against the bunk and shut my eyes, as if I was very tired, as if sleep was all I wanted – as indeed, bar Alison, it was. Suddenly she moved. I opened my eyes. She was naked beside me, the blanket thrown back.

'Alison. No.' But she knelt and began to undress me.

'Poor little boy.'

She straddled my legs and unbuttoned my shirt, pulled it out. I shut my eyes and let her make me barechested.

'It's so unfair.'

'You're so brown.'

She ran her hands up the side of my body, my shoulders, my neck, my lips; playing with me, examining me, like a child with a new toy. She knelt and kissed the side of my neck and the ends of her breasts brushed my skin.

I said, 'I'd never forgive myself if … '

'Don't talk. Just lie still.'

She undressed me completely, then led my hands all over her body, to know it all again, soft skin, small curves, slimness, her always natural nakedness. Her hands. As she caressed me, I thought, it's like being with a prostitute, hands as adept as a prostitute's, nothing but a matter of pleasure … and I gave way to the pleasure she gave me. After a while she lay on top of me, her head on my chest. A long silence. The fire crackled, burnt our legs a little. I stroked her back, her hair, her small neck, surrendered to the nerve-ends in my flesh. I imagined lying in the same position with Julie, and I thought I knew it would be infinitely disturbing and infinitely more passionate; not familiar, not aching with fatigue, hot, a bit sweaty ... some cheapened word like randy; but white-hot, mysterious, overwhelming passion.

Alison murmured, shifted, bit me, swayed over me in a caress she called the pasha caress, that she knew I liked, all men liked; my mistress and my slave.

I remember our dropping into the bunk, a coarse straw mattress, the harsh blankets, her holding me a moment, kissing me once on the mouth before I could pull away, then turning her back; my hand on the wet breasts, and her hand holding it there, the small smooth belly, the faint washed and rainwashed smell of her hair; and then, in seconds, too soon to analyse anything, sleep.

I woke up some time in the night, and went and drank some water from the pail. Small pencils of late-risen moon came through the old bullet-holes. I went back and leant over Alison. She had thrown back the blanket a little and her skin was a deep shadowed red in the ember-light; one breast bare and slightly slumped, her mouth half open, a slight snore. Young and ancient; innocent and corrupt; in every woman, all woman.

The wave of affection and tenderness I felt made me determine, with that sort of revelationary shock ideas about courses of action sometimes have when one wakes up drugged with sleep, that tomorrow I must tell her the truth; and not as a confession, but as a means of letting her see the truth, that my real disease was not something curable like syphilis, but far more banal and far more terrible, a congenital promiscuity. I stood over her, almost touching her, almost tearing the blanket back and sinking on her, entering her, making love to her as she wanted me to; but not. I gently covered the bare breast, then picked up some blankets and went to the next bunk.

42

We were woken by someone knocking on the door, then half opening it. Sunlight slashed through. He withdrew when he saw we were
still in the bunks. I looked at my watch. It was ten o'clock. I pulled
on my clothes and went out. A shepherd. Somewhere in the distance
I could hear the bells of his flock. He struck back with his crook the
two enormous dogs that bared their teeth at me and produced from
the pockets of his greatcoat a cheese wrapped in sorrel-leaves, which
he had brought for our breakfast. After a few minutes Alison came
out, tucking her shirt into her jeans and screwing up her eyes against
the sun. We shared what was left of the rusks and the oranges with
the shepherd; used up the last of the film. I was glad he was there. I
could see, as clear as printed words in Alison's eyes, that she thought
we had crossed back into the old relationship. She had broken the
ice; but it was for me to jump into the water.

The shepherd stood up, shook hands and strode off with his two
savage dogs and left us alone. Alison stretched back in the sun across
the great slab of rock we had used as a table. It was a much less windy
day, April-warm, a dazzling blue sky. The sheep-bells sounded in the
distance and some bird like a lark sang high up the slope above us.

'I wish we could stay here for ever.'

'I've got to get the car back.'

'Just wishing.' She looked at me. 'Come and sit here.' She patted
the rock by her side. Her grey eyes stared up at me, at their most
candid. 'Do you forgive me?'

I bent and kissed her cheek and she put her arms round me so that
I lay half across her, and we had a whispered conversation, mouths to
each other's left ears.

'Say you wanted to.'

'I wanted to.'

'Say you love me a little still.'

'I love you a little still.' She pinched my back. 'A lot still.'

'And you'll get better.'

'Mm.'

'And never go with those nasty women again.'

'Never.'

'It's silly when you can have it for free. With love.'

'I know.'

I was staring at the ends of her hair against the rock, an inch or two from my eyes, and trying to bring myself to the point of confession. But it seemed like treading on a flower because one can't be bothered to step aside. I pushed up, but she held me by the shoulders, so that I had to stare down at her. I sustained her look, its honesty, for a moment, then I turned and sat with my back to her.

'What's wrong?'

'Nothing. I just wondered what malicious god made a nice kid like you see anything in a shit like me.'

'That reminds me. A crossword clue. I saw it months ago. Ready?' I nodded, '"She's all mixed up, but the better part of Nicholas" ... six letters.'

I worked it out, smiled at her. 'Did the clue end in a full-stop or a question-mark?'

'It ended in my crying. As usual.'

And the bird above us sang in the silence.

We set off down. As we came lower, it grew warmer and warmer. Summer rose to meet us.

Alison led the way, and so she could rarely see my face. I tried to sort out my feelings about her. It irritated me still that she put so much reliance on the body thing, the shared orgasm. Her mistaking that for love, her not seeing that love was something other ... the mystery of withdrawal, reserve, walking away through the trees, turning the mouth away at the last moment. On Parnassus of all mountains, it occurred to me, her unsubtlety, her inability to hide behind metaphor, ought to offend me; to bore me as uncomplex poetry normally bored me. And yet in some way I couldn't define she had, had always had, this secret trick of slipping through all the obstacles I put between us; as if she were really my sister, had access to unfair pressures and could always evoke deep similarities to annul, or to make seem irrelevant, the differences in taste or feeling.

She began to talk about being an air hostess; about herself.

'Oh Jesus, excitement. That lasts about a couple of duties. New faces, new cities, new romances with handsome pilots. Most of the pilots think we're part of the aircrew amenities. Just queueing up to be blessed by their miserable old Battle-of-Britain cocks.'

I laughed.

'Nicko, it's not funny. It destroys you. That bloody tin pipe. And all that freedom, that space outside. Sometimes I just want to pull the safety handle and be sucked out. Just falling, a minute of wonderful lovely passengerless falling ... '

'You're not serious.'

'More serious than you think. We call it charm depression. When you get so penny-in-the-slot charming that you stop being human any more. It's like ... sometimes we're so busy after take-off we don't realize how far the plane's climbed and you look out and it's a shock ... it's like that, you suddenly realize how far you are from what you really are. Or you were, or something. I don't explain it well.'

'Yes, you do. Very well.'

'You begin to feel you don't belong anywhere any more. You know, as if I didn't have enough problems that way already. I mean England's impossible, it becomes more *honi soit qui* smelly pants every day, it's a graveyard. And Australia ... Australia. God, how I hate my country. The meanest stupidest blindest ... ' She gave up.

We walked on a way, then she said, 'It's just I haven't roots anywhere any more, I don't belong anywhere. They're all places I fly to or from. Or over. I just have people I like. Or love. They're the only homeland I have left.'

She threw a look back, a shy one, as if she had been saving up this truth about herself, this rootlessness, homelandlessness, which she knew was also a truth about me.

'At least we've got rid of a lot of useless illusions as well.'

'Clever us.'

She fell silent and I swallowed her reproach. In spite of her superficial independence, her fundamental need was to cling. All her life was an attempt to disprove it; and so proved it. She was like a sea-anemone – had only to be touched to adhere to what touched her.

She stopped. We both noticed it at the same time. Below us to our right, the sound of water, a rush of water.

'I'd love to bathe my feet. Could we get down?'

We struck off the path through the trees and after a while came on a faint trail. It led us down, down and finally out into a clearing. At one end was a waterfall some ten feet or so high. A pool of limpid water had formed beneath it. The clearing was dense with flowers and butterflies, a tiny trough of green-gold luxuriance after the dark forest we had been walking through. At the upper edge of the clearing there was a little cliff with a shallow cave, outside which some shepherd had pleached an arbour of fir-branches. There were sheep droppings on the floor, but they were old. No one could have been there since summer began.

'Let's have a swim.'

'It'll be like ice.'

'Yah.'

She pulled her shirt over her head, and unhooked her bra, grinning at me in the flecked shadow of the arbour.

'The place is probably alive with snakes.'

'Like Eden.'

She stepped out of her jeans and her white pants. Then she reached up and snapped a dead cone off one of the arbour branches and held it out to me. I watched her run nakedly through the long grass to the pool, try the water, groan. Then she waded forwards and swanned in with a scream. The water was jade-green, melted snow, and it made my heart jolt with shock when I plunged beside her. And yet it was beautiful, the shadow of the trees, the sunlight on the glade, the white roar of the little fall, the iciness, the solitude, the laughing, the nakedness; moments one knows only death will obliterate.

Sitting in the grass beside the arbour we let the sun and the small breeze dry us and ate the last of the chocolate. Then Alison lay on her back, her arms thrown out, her legs a little open, abandoned to the sun – and, I knew, to me. For a time I lay like her, with my eyes closed.

Then she said, 'I'm Queen of the May.'

She was sitting up, turned to me, propped on one arm. She had woven a rough crown out of the oxeyes and wild pinks that grew in the grass around us. It sat lopsidedly on her uncombed hair; and she wore a smile of touching innocence. She did not know it, but it was was at first for me an intensely literary moment. I could place it exactly: *England's Helicon*. I had forgotten that there are metaphors and metaphors, and that the greatest lyrics are very rarely anything but direct and unmetaphysical. Suddenly she was like such a poem and I felt a passionate wave of desire for her. It was not only lust, not only because she looked, as she did in her periodic fashion, disturbingly pretty, small-breasted, small-waisted, leaning on one hand, dimpled then grave; a child of sixteen, not a girl of twenty-four; but because I was seeing through all the ugly, the unpoetic accretions of modern life to the naked real self of her – a vision of her as naked in that way as she was in body; Eve glimpsed again through ten thousand generations.

It rushed on me, it was quite simple, I did love her, I wanted to keep her *and* I wanted to keep – or to find – Julie. It wasn't that I wanted one more than the other, I wanted both. I had to have both; there was no emotional dishonesty in it. The only dishonesty was in my feeling dishonest, concealing ... it was love that finally drove me to confess, not cruelty, not a wish to be free, to be callous and clear, but simply love. I think, in those few long moments, that Alison saw that. She must have seen something torn and sad in my face, because she said, very gently, 'What's wrong?'

'I haven't had syphilis. It's all a lie.'

She gave me an intense look, then sank back on the grass.

'Oh Nicholas.'

'I want to tell you – '

'Not now. Please not now. Whatever's happened, come and make love to me.'

And we did make love; not sex, but love; though sex would have been far wiser.

Lying beside her I began to try to describe what had happened at Bourani. The ancient Greeks said that if one slept a night on Parnassus either one became inspired or one went mad, and there was no doubt which happened to me; even as I spoke I knew it would have been better to say nothing, to have made something up ... but love, that need to be naked. I had chosen the worst of all possible moments to be honest, and like most people who have spent much of their adult life being emotionally dishonest, I overcalculated the sympathy a final being honest would bring ... but love, that need to be understood. And Parnassus was also to blame, for being so Greek; a place that made anything but the truth a mindsore.

Of course she wanted first to know the reason for the bizarre pretext I had hit on, but I wanted her to understand the strangeness of Bourani before I mentioned its deepest attraction. I didn't deliberately hide anything else about Conchis, but I still left great gaps.

'It's not that I believe any of these things in the way he tries to make me believe them. But even there ... since he hypnotized me, I don't absolutely know. It's simply that when I'm with him I feel he does have access to some kind of power. Not occult. I can't explain.'

'But it must be all faked.'

'All right. But why me? How did he know I would go there? I'm nothing to him, he obviously doesn't even think very much of me. As a person. He's always laughing at me.'

'I still don't understand ... ' but then she did. She looked at me. 'There's someone else there.'

'Alison darling, for God's sake try to understand. Listen.'

'I'm listening.' But her face was averted.

So at last I told her. I made it out to be an asexual thing, a fascination of the mind.

'But she attracts you the other way.'

'Allie, I can't tell you how much I've hated myself this week-end. And tried to tell you everything a dozen times before. I don't want to be attracted by her. In any way. A month, three weeks ago I couldn't have believed it. I still don't know what it is about her. Honestly. I only know I'm haunted, possessed by everything over there. Not just her. Something so strange is going on. And I'm ... involved.' She looked unimpressed. 'I've got to go back to the island. Because of the job. There are so many ways in which I'm not a free agent.'

'But this girl.' She was staring at the ground, picking seeds off grassheads.

'She's irrelevant. Really. Just a very small part of it.'

'Then why all the performance?'

'You can't understand, I'm being pulled in two.'

'Is she pretty?'

'If I still didn't care like hell for you deep down it would all have been so easy.'

'Is she pretty?'

'Yes.'

'Very pretty.'

I said nothing. She buried her face in her arms. I stroked her warm shoulder.

'She's totally unlike you. Unlike any modern girl. I can't explain.' She turned her head away. 'Alison.'

'I must seem just ... ' but she didn't finish.

'Now you're being ridiculous.'

'Am I?'

There was a tense silence.

'Look, I'm trying desperately, for once in my miserable life, to be honest. I have no excuses. If I met this girl tomorrow, okay, I could say, I love Alison, Alison loves me, nothing doing. But I met her a fortnight ago. And I've got to meet her again.'

'And you don't love Alison.' She stared away. 'Or you love me till you see a better bit of tail.'

'Don't be crude.'

'I am crude. I think crude. I talk crude. I *am* crude.' She knelt, took a breath. 'So what now? I curtsy and withdraw?'

'I wish to God I wasn't so complicated – '

'Complicated!' She snorted.

'Selfish.'

'That's better.'

We were silent. Two coupled yellow butterflies flitted heavily, saggingly, past.

'All I wanted was that you should know what I am.'

'I know what you are.'

'If you did you'd have cut me out right at the beginning.'

'I still know what you are.'

And her cold grey eyes went through me, till I had to look down. She stood up and went to wash. It was hopeless. I couldn't manage it, I couldn't explain, and she could never understand. I put my clothes on and turned my back while she dressed in silence.

When she was ready, she said, 'Don't for God's sake say any more. I can't bear it.'

We got to Arachova about five and set off to drive back to Athens. I twice tried to discuss everything again with her, but she wouldn't allow it. We had said all that could be said; and she sat brooding, wordless, all the way.

We came over the pass at Daphni at about eight-thirty, with the last light over the pink and amber city, the first neon signs round Syntagma and Ommonia like distant jewels. I thought of where we had been that time the night before, and glanced at Alison. She was putting on lipstick. Perhaps after all there was a solution; to get her back into the hotel, make love to her, prove to her through the loins that I did love her ... and why not, let her see that I might be worth suffering, just as I was and always would be. I began to talk a little, casually, about Athens; but her answers were so uninterested, so curt, that it sounded as ridiculous as it was, and I fell silent. The pink turned to violet, and soon it was night.

We arrived at the hotel in the Piraeus – I had reserved the same rooms. Alison went up while I took the car round to the garage. On the way back I saw a flower-seller and bought a dozen carnations from him. I went straight to her room, and knocked on the door. I had to knock three times before she unlocked it. She had been crying.

'I brought you some flowers.'

'I don't want your bloody flowers.'

'Look, Alison, it's not the end of the world.'

'Just the end of the affaire.'

I broke the silence. 'Aren't you going to let me in?'

'Why the hell should I?'

She stood holding the door half shut, the room in darkness behind her. Her face was terrible; puffed and unforgiving; nakedly hurt.

'Just let me come in and talk to you.'

'No.'

'Please.'

'Go away.'

I pushed in past her and closed the door. She stood against the wall, staring at me. Light came up from the street, and I could see her eyes. I offered the flowers. She snatched them from my hand, went to the window and hurled them, pink heads, green stems, out into the night; remained there with her back to me.

'This experience. It's like being halfway through a book. I can't just throw it in the dustbin.'

'So you throw me instead.'

I went behind her to try to put my hands on her shoulders, but she jerked angrily away.

'Fuck off. Just fuck off.'

I sat on the bed and lit a cigarette. Down in the street monotonous Macedonian folk-music skirled from some café loudspeaker; but we sat and stood in a strange cocoon of remoteness from even the nearest outside things.

'I came to Athens knowing I ought not to meet you. I did my damnedest that first evening and yesterday to prove to myself that I don't have any special feeling for you any more. But it didn't work. That's why I talked. So ineptly. So at the wrong time.' She gave no sign of listening; I produced my trump. 'Talked when I could have kept quiet. Could still be deceiving you.'

'I'm not the one who's deceived.'

'Look – '

'And what the hell does "special feeling" mean?' I was silent. 'Christ, you're not just afraid of the *thing* love. You're even afraid of using the word now.'

'I don't know what love is.'

She spun round. 'Well let me tell you. Love isn't only what I said it was in that letter. Not turning back to look. Love is pretending to go to work but going to Victoria. To give you one last surprise, one last kiss, one last ... it doesn't matter, I saw you buying magazines. That morning I couldn't have laughed with anyone in the world. And yet you laughed. You fucking well stood with a porter and laughed about something. That's when I found out what love was. Seeing the one person you want to live with happy to have escaped from you.'

'But why didn't you – '

'You know what I did? I crept away. And spent the whole god-awful day curled up on *our* bed. Not because I loved you. Because I was so mad with rage and shame that I loved you.'

'I wasn't to know.'

She turned away. 'I wasn't to know. Christ!' Violence hung in the air like static electricity. 'Another thing. You think love is sex. Let me tell you something. If I'd wanted you just for that, I'd have left you straight after the first night.'

'My apologies.'

She looked at me, took a breath, gave a bitter little smile. 'Oh God, now he's hurt. I'm trying to tell you that I loved you for you. Not for your blasted prick.' She stared back out into the night. 'Of course you're all right in bed. But you're not the ... '

Silence.

'Best you've had.'

'If that was what mattered.' She came to the end of the bed and leant against it, looking down at me. 'I think you're so blind you probably don't even know you don't love me. You don't even know you're a filthy selfish bastard who can't, can't like being impotent, can't *ever* think of anything except number one. Because nothing can hurt you, Nicko. Deep down, where it counts. You've built your life so that nothing can ever reach you. So whatever you do you can say, I couldn't help it. You can't lose. You can always have your next adventure. Your next bloody affaire.'

'You always twist – '

'Twist! Holy Jesus, don't you talk of twisting. You can't even tell a simple fact straight.'

I looked round at her. 'Meaning?'

'All that mystery balls. You think I fall for that? There's some girl on your island and you want to lay her. That's all. But of course that's nasty, that's crude. So you tart it up. As usual. Tart it up so it makes you seem the innocent one, the great intellectual who must have his experience. Always both ways. Always cake and eat it. Always – '

'I swear ... ' But her impatient jerk away silenced me. She walked up and down the room. I tried another excuse. 'Because I don't want to marry you – or anyone – it doesn't mean I don't love you.'

'That reminds me. That child. You thought I didn't notice. That little girl with the boil. It made you furious. Alison showing how good she is with kids. Doing the mother act. And shall I tell you something? I was doing the mother act. Just for a moment, when she smiled, I did think that. I did think how I'd like to have your children and ... have my arm round them and have you near me. Isn't that terrible? I have this filthy disgusting stinking-taste thing called

274

love … God, syphilis is *nice* compared to love … and I'm so depraved, so colonial, so degenerate that I actually dare show you … '

'Alison.'

She took a shuddery breath; near tears.

' I realized as soon as we met on Friday. For you I'll always be Alison who slept around. That Australian girl who had an abortion. The human boomerang. Throw her away and she'll always come back for another week-end of cheap knock.'

'That's a long way below the belt.'

She lit a cigarette. I went and stood by the window and she spoke at my back, across the bed and the room, from the door. 'All that time, last autumn … I didn't realize then. I didn't realize you can get softer. I thought you went on getting harder. God only knows why, I felt closer to you than I've ever felt to any other man. God only knows why. In spite of all your smart-alec Pommie ways. Your bloody class mania. So I never really got over your going. I tried Pete, I tried another man, but it didn't work. Always this stupid, pathetic little dream. That one day you'd write … so I went mad trying to organize these three days. Betting everything on them. Even though I could see, God how I could see you were just bored.'

'That's not true. I wasn't bored.'

'Thinking about this bit on Phraxos.'

'I missed you too. Hellishly, those first months.'

Suddenly she switched the lights on.

'Turn round and look at me.'

I did. She was standing by the door, still in her blue jeans and the dark-blue shirt; her face a grey-and-white mask.

'I've saved some money. And you can't be exactly broke. If you say the word, I'll walk out of my job tomorrow. I'll come on your island and live with you. I said a cottage in Ireland. But I'll take a cottage on Phraxos. You can have that. The dreadful responsibility of having to live with someone who loves you.'

It was vile, but my one reaction when she said 'a cottage on Phraxos' was of profound relief that I hadn't told her of Conchis's offer.

'Or?'

'You can say no.'

'An ultimatum.'

'No sliding. Yes or no.'

'Alison, if – '

'Yes or no.'

'You can't decide these things … '

Her voice sharpened a pitch. 'Yes or no.'

I stared at her. She gave a tiny humourless twist of her lips and answered for me.

'No.'

'Only because … '

She ran straight to the door and opened it. I felt angry, trapped into this ridiculous either-or choice, this brutal demand for total commitment. I went round the bed towards her, yanked the door away from her grip and slammed it shut again; then caught her and tried to kiss her, reaching past her at the same time to flick off the light. The room was plunged into darkness again, but she struggled wildly, jerking her head from side to side. I pulled her back towards the bed and fell with her across it, making it roll and knock both lamp and ashtray off the bedside table. I thought she would give in, she must give in, but suddenly she screamed, so loud that it must have pierced all through the hotel and echoed over on the other side of the port.

'LET ME GO!'

I sat back a little and she hit me with her clubbed fists. I caught her wrists.

'For God's sake.'

'I HATE YOU!'

'Keep quiet!'

I forced her on her side. Someone in the next room banged on the wall. Another nerve-splitting scream.

'I HATE YOU!'

I slapped the side of her face. She began to sob violently, twisted sideways against the bed-end, fragments of words howled at me between gasps for air and tears.

'Leave me alone … leave me alone … you shit … you fucking selfish … ' Explosion of sobs, her shoulders racked. I stood and went to the window.

She began to bang the bedrail with her fists, as if she was beyond words. I hated her then; her lack of control, her hysteria. I remem-

bered that there was a bottle of Scotch downstairs in my room – she
had brought it for me as a present, the first day.

'Look, I'm going to get you a drink. Now stop wailing.'

I hovered over her. She took no notice, went on beating the bedrail. I got to the door, hesitated, looked back, then went out. Three
Greeks, a man and woman and an elder man, were standing two
open doors away, staring at me as if I were a murderer. I went downstairs, opened the bottle, swallowed a stiff shot straight out of it, then
went back.

The door was locked. The three spectators continued to stare;
watched me try it, knock, try it again, knock, then call her name.

The older man came up to me.

Was anything wrong?

I grimaced and muttered. The heat.

He repeated it unnecessarily back to the other two. Ah, the heat,
said the woman, as if that explained everything. They did not move.

I tried once more; called her name through the wooden panels. I
could hear nothing. I shrugged for the benefit of the Greeks, and
went back downstairs. Ten minutes later I returned; I returned four
or five times more during the next hour; and always the door, to my
secret relief, was shut.

I had asked to be and was woken at eight, and I dressed at once and
went to her room. I knocked; no answer. When I tried the handle,
the door opened. The bed had been slept in, but Alison and all her
belongings were gone. I ran straight down to the reception desk. A
rabbity old man with spectacles, the father of the proprietor, sat
behind it. He'd been in America, and spoke English quite well.

'You know that girl I was with last night – has she gone out this
morning?'

'Oh yeah. She wen' out.'

'When?'

He looked up at the clock. 'About one hour since. She lef' this.
She said give it you when you came down.'

An envelope. My scrawled name: *N. Urfe*.

'She didn't say where she was going?'

'Just paid her check and went.' I knew by the way he was watching

me that he had heard, or heard about, the screaming the evening
before.

'But I said I'd pay.'

'I said. I told her.'

'Damn.'

As I turned to go he said, 'Hey, you know what they say in the
States? Always plenny more fish in the sea. Know that one? Plenny
more fish in the sea.'

I went back to my room and opened her letter. It was a scrawl, a
last-moment decision not to go in silence.

Think what it would be like if you got back to your island
and there was no old man, no girl any more. No mysterious
fun and games. The whole place locked up for ever.

It's finished finished *finished*.

About ten I telephoned the airport. Alison had not returned, and was
not due to return until her flight to London at five that afternoon. I
tried again at eleven thirty, just before the boat sailed; the same
answer. As the ship, which was filled with returning boys, drew out
from the quay I scanned the crowds of parents and relations and
idlers. I had some idea that she was there among them, watching;
but if she was, she was invisible.

The ugly industrial seafront of the Piraeus receded and the boat
headed south for the svelte blue peak of Aegina. I went to the bar
and ordered a large ouzo; it was the only place the boys were not
allowed. I drank a mouthful neat, and made a sort of bitter inner
toast. I had chosen my own way; the difficult, hazardous, poetic way;
all on one number; though even then I heard Alison bitterly reverse
those last two words.

Someone slipped on to the stool beside me. It was Demetriades.
He clapped his hands for the barman.

'Buy me a drink, you perverted Englishman. And I will tell you
how I spent a most amusing week-end.'

43

Think what it would be like if you got back to your island and ... I had all
Tuesday to think nothing but that; to see myself as Alison saw me. I
drafted a long letter, several letters, to her that evening, but none of
them said what I wanted: that I hated what I had done to her, but
couldn't do otherwise. I was like one of Ulysses' sailors – turned into
a swine, and able now only to be my new self. I tore the pages up.
What I really wanted to say was that I was enchanted and that I had,
absurd though it was, to be free to be enchanted.

It was a help to teach hard, conscientiously for once, to get
through the suspense. On Wednesday evening, when I returned from
the last lesson of the day to my room, I found a note on my desk. My
heart leapt. I recognized the handwriting at once. The note said:
'We look forward to seeing you on Saturday. If I do not hear to the
contrary I shall know that you are coming. Maurice Conchis.' It
was dated above 'Wednesday morning'. I felt an enormous relief, a
surge of renewed excitement; and suddenly everything during that
last week-end seemed, if not justified, necessary.

I had marking to do, but I couldn't stay in. I walked up to the
main ridge, to my natural gazebo. I had to see the roof of Bourani,
the south of the island, the sea, the mountains, all the reality of the
unreality. There was none of the burning need to go down and spy
that had possessed me the previous week, but a balancing mixture of
expectation and reassurance, a certainty of the health of the symbiosis. I was their still; they were mine.

For some extraordinary reason, on the way back to the school, my
own happiness made me think of Alison again; almost to pity her
her ignorance of her real rival. On impulse, before I started on the
marking, I scribbled her a note.

Allie darling, you *can't* say to someone 'I've decided I ought
to love you'. I can see a million *reasons* why I ought to love you,
because (as I tried to explain) in my fashion, my perfect-bastard
fashion, I do love you. Parnassus was beautiful, please don't

think it was nothing to me, only the body, or could ever be anything but unforgettable, always, for me. Let's for God's sake keep that. I know it's over. But a moment or two, beside that pool, however many other lovers we both have, will never be over.

It relieved my conscience a little, and I posted it the next morning. The only conscious exaggeration was in the last sentence.

At ten to four on Saturday I was at the gate of Bourani; and there, walking along the track towards me, was Conchis. He had on a black shirt, long khaki shorts; dark brown shoes and faded green stockings. He was walking purposefully, almost in a hurry, as if he had wanted to be out of the way before I arrived. But he raised his arm as soon as he saw me. We stopped in mid-track, six feet apart.

'Nicholas.'

'Hallo.'

He gave his little headshake.

'A pleasant half-term?'

'Not particularly.'

'You went to Athens?'

I had already decided on my story there. He might know, through Hermes or Patarescu, that I had been away.

'My friend couldn't make it. Her airline have put her on another route.'

'Ah. I am sorry. A shame.'

I shrugged, then eyed him. 'I spent most of it wondering whether I should come here again. I haven't been hypnotized before.'

He smiled, he knew what I was really asking.

'It is for you to reject or accept what was suggested.'

I remembered, as I smiled thinly in return, that I was back in a polysemantic world. 'I'm grateful for that part of it.'

'There was no other part.' He did not take kindly to my sceptical look, and went on with some asperity. 'I am a doctor, therefore under the Hippocratic oath. If I ever wished to ask you questions under hypnosis, I should most certainly ask your permission first. Apart from anything else, it is a very unsatisfactory method. It has been demonstrated again and again that patients are quite capable of lying under hypnosis.'

'All those stories about sinister mesmerists forcing – '

'A hypnotist can force you to do foolish and incongruous things. But he is powerless against the super-ego. I can assure you of that.'

I let a few moments pass.

'You're going out?'

'I have been writing all day. I must walk. But I hoped to meet you first. Someone is waiting to serve you tea.'

'How do you want me to behave?'

He glanced back towards the invisible house, then took my arm and made me stroll back beside him towards the gate.

'Our patient is in mixed spirits. She cannot quite hide her excitement at your return. Nor her disappointment that I am in the little secret between you.'

'What little secret is that?'

He gave me a look under his eyebrows. 'Investigative hypnosis is a regular part of my treatment of *her*, Nicholas.'

'With her permission?'

'In this case, her parents'.'

'I see.'

'I know she is pretending to be an actress now. And I know why. She wishes to please you.'

'Please me?'

'You accused her of acting, or so I understand. And she has gratefully embraced the accusation.' He squeezed my elbow. 'But I have set her a problem. I have told her I know her new disguise. Not through hypnosis. But because you have told me.'

'Then now she won't trust me.'

'She never trusted you. She also revealed under hypnosis that from the first she suspected you to be a doctor – someone working with me.'

I recalled what she had said about being spun round in blind-man's-buff.

'But rightly suspicious – now that you've told me the ... truth?'

He raised a delighted finger. 'Precisely.' It was as if he were congratulating an especially bright pupil; and was blind, as nonsensically blind as one of Lewis Carroll's queens before Alice, to my obvious bewilderment. 'Therefore your task is now to gain her confidence. By all means share any suspicion she shows of my motives. Give them credence. But be careful. She may set traps. You must make objections if she becomes too farfetched. Always remember that one side of her split mentality is quite capable of rational assessment – and has a great deal of experience in making fools of doctors whose technique is to humour *ad absurdum*. I am sure some story of persecution will come. She will try to gain you to her side. Against me.'

Metaphorically, if not literally, I bit my lips.

'But surely if we all know now that she can't be Lily … ?'

'That is dropped. I am become an eccentric millionaire. She and her sister are a pair of young actresses I have brought here – she will no doubt invent some outlandish reason – for what she will perhaps lead you to believe are very wicked purposes. They may well be of some suspect sexual nature. You will demand evidence, proof … ' he waved his hand, as if my part in all this was too manifest now to need specifying in detail.

'What happens if she tries a repeat of last year – tries to make me help her escape?'

He gave me a briskly warning look. 'You must tell me at once. But I do not think it is likely. She learnt her lesson with Mitford. And remember, however much she may appear to trust you, she does not. You will of course maintain that you never told me a word of what happened on your last visit.'

I smiled. 'Of course.'

'I am sure you see where I am driving. I wish to bring the poor child to a realization of her own true problem by forcing her to recognize the nature of the artificial situation we are creating together here. She will make her first valid step back towards normality when one day she stops and says, This is not the real world. These are not real relationships.'

'What are her chances?'

'Small. But they exist. Especially if you play your part well. She may not trust you. But she is attracted to you.'

'I'll do my best.'

'Thank you. I have great confidence in you, Nicholas.' He held out his hand. 'I am delighted to have you back.'

We parted, but I looked back after a few steps to see which way he had taken. It was apparently down towards Moutsa. I did not believe he was going for a constitutional. He walked far too much like a man with someone else to meet, something to arrange. Once again I was shaken. I had come to Bourani determined, after so many useless hours of speculation, to be equally doubting of both him and Julie. But I knew I would have to watch her like a hawk now. The old man had been involved in psychiatry, he could hypnotize – those were proven facts; and nothing she had said about herself had been backed by any hard evidence. There was also the increasingly strong possibility that they were acting in league to gull me; in which case Julie Holmes was no more her real self than Lily Montgomery had been.

No one was visible as I approached the house, as I crossed the gravel. I leapt up the steps and walked quietly round the corner on to the wide tiling under the front of the colonnade.

She was standing in one of the arches facing the sea, half in sun, half in shadow; and – it was a shock, though I might have guessed – in contemporary clothes. A navy blue short-sleeved shirt, a pair of white beach trousers with a red belt – she was barefooted, her long hair down, a girl who might have adorned the terrace of any smart Mediterranean hotel. One thing was decided at once: she was as desirable in modern dress as in costume, an arrestingly beautiful young woman; in no way less attractive for being less artificial now.

She turned as I appeared, and there was a strange silence, a doubt in both our looks across the space between us. She seemed faintly surprised, as if she had half decided I would not come; was relieved, yet almost at once distancing. There was a tiny air about her of having been caught out of costume, and not being sure of my reaction to this new appearance – like a woman showing a new dress for the first time to the man who has to pay for it. She looked down from my eyes. On my side I knew the ghost of Alison, of what had happened on Parnassus; a flicker of adultery, a moment's guilt. We remained like that for several seconds. Then she looked up again to where I stood twenty feet away, with the duffel-bag in my hand. I noticed something else new about her; the beginning of a tan, a honeyed skin now. I tried to read her psychologically, psychiatrically; and gave up.

I said, 'They suit you. Modern clothes.'

Still she seemed at a loss, as if the days apart had given her countless second thoughts.

'Did you meet him?'

'Meet who?' But that was a mistake, there was something impatient in her stare. 'The old man? Yes. He was just going for a walk.'

Her suspicion was not assuaged, and she stared at me a moment more. Then she said, with a perceptible indifference, 'Do you want some tea?'

'That'd be nice.'

She moved in barefooted silence across the tiles to the table. I saw a pair of red espadrilles by the music-room doors. I watched her strike a match and light the spirit-lamp, then set the kettle on its stand. She avoided my eyes, fiddling with the muslin covers over the food; the scar on her wrist. There was almost a sullenness about her. I dropped my bag by the wall and went closer.

'What's wrong?'

'Nothing.'

'I haven't betrayed you in any way. Whatever he may have said.' She gave me the briefest glance, but then stared down at the table again. I tried small talk. 'Where've you been?'

'On the yacht.'

'Where?'

'Cruising. In the Cyclades.'

'I've missed you.'

She said nothing. She would not look at me. I had anticipated various kinds of reception, but not this apparent wishing that I hadn't come at all. There stole through me a little chill of fear – something fraught about her, lost; and with a girl as pretty as this, only the reason I did not want to believe could account for the apparent lack of other men in her life.

'I gather Lily's dead.'

She spoke to the table. 'You don't seem very surprised.'

'Nothing surprises me here. Any more.' She drew a breath; I had made another wrong answer. 'So what are you officially playing now?'

She sat down. The kettle must have been boiled once already, because it began to hiss. Suddenly she looked up at me. The question was transparently accusing.

'Did you enjoy Athens?'

'No. And I didn't meet my friend.'

'Maurice told us you had.'

I silently cursed him, and had a touch of liar's nightmare. 'That's odd. He didn't know five minutes ago. Since he asked me himself if I'd met her.'

She looked down. 'Why didn't you?'

'For the reasons I told you. It's all over.'

She tipped a little hot water into the tea-pot, then crossed the colonnade to empty it over the edge. As she came back, I said, 'And because I knew I was going to see you again.'

She sat, and spooned some tea from a caddy into the pot. 'Start eating. If you're hungry.'

'I'm much more hungry to know why we're behaving like total strangers.'

'Because that's precisely what we are.'

'Why won't you answer my question about your new role?'

'Because you already know the answer.'

Her grey-hyacinth eyes were on me, and they were very direct. The kettle boiled, and she lifted it and filled the pot. As she put it back on its stand and turned out the flame beneath, she said, 'I wouldn't really blame you for thinking I was mad. I begin to wonder increasingly myself if I'm not.' Her voice grew drier still. 'Sorry if I've spoilt a prepared scene.' Then she smiled up without humour. 'Do you want this foul goat's milk or lemon?'

'Lemon.'

I felt a great relief then. She had just done the one thing she would never do, if the old man had been telling me the truth – unless she was so insanely cunning, or cunningly insane, that she was beating him at his own game. I remembered Occam's razor: always believe the simplest of several explanations. But I played safe.

'Why should I think you're mad?'

'Why should I think you're not what you say you are?'

'Why indeed?'

'Because the question you've just asked proves you aren't.' She pushed a cup towards me. 'Your tea.'

I stared at it, then up at her. 'Okay. I don't believe you're a famous case of schizophrenia.'

She eyed me, still unwon. 'Will you not partake of a sandwich ... Mr Urfe?'

I did not smile, and I left a silence.

'Julie, this is absurd. We're falling into every trap he sets. I thought we agreed last time. We don't have to lie to each other out of his hearing.'

Without warning she stood and walked slowly to the far end of the colonnade, where steps led down to the vegetable terrace to the west. She leant against the wall of the house, her back to me, staring out towards the distant mountains of the Peloponnesus. After a moment I stood and went behind her. She did not turn to look at me.

'I'm not blaming you. If he's told you as many lies about me as he has me about you ... ' I reached and touched her shoulder. 'Come on. We did establish some sort of trust last time.' There was no response to my hand, and I let it drop.

'I suppose you want to kiss me again.'

The naïve abruptness of that took me by surprise.

'Is that a crime?'

Suddenly she folded her arms, turned her back to the wall, faced me with an intense look.

'And get me into bed?'

'Only if you wanted.'

She explored my eyes, then looked down.

'And if I don't?'

'Then obviously.'

'So perhaps it's not worth your going on.'

'That's bloody insulting.'

I said it with enough force to check her. She bowed her head, her arms still folded.

I spoke in a gentler voice. 'Look, what the hell's he been telling you?'

There was a long silence, then she murmured, 'If only I knew what to believe.'

'Try your instincts.'

'I seem to have mislaid them since I came here.' There was another silence, then she made a little sideways movement of her bent head.

Her voice was a shade less accusing. 'He said something foul, after last time. That you ... that you went to brothels and that Greek brothels weren't safe and that I mustn't let you kiss me again.'

'Is that where you think I've been?'

'I don't know where you've just been.'

'So you believe him?' She said nothing. I felt furious with Conchis; the damned gall he had, talking about the Hippocratic oath. I stared at the bent head, then spoke. 'I've had enough of this. I'm clearing out.'

I didn't really mean it, but I turned back towards the table as if I did. She said quickly, 'Please.' A tiny pause. 'I didn't say I believed it.'

I stopped and looked back at her. At last there was something less hostile in her eyes.

'But you're behaving as if you did.'

'I'm behaving as I am because I don't understand why he keeps telling me things he knows I can't believe.'

'If it was true, he ought to have warned you at the beginning.'

'That did occur to us.'

'Didn't you ask him why not?'

'He said he'd only just found out.' Then she said, in her gentlest voice yet, 'Please don't go away.'

Though she looked down in the end, she held my eyes long enough for me to believe the request was sincere. I went back in front of her.

'Are we still so convinced of his essential goodness?'

'In a kind of way, yes.' She added, 'In spite of everything.'

'I had the universal telepathy experience.'

'Yes, he told us.'

'He has hypnotized you?'

'Yes, several times.'

'He claims that's how he knows everything that's going on in your mind.'

That shocked her momentarily, she looked up, but then she gave a little puff of protest. 'It's ridiculous. I'd never let him do it. June's always been there, he insists on that himself. It's just a technique, actually rather a marvellous one, for helping you get into a part. She says he just talks and talks ... and somehow I absorb it all.'

'Is Julie just another part?'

'I'll show you my passport. I haven't got it with me, but … next time. I promise.'

'That last time … you might have warned me the schizophrenia thing was coming.'

'I did warn you something was coming. As much as I dared.'

I could feel our doubts and suspicions mounting once more, and I had to concede that yes, she had warned me in her fashion. There was something much more submissive about her now, on the defensive.

'All right … but whatever he isn't, he *is* a psychiatrist?'

'We've known that for some time.'

'So the whole thing here is along those lines?'

Again I was assessed. Then she looked sideways down at the tiles. 'He talks a lot about experimental situations. About the behaviour patterns of people faced with situations they don't understand. A lot about schizophrenia.' She shrugged. 'How people split themselves … ethically, all sorts of ways, before the unknown. One day he said something about the unknown being the great motivating factor in all human existence. He meant not knowing why we're here. Why we exist. Death. The after-life. All that.'

'But what does he actually want us to prove for him?'

She still looked at the ground; now shook her head.

'Honestly, we've tried and tried to pin him down, but he … he always comes up with the same argument – if we know the final purpose, what he expects, then obviously it will effect how we behave.' She let out a reluctant breath. 'It does have a sort of logic.'

'I've had that line. When I asked to know your supposed case-history.'

Her eyes met mine. 'It does exist. I've had to learn it by heart. What he's invented.'

'One thing's clear. For some reason he's feeding us every lie under the sun. But we don't have to be what he wants us to imagine. I'm no more a syphilitic than you're a schizophrenic.'

She bowed her head. 'I really didn't believe it.'

'I mean, if it's a part of his game, experiment, whatever it is, I don't care a damn how many lies he tells you about me. But I do care if you start believing them.'

There was a silence. Her eyes, it seemed almost against her will, rose to meet mine again. They said something beyond the present situation, in a much older language than that of words. A doubt dissolved in them, a candour was restored; and they tacitly accepted my judgment. For a fleeting moment there was the tiniest conceding curl, a wry admission, at the corners of her mouth. She lowered her eyes again, and then her hands slipped behind her back. Silence, a hint of little girl's penitence, a timid waiting to be forgiven.

This time it was a shared thing. The lips were warm and they moved under mine, and I was allowed to hold her body close, to know its curves, its slenderness ... and also to know, with a delicious certainty, that all was much less complicated than it seemed. She wanted to be kissed. The tips of our tongues touched, for a few seconds the embrace became tight, passionate. But then she abruptly pulled her mouth away and turned her head against my shoulder, though she stayed close against my body. I kissed the crown of her hair.

'I've nearly gone mad thinking about you.'

She whispered, 'I'd have died if you hadn't come today.'

'This is real. Whatever else is unreal.'

'That's what frightens me.'

'Why?'

'Wanting to be sure. But not being sure.'

I tightened my arms a little round her. 'Can't we meet tonight? Alone somewhere?' She was silent and I said quickly, 'For God's sake trust me. I'd never hurt you.'

She detached herself gently, took my hands, still looked down. 'It's not that. Just that there are more people about than you imagine.'

'Where do you sleep here?'

'There's a ... a sort of hiding-place.' She said quickly, 'I will show you. I promise.'

'Is there something planned for tonight?'

'He's telling us another supposed episode from his life. I'm going to join you after dinner.' She smiled up. 'And I honestly don't know what it is.'

'Then we could meet after that?'

'I'll try. But I can't ... '

'How about midnight? By the statue?'

'If I possibly can.' She glanced back towards the table, and pressed my hands. 'Now your tea's cold.'

We went back to the table and sat. I stopped her making any fresh tea, and we drank it tepid. I ate a sandwich or two, she smoked, and we talked. Like myself neither she nor her sister could understand the old man's paradoxical determination to lure us into his game, yet seeming preparedness to abandon it.

'Every time we show qualms, he offers to fly us straight back to England. One evening on the cruise we went at him – what *was* he doing, couldn't he *please* ... all the rest. In the end he was as near being upset as I've seen. We almost had to plead with him the next morning. Ask his forgiveness for being so nosy.'

'He's obviously using the same technique on all of us.'

'He keeps saying I must keep you at arm's length. Runs you down.' She flicked ash on the tiles, and smiled. 'He even apologized for your being so slow-witted the other day. I thought that was rather rich, considering you'd seen through the Lily thing in the first five seconds.'

'He hasn't tried to sell you the idea that I'm some kind of assistant – a young psychiatrist?'

I could see that that both surprised and unsettled her. She hesitated. 'No. But it had crossed our minds.' Then she added, 'Are you?'

I grinned. 'He told me just now that he'd extracted it from you under hypnosis. That it's what you suspect. We must watch it, Julie. He wants us on a quicksand.'

She put out her cigarette. 'And also to realize we are?'

'The last thing he can really want is to drive us apart.'

'Yes, that's what we feel.'

'So the enigma is why?' She gave a little nod of the head. 'And also why you have any remaining doubts about me.'

'No more than you must feel about me.'

'But you said it last time. We ought to behave as if we'd met naturally away from here. The more we know about each other the safer we are. The surer.' I gave her a small smile. 'So far as I'm concerned, the most incredible thing about you is that you got away from Cambridge unmarried.'

She looked down. 'I very nearly didn't.'

'But past now?'

'Yes. Very past.'

'There are so many things I want to know about the real you.'

'The real me's a lot less exciting than the imaginary one.'

'Where do you live at home?'

'Real home's Dorset. My mother. My father's dead.'

'What was he?'

But I never got an answer. She gave a lightning shocked look behind me. I twisted round. It was Conchis. He must have crept up on us, I hadn't heard a sound. In his hands he held poised a four-foot axe, exactly as if he were in two minds about raising and sinking it in my skull. I heard Julie's sharp voice.

'Maurice, that's not funny!'

He ignored her, staring at me.

'Have you had your tea?'

'Yes.'

'I have found a dead pine. I wish it chopped up.'

His voice was ludicrously abrupt and peremptory. I threw a glance back at Julie. She was on her feet and staring furiously at the old man. I knew at once that something was very wrong. It was as if I was no longer there. Conchis said, with a bizarrely grim irrelevance, 'Maria needs wood for her stove.'

Julie's voice was scalding, very nearly hysterical.

'You gave me a shock! How *could* you do that!'

I jerked another look back at her. Her eyes were dilated, as if mesmerized by Conchis. She almost spat her next words at him.

'I *hate* you!'

'My dear, you are over-excited. Go and rest.'

'No!'

'I insist.'

'I *hate* you.'

It was said with a mixture of venom and despair that sent all my newly acquired confidence in her crashing to the ground. I looked in a panic from one face to the other, trying to see some sign of collusion. Conchis lowered the axe.

'I insist, Julie.'

There was a brief battle of wills over my head. Then abruptly she turned and kicked into the espadrilles by the doors of the music-room. As she came back past the table – through all this she had not given me one look – apparently to go away from the house, she suddenly snatched up the cup of tea in front of me and dashed it in my face. There was hardly any liquid left, and it was nearly cold, but the gesture had a terrible infantile spitefulness. It took me totally by surprise. She had moved on at once. Conchis spoke sharply.

'Julie!'

She stopped at the eastern edge of the colonnade, but kept a resentful back turned to us.

'You are behaving like a spoilt child. That was unforgivable.' She did not move. He took a few steps towards her and spoke in a lower voice, but I heard his words. 'Actresses may show temperament. But not to innocent bystanders. Now go and apologize to our guest.'

She wavered, then swivelled round and marched back past him to where I sat. Her cheeks were faintly flushed and her eyes still avoided mine. She stopped in front of me, but stared mutinously at the ground. I searched her face, her downcast eyes, then in desperation looked past her at Conchis.

'You did give us a shock.'

Unseen by her, he raised a pacifying hand for my benefit, then addressed her back.

'We await your apology, Julie.'

Suddenly her eyes were on mine.

'I hate *you*, too!'

The voice was petulant, exactly that of a spoilt child. But miraculously, or so it seemed to me, her right eyelid fluttered: I was not to believe a word of all this little scene. I had difficulty in keeping a straight face. Meanwhile she had turned and was walking past the old man again. He reached out a detaining hand, but she brushed it angrily aside and ran down the steps and then across the gravel; after some twenty yards she stopped running and her hands rose to her face, as if in self-dismay, as she went on at a fast walk. Conchis turned back to me and smiled at the face of concern I had managed to assume.

'You must not take that tantrum too seriously. A part of her is always on the brink of acutely regressive behaviour. She was pretending a little.'

'She could have fooled me.'

'That was her hope. To demonstrate what a tyrant I am.'

'And a scandal-monger. Or so it seems.' He eyed me. I said, 'I don't mind a drop of tea in my face. But I draw the line at being given syphilis. Especially when you know the facts about that.'

He smiled. 'But you have surely guessed why?'

'Not yet.'

'I also told her you had met your friend last week. Perhaps that is a clue?' He must have seen by my face that it wasn't. He hesitated, then offered me the axe to carry. 'Come. I will explain.'

I stood and took the axe and we set off back towards the gate.

'There must arrive a time this summer when all this is ended. I must therefore provide for, how shall I put it, exits that will not cause Julie too much pain. This false information I provide about you offers two such exits. She knows there is someone else in your life. That perhaps you are not such a desirable young man as you seem at first sight. In addition schizophrenics, as you have just seen, are emotionally unstable. I know I can trust you not to take sexual advantage of a very sick girl. But it will help relieve the situation for you if there are additional obstacles implanted in her mind.'

I felt a purr inside me. That one shadow of a wink had made all his deceptions hollow – and tolerable; it also allowed me to deceive in return.

'On that level ... of course. I understand.'

'That is why I interrupted your *tête-à-tête*. She needs little set-backs, problems to overcome. As people with broken limbs need exercise.' He said, 'And how did you find her, Nicholas?'

'Very suspicious of me. As you said.'

'But you managed ... ?'

'I was beginning to.'

'Good. Tomorrow I am going to disappear. Or at least I shall lead her to believe that. You will have all day with her in apparent solitude. We will see what she makes of it.'

'I'm delighted you trust me so much.'

He touched my arm. 'I confess also that I did wish to provoke a somewhat excessive reaction in her. For your benefit. In case you had any remaining doubts about her abnormality.'

'I have none now. Whatever.'

He inclined his head, and I grinned in my mind. We came to the tree, which was already on its side. He wanted it hacked into manageable lengths. Hermes would carry the wood to the house, I had only to pile it in readiness. He went off as soon as I started swinging the axe. I enjoyed the work much better than the previous time. The smaller stems were so dry and brittle that they broke at one stroke; and I felt each stroke was symbolic. Something more than wood was being hewn into manageable lengths. As I neatly stacked the branches, I felt I was also beginning to neatly stack the mystery of Bourani and Conchis. I was going to discover all about Julie, and I had already discovered the essential thing: that she was on my side. In some way he was using us as personifications of his irony, as his partners in exploring ambivalence. Every truth in his world was a sort of lie; and every lie a sort of truth. Like Julie I began, despite the traps and tricks and their seeming malice, to accept his fundamental benevolence. I remembered that smiling stone head he had shown me: his ultimate truth.

He was in any case far too intelligent to expect us not to see through the surface aspect of his masques; secretly he must want us to … and as for whatever deeper purpose, inner meaning they had, I was content to wait now.

Swinging the axe in the afternoon sun, enjoying the physical exercise, feeling in command again, thinking of midnight, tomorrow, Julie, the kiss, Alison forgotten, I was content to wait all summer if he wanted; and for the summer itself to wait all time.

44

She came towards us in the lamplight, towards the table in the southeast corner of the upstairs terrace. It was the antithesis of her first entrance there, the night I had formally met her as Lily. She wore almost the same clothes as that afternoon … the same white trousers, though she had changed into a white shirt, slightly loose-sleeved, as some sort of concession to evening formality. A coral necklace, the red belt and espadrilles; a hint of eye-shadow, a touch of lipstick. Conchis and I stood for her. She hesitated in front of me, then gave me a charged look, faintly desperate, staring.

'I feel awful about this afternoon. Will you please forgive me?'

'Forget it. It was nothing.'

She glanced then at Conchis, as if to see whether she had his approval. He smiled, indicated the chair between us. But she reached where her white shirt was buttoned and held out a sprig of jasmine.

'A peace offering.'

I smelt it. 'That's sweet of you.'

She sat. Conchis poured her a cup of coffee, while I offered her a cigarette and then lit it. She seemed chastened, and carefully avoided my eyes after that first look.

Conchis said, 'Nicholas and I have been discussing religion.'

It was true. He had brought a Bible to table, with two reference slips in it; and we had got on to God and no-God.

'Oh.' She stared down at her coffee, then raised the cup and sipped; but at the same time I felt a minute pressure on my foot, under the long table-cloth.

'Nicholas calls himself an agnostic. But then he went on to say that he does not care.'

She raised her eyes politely at me. 'No?'

'More important things.'

She touched the small spoon in the saucer beside her cup. 'I should have thought nothing was more important.'

'Than one's attitude to what one will never know? It seems to me a waste of time.' I felt for her foot, but it had disappeared. She leant forward and picked up the box of matches I had left on the table between us, and shook out a dozen matchsticks on the white cloth.

'Perhaps you're afraid to think about God?'

She was not being natural, and I realized that this was some kind of pre-arranged scene ... she was saying what Conchis wanted.

'One can't *think* about what cannot be known.'

'You never *think* about tomorrow? About next year?'

'Of course. I can make reasonable prophecies about them.'

She played with the matches, pushing them idly into patterns with her fingers. I watched her mouth, wished I could end the cold dialogue.

'I can make reasonable prophecies about God.'

'Such as?'

'He is very intelligent.'

'How do you know that?'

'Because I don't understand Him. Why He is, who He is, or how He is. And Maurice tells me I am quite intelligent. I think God must be very intelligent to be so much more intelligent than I am. To give me no clues. No certainties. No sights. No reasons. No motives.' She stared briefly up at me from her matches; her eyes had a kind of dry query that I recognized from Conchis.

'Very intelligent – or very unkind?'

'Very wise. If I prayed, I'd ask God never to reveal Himself to me. Because if He did I should know that He was not God. But a liar.'

Now she glanced at Conchis, who was facing out to sea; waiting for her, I thought, to finish her part of the act. But then I saw her forefinger silently tap the table twice. Her eyes flicked sideways again at Conchis and then back to me. I looked down. She had laid two matches diagonally across each other and two others beside them: XII. She avoided my suddenly comprehending eyes; and then, pushing the matchsticks into a little heap, she leant back out of the pool of light from the lamp and turned to Conchis. 'You're very silent, Maurice. Am I right?'

'I sympathize with you, Nicholas.' He smiled at me. 'I felt very much as you do when I was older and more experienced than you are. Neither of us has the intuitive humanity of womankind, so we are not to blame.' He said it quite without gallantry, as a simple statement. Julie would not meet my eyes. Her face was in shadow. 'But then I had an experience that led me to understand what Julie has just said to you. Just then she paid us the compliment of making God male. But I think she knows, as all true women do, that all profound definitions of God are essentially definitions of the mother. Of giving things. Sometimes the strangest gifts. Because the religious instinct is really the instinct to define whatever gives each situation.'

He settled back in his chair.

'I think I told you that when modern history – because that chauffeur stood for democracy, equality, progress – struck de Deukans down in 1922 I was abroad. I was in fact in the remote north of Norway, in pursuit of birds – or to be more exact, bird-sounds. You know perhaps that countless rare birds breed up there on the Arctic tundra. I am lucky. I have perfect pitch. I had by that time published one or two papers on the problems of accurately notating birds' cries and songs. I had even begun a small scientific correspondence with men like Dr Van Oort of Leiden, the American A. A. Saunders, the Alexanders in England. So in the summer of 1922 I left Paris for three months in the Arctic.'

Julie shifted slightly and I felt another small pressure on my foot; a very soft, naked pressure. I was wearing sandals myself, and without distracting Conchis, I forced the heel of the left one against the ground until I was free of it; then felt a bare sole slide gently down the side of my own naked foot. Her toes curled and brushed the top of mine. It was innocent, but erotic. I tried to get my foot on top of hers, but this time the pressure was reproving. We could stay in contact, but no more. Meanwhile Conchis had gone on.

'On my way north a professor at Oslo University told me of an educated farmer who lived in the heart of the vast fir-forests that run from Norway and Finland into Russia. It seemed this man had some knowledge of birds. He sent migration records to my professor, who had never actually met him. The fir-forest had several rare species I wanted to hear, so I decided to visit this farmer. As soon as I had ornithologically exhausted the tundra of the extreme north I crossed the Varangerfjord and went to the little town of Kirkenes. From there, armed with my letter of introduction, I set out for Seidevarre.

'It took me four days to cover ninety miles. There was a road through the forest for the first twenty, but after that I had to travel by rowing-boat from isolated farm to farm along the river Pasvik. Endless forest. Huge, dark firs for mile after mile after mile. The river as broad and silent as a lake in a fairy-tale. Like a mirror unlooked-in since time began.

'On the fourth day two men rowed me all day, and we did not pass a single farm or see a single sign of man. Only the silver-blue sheen of the endless river, the endless trees. Towards evening we came in sight of a house and a clearing. Two small meadows carpeted with buttercups, like slabs of gold in the sombre forest. We had arrived at Seidevarre.

'Three buildings stood facing each other. There was a small wooden farmhouse by the water's edge, half hidden among a grove of silver birches. Then a long turf-roofed barn. And a storehouse built on stilts to keep the rats out. A boat lay moored to a post by the house, and there were fishing nets hung out to dry.

'The farmer was a smallish man with quick brown eyes – about fifty years old, I suppose. I jumped ashore and he read my letter. A woman some five years younger appeared and stood behind him. She had a severe but striking face, and though I could not understand what she and the farmer were saying I knew she did not want me to stay there. I noticed she ignored the two boatmen. And they in their turn gave her curious looks, as if she was as much a stranger to them as myself. Very soon she went back indoors.

'However, the farmer bade me welcome. As I had been told, he spoke halting, but quite good, English. I asked him where he had learnt it. And he said that as a young man he had trained as a veterinary surgeon – and had studied for a year in London. This made me look at him again. I could not imagine how he had ended up in that remotest corner of Europe.

'The woman was not, as I expected, his wife, but his sister-in-law. She had two children, both in their late adolescence. Neither the children nor their mother spoke any English, and without being rude, she made it silently clear to me that I was there against her choice. But Gustav Nygaard and I took to each other on sight. He showed me his books on birds, his notebooks. He was an enthusiast. I was an enthusiast.

'Of course one of the early questions I asked concerned his brother. Nygaard seemed embarrassed. He said he had gone away. Then as if to explain and to stop any further questions, he said, "Many years ago."

'The farmhouse was very small and a space was cleared in the hay-loft above the barn for my camp-bed. I took my meals with the family. Nygaard talked only with me. His sister-in-law remained silent. Her chlorotic daughter the same. I think the inhibited boy would have liked to join in, but his uncle could rarely be bothered to translate what we said. Those first days none of this little Norwegian domestic situation seemed important to me, because the beauty of the place and the extraordinary richness of its bird life overwhelmed me. I spent each day looking and listening to the rare duck and geese, the divers, the wild swans, that abounded in all the inlets and lagoons along the shore. It was a place where nature was triumphant over man. Not savagely triumphant, as one may feel in the tropics. But calmly, nobly triumphant. It is sentimental to talk of a landscape having a soul, but that one possessed a stronger character than any other I have seen, before or since. It ignored man. Man was nothing in it. It was not so bleak that he could not survive in it – the river was full of salmon and other fish and the summer was long and warm enough to grow potatoes and a crop of hay – but so vast that he could not equal or tame it. I make it sound forbidding, perhaps. However, from being rather frightened by the solitude when I first arrived at the farm, I realized in two or three days that I had fallen in love with it. Above all, with its silences. The evenings. Such peace. Sounds like the splash of a duck landing on the water, the scream of an osprey, came across miles with a clarity that was first incredible – and then mysterious because, like a cry in an empty house, it seemed to make the silence, the peace, more intense. Almost as if sounds were there to distinguish the silence, and not the reverse.

'I think it was on the third day that I discovered their secret. The very first morning Nygaard had pointed out a long tree-covered spit of land that ran into the river some half a mile south of the farm, and asked me not to go on it. He said he had hung many nesting-boxes there and started a thriving colony of smew and goldeneye, and he did not want them disturbed. Of course I agreed, though it seemed late, even at that latitude, for duck to be sitting their eggs.

'I then noticed that when we had our evening meal, we were never all present. On the first evening, the girl was away. On the second the boy appeared only when we had finished – even though I had seen him sitting gloomily by the shore only a few minutes before Nygaard came and called me to eat. The third day it so happened that I came back late myself to the farm. As I was walking back through the firs some way inland I stopped to watch a bird. I did not mean to hide, but I was hidden.'

Conchis paused, and I remembered how he had been standing two weeks before, when I left Julie; like a pre-echo of this.

'Suddenly about two hundred yards away I saw the girl going through the trees by the shore. In one hand she held a pail covered with a cloth, in the other a milk-can. I remained behind a tree and watched her walk on. To my surprise she followed the shore and went on to the forbidden promontory. I watched her through glasses until I saw her disappear.

'Nygaard disliked having to sit in the same room with both his relations and myself. Their disapproving silence irked him. So he took to coming with me when I went to my "bedroom" in the barn, to smoke a pipe and talk. That evening I told him I had seen his niece carrying what must have been food and drink on to the point. I asked him who was living there. He made no effort to hide the truth. The fact was this. His brother was living there. And he was insane.'

I glanced from Conchis to Julie and back; but neither of them showed any sign of noticing the oddness of this weaving of the past and the alleged present. I pressed against her foot. She returned the touch, but then moved her foot away. The story caught her, she was not to be distracted.

'I asked at once if a doctor had ever seen him. Nygaard shook his head, as if his opinion of doctors, at least in this case, was not very high. I reminded him that I was a doctor myself. After a silence he said, "I think we are all insane here." He got up then and went out. However, it was only to return a few minutes later. He had fetched a small sack. He shook its contents out on my camp-bed. I saw a litter of rounded stones and flints, of shards of primitive pottery with bands of incised ornament, and I knew I was looking at a collection of Stone Age articles. I asked him where he had found them. He said, at Seidevarre. And he then explained that the farm took its name from the point of land. That Seidevarre was a Lapp name, and meant "hill of the holy stone", the dolmen. The spit had once been a holy place for the Polmak Lapps, who combine a fisher culture with the reindeer-herding one. But even they had only superseded far earlier cultures.

'Originally the farm had been no more than a summer *dacha*, a hunting and fishing lodge, built by his father – an eccentric priest, who by a fortunate marriage had got enough money to indulge his multiple interests. A fierce old Lutheran pastor in one aspect. An upholder of the traditional Norwegian ways of rural life in another. A natural historian and scholar of some local eminence. And a fanatical lover of hunting and fishing – of returning to the wild. Both his sons had, at least in youth, revolted against his religious side. Henrik, the elder, had gone to sea, a ship's engineer. Gustav had taken to veterinary work. The father had died, and left almost all his money to the Church. While staying with Gustav, who had by then begun to practise in Trondheim, Henrik met Ragna, and married her. I think he went to sea again for a short time, but very soon after his marriage he went through a nervous crisis, gave up his career, and retired to Seidevarre.

'All went well for a year or two, but then his behaviour grew stranger and stranger. Finally Ragna wrote Gustav a letter. What it said made him catch the next boat north. He found that for nearly nine months she had managed the farm single-handed – what is more, with two babies to look after. He returned briefly to Trondheim to clear up his affairs, and from then on assumed the responsibility of the farm and his brother's family.

'He said, "I had no choice." I had already suspected it in the strain between them. He was, or had been, in love with Ragna. Now they were locked together more tightly than love can ever lock – in a state of total unrequitedness on his side and one of total fidelity on hers.

'I wanted to know what form the brother's madness had taken. And then, nodding at the stones, Gustav went back to Seidevarre. To begin with, his brother had taken to going there for short periods to "meditate". Then he had become convinced that one day he – or at any rate the place – was to be visited by God. For twelve years he had lived as a hermit, waiting for this visit.

'He never returned to the farm. Barely a hundred words had passed between the brothers those last two years. Ragna never went near him. He was of course dependent for all his needs on them. Especially since, by a *surcroît de malheur*, he was almost blind. Gustav believed that he no longer fully realized what they did for him. He took it as manna fallen from heaven, without question or human gratitude. I asked Gustav when he had last spoken to his brother – remember we were then at the beginning of August. And he said shamefacedly but with a hopeless shrug, "In May."

'I now found myself more interested in the four people at the farm than in my birds. I looked at Ragna again, and thought I saw in her a tragic dimension. She had fine eyes. Euripidean eyes, as hard and dark as obsidian. I felt sorry for the children too. Brought up, like bacilli in a test-tube, on a culture of such pure Strindbergian melancholia. Never to be able to escape the situation. To have no neighbours within twenty miles. No village within fifty. I realized why Gustav had welcomed my arrival. In a way he had kept his sanity, his sense of perspective. *His* insanity, of course, lay in his doomed love for his sister-in-law.

'Like all young men I saw myself as a catalyst, as a solver of situations. And I had my medical training, my knowledge of the still then not ubiquitously familiar gentleman from Vienna. I recognized Henrik's syndrome at once – it was a textbook example of anal over-training. With an obsessive father identification. The whole exacerbated by the solitude in which they lived. It seemed as clear to me as the behaviour of the birds I watched each day. Now that the secret was revealed, Gustav was not unreluctant to talk. And the next evening he told me more, which confirmed my diagnosis.

'It seemed Henrik had always loved the sea. This was why he had studied engineering. But gradually he realized that he did not like machinery, and he did not like other men. It began with miso-mechanism. The misanthropism took longer to develop, and his marriage was probably at least partly an attempt to prevent its development. He had always loved space, solitude. That is why he loved the sea, and no doubt why he came to hate being cramped aboard a ship, in the grease and clangour of an engine-room. If he could have sailed round the world alone ... But instead he came to live at Seidevarre where the land was like the sea. His children were born. And then his eyesight began to fail. He knocked glasses over at table, stumbled over roots in the forest. His mania began.

'Henrik was a Jansenist, he believed in a divine cruelty. In his system, he was elect, especially chosen to be punished and tormented. To sweat out his youth in bad ships in filthy climates so that his reward, his paradise should be snatched out of his hands when he came to enjoy it. He could not see the objective truth, that destiny is hazard: nothing is unjust to all, though many things may be unjust to each. This sense of God's injustice smouldered in him. He refused to go to hospital to have his eyes looked at. He became red-hot for lack of the oil of objectivity, and so his soul both burnt in him and burnt him. He did not go to Seidevarre to meditate. But to hate.

'Needless to say, I was eager to have a look at this religious maniac. And not altogether out of medical curiosity, because I had grown to like Gustav very much. I even tried to explain to him what psychiatry was, but he seemed uninterested. It is best left alone, was all he said.

I promised him still to avoid the promontory. And there the matter was left.

'One windy day soon after, I had gone three or four miles south along the river when I heard someone calling my name. It was Gustav in his boat. I stood out from the trees and he rowed towards me. I thought he had been netting grayling, but he had come to find me. He wanted me after all to look at his brother. We were to remain hidden, to stalk and watch Henrik like a bird. Gustav explained that it was the right day. Like many afflicted with near-blindness, his brother had developed very sharp hearing and so the wind was in our favour.

'I got into the boat and we rowed to a little beach near the end of the point. Gustav disappeared and then came back. He said Henrik was waiting near the *seide*, the Lapp dolmen. It was safe for us to visit his hut. We made our way through the trees up a small slope, passed over to the southern side, and there, where the trees were thickest, in a depression, was a curious cabin. It had been sunk into the ground, so that only the turf roof showed on three sides. On the fourth, where the ground fell away, there was a door and a small window. A stack of wood lay beside the house. But no other sign of any employment.

'Gustav made me go in while he stayed on watch outside. It was very dark. As bare as a monastic cell. A truckle bed. A rough table. A tin with a bundle of candles. The only concession to comfort, an old stove. There was no carpet, no curtain. The lived-in parts of the room were fairly clean. But the corners were full of refuse. Old leaves, dirt, spiders' webs. An odour of unwashed clothes. There was one book, on the table by the one small window. A huge black Bible, with enormous print. Beside it, a magnifying glass. Pools of candle-wax.

'I lit one of the candles to look at the ceiling. Five or six beams that supported the roof had been scraped pale and along them had been carved two long brown-lettered texts from the Bible. They were in Norwegian, of course, but I noted down the references. And on a cross-beam facing the door there was another sentence in Norwegian.

'When I came out into the sunlight again I asked Gustav what the Norwegian sentence meant. He said "Henrik Nygaard, cursed by

God, wrote us in his own blood in the year 1912." That was ten years before. Now I will read you the other two texts he had cut and then stained in with blood.'

Conchis opened the book beside him.

'One was from Exodus: *They encamped in the edge of the wilderness. And the Lord went before them by day in a pillar of cloud, and by night in a pillar of fire.* The other was an echo of the same text in the Apocrypha. Here. From Esdras: *I gave you light in a pillar of fire, yet have you forgotten me, saith the Lord.*

'These texts reminded me of Montaigne. You know he had forty-two proverbs and quotations painted across the beams of his study roof. But there was none of the sanity of Montaigne in Henrik. More the intensity of Pascal's famous *Mémorial* – those two crucial hours in his life that he could afterwards describe only by one word: *feu*. Sometimes rooms seem to imbibe the spirit of the people who have lived in them – think of Savonarola's cell in Florence. And this was such a place. One did not have to know the occupant's past. The suffering, the agony, the mental sickness were as palpable as tumours.

'I left the cabin and we went cautiously towards the *seide*. It came in sight through the trees. It was not a true dolmen, but simply a tall boulder that wind and frost had weathered into a picturesque shape. Gustav pointed. Some fifty yards away, on the far side of a clump of birches, hidden from the *seide*, stood a man. I focused my glasses on him. He was taller than Gustav, a thin man with rough-cut dark-grey hair and beard and an aquiline nose. He turned by chance and faced us and I had a full view of his gaunt face. What surprised me was its fierceness. A severity that was almost savagery. I had never seen a face that expressed such violent determination never to compromise, never to deviate. Never to smile. And what eyes! They were slightly exophthalmic, of the most startling cold blue. Beyond any doubt, insane eyes. Even at fifty yards I could see that. He wore an old indigo Lapp smock with faded red braid round its edges. Dark trousers and heavy snout-ended Lapp boots. And in his hand he held a staff.

'I watched this rare specimen of humanity for some time. I had expected to see some furtive creature, someone who mumbled to himself as he crept through the trees. Not this fierce blinded hawk of a man. Gustav nudged my arm again. The nephew appeared by the *seide* with a bucket and the milk-can. He put them down, picked up another empty bucket that must have been set there by Henrik, looked round, and then cried something in Norwegian. Not very loud. He evidently knew where his father was, for he faced the clump of birches. Then he disappeared back through the trees. After five minutes Henrik began to walk up towards the *seide*. Quite confidently, but feeling his way with the end of the staff. He picked up the bucket and can, placing the staff under his arm, and then started back along the familiar path to his cabin. The path brought him within twenty yards of the birch-scrub behind which we were standing. Just as he passed us I heard high overhead one of the frequent sounds of the river, a very beautiful one, like the calling of Tutankhamen's trumpets. The flight cry of a black-throated diver. Henrik stopped, although the sound must have been as banal to him as the wind in the trees. He stood there, his face turned up towards the sky. Without emotion, without despair. But listening, waiting, as if it might be the first notes of the herald angels telling him the great visit was near.

'He went on out of sight and I returned to the farmstead with Gustav. I did not know what to say. I did not like to disappoint him, to admit defeat. I had my own foolish pride. After all, I was a founder-member of the Society of Reason. In the end I concocted a plan. I would visit Henrik alone. I would tell him I was a doctor and that I would like to look at his eyes. And while I looked at his eyes, I would try to look at his mind.

'I arrived outside Henrik's hut at midday the next morning. It was raining slightly. A grey day. I knocked on the cabin door and stood back a few steps. There was a long pause. Then he appeared, dressed exactly as he had been the evening before. Face to face and close to him I was struck more than ever by his fierceness. It was very difficult to believe that he was nearly blind, because his eyes had such a pale, staring blueness. But now I was close to him I could see that it was a poorly focused stare; and I could also see the characteristic opacity of cataract in both eyes. He must have been very shocked, but he gave no sign of it. I asked him if he understood English – I knew from Gustav that he in fact did, but I wanted him to answer. All he did was to raise his staff, as if to keep me at bay. It was a warning rather than a threatening gesture. So I took it to mean that I could go on provided that I kept my distance.

'I explained that I was a doctor, that I was interested in birds, I had come to Seidevarre to study them – and so on. I spoke very slowly, remembering that he could not have heard the language for fifteen years or more. He listened to me without expression. I began to talk about modern methods of treatment for cataract. I was sure that a hospital could do something for him. All the time, not a single word. At last I fell silent.

'He turned and went back into the hut. He left the door open, so I waited. Suddenly he appeared again. In his hand he held what I held, Nicholas, when I came on you this afternoon. A long axe. But I knew at once that he was no more thinking of chopping wood than a berserk about to enter battle. He hesitated a moment, then rushed at me, swinging the axe up as he ran. If he had not been nearly blind he would beyond any doubt have killed me. As it was I sprang back only just in time. The axe head went deep into the soil. The two moments he took to jerk it free gave me the time to run.

'He came stumbling after me across the little clearing in front of the hut. I ran some thirty yards into the trees, but he stopped by the first one. At twenty feet he probably could not have told me from a tree-trunk. He stood with the axe poised in his hands, listening, straining his eyes. He must have known I was watching him, for without warning he turned and swung the axe with all his strength into a silver birch just in front of him. It was a fair-sized tree. But it shook from top to bottom with the blow. And that was his answer. I was too frightened by the violence of the man to move. He stared a moment into the trees where I stood and then turned and walked into the hut, leaving the axe where it had struck.

'I went back to the farmstead a wiser young man. It seemed incredible to me that a man should reject medicine, reason, science so violently. But I felt that this man would have rejected everything else about me as well if he had known it – the pursuit of pleasure, of music, of reason, of medicine. That axe would have driven right through the skull of all our pleasure-orientated civilization. Our science, our psycho-analysis. To him all that was not the great meeting was what the Buddhists call *lilas* – the futile pursuit of triviality. And of course to have been concerned about his blindness would have been for him more futility. He wanted to be blind. It made it more likely that one day he would see.

'Some days afterwards I was due to leave. On my last evening Gustav kept me talking very late. I had said nothing to him of my visit. It was a windless night, but in August up there it begins to get cold. I went out of the barn to urinate when Gustav left. There was a brilliant moon, but in one of those late summer skies of the extreme north, when day lingers even in the darkness and the sky has strange depths. Nights when new worlds seem always about to begin. I heard from across the water, from Seidevarre, a cry. For a moment I thought it must be some bird, but then I knew it could only be Henrik. I looked towards the farmstead. I could see Gustav had stopped, was standing outside, listening. Another cry came. It was dragged out, the cry of someone who is calling a great distance. I walked across the grass to Gustav. "Is he in trouble?" I asked. He shook his head, and remained staring out at the dark shadow of Seidevarre across the moon-grey water. What was he calling? Gustav said, "Do you hear me? I am here." And then the two cries, with an interval between, came again and I could make out the Norwegian words. "*Hører du mig? Jeg er her.*" Henrik was calling to God.

'I told you how sounds carried at Seidevarre. Each time he called the cry seemed to stretch out infinitely, through the forest, over the water, into the stars. Then there were receding echoes. One or two shrill cries from distant disturbed birds. There was a noise from the farmstead behind us. I looked up, and saw a white figure at one of the upper windows – whether Ragna or her daughter, I could not see. It was as if we were all under a spell.

'To break it, I began to question Gustav. Did he often call like this? He said, not often – three or four times a year, when there was no wind and a full moon. Did he ever cry other phrases? Gustav thought back. Yes – "I am waiting" was one. "I am purified", another. "I am prepared", another. But the two phrases we had heard were the ones he used most.

'I turned to Gustav and asked him if we could go again and see what Henrik was doing. Without answering, he nodded, and we set off. It took us some ten or fifteen minutes to get to the base of the point. Every so often we heard the cries. We came to the *seide*, but the cries were still some way off. Gustav said, "He is at the end." We passed the cabin, and walking as quietly as we could, made our way to the end of the point. At last we came through the trees.

'Beyond them there ran out a beach. Some thirty or forty yards of shingle. The river narrowed a little and the point took the force of what current there was. Even on a night as calm as that there was a murmur over the shallow stones. Henrik was standing at the very tip of the shingle spit, in about a foot of water. He was facing out to the north-east, to where the river widened. The moonlight covered it in a grey satin sheen. Out in midstream there were long low banks of mist. As we watched, he called. *"Hører du mig?"* With great force. As if to someone several miles away, on the invisible far bank. A long pause. Then, *"Jeg er her."* I trained my glasses on him. He was standing legs astride, his staff in his hand, biblically. There was silence. A black silhouette in the glittering current.

'Then we heard Henrik say one word. Much more quietly. It was *"Takk."* The Norwegian for "thanks". I watched him. He stepped back a pace or two out of the water, and knelt on the shingle. We heard the sound of the stones as he moved. He still faced the same way. His hands by his side. It was not an attitude of prayer, but a watching on his knees. Something was very close to him, as visible to him as Gustav's dark head, the trees, the moonlight on the leaves around us, was to me. I would have given ten years of my life to have been able to look out there to the north, from inside his mind. I did not know what he was seeing, but I knew it was something of such power, such mystery, that it explained all. And of course Henrik's secret dawned on me, almost like some reflection of the illumination that shone over him. He was not waiting to meet God. He was meeting God; and had been meeting him probably for many years. He was not waiting for some certainty. He lived in it.

'Up to this point in my life you will have realized that my whole approach was scientific, medical, classifying. I was conditioned by a kind of ornithological approach to man. I thought in terms of species, behaviours, observations. Here for the first time in my life I was unsure of my standards, my beliefs, my prejudices. I knew the man out there on the point was having an experience beyond the scope of all my science and all my reason, and I knew that my science and reason would always be defective until they could comprehend what was happening in Henrik's mind. I knew that Henrik was seeing a pillar of fire out there over the water, I knew that there was no pillar of fire there, that it could be demonstrated that the only pillar of fire was in Henrik's mind.

'But in a flash, as of lightning, all our explanations, all our classifications and derivations, our aetiologies, suddenly appeared to me like a thin net. That great passive monster, reality, was no longer dead, easy to handle. It was full of a mysterious vigour, new forms, new possibilities. The net was nothing, reality burst through it. Perhaps something telepathic passed between Henrik and myself. I do not know.

'That simple phrase, I do not know, was my own pillar of fire. For me, too, it revealed a world beyond that in which I lived. For me, too, it brought a new humility akin to fierceness. For me too a profound mystery. For me too a sense of the vanity of so many things our age considers important. I do not say I should not have arrived at such an insight one day. But in that night I bridged a dozen years. Whatever else, I know that.

'In a short time we saw Henrik walk back into the trees. I could not see his face. But I think the fierceness it wore in daylight was the fierceness that came from his contact with the pillar of fire. Perhaps for him the pillar of fire was no longer enough, and in that sense he was still waiting to meet God. Living is an eternal wanting more, in the coarsest grocer and in the sublimest mystic. But of one thing I am certain. If he still lacked God, he had the Holy Spirit.

'The next day I left. I said goodbye to Ragna. There was no lessening of her hostility. I think that unlike Gustav she had divined her husband's secret, that any attempt to cure him would kill him. Gustav and his nephew rowed me the twenty miles north to the next farm. We shook hands, we promised to write. I could offer no consolation and I do not think he wanted any. There are situations in which consolation only threatens the equilibrium that time has instituted. And so I returned to France.'

45

Julie glanced at me, as if asking tacitly whether this didn't prove that we must ultimately be in safe hands. I didn't dispute it, and not only because I could see she didn't want me to. I half expected to hear a voice calling in Norwegian from Moutsa, or to see some brilliantly contrived pillar of fire rise out of the trees. But there was a long silence; only the crickets cheeping.

'You never went back there?'

'Sometimes to return is a vulgarity.'

'But you must have been curious to know how it all ended?'

'Not at all. Perhaps one day, Nicholas, you will have an experience that means a great deal to you.' I could hear no irony in his voice, but it was implicit. 'You will then realize what I mean when I say that some experiences so possess you that the one thing you cannot tolerate is the thought of their not being in some way for ever present. Seidevarre is a place I do not want time to touch. So I am not interested in what it is now. Or what they are now. If they still are.'

Julie spoke. 'But you said you would write to Gustav?'

'So I did. He wrote to me. He wrote for two years with regularity, at least once a season. But he never referred to what interests you – except to say that the situation was unchanged. His letters were full of ornithological notes. They became very dull reading, because I had lost most of my interest in the classifying aspects of natural history. Our letters became very infrequent. I think I had a Christmas card from him in 1926 or 1927. Since then, no sound. He is dead now. Henrik is dead, Ragna is dead.'

'What happened to you when you got back to France?'

'I saw Henrik meet his pillar of fire at about midnight on August 17th, 1922. The fire at Givray-le-Duc began at the same hour of the same night.'

Julie was more nakedly incredulous than I was. He sat turned away, and our eyes met. She lowered heis with a little grimace, like someone disappointed.

said, 'You're not suggesting ... '

'I am suggesting nothing. There was no connection between the events. No connection is possible. Or rather, I am the connection, I am whatever meaning the coincidence has.'

There was an unusual shade of vanity in his voice, as if in fact he believed he had in some way precipitated both events and their common timing. I sensed that the coincidence was not literally true, but something he had invented, which held another, metaphorical, meaning; that the two episodes were linked in significance, that we were to use both to interpret him. Just as the story of de Deukans had thrown light on Conchis himself, this threw light on the hypnosis – that image he had used, '*reality breaking through the thin net of science*' ... I had myself recalled something too similar from the hypnosis for it to be coincidence. Everywhere in the masque, these inter-relationships, threads between circumstance.

He turned parentally to Julie. 'My dear, I think it is your bedtime.' I glanced at my watch. It was just after eleven. Julie gave a little shrug, as if the question of bedtime was unimportant.

She said, 'Why have you told us this, Maurice?'

'All that is past possesses our present. Seidevarre possesses Bourani. Whatever happens here now, whatever governs what happens, is partly, no, is essentially what happened thirty years ago in that Norwegian forest.'

He spoke to her then as he often spoke to me. The pretence that Julie was basically any different, any more understanding of what was going on, was wearing very thin. I knew he was initiating another shift in our relationships, or the conventions that ruled them. In some way we were both cast now as his students, his disciples. I remembered that favourite Victorian picture of the bearded Elizabethan seaman pointing to sea and telling a story to two goggle-eyed little boys. Another surreptitious look passed between Julie and myself. It was clear to both of us that we were moving into new territory. Then I felt her foot: a fleeting touch like a snatched kiss.

'Well. I suppose I must go.' The mask of formality was reassumed. We all stood. 'Maurice, that was so remarkable and interesting.'

She moved and kissed him briefly on the cheek. Then she offered me her hand. One shadow of conspiracy in her eyes, one minute extra pressure of her fingers. She turned to go; stopped.

'I'm sorry. I forgot to replace your matches.'

'It doesn't matter.'

Conchis and I sat again, in silence. A few moments later I heard light footsteps going across the gravel towards the sea. I smiled across the table at his unrevealing face. The pupils of his eyes seemed black in their clear whites – a mask that watched me, watched me.

'No illustrations in the text tonight?'

'Does it need them?'

'No. You told it ... very well.'

He shrugged dismissively, then waved his arm briefly round: at house, at trees, at sea.

'This is the illustration. Things as they are. In my small domaine.'

At any point before that day I should have argued with him. His not so small domaine held a lot more mystification than mysticism; and the one sure feature of 'things' there was that they were not what they seemed. He might have his profound side, but another was that of a cunning old charlatan.

I said lightly, 'Your patient seemed much more normal this evening.'

'She may appear more normal tomorrow. You must not let that deceive you.'

'There's no chance of that.'

'As I told you, I shall keep myself out of sight tomorrow. But if we do not see each other again ... I shall see you next week-end?'

'I'll be here.'

'Good. Well ... ' He stood up, as if he had really only been waiting for a certain time, I presumed the time for Julie to 'disappear', to pass.

As I stood as well I said, 'Thank you. Once again. For possessing me.'

He inclined his head, like some seasoned impresario too accustomed to first-night compliments to take them very seriously. We walked indoors. The two Bonnards glowed gently from the inner wall of his bedroom. On the landing outside I came to a decision.

'I think I'll go for a stroll, Mr Conchis. I don't feel very sleepy. Just down to Moutsa.'

I knew he might say he would come with me and so make it impossible to be at the statue at midnight; but it was a counter-trap for him, an insurance for me. If we were caught, I could claim the assignation was an accident. At least I hadn't concealed that I was going out.

'As you wish.'

He put out his hand and clasped mine, then watched me for a moment as I went downstairs. But before I reached the bottom I heard his door close. He might have been out on the terrace listening, so I crunched noisily on the gravel as I walked north towards the track out of Bourani. But at the gate, instead of turning down to Moutsa, I went on up the hill for fifty yards or so and sat down against a tree-trunk, from where I could watch the entrance and the track. It was a dark night, no moon, but the stars diffused a very faint luminescence over everything, a light like the softest sound, touch of fur on ebony.

My heart was beating faster than it should. It was partly at the thought of meeting Julie, partly at something far more mysterious, the sense that I was now deep in the strangest maze in Europe. Now I really was Theseus; somewhere in the darkness Ariadne waited; and perhaps the Minotaur.

I sat there for a quarter of an hour, smoking but shielding the red tip from view, ears alert and eyes alert. Nobody came; and nobody went.

At five to twelve I slipped back through the gate and struck off eastwards through the trees to the gulley. I moved slowly, stopping frequently. I reached the gulley, waited, then crossed it and walked as silently as I could up the path to the clearing with the statue. It came, majestic shadow, into sight. The seat under the almond tree was deserted. I stood in the starlight at the edge of the clearing, very tense, certain that something was about to happen, straining to see if there was anyone in the dense black background. I had an idea it might be a man with blue eyes and an axe.

There was a loud ching. Someone had thrown a stone and hit the statue. I stepped into the darkness of the pine trees beside me. Then I saw a movement, and an instant later another stone, a pebble, rolled across the ground in front of me. The movement showed a gleam of white, and it came from behind a tree on my side of the clearing, higher up. I knew it was Julie.

I ran up the steep slope, stumbled once, then stood. She was standing beside the tree, in the thickest shadow. I could see her white shirt and trousers, her blonde hair, and she reached forward with both hands. In four long strides I got to her and her arms went round me, and we were kissing, one long wild kiss that lasted, with one or two gulps for air, for a fevered readjustment of the embrace, and lasted … in that time I thought I finally knew her. She had abandoned all pretence, she was passionate, almost hungry. She let me crush her body; met mine. I murmured one or two torn endearments, but she stopped my mouth. I turned to kiss her hand; caught it; and brushed my lips down its side and round the wrist to the scar on the back.

A second later I had let go of her and was reaching in my pocket for the matches. I struck one and lifted her left hand. It was scarless. I raised the match. The eyes, the mouth, the shape of the chin, everything about her was like Julie. But she was not Julie. There were little puckers at the corner of her mouth, a slight over-alertness in the look, a sort of calculated impudence; above all, there was a deep suntan. She sustained my stare, then looked down, then up again under her eyelashes.

'Damn.' I flicked the match away, and struck another. She promptly blew it out.

'Nicholas.' A low, reproachful – and strange – voice.

'There must be some mistake. Nicholas is my twin brother.'

'I thought midnight would never come.'

'Where is she?'

I spoke angrily, and I was angry, but not quite as much as I sounded. It was so neat a modulation into the world of Beaumarchais, of Restoration comedy; and I knew the height the dupe has fallen is measured by his anger.

'She?'

'You forgot your scar.'

'How clever of you to see it was make-up before.'

'And your voice.'

'It's the night air.' She coughed.

I caught hold of her hand and pulled her over to the seat under the almond tree.

'Now. Where is she?'

'She couldn't come. And don't be so rough.'

'Well, where is she?' The girl was silent. I said, 'That wasn't funny.'

'I thought it was rather exciting.' She sat, then glanced up at me. 'And so did you.'

'For Christ's sake I thought you ... ' but I didn't bother to finish the sentence. 'You're June?'

'Yes. If you're Nicholas.'

I sat down beside her and fished out a packet of Papastratos. She took one, and I gave her a good long look in the match-flare. In return she examined me, with eyes markedly less frivolous than her voice till then.

The striking facial similarity with her sister upset me in some un-expected way. It seemed a hitherto unrealized aspect of Julie that I could do without, an unnecessary complication. Perhaps it was the tan on this other girl's skin, a general air of living a more outdoor, physical life, of being healthier, a fraction more rounded in the cheeks ... indeed of being what Julie herself must look like in nor-mal circumstances. I leant forward, elbows on knees.

'Why didn't she come herself?'

'I thought Maurice had told you why.'

I didn't show it, but I felt like an over-confident chess-player who suddenly sees that his supposedly impregnable queen is only one move from extinction. Once again I thought frantically back – per-haps the old man had been right about the high intelligence of some schizophrenics. The tea-throwing scene had seemed too far out of character if she was cunning-mad; but cunning-madder still might have precipitated it just to plant the wink at the end; then those collu-sive bare feet under the table, the message with the matches ... per-haps he had been less oblivious than he had seemed.

'We don't blame you. Julie's misled far greater experts than you.'

'Why are you so sure I'm misled?'

'Because you wouldn't have kissed someone you really thought was mentally unbalanced like that.' She added, 'At least I hope you wouldn't.' I said nothing. 'Honestly, we're not blaming you. I know how clever she is at suggesting that the madness is in everyone around her. The damsel-in-distress line.'

But there was something faintly interrogative behind her tone of voice in that last little phrase, as if she wasn't quite certain how I would react – how far I could be pushed.

'She's certainly cleverer at that than the line you're taking.'

She was silent a long moment. 'You don't believe me?'

'You know I don't believe you. And I think your sister's mean to still doubt me.'

She left a longer silence still.

'We couldn't both get away together.' She added in a lower voice, 'I wanted to be sure, too.'

'Sure of what?'

'That you are what you claim.'

'I've told her the truth.'

'As she keeps claiming. With a little too much enthusiasm to make me feel she's in a fit state to judge.' She added drily, 'Which I now begin to understand. At least physically.'

'You can easily check that I work at a school on the other side of the island.'

'We know there's a school. I don't suppose you have any means of identification on you?'

'This is ridiculous.'

'Not so ridiculous, in present circumstances, as my not asking.'

I had to grant some justice to that. 'I haven't got my passport. A Greek *permis de séjour*, if that's any good.'

'May I see it? Please?'

I fished in my back pocket, then struck three or four matches while she examined the *permis*. It gave my name, address and profession. She handed it back.

'Satisfied?'

Her voice was serious. 'You swear you're not working for him?'

'Only in the sense you know. That I've been told Julie is undergoing some kind of experimental cure for schizophrenia. Which I've never believed. Or never face-to-face with her.'

'You never met Maurice before you came here a month ago?'

'Categorically not.'

'Or signed a contract of any sort with him?'

I looked at her. 'Meaning you have?'

'Yes. But not for what's happening.'

She hesitated. 'Julie will tell you tomorrow.'

'I wouldn't mind seeing some documentary evidence either.'

'All right. That's fair enough.' She dropped her cigarette and screwed it out. Her next question came out of the blue. 'Are there any police on the island?'

'A sergeant, two men. Why do you ask?'

'I just wondered.'

I drew a breath. 'Let me get this straight. First of all you were ghosts. Then you were schizophrenics. Now you're next week's consignment to the seraglio.'

'Sometimes I almost wish we were. It would be simpler.' She said quickly, 'Nicholas, I'm notorious for never taking anything very seriously, and that's partly why we're here, and even now it's fun in a way – but we really are just two English girls who've got themselves into such deep waters these last two months that … ' she broke off, and there was a silence between us.

'Do you share Julie's fascination for Maurice?'

She didn't answer for a moment, and I looked at her. She had a wry smile.

'I have a suspicion that you and I are going to understand each other.'

'You don't share it?'

She looked down. 'She's academically much brighter than I am, but … I do have a sort of basic common-sense she lacks. I smell a rat if I don't understand what's going on. Julie tends to be all starry-eyed about it.'

'Why did you bring up the police?'

'Because we're prisoners here. Oh, very subtle prisoners. No expense spared, there aren't any bars – I gather she's told you we're constantly being assured we can go home whenever we like. Except that somehow we're always being shepherded and watched.'

'Are we safe at the moment?'

'I hope so. But I must go soon.'

'I can easily get the police. If you want.'

'That's a relief.'

'And what's *your* theory about what's going on?'

She gave me a rueful smile. 'I was going to ask you that.'

'I accept he has been genuinely connected with psychiatry.'

'He questions Julie for hours after you've been here. What you said, how you behaved, what lies she told you … all the rest of it. It's as if he gets some vicarious thrill from knowing every detail.'

'And he does hypnotize her?'

'He's done us both – me only once. That extraordinary ... you had it?'

'Yes.'

'And Julie several times. To help her learn her parts. All the facts about the Lily thing. Then a whole session on how a schizophrenic would behave.'

'Does he question her while she's under?'

'To be fair, no. He's always scrupulous about whichever one of us isn't being hypnotized being present. I've always been there listening.'

'But you have doubts?'

She hesitated again. 'There's something that worries us. A sort of voyeuristic side. The feeling we have that he's watching you two falling for each other.' She looked at me. 'Has Julie told you about three hearts?' She must have seen by my face that the answer was no. 'I'd rather she told you. Tomorrow.'

'What three hearts?'

'The original idea wasn't that I should always stay in the background.'

'And?'

'I'd rather she told you.'

I made a guess. 'You and me?'

She hesitated. 'It has been dropped now. Because of what's happened. But we suspect it was always meant to be dropped. Which leaves me wondering why I'm here at all.'

'But it's vile. We're not just pawns on a chessboard.'

'As he knows full well, Nicholas. It's not just that he wants to be mysterious to us. He wants us to be mysterious to him.' She smiled and murmured, 'Anyway, speaking for myself, I'm not sure I don't wish it hadn't been dropped.'

'Can I tell your sister that?'

She grinned and looked down. 'You mustn't take me too seriously.'

'I've already begun to realize that.'

She let a little silence pass. 'Julie's only just got over a particularly messy affair, Nicholas. That's one reason she wanted to be out of England.'

'She has my sympathies.'

'So I understand. What I'm trying to say is that I don't want to see her hurt again.'

'She won't be hurt by me.'

She leant forward. 'She has a kind of genius for picking the wrong men. I don't know you, so that's not meant personally at all. Simply that her past record doesn't give me much confidence.' She said, 'I'm being over-protective.'

'She doesn't need protecting from me.'

'I just mean that she's always looking for poetry and passion and sensitivity, the whole Romantic kitchen. I live on a rather simpler diet.'

'Prose and pudding?'

'I don't expect attractive men necessarily to have attractive souls.'

She said it with a dryness tinged with wistfulness that I liked. I looked secretly at her profiled face; and had a glimpse of a world where they did both play the same part, where I had both, the dark and the pale; Renaissance bawdy stories about girls who changed places in the night. I saw a future where, all right, of course, I married Julie, but this equally attractive and evidently rather different sister-in-law accompanied, if only aesthetically, the marriage. With twins there must always be nuances, suggestions, blendings of identity, souls and bodies that became indistinguishable and reciprocally haunting.

She murmured, 'I must go now.'

'Have I convinced you?'

'As much as you can.'

'Can't I walk back with you to wherever you hide?'

'You can't come in.'

'All right. But I need reassurance, too.'

She hesitated. 'If you'll promise to turn back when I say.'

'Agreed.'

We stood up and went down towards the statue of Poseidon in the starlight. We had hardly reached it when we saw we hadn't been alone. We both froze. A white figure had stood out, some twenty-five yards away, from among the bushes at the bottom, seaward side of the clearing round the statue. We had spoken in voices too low to be overheard, but it was still a shock.

June whispered, 'Oh God. Damn.'

'Who is it?'

She caught my hand and made me turn away.

'It's our beloved watchdog. Don't do anything. I'll have to leave you here.'

I looked over my shoulder and made him out better – a man in a white medical coat, a would-be male nurse with some kind of dark mask over his face, whose features I couldn't distinguish. June pressed my hand and sought my eyes, a look as direct as her sister's.

'I do trust you. Please trust us.'

'What's going to happen now?'

'I don't know. But don't start arguing. Just go back to the house.'

She leant quickly forward, pulling me a little towards her, and kissed my cheek. Then she was walking down towards the white coat. When she was near the man, I followed her. He stood silently aside to let her pass into the deeper darkness between the trees, but then blocked the opening between the bushes again. With a shock, almost greater than seeing him in the first place, I suddenly realized as I came down to him that he wasn't wearing a mask. He was a Negro: a big, tall man, perhaps five years older than myself. He stared at me without expression. I came to within some ten feet of him. He extended his arms, warning, forbidding the way. I could see he was lighter-skinned than some black men, a smooth face, intent eyes, somehow liquid and animal, concentrated purely on the physical problem of my next move. He stood poised yet coiled, like an athlete, a boxer.

I stopped and said, 'You look prettier with your jackal mask on.'

He did not move. But June's face reappeared behind him. It was anxious, beseeching.

'Nicholas. Go back to the house. *Please*.' I looked from her concerned eyes to his. She said, 'He can't speak. He's a mute.'

'I thought black eunuchs went out with the Ottoman Empire.'

His expression did not change a millimetre, and I had the impression that he hadn't even understood my words. But after a moment he folded his arms and widened his stance. I could see a black polo-neck jumper under the medical coat. I knew he wanted me to come at him, and I was tempted to take him on.

I let June decide. I looked past him at her. 'Will you be all right?'

'Yes. Please go.'

'I'll wait by the statue.'

She nodded and turned away. I went back to the sea-god, and sat on the rock he stood on; for some reason, I don't know why, reached out a hand and grasped his bronze ankle. The Negro stood with folded arms, like a bored attendant in a museum – or perhaps indeed like some scimitared janissary at the gates of the imperial harem. I relinquished the ankle and lit a cigarette to counter the released adrenalin. A minute passed, two. I listened, despite the sisters' talk of a hiding-place, for a boat engine. But there was silence. I felt, beyond the insult to my virility before an attractive girl, ill-at-ease and guilty. The news of the clandestine meeting would obviously go straight back to Conchis now. Perhaps he would appear. It wasn't so much that I was frightened of having a show-down over the schizophrenia nonsense; but that having broken his rules so signally, I would be sent off the field for good. I contemplated trying to suborn the Negro in some way, argue with him, plead. But he simply waited in the shadows, a doubly, both racially and personally, anonymous face.

From somewhere down by the sea there was a whistle. Things happened very fast then.

The white figure strode swiftly up towards me. I stood and said, 'Now wait a minute.' But he was strong and quick as a leopard, two inches taller than I am. An obviously humourless face, and an angry one. It was no good – I was frightened – there was something insanely violent about his eyes, and it flashed through my mind that he was a black surrogate of Henrik Nygaard. Without warning he spat full in my face and then palm-pushed me sharply back on to the rock pedestal of the statue. The edge caught the back of my knees and I had to sit. As I wiped the spittle off my nose and cheek I saw him already walking away down the slope. I opened my mouth to shout something after him, then swallowed it. I pulled out a handkerchief, kept wiping my face. It was filthy, defiled. I would have murdered Conchis if he had stood in front of me then.

But in fact I went back to the gate and down the path to Moutsa; I had to be outside the domaine. There I stripped off my clothes and plunged into the sea; rubbed my face in the salt water, then swam a hundred yards out. The sea was alive with phosphorescent diatoms that swirled in long trails from my hands and feet. I dived and seal-turned on my back and looked up through the water at the blurred white specks of the stars. The sea cooled, calmed, silked round my genitals. I felt safe out there, and sane, out of their reach, all their reaches.

I had long suspected there was some hidden significance in the story of de Deukans and his gallery of automata. What Conchis had done, or was trying to do, was to turn Bourani into such a gallery, and real human beings into *his* puppets ... and I was not going to stand much more of it. June had impressed me, her common-sense view of the situation. I was clearly the only male around that they could trust; and quite apart from anything else, they needed my help, my strength. I knew it would be no good storming into the house and having it out with the old man – he would only feed me more lies. He was like some animal in a den, he had to be coaxed out a little more before he could be trapped and destroyed.

I slowly trod water, with the dark slope of Bourani across the silent water to the east; and gradually I quietened down. It might have been worse than just that spit; and I had insulted the man. I possessed a lot of faults, but racialism wasn't one of them ... or at least I liked to think racialism wasn't one of them. Besides, the ball was now firmly in the old man's court; however he reacted, I would discover something about him. I must wait to see what change this brought to tomorrow's 'script'. There returned that old excitement – let it all come, even the black Minotaur, so long as it came; so long as I might reach the centre, and have the final prize I coveted.

I went ashore and dried myself with my shirt. Then I pulled on the rest of my clothes and walked back to the house. It was silent. I listened, without bothering to conceal it from anyone who might have been listening in return, outside Conchis's bedroom door. There was no sound.

46

I woke up feeling more slugged, more beaten-steak – the heat does it in Greece – than usual. It was nearly ten o'clock. I soaked my head in cold water, dragged on my clothes, and went downstairs under the colonnade. I looked under the muslin on the table; my breakfast, the spirit-stove to heat up the usual brass *vriki* of coffee. I waited a moment, but no one appeared. There was a deserted silence about the house that puzzled me. I had expected Conchis, more comedy; not an empty stage. I sat down and ate my breakfast.

Afterwards I carried the breakfast things round to Maria's cottage, on the pretext of being helpful; but her door was locked. First failure. I went upstairs, knocked on Conchis's door, tried it: second failure. Then I went round all the ground-floor rooms in the house. I even cursorily searched the book-cases in the music-room for his psychiatric papers, also without success. I knew a sudden fear: because of last night, it was all over. They were all vanished for good.

I walked to the statue, all round the domaine, like a man searching for a lost key – then back to the house, nearly an hour had passed. It remained as deserted as before. I began to feel desperate and at a loss – what should I do now? Go to the village, tell the police? In the end I went down to the private beach. The boat was gone. I swam out of the little cove and round its eastern headland. There some of the tallest cliffs on the island, a hundred feet or more high, fell into the sea among a litter of boulders and broken rocks. The cliffs curved in a very flat concave arc half a mile eastwards, not really making a bay, but finally jutting sufficiently from the coast to hide the beach where the three cottages were. I examined every yard of the cliffs: no way down, no place where even a small boat could land. Yet this was the area the two sisters supposedly headed for when they went 'home'. There was only low scrub on the abrupt-sloping cliff-tops after the pines ended, manifestly impossible to hide in. That left only one solution. They made their way along the top of the cliffs, then circled inland and down past the cottages.

I swam a little further out to sea, but then a colder vein of water made me turn back. I saw at once. A girl in a pale pink summer dress was standing under the edge of the pines on top of the cliff, some hundred yards to the east of where I was; in shadow, but brilliantly, exuberantly conspicuous. She waved down and I waved back. She walked a few yards along under the green wall of trees, the sunlight between the pines dappling the pale rose of the dress; and then, with a leap of surprise, I saw another flash of pink, a second girl. They stood, each replica of each, and the closer waved again, beckoning me ashore. They both turned and disappeared, as if they were setting off to meet me half-way.

Five or six minutes later I arrived, very out of breath, with a shirt pulled over my wet trunks, at the far side of the gulley. They weren't by the statue, and I had a few moments' angry suspicion that I was being teased again – shown them only to lose them. But I went down towards the cliffs, past the carob. The sea seared blue through the furthermost pines. Suddenly I saw their two figures. They were sitting on a shaded hummock of earth and rock, to the east. I walked more slowly, sure of them now. The identical dresses were very simple, with short faintly puffed sleeves, scalloped deep above the breast; they wore powder-blue stockings, pale grey shoes. They looked very feminine, pretty, a pair of nineteen-year-olds in their Summer Sunday best ... yet to my mind vaguely over-dressed, towny – even, weirdly, there was a rush basket beside June, as if they were still students at Cambridge.

June stood as I got near and came to meet me. She had her hair down, like her sister; golden skin, an even deeper tan than I had realized the previous night; and there was a facial difference at close range, a greater openness, even a touch of impudent tomboyishness. Behind her Julie watched us meet. She was noticeably unsmiling and holding herself aloof. June grinned.

'I told her you said you didn't care which of us you met this morning.'

'That was kind of you.'

She took my hand and led me to the foot of the hummock.

'Here's your knight in shining armour.'

Julie looked coolly down at me. 'Hallo.'

Her sister said, 'She knows all.'

Julie slid a look at her. 'I also know whose fault it was.'

But then she stood and came down beside us. The reproof in her eyes gave way to concern.

'Did you get back all right?'

I told them what had happened, the spitting. The first moments of sisterly banter rapidly disappeared. I had the benefit of two pairs of disturbed blue-grey eyes. Then they looked at each other, as if this confirmed something they had been discussing. Julie spoke first.

'Have you seen Maurice this morning?'

'Not a sign.'

There was another exchanged glance.

June said, 'Nor have we.'

'The whole place seems deserted. I've been looking everywhere for you.'

June glanced behind me, into the trees. 'It may seem. But I bet it isn't.'

'Who is that damned black man?'

'Maurice calls him his valet. When you're not here he even serves at table. He's supposed to look after us when we're in hiding. Actually he gives us both the creeps.'

'Is he really a mute?'

'You may well ask. We suspect not. He just sits and stares. As if he could say worlds.'

'He's never … ?'

Julie shook her head. 'He hardly even seems aware we're female.'

'He must be blind as well.'

June made a little grimace. 'It would be insulting if it wasn't such a relief.'

'The old man must know what happened last night.'

'That's what we're trying to work out.'

June added, 'The mystery of the dog that *didn't* bark in the night.'

I looked at her. 'I thought you and I weren't supposed to meet officially.'

'We were always going to, today. I was supposed to back Maurice's story.'

Julie added, 'After I'd put on another of my celebrated madwoman acts.'

'But he must … '

'That's what puzzles us. The trouble is he hasn't told us the next chapter. What we're supposed to be when you've seen through the schizophrenia.'

June said, 'So we've decided to be ourselves. And see what happens.'

'You must tell me all you know now.'

Julie gave her sister a dry look. June gave a little start of mock surprise.

'I'm not *de trop* by any chance?'

'You can go and improve your nauseating tan. We'll perhaps tolerate you at lunch.'

June made a little curtsey, then went and picked up the basket; but as she came back, she raised a warning finger. 'I shall want to hear all that concerns me.'

I smiled, then belatedly realized, as June walked away, that I was getting a cool and wide-eyed look from Julie.

'It was so dark. The same clothes, I … '

'I'm very angry with her. Things are quite complicated enough without that.'

'She's very different from you.'

'We've rather cultivated that.' But then her voice was gentler, more honest. 'We're very close, really.'

I took her hand. 'I prefer you.'

But she wouldn't let me pull her close, though the hand was not withdrawn. 'I've found a place along the cliff. Where at least we can talk without being seen.'

We went through the trees to the east.

'You're not seriously angry?'

'Did you enjoy kissing her?'

'Only because I thought it was you.'

'How long did it last?'

'A few seconds.'

She jerked on my hand. 'Liar.'

But there was a hidden smile on her face. She led the way round an outcrop of rock; a solitary pine, then the steep slope down to the cliff-edge. The outcrop formed a natural wall shielding us from eyes inland, behind us. Another basket stood on a dark green rug spread in the thin shade of the wind-bent tree. I glanced round, then took

Julie in my arms. This time she let me kiss her, but only briefly before she turned her head away.

'I so wanted to come last night.'

'It was awful.'

'I had to let her meet you.' There was a little outbreath. 'She complains I have all the excitement, apart from anything else.'

'It doesn't matter. Now we've got all day.'

She kissed my shoulder through my damp shirt. 'We must talk.'

She slipped out of her flat-heeled shoes, then sat down on the rug with her legs curled beside her. The pale-blue stockings ended just below her bare knees. The dress was really white, but thick-sewn with a close pattern of tiny roses. It was cut deep round the neck, to where the breasts began to swell apart. The clothes gave her a kind of sensual innocence, a schoolgirlishness. The sun-wind teased the ends of her hair against her back, as when she had been 'Lily' on the beach – but all that side of her had drained away, like water between stones. I sat beside her, and she turned away and reached for the basket. The fabric tightened over the breasts, the small waist. She faced back and our eyes met; those fine grey-hyacinth eyes, tilted corners, lingering a little in mine.

'Go on. Ask me anything.'

'What did you read at Cambridge?'

'Classics.' She saw my surprise. 'My father's subject. He was like you. A schoolmaster.'

'Was?'

'He died in the war. In India.'

'And June as well?'

She smiled. 'I was the sacrificial lamb. She was allowed to do what she liked. Modern languages.'

'When did you come down?'

'Last year.' She opened her mouth, then changed her mind, and set the basket between us. 'I've brought all I could. I'm so scared they'll see what I'm doing.' I looked round, but the natural wall protected us completely. Only someone on top of it could have observed us. She produced a book. It was small, half bound in black leather, with green marbled-paper sides; rubbed and worn. I looked at the title-page: *Quintus Horatius Flaccus, Parisiis*.

'It's a Didot Aîné.'

'Who's he?' I saw the date 1800.

'A famous French printer.'

She turned me back to the fly-leaf. On it, in very neat writing, was an inscription: *From the 'idiots' of IVB to their lovely teacher, Miss Julia Holmes.* Underneath were fifteen or so signatures: *Penny O'Brien, Susan Smith, Susan Mowbray, Jane Willings, Lea Gluckstein, Jean Ann Moffat ...*

'Where was this?'

'Please look at these first.'

Six or seven envelopes. Three were addressed to 'Miss Julia and Miss June Holmes, c/o Maurice Conchis, Esquire, Bourani, Phraxos, Greece'. They had English stamps and recent postmarks, all from Dorset.

'Read one.'

I took out a letter from the top envelope. It was on headed paper, *Ansty Cottage, Cerne Abbas, Dorset.* It began in a rapid scrawl:

Darlings, I've been frantically busy with all the doodah for the Show, on top of that Mr Arnold's been in and he wants to do the painting as soon as possible. Also guess who – Roger rang up, he's at Bovington now, and asked himself over for the week-end. He was so disappointed you were both abroad – hadn't heard. I think he's much nicer – not nearly so pompous. And a captain!! I didn't know what on earth to do with him so I asked the Drayton girl and her brother round for supper and I think it went off rather well. Billy is getting so fat, old Tom says it's all the grass, so I asked the D. girl if she'd like to give him a ride or two, I knew you wouldn't mind ...

I turned to the end. The letter was signed *Mummy*. I looked up and she pulled a face. 'Sorry.'

She handed me three other letters. One was evidently from a former fellow-teacher – news about people, school activities. Another from a friend who signed herself Claire. One from a bank in London, to June, advising her that 'a remittance of £100' had been received on May 31st. I memorized the address: Barclay's Bank, Englands Lane, London NW3. The manager's name was P. J. Fearn.

'And this.'

It was her passport. Miss J. N. Holmes.

'N?'

'Neilson. My mother's family name.'

I read the *signalement* opposite her photograph. *Profession*: teacher. *Date of birth*: 16.1.1929. *Place of birth*: Winchester.

'Is Winchester where your father taught?'

'He was the senior classics master there.'

Country of residence: England. *Height*: 5 ft. 8 in. *Colour of eyes*: grey. *Hair*: fair. *Special peculiarities*: scar on left wrist (twin sister). At the bottom she had signed her name, a neat italic hand. I flicked through the visa pages. Two journeys to France, one to Italy the summer before. An entry visa to Greece made out in April; an entry stamp, May 2nd, Athens. There was none for the year before. I thought back to May 2nd – that all this had been preparing, even then.

'Which college were you at?'

'Girton.'

'You must know old Miss Wainwright. Doctor Wainwright.'

'At Girton?'

'Chaucer expert. Langland.' She stared at me, then looked down, then up again with a little smile: she wasn't falling for that. 'Sorry. Okay. You were at Girton. Then a teacher?'

She mentioned the name of a famous girls' grammar school in North London.

'That's not very plausible.'

'Why not?'

'Not enough *cachet*.'

'I didn't want *cachet*. I wanted to be in London.' She picked at her skirt. 'You mustn't think I was born to this sort of life.'

'Why did you want to be in London?'

'June and I did act quite a lot at Cambridge. We both had careers, but – '

'What was hers?'

'She was in advertising. Copy-writing. Not a world I liked very much. Or its men, anyway.'

'I interrupted.'

'I'm just saying that neither of us was mad about what we were doing. We got involved with a London amateur company called the Tavistock Rep. They have a little theatre in Canonbury?'

'I've heard of it.'

I leant back on an elbow, she sat propped on an arm. Beyond her the deep blue sea merged into the sky's azure. A breeze blew through the pine-branches above us, caressed the skin like a current of warm water. I found her new, her real self, a simplicity and seriousness in her expression, even more delectable than the previous ones. I realized that it was what had been lacking: a sense of her ordinariness, that she was attainable.

'Well, last November they put on *Lysistrata*.'

'Tell me first why you weren't happy teaching.'

'Are you?'

'No. Or not until I met you.'

'Just ... not feeling my heart was in it. The rather prim façade one has to wear?'

I smiled, and nodded. '*Lysistrata*.'

'I thought you might have read about it. No? Anyway, a rather clever producer there called Tony Hill put us both, June and I, in the main part. I stood in front of the stage and spoke the lines, some in Greek, and June did all the acting in mime. It was ... in some of the papers, quite a lot of real theatre people came to see it. The production. Not us.'

She reached in her basket and found a packet of cigarettes. I lit them both and she went straight on.

'One day near the end of the run a man came backstage and told us he was a theatrical agent and he had someone who wanted to meet us. A film producer.' She smiled at my raised eyebrows. 'Of course. And he was so secretive about who it was that it seemed too clumsy and obvious for words. But then two days later we both got enormous bouquets and an invitation to have lunch at Claridge's from someone who signed himself – '

'Don't bother. I can guess.'

She bowed her head drily. 'We talked it over, then – really just for fun – went along.' She paused. 'I suppose he dazzled us. We were so sure it was going to be some dreadful pseudo-Hollywood type. Instead there was this ... he seemed perfectly open. Obviously very rich, he told us he had business interests all over Europe. He gave us a card, some Swiss address, but he said he lived mainly in France and Greece. He even described Bourani and the island. Everything here. Exactly as it is ... as a place.'

'Nothing about his past?'

'We did ask about his English. He said he'd wanted to be a doctor as a young man and had studied medicine in London.' She shrugged. 'I know countless things he told us then were so much eyewash, but putting together all the bits of jigsaw we've been handed since – I think he must have spent a lot of his youth in England. Perhaps he even went to boarding-school at home – he was very sarcastic about the English public-school system the other day. It did rather sound from the heart.' She put out her cigarette. 'I'm sure that at some time in his life he rebelled against money. And his father.'

'You've not discovered … ?'

'That very first time. We did politely ask. I remember exactly what he said. "My father was the dullest of human beings. A millionaire with the mind of a shopkeeper." End of subject. We've never really got any closer than that. Except that he did once say he was born in Alexandria – Maurice himself. There is a rich Greek colony there.'

'So something really the opposite of the de Deukans story?'

'I suspect that may have been a temptation Maurice himself underwent at some point. A way he might have used the fortune he inherited.'

'That's how I read it. But you didn't finish at Claridge's.'

'It did all rather bear this out. He was so anxious to put himself across as a cosmopolitan man of culture. Not a mere millionaire. He asked us what we'd read at Cambridge – which of course allowed him to demonstrate his own reading. Then the contemporary theatre, he obviously knows that very well. What's going on in the rest of Europe. He said he was backing a small experimental theatre in Paris.' She took a breath. 'Anyway. Cultural credentials thoroughly established. More than thoroughly, we were beginning to wonder why we were there. In the end June, in her usual way, asked point-blank. Whereupon he announced that he was the major shareholder in a film company in the Lebanon.' Her grey eyes opened wide at me. 'Then. In the next breath. Absolutely out of the blue.' She paused. 'He wanted us to star in a film this summer.'

'But you must have … '

'Actually we nearly had the giggles. We knew he must really be suggesting something else – what we'd suspected in the first place.

331

But then he said the terms.' She showed me a still amazed face. 'A thousand pounds each when we signed a contract. A thousand more when we finished the making. Plus a hundred pounds a month each for expenses. Of which, it's turned out, we have virtually none.'

'Christ. Have you seen any of it?'

'The contract money. And the expenses ... that letter.' She looked down, as if I must think her mercenary, and smoothed the nap of the rug. 'It's one major reason we've stuck it here, Nicholas. It's so absurd. We've done so little to earn it.'

'What was the film supposed to be about?'

'It was to be shot here in Greece. I'll explain in a minute.' She gave me an uncertain look. 'You mustn't think we were totally innocent. We didn't at all say yes at once. Rather the opposite. And he played his cards so well. He was almost paternal. Of course we couldn't decide at once, we'd want to make enquiries, consult our agent – not that we actually even had one at that point.'

'Go on.'

'We were driven home – in a hired Rolls – to think it over. You know, to a pokey top-floor flat in Belsize Park. Like two Cinderellas. He was so clever, he never put any suspicious kind of pressure on us. We saw him, oh – twice, three times more. He took us out. Theatre. Opera. Never any attempt to get either of us on our own. I'm missing out so many things. But you know what he can be like when he wants to charm you. That feeling he can give of knowing what life's about.'

'What did everyone else think? Your friends – this producer man?'

'They thought we ought to be very careful. We found ourselves an agent. He hadn't heard of Maurice or the film company in Beirut. But he soon tracked it down. It makes bread-and-butter pictures for the Arab market. Iraq and Egypt. As Maurice had already told us. He'd explained that they wanted to get into the European market. Our film was only to be financed by the Lebanese company for some tax reason.'

'What was it called?'

'Polymus Films.' She spelt it. 'It's in whatever they list film companies in. The trade directory. Perfectly respectable and rather successful, so far as our agent could tell. Like the contract, when we got to that – also absolutely normal.'

'Could he have fixed the agent?'

She let out a breath. 'We've wondered. But I don't think he had to. I suppose it was the money. There it was, in the bank. Money must be true. I mean, we realized it was a kind of risk. Perhaps if it had just been the one of us. But being two.' She gave me a wry little interrogative glance under her eyebrows. 'Are you believing any of this?'

'Shouldn't I be?'

'I feel I'm not explaining it very well.'

'You're doing fine.'

But she gave me another look, still doubtful about how I was reacting to such apparent gullibility; then lowered her eyes.

'There's something else. Greece. Having done classics. I've always had this longing to come here. That was part of the inducement. Maurice kept promising we'd have time to see everything. Which he hasn't welshed on. I mean there's this, but the rest of it has been like one long holiday.' Again she seemed almost embarrassed at the knowledge that their rewards had been much greater than mine. 'He's got a fabulous yacht. We live like princesses on it.'

'Your mother?'

'Oh Maurice saw to that. He insisted on meeting her one day when she'd come up to see us in London. Bowled her over with his gentlemanliness.' She grinned ruefully. 'And his money.'

'She knows what's happened?'

'We've told her we're still rehearsing. We don't want to worry her.' She pulled a face. 'She's an expert at the useless tizzy.'

'This film?'

'It was taken from a demotic Greek story by a writer called Theodoritis – have you ever heard of him? *Three Hearts*?' I shook my head. 'Apparently it's never been translated. It was written in the early 'twenties. It's about two English girls, they're supposed to be the British ambassador at Athens's daughters, though not twins in the original, who go for a holiday on a Greek island during the First World War and – '

'One doesn't happen to be called Lily Montgomery, by any chance?'

'No, but wait. This island. They meet a Greek writer there – a poet, he's got tuberculosis, dying ... and he falls in love with each sister in turn, and they fall in love with him and everyone's terribly miserable and it all ends – you can guess. Actually it's not quite as silly as that. It does have a certain period charm.'

'You've read it?'

'What I can. It's quite short.'

I spoke in Greek. '*Xerete kala ta nea ellenika?*'

She answered, in a much more fluent and better accented demotic than my own, that she was learning some modern Greek, though knowing the ancient language was less help than people imagined; and gave me a steady look. I touched my forehead in obeisance.

'He also showed us a script in London.'

'In English?'

'He said he was hoping to distribute two versions. Greek and English. Dubbing voices both ways.' She gave a little shrug. 'It seemed playable. Though it was really just a cunning rehearsal.'

'But how – '

'Wait a minute. More evidence.'

She delved in the bag, then swivelled round so that we were sitting facing in opposite directions. She came out with a wallet; produced two cuttings from it. One showed the two sisters standing in a London street, in overcoats and woollen hats, laughing. I knew the paper by the print but it was in any case gummed on to a grey cuttings-agency tag: *Evening Standard, January 8th, 1953.* The paragraph underneath ran:

AND BRAINS AS WELL!

Two lucky twins, June and Julie (on right) Holmes, who will star in a film this summer to be shot in Greece. The twins both have Cambridge degrees, acted a lot at varsity, speak eight languages between them. Unfair note for bachelors: neither wants to marry yet.

'We didn't write the caption.'

'So I deduced.'

The other cutting was from the *Cinema Trade News.* It repeated, in Americanese, what she had just told me.

'Oh and while I'm at it. My mother.' She showed me a snapshot from the wallet; a woman with fluffy hair in a deckchair in a garden, a clumber spaniel beside her. I could see another photograph, and made her show me that as well: a man in a sports shirt, a nervous and intelligent face. He seemed in his early thirties.

'This is … ?'

'Yes.' She added, 'Was.'

She took the photo back. There was something closed in her face, and I did not press. She went quickly on.

'Of course we realize now it was a perfect cover for Maurice. If we were to play well-brought-up young ambassador's daughters in 1914 … we innocently trotted off for lessons in deportment. Had clothes fittings. All the Lily costumes were made in London. Then in May we came out. He met us in Athens and said the rest of the company wouldn't assemble for a fortnight. He had warned us, so we weren't surprised. He took us on a cruise with him. To Rhodes and Crete. On the *Arethusa*. His yacht.'

'Which he never brings here?'

'It's usually at Nauplia.'

'In Athens – you stayed in his house?'

'I don't think he's got one there. He says he hasn't. We stayed at the Grande Bretagne.'

'No office?'

'I know.' She contracted her mouth self-accusingly. 'But we'd been told only the location shooting would take place here. And the interiors in Beirut. He showed us set designs.' She hesitated. 'It was a new world for us, Nicholas. If we hadn't been so green. And so excited. And he did introduce us to two people. The Greek actor he said was going to play the poet. And the director. Another Greek. We all had dinner … actually we rather liked them both. There was lots of talk about the film.'

'You didn't check on them?'

'We were only there a couple of nights – then off in the yacht with Maurice. They were to come straight here.'

'But never did?'

'We've never seen them again.' She picked a loose thread from the hem of her skirt. 'As a matter of fact we did think it was odd there was no publicity, but they even had a reason for that. Apparently here if you say you're going to make a film you get hundreds of extras turning up in hope of a job.'

By chance I knew that was true. Some three months before a

Greek film unit had been working on Hydra. Two of the school waiters had run away in the hope of being hired by them. It had been a minor scandal for a couple of days. I didn't tell Julie, but smiled with the secret knowledge.

'You came here.'

'After a lovely cruise. But that's when the madness began. Hardly forty-eight hours. Already we'd both realized there was something subtly different about Maurice. Because of the cruise, in so many ways we felt closer to him ... I suppose we've both missed not having a father since 1943. He couldn't be that, but it was a little like finding a kind of fairy uncle. Being alone with him so much, knowing we could trust him. And we had fascinating evenings. Enormous arguments. About life, love, literature, the theatre ... everything. Except when we tried to discover his past, then a sort of curtain came down. You know how it is. Things you really only see in retrospect. How shall I put it – it was all so civilized on the boat. Then suddenly here it was as if he owned us. We somehow weren't his guests any more.'

Again she sought my eyes, as if I must be blaming her for liking anything about the old man. She had lain back on an elbow, and her voice had dropped. Now and then she would touch her hair back from where the breeze carried it across her cheek.

'I know the feeling.'

'The first thing was ... we wanted to go and see the village. But he said no, he wanted to make the film as quietly as possible. But it was too quiet. No one else here, no sign of generators, lights, kliegs, all the things they'd need. No production unit. And this feeling that Maurice was watching us. There was something in the way he began to smile. As if he knew something we didn't. And didn't have to hide it any more.'

'I know that exactly.'

'It was our second afternoon here. June – I was sleeping– tried to go for a walk. She got to the gate and suddenly this silent Negro – we'd never seen him before – stepped out in the path and stopped her. He wouldn't let her pass, wouldn't answer her. Of course she was petrified. She came back at once and we marched off to Maurice.' Her eyes lingered a dry moment on mine. 'Then he told us.' She looked down at the rug. 'Not quite straight out. He could see we were ... obviously. He put us through a sort of catechism. Had he

336

ever behaved improperly, had he not honoured all that the contracts stipulated in financial terms, didn't the relationship we'd established on the cruise ... you know. Then he did come out with it. Yes, he had misled us about the film, but not totally. He did need the services of two accomplished and highly intelligent – his adjectives – young actresses. We must please listen. He swore blind that if, having listened, we were unconvinced, then ... '

'You could go.'

She nodded. 'So we made the mistake of listening. It went on for hours, in the end. The gist of it was that though he was truly interested in the theatre – really does own this film studio in the Lebanon – he had remained much more the doctor than he'd led us to believe. That his field had been psychiatry. He even said that he'd studied under Jung.'

'I've had that.'

'I know so little about Jung. Did you think ... ?'

'I was convinced at the time.'

'So were we. In the end, and rather against our will. But that day. He kept talking about our helping him cross a frontier to a new world that was half art and half science. A unique psychological and philosophical adventure. What might be an extraordinary voyage into the human unconscious. Those were all phrases he used. Of course we wanted to know what lay behind all the fine words – what we were actually expected to do. Then for the first time he mentioned you. That he wanted to mount a situation in which we two were to play parts rather like the ones in the original *Three Hearts* story. And you, without realizing it, would play the Greek poet.'

'But Christ Almighty, you must have – '

She tilted her head, looked away a moment, beyond the words to express it. 'Nicholas, we were flabbergasted. And yet in some way ... I don't know, it had somehow always been there. You know, real theatre people are generally rather silly and superficial offstage. And Maurice ... I remember June said something about feeling insulted. How dare he think he could buy people just because he was so rich. It was the nearest I've ever seen him to being caught on the raw. Hurt. He made a long speech, and I know for once it was sincere, about the guilt he'd always felt over his money. How his only real passion was to know, to extend human knowledge. How his one dream was to realize a long-held theory, how it was not a selfishness, a mere strange whim ... as far as genuineness in that way was concerned, he really was rather impressive. He even silenced June in the end.'

'You must have asked what the theory was.'

'Over and over again. But he came up with the same old thing. If we knew, we would contaminate the purity of the experiment. His words again. He did give us more analogies than we've ever had since. In one way it was to be a sort of fantastic extension of the Stanislavski method. Improvising realities more real than reality. You were to be like a man following a mysterious voice, several voices, through a forest of alternative possibilities – who wouldn't even know themselves ... since they were us ... what their alternatives really meant. Another parallel was a play, but without a writer or an audience. Only actors.'

'And in the end – can we be told then?'

'He's promised that from the beginning.'

'Me as well?'

'He must be dying to know what you're really feeling and thinking. Since you're at the centre of it all. The chief guinea-pig.'

'Obviously he won you over that day.'

'We spent a night talking it over alone. One minute we would, the next we wouldn't. In the end June decided to make a little test. We came down the next morning and said we wanted to go home, as soon as possible. He argued and argued, but we were adamant. In the end he said very well, he'd have the yacht come from Nauplia and take us to Athens. But we said no. This day, now. We'd catch the steamer back to Athens.'

'And he let you go?'

'We packed, he took us and our luggage round the island in the boat. He was absolutely silent, he didn't say a word. All I could think about was losing the sunlight, everything around us. Dreary old London. It came to the point when we were only a hundred yards from the steamer. I looked at June ... '

'And bit the apple.' She nodded. 'Had he wanted the money back?'

'No. That was another thing. And he was so delighted. He didn't blame us at all.' She sighed. 'He said it proved his choice was right.'

Through all this I had waited for a reference to the past, to my own

338

certain knowledge that Conchis had now devoted at least three summers to his 'long-held theory', whatever it really was. But I held my tongue. Perhaps Julie sensed that I remained sceptical.

'That story last night. About Seidevarre. I think that's some kind of clue. The place of mystery in life. Not taking anything for granted. A world where nothing is certain. That's what he's trying to create here.'

'With himself cast as God.'

'But not out of vanity. Out of intellectual curiosity. As a hypothesis. To see how we react. And not one kind of god. Several.'

'He keeps telling me hazard rules everything. But you can't knowingly pretend to be God as Hazard.'

'I think he means us to realize that.' She added, 'He even jokes about it sometimes. We see far less of him, ever since you appeared. Much more only to do with whatever's happening. It's as if he's withdrawn. He says it. We can't expect to question God.'

I surveyed her bent head, the line of her body, her closeness; and almost heard Conchis's voice answering my doubt of hazard. Then why are you here with this girl? Or, Does it matter, as long as you are here with her?

'June says he questions you about me.'

Her eyes went skywards a moment. 'You've no idea. It's not only you. What *I* feel. Whether I believe you … even what I think's going on in his, Maurice's, mind. You can't imagine.'

'It must have been obvious I was no actor.'

'It wasn't at all. I thought you were brillant. Acting as if you couldn't act.' She turned and lay on her stomach, head towards me. 'We've long realized that the first line he gave us – that we should mystify you – was a blind. According to the script we deceive you. But the deceiving deceives us even more.'

'This script?'

'"Script" is a joke. He tells us roughly when to appear and disappear – in terms of exits and entries. The sort of atmosphere to create. Sometimes lines.'

'That theological talk last night?'

'Yes. He asked me to say that.' She gave a little half-apologetic glance up. 'And I do believe it a little, anyway.'

'But otherwise you improvise?'

'All along he says that if things don't go quite as planned it doesn't matter. As long as we keep to the main development.' She said, 'It's also all about role-playing. How people behave in situations they don't understand. I told you. He has said that's part of it.'

'One thing's obvious. He wants us to think he's putting all sorts of obstacles between us. Then gives us all these opportunities to destroy them.'

'To begin with there was no talk of getting you to fall in love with me except in a very distant nineteen-fifteeny sort of way. Then by that second week he persuaded me that I had to make some compromise between my 1915 false self and your 1953 true one. He asked me what I'd do if you wanted to kiss me.' She shrugged. 'One's kissed men on stage. In the end I said, If it was absolutely necessary. That second Sunday I hadn't decided. That's why I put on that dreadful act.'

'It was a nice act.'

'That first conversation with you. I had terrible *trac*. Far worse than I've ever had on a real stage.'

'But you forced yourself to let me kiss you.'

'Only because I thought I had to.' I followed the hollow of her arched back. She had raised one blue-stockinged foot backwards in the air and, chin cupped in her hands, was avoiding my eyes. She said, 'I think for him it's like some mathematical proposition. Except that we're all x, and he can put us where he likes in his equation.' There was a little silence. 'I'm not being honest. I wanted to know what it was like being kissed by you.'

'Despite the adverse propaganda.'

'That didn't begin till after that Sunday afternoon. Though he had said all along that I mustn't get emotionally involved with you.'

She stared at the rug. A yellow butterfly hovered over us, then glided away.

'Did he give a reason?'

'Yes. That one day I might have to make you … dislike me.' She stared down. 'Because you'd have to start feeling attracted to June. It all goes back to the ridiculous *Three Hearts* thing again. The poet character did transfer his affections. One sister was fickle, the other caught him on the rebound … you know.' She added, 'He does keep running you down terribly. To both of us. As if he's apologizing to the hounds for having provided such an awful fox. Which is palp-ably absurd. Especially when you've done all the hunting.' She looked up. 'Do you remember that speech he gave me, when I was Lily, about your having no poetry? No humour, and all the rest? I'm sure it was meant just as much for me as for you.'

'But why should he drive us together?'

She said nothing for a moment. 'I don't think the *Three Hearts* story means anything. But there's a much greater work of literature that may.' She left a pause for me to guess, then murmured, 'Yester-day afternoon, after my little scene. Another magician once sent a young man hewing wood.'

'I missed that. Prospero and Ferdinand.'

'Those lines I recited.'

'He also brought it up on my very first visit here. Before I even knew you existed.' I noticed she was avoiding my eyes. It was not, given the end of *The Tempest*, difficult to guess why. I murmured, 'He can't have known we'd … '

'I know. It's just … ' she shook her head. 'That I'm his to give.' She added, 'Not you.'

'And he certainly has a Caliban.'

She sighed. 'I know.'

'Which reminds me. This hiding-place of yours.'

'Nicholas, I can't show you. If we are being watched, they'll see.'

'It's close to here?'

'Yes.'

'At least you can tell me where.' She seemed embarrassed in a different way now; again avoided my eyes. 'Supposing you were in trouble.'

She smiled. 'If we were earmarked for a fate worse than death … I think it would have happened by now.'

'But why can't I know? You promised.'

'I still promise. But please not now.' She must have heard the sharpness in my voice, because she reached out and touched my hand. 'I'm sorry. I've broken so many other promises to Maurice this last hour. I feel I ought to keep one.'

'Is it so important?'

'Not at all. Except he says he wants to surprise you with it one day. I don't know how.'

I was puzzled, yet in a way it was additional proof of her story; a contrariness that confirmed it. I left a little silence, as a test, knowing that liars hate silence. But she passed that.

'Have you talked with the other people here?'

'We've never seen the others to talk to. There's Maria, but she's hopeless. As impossible to get anything out of as Joe.'

'The crew on the yacht?'

'They're just Greeks. I don't think they know what goes on here.' She suddenly said, 'Did June tell you we suspect there's a spy at your school?'

'Who?'

'Maurice told us one day you were very stand-offish with the other masters. That they didn't like you.'

I thought at once of Demetriades; of how, when I reflected, it was odd that such a natural gossip should have kept my trips to Bourani so secret. Besides, I *was* stand-offish. He was the only other master I was ever frequently with, outside the common-room. I remembered, with a flash of relief, that I had lied to him about meeting Alison – not out of cunning, but to avoid his wretched jokes.

'I can guess who it would be.'

'It's the one side of Maurice I can't stand. All this spying. He's got a cine-camera on the yacht. With a telephoto lens. He claims it's for birds.'

'If I ever caught the old bastard … '

'I've never seen it here. I think it's just another of his fifty-seven varieties of red herring.'

I watched her, I knew there was some conflict in her, some in-decision, some admission she wanted to coax out of me that ran contrary to most of what we had been saying. I remembered what her sister had told me about her the night before; and made a guess.

'In spite of everything, you want to go on?'

She shook her head. 'Nicholas, I don't know. Today, now, yes. Tomorrow, probably not. Nothing like this has ever happened to me before. I suppose if I have a clear instinct, it's that if we walked out on it, nothing like it would ever happen again. Do you feel that?'

I had her eyes, and the moment seemed right. I sprang my final test.

'Not really. Since I know it's happened at least twice before this year.'

She was so surprised that she did not understand. She stared at my faint smile, then pushed off her stomach and sat back on her heels.

'You mean you've been ... this isn't your first ... '

She was transparently set back. Her eyes, both hurt and lost, accused mine.

'My two predecessors at the school.'

Still she didn't understand. 'They told you? You knew all along?'

'Just that something odd happened here last year. And the one before.' I explained how I had found out; and how little; and that the old man had admitted it. Again I watched to see how she would react. 'He also told me you'd both been here before. And met them.'

She stared at me, outraged. 'But we've never set foot ... '

'I know.'

She sat sideways and looked out to sea. 'Oh he's impossible.' Then her eyes were back on mine. 'So all the time you've been thinking we –'

'Not really. I knew he was lying about one thing.' I described Mitford, and the old man's tale of his supposed attraction for her. She asked questions, she wanted to know every detail.

'And you've really no idea what happened with them?'

'They certainly never told anyone at the school. Mitford gave me that one hint. I have written to him. No answer yet.'

She searched my eyes one last time, then looked down. 'I suppose it argues that it can't be too awful in the end.'

'That's what I try to tell myself.'

'How extraordinary.'

'You'd better not tell him.'

'No, of course not.' After a moment she smiled wrily up. 'Do you think he has an endless supply of twin sisters?'

'Like you, no. Not even him.'

She looked down from my unambiguous eyes.

'What do you think we should do?'

'When's he due back? Or pretending to be back?'

'This evening. Or so we were told yesterday.'

'It could be an interesting meeting.'

'I may get the sack for incompetence.'

I said softly, 'I'll find you a job.'

There was a little silence, then she met my look. I reached a hand, and it too was met; I pulled her towards me, and we lay side by side, a little apart. I began to trace the lines of her face ... the eyes, which she closed, the nose to its tip, then the contour of the mouth. She kissed the finger. I drew her closer and kissed the mouth. She responded, yet I sensed a reserve still; a wanting, and not wanting. We separated a little, I stared at that face. It seemed to me one I could never tire of, an eternal source of desire, of the will to protect; without either physical or psychological flaw. She opened her eyes and gave me a gentle, but reticent, smile.

'What are you thinking?'

'How beautiful you are.'

'Did you really not meet your friend in Athens?'

'Would you be jealous if I had?'

'Yes.'

'Then I didn't.'

'I bet you did really.'

'Honestly. She couldn't make it.'

'Then you did want to meet her?'

'Out of some sort of kindness to dumb animals. Only to tell her it was no good. I'd given my soul to a witch.'

'Some witch.'

I raised her hand and kissed it, then the scar.

'How did you get that?'

She cocked the wrist and looked at it. 'When I was ten. Playing hide-and-seek.' She made a fleeting duck's mouth, mocking herself. 'I should have learnt my lesson. I hid in a garden shed and knocked this what looked like a long stick off a peg ... and put up my arm to shield myself.' She mimed it. 'It was a scythe.'

'You poor thing.' I kissed the wrist again, then once more drew us close, but after a while left her mouth, kissed the eyes, the neck, the throat, along the curve of the dress above the breasts; then found the mouth again. We explored each other's eyes. There was something still uncertain in hers; yet something melted as well. Suddenly they closed, and her mouth reached towards mine, as if she could speak better with lips now than in words. But just as we were be-

344

coming drowned in each other, unaware of anything but our joined mouths and close-pressed bodies, we were stopped.

It was the bell from the house, a monotonous regular ringing, but insistent, like a tocsin. We sat up and looked guiltily round: we seemed alone. Julie lifted my hand to see my wrist-watch.

'It's probably June. Lunch.'

I leant and kissed her head. 'I'd rather stay here.'

'She'll only come and look for us.' She flicked me a would-be dry glance. 'Most men find her more attractive than me.'

'Then most men are idiots.'

The bell stopped. She kept my hand, and looked at it as we sat side by side. 'Perhaps they just want something she finds it easier to give than I do.'

'Any girl can give you that.' Still she examined my hand, as if it was some object dissociated from me. 'Did you give it to this other man?'

'I tried to.'

'What went wrong?'

She shook her head, as if it was too complicated. But then she said, 'I'm not a virgin, Nicholas. It's not that.'

'But being hurt again?'

'Being ... used again.'

'How was he using you?'

The bell started afresh. She smiled up at me. 'It's a long story. Not now.'

She kissed me quickly, then stood and picked up her basket, while I folded the rug and put it over my arm. We set off back for the house. We had hardly gone a few steps into the pines when I caught a movement to the east in the corner of my eyes: a glimpse of a black shape drawing back behind intervening low branches some seventy or eighty yards away. I barely saw the man, but there was something unmistakable in the way he moved.

'We are being watched. That Joe character.'

We didn't stop, though she glanced past me. 'We can't do anything about it. Except ignore him.'

But the presence of that hidden pair of eyes in the trees behind us could not really be ignored. From then on we walked rather self-consciously apart; almost guiltily. It was a guilt one part of me despised, since the better I knew the real girl beside me the more artificial became the situation that kept us apart; and yet which another side of me, the eternal deception-relishing child, tolerated. There is something erotic in all collusion. Perhaps I should have known a more real guilt and remembered a more deeply hidden pair of eyes in the forest of my unconscious; perhaps I did know them, for all my outward oblivion, and found an extra relish still. Long afterwards I realized why some men, racing drivers and their like, become addicted to speed. There are those of us who never see death ahead, but eternally behind: in any moment that stops and thinks.

47

As we approached the colonnade, a barelegged figure in a brick-red shirt stood from the steps in the sun where she had been sitting.

'I nearly started without you. I'm hungry.'

The shirt was unbuttoned, and underneath I could see a dark blue bikini. The word, like the fashion, was very new then: in fact it was the first bikini I had ever seen outside a newspaper photograph and it gave me something of a shock ... the bare navel, the slender legs, brown-gold skin, a pair of amusedly questioning eyes. I caught Julie wrinkling her nose at this young Mediterranean goddess, who only widened her smile. As we followed her to the table set back in the shade beneath the arches, I remembered the story of *Three Hearts* ... but banned the thought before it grew. June went to the corner of the colonnade and called for Maria, then turned to her sister.

'She's been trying to tell me something about the yacht. I couldn't work it out.'

We sat, and Maria appeared. She spoke to Julie. I followed well enough. The yacht was arriving at five, to take the girls away. Hermes was coming to take Maria herself back to the village for a night. She had to see the dentist there. The 'young gentleman' must return to the school, as the house would be locked up. I heard Julie ask where the yacht was going. *Then xero, despoina.* I don't know, miss. She repeated, as if that was the nub of her message, At five o'clock? Then she bobbed in her usual way, and disappeared back to her cottage.

Julie translated for June's benefit.

I said, 'This wasn't planned?'

'I thought we were staying here.' She looked doubtfully at her sister, who in turn eyed me, then drily queried Julie back.

'Do we trust him? Does he trust us?'

'Yes.'

June gave me a little grin. 'Then welcome, Pip.'

I looked to Julie for help. She murmured, 'I thought you claimed to have read English at Oxford.'

There was suddenly a shadow of reawakened suspicion between us. Then I woke up, and took a breath. 'All these literary references.' I smiled. 'Miss Havisham rides again?'

'And Estella.'

I looked from one to the other. 'You're not serious?'

'Just our little joke.'

Julie regarded her sister. '*Your* little joke.'

June spoke to me. 'Which I've tried to get Maurice to share. With total unsuccess.' She leant her elbows on the table. 'But come on. Tell me what great conclusions you've reached.'

'Nicholas has told me something extraordinary.'

I was given one more chance to test a reaction; and found myself once more convinced, though June seemed more outraged than amused by the new evidence of the old man's duplicity. As we went over it all again, I discovered (and might have already deduced from their names) that in terms of delivery June was the older twin. She also seemed it in other ways. I detected a protectiveness in her towards Julie, which sprang from a more open personality, greater experience of men. There was a shadow of reality in the casting of the masque: a more normal and a less normal sister, or one more assertive, the other more fragile. I sat between them, facing the sea, keeping an eye open for the hidden watcher – though he stayed hidden, if he was still spying on us. The girls started questioning me, my own background and past.

So we talked about Nicholas: his family, his ambitions, his failings. The third person is apt, because I presented a sort of fictional self to them, a victim of circumstances, a mixture of attractive raffishness and essential inner decency. Alison came up again briefly. I put the main blame there on hazard, on fate, on elective affinity, one's knowing one sought more; and let them feel, copying Julie, that I didn't want to talk in detail about all that. It was over and done with, pale and sour beside the present.

Something about that long lunch, the enjoyable food and the *retsina*, all the debating and speculating, the questions they asked, the being between the two of them, the dressed and the near-naked, feeling closer to them both all the time – we got on to their father, their having lived their childhood in the shadow of a boys' boarding-school, then their mother, they kept capping each other's affectionate stories about her silliness ... it was like entering a deliciously warm room after a long, cold journey; an erotically warm room, as well. Towards the end of the meal June slipped out of her shirt. In return Julie slipped out a sisterly tongue, which was met by an impervious little smile. I began to have trouble keeping my eyes off that body. The bikini top barely covered the breasts; and the bottom half was tied at the hips by white laces that let the skin show through. I knew I was being visually teased a little, innocently flirted with ... some small revenge, perhaps, on June's part for having been kept so long in the wings. If human beings could purr, I should have done so then.

About half past two we decided to go out of Bourani and down to Moutsa to swim – partly to see whether we should be allowed to. If Joe blocked our way, I promised not to challenge him. The girls seemed to share my own view of his physical strength. So we strolled down the track, expecting to be stopped, as June had been once. But there was no one there; only the pines, the heat, the racket of the cicadas. We installed ourselves halfway down the beach, near the little chapel in the trees. I spread two rugs where the needled earth ran into the shingle. Julie, who had disappeared for a minute before we left the house, peeled off her schoolgirl stockings, then pulled her dress over her head. She was wearing a white one-piece bare-backed costume underneath, and she managed to look shyly ashamed at the weakness of her own tan.

Her sister grinned. 'If only Maurice could provide the seven dwarfs as well.'

'Shut up. It's not fair. I'll never catch up now.' She gave me what was almost a scowl. 'Honestly I've been sitting on that wretched yacht under an awning while all she does is … ' she turned away and folded her dress.

They both did up their hair, we went down the burning shingle and into the water, and swam a little way out. I looked down the beach towards Bourani, but saw no one. We were alone in the world, in the cool blue water, three heads; and again I felt a near-absolute happiness, a being poised, not sure how all this would turn out, but also not wanting to know, totally identified with the moment: with Greece, this lost place, these two real-life nymphs. We came back ashore, dried, lay on the rugs; myself beside Julie on one of them, she was anointing herself with sun-tan oil; June on the far side on the other rug, flat on her stomach, her head couched on her hands and turned towards us. I thought of the school, its repressed boys and sour masters, the unendurable lack of femininity and natural sexuality in its life. We began to talk about Maurice again. Julie put on sunglasses, lay on her back, while I still lay propped on an elbow.

There came in the end a little silence; the wine at lunch, the soporific sun. June reached back and undid the hook at the back of her bikini top, then stretched up and eased it away to dry on the stones beside her. I glimpsed her bare breasts as she reached an arm to do it; and the long golden back, divided by the taut little strip of dark blue from the long golden legs. There was no white bar on her skin, the breasts were the same colour as the rest; she must have tanned a lot like that. It had been done casually and naturally, but I made sure my eyes were looking out to sea when she lay flat again, turned towards us as before. Once more I was shocked: this was not just the latest clothes fashion, but behaviour years ahead of its time. I was also uncomfortably aware that she was staring at me, that a comparison was being invited – or a reaction, observed. After a few moments she shifted a little and moved her head to face the other way. I looked at her brown figure, then down at Julie; then lay on my back myself and felt for the hand of the girl beside me. Her fingers curled through mine, played, contracted. I closed my eyes. Darkness, both; the old wickedness of Greece.

But I was soon punished for my day-dreaming. Out of nowhere, a minute or two later, there was an abrupt approaching roar. For a wild first second I thought it was something to do with Bourani. Then I realized it was a sound I had not heard since I had been on the island: a low-flying plane, a fighter by the sound of it. Julie and I sat up, June leant round on an elbow, her back to us. The plane was very low. It shot out from behind the Bourani cape, some four hundred yards to sea of it, and scorched like an angry hornet over the water towards the Peloponnesus. In a few seconds it had passed out of sight behind the headland to the west; but not before we had seen the American markings – or at least I had. Julie seemed more interested in her sister's bare back.

June said, 'What a cheek.'

'He'll probably be back, now he's seen you like that.'

'Don't be such a prude.'

'Nicholas is perfectly well aware of what beautiful bodies we both have.'

June turned to us then, on her elbows, a small pendant breast visible past the nearer bent arm. She was biting her lips. 'I didn't realize things had gone that far.'

Julie stared fixedly out to sea. 'We are not amused.'

'Nicholas seems to be.'

'You're showing off.'

'Since he's already had the divine good luck to see me –'

'*June.*'

Through all this little spat Julie hadn't looked at me. But now she did, and made it clear whose side I was to be on. It was delicious: she was both embarrassed and piqued, like still water ruffled. She surveyed me reproachfully, as if it was all my fault.

'Let's go and look at the chapel.'

I glanced at June as I obediently stood, and received a sarcastic and impudent little cast skywards of her eyes. Now I had to bite my lips. Julie and I strolled away into the trees, the shade, in bare feet. There was a charming pinkness about her cheeks, and a setness of mouth.

'She's only teasing you.'

'I could scratch her eyes out sometimes.'

'A classicist shouldn't be shocked by nakedness in Greece.'

'I'm not a classicist at the moment. Just a girl who feels at a disadvantage.'

I leant and kissed the side of her head. I was pushed away, but without force.

We came to the whitewashed chapel. I thought it would be locked, as it had been when I had tried to get in before. But the primitive wooden latch gave – someone must have been there, and forgotten to relock the place. There was no window, only the light from the door. It was bare of chairs; an iron candle-holder with one or two ancient stumps on its spikes, a naïvely painted iconostasis spanning the far end, a very faint aroma of incense. We went and looked at the crudely figured saints on the worm-eaten wall of wood, but I knew we were both less aware of them than of the darkness and seclusion of the little place. I put an arm round her shoulders. A moment later she had turned and we were kissing. She twisted her mouth away and turned her cheek against my shoulder. I looked at the open door, then drew her back towards it; pushed it to, leant against the wall on the hinge side and coaxed her to me. I began to kiss her throat, her shoulder, then reached up to the straps of her costume.

'No. You mustn't.'

But her voice had that peculiar feminine tone that invites you to go on as much as to stop. I gently eased the straps off her shoulders, then down, till she was bare to the waist; caressed the waist, then up, slowly, to the firm small breasts, still a little damp from the sea-water, but warm, excited. I bent and licked the salt from the nipples. Her hands began to stroke down my back, in my hair. I let my own wander down to the waist again, to where the costume hung, but then her hands were abruptly on mine.

She whispered. 'Please. Not yet.'

I brushed my lips against her mouth. 'I want you so much.'

'I know.'

'You're so beautiful.'

'But we can't. Not here.'

I moved my hands up to her breasts.

'Do you want me to?'

'You know I do. But not now.'

Her arms slipped round my neck and we kissed again, crushing each other. I slid a hand down her back, slipped the fingers inside the edge of the costume, appled a curved cheek, pulled her closer still, against the hardness in my loins, made sure she could feel it and know she was wanted. Our mouths twisted, our tongues explored wildly, she began to rock against me and I could sense she was losing control, that this nakedness, darkness, pent-up emotion, repressed need ...

351

There was a sound. It was minute, and gave no indication of what had caused it. But it came beyond any doubt from the far end of, and inside, the chapel. We clung in petrified horror for a long second. Julie's head twisted round to look where I was looking, but the few glints of light through the sides of the closed door made it difficult to see. Instinctively we both reached for her costume and slipped it back on over her arms. Then I gripped her hand, moved her against the wall beside me, and reached for the door. I jerked it open, light flooded in. The iconostasis stared at us, the black iron candlestand in front of it. There was nothing else. But I could see that the iconostasis, as in all such Greek chapels, stood some three or four feet off the back wall; and there was a narrow door at one end. Suddenly Julie was in front of me, mutely but violently shaking her head – she must have seen my instinct was to rush down there. I had guessed at once who it was: that accursed Negro. He could have sneaked in easily enough when we were swimming, and had probably assumed we would not leave the beach and the sea.

Julie pulled my hand urgently, casting a quick look back at the far end. I hesitated, then let her drag me out into the open air. I slammed the door shut, then looked at her.

'The bastard.'

'He can't have known we were going in there.'

'But he could damn well have warned us earlier.'

We spoke in whispers. She made me walk a few steps away. Beyond, in the sun, I could see June with her head raised, looking at us. She must have heard the sharp bang of the door.

Julie said, 'Maurice will know for sure now.'

'That no longer worries me. It's about bloody time he did.'

June called. 'Is something wrong?'

Julie raised a finger to her mouth. Her sister turned, sat up, put her bikini top on, then came to meet us.

'Joe's in there. Hidden.'

June looked past us at the white walls of the chapel, then at our faces – no longer teasing, but concerned.

Julie said, 'I'm going to have it out with Maurice. Either Joe goes, or we do.'

'I suggested that weeks ago.'

'I know.'

'Were you talking? Did he hear anything?'

Julie looked down. 'It's not that.' Her cheeks were flushed. June gave me a sympathetic little smile, but had the grace to look down as well.

I said, 'I'm only too happy to go in there and ... '

But they were firmly against that. We walked back to our things and talked it over for a few minutes, covertly watching the chapel door. It stayed as it was, but somehow the place was spoilt now. That invisible black presence in the little building seeped into the land-scape, the sunlight, the whole afternoon. I also felt a violent sexual frustration ... but there was nothing now to be done about that. We decided to go back to the house.

There we found Maria sitting impassively outside her cottage, talking to the donkeyman, Hermes. She said tea was waiting for us, on the table. The two peasants stared at us from their wooden chairs, as if we were so remote from their simple world, so foreign, that all communication was impossible. But then Maria pointed mysteriously out to sea and said two or three words in Greek that I didn't under-stand. We looked, but saw nothing.

Julie said, 'She says a fleet of warships.'

We went to the edge of the gravel to the south of the house; and there, almost hull down, a line of grey ships steamed east across the Aegean between Malea and Skyli: a carrier, a cruiser, four destroyers, another ship, intent on some new Troy. The harsh irruption of the fighter plane into our peace was explained.

June said, 'Perhaps it's Maurice's last trick. To bombard us to death.'

We laughed, but were held by those cloud-grey shapes on the world's blue rim. Death machines holding thousands of gum-chewing, contraceptive-carrying men, for some reason more thirty years away than thirty miles; as if we were looking into the future, not the south; into a world where there were no more Prosperos, no private domaines, no poetries, fantasies, tender sexual promises ... I stood between the two girls and felt acutely the fragility not only of the old man's extraordinary enterprise, but of time itself. I knew I would never have another adventure like this. I would have sacrificed all the rest of my days to have this one afternoon endless, endlessly repeated, a closed circle, instead of what it was: a brief and tiny step that could never be retraced.

My previous euphoria waned further over the tea. The girls had gone indoors, then re-appeared in their dresses of that morning. The yacht was due so soon, and there was a hurried confusion over all we said. They were in two minds over what they should do; there was even a moment when we talked of their coming back with me to the other side of the island – they could put up at the hotel. But in the end we decided to give Conchis one more chance, one last week-end to declare himself. We were still discussing that when something else out to sea caught my eye. It came round the headland from the direction of Nauplia.

They had told me about the yacht, how luxurious it was, how much proof, if any more were needed, that one thing the old man must be was rich. It still took my breath away a little. We all went again to the edge of the gravel, where we could see better. A two-master, it was moving very slowly, under engine power, its sails furled; a long white hull, cabins rising out of the deck both fore and aft. The Greek flag hung lazily at a small mast at the stern. I saw half a dozen blue and white figures, presumably the crew. It was too far out, nearly half a mile, to distinguish a face.

I said, 'Well. As prisons go ... '

June said, 'You should see below decks. There are eight brands of French scent on our cabin table.'

The yacht almost ceased to move. Three men were at a davit, getting ready to lower a small boat. A siren moaned, to be sure we knew of the arrival. I felt, in characteristic English fashion, both a stab of envy and a contempt. The yacht itself was not vulgar, but I smelt something vulgar about owning it. I also saw myself aboard it one day. Nothing in my life before had taken me into the world of the very rich – I had had one or two rich acquaintances at Oxford, people like Billie Whyte, but had never experienced their home backgrounds. I did envy the two girls then; it was easier for them, good looks were the only passports they needed to enter that world. Money-getting was a male thing, sublimated virility. Perhaps Julie sensed all this. At any rate, when we went back to the colonnade for them to collect their things, she suddenly caught my hand and drew me indoors out of June's sight and hearing.

'It's only a few days.'

'Which are going to seem like a few years.'

'And for me.'

I said, 'I've been waiting to meet you all my life.'

She looked down, we were standing very close. 'I know.'

'Do you feel the same?'

'I don't know what I feel, Nicholas. Except that I want you to feel like that.'

'If you come back, could you get away one evening during the week?'

She glanced round through the open doors, then into my eyes. 'It's not that I wouldn't love to, but –'

'I could make Wednesday. We could meet down by the chapel.' I added, 'Not in it.'

She appealed for understanding. 'We may not even be here.'

'I'll come anyway. After dark. I'll wait till midnight. It'll be better than biting my fingernails in that damned school.'

'I will try. If I possibly can. If we're here.'

We kissed, but there was something torn, already too late, about it.

We went outside. June waited by the tea-table and immediately nodded across the gravel. There, standing on the path that led down to the private beach, was the Negro. He was in black trousers and a polo-necked jumper, and he wore dark glasses; waiting. The yacht's siren moaned again. I could hear the sound of a small outboard engine coming fast ashore.

June reached out a hand, and I wished them both good luck. Then I stood watching them walk across the gravel, in their pink dresses and blue stockings, baskets in hand. The Negro turned long before they reached him and started to walk down the path, as if he was too sure they would follow him to bother any more. When their heads had disappeared, I went to the top of the path. The power dinghy entered the little cove and came alongside the jetty. A minute later, the black figure, with the two pale pink ones of the girls just behind, walked down it. There was a sailor in the boat, white shorts, a dark blue shortsleeved singlet with a name in red across the breast. I couldn't read it at that range, but it was obviously *Arethusa*. The sailor helped the two girls into the boat, then the Negro got in. I noticed he sat in the bows, behind their backs. They started out to sea. After a few yards, they must have seen me standing up above, the girls waved; then again, when they left the cove and began to head faster towards the waiting yacht.

The afternoon sea stretched down to Crete, ninety miles away. The fleet had almost disappeared. The black shadow of a cypress halfway down the cliff stabbed across a patch of parched red-grey earth, already lengthening. The day died. I felt both sexually and socially deprived, I did not expect we should be able to meet during the week; but yet a deep excitement buoyed me on, a knowledge like that of the poker-player who needs only one more card to have an unbeatable hand.

I turned back to the house, where Maria was now waiting to lock up. I didn't try to pump her, I knew it was useless, but went up to my bedroom and packed my things in the duffel-bag. When I came down again, the small boat was already being hauled inboard and the huge yacht was under way. It began a long turn, then held course towards the southern end of the Peloponnesus. I was tempted to watch it out of sight; but then, knowing I was probably being watched as well from out there, decided that I did not want to play the wistful marooned man.

A few moments later I set off back to my dull, daily penal colony on the far side of the dream; as Adam left the Garden of Eden, perhaps ... except that I knew there were no gods, and nothing was going to bar my return.

48

During the long climb back I suffered, perhaps inevitably, a reaction from the day's events. I couldn't doubt the physical proof Julie had given me that she was to be emotionally trusted, but I kept on thinking of additional questions I ought to have asked her – and I also kept remembering how near I had been, on more than one occasion, to swallowing the story about schizophrenia. But that had been impossible to check on; this circumstantial new account was not. It was just conceivable that the sisters were in some way still running with the hare and hunting with the hounds – that is, Julie might find me physically attractive and yet still be prepared to mislead me about her real background. There was also my next meeting with Conchis: a little hard evidence that not only did I now know the truth about the sisters, but had had it confirmed away from the island, might prove very useful.

That same Sunday evening, back in my room, I composed letters to Mrs Holmes at Cerne Abbas, to Mr P. J. Fearn of Barclay's Bank, and to the headmistress of the grammar school where Julie had taught. To the first I explained that I had met her two daughters in connection with their film; that the local village schoolmaster had asked me to find a rural school in England that would provide 'pen pals'; and that the two girls had suggested that I should write to their mother and ask her to put me in touch with the primary school at Cerne Abbas – and as soon as possible, as our term was ending shortly. In the second I said that I wanted to open an account and that I had been recommended by two customers at the branch. In the third I gave myself the principalship of a language school opening in the autumn in Athens; a Miss Julia Holmes had applied for a post.

On Monday I read the drafts through, altered a word or two, then wrote the first two in longhand and laboriously typed the last in the bursar's office, where there was an ancient English-character machine. I knew the third letter was a bit far-fetched; film stars do not normally become down-and-out teachers abroad. But any sort of reply would serve.

And then, deciding I might as well be hung for a suspicious sheep as for a suspicious lamb, I wrote two more letters, one to the Tavistock Rep., and another to Girton, at Cambridge.

I posted those five letters; and with them one to Leverrier. I had half hoped that there might be a letter waiting for me from Mitford. But I knew mine to him had probably to be forwarded; and even then he might well not answer it. I made the letter to Leverrier, very brief, merely explaining who I was and then saying:

My real reason for writing is that I have got into a rather complicated situation at Bourani. I understand that you used to visit Mr Conchis over there – he told me this himself. I really need the benefit of someone else's advice and experience at the moment. I'd better add that this is not only for myself. Others are involved. We should be very grateful for any sort of reply from you, for reasons that I have a feeling you will appreciate.

Even as I sealed that letter I knew that Mitford's and Leverrier's silence was the best possible augury of what would happen to me. If in previous years something truly unpleasant had happened at Bourani, they would surely have talked; and if they were silent, then it must be with the silence of gratitude. I had not forgotten Mitford's story of his row with Conchis; or his warning. But I began to doubt his motives.

The more I thought about it the surer I was that Demetriades was the spy. The first rule of counter-espionage is to look fooled, so I was especially friendly with him after supper on Sunday. We strolled for ten minutes on the school jetty to find what breaths of air still moved in the oppressive night heat. Yes thank you, Méli, I said, I had a nice week-end at Bourani. Reading and swimming and listening to music. I even laughed at his obscene guesses – though I now suspected their obscenity had a purpose, he was checking for Conchis on my ability to keep my mouth shut – as to how I really passed my time there. I also thanked him for keeping so quiet about it all with the other masters.

As we walked idly up and down I looked across the dark water of the straits between the island and the Argolian mainland; and wondered what the sisters were doing at that moment, what other dark water they rode ... the silent sea, with all its secrets and its endless patience; yet not hostile. I understood its mysteries now.

I understood them even better after morning break the next day. I found an opportunity to get the deputy headmaster, who was also the senior teacher of Modern Greek, on one side. Someone had told me I should read a story by a writer called Theodoritis ... *Three Hearts*, had he ever heard of it? He had. He spoke no French or English, and I couldn't follow all he said. Apparently Theodoritis had been some sort of Greek disciple of Maupassant. Of the story I gathered enought to guess that it did conform with what Julie had told me. Any last doubt was removed when I went into lunch. A boy came over from the deputy headmaster's table to my own and laid a book by my side. *Three Hearts* was the long final story of a collection. It was written in *katharevousa*, the 'literary' and anti-demotic form of the modern language, and I found it a long way beyond my powers; and I could not go to Demetriades for help. But every passage I worked through with a dictionary at my side bore out the truth of Julie's account.

Wednesday …Wednesday. I couldn't even wait till then. After school on the Tuesday evening, I climbed to the central crest. I had convinced myself that it was a journey in vain. But I was wrong. There far below, anchored like a toy in the lavender sea of the Moutsa bay, I saw what made my heart leap: the unmistakable white shape of the *Arethusa*. I knew then. The old man had surrendered.

49

I came to the gate about half past nine, waited a few moments to listen, heard nothing, and went off the track through the trees to where I could observe the house. It lay in silence, black against the last light from the west. There was one lamp on, in the music room; a resinous smell of burning wood, from Maria's cottage. The scops owl called from somewhere nearby. As I returned to the gate a small black shape slipped overhead and dipped towards the sea between the pines: Conchis perhaps, the wizard as owl.

I walked quickly down, outside the domaine, to the beach at Moutsa: the forest was dark, the water dim, the faintest night lap. Five hundred yards away, out to sea, I saw the red port light of the anchored yacht. There were no other lights visible, no sign of life aboard it. I walked quickly through the edge of the trees towards the chapel.

Julie was waiting under its east wall, a shadow against its white-wash, and moved forward as soon as she saw me coming. She had on one of the dark-blue short-sleeved singlets worn by the *Arethusa* crew, a pale skirt. Her hair was tied back with a ribbon, which gave her a faintly severe, schoolmarmish look. We halted a yard from each other, suddenly shy.

'You got away?'

'It's all right. Maurice knows I'm here.' She smiled. 'And no more spying. We've had it all out.'

'You mean ... ?'

'He knows about us. I told him. And that I might be a schizophrenic in his plot, but I wasn't in reality.'

Still she smiled. I stepped forward and she came into my arms. But when, during the kiss, I tried to tighten the embrace, she pushed away a little, with her head down.

'Julie?'

She lifted one of my hands and kissed it.

'You must be kind. The wretched calendar. I didn't know how to tell you on Sunday.'

I had come prepared for every eventuality but this most banal and frequent of all. I touched my mouth against her hair: a faint melony scent in it.

'What a shame.'

'I so wanted you to come.'

'Let's walk towards the far end.'

I took her hand and we began to stroll past the chapel and through the trees to the west. They had had it out with the old man almost as soon as they had gone aboard the previous Sunday afternoon. Apparently he had played the innocent a little, but then June had let fly at him about the Negro and the spying in the chapel. They had had enough, either he told them what he was doing or ... Julie gave a little breath of still incredulous amusement, looked at me.

'Do you know what he said? As coolly as if we'd told him a tap needed mending?' I shook my head. '"Good. Exactly as I hoped and expected." Then before we could even get our breath back, he informed us that all that had happened so far was merely a rehearsal. Honestly, you should have seen his smile. It was so smug. Just as if we were two students who'd passed some preliminary examination.'

'A rehearsal for what?'

'Firstly, all *is* to be explained to us. To you as well, this coming week-end. From now on, we shall all work together under his direction. Someone else is coming here soon – he said "people", so it must be more than one or two. And they are to have our roles up to now. The being spun round and round. But this time, by us.'

'What people?'

'He wouldn't say. Nor what this all that's to be explained is. He said he wanted you to be there as well.'

'You're to vamp someone else?'

'That was the first thing I said. That I'd had enough of making eyes at strange men. Especially now.'

'You told him about us?'

She pressed my hand. 'Yes.' She let out a little breath. 'Actually he said he'd feared the worst as soon as he set eyes on you.'

'What worst?'

'That the cheese on his trap might fall for the mouse.'

'And he accepts … '

'He swore blind.'

'Did you believe him?'

She hesitated. 'As much as one can ever believe him. I've even been given a carrot to dangle in front of your nose.'

'Apart from the one whose hand I'm holding.'

She touched the side of her head against my shoulder. 'He wouldn't expect you to do it for nothing … you'd be paid. Whatever it is, it wouldn't start before your term ended. And he'd want us three to live, sleep anyway, at the house in the village. Initially as if we'd never met Maurice.'

'Are you tempted?'

She left a pause. 'There's one other tiny snag. He'd like you and me to pretend we're man and wife before whoever it is who's coming.'

'I couldn't possibly pretend. I don't have your acting ability.'

'Be serious.'

'I am. More than you think.'

Again her head turned against my shoulder. 'Tell me what you feel.'

'It all depends on next week-end. When we know what's really at stake.'

'That's what we think.'

'He must have given some clue.'

'He did say we can definitely think of it as psychiatric. Then in his usual helpful way added that it was really about something there's no word for. He said … a science yet to be discovered and named. He was terribly curious to know why I finally came to trust you.'

'What did you tell him?'

'That certain feelings between people can't be faked.'

'How's he been otherwise?'

'Actually rather sweet. Much more as he was in the beginning. Full of compliments about how brave, intelligent, all the rest, we've been.'

'Fear the Greeks … '

'I know. But we've made it absolutely clear. One more trick from him – and that's it.'

I looked out towards the silent yacht. 'Where did you go?'

'Down to Kythera. We came back yesterday.'

I thought of my own three days: catching up with the eternal backlog of marking, two prep duties, the smell of chalk, of boys … and then of term being ended, the secluded village house, the constant presence of the two girls.

'I got hold of a copy of *Three Hearts*.'

'Could you read it?'

'Enough to believe that part of it.'

She left a little silence.

'Someone said something about trusting one's instincts. Only three days ago.'

'It's just that over there … I sit in class and wonder whether this side of the island even exists. If it isn't all a dream.'

'You haven't heard from the man before you?'

'Not a word.'

Again she left a silence.

'Nicholas, I'll do whatever you say.' She stopped me, took my other hand, looked me in the eyes. 'We'll go straight back now and tell him. Seriously.'

I hesitated, then smiled. 'Can I hold you to that if I don't like the sound of his next chapter?'

'You know you can.'

A moment, and her arms came round me. Mouth confirmed eyes. Then we strolled on, very close. We came to the far end of the bay. It was tropically airless.

She said, 'I love the nights here. More than the day.'

'Me too.'

'Shall we paddle?'

362

We went down over the shingle to the water. She kicked off her shoes, I got free of mine. Then we stood in the tepid sea, and she let me kiss her again; her mouth, her throat. I held her lightly, protectively; then murmured in her ear.

'Beastly female physiology.'

She moved a little against me in sympathy.

'I know. I'm so sorry.'

'I've kept remembering how you were in the chapel.'

'I felt undone.'

'That's strictly for maidens.'

'It's how you made me feel.'

'Haven't other men?'

'One or two.'

'This one particular other man?' She said nothing. 'I wish you'd tell me about him.'

'There's nothing much to tell.'

'Let's go and sit down.'

We went back into the trees, a little way up the slope where the spine of the western headland rose. One or two large boulders had fallen in the past, and we installed ourselves where one had lodged. I sat with my back to it, and Julie leant against me. I reached up and undid the bow in the ribbon round her long hair, loosed it.

He had been a young don at Cambridge, a mathematician, nearly ten years older than she: very intelligent, sensitive, well-read, 'not at all a monomaniac'. They had met in her second year, but it had stayed 'demi-platonic' until well into her last.

'I don't know what it was, perhaps realizing I had only two terms to go, but Andrew started getting very hurt if I went out with anyone else. He hated the university drama set June and I were involved with. He seemed to sort of make up his mind that he ought to be in love with me. He was always very gentle – even funny about it, in a way – how I'd corrupted a born bachelor. I did like being with him, we used to go out in the country a lot, he was very generous, always flowers, books … you know. He wasn't a born bachelor at all in that way. But even then, it was never really a physical thing for me. You know how it is, you like someone in every other way, you feel flattered, even a tiny bit embarrassed to have a tame don as your escort everywhere. You admire them intellectually and … '

'Acquire a blind spot?'

'He insisted we got informally engaged. This was at the beginning of the summer term. I was working like mad. We hadn't been to bed, and I thought he was being very considerate ... the understanding was that we were going to have a holiday in Italy, then get married in the autumn.'

She was silent. 'What happened?'

'It's so embarrassing.'

I stroked her hair. 'Better than keeping it bottled up.'

She hesitated, then spoke in an even lower voice.

'I'd always realized there was something, I can't really describe it, not quite natural about him when we ... always a little bit of an air of going through the motions. Kissing me because he knew girls expected to be kissed. I never felt any real desire in him. On that side.' She smoothed her skirt over her knees. 'Quite simply in Italy it turned out that he did have ... rather serious problems. He'd never told me before, but he'd had homosexual experiences at school. Even when he was a student himself at Cambridge before the war.' She paused. 'I must sound appallingly innocent.'

'No. Just innocent.'

'He honestly didn't have any of the outward signs. He wanted so desperately to be absolutely normal. Perhaps too desperately.'

'I understand.'

'I kept saying it didn't matter, to myself as well. It only needed patience. And there were ... times. And out of bed he was still a terribly nice man to be with.' She was silent a long moment. 'I did something terrible, Nicholas. I walked out of the *pension* in Sienna where we were staying and caught a train back to England. Just like that, without warning him. Something in me snapped. I somehow knew there would always be that problem between us. We used to go out after ... it hadn't worked, and I used to look at the Italian boys and think – ' she broke off, as if she were still ashamed at what she had thought. She said, 'What you made me feel in the chapel. How simple it can be.'

'You haven't seen him since?'

'Yes. That's the trouble.'

'Tell me.'

'I fled home to Dorset. I couldn't tell my mother what had really

364

happened. Andrew came back, insisted we met in London.' She shook her head in memory. 'He was in such distress, nearly suicidal, I ... I gave in in the end. I won't go into all the grisly details. I wouldn't go through with the marriage, I took the London teaching job really so that I could be away from Cambridge. But ... well, we tried again on the physical side and ... oh, it dragged on for several months. Two supposedly intelligent human beings slowly destroying each other. He'd ring and say he couldn't get down to London the next week-end and all I'd feel was relief.' She stopped once more, then took courage in the darkness and her averted face. 'It really worked best if I played boy to him ... and I hated that. He hated it himself, really.' I felt her take a breath against me. 'In the end June made me do what I ought to have done months before. He writes to me occasionally. But that's all now.' There was a silence. 'End of sad little story.'

'It is sad.'

'I'm honestly not a prude. It's just that ... '

'It wasn't your fault.'

'It became a masochistic thing with me in the end. The more awful it got, the nobler I was being.'

'There's been no one since?'

'I was going out with someone at the Tavistock earlier this year. But he was already deciding I was a bad job.'

I kept running skeins of her hair through my fingers.

'Why?'

'Because I wouldn't go to bed with him.'

'As a matter of general policy?'

'There was someone else at Cambridge. In my first year.'

'What happened to that?'

'It was the reverse, absurdly enough. He was much nicer in bed than out of it.' She added drily, 'Unfortunately he knew it. I discovered one day I wasn't the only string to his bow.'

'He must have been a fool.'

'I know it's different for men. Or for men like that. I just felt so humiliated. One more stuffed head on the wall.'

I kissed her hair. 'At least I approve his taste in stuffed heads.'

There was a little silence. Her voice dropped, was shy, almost naïve.

'Have you slept with many girls?'

'None like you. And I've never two-timed.'

She must have belatedly realized the question had been gauche. 'I didn't mean ... you know.' It was not a subject I wanted to linger over, but it obviously held a certain fascination for her, now it was broached. 'It's just that I can't be as clinical about it as June is.'

'Is she clinical about me?'

'You have her approval. For what it's worth.'

'You might sound as if you put more value on it.'

'I hated her on Sunday.' An elbow nudged back. 'And you for not hating her as well.'

'Only because it helped me imagine you like that.'

'She's been teasing me about it ever since. How she's really much more your type.'

I held her a little closer. 'I know which mind I prefer. By a long chalk.'

There was a silence. She took my hand and traced its fingers.

'We came down here last night.'

'Why?'

'It was so hot. We couldn't sleep. To swim. She was hoping some lovely Greek shepherd would spring from the trees.'

'And you?'

'I thought about my English one.'

'What a pity we haven't got costumes.'

Still she traced the backs of my fingers.

'We didn't last night.'

'Is that a suggestion?'

She left a little pause. 'June bet me I wouldn't dare.'

'We can't let her get away with that.'

'Just to swim.'

'But only because ... ?'

She said nothing for a moment, yet I could sense that she was smiling. Then she leant up and whispered in my ear.

'Why do men always want to know in words?'

The next second she was on her feet and pulling me to mine. We went back to the beach. The red light floated on the side of the ghostly white yacht, shimmering a little in the water. There was a glint of light through the highest trees opposite us, from the house.

Someone there was still awake. I took the sides of her singlet and she raised her arms for me to peel it off; then turned her back for me to unhook her bra, while she fiddled at the side of her skirt. I slipped my hands to the front. The skirt fell. For a moment she rested back against me, and her hands covered mine, to still them, on the bare breasts. I kissed the curve of her neck. Then she was gone down towards the water, long-haired, a slim pale figure with a narrow white band around her waist; a nocturnal echo of her sister on the same beach, in the sun, three days before. I stripped off my clothes. Without looking back she waded in to her waist, then plunged forward with a small splash and began to swim, a breast-stroke, out towards the yacht. Half a minute later I was beside her and we swam out together a little further. She stopped first, trod water, grinned at me – it was suddenly a jape, a little piece of daring achieved.

She began to speak in Greek, but not the Greek I knew; something much more archaic, less lisping, unelided.

'What was that?'

'Sophocles.'

'What did it say?'

'Just the sound.' She said, 'When I first arrived, I couldn't believe it. Thousands and thousands of little black squiggles suddenly alive. Not past, but present.'

'I can imagine.'

'Like someone who's always lived in exile. But never realized it.'

'I've felt that.'

'Do you miss England at all?'

'No.'

I saw her smile. 'There must be something we don't agree on.'

'In some other life. Not this.'

'I'm going to float. I've only just learnt how to do it.'

She extended her arms and floated on her back, like a child showing off. I swam a stroke or two closer. She lay with her eyes closed, a small smile on her lips, and her wet hair made her look younger. The sea was absolutely calm, like black glass.

'You look like Ophelia.'

'Shall I get me to a nunnery?'

'I never felt less like Hamlet.'

'Perhaps you're the fool he advised me to marry.'

I smiled in the darkness. 'Have you played her?'

'At school. Just those scenes. Against a ghastly repressed lesbian girl who revelled in every minute of being in male drag.'

'Right down to the codpiece?'

Her voice sank in reproach. 'Mr Urfe! I thought you were above such vulgarity.'

I pushed myself a little closer still and kissed the side of her body, then attempted to peck up it; but was pushed away as she twisted and sank beneath the water again. There was a little struggle, a flurry of water, a splashing, as I tried to embrace her. I was allowed one fleeting pressure of her mouth, but then she had twisted away again and was doing her old-fashioned breast-stroke back towards the beach.

However, she slowed, as if the effort had exhausted her, when we came near the shore, and stood with the water up to her armpits. I stood beside her, our hands met again under the water, this time she let herself be drawn towards me, then my hands were on her waist. She raised her arms and put them round my neck, and then lowered her eyes as I gently explored under the water – the curves, the breasts, the armpits. I coaxed her closer still and felt the soles of her feet inch over the top of mine. Our bodies pressed, her face came up, the eyes closed, to meet mine. I eased a hand behind beneath the wet band of cloth round her hips, cupped the other round the side of a breast. It was cool, liquid, restrained in comparison to the fever of our nakedness in the chapel.

I had guessed, as she had talked, what was missing from her account of her abortive love affaire: the delicate balance in her of physical timidity and sensual imagination ... the first must have made the man attractive to her initially, the second had condemned him when it came to the point – all of which gave her a genuinely nymphlike quality; one her sister, despite her playing of the part that night, lacked. This girl did quite literally flee the satyr and invite him on. There was a wild animal in her, but a true wild animal, intensely suspicious of wrong moves, of too obvious attempts to tame. She set little boundaries, almost like snares, to see if one understood – behaved, advanced, withdrew, as she wanted. Yet behind it all I foresaw an eventual place without boundaries, where she would one day allow me anything ... and one day soon, for she clung to me now, succumbed, her femaleness against my maleness, and our tongues interlaced, aped what out loins wanted.

The silence, the dark water, the brilliant canopy of stars; and my sexual excitement, which she must have felt. Suddenly she turned her head away, almost with violence, though she still clung to me. After a moment I heard her whisper.

'You poor thing. It's not fair.'

'I can't help it. You excite me so much.'

'I don't want you to help it.'

She pulled away a little and a hand slipped down through the water between us. She brought me gently up, curled her fingers round me; timidly, with a return of that naïvety she had shown earlier.

'Poor little eel.'

'With nowhere to swim.'

She began to brush and tease her fingers through the water; then whispered again.

'Do you like me to do this?'

'Idiot.'

She hesitated, then turned, slipped her right arm round my waist, while I put my left one over her shoulder and drew her close against my side. Her left hand felt lower, all round my loins, caressed, lifted and let fall, touched; then silked its way up the shaft, gripped, gently squeezed. The fingers seemed inexperienced, afraid of hurting. I slid my own free hand down and gave hers a little lesson, then left it, and raised her head, found her mouth. I began to lose all sense of everything around us. There was nothing but her tongue, her pressed nakedness, the wet hair, the gentle rhythm of the underwater hand. I would have had it go on all night, this being seduced that was also a seduction, this sudden conversion of the aloof, the fastidious, the voice that quoted Sophocles, into an obedient geisha, an adorable mermaid – though not physiologically the latter. I had shifted my own feet wider to stand more firmly, and one of her legs had curled round mine. The one little garment she wore was pressed very hard against my hip. I slid a hand down from the breast it was holding towards the place; but it was caught, discreetly returned to where it had left.

All night; but it was too erotic. She seemed to know by instinct that I no longer wanted her gentle; clung tighter still, began to show herself less of a novice; and as I racked quietly beneath the water, she bent her head and bit into the side of my armpit, as if she too had her orgasm, though only in the mind.

It was done. Her hand left me, then stroked gently up my stomach. I forced her round and kissed her, a little stunned by how complete and quick this descent from prudishness had been. I suspected that I had her sister's teasing partly to thank for it; but something in Julie herself as well, perhaps always a secret willingness for something like this to happen. We stood clung together, as before, not needing to say anything, the final barrier between us broken. She kissed my skin softly; an unspoken promise.

'I must go. June's waiting up for me.'

One last quick kiss, then we swam a few strokes to where the beach shelved to land. Hand in hand to where our clothes lay. We didn't bother to dry. She stepped into her skirt, twisted to fasten it. I kissed the wet breasts, then hooked her bra for her, helped her back into the singlet; was in turn helped to dress by her. We walked back along beside the water to Bourani, arms enlaced. I had an intuition it had meant more for her ... it was a kind of discovery, or redis-covery, of her own latent sexuality, through the satisfaction of mine – and through the night, the warmth, the old magic of wild Greece. Her face seemed softer, simpler, maskless now. I also knew, with an inwardly crowning elation, that it had destroyed whatever last traces had remained of the suspicion Conchis had tried to sow between us. I needed no answers to my letters now. It might on the surface – or under the water – be a trivial little moment of wickedness, but it was a shared one, wanted on both sides; and a little to test that, I suddenly pulled her round as we walked. She turned and raised her mouth as eagerly as if she had been inside my mind and read my thoughts. All was transparent between us.

I accompanied her back inside the grounds, to within sight of the house. The light in the music-room was off, but I could see one in the back, in the window of the bedroom I used myself. Apparently another bed was brought in, she and June slept there when I was not visiting – and that seemed a perfect symbolic ending to the night, that she was going to sleep in 'my' bed. We had one last brief whispered discussion about the following week-end; but all that had receded now. The old man had been as good as his word, we had not been spied on, I was at last sanctioned as the Ferdinand to his salt-haired, clinging, warm-mouthed Miranda. Whatever happened, the summer ahead, all life ahead, was ours.

She kissed and left me, then after a few steps, turned quickly and ran back and kissed me once more. I waited until I saw her slip under the colonnade and disappear.

Though I felt tired, I walked the uphill path to the central crest quickly, to dry my damp clothes. I hardly thought about the day to come, the lack of sleep, the dread struggle to stay awake in class; all that was now tolerable. Julie entranced me. It was as if I had stumbled on a sleeping princess and found her, once woken, not merely in love with me, but erotically starved, deliciously eager to exorcize whatever sour and perverse lovemaking had gone on with her ill-starred choice of the previous year. I imagined a Julie who had acquired all Alison's experience and adeptness, her quick passions, her slow lubricities, but enhanced, enriched, diversified by superior taste, intelligence, poetry ... I kept smiling to myself as I walked. There was a thin new moon, the starlight, and I now knew almost by heart my way up through the ghostly, silent forest of Aleppo pines. I saw nothing in the present, only the endless seduction and surrender of that willing body: nights in the village house, indolent naked siestas on some shadowed bed ... and when we were satiated, that other, golden, lapping presence, June, implicit two for the price of one. Of course it was Julie I loved, but all love needs a teasing, a testing dry relief.

I began to review the miracle-mystery that had brought us together – Conchis, and his purposes. If you have a private menagerie, your concern is to keep the animals in, not to dictate exactly what they do inside the cage. He constructed bars around us, subtle psycho-sexual bars that kept us chained to Bourani. He was like some Elizabethan nobleman. We were his Earl of Leicester's troupe, his very private company; but he might well have incorporated the Heisenberg principle into his 'experiment', so that much of it was indeterminate, both to him as observer-voyeur and to us as observed human particles. I guessed that he partly wanted to taunt us with a false contrast between an all-wise Europe and a callow England. In spite of all his gnomic cant he was like so many other Europeans, quite unable to understand the emotional depths and subtleties of the English attitude to life. He thought the girls and I were green, innocents; but we could outperfidy his perfidy, and precisely because we were English: born with masks and bred to lie.

I came towards the main ridge. As I walked I overturned a loose stone here and there, but otherwise the landscape was totally silent. Far below, over the crumpled grey velvet of the outstretched pine-tops, the sea glistened obscurely under the spangled sky. The world belonged to night.

The trees thinned out where the ground rose steeply to the small bluff that marked the south side of the main ridge. I paused a moment for breath and turned to look back down towards Bourani; glanced at my watch. It was just after midnight. The whole island was asleep. Under the silver nailparing of a moon, I felt, though without any melancholy at all, that sense of existential solitude, the being and being alone in a universe, that still nights sometimes give.

Then from behind me, from somewhere up on the ridge, I heard a sound. A very small sound, but enough to make me step swiftly off the path into the cover of a pine. Someone or something up there had overturned a stone. A pause of fifteen seconds or more. Then I froze; both with shock and as a precaution.

A man was standing on top of the bluff, ashily silhouetted against the night sky. Then a second man, and a third. I could hear the faint noise of their feet on the rock, the muffled clink of something metallic. Then, like magic, there were six. Six grey shadows standing along the skyline. One of them raised an arm and pointed; but I heard no sound of voices. Islanders? But they hardly ever used the central ridge in summer; and never at that time of night. In any case I suddenly realized what they were. They were soldiers. I could just see the indistinct outlines of guns, the dull sheen of a helmet.

There had been Greek army manoeuvres on the mainland a month before, and a coming and going of landing-craft in the strait. These men must be on some similar commando-type exercise. But I didn't move.

One of the men turned back, and the others followed. I thought I knew what had happened. They had come along the central ridge and overshot the transverse path that led down to Bourani and Moutsa. As if to confirm my guess there was a distant pop, like a firework. I saw, from somewhere west of Bourani, a shimmering Very light hanging in the sky. It was one of the starshell variety and fell in a slow parabola. I had fired dozens myself, on night exercises. The six were evidently on their way to 'attack' some point on the other side of Moutsa.

For all that, I looked round. Twenty yards away there was a group of rocks with enough small shrubs to give cover. I ran silently under the trees and, forgetting my clean trousers and shirt, dropped down in a natural trough between two of the rocks. They were still warm from the sun. I watched the cleft in the skyline down which the path lay.

In a few seconds a pale movement told me I was right. The men were coming down. They were probably just a group of friendly lads from the Epirus or somewhere. But I pressed myself as flat as I could. When I could hear that they had come abreast, about thirty yards away, I sneaked a facedown look through the twigs that shielded me.

My heart jumped. They were in German uniforms. For a moment I thought that perhaps they were dressed up to be the 'enemy' on the manoeuvres; but it was unthinkable, after the atrocities of the Occupation, that any Greek soldier would put on a German uniform, even for an exercise; and from then on I knew. The masque had moved outside the domaine, and the old devil had not given in one bit.

The last man was carrying a much bulkier pack than the others; a pack with a thin, just visible rod rising from it. The truth flashed in on me. In an instant I knew Demetriades had a fellow-spy at the school. He was a very Turkish-looking Greek, a compact, taciturn man with a close-cropped head, one of the science masters. He never came into the common-room; lived in his laboratory. His colleagues nick-named him 'o Alchemikos', the alchemist. With a grim realization of new depths of treachery, I remembered that he was one of Patarescu's closest cronies. But what I had remembered first was that there was a transmitter in his laboratory, since some of the boys wanted to become radio officers. The school even had a ham radio station sign. I hit the ground with my fist. It had all been so obvious. That was why they always knew I was coming. There was only the one gate; the old gatekeeper was always on duty.

The men had gone. They must have been wearing rubber-soled boots; and they must have wadded their equipment well to make so little noise. But the fact that I had walked fast had evidently upset their calculations. The flare could only have been a belated signal that I was on my way. For a moment I accused Julie, then exonerated her. Suspicion of her was far too obviously now what Conchis hoped for; but he had not allowed for the way his 'bait' would prove she was on the mouse's side. I knew she must be totally innocent of this new trap; and the mouse was turned fox, not to be tricked so easily.

I was even half-tempted to follow the men down to see where they went, but I remembered old lessons from my own military training. Never patrol on a windless night if you can avoid it; remember the man nearer the moon sees you better than you see him. Already, within thirty seconds of the passing, I could hardly hear them. A stone was sent scuttering, then silence; then another, very faintly. I gave them another thirty seconds, then I pushed myself up and began to climb the path as fast as I could.

At the top of the cleft where the ridge flattened out I had to cross fifty yards or so of open space before the ground dipped down to the northern side. It was a windswept area littered with stones, a few lone bushes. On the far side lay a large patch, an acre or so, of high tamarisk. I could see the black opening in the feathery branches where my path went in. I stood and listened. Silence. I began to lope across the open space.

I had got halfway across when I heard a bang. A second later a Very flare burst open some two hundred yards to the right. It flooded the ridge with light. I dropped, my face averted. The light died down. The moment it hissed into darkness I was on my feet and racing, careless of noise, for the tamarisks. I got into them safely, stopped a moment, trying to work out what insane new trick Conchis was playing. Then I heard footsteps running along the ridge, from the direction the flare had come. I began to sprint down the path between the seven-foot bushes.

I came to a flat, wider curve in the path, where I could run faster. Then terrifyingly, without any warning, my foot was caught and I was plunging headlong forward. A searing jab as my flung-out hand hit the sharp edge of a stone. An agonizing bang in the ribs. I heard my breath blasted out of my lungs with the impact and my shocked voice saying 'Oh Christ'. I was too dazed for a moment to realize what had happened. Then came a sharp low command from behind the tamarisks to the right. I spoke only a word or two of the language. But the voice sounded authentically German.

There were sounds all around me, on both sides of the path. I was surrounded by men dressed as German soldiers. There were seven of them.

'What the bloody hell's the game?'

I scrambled on to my knees, rubbing the grit off the palms of my hands. Blood covered the knuckles of one of them. Two men came behind me and seized me by the arms, jerked me up. Another man stood in the centre of the path. He was apparently in charge. He had no rifle or sub-machine-gun, like the others, but only a revolver. I looked sideways at the rifle the man to my left had slung over his shoulder. It looked real; not a stage property. He also looked really German: not Greek.

The man with the revolver, evidently some kind of N.C.O., spoke again in German. Two men bent, one on either side of the path, and fiddled by the tamarisk stems: a tripwire. The man with the revolver blew a whistle quietly. I looked at the two men beside me.

'You speak English? *Sprechen Sie Englisch?*'

They took not the slightest notice, except to jerk my arms for silence. I thought, Christ, wait till I see Conchis again. The N.C.O. stood in the path with his back to me, and the other four men gathered beyond him. Two of them sat down.

One evidently asked if they could smoke. The N.C.O. gave permission.

They lit up, helmeted faces in matchflares, and began to talk in a low murmur of voices. They seemed all German. Not just Greeks who knew a few words of German; but Germans. I spoke to the sergeant.

'When you've finished the clowning perhaps you'll tell me what we're waiting for.'

The man pivoted round and came up to me. He was a man of about forty-five, long-cheeked. He stood with his face about two feet from mine. He did not look particularly brutal; but he looked his part. I expected another spit routine, but he simply said quietly, '*Was sagen Sie?*'

'Oh go to hell.'

He remained staring at me, as if he did not understand, but was interested to see me at last; then expressionlessly turned away. The grip of the soldiers relaxed a little. If I had felt less battered, I might have run for it. But then I heard footsteps from the ridge above. A few seconds later the six men I had first seen came marching down the path in a loose single file. But before they came to us, they fell out by the group of smoking men.

The boy who was holding me on the right was only about twenty. He began siss-whistling under his breath; and in what had been, in spite of my remark about clowning, a pretty convincing performance until then, he struck a rather obvious note, for the tune was the most famous of all, 'Lili Marlene'. Or was it a very bad pun? He had a huge acne-covered jaw and small eyelashless eyes; specially chosen, I suppose, because he appeared so Teutonic, with a curious machine-like indifference, as if he didn't know why he was there, who I was; and didn't care; just carried out orders.

I calculated: thirteen men, at least half of whom were German. Cost of getting them to Greece, from Athens to the island. Equipment. Training-rehearsing. Cost of getting them off the island, back to Germany. It couldn't be done under five hundred pounds. And for what? To frighten – or perhaps to impress – one unimportant person. At the same time, now that the first adrenalin panic had subsided, I felt my attitude changed. This scene was so well organized, so elaborate. I fell under the spell of Conchis the magician again. Frightened, but fascinated; and then there were more footsteps.

Two more men appeared. One was short and slim. He came striding down the path with a taller man behind him. Both had the peaked hats of officers. Eagle badges. The soldiers he passed stood hurriedly, but he made a brisk movement of his hand to put them at ease. He came straight to me. He was obviously an actor who had specialized in German colonel roles; a hard face, a thin mouth; all he lacked were spectacles with oblong lenses and steel frames.

'Hallo.'

He did not answer, but looked at me rather as the sergeant, who was now standing stiffly some way behind him, had. The other officer was apparently a lieutenant, an aide. I noticed he had a slight limp; an Italian-looking face, very dark eyebrows, round tanned cheeks; handsome.

'Where's the producer?'

The 'colonel' took a cigarette case out of his inside pocket and selected a cigarette. The 'lieutenant' reached forward with a light. Beyond them I saw one of the soldiers cross the path with something in loose paper – food of some sort. They were eating.

'I must say you look the part.'

He said one word, carefully pursed in his mouth, spat out like a grape pip.

'*Gut.*'

He turned away; said something in German. The sergeant went up the path and came back with a hurricane lamp, which he lit, then set behind me.

The 'colonel' moved up the path to where the 'sergeant' was standing, and I was left staring at the 'lieutenant'. There was something strange in his look, as if he would like to tell me something, but couldn't; searching my face for some answer. His eyes flicked away, and he turned abruptly, though awkwardly, on his heel and rejoined the colonel. I heard low German voices, then the sergeant's laconic command.

The men stood to, and for some reason I couldn't understand lined up on both sides of the path, facing inwards, irregularly, not standing to attention, as if waiting for someone to pass. I thought they were going to take me somewhere, I had to pass through them. But I was pulled back by my two guards in line with the others. Only the sergeant and the two officers stood in the centre of the path. The lamp threw a circle of light round me. I realized it had a dramatic function.

There was a tense silence. I was cast as a spectator in some way, not as the protagonist. At last I heard more people coming. A different, unmilitary figure came into sight. For a second I thought he was drunk. But then I realized he had his hands tied behind his back; like me, a prisoner. He wore dark trousers, but was bare above the waist. Behind him came two more soldiers. One of them seemed to prod him, and he groaned. As he came closer to me I saw, with a sharp sense that the masque was running out of control, that he was barefoot. His stumbling, ginger walk was real, not acted.

He came abreast of me. A young man, evidently Greek, rather short. His face was atrociously bruised, puffed, the whole of one side covered in blood from a gash near the right eye. He appeared stunned, hardly able to walk. He didn't notice me until the last moment, when he stopped, looked at me wildly. I had a swift stab of terror, that this really was some village boy they had got hold of and beaten up – not someone to look the part, but be the part. Without warning the soldier behind jabbed him savagely in the small of the back. I saw it, I saw his spasmic jerk forward, and the – or so it sounded – absolutely authentic gasp of pain the jab caused. He stumbled on another five or six yards. Then the colonel spat one word. The guards reached roughly out and brought him to a halt. The three men stood there in the path facing downhill. The colonel moved down to just in front of me, his lieutenant limping beside him; both backs to me.

Another silence; the panting of the man. Then almost at once came another figure, exactly the same, hands tied behind his back, two soldiers behind him. I knew by then where I was. I was back in 1943, and looking at captured resistance fighters.

The second man was obviously the *kapetan*, the leader – heavily built, about forty, some six feet tall. He had one naked arm in a rope sling, a rough bandage covered in blood round his upper arm. It seemed to have been made from the sleeve torn off his shirt; was too thin to staunch the blood. He came down the path towards me; a magnificent *klepht* face with a heavy black moustache, an accipitral nose. I had seen such faces one or twice in the Peloponnesus, but I knew where this man came from, because over his forehead he still wore the fringed black headband of the Cretan mountaineer. I could see him standing in some early-nineteenth-century print, in folk-costume, silver-handled yataghan and pistols in his belt, the noble brigand of the Byronic myth. He was actually wearing what looked like British Army battledress trousers, a khaki shirt. And he too was barefooted. But he seemed to refuse to stumble. He was less battered than the other man, perhaps because of the wound.

As he came up level with me, he stopped and then looked past the colonel and the lieutenant straight at me. I understood that he was meant to know me, that I had once known him. It was a look of the most violent loathing. Contempt. At the same time of a raging despair. He said nothing for a moment. Then he hissed in Greek one word.

'*Prodotis.*' His lips snarled on the *v*-sounding demotic Greek *delta*. Traitor.

He had great power, he was completely in his role; and in a barely conscious way, as if I sensed that I must be an actor too, I did not come out with another flip remark but took his look and his hatred in silence. For a moment, I was the traitor.

He was kicked on, but he turned and gave me one last burning look back across the ten feet of lamplight. Then again that word, as if I might not have heard it the first time.

'*Prodotis.*'

As he did so there was a cry, an exclamation. The colonel's rapped command: *Nicht schiessen*! My guards gripped me vice tight. The first man had bolted, diving headlong sideways into the tamarisks. His two guards plunged after him, then three or four of the soldiers lining the path. He can't have got more than ten yards. There was a cry, German words, then a sickening scream of pain and another. The sound of a body being kicked, butt-ended.

At the second cry the lieutenant, who had been standing watching just in front of me, turned and looked past me into the night. I was meant to understand he was revolted by this, by brutality; his other first look at me was explained. The colonel was aware that he had turned away. He gave the lieutenant a quick stare round, flicked a look at the guards holding me, then spoke – in French; so that the guards could not understand … and no doubt, so that I could.

'*Mon lieutenant, voilà pour moi la plus belle musique dans le monde.*'

His French was heavily German; and he gave a sort of mincing lip-grimacing sarcasm to the word *musique* that explained the situation. He was a stock German sadist; the lieutenant, a stock good German.

The lieutenant seemed about to say something, but suddenly the night was torn open by a tremendous cry. It came from the other man, the noble brigand, from the very depths of his lungs and it must have been heard, if anyone had been awake to hear it, from one side of the island to the other. It was just one word, but the most Greek of all words.

I knew it was acting, but it was magnificent acting. It came out harsh as fire, more a diabolical howl than anything else, but electrifying, right from the very inmost core.

It jagged into the colonel like the rowel of a spur. He whipped round like a steel spring. In three strides he was in front of the Cretan and had delivered a savage smashing slap across his face. It knocked the man's head sideways, but he straightened up at once. Again it shocked me almost as if I was the one hit. The beating-up, the bloody arm could be faked, but not that blow.

Lower down the path they came dragging the other man out of the bushes. He could not stand and they were pulling him by the arms. They dropped him in mid-path and he lay on his side, groaning. The sergeant went down, took a water-bottle from one of the soldiers and poured it over his face. The man made an attempt to stand. The sergeant said something and the original guards hauled him to his feet.

The colonel spoke.

The soldiers split into two sections, the prisoners in the middle, and began to move off. In under a minute the last back disappeared. I was alone with my two guards, the colonel and the lieutenant.

The colonel came up to me. His face had a basilisk coldness. He spoke in a punctiliously over-distinct English.

'It. Is. Not. Ended.'

There was just the trace of a humourless smile on his face; and more than a trace of menace. As if he meant something more than that there was a sequel to this scene; but that the whole Nazi *Weltanschauung* would one day be resurrected and realized. He was an impressively iron man. As soon as he spoke he turned and began to follow the soldiers down the path. The lieutenant went with him. I called out.

'What isn't ended?'

But there was no reply. The two dark figures, the taller limping, disappeared between the pale, soft walls of the tamarisk. I turned to my guards.

'What now?'

For answer I found myself jerked forward and then back, and so forced to sit. There were a ridiculous few moments of struggle, which they easily won. A minute later they had roped my ankles together tightly, then hoisted me back against a boulder, so that I had support for my back. The younger soldier felt in his tunic top-pocket and tossed me down three cigarettes. In the flare of the match I lit I looked at them. They were rather cheap-looking. Along each one was printed in red, between little black swastikas, the words *Leipzig dankt euch*. The one I smoked tasted very stale, at least ten years old, as if they had been overthorough and actually used cigarettes from some war-issue tin. In 1943 it would have tasted fresh.

I made attempt after attempt to speak with them. In English, then in my exiguous German; French, Greek. But they sat stolidly opposite me, on the other side of the path. They hardly spoke ten words to each other; and were obviously under orders not to speak to me.

I had looked at my watch when they first tied me. It had said twelve thirty-five. Now it was one thirty. Somewhere on the north coast of the island, a mile or two west of the school, I heard the first faint pump of an engine. It sounded more like the diesel of a large coastal caïque than that of the yacht. The cast had re-embarked. My two guards must have been waiting for the sound. They stood, and the elder one held a table-knife up for me to see, then threw it down where they had been sitting. Then without a word they began to walk away – but not in the direction the others had taken. They climbed the path back to the ridge, and down to Bourani.

As soon as I was sure they had gone I crawled over the stones to the knife. It was blunt, the rope was new, and I wasn't free for another twenty exasperating minutes. I climbed back to the ridge, to where I could look down over the south coast. Of course it was quiet, serene, a landscape tilted to the stars, an Aegean island lying in its classical nocturnal peace. The yacht still rode at anchor. I could hear the caïque, whatever it was, heading away behind me towards Nauplia. I thought of storming down to Bourani, of waking the girls, bearding Conchis, demanding explanation at once. But I felt exhausted, I felt sure of the girls' innocence and I was far from sure I would be allowed anywhere near the villa … they would have anticipated such a reaction on my part, and I was hopelessly outnumbered in mere physical terms. I also felt, beneath my anger, a return of the old awe for what Conchis was doing. Once more I was a man in a myth, incapable of understanding it, but somehow aware that understanding it meant it must continue, however sinister its peripateia.

50

Morning school began at seven, so I had had less than five hours' sleep when I appeared in class. It was ugly weather, too, without wind, remorselessly hot and stagnant. All the colour was burnt out of the land, what few remaining greens there were looked parched and defeated. Processional caterpillars had massacred the pines; the oleander flowers were brown at the edges. Only the sea lived, and I did not begin to think coherently until school was over at noon and I could plunge into the water and lie in its blue relief.

One thing had occurred to me during the morning. Except for the main actors, almost all the German 'soldiers' had looked very young – between eighteen and twenty. It was the beginning of July; the German and the Greek university terms would probably be over. If Conchis really had some connection with film-producing he could probably have got Germans students to come easily enough – to work for a few days for him and then holiday in Greece. What I could not believe was that having got them to Greece he would use them only once. More sadism was, as the colonel warned, to come.

I floated on my back with my arms out and my eyes shut, crucified in the water. I had already cooled down enough in other ways to know that I wasn't going to write the angry and sarcastic letter I had been phrasing on the return from the ridge. Apart from anything else it was what the old man would be expecting – I had that morning in school detected something speculative and inquisitive in Demetriades' eyes – and my one sure good move was not to do what was expected. Nor on reflection did I think there was any great danger for the sisters; as long as he believed them misled, they were safe, or as safe as they always had been. If I was to get them out of it, it was better to wait till they were in front of me; not to warn him of what I intended. And then he had the enormous advantage of giving the entertainment – and such entertainment. It seemed, in some peculiar way, foolish to be angry about the way the thing had been done when the staggering fact was that it had been done at all.

The post came on the noon boat and was distributed during lunch. I had three letters; one of the rare ones from my uncle in Rhodesia, another with one of the information bulletins sent out by the British Council in Athens; and the third ... I knew the handwriting, round, a bit loose, big letters. I slit it. My letter to Alison fell out, unopened. There was nothing else. A few minutes later, back in my room, I put it on an ashtray, still unopened, and burnt it.

The next day was Friday. I had another letter at lunch. It had been delivered by hand and I knew the writing. I didn't open it until I had escaped from the dining-room – which was as well, because its brief contents made me swear aloud. It was as brutal and unexpected as a slap across the face; dateless, placeless, without superscription.

> Any further visits to Bourani will be in vain. I do not think I have to explain why. You have gravely disappointed me.
>
> MAURICE CONCHIS

I knew a stunned plunge of disappointment and a bitter anger. What right had he to issue such an arbitrary ukase? It was incomprehensible, it contradicted everything I had learnt from Julie; but not, as I soon saw, what had happened after I left her ... that accusation of treachery gained a fresh significance. I chillingly realized that the Occupation episode could also have been a finale, a notice of dismissal – he had no more time for me. But then there were the girls. What story could he have told them? Or could tell them, when they knew he had been lying to them?

All through that day I half expected to see them appear at the school. They must have seen through him now. I had notions of going to the police, of contacting the British Embassy in Athens. But slowly I came back on a more even keel. I recalled the parallels with *The Tempest*, and that old man's trial of the young usurper in *his* domaine. I recalled the constant past occasions when Conchis had said the opposite of what he meant; and above all, I remembered Julie ... not only the naked body in the sea, but her intuitive trust in our Prospero. I decided by the time I went to bed that it must be taken as some last black joke on his part, some testing trick analogous to the dice-game and the suicide pill. I refused to believe that he would

383

really keep either Julie or the truth from me for another week. He must know I should go over to Bourani on the morrow. He might carry on with some comedy of intense disapproval, but he would be there; and his other puppet would also be there to help me finally call his bluff.

Soon after two o'clock on Saturday, I was on my way up into the hills. At three, I entered the clump of tamarisk. In the blazing heat – the weather remained windless, stagnant – it was difficult to believe that what I had seen had happened. But there were two or three recently broken twigs and branches; and where the 'prisoner' had dived away there were several overturned stones, their bottoms stained ruddy from the island earth; and more broken sprays of tamarisk. A little higher I picked up several screwed-out cigarette-ends. One was only half-smoked and had the beginnings of the same phrase: *Leipzig da* ...

I stood on the bluff looking down over the other side of the island. I saw at once that the yacht wasn't there; yet I wouldn't let that kill all hope.

I arrived at the gate and walked straight to the house. It lay with the cottage in the sun, closed and deserted. I rattled the french window shutters hard, and tried the others. But none of them gave. All the time I kept looking round, not because I actually felt I was being watched so much as because I felt I ought to be feeling it. They must be watching me; might even be inside the house, smiling in the darkness just behind the shutters, only four or five feet away. I went and gazed down at the private beach. It lay in the heat; the jetty, the pump-house, the old baulk, the shadowed mouth of the little cave; but no boat. Then to the Poseidon statue. Silent statue, silent trees. To the cliff, to where I had sat with Julie the Sunday before.

The lifeless sea was ruffled here and there by a lost zephyr, by a stippling shoal of sardines, dark ash-blue lines that snaked, broad then narrow, in slow motion across the shimmering mirageous surface, as if the water was breeding corruption.

I began to walk along towards the bay with the three cottages. The landscape to the east came into view, and then I came on the boundary wire of Bourani. As everywhere else it was rusty, a token barrier, not a real one; shortly beyond it the inland cliff fell sixty or seventy feet to lower ground. I bent through the wire and walked inland along the edge. There were one or two places where one could clamber down; but at the bottom there was an impenetrable jungle of scrub and thorn-ivy. I came to where the fence turned west towards the gate. There were no tell-tale overturned stones; no obvious gaps in the wire. Following the cliff to where it levelled out, I eventually came on the seldom used path I had taken on my previous visit to the cottages.

Shortly afterwards I was walking through the small olive-orchard that surrounded them. I watched the three whitewashed houses as I approached through the trees. Strange that there was not even a chicken or a donkey. Or a dog. There had been two or three dogs before.

Two of the one-storey cottages were adjoining. Both front doors were bolted, with bolt-handles padlocked down. The third looked more openable, but it gave only an inch before coming up hard. There was a wooden bar inside. I went round the back. The door there was also padlocked. But on the last side I came to, over a hen-coop, I found two of the shutters were loose. I peered in through the dirty windows. An old brass bed, a cube of folded bedclothes in the middle of it. A wall of photographs and ikons. Two cane-bottomed wooden chairs, a cot beneath the window, an old trunk On the window-sill in front of me was a brown candle in a retsina bottle, a broken garland of *immortelles*, a rusty sprocket-wheel, and a month of dust. I closed the shutters.

The second cottage had another padlocked bolt on its back door; but though the last one had the bolt, it was simply tied down with a piece of fishing-twine. I struck a match. Half a minute later I was standing inside the cottage, in another bedroom. Nothing in the darkened room looked in the least suspicious. I went through to the kitchen and living-room in front. From it a door led straight through into the cottage next door; another kitchen; beyond it, another musty bedroom. I opened one or two drawers, a cupboard. The cottages were, beyond any possibility of faking, typical impoverished islanders' homes. The one strange thing was that they were empty.

I came out and fastened the bolt handle with a bit of wire. Fifty yards or so away among the olives I saw a whitewashed privy. I went over to it. A spider's web stretched across the hole in the ground. A collection of torn squares of yellowing Greek newspaper hung from a rusty nail.

Defeat.

I went to the cistern beside the double cottage, took off the wooden lid and let down an old bucket on a rope that stood beside the white washed neck. Cool air rushed up, like an imprisoned snake. I sat on the neck and swallowed great mouthfuls of the water. It had that living, stony freshness of cistern water, so incomparably sweeter than the neutral flavour of tap-water.

A brilliant red-and-black jumping spider edged along the puteal towards me. I laid my hand in its path and it jumped on to it; holding it up close I could see its minute black eyes, like gig-lamps. It swivelled its massive square head from side to side in an arachnoidal parody of Conchis's quizzing; and once again, as with the owl, I had an uncanny apprehension of a reality of witchcraft; Conchis's haunting, brooding omnipresence.

What really defeated me was this proof that I was not indispensable. I had assumed the 'experiment' needed my presence above all; but perhaps it didn't, and I had been a mere side-plot, discarded as soon as I had tried to gain too much prominence. What riled me most was to find myself apparently in the same category as Mitford, and for no clear reason at all. I felt fear as well, a sharp paranoia. Although he might have found some lie to tell the girls, some reason for my not being able to come that week-end, there remained the possibility that they were all three deceiving me. But how could I believe that now? All those kisses, franknesses, caresses, that token coupling in the night water ... no girl could pretend to want and to enjoy such things unless she was a prostitute. It was unthinkable. Perhaps the clue lay in dispensability. I was being taught some obscure metaphysical lesson about the place of man in existence, about the limitations of the egocentric view. But it seemed much more like a piece of gratuitous cruelty, closer to tormenting dumb animals than any true teaching. I was drowned in a sea of mistrust – not only of outward appearances but of deeper motives as well. For weeks I had had a sense of being taken apart, disconnected from a previous self – or the linked structures of ideas and conscious feeling that constitute self; and now it was like lying on the workshop bench, a litter of parts, the engineer gone ... and not being quite sure how one put oneself together again.

I found myself thinking of Alison, for the first time less with guilt than regret. I almost wished she was there, beside me, for companionship. To talk to, nothing more, like a man friend. I had hardly given her a thought since the return of my unopened letter. Events had already swept her into the past. But now I recalled those moments on Parnassus: the sound of the waterfall, the sun on my back, her closed eyes, her whole body arched to have me deeper ... that strange certainty I had always had of knowing, even when she lied, how and why she lied; that she couldn't lie, in simple fact. Of course it made her, in daily terms, dull and predictable, rather tediously transparent. What had always attracted me in the opposite sex was what they tried to hide, what provoked all the metaphorical equivalents of seducing them out of their clothes into nakedness. That had always been too easy with Alison. And anyway ... I stood up and screwed out my promiscuity of mind with my cigarette. She was spilt milk; or spilt semen. I wanted Julie ten times more.

I spent the rest of that afternoon searching the coast eastward of the three cottages, then came back past them to Bourani again, nicely timed for tea under the colonnade. But the place remained as deserted as before. I spent a further hour searching for a note, a sign, anything; it became like the idiot ransacking of a drawer already ten times searched.

At six I set off back to the school, with nothing but a useless rage of frustration. With Conchis; with Julie; with everything.

On the far side of the village there was another harbour, used exclusively by the local fishermen. It was avoided by everyone from the school, and by everyone with any claim to social *ton* in the village. Many of the houses had been ruthlessly dilapidated. Some were no more than the carious stumps of walls; and the ones that still stood along the broken quays had corrugated iron roofs, concrete patches and other unsightly evidence of frequent mending. There were three tavernas, but only one was of any size. It had a few rough wooden tables outside its doors.

Once before, coming back from one of my solitary winter walks, I had gone there for a drink; I remembered the taverna-keeper was loquacious and comparatively easy to understand. By island standards, and perhaps because he was Anatolian by birth, conversable. His name was Georgiou; rather foxy-faced, with a lick of grey-black hair and a small moustache that gave him a comic resemblance to Hitler. On Sunday morning I sat under a catalpa and he came up, obsequiously delighted to have caught a rich customer. Yes, he said, of course he would be honoured to have an ouzo with me. He called one of his children to serve us ... the best ouzo, the best olives. Did things go well at the school, did I like Greece ... ? I let him ask the usual questions. Then I set to work. Twelve or so faded carmine and green caïques floated in the still blue water in front of us. I pointed to them.

'It's a pity you do not have any foreign tourists here. Yachts.'

'Ech.' He spat out an olive-stone. 'Phraxos is dead.'

'I thought Mr Conchis from Bourani kept his yacht over here sometimes.'

'That man.' I knew at once that Georgiou was one of the village enemies of Conchis. 'You have met him?'

I said no, but I was thinking of visiting him. He did have a yacht then?

Yes. But it never came to this side of the island.

Had *he* ever met Conchis?

'*Ochi.*' No.

'Does he have houses in the village?'

Only the one where Hermes lived. It was near a church called St Elias, at the back of the village. As if changing the subject I asked idly about the three cottages near Bourani. Where had the families gone?

He shook his hand to the south. 'To the mainland. For the summer.' He explained that a minority of the island fishermen were semi-nomadic. In winter they fished in the protected waters off Phraxos; but in summer, taking their families with them, they wandered round the Peloponnesus, even as far as Crete, in search of better fishing. He returned to the cottages.

He pointed down and then made drinking gestures. 'The cisterns are bad. No good water in summer.'

'Really – no good water?'

'No.'

'What a shame.'

'It is his fault. He of Bourani. He could make better cisterns. But he is too mean.'

'He owns the cottages then?'

'*Vevaios.*' Of course. 'On that side of the island, all is his.'

'All the land?'

He ticked off his stubby fingers: Korbi, Stremi, Bourani, Moutsa, Pigadi, Zastena ... all names of bays and capes around Bourani; and apparently this was another complaint against Conchis. Various Athenians, 'rich people', would have liked to build villas over there. But Conchis refused to sell one metre; deprived the island of badly needed wealth. A donkey loaded with wood tripped down the quay towards us; rubbing its legs together, picking its fastidious way like a model. This news proved Demetriades's complicity. It must have been common gossip.

'I suppose you see his guests in the village?'

He raised his head, negatively, uninterestedly; it was nothing to him whether there were guests or not. I persisted. Did he know if there were foreigners staying over there?

But he shrugged. '*Isos.*' Perhaps. He did not know.

Then I had a piece of luck. A little old man appeared from a side-alley and came behind Georgiou's back; a battered old seaman's cap, a blue canvas suit so faded with washing that it was almost white in the sunlight. Georgiou threw him a glance as he passed our table, then called.

'*Eh, Barba Dimitraki*! *Ela.*' Come. Come and speak with the English professor.

The old man stopped. He must have been about eighty; very shaky, unshaven, but not totally senile. Georgiou turned to me.

'Before the war. He was the same as Hermes. He took the mail to Bourani.'

I pressed the old man to take a seat, ordered more ouzo and another *mezé*.

'You know Bourani well?'

He waved his old hand; he meant, very well, more than he could express. He said something I didn't understand. Georgiou, who had some linguistic resourcefulness, piled our cigarette boxes and matches together like bricks. Building.

'I understand. In 1929?'

The old man nodded.

'Did Mr Conchis have many guests before the war?'

'Many, many guests.' This surprised Georgiou; he even repeated my question, and got the same answer.

'Foreigners?'

'Many foreigners. Frenchmen, Englishmen, all.'

'What about the English masters at the school? Did they go there?'

'*Ne, ne. Oloi.*' Yes, all of them.

'You can't remember their names?' He smiled at the ridiculousness of the question. He couldn't even remember what they looked like. Except one who was very tall.

'Did you meet them in the village?'

'Sometimes. Sometimes.'

'What did they do at Bourani, before the war?'

'They were foreigners.'

Georgiou was impatient at this exhibition of village logic. '*Ne, Barba. Xenoi. Ma ti ekanon?*'

'Music. Singing. Dancing.' Once again Georgiou didn't believe him; he winked at me, as if to say, the old man is soft in the head. But I knew he wasn't; and that Georgiou had not come to the island till 1946.

'What kind of singing and dancing?'

He didn't know; his rheumy eyes seemed to search for the past, and lose it. But he said, 'And other things. They acted in plays.' Georgiou laughed out loud, but the old man shrugged and said indifferently, 'It is true.'

Georgiou leant forward with a grin. 'And what were you, Barba Dimitraki? Karayozis?' He was talking about the Greek shadowplay Punch.

I made the old man see I believed him. 'What kind of plays?'

But his face said he didn't know. 'There was a theatre in the garden.'

'Where in the garden?'

'Behind the house. With curtains. A real theatre.'

'You know Maria?'

But it seemed that before the war it had been another house-keeper, called Soula, now dead.

'When were you last there?'

'Many years. Before the war.'

'Do you still like Mr Conchis?'

The old man nodded, but it was a brief, qualified nod. Georgiou chipped in.

'His eldest son was killed in the execution.'

'Ah. I am very sorry. Very sorry.'

The old man shrugged; kismet. He said, 'He is not a bad man.'

'Did he work with the Germans in the Occupation?'

The old man raised his head, a firm no. Georgiou made a hawk of violent disagreement. They began to argue, talking so fast that I couldn't follow them. But I heard the old man say, 'I was here. You were not here.'

Georgiou turned to me with a wink. 'He has given the old man a house. And money every year. The old man cannot say what he really thinks.'

'Does he do that for the other relatives?'

'Bah. One or two. The old ones. Why not? He has millions.' He made the corruption gesture, meaning conscience money.

Suddenly the old man said to me, '*Mia phora* ... once there was a big *paneyiri* with many lights and music and fireworks. Many fire-works and many guests.'

I had an absurd vision of a garden party: hundreds of elegant women, and men in morning-dress.

'When was that?'

'Three, five years before the war.'

'Why was this celebration?'

But he didn't know.

'Were you there?'

I was with my son. We were fishing. We saw it up in Bourani. Many lights, many voices. *Kai ta pyrotechnimata.*' And the fireworks.

Georgiou said, 'Yah. You were drunk, Barba.'

'No. I was not drunk.'

Try as I did, I could get nothing more out of the old man. So in the end I shook them both by the hand, paid the small bill, tipped Georgiou heavily, and walked back to the school.

One thing was clear. There had been Leverrier, Mitford, and myself; but then others whose names I did not yet know back in the 'thirties; a long line. It gave me a return of great expectations; and the courage to face whatever new was being prepared in that now uncurtained theatre over on the far side.

I returned to the village that evening, and climbed up the narrow cobbled streets that led to the back of the village; past warrens of whitewashed walls, peasant interiors, through tiny squares shaded by almond trees. Great magenta sprays of bougainvillaea flamed in the sun or glowed in the pale evening shadows. It was a sort of kasbah area of the village, a very pretty kasbah, with its cross-glimpses of the plumbago-blue six-o'clock sea below, and the gold-green pine-covered hills above. People sitting outside their cottages greeted me, and I collected the inevitable small Pied Piper chain of children, who subsided into giggles if I looked at them and waved them away. When I came to the church I went in. I wanted to justify my presence in the quarter. It was densely gloomy, with a miasma of incense over everything; a row of ikons, sombre silhouettes set in smoky gold, stared down at me, as if they knew what an alien I was in their cryptlike Byzantine world.

After five minutes I came out. The children had mercifully disappeared, and I could take the alley to the right of the church. On one side there were the round cylinders of the church apses, on the other a wall eight or nine feet high. The alley turned and the wall continued. But halfway along it there was an arched gateway: a keystone with the date 1823 on it, and above that a place where there had once been a coat of arms. I guessed that the house inside had been built by one of the pirate 'admirals' of the War of Independence. There was a narrow door let into the right-hand of the two gate-doors, with a slit for letters. Above it, stencilled white on black on an old bit of sheet metal, was the name 'Hermes Ambelas'. To the left the ground fell away behind the church. There was no way of looking over the wall from that side. I went to the small door and pushed it gently to see if it gave. But it was locked. The islanders were notoriously honest, thieves unknown; and I could not remember having seen an outer gate locked like that anywhere else on Phraxos.

The rocky lane dipped abruptly down between two cottages. The roof of the one on the right was below the wall of the house. At the bottom a cross alley took me back and round to the other side. There the ground fell away even more precipitously and I found myself looking up ten feet of vertical rock even before the wall foundation started. The house and its garden walls on this side continued the rock face, and I could see that in fact it was not a very big house, though still by village standards much too grandiose for a donkey-driver.

Two ground-floor windows, three upstairs, all shuttered. They were still in the last sunlight and must have given a fine view west over the village and the straits to the Argolian mainland. Was it a view Julie knew well? I felt like Blondel beneath Richard Cœur-de-Lion's window; but not even able to pass messages by song. Down in a small square below I could see two or three women interestedly watching me. I waved, strolled on, as if my look upwards had been idle curiosity. I came to yet another cross alley, and climbed up it to my starting-point outside Agios Elias. The house was impregnable to passing eyes.

Later, down in front of the Hotel Philadelphia, I looked back. I could see over all the intervening roofs the church and the house to the right of it, the five windows staring out.

They seemed defiant, but blind.

5 1

Monday was a day of academic chores; catching up on the Sisyphean piles of marking that seemed always to roll down on my desk; finalizing – miserable word for a miserable prospect – the end-of-term examination papers; and trying all the time not to think about Julie.

I knew it was useless asking Demetriades to help me find out the names of the English masters at the school before the war. If he knew them he wouldn't tell them; and very probably he genuinely did not know them. I went to the school bursar, but this time he could not help me; all the bursary records had gone with the wind of 1940. On

Tuesday I tried the master who ran the school library. He went at once to a shelf and pulled down a bound volume of Founder's Day programmes – one for each year before the war. These programmes were lavishly got up to impress visiting parents and in the back contained class-lists – as well as a list of 'professors'. In ten minutes I had the names of the six who had taught between 1930 and 1939. But I was still stuck for their addresses.

The week ground slowly past. Each lunch-time I watched the village postman come in with letters and give them to the duty prefect, who then made a slow, slow tour of the tables. None came for me. I now expected no mercy from Conchis; but I found it hard to forgive Julie.

The first and most obvious possibility was that they had flown back to England; in which case I couldn't believe she would not have written at once – at least to tell me. The second was that she had had to accept the cancellation of the weekend; but she could still have written to console me, to explain why. The third was that she was being held prisoner, or at any rate *incommunicado* to the extent that she could not post a letter to me. I couldn't really believe that, though I still had angry moments when I thought of going to the police.

The days dragged on, redeemed only by one little piece of information that fell into my hands by chance. Looking through the books in the English bay in the library for a suitable 'unseen' for the exams, I took down a Conrad. There was a name on the flyleaf, D. P. R. Nevinson. I knew he had been at the school before the war. Underneath was written 'Balliol College, 1930'. I started looking through the other books. Nevinson had left a good number; but there was no other address besides Balliol. The name W. A. Hughes, another prewar master's, appeared on two poetry volume flyleafs, without address.

I left lunch early on the Thursday, asking a boy to bring me any letters that might be distributed later. I had come not to expect any. But about ten minutes afterwards, when I was already in pyjamas for the siesta, the boy knocked on my door. Two letters. One from London, a typewritten address, some educational publisher's catalogue. But the other …

A Greek stamp. Indecipherable postmark. Neat italic handwriting. In English.

My dear sweet Nicholas,

1 know you must be terribly disappointed about the week-end, and I do hope you're better now. Maurice gave me your letter. I'm so sorry for you. I used to be the same, catch every disease my wretched little brats brought into class. I couldn't write earlier, we've been at sea and today is our first sight of a post-box. I must be quick – they've just told me the boat that takes the mail to Athens goes in half an hour. I'm scribbling this in a café by the harbour.

Maurice has actually been rather an angel, though still a mute one. He insists on waiting till you're with us this coming week-end, if you're better. (*Please* be better! Not just for that.) M. has actually been playing a tiny bit hurt as well because we, unreasonable creatures, still won't promise to go on with his new plan until we know what it entails. We've really given up trying to get it out of him – it's such a waste of time, and he positively enjoys being dark and enigmatic.

Which reminds me, I forgot, he *has* let slip that he wants to tell you the 'last chapter' (his words) of his life and also that you will be expecting it now ... he said the last bit with a sort of smirk, as if something had happened we don't know about. He's terrible, he won't stop playing games. Anyway, 1 hope you know what it's all about.

I'm saving the best to the last. He's sworn we shan't be whisked away again any more, if we want to stay on the is-land in his village house we can ... perhaps you won't like me any more if you can see me every day. That's June, she's fed up because I'm at last getting some sort of tan.

It will be only two or three days more when you get this. He may play some last Maurician trick, so please pretend, re-member you haven't heard about the last chapter thing, let him have one last little bit of teasing you if he wants it. I think there is a tiny bit of jealousy. He keeps saying how lucky *you* are ... and not listening when I say – you know what I say.

Nicholas.

Night water. You were sweet.

I must finish.

I love you.

YOUR JULIE

I read the letter twice, three times. Obviously the old devil was still up to his tricks. She had never seen my hand-writing, it would have been simple to forge something – Demetriades could have got him specimens of my hand, if he wanted to be exact. Why he should still want to delay, still throw up these last obstacles, I couldn't imagine. But her letter, those last five words, the thought of having her in the village – all that made everything else seem unimportant. I felt completely buoyant again, able to cope; as long as she was still in Greece, waiting for me, wanting me ...

I was woken at four by the end-of-siesta bell that a prefect always came across and rang with vindictive violence in the wide stone corridor outside our rooms. There was the usual chorus of angry shouts from my colleagues. I lay on my elbow and read Julie's letter again. Then I remembered the other one I had thrown on my desk and went yawning to open that.

Inside was a typewritten note and another, airmail, envelope slit open, but I hardly looked at them because two newspaper cuttings were pinned on to the top of the note. I had to read them first.

The first words.

The first words.

The whole thing had happened to me before, the same sensations, the same feeling that it could not be true and was true, of vertiginous shock and superficial calm. Coming out of the Randolph in Oxford with two or three other people, walking up to Carfax, a man under the tower selling the *Evening News*. Standing there, a silly girl saying 'Look at Nicholas, he's pretending he can read.' And I looked up with the news of the Karachi air crash and the death of my parents in my face and said 'My mother and father.' As if I had just for the first time discovered that such people existed.

The top cutting was from some London local newspaper, from the bottom of a column. It said:

AIR HOSTESS SUICIDE
Australian air hostess Alison Kelly, 24, was yesterday found lying on her bed in the Russell Square flat they both share by her friend Ann Taylor, also Australian, when she returned from

a week-end in Stratford-on-Avon. She was rushed to the Middlesex Hospital but found to be dead on admission. Miss Taylor was treated for shock. Inquest next week.

The second cutting said:

UNHAPPY IN LOVE SO KILLS HERSELF

P.C. Henry Davis told the deputy Holborn coroner on Tuesday how on the evening of Sunday, June 29th, he found a young woman lying on her bed with an empty bottle of sleeping tablets by her side. He had been called by the dead girl's flat-mate, Australian physiotherapist Ann Taylor, who found the deceased, Alison Kelly, air hostess, aged 24, on her return from a week-end at Stratford-on-Avon.

A verdict of suicide was recorded.

Miss Taylor said that although her friend had been subject to fits of depression and said she could not sleep properly she had had no reason to suppose the deceased was in a suicidal frame of mind. In answer to questions, Miss Taylor said, 'My friend was recently depressed because of an unhappy love affair, but I thought she had got over it.'

Dr Behrens, the deceased's doctor, told the coroner that Miss Kelly had led her to believe that it was her work which gave her insomnia. Asked by the coroner whether she normally prescribed such large quantities of tablets, Dr Behrens replied that she took into account the difficulty the deceased might have in getting to a chemist frequently. She had no reason to suspect suicide.

The coroner stated that two notes found by the police threw no light on the real motive of this tragic business.

The typewritten note was from Ann Taylor.

Dear Nicholas Urfe,

The enclosed cuttings will explain why I am writing. I am sorry, it will be a great shock, but I don't know how else to break it. She was very depressed when she came back from Athens, but she wouldn't talk about it, so I don't know whose fault it was. She used to talk a lot about suicide at one time but we always thought it was a joke.

She left this envelope for you. The police opened it. There was no note inside. There was a note for me, but it said nothing – just apologies.

We are all heartbroken about it. I feel I am to blame. Now she is gone we realize what she was. I can't understand any man not realizing what she really was underneath and not wanting to marry her. But I don't understand men, I suppose.

Yours very sadly,

ANN TAYLOR

P.S. I don't know if you want to write to her mother. The ashes are being sent home. Her address is – Mrs Mary Kelly, 19 Liverpool Avenue, Goulburn, N.S.W.

I looked at the airmail envelope. It had my name outside, in Alison's handwriting. I tipped the contents out on the desk. A tangle of clumsily pressed flowers: two or three violets, some pinks. Two of the pinks were still woven together.

Three weeks.

To my horror I began to cry.

My tears did not last very long. I had no privacy. The bell for class rang, and Demetriades was tapping at my door. I brushed my eyes with the back of my wrist and went and opened it. I was still in pyjamas.

'Eh! What are you doing? We are late.'

'I don't feel very well.'

'You look strange, my dear fellow.' He put on a look of concern. I turned away.

'Just tell the first lot to revise for the exam. And tell the others to do the same.'

'But –'

'Leave me alone, will you?'

'What shall I say?'

'Anything.' I shoved him out.

As soon as the sound of footsteps and voices had died down and I knew school had begun I pulled on my clothes and went out. I wanted to get away from the school, the village, from Bourani, from everything. I went along the north coast to a deserted cove and sat there on a stone and pulled out the cuttings again and re-read them. June 29th. One of the last things she must have done was to post my letter back unopened. Perhaps the last thing. For a moment I felt angry with the other girl; but I remembered her, her flat, prim face, and her kind eyes. She wrote stilted English, but she would never deliberately leave anyone in the lurch. That sort never did. And I knew those two sides of Alison – the hard practical side that misled one into believing she could get over anything; and the other apparently rather histrionic Alison that one could never quite take seriously. In a tragic way these two sides had finally combined: there would have been no fake suicides with her, no swallowing a few tablets when she knew someone would come in an hour's time. But a week-end to die.

It was not only that I felt guilty of jettisoning Alison. I knew, with one of those secret knowledges that can exist between two people, that her suicide was a direct result of my having told her of my own attempt – I had told it with a curt meiosis that was meant to conceal depths; and she had called my bluff one final time. *I don't think you know what sadness means.*

I remembered those hysterical scenes in the Piraeus hotel; that much earlier 'suicide note' she had composed, to blackmail me, as I then thought, just before I left London. I thought of her on Parnassus; I thought of her in Russell Square; things she said, she did, she was. And a great cloud of black guilt, knowledge of my atrocious selfishness, settled on me. All those bitter home truths she had flung at me, right from the beginning ... and still loved me; was so blind that she still loved me. One day she had said: *When you love me* (and she had not meant 'make love to me') *it's as if God forgave me for being the mess I am*; and I took it as a chicanery, another emotional blackmail, to make me feel essential and so give me a sense of responsibility towards her. In a way her death was the final act of blackmail; but the blackmailed should feel innocent, and I felt guilty. It was as if at this moment, when I most wanted to be clean, I had fallen into the deepest filth; most free for the future yet most chained to the past.

And Julie; she now became a total necessity.

Not only marriage with her, but confession *to* her. If she had been beside me then, I could have poured out everything, made a clean start. I needed desperately to throw myself on her mercy, to be for-given by her. Her forgiveness was the only possible justification now. I was tired, tired, tired of deception; tired of being deceived; tired of deceiving others; and most tired of all of being self-tricked, of being endlessly at the mercy of my own loins; the craving for the best, that made the very worst of me.

Those flowers, those intolerable flowers.

My monstrous crime was Adam's, the oldest and most vicious of all male selfishnesses: to have imposed the role I needed from Alison on her real self. Something far worse than *lèse-majesté*. *Lèse-humanité*. What had she said about that muleteer? *I felt two packets fond of him*.

And one death fond of me.

When I got back that evening I wrote two letters, one to Ann Taylor, the other to Alison's mother. I thanked Ann and true to my new resolve took as much blame as I could; to the mother (Goulburn, N.S.W. – I remembered Alison screwing up her face: *Goulburn, the first half's all it's fit for, the second's what they ought to do with it*), to the mother, a difficult, because I didn't know how much Alison had said about me, letter of condolence.

Before I went to bed I took out *England's Helicon*; turned to Marlowe.

> Come live with mee, and be my love,
> And we will all the pleasures prove,
> That Vallies, groves, hills and fieldes,
> Woods or steepie mountaine yeeldes.
>
> And wee will sit upon the Rocks,
> Seeing the sheepheards feede theyr flocks,
> By shallow Rivers, to whose falls
> Melodious byrds sing Madrigalls.
>
> And I will make thee beds of Roses,
> And a thousand fragrant poesies,
> A cap of flowers, and a kirtle,
> Imbroydred all with leaves of Mirtle ...

52

I had another letter from England on Saturday morning. There was a small black eagle on the flap: Barclay's Bank.

> Dear Mr Urfe,
>
> Thank you for writing to me upon the recommendation of the Misses Holmes. I have pleasure in enclosing a form which I hope you will kindly fill in and return to me and also a small booklet with details of the special services we can offer overseas customers.
>
> Yours truly,
> P. J. FEARN
> Manager

I looked up from reading it into the eyes of the boy who sat opposite me at table, and gave him a small smile; the unsuppressed smile of the bad poker-player.

Half an hour later I was climbing through the windless forest to the central ridge. The mountains were reduced to a pale insubstantiality by the heat, and the islands to the east rose and trembled shimmeringly over the sea, a strange optical illusion, like spinning tops. I came to where I could see down to the south; and my heart leapt. The yacht was there, like a reprieve. I moved along to a place where there was shade and a view down over Bourani; and sat there for half an hour, in limbo, with the death of Alison still dark inside me and the hope of Julie, Julie now confirmed as Julie, there below me in the sun. Gradually, those last two days, l had begun to absorb the fact of Alison's death; that is, had begun to edge it out of the moral world into the aesthetic, where it was easier to live with.

By this sinister elision, this slipping from true remorse, the belief that the suffering we have precipitated ought to ennoble *us*, or at least make us less ignoble from then on, to disguised self-forgiveness, the belief that suffering in some way ennobles *life*, so that the precipitation of pain comes, by such a cockeyed algebra, to equal the ennoblement, or at any rate the enrichment, of life, by this characteristically twentieth-century retreat from content into form, from meaning into appearance, from ethics into aesthetics, from *aqua* into *unda*, I dulled the pain of that accusing death; and hardened myself to say nothing of it at Bourani. I was still determined to tell Julie, but at the right time and place, when the exchange rate between confession and the sympathy it evoked looked likely to be high.

Before I moved off I took out the headed Barclays letter and read it again. It had the effect of making me feel more indulgent towards Conchis than I had intended to be. I saw no objection now to a few small last dissimulations – on both sides.

It was like the first day. The being uninvited, unsure; the going through the gate, approaching the house in its silent sunlit mystery, going round the colonnade; and there too it was the same, the tea-table covered in muslin. No one present. The sea and the heat through the arches, the tiled floor, the silence, the waiting.

And although I was nervous for different reasons, even that was the same. I put my duffel-bag on the cane settee and went into the music-room. A figure rose from behind the harpsichord, as if it had been sitting there in wait. Neither of us said anything.

'I am expected?'

'Yes.'

'In spite of your note?'

He stared at me, then down at my hand – my battle-wound from the Nazi incident ten days previously. It was scarred and still red from the daubings of mercurochrome the school nurse had put on it.

'You must be careful. There is always the danger of tetanus.'

I smiled grimly. 'I intend to be.'

No apologies, no explanations, not even answers to questions: it was very clear that whatever he might have told the girls, he was not finished with trying to bamboozle me. Behind him, through the window, I saw Maria pass with a tray. I also saw something else. The old photograph of 'Lily' had disappeared from the cabinet of obscene antiquities. I put my duffel-bag on the floor, then folded my arms and gave him another thin smile.

'I had a talk with Barba Dimitraki the other day.'

'Indeed.'

'I understand I have more fellow-victims than I thought.'

'Victims?'

'Whatever you call people who are made to suffer without being given the choice.'

'That sounds like an excellent definition of man.'

'I'm more interested in a definition of someone who seems to think he is God.'

At last he smiled, as if he took as a compliment what had clearly been said sarcastically. Then he came round the harpsichord towards me.

'Let me see this hand of yours.' I lifted it impatiently. It had been badly grazed along the knuckles, but it was largely healed now. He examined it, asked if there had been any septicaemia. Then he looked me in the eyes. 'This was not intended. At least you will accept that?'

'I'm not accepting anything any more, Mr Conchis. Except the truth.'

'You may find you were happier not knowing it.'

'I'll risk that.'

He measured the look in my eyes, then gave a little shrug.

'Very well. Let us have tea.'

I followed him out under the colonnade. He stood to pour, waved me rather impatiently to my chair opposite. I sat. He waved again at the food. 'Please.' I took a sandwich, but spoke before I started eating it.

'I thought the girls were going to hear the truth with me.'

'They know it already.' He sat down.

'Including the fact that you forged a letter from me to Julie?'

'It is her letters to you that are the forgeries.'

I noted that plural. He must have guessed she had been writing, but had guessed wrong as to the quantity. I smiled. 'Sorry. I've been bitten once too often.'

He looked down, then smoothed, I fancied a shade uneasily, obviously not knowing the full extent of the rapport between Julie and myself, the edge of the table-cloth. He gave me his grave eyes.

'What do you think I am doing?'

'Taking some infernal liberties.'

'Were you ever forced to return here? To come here in the first place?'

'Now you're being naïve. You know damn well that no normal person could have stayed away.' I raised my scarred hand. 'And in spite of this, I'm very far from being ungrateful. But stage one of the masque, experiment, whatever you call it, is over.' I smiled at him. 'Your tame white rats have tumbled.' I could see he didn't understand the slang use of that last word. I said, 'Fallen flat on their faces. But see no reason for repeating the process until they know why.'

Again he searched my eyes. I remembered something June had said: *He wants us to be mysteries to him as well.* But it was only too clearly a very limited freedom and mystery he wanted in us; however large a maze the scientist builds, its purpose is still to allow him to watch every move. He seemed to come to a decision.

'You learnt from Barba Dimitraki that I had a small private theatre here before the war?'

'Yes.'

He leant back. 'During the war, when I had a great deal of time to think, and no friends to amuse me, I conceived a new kind of drama. One in which the conventional separation between actors and audience was abolished. In which the conventional scenic geography, the notions of proscenium, stage, auditorium, were completely discarded. In which continuity of performance, either in time or place, was ignored. And in which the action, the narrative was fluid, with only a point of departure and a fixed point of conclusion. Between those points the participants invent their own drama.' His mesmeric eyes pinned mine. 'You will find that Artaud and Pirandello and Brecht were all thinking, in their different ways, along similar lines. But they had neither the money nor the will – and doubtless, not the time – to think as far as I did. The element they could not bring themselves to discard was the audience.'

I gave him an openly sceptical smile. This did make slightly more sense than his previous 'explanations', but he apparently remained ludicrously blind to the fact that he had destroyed even the remotest hope of my ever believing anything he said again – that is, he trotted out this new story with his habitual conviction, as if I could not possibly not swallow it.

'I see.'

'We are all actors here, my friend. None of us is what we really are. We all lie some of the time, and some of us all the time.'

'Except me.'

'You have much to learn. You are as far from your true self as that Egyptian mask our American friend wore is from his true face.'

I gave him a warning look. 'He's not *my* American friend.'

'If you had seen him play Othello, you would not say that. He is a very accomplished young actor.'

'He must be. I thought he was meant to be a mute.'

'Then I have proved my praise.'

'Rather a waste of such talent.' He sat watching me: the old humourlessly amused look. I said, 'Your bank balance must get some surprises.'

'The tragedy of being very rich is that one's bank balance is incapable of giving one surprises. Pleasant or otherwise. But I confess that this was to be the most ambitious of our creations.' He added, 'For the reason that for me there may not be another year.'

'Your heart?'

'My heart.'

But he looked immortally tanned and fit; in any case, distanced any sympathy.

'Why do you say "was to be"?'

'Because you have proved incapable of playing your part properly.'

I grinned; it was becoming absurd. 'It might have helped if I'd known what it was.'

'You were given many indications.'

'Look, Mr Conchis, I know what you've been saying to Julie about the rest of this summer. I didn't come here to be provoked into a quarrel with you. So can we drop this ridiculous nonsense about my having failed you in some way? Either you meant me to fail or I haven't failed. There's no other alternative.'

'I am telling you, as the director, if you like, that you have failed to gain a part. But if it is any consolation, I will also tell you that even if you had gained it, it would not have brought you what you wish … the young woman you find so seductive. That was always to be the fixed point of conclusion this summer.'

'I'd like to hear that from her.'

'It is you who would not have wanted to see her again. The comedy is over.'

'But I intend to see the actress home afterwards.'

'She has promised that, no doubt.'

'In ways infinitely more credible than yours.'

'Her promises are worth nothing. All here is artifice. She is acting, amusing herself with you. Playing Olivia to your Malvolio.'

'And I suppose her name is not Julie Holmes?'

'Her real first name is Lily.'

I grinned so broadly that I had once again to admire his ability to keep a straight face. In the end I looked down.

'Where are they? Can I see them now?'

'They are in Athens. You will not see either Lily or Rose again.'

'Rose?' I said it with a sarcastic incredulity, but he simply nodded. 'You're out of touch. No one calls girls of their age by names like that any more.'

'You will not see them again.'

'Oh yes I will. One, you want me to see them again. Two, even if for some reason you didn't, and whatever lies you've cooked up to keep them in Athens this weekend, nothing can prevent me from seeing Julie finally. And three, you have absolutely no business meddling in our private feelings about each other.'

'I agree. If they were equally real on both sides.'

I made myself sound less aggressive.

'I also know you're far too humane a man to think you can command people's emotions so easily.'

'It is simpler than you think. When you know the plot.'

'The present plot's ruined. The *Three Hearts* thing. You know that even better.' I tried one last appeal to him. 'I know you've admitted as much to the girls, so what's the point of trying to make me think you haven't?' He said nothing. I put on my most reasonable voice. 'Mr Conchis, we need hardly any convincing. We're all happy to admit that we're a little bit under your spell. Within limits we're only too delighted to go on with whatever you have planned next.'

'There is no place for limits in the meta-theatre.'

'Then you shouldn't involve ordinary human beings in it.'

That seemed to register. He looked down at the table between us, and for a few moments I felt that I had won. But then his eyes were on me again, and I knew I hadn't.

'Take my advice. Go back to England and make it up with this girl you spoke of. Marry her and have a family and learn to be what you are.' I looked away. I wanted to shout at him that Alison was dead; and largely because he had woven Julie's life into mine. I trembled on the brink of telling him that I wanted no more deceptions, no more of this futile double-talk ... but I kept quiet. I knew my conduct there did not want his inevitable examination.

'Is that how you learn what you are? Marrying and having a family?'

'Why not?'

'A steady job and a house in the suburbs?'

'It is how most people live.'

'I'd rather die.'

He gave a shrug of regret, but as if he didn't really care any longer who I was or what I felt. Suddenly he stood.

'We will meet again for dinner.'

'I'd like to see your yacht.'

'That is not possible.'

'I want to talk to the girls.'

'I have told you. They are in Athens.' Then he said, 'Tonight I intend to tell you something that is for our sex alone. Womankind has no place in it.'

The last chapter: I had already guessed what that meant.

'What happened in the war?'

'What happened in the war.' He gave me a little nod. 'Until dinner.'

He turned and marched indoors, and that was that. I was angry with him, yet it was more an anger of impatience than an anger of fear. I supposed Julie and I had between us in some way spoilt his fun, had seen through him in a way he did not like – perhaps more quickly than he had expected; and given rise to this infantile old man's pique. I knew the girls were on the yacht; that even if I didn't see them this evening, I would see them the next day. I picked up a cake and ate it thoughtfully. On top of everything else, there was my old sense of gravity, of the nature of probability ... one didn't make such elaborate preparations for a summer's entertainment, only to call it off when it was getting interesting. We must continue; all I had just experienced was a bout of bluffing in the early part of a poker-game. The real betting was still to come.

I remembered the lunch, at this same table, a fortnight before, then looked round outside the colonnade. Perhaps the sisters were waiting there now, somewhere in the pines ... it might all have been no more than his perverse way of making me look. I took my things upstairs to my room; searched under the pillow, in the wardrobe, thinking that Julie might have left some little message. But there was nothing. Then I went out.

I strolled all round the domaine, in the windless air. I waited in all the previous places. I kept on turning, looking backwards, sideways, listening. But the landscape seemed silent, and nothing and no one appeared. Even on the yacht there was no sign of life, though I noticed that the little power-boat was in the water, moored by a rope ladder amidships. The theatre seemed truly empty; and like all empty theatres, as the old devil no doubt intended, it became in the end both flat and a little frightening.

We were to have dinner under the colonnade, not upstairs as usual. The table, laid for two, had been placed at its western end, looking out over the trees and Moutsa down below. Another table stood at the front, by the central steps, with sherry and ouzo, water and a bowl of olives. I had almost finished my second glass when the old man appeared. Dusk was fading into night. It was very still, dead air over everything.

I had decided while I waited to be more diplomatic. I suspected that the angrier I became, the more pleased he secretly was. I resigned myself to not seeing the girls; and to pretending that I accepted his explanation. He came silently to where I stood, and I smiled at him.

'May I get you something?'

'A little sherry. Thank you.'

I poured half a glass and handed it to him.

'I'm sincerely sorry if we have spoilt your plans.'

'My plans are whatever happens.' He silently toasted me. 'You cannot spoil that.'

'But you must have known we would see through the parts you gave us.'

He looked out to sea. 'The object of the meta-theatre is precisely that – to allow the participants to see through their first roles in it. But that is only the catastasis.'

'I'm afraid I don't know what that word means.'

'It is what precedes the final act, or catastrophe, in classical tragedy.' He added, 'Or comedy. As the case may be.'

'The case depending on?'

'Whether we learn to see through the roles we give ourselves in ordinary life.'

I sprang my next question on him, out of a silence, in his own style. 'To what extent is your dislike of me a part of *your* part?'

He was undisconcerted. 'Liking is not important. Between men.'

I felt the ouzo in me. 'Even so, you don't like me?'

His dark eyes turned on mine. 'I am to answer?' I nodded. 'Then no. But I like very few people. And even fewer of your age and sex. Liking other people is an illusion we have to cherish in ourselves if we are to live in society. It is one I have long banished, at least from my life here. You wish to be liked. I wish simply to be. One day you will know what that means, perhaps. And you will smile. Not against me. But with me.'

I left a pause. 'You sound like a certain kind of surgeon. A lot more interested in the operation than the patient.'

'I should not like to be in the hands of a surgeon who did not take that view.'

'Then your … meta-theatre is really a medical one?'

Maria's shadow appeared behind him as she brought a soup-tureen to the white-and-silver table in its pool of lamplight.

'You may see it so. I prefer to think of it as a metaphysical one.' Maria announced that we could take our seats. He acknowledged her words with a little bow, but did not move. 'It is above all an attempt to escape from such categories.'

'More an art than a science?'

'All good science is art. And all good art is science.'

With this fine-sounding but hollow apophthegm he put down his glass and moved towards the table. I spoke at his back as I followed.

'My guess is that, in your view, I'm the real schizophrenic here.'

He did not answer until he was at his chair.

'Real schizophrenics have no choice in what they are.'

I stood opposite him. 'Then I'm an unreal schizophrenic?'

Just for a moment he relaxed a little, as if I had said something childish but amusing. He gestured.

'It does not matter now. Let us eat.'

Almost as soon as we had started I heard the footsteps of two or three people behind me on the gravel round by Maria's cottage. I glanced back from my egg-lemon soup, but the table had been placed, no doubt deliberately, where it was impossible to see.

'Tonight I wish to illustrate my story,' said Conchis.

'I thought you'd done that already. And only too vividly.'

'These are real documents.'

He indicated that I should go on eating, he would say nothing more. Then I heard footsteps on the terrace outside his bedroom, above our heads. There was a tiny squeal, the scrape of metal. I finished my soup, and while we waited for Maria, tried again to mollify him.

'I'm sorry I'm not going to hear more of your life before the war.'

'You have heard the essential.'

'As I understood the Norwegian story, you rejected science. Yet apparently you went into psychiatry.'

He gave a little shrug. 'I dabbled in it.'

'That glimpse I had of your papers suggested more than dabbling.'

'They were not by me. The title pages were not genuine.'

I had to smile at him then: the curtly dismissive way in which he made such statements had become an almost sure sign that they were not to be believed. Of course he did not smile back, but he evidently felt that I needed reminding of his more serious self.

'There is some truth in what I have told you. To that extent your question is fair. There was an event in my life analogous to the story I invented.' He paused, then decided to go on. 'There had always been a conflict in me between mystery and meaning. I had pursued the latter, worshipped the latter as a doctor. As a socialist and rationalist. But then I saw that the attempt to scientize reality, to name it and categorize it and vivisect it out of existence, was like trying to remove the air from the atmosphere. In the creating of the vacuum it was the experimenter who died, because he was inside the vacuum.'

'Was your coming into wealth something like the de Deukans story?'

'No.' He added, 'I was born rich. And not in England.'

'Then the First World War ... '

'Pure invention.'

I took a breath; for once he was avoiding my eyes.

'You must have been born somewhere.'

'I have long ceased to care what I am, in those terms.'

'And you must have lived in England.'

He glanced up; searching, unsmiling, yet somewhere beneath there was a hint of irony. 'Does your appetite for invention never end?'

'At least I know you have a house in Greece.'

He looked beyond me, and past the sarcasm, into the night. 'I have always craved for territory. In the technical ornithological sense. A fixed domaine on which no others of my species may trespass without my permission.'

'Yet you live very little here.'

He hesitated, as if he began to find this interrogation tedious. 'Life is more complicated for human beings than for birds. And human territory is defined least of all by physical frontiers.'

Maria brought a dish of stewed kid and removed our soup-plates, and there was a little silence. But unexpectedly, when she left, he looked at me. He had something more to say.

'Wealth is a monster. It takes a month to learn to control it financially. And many years to learn to control it psychologically. For those many years I lived a selfish life. I offered myself every pleasure. I travelled a great deal. I lost some money in the theatre, but I made much more on the stock market. I gained a great many friends, some of whom are now quite famous. But I was never very happy. However, in the end I did discover what some rich people never discover – that we all have a certain capacity for happiness and unhappiness. And that the economic hazards of life do not seriously affect it.'

'When did you start your theatre here?'

'Friends used to come. They were bored. Very often they bored me. An amusing person in London or Paris can become insufferable on an Aegean island. We had a little fixed theatre, a stage. Where the Priapus is now. *Et voilà.*'

'Have you kept in touch with any of my predecessors?'

He was serving himself a little of the stew. 'Before the war it was not like this. We acted other men's plays. Or versions of them. Not our own.'

'Barba Dimitraki talked about a firework display. He saw it from the sea.'

He gave a little nod. 'Then without knowing it he saw an important night in my life.'

'He couldn't remember when it was.'

'1938.' He kept me waiting a moment. 'I set a match to my theatre. The building. The fireworks were in celebration.'

I remembered that story about burning every novel he owned; and was going to remind him, but suddenly he gestured with his knife.

'No more. Let us eat.'

He ate very little of the excellent stew and long before I had cleared my own plate he was on his feet.

'Finish your dinner. I will return.'

He disappeared indoors. Soon after that I heard low voices, Greek voices, upstairs; then silence. Maria brought dessert, then coffee, and I waited, smoking. I still hoped against hope that Julie and her sister would arrive; I badly needed their warmth, normality, Englishness, again. All through the meal, his talking, there had been something sombre and withdrawn about him, as if more than one comedy was over; so many pretences were being dropped – and yet the one that concerned me showed no sign at all of being jettisoned. I had believed him when he said he did not like me. I somehow knew now that he would not keep the girls away from me by force; but a man with such formidable powers of lying ... I nursed a tiny terror that he knew I had met Alison in Athens, had somehow got proof for them that I too was a liar, and of a much more banal kind.

He re-appeared in the open doors of the music-room, a thin cardboard folder in his hand.

'I should like us to sit there.' He pointed towards the drinks table, now cleared by Maria, by the central arch of the front of the colonnade. 'If you would bring two chairs. And the lamp.'

I carried the chairs over. As I brought the lamp, somebody came round the corner of the colonnade. My heart leapt a fraction of a moment, because I thought it was finally Julie, that we had been waiting for her. But it was the Negro, dressed in black. He carried a long cylinder; went over the gravel in front of us and then, a few yards out, set the cylinder on its tripod end. I realized what it was – a small cinema-screen. There was a harsh ratcheting noise as he unfurled the white square and hooked it up, adjusted its angle. Someone called quietly from above.

'*Entaxi*.' All right. A Greek voice I didn't recognize.

The Negro went silently back the way he had come, without looking at us. Conchis turned down the lamp to its lowest glimmer, then made me sit beside him, facing the screen. There was a long pause.

'What I am now about to tell you may help you understand why I am bringing your visits here to an end tomorrow. And for once it is a true story.' I said nothing, though he left a little pause as if he expected me to object. 'I should like you also to reflect that its events could have taken place only in a world where man considers himself superior to woman. In what the Americans call "a man's world". That is, a world governed by brute force, humourless arrogance, illusory prestige and primeval stupidity.' He stared at the screen. 'Men love war because it allows them to look serious. Because they imagine it is the one thing that stops women laughing at them. In it they can reduce women to the status of objects. That is the great distinction between the sexes. Men see objects, women see the relationship between objects. Whether the objects need each other, love each other, match each other. It is an extra dimension of feeling we men are without and one that makes war abhorrent to all real women – and absurd. I will tell you what war is. War is a psychosis caused by an inability to see relationships. Our relationship with our fellowmen. Our relationship with our economic and historical situation. And above all our relationship to nothingness. To death.'

He paused. His mask-face looked as concentrated, as inward, as I could remember having seen it. Then he said, 'I will begin.'

53

'When the Italians invaded Greece in 1940, I had already decided that I would not run away. I cannot tell you why. Perhaps it was curiosity, perhaps it was guilt, perhaps it was indifference. And here, on a remote corner of a remote island, it did not require great courage. The Germans took over from the Italians on April 6th, 1941. By April 27th they were in Athens. In June they started the invasion of Crete and for a time we were in the thick of the war. Transport aeroplanes passed over all day long, German landing-craft filled the harbours. But after that peace soon alighted back on the island. It had no strategic value, either to the Axis or to the Resistance. The garrison here was very small. Forty Austrians – the Nazis gave the Austrians and the Italians all the easy Occupation posts – commanded by a lieutenant who had been wounded during the invasion of France.

'Already, during the invasion of Crete, I had been ordered out of Bourani. A permanent look-out section was posted here, and the maintenance of this observation point was the real reason we had a garrison at all. Fortunately 1 had the house in the village. The Germans were not unpleasant. They carried all my portable possessions over there for me; and even paid me a small billeting rent for Bourani. Then just when things were settling down, it happened that the *proedros*, the mayor of the village that year, had a fatal thrombosis. Two days later I was summoned to meet the newly arrived commandant of the island. He and his men were installed in your school, which had been closed since Christmas.

'I was expecting to meet some promoted quartermaster type of officer. Instead I found myself with a very handsome young man of twenty-seven or eight, who said, in excellent French, that he understood I could speak the language fluently. He was extremely polite, more than a little apologetic, and inasmuch as one can in such circumstances we took to each other. He soon came to the point. He wanted me to be the new mayor of the village. I refused at once; I wanted no involvement in the war. He then sent out for two or three of the leading villagers. When they came he left me alone with them, and I discovered that it was they who had proposed my name. Of course the fact was that none of them wanted the job, the odium of collaboration, and I was the ideal *bouc émissaire*. They put the matter to me in highly moral and complimentary terms, and I still refused. Then they were frank – promised their tacit support ... in short, in the end I said, very well, I will do it.

'My new but dubious glory meant that I came into frequent contact with Lieutenant Kluber. Five or six weeks after our first meeting he said one evening that he would like me to call him Anton when we were alone. That will tell you that we often were alone; and that we had confirmed our liking of each other. Our first link was through music. He had a fine tenor voice. Like many really gifted amateurs, he sang Schubert and Wolf better – in some way more feelingly – than any but the very greatest professional *lieder* singers. That is, to my ear. On his very first visit to my house he saw my harpsichord. And rather maliciously I played him the Goldberg Variations. If one wishes to reduce a sensitive German to tears there is no surer lachrymatory. I must not suggest that Anton was a hard subject to conquer. He was more than disposed to be ashamed of his role and to find a convenient anti-Nazi figure to worship. The next time I visited the school he begged me to accompany him at the school piano, which he had had moved to his quarters. Then it was my turn to be sentimentally impressed. Not to tears, of course. But he sang very well. And I have always had a softness for Schubert.

'One of the first things I wanted to know was why Anton, with his excellent French, was not in Occupied France. It seemed "certain compatriots" considered him not sufficiently "German" in his attitude to the French. No doubt he had spoken once too often in the mess in defence of Gallic culture. And that was why he had been relegated to this backwater. I forgot to say he had been shot in the kneecap during the 1940 invasion and had a limp, unfitting him for active military duties. He was German, not Austrian. His family was rich, and he had spent a year before the war studying at the Sorbonne. Finally he had decided that he would become an architect. But of course his training was interrupted by the war.'

He stopped and turned up the lamp; then opening the file,

unfolded a large plan. Two or three sketches – perspectives and elevations, all glass and glittering concrete.

'He was very rude about this house. And he promised he would come back after the war and build me something new. After the best Bauhaus principles.'

All the notes were written in French; not a word of German anywhere. The plan was signed: *Anton Kluber, le sept juin, l'an 4 de la Grande Folie*. He let me look a few moments longer, then he turned down the lamp again.

'For a year during the Occupation everything was tolerable. We were very short of food, but Anton – and his men – shut their eyes to countless irregularities. The idea that the Occupation was all a matter of jackbooted stormtroopers and sullen natives is absurd. Most of the Austrian soldiers were over forty and fathers themselves – easy meat for the village children. One summer dawn, in 1942, an Allied plane came and torpedoed a German supply landing-craft that had anchored in the old harbour on its way to Crete. It sank. Hundreds of crates of food came bobbing to the surface. By then the islanders had had a year of nothing but fish and bad bread. The sight of all this meat, milk, rice and other luxuries was too much. They swarmed out in anything that would float. Somebody told me what was happening and I hurried down to the harbour. The garrison had a machine-gun on the point, it had fired furiously at the Allied plane, and I had terrible visions of a revengeful massacre. But when I got there I saw islanders busily hauling in crates not a hundred yards from where the machine-gun was. Outside the post stood Anton and the duty section. Not a shot was fired.

'Later that morning Anton summoned me. Of course, I thanked him profusely. He said that he was going to report that several of the crew of the landing-craft had been saved by the prompt action of the villagers who had rowed to their help. He must now have a few crates handed back to show as salvage. I was to see to that. The rest would be considered "sunk and destroyed". What little hostility that remained against him and his men among the villagers disappeared.

'I remember one evening, it must have been about a month after that, a group of Austrian soldiers, a little drunk, began to sing down by the harbour. And then suddenly the islanders began to sing as well. In turn. First the Austrians, then the islanders. German and Greek. A

Tyrolean carol. Then a *kalamatiano*. It was very strange. In the end they were all singing each other's songs.

'But that was the zenith of our small golden age. Somewhere among the Austrian soldiers there must have been a spy. About a week after the singing, a section of German troops was added to Anton's garrison to "stiffen morale". He came to me one day like an angry child and said, "I have been told I am in danger of becoming a discredit to the Wehrmacht. I must mend my ways." His troops were forbidden to give food to the islanders, and we saw them far less frequently in the village. In November of that year the Gorgopotamos exploit created a new strain. Fortunately I had been given more credit than I deserved by the villagers for the easiness of the regime, and they accepted the stricter situation as well as could be expected.'

Conchis stopped speaking, then clapped his hands twice.

'I should like you to see Anton.'

'I think I've seen him already.'

'No. Anton is dead. You have seen an actor who looks like him. But this is the real Anton. During the war I had a small cine-camera and two reels of film. Which I kept until 1944, when I could get them developed. The quality is very poor.'

I heard the faint whir of a projector. A beam of light came from above, was adjusted, centred on the screen. A blur, hasty focusing.

I saw a handsome young man of about my own age. He was not the one I had seen the week before, though in one feature, the heavy dark eyebrows, they were very similar. But this was unmistakably a wartime officer. He didn't look particularly soft; but more like a Battle of Britain pilot, stylishly insouciant. He was walking down a path beside a high wall, the wall of Hermes Ambelas's house, perhaps. Smiling. He struck a sort of heroic tenor attitude, laughed self-consciously; and abruptly the ten-second sequence was over. In the next he was drinking coffee, playing with a cat at his feet; looked sideways up at the camera, a serious, shy look, as if someone had told him not to smile. The film was very fuzzy, jerky, amateurish. Another sequence. A file of men marching round the island harbour; apparently shot from above, out of some upper-storey window.

'That is Anton in the rear.'

He had a slight limp. And I also knew that I was for a moment watching the unfakable truth. Beyond the men I could see a broad quay, on which there stood the little island customs and coastguard house. I knew it had been built since the war. On this film the quay was bare.

The beam was extinguished.

'There. I took other scenes, but one reel deteriorated. Those were all I could salvage.' He paused, then went on. 'The officer responsible for "stiffening morale" in this area of Greece was an S.S. colonel called Wimmel. Dietrich Wimmel. By the time I am now speaking of resistance movements had begun in Greece. Wherever the terrain permitted. Among the islands, of course, only Crete allowed *maquis* operations. But up in the north and over there in the Peloponnesus ELAS and the other groups had begun to organize themselves. Arms were dropped to them. Trained saboteurs. Wimmel was brought to Nauplia, late in 1942, from Poland, where he had had a great deal of success. He was responsible for the south-west of Greece, in which we were included. His technique was simple. He had a price-list. For every German wounded, ten hostages were executed; for every German killed, twenty. As you may imagine, it was a system that worked.

'He had a handpicked company of Teutonic monsters under him, who did the interrogating, torturing, executing, and the rest. They were known, after the badge they wore, as *die Raben*. The ravens.

'I met him before his infamies had become widely known. I heard one winter morning that a German motor-launch had unexpectedly brought an important officer to the island. Later that day, Anton sent for me. In his office I was introduced to a small, thin man. My own height, my own age. Immaculately neat. Scrupulously polite. He stood to shake my hand. He spoke some English, enough to know that I spoke it much better than he did. And when I confessed that I had many cultural attachments to England, had been partly educated there, he said, "The great tragedy of our time is that England and Germany should have quarrelled." Anton explained that he had told the colonel about our musical evenings and that the colonel hoped that I would join them for lunch and afterwards accompany Anton in one or two songs. Of course I had, *à titre d'office*, to accept.

'I did not like the colonel at all. He had eyes like razors. I think the most unpleasant eyes I have ever seen in a human being. They were without a grain of sympathy for what they saw. Nothing but assessment and calculation. If they had been brutal, or lecherous, or sadistic, they would have been better. But they were the eyes of a machine.

'An educated machine. The colonel had brought some bottles of hock with him and we had the best lunch I had eaten for many months. We discussed the war very briefly, rather as one might discuss the weather. It was the colonel himself who changed the subject to literature. He was obviously a well-read man. Knew Shakespeare well, and Goethe and Schiller extremely well. He even drew some interesting parallels between English and German literature, and not all in Germany's favour. I realized that he was drinking less than we were. Also that Anton was careless with his tongue. We were both in fact being watched. I knew that halfway through the meal; and the colonel knew that I knew it. We two older men polarized the situation. Anton became an irrelevance. The colonel would have had nothing but contempt for the ordinary Greek official, and I was highly honoured to be treated by him as a gentleman and equal. But I was not misled.

'After lunch we performed a few *lieder* for him, and he was full of compliments. He then announced that he wished to inspect the lookout post on the far side of the island, and invited me to accompany him – the place was of no great military importance. So I travelled round with them in his launch to Moutsa and we climbed up to the house here. There was a great deal of military paraphernalia about – wire everywhere and some pill-boxes. But I was happy to find that the house had not been damaged at all. The men were paraded and briefly addressed by the colonel in my presence – in German. He referred to me as "this gentleman" and insisted that my property should be respected. But I remember this. As we left he stopped to correct some minor fault in the way the man on guard at the gate was wearing his equipment. He pointed it out to Anton and said to him, "*Schlamperei, Herr Leutnant. Sehen Sie?*" Now *schlamperei* means something like sloppiness. It is the kind of word Prussians use of Bavarians. And of Austrians. He was evidently referring to some previous conversation. But it gave me a key to his character.

'We did not see him again for nine months. The autumn of 1943.

'It was the end of September. I was in my house one beautiful late afternoon when Anton strode in. I knew that something terrible had happened. He had just come back from Bourani. About twelve men were stationed there at a time. That morning four who were not on duty had gone down to Moutsa to swim. They must have grown careless, more *schlamperei*, because they all got into the water together. They came out, one by one, and sat throwing a ball and sunning on the beach. Then three men stood out of the trees behind them. One had a sub-machine-gun. The Germans had no chance. The *Unteroffizier* in charge heard the shots from here, the house, wirelessed Anton, then went down to look. He found three corpses, and one man who lived long enough to say what had happened. The guerillas had disappeared – and with the soldiers' guns. Anton immediately set out round the island in a launch.

'Poor Anton. He was torn between doing his duty and trying to delay the news from reaching the dreaded Colonel Wimmel. Of course he knew that he had to report the incident. He did so, but not until that evening, after he had seen me. He told me that that morning he had reasoned that he had to deal with *andarte* from the mainland, who must have slipped over by night and who would certainly not risk going back again before darkness. He therefore went round the island very slowly, searching every place where a boat might be hidden. And he found one, drawn up in the trees over there at the end of the island facing Petrocaravi. He had no alternative. The guerillas must have heard and seen him searching. There were strict High Command instructions in such a contingency. One destroyed the means of retreat. He set the boat on fire. The mice were trapped.

'He had come to explain all this to me; by this time Wimmel's price-list was well known. We owed him eighty men. Anton thought we had one chance. To capture the guerillas and have them waiting for Wimmel when he arrived, as he was almost certain to, the following day. At least we should thus prove that they were not islanders, but *agents provocateur*. We know they must be Communists, ELAS men, because their policy was the deliberate instigation of German reprisals – in order to stiffen morale on the Greek side. The eighteenth-century klephts used exactly the same tactics to raise the passive peasantry against the Turks.

'At eight that evening I called all the leading villagers together and explained the situation to them. It was too late to do anything that night. Our only chance was to co-operate with Anton's troops in combing the island the next day. Of course they were passionately angry at having their peace – and their lives – put into such jeopardy. They promised to stand guard all night over their boats and cisterns and to be out at dawn to track the guerillas down.

'But at midnight I was woken by the sound of marching feet and a knocking at the outside gates. Once again it was Anton. He came to tell me that it was too late. He had received orders. He was to take no more action on his own initiative. Wimmel would arrive with a company of *die Raben* in the morning. I was to be placed under immediate arrest. Every male in the village between the ages of four-teen and seventy-five was to be rounded up at dawn. Anton told me all this in my bedroom. He paced up and down, almost in tears, while I sat on the side of my bed, and listened to him say he was ashamed to be German, ashamed to have been born. That he would have killed himself if he did not feel it his duty to try to intercede with the colonel the next day. We talked for a long time. He told me more than he had before about Wimmel. We were so cut off here, and there were many things I had not heard. In the end he said, there is one good thing in this war. It has allowed me to meet you. We shook hands.

'Then I went with him back to the school, where I slept under guard.

'When I was taken down to the harbour the next morning at nine, all the men and most of the women in the village were there. Anton's troops guarded all the exits. Needless to say, the guerillas had not been seen. The villagers were in despair. But there was noth-ing they could do.

'At ten *die Raben* arrived in a landing-craft. One could see at once the difference between them and the Austrians. Better drilled, better disciplined, far better insulated against feelings of humanity. And so young. I found that the most terrifying aspect of them, their fanatical youth. Ten minutes later a seaplane landed. I remember the shadows of its wings falling on the whitewashed houses. Like a black scythe. A young fisherman near me picked a hibiscus and put the blood-red flower against his heart. We all knew what he meant.

'Wimmel came ashore. The first thing he did was to have all of us men herded on to a quay, and for the first time the islanders knew what it was like to be kicked and struck by foreign troops. The women were driven back into the adjoining streets and alleys. Then Wimmel disappeared into a taverna with Anton. Soon after I was called for. All the villagers crossed themselves, and I was roughly marched in to see him by two of his men. He did not stand to greet me, and when he spoke to me, it was as if to a total stranger. He even refused to speak English. He had brought a Greek collaborationist interpreter with him. I could see that Anton was lost. In the shock of the event he did not know what to do.

'Wimmel's terms were made known. Eighty hostages were to be chosen at once. The rest of the men would comb the island, find the guerillas, and bring them back – with the stolen weapons. It was not sufficient to produce the corpses of three brave volunteers. If we did this within the next twenty-four hours the hostages would be deported to labour camps. If we did not, they would be shot.

'I asked how we were to capture, even if we could find them, three desperate armed men. He simply looked at his watch and said, in German, "It is eleven o'clock. You have until noon tomorrow."

'At the quay I was made to repeat in Greek what I had been told. The men all began to shout suggestions, to complain, to demand weapons. In the end the colonel fired a shot from his pistol in the air, and there was quiet. The roll of the village men was called. Wimmel himself picked out the hostages as they filed forward. I noticed that he picked the healthiest, the ones between twenty and forty, as if he were thinking of the labour camp. But I think that he was choosing the best specimens for death. He chose seventy-nine like that, and then pointed at me. I was the eightieth hostage.

'So the eighty of us were marched off to the school and put under close guard. We were crammed in one classroom, without sanitation, given nothing to eat or drink – *die Raben* were guarding us – and even worse, no news. It was only much later that I found out what happened during that time.

'The remaining men rushed to their homes – poles, sickles, knives, they picked up what they could and then met again on a hill above the village. Men so old they could hardly walk, boys of ten and twelve. Some women tried to join them but they were pushed back. To be guarantors of their men's return.

'This sad regiment argued, as Greeks always will. They decided on one plan, then on another. In the end someone took charge and allotted positions and areas to search. They set out – one hundred and twenty of them. They were not to know that they were searching in vain even before they began. But even if the guerillas had been in the pine-forest I do not think they would have found them – let alone captured them. So many trees, so many ravines, so many rocks.

'They stayed out all night on the hills in a loose cordon across the island, hoping that the guerillas might try and break through to the village. They searched wildly the next morning. At ten they met and tried to make up their minds to launch a desperate attack on the troops down in the village. But the wiser heads knew it could only end in an even greater tragedy. There was a village in the Mani where two months before the Germans had killed every man, woman, and child for far less provocation.

'At noon they came, carrying a cross and ikons, down to the village. Wimmel was waiting for them. Their spokesman, an old sailor, in a last vain lie told him they had seen the guerillas escape in a small boat. Wimmel smiled, shook his head and had the old man put under arrest – an eighty-first hostage. What had happened was simple. The Germans themselves had already captured the guerillas. In the village. But let us look at Wimmel.'

Conchis clapped his hands again.

'This is him, in Athens. One of the resistance groups took it so that we should have his face recorded.'

The screen filled with light again. A town street. A German jeep-like vehicle drew up in the shade on the opposite side of the street. Three officers got out and walked in the hard sunlight diagonally across the camera, which must have been in the ground-floor room of the house next to the one they were entering. The head of someone passing blocked the view. A shorter, trimmer man led the way. I could see he had an air of curt, invincible authority. The other two men existed in his wake. Something, a shutter or a screen, obscured the view. Darkness. Then came a still of a man in civilian clothes.

'That is the only known photograph of him before the war.'

An unexceptional face; but a mean mouth. I remembered there were other sorts of humourlessness and fixed stare besides Conchis's; and much more unpleasant ones. There was a certain similarity with the face of the 'colonel' on the central ridge; but they were different men.

'And these are excerpts from newsreels taken in Poland.'

As they came on, Conchis said, 'That is him, behind the general'; or 'Wimmel is on the extreme left.' Though I could see the film was genuine, I had the same feeling that films of the Nazis had always given me; of unreality, of the distance, enormous, between a Europe that could breed such monsters and an England that could not. And I felt that Conchis was trying to enweb me, to make me too innocent, too historically green. Yet when I glanced at his face reflected in the light from the screen, he seemed even more absorbed in what he saw than I was myself; more a victim of the past.

'What the guerillas must have done is this. As soon as they realized their boat had been burned they doubled back towards the village. They were probably already only just outside it when Anton came to see me. What we did not know was that one of them had relations on the outskirts of the village – a family called Tsatsos. It consisted of two sisters of eighteen and twenty, a father and a brother. But the men happened to have left two days before for the Piraeus with a cargo of olive-oil – they had a small caïque and the Germans allowed a certain amount of coastal traffic. One of the guerillas was a cousin of these girls – probably in love with the elder one.

'The guerillas came to the cottage unseen, before anyone in the village knew of the catastrophe. They were no doubt counting on using the family caïque. But it was away. Later a weeping neighbour arrived to tell the sisters the news of the killing and all that I had told the village men. By then the guerillas were in hiding. We do not know where they spent that night. Probably in an empty cistern. Parties of hastily constituted vigilantes searched every cottage and villa, empty and lived-in, in the village, including the Tsatsos's, and found nothing. Whether the girls were simply frightened or unusually patriotic we shall never know. But they had no blood relations in the village – and of course their father and brother were safely out of it.

'The guerillas must that next day have decided to split up. At any rate the girls started baking bread. A sharp-eyed neighbour noticed it, and remembered that they had been baking only two days before. Bread for the brother and father to take on the voyage. Apparently she did not suspect anything at once. But about five o'clock she went to the school and told the Germans. She had three relations among the hostages.

424

'A squad of *die Raben* arrived at the cottage. Only the cousin was there. He threw himself into a cupboard. He heard the two girls being struck, and screaming. He knew his time was up, so he leapt out, pistol in hand, fired before the Germans could move – and nothing happened. The pistol had jammed.

'They took the three to the school, where they were interrogated. The girls were tortured, the cousin was quickly made to co-operate. Two hours later – when night had come – he led the way down the coast road to an empty villa, knocked on the shutter and whispered to his two comrades that the sisters had managed to find a boat. As they came through the gate the Germans pounced. The leader was shot in the arm, but no one else was hurt.'

I interrupted. 'And he was a Cretan?'

'Yes. Quite like the man you saw. Only shorter and broader. All that time we hostages had been up in the classroom. It faced over the pine-forest, so we could not see any of the comings and goings. But about nine we heard two terrible screams of pain and a fraction later a tremendous cry. The one Greek word: *eleutheria*.

'You may think that we cried in return, but we did not. Instead we felt hope – that the guerillas had been caught. Not long after that there were two bursts of automatic fire. And some time after that the door of our room was thrown open. I was called out, and another man: the local butcher.

'We were marched downstairs and out in front of the school to the wing where I believe you masters live now – the western. Wimmel was standing at the entrance there with one of his lieutenants.

'On the side of the steps behind them the collaborationist interpreter was sitting, with his head in his hands. He looked white, in a state of shock. Some twenty yards away, by the wall, I saw two dead female bodies. Soldiers rolled them on to stretchers as we approached. The lieutenant stepped forward and signalled to the butcher to follow him.

'Wimmel turned and went into the building. I saw his back going down the dark stone corridor and then I was pushed forward after him. He stood outside a door at the far end and waited for me. Light poured from it. When I got there he gestured for me to go in.

'I think anyone but a doctor would have fainted. I should have liked to have fainted. The room was bare. In the middle was a table. Roped to the table was a young man. The cousin. He was naked except for a bloodstained singlet, and he had been badly burnt about the mouth and eyes. But I could see only one thing. Where his genitals should have been, there was nothing but a black-red hole. They had cut off his penis and scrotal sac. With a pair of wire-cutting shears.

'In one of the far corners another naked man lay on the floor. His face was to the ground and I could not see what they had done to him. He too was apparently unconscious. I shall never forget the stillness of that room. There were three or four soldiers – soldiers! of course torturers, psychopathic sadists – in the room. One of them held a long iron stake. An electric fire was burning, lying on its back. Three of the men wore leather aprons like blacksmith's aprons, to keep their uniforms clean. There was a disgusting smell of excrement and urine.

'And there was one other man, bound to a chair in the corner. He had been gagged. A great bull of a man. Badly bruised and wounded in one arm, but evidently not tortured yet. Wimmel had started first on the ones most likely to break.

'I have seen films – like Rossellini's – of the good human's re-actions to such scenes. How he turns on the Fascist monsters and delivers himself of some terse yet magnificent condemnation. How he speaks for history and humanity and for ever puts them in their place. I confess my own feelings were of immediate and intense personal fear. You see, Nicholas, I thought, and Wimmel left a long silence to let me think, that I was now going to be tortured as well. I did not know why. But there was no reason left in the world. When human beings could do such things to one another ...

'I turned round and looked at Wimmel. The extraordinary thing was that he seemed the most human other person in the room. He looked tired and angry. Even a little disgusted. Ashamed at the mess his men had created.

'He said in English, "These men do this for pleasure. I do not. I wish, before they start on that murderer there, that you will speak to him."

'I said, "What must I say?"

'"I want the names of his friends. I want the names of the people who help him. I want the positions of hiding-places and arms places. If he gives me these I give him my word he will be executed in a correct military manner."

'I said, "Did *they* not tell you enough?"

'Wimmel said, "All they knew. But he knows more. He is a man I have long wished to meet. His friends could not make him speak. I do not think we shall make him speak. Perhaps you can. You will say this. The truth. You do not like us Germans. You are an educated man. You wish only to stop these … procedures. You will advise him to speak what he knows. It is no guilt now that he is caught to speak. You understand? Come with me."

'We went into another bare room next door. A few moments later the wounded man was dragged in, still tied to his chair, and set in the centre of the room. I was given a chair facing him. The colonel sat in the background and waved the torturers outside. I began to talk.

'I did exactly as the colonel had ordered. That is, I begged the man to give all the information he could. You will say it was dishonourable of me, because you are thinking of the families and other men he could have betrayed. But that night I lived in those two rooms. They were the only reality. The outside world did not exist. I felt passionately that it was my duty to stop any more of this atrocious degradation of human intelligence. And that the Cretan's obsessive obstinacy seemed to contribute so directly to the degradation that it in part constituted it.

'I told him I was not a collaborationist, that I was a doctor, that my enemy was human suffering. That I spoke for Greece when I said that God would forgive him if he spoke now – his friends had suffered enough. There was a point beyond which no man could be expected to suffer … and so on. Every argument I could think of.

'But his expression was one of unchanging hostility to me. Hatred of me. I doubt if he even listened to what I was saying. He must have assumed that I was a collaborationist, that all the things I told him were lies.

'In the end I fell silent and looked back at the colonel. I could not hide the fact that I thought I had failed. He must have signalled to the guards outside, because one of them came in, went behind the Cretan and unfastened the gag. At once the man roared, all the chords in his throat standing out, that same word, that one word: *eleutheria*. There was nothing noble in it. It was pure savagery, as if he was throwing a can of lighted petrol over us. The guard brutally twisted the gag back over his mouth and retied it.

'Of course the word was not for him a concept or an ideal. It was simply his last weapon, and he used it as a weapon.

'The colonel said, "Take him back and await my orders." The man was dragged away again into that sinister room. The colonel walked to the shuttered window, opened it on to darkness and stood there for a minute, then turned to me. He said, "Now you see why I must speak the language that I do."

'I said, "I see nothing any more." Wimmel replied: "Perhaps I should make you watch the dialogue between my men and that animal." I said, "I beg you not to." He asked me if I thought he enjoyed such scenes. I did not answer. Then he said, "I should be very happy to sit at my headquarters. To have nothing to do but sign papers and enjoy the beautiful classical monuments. You do not believe me. You think I am a sadist. I am not. I am a realist."

'Still I sat in silence. He planted himself in front of me, and said, "You will be placed under guard in a separate room. I will give orders that you have something to eat and drink. As one civilized man to another, I regret the incidents of today and the incidents in the next room. You will not, of course, be one of the hostages."

'I looked up at him, I suppose with a shocked gratitude.

'He said, "You will please remember that like every other officer I have only one supreme purpose in my life, the German historical purpose – to bring order into the chaos of Europe. When that is done – then is the time for lieder-singing."

'I cannot tell you how, but I knew he was lying. One of the great fallacies of our time is that the Nazis rose to power because they imposed order on chaos. Precisely the opposite is true – they were successful because they imposed chaos on order. They tore up the commandments, they denied the super-ego, what you will. They said, "You may persecute the minority, you may kill, you may torture, you may couple and breed without love." They offered humanity all its great temptations. Nothing is true, everything is permitted.

'I believe that unlike most Germans, Wimmel knew, had always known, this. What he was. What he was doing. And that he was playing with me. It did not seem so at first. He gave me one last look and then went out, and I heard him speak to one of the guards who had brought me. I was taken to a room on another floor and given something to eat and a bottle of German beer. I had many feelings, but the dominant one was that I was going to survive. I was still going to see the sun shining. To breathe, to eat bread, to touch a keyboard.

'The night passed. I was brought coffee in the morning, allowed to wash. Then at half past ten I was made to go out. I found all the other hostages waiting. They had not been given anything to drink or eat and I was forbidden to speak to them. There was no sign of Wimmel or of Anton.

'We were marched to the harbour. The entire village was there, some four or five hundred people, black and grey and faded blue, crammed on to the quays with a line of *die Raben* watching them. The village priests, the women, even little boys and girls. They screamed as we came into sight. Like some amorphous protoplasm. Trying to break bounds, but unable to.

'We went on marching. There is a large house with huge Attic acroteria facing the harbour – you know it? – in those days there was a taverna on the ground-floor. On the balcony above I saw Wimmel and behind him Anton, flanked by men with machine-guns. 1 was taken from the column and made to stand against the wall under the balcony, among the chairs and tables. The hostages went marching on. Up a street and out of sight.

'It was very hot. A perfect blue day. The villagers were driven from the quay to the terrace with the old cannons in front of the taverna. They stood crowded there. Brown faces upturned in the sunlight, black kerchiefs of the women fluttering in the breeze. I could not see the balcony, but the colonel waited above, impressing his silence on them, his presence. And gradually they fell absolutely quiet, a wall of expectant faces. Up in the sky I saw swallows and martins. Like children playing in a house where some tragedy is taking place among the adults. Strange, to see so many Greeks ... and not a sound. Only the tranquil cries of little birds.

'Wimmel began to speak. The collaborationist interpreted.

'"You will now see what happens to those ... those who are the enemies of Germany ... and to those who help the enemies of

Germany ... by order of a court martial of the German High Command held last night ... three have been executed ... two more will now be executed ... "

'All the brown hands darted up, made the four taps of the Cross. Wimmel paused. German is to death what Latin is to ritual religion – entirely appropriate.

'"Following that ... the eighty hostages ... taken under Occupation law ... in retaliation for the brutal murder ... of four innocent members of the German Armed Forces ... " and yet again he paused ... "will be executed."

'When the interpreter interpreted the last phrase, there was an exhaled groan, as if they had all been struck in the stomach. Many of the women, some of the men, fell to their knees, imploring the balcony. Humanity groping for the non-existent pity of a *deus vindicans*. Wimmel must have withdrawn, because the beseechings turned to lamentations.

'Now I was forced out from the wall and marched after the hostages. Soldiers, the Austrians, stood at every entrance to the harbour and forced the villagers back. It horrified me that they could help *die Raben*, could obey Wimmel, could stand there with impassive faces and roughly force back people that I knew, only a day or two before, they did not hate.

'The alley curved up between the houses to the square beside the village school. It is a natural stage, inclined slightly to the north, with the sea and the mainland over the lower roofs. With the wall of the village school on the uphill side, and high walls to east and west. If you remember, there is a large plane tree in the garden of the house to the west. The branches come over the wall. As I came to the square that was the first thing I saw. Three bodies hung from the branches, pale in the shadow, as monstrous as Goya etchings. There was the naked body of the cousin with its terrible wound. And there were the naked bodies of the two girls. They had been disembowelled. A slit cut from their breastbones down to their pubic hair and the intestines pulled out. Half-gutted carcasses, swaying slightly in the noon wind.

'Beyond those three atrocious shapes I saw the hostages. They had been herded against the school in a pen of barbed wire. The men at the back were just in the shadow of the wall, the front ones in sunlight. As soon as they saw me they began to shout. There were insults of the obvious kind to me, confused cries of appeal – as if anything I could say then would have touched the colonel. He was there, in the centre of the square, with Anton and some twenty of *die Raben*. On the third side of the square, to the east, there is a long wall. You know it? In the middle a gate. Iron grilles. The two surviving guerillas were lashed to the bars. Not with rope – with barbed wire.

'I was halted behind the two lines of men, some twenty yards away from where Wimmel was standing. Anton would not look at me, though Wimmel turned briefly. Anton – staring into space, as if he had hypnotized himself into believing that none of what he saw existed. As if he no longer existed himself. The colonel beckoned the collaborationist to him. I suppose he wanted to know what the hostages were shouting. He appeared to think for a moment and then he went towards them. They fell silent. Of course they did not know he had already pronounced sentence on them. He said something that was translated to them. What, I could not hear, except that it reduced the villagers to silence. So it was not the death sentence. The colonel marched back to me.

'He said, "I have made an offer to these peasants." I looked at his face. It was absolutely without nervousness, excitation; a man in complete command of himself. He went on, "I will permit them not to be executed. To go to a labour camp. On one condition. That is that you, as mayor of this village, carry out in front of them the execution of the two murderers."

'I said, "I am not an executioner."

'The village men began to shout frantically at me.

'He looked at his watch, and said, "You have thirty seconds to decide."

'Of course in such situations one cannot think. All coherence is crowded out of one's mind. You must remember this. From this point on I acted without reason. Beyond reason.

'I said, "I have no choice."

'He went to the end of one of the ranks of men in front of me. He took a sub-machine-gun from a man's shoulder, appeared to make sure that it was correctly loaded, then came back with it and presented it to me with both hands. As if it was a prize I had won. The hostages cheered, crossed themselves. And then were silent. The colonel watched me. I had a wild idea that I might turn the gun on him. But of course the massacre of the entire village would then have been inevitable.

'I walked towards the men wired to the iron gates. I knew why he had done this. It would be widely publicized by the German-controlled newspapers. The pressure on me would not be mentioned, and I would be presented as a Greek who co-operated in the German theory of order. A warning to other mayors. An example to other frightened Greeks everywhere. But those eighty men – how could I condemn them?

'I came within about fifteen feet of the two guerillas. So close, because I had not fired a gun for very many years. For some reason I had not looked them in the face till then. I had looked at the high wall with its tiled top, at a pair of vulgar ornamental urns on top of the pillars that flanked the gate, at the fronds of a pepper tree beyond. But then I had to look at them. The younger of the two might have been dead. His head had fallen forward. They had done something to his hands, I could not see what, but there was blood all over the fingers. He was not dead. I heard him groan. Mutter something. He was delirious.

'And the other. His mouth had been struck or kicked. The lips were severely contused, reddened. As I stood there and raised the gun he drew back what remained of those lips. All his teeth had been smashed in. The inside of his mouth was like a blackened vulva. But I was too desperate to finish to realize the real cause. He too had had his fingers crushed, or his nails torn out, and I could see multiple burns on his body. But the Germans had made one terrible error. They had not gouged out his eyes.

'I raised the gun blindly and pressed the trigger. Nothing happened. A click. I pressed it again. And again, an empty click.

'I turned and looked round. Wimmel and my two guards were standing thirty feet or so away, watching. The hostages suddenly began to call. They thought I had lost the will to shoot. I turned back and tried once more. Again, nothing. I turned to the colonel, and gestured with the gun, to show that it would not fire. I felt faint in the heat. Nausea. Yet unable to faint.

'He said, "Is something wrong?"

'I answered, "The gun will not fire."

' "It is a Schmeisser. An excellent weapon."

' "I have tried three times."

' "It will not fire because it is not loaded. It is strictly forbidden for the civilian population to possess loaded weapons."

'I stared at him, then at the gun. Still not understanding. The hostages were silent again.

'I said, very helplessly, "How can I kill them?"

'He smiled, a smile as thin as a sabre-slash. Then he said, "I am waiting."

'I understood then. I was to club them to death. I understood many things. His real self, his real position. And from that came the realization that he was mad, and that he was therefore innocent, as all mad people, even the most cruel, are innocent. He was what life could do if it wanted – an extreme possibility made hideously mind and flesh. Perhaps that was why he could impose himself so strongly, like a black divinity. For there was something superhuman in the spell he cast. And therefore the real evil, the real monstrosity in the situation lay in the other Germans, those less-than-mad lieutenants and corporals and privates who stood silently there watching this exchange.

'I walked towards him. The two guards thought I was going to attack him because they sharply raised their guns. But he said something to them and stood perfectly still. I stopped some six feet from him. We stared at each other.

' "I beg you in the name of European civilization to stop this barbarity."

' "And I command you to continue this punishment."

'Without looking down he said, "Refusal to carry out this order will result in your own immediate execution."

'I walked back over the dry earth to that gate. I stood in front of those two men. I was going to say to the one who seemed capable of understanding that I had no choice, I must do this terrible thing to him. But I left a fatal pause of a second to elapse. Perhaps because I realized, close to him, what had happened to his mouth. It had been burnt, not simply bludgeoned or kicked. I remembered that man with the iron stake, the electric fire. They had broken in his teeth and branded his tongue, burnt his tongue right down to the roots with red-hot iron. That word he shouted must finally have driven them beyond endurance. And in those astounding five seconds, the most momentous of my life, I understood this guerilla. I mean that I understood far better than he did himself what he was. He helped me. He managed to stretch his head towards me and say the word he could not say. It was almost not a sound, but a contortion in his throat, a five-syllabled choking. But once again, one last time, it was unmistakably that word. And the word was in his eyes, in his being, totally in his being. What did Christ say on the cross? Why hast thou forsaken me? What this man said was something far less sympathetic, far less pitiful, even far less human, but far profounder. He spoke out of a world the very opposite of mine. In mine life had no price. It was so valuable that it was literally priceless. In his, only one thing had that quality of pricelessness. It was *eleutheria*: freedom. He was the immalleable, the essence, the beyond reason, beyond logic, beyond civilization, beyond history. He was not God, because there is no God we can know. But he was a proof that there is a God that we can never know. He was the final right to deny. To be free to choose. He, or what manifested itself through him, even included the insane Wimmel, the despicable German and Austrian troops. He was every freedom, from the very worst to the very best. The freedom to desert on the battlefield of Neuve Chapelle. The freedom to confront a primitive God at Seidevarre. The freedom to disembowel peasant girls and castrate with wire-cutters. He was something that passed beyond morality but sprang out of the very essence of things – that comprehended all, the freedom to do all, and stood against only one thing – the prohibition not to do all.

'All this takes many words to say to you. And I have said nothing about how I felt this immalleability, this refusal to cohere, was essentially Greek. That is, I finally assumed my Greekness. All I saw I saw in a matter of seconds, perhaps not in time at all. Saw that I was the only person left in that square who had the freedom left to choose, and that the annunciation and defence of that freedom was more important than common sense, self-preservation, yes, than my own life, than the lives of the eighty hostages. Again and again, since then, those eighty men have risen in the night and accused me. You must remember that I was certain I was going to die too. But all I have to set against their crucified faces are those few transcendent seconds of knowledge. But knowledge like a white heat. My reason has repeatedly told me I was wrong. Yet my total being still tells me I was right.

'I stood there perhaps fifteen seconds – I could not tell you, time means nothing in such situations – and then I dropped the gun and stepped beside the guerilla leader. I saw the colonel watching me, and I said, for him and so also for the remnant of a man beside me to hear, the one word that remained to be said.

'Somewhere beyond Wimmel I saw Anton moving, walking quickly towards him. But it was too late. The colonel spoke, the sub-machine-guns flashed and I closed my eyes at exactly the moment the first bullets hit me.'

54

He leant forward, after a long silence, and turned up the lamp; then stared at me. Deep in him I sensed something was finally moved; but after a moment the stare became its old, dry self.

'The disadvantage of our new drama is that in your role you do not know what you can believe and what you cannot. There is no one on the island who was in the square. But many can confirm for you every other incident I have told you.'

I thought of the scene on the central ridge; by not being insertible in the real story, it verified. Not that I doubted Conchis; I knew I had been listening to the history of events that happened; that in the story of his life he had saved the certain truth to the end.

'After you were shot?'

'I was hit and I fell and I knew no more because I fainted. I believe I heard the uproar from the hostages before darkness came. And possibly that saved me. I imagine the men firing were distracted. Other orders were being given to fire at the hostages. I am told that half an hour later, when the villagers were allowed to wail over their dead, I was found lying in a pool of blood at the feet of the guerillas. I was found by my housekeeper Soula – before the days of Maria – and Hermes. When they moved me I showed faint signs of life. They carried me home and hid me in Soula's room. Patarescu came and looked after me.'

'Patarescu?'

'Patarescu.' I tried to read his look; understood, by something in it, that he fully admitted that guilt, and did not consider it a guilt; and that he was prepared to justify it if I should press for the truth.

'The colonel?'

'By the end of the war he was wanted for countless atrocities. Several of them showed the same feature. An apparent reprieve at the last moment – which turned out to be a mere prolongation of the agony for the hostages. The War Crimes Commission have done their best. But he is in South America. Or Cairo, perhaps.'

'And Anton?'

'Anton believed that I had been killed. My servants let no one but Patarescu into the secret. I was buried. Or rather an empty coffin was buried. Wimmel left the island that same afternoon, leaving Anton in the middle of all the carnage of flesh, to say nothing of that of the good relations he had established. He must have spent all evening, perhaps night, writing a detailed report of the whole incident. He typed it himself – seven copies. He stated that fact in the report. I presume they were all he could get on the typewriter at one time. He hid nothing and excused no one, least of all himself. I will show you, in a moment.'

The Negro came across the gravel and began to dismantle the screen. Upstairs I could hear movements.

'What happened to him?'

'Two days later his body was found under the wall of the village school, where the ground was already dark with blood. He had shot himself. It was an act of contrition, of course, and he wanted the villagers to know. The Germans hushed the matter up. Not long afterwards the garrison was changed. The report explains that.'

'What happened to all the copies?'

'One was given to Hermes by Anton himself the next day, and he was asked to give it to the first of my foreign friends to inquire for me after the war. Another was given to one of the village priests with the same instructions. Another was left on his desk when he shot himself. It was open – no doubt for all his men and the German High Command to read. Three copies completely disappeared. Probably they were sent to relations or friends in Germany. They may have been intercepted. We shall never know now. And the last copy turned up after the war. It was sent to Athens, to one of the newspapers, with a small sum of money. For charity. A Viennese postmark. Plainly he gave a copy to one of his men.'

'It was published?'

'Yes. Certain parts of it.'

'Was he buried here?'

'His family cemetery – near Leipzig.'

Those cigarettes.

'And the villagers never knew that you had the choice?'

'The report came out. Some believe it, some do not. Of course I have seen that no helpless dependants of the hostages suffered financially.'

'And the guerillas – did you ever find out about them?'

'The cousin and the other man – yes, we know their names. There is a monument to them in the village cemetery. But their leader … I had his life investigated. Before the war he spent six years in prison. On one occasion for murder – a *crime passionnel*. On two or three others for violence and larceny. He was generally believed in Crete to have been involved in at least four other murders. One was particularly savage. He was on the run when the Germans invaded. Then he performed a number of wild exploits in the Southern Peloponnesus. He seems to have belonged to no organized resistance group, but to have roamed about killing and robbing. In at least two proven cases, not Germans, but other Greeks. We traced several men who had fought beside him. Some of them said they had been frightened of him, others evidently admired his courage, but not much else. I found an old farmer in the Mani who had sheltered him several times. And he said, *Kakourgos, ma Ellenas.* A bad man, but a Greek. I keep that as his epitaph.'

A silence fell between us.

'Those years must have strained your philosophy. The smile.'

'On the contrary. That experience made me fully realize what humour is. It is a manifestation of freedom. It is because there is freedom that there is the smile. Only a totally predetermined universe could be without it. In the end it is only by becoming the victim that one escapes the ultimate joke – which is precisely to discover that by constantly slipping away one has slipped away. One exists no more, one is no longer free. That is what the great majority of our fellow-men have always to discover. And will have always to discover.' He turned to the file. 'But let me finish by showing you the report that Anton wrote.'

I saw a thin stitched sheaf of paper. A title-page: *Bericht über die von deutschen Besetzsungstruppen unmenschliche Grausamkeiten* ...

'There is an English translation at the back.'

I turned to it, and read:

Report of the inhuman atrocities committed by German Occupation troops under the command of Colonel Dietrich Wimmel on the island of Phraxos between September 30th and October 2nd, 1943.

I turned a page.

On the morning of September 29th, 1943, four soldiers of No. 10 Observation-post, Argolis Command, situated on the cape known as Bourani on the south coast of the island of Phraxos, being off duty, were given permission to swim. At 12.45 ...

Conchis spoke. 'Read the last paragraph.'

I swear by God and by all that is sacred to me that the above events have been exactly and truthfully described. I observed them all with my own eyes and I did not intervene. For this reason I condemn myself to death.

I looked up. 'A good German.'

'No. Unless you think suicide is good. It is not. Despair is a disease, and as evil as Wimmel's disease.' I suddenly remembered Blake – what was it, 'Sooner murder an infant in its cradle than nurse un-acted desires.' A text I had once often used to seduce – myself as well as others. Conchis went on. 'You must make up your mind, Nicholas. Either you enlist under the *kapetan*, that murderer who knew only one word, but the only word, or you enlist under Anton. You watch and you despair. Or you despair and you watch. In the first case, you commit physical suicide; in the second, moral.'

'I can still feel pity for him.'

'You *can*. But ought you to?'

I was thinking of Alison, and I knew I had no choice. I felt pity for her as I felt pity for that unknown German's face on a few feet of flickering film. And perhaps an admiration, that admiration which is really envy of those who have gone farther along one's own road: they had both despaired enough to watch no more. While mine was the moral suicide.

I said, 'Yes. He couldn't help himself.'

'Then you are sick. You live by death. Not by life.'

'That's a matter of opinion.'

'No. Of conviction. Because the event I have told you is the only European story. It is what Europe is. A Colonel Wimmel. A rebel without a name. An Anton torn between them, killing himself when it is too late. Like a child.'

'Perhaps I have no choice.'

He looked at me, but said nothing. I felt all his energy then, his fierceness, his heartlessness, his impatience with my stupidity, my melancholy, my selfishness. His hatred not only of me, but of all he had decided I stood for: something passive, abdicating, English, in life. He was like a man who wanted to change all; and could not; so burned with his impotence; and had only me, an infinitely small microcosm, to convert or detest.

I looked down at last. 'Then you think I'm another Anton. Is that what I'm meant to understand?'

'You are someone who does not understand what freedom is. And above all that the better you understand it, the less you possess of it.'

I tried to absorb that paradox. 'I've shown too much to please you?'

'To be of further significance to me.' He picked up the file. 'Now I suggest we go to bed.'

I spoke sharply. 'You can't treat people like this. As if we're all just villagers to be shot so that you can prove some abstract theory of freedom.'

He stood up and stared down at me. 'For as long as you cherish your present view of freedom, it is you who holds the executioner's gun.'

I thought again of Alison; suppressed the thought.

'What makes you so sure you know my real self?'

'I do not claim that. My decision is based on the certain knowledge that you are incapable of knowing it yourself.'

'You honestly do think you're God, don't you?'

Incredibly, he did not answer; and his eyes said that that was what I might be left to believe. I let out a little snort of air, to show him what I thought, then went on.

'So what do you want me to do now? Collect my bag and walk back to the school?'

This seemed, unexpectedly, to set him back a little. There was a minute, but telltale, hesitation before he answered.

'As you wish. There was to be a little final ceremony tomorrow morning. But it is not of importance.'

'Ah. Well. I'd hate to miss that.'

He contemplated my humourless smile up at him, then gave a little nod.

'I wish you good night.' I turned my back, and his footsteps receded. But he stopped at the music-room doors. 'I repeat. No one will come.'

I didn't acknowledge that, either, and he went on inside. I believed him, as regards no one coming, but I had begun to smile to myself in the darkness. I knew that the threat to walk out at once had secretly alarmed him; had forced him to toss me another hasty carrot, a reason to stay. It must all have been a test, some sort of ordeal to be passed before I entered the inner circle ... at any rate, I felt more than ever certain that the girls were on the yacht. I had, so to speak, been brought before the execution squad, but this time there was to be a last-minute reprieve. The longer he denied me Julie now, the more he followed the philosophy of a Wimmel ... and at least I knew Conchis was a very different human being; if he was cruel it was, by his lights, to be kind.

I smoked one cigarette, another. There was a great stewing still-ness, an oppressiveness, a silence. The gibbous moon hung over the planet Earth, a dead thing over a dying thing. I got up and strolled across the gravel to the seat on the path down to the beach.

I had not expected such a finale: the statue of stone in the comic door. But then he couldn't have known of its secret relevance to me. He had simply guessed that for me freedom meant the freedom to satisfy personal desire, private ambition. Against that he set a free-dom that must be responsible for its actions; something much older than the existentialist freedom, I suspected – a moral imperative, an almost Christian concept, certainly not a political or democratic one. I thought back over the last few years of my life, the striving for individuality that had obsessed all my generation after the limiting and conforming years of the war, our retreat from society, nation, into self. I knew I couldn't really answer his charge, the question his story posed; and that I could not get off by claiming that I was a historical victim, powerless to be anything else but selfish – or I should not be able to get off from now on. It was as if he had planted a bandillera in my shoulder, or a succubus on my back: a knowledge I did not want.

Once more my mind wandered, in the grey silences of the night, not to Julie, but to Alison. Staring out to sea, I finally forced myself to stop thinking of her as someone still somewhere, if only in memory, still obscurely alive, breathing, doing, moving, but as a shovelful of ashes already scattered; as a broken link, a biological dead end, an eternal withdrawal from reality, a once complex object that now dwindled, dwindled, left nothing behind except a smudge like a fallen speck of soot on a blank sheet of paper.

As something too small to mourn; the very word was archaic and superstitious, of the age of Browne, or Hervey; yet Donne was right, her death detracted, would for ever detract, from my own life. Each death laid a dreadful charge of complicity on the living; each death was incongenerous, its guilt irreducible, its sadness immortal; a bracelet of bright hair about the bone.

I did not pray for her, because prayer has no efficacy; I did not cry for her, or for myself, because only extraverts cry twice; but I sat in the silence of that night, that infinite hostility to man, to permanence, to love, remembering her, remembering her.

55

Ten o'clock. I woke and swung out of bed, aware that I had overslept; shaved in a hurry. Somewhere below I could hear hammering, a man's voice, and what sounded like Maria's. But the colonnade was deserted when I came down. By the wall I saw four wooden crates. It was obvious that three of them had paintings inside. I looked back inside the music-room. The Modigliani had gone; so had the little Rodin and the Giacometti; and I guessed that the other two crates held the Bonnards from upstairs. My optimism of the night before swiftly vanished before this evidence that the 'theatre' was being dismantled. I had a dreadful intuition that Conchis meant exactly what he had said.

Maria appeared with coffee for me. I gestured at the crates.

'What's happening?'

'*Phygoume.*' We're going.

'*O kyrios Conchis?*'

'*Tha elthei.*'

He's coming. I gave up with her, swallowed a cup of coffee, another. There was a bright wind, it was a Dufy day, all bustle, movement, animated colour. I walked over to the edge of the gravel. The yacht was alive now, I could see several people on deck, but none seemed female. Then I glanced back to the house. Conchis stood under the colonnade, as if waiting for me to return.

He wore clothes that were somehow as incongruous as if he had been wearing fancy-dress. He looked exactly like some slightly intellectual businessman: a black leather brief-case; a dark blue summer suit, a cream shirt, a discreetly polka-dotted bow tie. It was perfect for Athens, but ridiculous on Phraxos … and unnecessary, since he would have had at least six hours on his yacht to change, except as a proof to me that his other world had already claimed him. He did not smile as I came up to him.

'I am leaving very shortly.' He glanced at his wrist-watch, an object I had never seen him wear before. 'This time tomorrow I shall be in Paris.'

The wind rattled the shimmering vegetal glass of the palm-fronds. The last act was to be played *presto*.

'A quick curtain?'

'No real play has a curtain. It is acted, and then it continues to act.'

We stared at each other.

'The girls?'

'Are accompanying me to Paris.' I took a breath, and gave him a little grimace of scepticism. He said, 'You are being very naïve.'

'In what way?'

'In supposing that rich men give up their toys.'

'Julie and June are not your toys.' He smiled without humour, and I said angrily, 'I don't swallow that one, either.'

'You think intelligence and good taste, to say nothing of good looks, cannot be bought? You are profoundly mistaken.'

'Then you have a very unfaithful pair of mistresses.'

I continued to amuse him. 'When you are older you will realize that infidelity of that sort is of no importance. I pay for their appearance, their presence, their conversation. Not their bodies. At my age, the demand there is easily met.'

'Are you really expecting me to – '

He cut me short. 'I know what you are thinking. I have them locked away in a cabin. Under duress somewhere – some such conclusion to the nonsense we have been feeding you.' He shook his head. 'We did not meet last week-end for a very simple reason. So that Lily might decide which she preferred – life with a penniless and, I suspect, ungifted schoolmaster ... or an existence in a much richer and more interesting world.'

'If she's what you say she is, she wouldn't have to think twice.'

He folded his arms. 'If it is any consolation to your self-esteem, she did. But she finally had the good sense to see that a long, dull and predictable future was an expensive price to pay for the satisfaction of a passing sexual attraction.'

I left a brief silence, then put down my coffee. 'Lily? And what did you say, Rose?'

'I told you last night.'

I stared at him, then took out my wallet, found the letter from Barclay's Bank and pushed it at him. He took it, but only gave it a cursory glance.

'A forgery. I am sorry.'

I snatched the letter back from his hands. 'Mr Conchis, I want to see those two girls. I also know the story of how you got them here in the first place. The police might be interested in that.'

'Then they must be interested in Athens. Since the girls are there – and will laugh your charge to ridicule in the first minute.'

'I don't believe you. They're on the yacht.'

'You may come aboard with me in a minute. If you insist. Look where you like. Question my crew. We will return you to shore before we sail.'

I knew he could be bluffing, but I had a strong idea that he wasn't – and anyway, if he was holding them under duress, he would not risk using such an obvious place.

'All right. I'll give you credit for being cleverer than that. But I'll have the whole matter in British Embassy hands as soon as I get to the village.'

'I do not think the Embassy will be amused. When they discover that their aid is being invoked by a mere disappointed lover.' He went on quickly, as if this display of futile threat was boring him. 'Now. Two of my cast wish to say goodbye to you.' He walked back to the corner of the house.

'Catherine!'

It was pronounced in the French way. He turned back to me.

'Maria – of course – is not a simple Greek peasant.'

But I was not to be diverted so easily. I accused him again.

'Quite apart from anything else, Julie ... even if she was what you claim ... would at least have the courage to tell me all this to my face.'

'Such scenes belong to the old drama. Not the new.'

'That's got nothing to do with what she is.'

'Perhaps one day you will meet her again. You may indulge your masochistic instincts then.'

We were saved all further argument by the appearance of Maria. She was still an elderly woman, still had a lined face; but she wore a well-cut black suit, a gilt-and-garnet brooch at one lapel. Stockings, shoes with the beginning of high heels, a touch of powder and rouge, lipstick ... the sort of middle-class matron of sixty one might see in any fashionable Athens street. She stood with a faint smile – the surprise, the quick-change entrance. Conchis watched me drily.

'This is Madame Catherine Athanasoulis, who has made a speciality of peasant roles. She has helped me many times before.'

He held out a hand politely for her to come nearer. She advanced with an open-palmed gesture, almost one of regret at having deceived me so completely. I gave her a cold and wide-eyed look; she wasn't going to have any compliments from me. She reached out a hand. I ignored it. After a moment, she gave a little mock bow of the head.

Conchis said, '*Les valises?*'

'*Tout est prêt.*' She eyed me. '*Eh bien, monsieur. Adieu.*'

She withdrew as composedly as she had come. I had begun to feel something like despair – or shock. I knew Conchis was lying, but he was lying at such length, so circumstantially; and I was to have no relief, because he looked across the gravel.

'Good. Here is Joe. This is what we call the *désintoxication*.'

It was the Negro, strolling up from the beach path in an elegant dark-tan suit, a pink shirt, a club tie, dark glasses. He raised an easy hand as he saw us waiting for him and came across the gravel; a smile at Conchis, a dry quirk of the mouth in my direction.

'This is Joe Harrison.'

'Hi.'

I said nothing. He gave a little side-glance at Conchis, then reached out a hand. 'Sorry, friend. Just did what master said.'

He was American, not West Indian. Once more I ignored the hand.

'With some conviction.'

'Yeah, well – of course we niggers are all first cousin to apes. You call us eunuchs, we just don't understand.' He said it lightly, as if it didn't matter any more.

'I didn't mean that.'

'Okay.'

We exchanged a wary look, then he turned to Conchis. 'They're coming to pick up the stuff.'

Conchis said, 'I have some last things upstairs.'

I was left standing there with Joe. More figures appeared on the path, four or five sailors in their navy-blue singlets and white shorts. Four looked like Greeks, but one, with pale blond hair, looked Scandinavian or German. The girls had hardly talked about the crew – they were just 'Greek sailors'. I felt a new prick of jealousy, and a deeper one of uncertainty – I truly began to feel now that I was discarded, a mere encumbrance ... and a fool. They all knew I was a fool. I eyed Joe, who was leaning idly against one of the arches. He seemed a poor bet, but my only one.

'Where are the girls?'

His dark glasses lazily surveyed me. 'In Athens.' But then his look swivelled briefly back towards the doors through which the old man had disappeared. He glanced at me again with the trace of a rueful smile. Then he shook his head, once, with a kind of shared sympathy.

'What does that mean?' He gave a small shrug: that was the way it was. I said, 'You're speaking from experience?'

He murmured softly, 'Could be.'

The sailors came up past us and went to the crates. Then Hermes appeared beside the house, carrying more suitcases over the gravel down towards the beach. Maria followed him in her finery, a few steps behind. Joe lounged away from the column and came a step or two towards me, holding out a packet of American cigarettes. I hesitated, then took one, bent to the light he offered. He spoke in a low voice.

'She said to say sorry.' I sought his eyes as they lifted from lighting his own cigarette. 'No bullshit. She meant it. Right?' Still I stared at him. Once again his eyes slipped past me towards the doors, as if he didn't want to be caught talking confidentially to me. 'Man, you're holding a lousy pair against a full house. No chance. *Compris*?'

Somehow that convinced me, though totally against my will, more than anything that the old man himself had said. I was almost tempted to give Joe some bitter message back, but before I could frame it, it was too late. Conchis stood in the doorway with a small suitcase. He spoke to one of the sailors in Greek. Joe touched my arm, again almost as if in secret sympathy, and then moved forward to take the case from Conchis's hand. As he came back past me, he pulled a face.

'Know the one about the white man's burden? They make it, we carry it.'

He raised a hand in casual farewell, then set off after Hermes and Maria. The sailors moved off with the crates, and I was left once more alone with Conchis. He opened his hands, unsmiling, almost taunting: I had better believe him now.

I said, 'You haven't heard the last of me.'

'I should not be foolish. Money goes a long way in this country.'

'And sadism, apparently.'

He examined me one last time. 'Hermes will return to lock up in a minute.' I said nothing. 'You had your chance. I suggest you reflect on what it is in you that caused you to miss it.'

'Go to hell.'

He said absolutely nothing, simply fixed my eyes, as if he could hypnotize me into a retraction.

446

I said, 'I mean that.'

A moment, then he slowly shook his head. 'You do not know your meaning yet. Or mine.'

Then – he must have known I should not have taken his hand – he moved past me. But at the steps he stopped and turned.

'I forgot. My sadism does not extend to your stomach. Hermes will give you a packed lunch. It is prepared.'

He was some way across the gravel before I could think of a parting shot. I shouted it after him.

'Hydrocyanic acid sandwiches?'

But he took no notice. I felt like running after him, catching his arm, detaining him by force, anything; and equally knew myself powerless. Hermes appeared on his way back from the beach, beyond Conchis. I heard the sound of the power dinghy going out on a first ferry to the yacht. The two men stopped, exchanged a word, shook hands, then the donkey-driver came on towards me. Conchis went down out of sight. Hermes stood at the foot of the steps and presented me with his morose wall eye; then lifted a bunch of keys. I spoke in Greek.

'The two girls – are they on the yacht?'

He frogged his mouth: he did not know.

'Have you seen them today?'

His chin went up: no.

I turned disgustedly away. Hermes followed me indoors, even up the stairs, but he abandoned me at the door of my bedroom and went off to lock windows and shutters elsewhere ... not that I noticed that, because I had no sooner entered my room when I saw that I had been left a parting present. It lay on the pillow: an envelope stuffed full of Greek currency notes. I counted them out: twenty million *drachmai*. Even allowing for the acute inflation of the time, that was well over two hundred pounds, more than a third of my annual salary. I knew then why the old man had slipped upstairs before he left. The money, with its implicit suggestion that I too could be bought, enraged me; it was the final humiliation. At the same time it was a lot of money. I thought of rushing down to the jetty and throwing it all in his face – there was still time, the power-boat had to unload and return; but I thought only. When I heard Hermes returning, I hastily stuffed the money inside my duffel-bag.

He watched in the doorway while I packed the rest of my few things; and once more followed me downstairs, as if my every movement had to be watched.

A last look round the music-room, at the nail, the mark on the empty wall, where the Modigliani had hung; a moment or two later I was standing alone under the colonnade listening to Hermes while he locked the music-room door from inside. I heard the boat returning below, I was still tempted to go and ... but I had to do something positive, rather than symbolic. With any luck I could talk the village police sergeant into letting me use the coastguard station radio. I was beyond caring whether I made a fool of myself. I nursed one last hope – that Conchis had told the twins some new story that made their absence from the island seem plausible to them. It occurred to me that they might have received some equivalent of what he had told me of them, had been persuaded that I was in his pay, lying to Julie throughout ... I had to get in touch with them, even if it was finally only to discover that they were as he claimed. But until I heard it straight from them, I would not believe it. I clung to my memory of Julie in the water, Julie at countless moments that must have been sincere; and to her Englishness, all that middle-class and university background we shared. To sell oneself, even to a Conchis, required a kind of humourlessness, a lack of objectivity, a shallowness that lost nothing if it traded decency for luxury, mind for body ... but it was no good. However much green English scepticism I tried to set against decadent European venality, I was still left with the mystery of how two such ravishing girls accepted the absence of admirers, kept themselves so in purdah for Conchis; then there was his seeming intellectual hold over Julie, his wealth, a certain air both girls betrayed of being more used to this life of luxury than they pretended. I gave up.

I heard Hermes come out by the seldom-used door with the dolphin knocker under the side-colonnade, and start locking it. I decided: the faster I set things in motion, the better. I turned and marched for the gate, jumping off the edge of the colonnade on to the gravel. Hermes called sharply from the door.

'The food, *kyrios!*'

I waved a hand at him without stopping: to hell with food also. I saw his donkey, bulging sacks already tied to its back, tethered beside the cottage door. As if in some idiotic fear of not carrying out Conchis's orders to the letter, the islander ran down the colonnade and over the bare earth to where the beast was tethered. I went on past, taking no notice of him, though I half saw that he snatched something from the shade inside the doorway. Then I heard his hurried footsteps on the gravel behind me. I turned to wave him angrily away again. But I stopped, my hand frozen.

What he held out was a rush basket. It was one I had seen before, beside Julie, during our long Sunday together. I stared slowly up from it to Hermes's eyes. He held it a shade closer, coaxingly, for me to take. Then he said in Greek, You must. For the first time since I had known him, there was the ghost of a smile on his face.

Still I hesitated. Then I dropped my duffel-bag and took the basket and pulled it open: two apples, two oranges, two packages wrapped in white paper and neatly tied – and beneath, half hidden, the gold foil of the neck of a bottle of French champagne. I shifted one of the sandwich packets to see the label: Krug. I looked up with what must have seemed a childish bewilderment. He said one word.

'Perimeni.'

She waits.

Then he nodded behind him, back towards the cliffs east of the private beach. I looked, expecting to see a figure. In the silence I heard the boat returning from the yacht. This time Hermes pointed, then repeated the same word.

You do not know my meaning yet.

To preserve some semblance of dignity, I walked as far as the steps across the gulley; but there I could hold back no longer and raced down them, and up the other side. The statue of Poseidon stood in the sun, but on this occasion somewhat less than majestically. A home-made notice, flapping in the breeze like a forgotten garment on a line, had been suspended from the outstretched arm. It showed only an indicating hand, but it pointed through the trees towards the cliffs. I strode down through the bushes into the pines.

56

Almost at once I spotted her through the thin trees. She stood at the cliff-edge, in pale blue trousers, a dark-blue shirt, a pink sun-hat, and she was looking towards me. I waved, and she waved back – but then, to my surprise, instead of coming towards me, she turned and went out of sight down the steep slope immediately above the sheer cliff. I was too relieved, too elated, to think much of it – perhaps she wanted to signal to the yacht that all was well. I broke into a run. Not twenty-five seconds passed between my first seeing her and my arrival at where she had stood ... and where I now stood myself incredulously. The ground fell away steeply for some twenty yards before it came to the lip of the cliff proper. There was nowhere to hide, a litter of small rocks and scree, a few patches of scrub not a foot high; but she had completely disappeared. No one as conspicuously dressed ... I dropped the basket and my duffel-bag and went along the top of the slope in the direction she had taken ... but it was pointless. There were no large rocks, no secret gulleys. I scrambled down to the very edge of the cliff, but only a trained climber could have descended there, and then only with a rope.

It was a reversal of all physical reason. She had vanished into thin air. I stared down at the yacht. The dinghy was being hoisted aboard, I could see at least ten people on deck, crew and passengers; the long hull was already on the move and heading slowly along to where I stood, as if I was to be publicly mocked one last time.

Then without warning there was a stage cough behind me. I jerked round – to an extraordinary sight. Some fifteen yards behind me, half way up the slope, Julie's head and shoulders had emerged from the ground. Her elbows were on the ground itself and behind her head, like some sinister and grotesque black halo, was a jagged circle. But there was nothing sinister about her mischievous face.

'Have you lost something? Can I help you?'

'Christ almighty.'

I climbed closer, stopped six feet from where she still grinned up at me. Her skin was much browner, now approached her sister's degree of tan. I could see the circle behind her was an iron lid, like a hinged drain-cover. Stones had been cemented all round its upper rim. Julie herself was in a vertical iron tube sunk into the ground. Two wire hawsers ran down from the lid, some counterbalance system. She bit her lips, and curled a beckoning finger.

'Won't you come into my parlour, said the ... '

It was apt. There was a real spider on the island that made neat little trap-doors on every bank; I'd watched the boys trying to entice them out. But suddenly her voice and expression changed.

'Oh you poor thing – what's happened to your hand!'

'He didn't tell you?' She shook her head, concerned. 'Not to worry. It's past history now.'

'It looks horrid.'

She climbed out. We stood a moment, then she reached, took the scarred hand and examined it, looked solicitously up into my eyes. I smiled.

'That's nothing. Wait till you hear the dance he's led me over this last twenty-four hours.'

'I rather thought he might.' She looked down at the hand again. 'But it's bearable now?'

'When I get over the shock.' I nodded at the hole in the ground. 'What the hell is it?'

'The Germans. In the war.'

'Oh God. I should have guessed.'

The observation post ... Conchis would have simply concealed the entrance, blocked off the front slits. We went beside it. The hole plunged down into darkness. I could see a ladder, massive counterweights at the end of the wires, a dim patch of concrete floor at the bottom. Julie reached and tipped the lid. It fell smoothly down to ground level, where the incrusted and projecting stones on the upper side fitted the surrounding ones like the pieces of a jigsaw puzzle. One would never have seen it; one might just, walking over the lid, have noticed an odd fixity about the stones – but even then the neck was in a little prominence one would ordinarily have skirted.

I said, 'I can't believe this is happening.'

'You surely didn't think I would – ' but she broke off.

'Just half an hour ago he told me you were his mistress. That I'd never see you again.'

'His *mistress*!'

'And June as well.'

It was her turn to be shocked. She stared at me as if I must be testing her in some way, then gave a little puff of protest.

'But you can't have believed him!' I received her first serious, or nearly serious, look. 'If you believed him for a moment I'll never speak to you again.'

A moment later my arms were round her and our mouths had met. It was brief, but agreeably convincing. She pulled her head gently away.

'I think we're being watched.'

I looked back down to the yacht; and released her body, but not her hands.

'Where's June?'

'Guess.'

'I'm beyond guessing.'

'I've had a long walk today. A lovely walk.'

'The village? Hermes's house?'

'We've been there since Friday. So close to you. It was awful.'

'Maurice ... ?'

'Has lent it to us for the summer.' Her smile deepened. 'I know. I've been pinching myself as well.'

'Good God. This other thing he was planning?'

'Abandoned. He suddenly announced one evening that he hadn't time for it. There was some talk about next year, but ... ' she gave a little shrug. That was to be the cost of our happiness. I sought her eyes.

'You still want to stay?'

She held my eyes a second, then bowed her head. 'If you think we could stand each other just as ordinary people. Without all the excitement.'

'That's so silly I'm not going to answer it.'

She smiled up. 'Then it looks as if you're stuck with me.'

The siren of the yacht sounded. We turned, hand in hand. It had come opposite us, some three hundred yards offshore. Julie raised an arm and waved; and after a moment I did the same. I could make out Conchis and Joe, with Maria's black figure between them. They raised their arms and waved back. Conchis called towards a man in the bows. There was an ascending plume of smoke, a report, a tiny black object hurtling skywards. It climbed, slowed, then burst. A shower of incandescent stars glittered for a few moments with an explosive crackle against the azure; then another, then a third. Fireworks, for the end of a theatre. A prolonged moan on the siren, more waving arms. Julie put her hands to her mouth and kissed them out to the yacht, I waved again. Then the long white hull began to curve away from the coast.

'Did he really say I was his kept woman?'

I told her *verbatim*. She stared after the yacht.

'What a cheek.'

'I knew it was a put-on. It's just that dear old poker-face of his.'

'I shall jolly well slap it next time I see him. June'll go mad.' But then she smiled at me. 'Still ... ' she pulled my hand. 'That walk. I'm famished.'

'I want to see where you lived.'

'Afterwards. Please let's eat.'

We climbed back to where I had left the basket, and installed ourselves under a pine-tree. She undid the sandwiches, I opened the champagne, and lost some of it, it had got too warm. But we toasted each other, then kissed again, and started eating. She wanted to know everything that had happened the day before, and I told her; then everything else, the night manoeuvres, the supposed letter to her from me the week before, my not having been ill ...

'You did get my real letter from Siphnos?'

'Yes.'

'Actually we wondered if it was some last trick. But he's been so sweet to us. Ever since our little show-down.'

I asked her what they'd been doing ... in Crete and cruising around. She grimaced. 'Lying in the sun and getting bored.'

'I can't think why there had to be the delay.'

Julie hesitated. 'He did make one attempt last week-end to sell us the idea of ... you know, pushing you off on to June. I suppose he couldn't quite give up hope on that.'

'Look at this.' I reached for my duffel-bag and showed her the envelope of money; told her how much it was, what I still felt inclined to do with it. But she was swift to disagree.

'No honestly, you must take it. You've earned it, and he's got so much.' She smiled. 'And you may have to start buying me meals soon. Now I'm out of work.'

'He didn't try and tempt you with more money?'

'He did actually. It was the house in the village and you against the completion of contract money.'

'A bit rough on June?'

Julie sniffed. 'She wasn't allowed a vote.'

'I adore that sun-hat.'

It was soft, childlike, short-brimmed. She took it off and contemplated it, again like a child, almost gauchely, as if no one had ever paid her physical compliments before. I leant across and kissed her cheek, then put an arm round her shoulders and drew her to me. The yacht was two or three miles away now, disappearing round the end of Phraxos to the east.

'And the grand enigma – not a clue?'

'You've no idea. We were almost on our knees to him the other day. But that's the other price. It was going on in that absurd way, or this. Being left in the dark.'

'I wish to God I knew what happened here last year – and the one before.'

'You haven't heard from them?'

'Not a word.' I added, 'I'd better confess.' I told her about the letters I had written checking on her, and showed her the one from her bank in London.

'I think that's absolutely foul of you, Nicholas. Fancy not trusting us.' She bit her lips. 'Nearly as foul as June's ringing up the British Council in Athens and checking on you.' I grinned. 'I made ten bob out of that.'

'Is that all I was worth?'

'All she was worth.'

I looked to the east. The yacht had disappeared, the sea was empty now, the wind blew gently through the pines above us, shifted wisps of her hair. She had slumped a little against me where I sat with my back to the pine-stem. I felt like one of those rockets, like the champagne we had drunk. I turned her face and we kissed, then lay, still kissing, side by side in the sun-flecked shade. I wanted her, but not so urgently, now that all summer lay ahead. So I contented myself with a hand beneath her shirt on her bare back, and her mouth. In the end she lay half across me, with her lips against my cheek, in silence.

I whispered, 'Have you missed me?'

'More than it's good for you to know.'

'I'd like to lie like this every night of my life.'

'I wouldn't. Not comfortable enough.'

'Don't be so literal-minded.' I held her a little tighter. 'Say I may. Tonight.'

She ran fingers through my shirt.

'Was she nice in bed? Your Australian friend?'

I lay there, chilled a moment, staring up through the pine-branches at the sky beyond, half inclined to tell her ... then no, it was better to wait.

'I'll tell you all about her one day.'

She pinched my skin gently. 'I thought you had.'

'Why do you ask, anyway?'

'Because.'

'Because what?'

'I'm probably not as ... you know.'

I turned and kissed her hair. 'You've already proved you're much cleverer.'

She was silent a moment, as if she wasn't fully reassured.

'I've never really been physically in love with anyone before.'

'It's not an illness.'

'An unknown place.'

'I promise you'll like it.'

Another little silence. 'I wish there was another you. For June.'

'She wants to stay?'

'A little while.' Then she murmured, 'That's the trouble with being twins. You always have the same tastes in everything.'

'I thought you didn't see eye to eye on men.'

She kissed my neck. 'We do on this one.'

'She's teasing you.'

'I bet you wish we had gone through with *Three Hearts*.'

'I'm gnashing my teeth in disappointment.'

There was another pinch, less gentle this time.

'Seriously.'

'You're like a little girl sometimes.'

'It's how I feel. *My* toy.'

'Who you're going to take to bed with you tonight?'

'It's only a single bed.'

'Then there won't be room for pyjamas.'

'Actually I've given up wearing them here.'

'You're driving me wild.'

'I drive myself wild. Lying naked there thinking about you.'

'What am I doing?'

'All sorts of wicked things.'

'Tell me.'

'I don't imagine them in words.'

'Gentle things or rough things?'

'Things.'

'Tell me just one.'

She hesitated, then whispered, 'I run away and you catch me.'

'What do I do then?' She said nothing. I reached my hand down her back. 'Put you over my knees and smack you?'

'Sometimes I have to be very, very slowly seduced.'

'Because you've never been made love to before?'

'Mm.'

'I want to undress you now.'

'Then you'd have to carry me back.'

'I wouldn't mind.'

She leant up on an elbow, then leant across and kissed me, a little smile.

'Tonight. I promise. And June's waiting for us.'

'Let me see your place first.'

'It's horrid. Like a tomb.'

'Just one quick dekko.'

She stared down into my eyes, as if for some reason she was inclined to argue me out of it; then smiled and stood and reached a hand for me. We went back down the steep slope over the sea. Julie stooped and pulled on a stone: the encrusted lid rose, the dark hole gaped. She turned and knelt, felt down with a foot for the top rung of the ladder, then began to clamber down. She reached the bottom some fifteen feet below and her face craned up.

'Be careful. Some of the rungs are worn.'

I turned and climbed down after her. It was unpleasantly claustro-phobic inside the tube. But at the bottom, opposite the ladder, a small square room opened out, about fifteen feet by fifteen. In the poor light I could make out a door in each sidewall and on the side towards the sea, the blocked apertures of what must have once been machine-gun, or observation, slits. A table, three wooden chairs, a small cupboard. There was a fusty staleness in the air, as if silence had a smell.

'Have you got a match?'

She held out a hurricane lamp, and I lit it. The left wall of the room was painted with a clumsy mural – a beer-cellar scene, foaming steins, bosomy girls with winking eyes. Dim traces showed that there had once been colours, but now it was only the black outlines that remained. It was as remote as an Etruscan wall-painting; of a culture long sunken under time. On the right-hand wall was some-thing more skilful – a perspective street vista that I guessed to be of some Austrian city ... Vienna, perhaps. I guessed, too, that Anton had helped to execute it. The two side-doors looked like bulkhead doors aboard a ship. There were massive padlocks on each.

Julie nodded. 'That was our room, in there. Joe used the other.'

'What a god-awful place. It smells.'

'We used to call it the Earth. Have you ever smelt a fox-earth?'

'Why are the doors locked?'

'I don't know. They never have been. I suppose there must be people on the island who know the place exists.' She gave a wry smile. 'You're not missing anything. Just costumes. Beds. More ghastly murals.'

I looked at her in the lamplight. 'You're a brave girl. To face this sort of thing.'

'We hated it. So many sour, unhappy men. Locked away here with all that sunlight outside.'

I touched her hand.

'Okay. I've seen enough.'

'Would you put out the lamp?'

I extinguished it, and Julie turned to climb the ladder to the out-side. Slim blue legs, the brilliant daylight dazzling down. I waited a moment at the bottom, to keep clear of her feet, then started after her. The top of her body disappeared.

457

And then she screamed my name.

Someone, perhaps two someones, had sprung from behind the lid and grabbed her arms. She seemed to be lifted, almost jerked bodily out and away – a leg kicked wildly sideways, as if she were trying to hook a foot behind the counterweight wires. My name again, but cut short; a scuffle of stones outside, out of my sight. I clawed violently up the remaining rungs. For one fraction of a second a face appeared in the opening above. A young man with crewcut blond hair, the sailor I had seen that morning at the house. He saw I was still two rungs from the top, and immediately slammed the lid down. The shocked counterweights rattled against the metal wall by my feet. I bellowed in the sudden pitch darkness.

'For God's sake! Hey! Wait a minute!'

I pushed with all my force on the underside of the lid. It gave infinitesimally, as if someone were sitting or standing on it. But it refused to budge at a second attempt. The tube was too narrow for me to apply much upward pressure.

Once more I strained to heave it up; then listened. Silence. I tried the lid one last time, then gave up and climbed down to the bottom. I struck a match, relit the hurricane-lamp; tried the two massive doors. They were impenetrable. I tore open the cupboard. It was as empty of objects as what had just happened was of reason. Snarling with rage, I remembered Conchis's fairy-godfather exit: the gay farewell, the fireworks, the bottle of Krug. Our revels now are ended. But this was Prospero turned insane, maniacally determined never to release his Miranda.

I stood at the foot of the ladder and seethed, trying to comprehend the sadistic old man's duplicities: to read his palimpsest. His 'theatre without an audience' made no sense, it couldn't be the explanation. The one thing all actors and actresses craved was an audience. Perhaps what he was doing did spring in part from some theory of the theatre, but he had said it himself: *The masque is only a metaphor.* So? Some incomprehensible new philosophy: metaphorism? Perhaps he saw himself as a professor in an impossible faculty of ambiguity, a sort of Empson of the event. I thought and thought, and thought again, and arrived at last at nothing but more doubt. It began to extend to Julie and June as well. I returned to the schizophrenia stage. That must be it, it was all planned from the beginning, I was never to have her, always to be tormented, mocked like Tantalus. Yet how could any girl do what she had done – I could still feel her kisses, remember every word of that deliberately erotic little whispered conversation she had initiated – and not mean an iota of it? Except someone who was indeed mentally deranged and in some way aware that her promises need never be met?

But how could a man who claimed to be a doctor allow such things to go on? It was inconceivable.

Half an hour and several attempts later the lid smoothly gave before my upthrust. Three seconds later I was in the sunlight again. The sea was empty, and the trees around me. I climbed the slope to where I could look further inland, but of course there was nothing. The wind blew through the Aleppo pines, indifferent, inhuman, on another planet. A scrap of white paper, a relic from our lunch, flapped idly where it had caught in a tangle of smilax some fifty yards away. The basket and the bag stood where we had left them; the pink hat where she had laid it when she took it off.

Two minutes later I was at the house. It was shuttered blind, exactly as I had last seen it. I started walking fast down the track towards the gate. And there, just as on my first visit to Bourani, I found that I had been left a clue.

57

Or rather, two clues.

They were hanging, from the branch of a pine tree near the gate, in the centre of the path, some six feet from the ground, swinging a little in the wind, innocent and idle, touched by sunlight. One was a doll. The other was a human skull.

The skull hung from a black cord, which passed through a neat hole drilled in the top, and the doll from a white one. Its neck was in a noose. It was hanging in both senses. About eighteen inches high, clumsily carved in wood and painted black, with a smiling mouth and eyes naïvely whitened in. Round its ankles were its only 'clothes' – two wisps of white rag. The doll was Julie, and said that she was evil, she was black, under the white innocence she wore.

I twisted the skull and made it spin. Shadows haunted the sockets, the mouth grinned grimly.

Alas, poor Yorick.

Disembowelled corpses?

Or Frazer ... *The Golden Bough*? I tried to remember. What was it? Hanging dolls in sacred woods.

I looked round the trees. Somewhere eyes were on me. But nothing moved. The dry trees in the sun, the scrub in the lifeless shadow. Once again fear, fear and mystery, swept over me. The thin net of reality, these trees, this sun. I was infinitely far from home. The profoundest distances are never geographical.

In the light, in the alley between the trees. And everywhere, a darkness beneath.

What it is, has no name.

The skull and his wife swayed in a rift of the breeze. Leaving them there, in their mysterious communion, I walked fast away.

Hypotheses pinned me down, as Gulliver was pinned by the countless threads of the Lilliputians. All I knew was that I ached for Julie, I was mad for her, the world that day had no other meaning; so I strode down to the school like some vengeance-brewing chieftain in an Icelandic saga, though with always the small last chance in mind that I should find Julie waiting for me. But when I flung my door open, I flung it open on to an empty room. Then I felt like going to Demetriades and trying to wring the truth out of him; forcing him to come with me to the science master. I half decided to go to Athens, and even got a suitcase down from the top of the wardrobe; then changed my mind. Probably the fact that there were another two weeks of term to run was the only significant one; two weeks more in which to torment us ... or me.

Finally I went down to the village, straight to the house behind the church. The gate was open; a garden green with lemon and orange trees, through which a cobbled path led to the door of the house. Though not large it had a certain elegance; a pilastered portico, windows with graceful pediments. The whitewashed façade was in shadow, a palest blue against the evening sky's pale blue. As I walked between the cool, dark walls of the trees Hermes came out at the front door. He looked behind me, as if surprised to see me alone.

I said in Greek, 'Is the young lady here?' He stared at me, then began to open his hands in incomprehension. I cut in impatiently. 'The other young lady – the sister?'

He raised his head. No.

'Where is she?'

With the yacht. After lunch.

'How do you know? You weren't here.'

His wife had told him.

'With Mr Conchis? To Athens?'

'*Nai.*' Yes.

The yacht could easily have called in at one of the village harbours after it had disappeared from our sight; and I supposed June might have gone aboard without fuss, if she had been told we were there. Or it might always have been planned so. I stared at Hermes a moment, then pushed past him and went into the house.

An airy hall, cool and bare, a fine Turkish carpet hanging on one wall; and on another an obscure coat-of-arms, rather like an English funeral hatchment. Through an open door to the left I saw the crates of pictures from Bourani. A small boy stood in the door, he must have been one of Hermes's children. The man said something to him and after a solemn brown stare the child turned away.

Hermes spoke behind my back. 'What do you want?'

'Which rooms were the girls in?'

He hesitated, then pointed up the stairs. I had a reluctant impression that he was genuinely out of his depth. I strode up the stairs. Passages led both left and right, the length of the building. I looked round at Hermes, who had followed me. Again he hesitated; then again he pointed. A door to the right. I found myself in a typical island room. A bed with a folkweave bedspread, a floor of polished planks, a chest of drawers, a fine *cassone*, some pleasant water-colours of island houses. They had the clean, stylish, shallow look of architectural perspectives and though they were unsigned I guessed that once more I was looking at Anton's work. The west-facing shutters were latched three-quarters closed. On the sill of the open windows stood a wet *kanati*, the porous jug the Greeks put there to cool both air and water. A small bowl of jasmine and plumbago flowers, creamy white and pale blue, sat on top of the *cassone*. A nice, simple, welcoming little scene.

I went and opened one of the shutters to let more light in. Hermes stood in the doorway, staring doubtfully at me. Once again he asked me what I was doing. I noticed he didn't bother to ask me where Julie was, and this time I ignored him. In a way I hoped he would try to stop me, since I felt a growing need for physical violence of some kind. But he made no move, and I had to vent my frustration on the chest-of-drawers. Apart from one half-drawer with toilet and cosmetic things, it contained nothing but clothes. I gave up, looked round the room. In one corner a rail had been fixed, and a curtain hung there. Ripped aside, it revealed a short row of dresses, skirts, a summer coat. I recognized the pink dress she had worn on the Sunday when I had been told the 'truth'; or what had then seemed the truth. On the floor were shoes, and behind them, against one of the angles of the wall, a suitcase. I picked it up and threw it on the bed and, without much hope, tried the catches. But they opened.

There were more clothes, two or three woollen jumpers, a heavy tweed skirt, seemingly things not needed in summer Greece; two Greek shoulder-bags, brand-new, there were price-tags still on, as if bought for presents. Underneath lay some books. A pre-war guide to Greece, with some postcards of classical sites and sculpture. None had been written on. A Greene novel. An American paperback on witchcraft, in which a place was marked by a letter. I slipped a printed card out of the envelope. It was an invitation to speech day, a week before, at the London school where Julie had told me she had worked. The envelope had been forwarded to Bourani from Cerne Abbas, her home in Dorset, nearly a month previously. There was also a text of the Palatine Anthology. I flicked it open. *Julia Holmes, Girton.* Some of the poems had little margin notes, English equivalents, in her neat handwriting.

Hermes spoke. 'What are you looking for?'

I muttered, 'Nothing.' I had a growing suspicion that Conchis operated on some principle like that of the espionage cell; one never told the lower echelons more than they needed to know ... and Hermes did not know very much: perhaps only that I might appear like this and seem angry, and was to be humoured. I gave up with the suitcase and looked at him.

'The other young lady's room?'

'Nothing. She took all her things.'

I made him show me the room, which was next-door, and similarly furnished. But that held no signs of occupation at all. Even a wastepaper-basket beside a table was empty. Once more I fixed Hermes.

'Why didn't she take her sister's things with her?'

He shrugged, as if I were being unreasonable. 'The master told me she would return. With you.'

Downstairs I made Hermes fetch his wife. She was an island woman of fifty or so, sallow-faced, in the ubiquitous black, but she seemed both less morose and more loquacious than her husband. Yes, the sailors had brought the boxes, the master had come. About two o'clock. The young lady had left with him. Had she looked unhappy? Not at all. She was laughing. Such a pretty young lady, the woman added. Had she ever seen her before this summer? Never. She added, as if I might not know, she is foreign. Did she say where she was going? To Athens. Did she say if she was coming back? The woman opened her hands, she did not know. Then she said, *Isos*. Perhaps. I asked more questions, but received no better answers. It was flagrantly odd that they asked me no questions in return, but I felt certain they were mere pawns; and even if they had known what was happening, they were very clearly not going to tell me.

Eyele. She was laughing. I think it was that one Greek word that stopped me going to the police. I could imagine June being tricked into going with Conchis, but she must have suspected something, she couldn't just have been laughing. It was somehow a false note, it confirmed all my worst doubts. Then all those things of Julie's still waiting in the room upstairs; that was another anomaly, though a more favourable one. All this leading me on, shutting me out, leading me on ... it was not over yet. I began to be sure that I had only to wait, however disappointed and thwarted I felt in the now.

I had a letter at lunch on the Monday. It was from Mrs Holmes, and had been posted in Cerne Abbas the previous Tuesday.

Dear Mr Urfe,

Of course I don't mind you writing. I've passed your letter on to Mr Vulliamy, who is headmaster of our primary, such a nice man, and he was very tickled by the idea, I think having pen-pals in France and America is getting rather old hat anyway, don't you. I'm sure he will be getting in touch with you.

I'm so glad you've met Julie and June and that there's someone else English on the island. It does sound so lovely. Do remind them to write. They are *awful* about it.

Yours most sincerely,
CONSTANCE HOLMES

That evening I was on duty, but I slipped out when the boys had gone to bed and went to Hermes's house. There were no lights on in the upper floor.

Tuesday came. I felt restless, futile, unable to decide anything. In the late afternoon I strolled up from the quay to the square of the execution. There was a plaque there against the wall of the village school. The walnut tree still stood on the right; but on the left the iron grilles had been replaced by wooden gates. Two or three small boys played football against the high wall beside it; and it was like the room, that torture room, which I had gone to see when I came back from the village on the Sunday evening – locked, but I went round outside and peered in. It was now used as a store-room, and had easels and blackboards, spare desks and other furniture; completely exorcized by circumstance. It should have been left as it had been, with the blood and the electric fire and the one terrible table in the centre.

Perhaps I was over-bitter about the school during those days. The examinations had taken place; and it promised in the prospectus that 'each student is examined personally in written English by the native English professor'. This meant that I had two hundred papers or so to correct. In one way I didn't mind. It kept other anxieties and suspenses at bay.

I realized a subtle but profound shift was taking place in me. I knew I could no longer trust the girls – the screw had been turned once too often for that. Julie's harking-back, just before she was 'kidnapped', to my supposed attraction for June was in retrospect the worst false note of all. If I hadn't been so besotted by her, I should have picked it up at the time. It seemed clear that they were still doing what Conchis wanted; which must mean that they knew, had known from the beginning, what lay behind it all. But if that was one reasonable assumption, I had to add another: that Julie did feel a very real attraction for me. Put the two together, and I had to conclude that she was in some way playing on both sides ... deceiving me for the old man's sake, but also deceiving him for mine. That in turn meant she must know I was not to be denied her in the end, that the teasing would one day stop. I regretted not having told her about Alison when I had had the chance, since that must, if her feeling for me had any decency at all, have brought the absurd hide-and-seek to an abrupt close. But at least my silence there killed one past fear. She could not have known the truth *and* continued with the charade.

Wednesday had been a sultry day with a veiled sun, an end-of-the-world day, very un-Aegean. That night I sat down for a really long session of correcting. Thursday was the deadline for handing in papers to the assistant headmaster. The air was very heavy, and about half past ten I heard distant rumbles. Rain was mercifully coming. An hour later, when I had worked about one-third of the way through the pile of foolscap, there was a knock on the door. I shouted. I thought it was one of the other masters or perhaps one of the sixth-form leavers who had come cadging advance results.

But it was Barba Vassili, from the gate. He was smiling under his white walrus moustache; and his first words made me jump from my desk.

'*Sygnomi, kyrie, ma mia thespoinis ...*'

58

'Excuse me, sir, but a young lady ... '

'Where?'

He gestured back towards the gate. I was tearing on a coat. 'A very beautiful young lady. A foreigner, she – '

But I was already past him and running down the corridor. I called back to his grinning face – '*To phos!*' – to make him turn out the light, then I leapt down the stairs, raced out of the building and along the path towards the gate. There was a bare bulb above Barba Vassili's window; a pool of white light. I expected to see her standing in it, but there was no one. The gate was locked at that time of night, since we masters all had pass-keys. I felt in my pockets and remembered that I had left mine in the old jacket I wore in class. I looked through the bars. There was no one in the road, no one on the thistly wasteland that ran down to the sea fifty yards away, no one by the water. I called in a low voice.

But no quick shape appeared from behind the walls. I turned exasperatedly. Barba Vassili was hobbling slowly down through the trees from the masters' block.

'Isn't she there?'

He seemed to take ages to unlock the side-gate used in the evening. We went out into the road. The old man pointed away from the village.

'That way?'

'I think.'

I began to smell more games. There was something in the old man's smile; the thundery air, the deserted road – and yet I didn't care what happened, as long as something happened.

'May I have your key, Barba?'

But he wouldn't let me have the one in his hand; had to return inside his lodge and rummage to find another. He seemed to be delaying me, and when he at last turned round with a spare key, I snatched it out of his hand.

I walked quickly down the road away from the village. To the east lightning shuddered. After seventy or eighty yards the school wall turned inland at right angles. I thought Julie might be waiting round the corner of it. She wasn't. The road did not go much more than a quarter of a mile farther; beyond the wall it looped a little away from the sea to cross a dried-out torrent. There was a small bridge and a hundred yards to the left and inland of that, another of the countless island chapels, linked to the road by an avenue of tall cypresses. The moon was completely obscured by a dense veil of high cloud, but there was a grey Palmeresque light over the landscape. I came to the bridge and hesitated, torn between following the road and turning back towards the village, the much more plausible way for her to have gone. Then I heard her call my name.

The voice came from the avenue of cypresses. I walked quickly up between them. Halfway to the chapel there was a movement to my left. She was standing ten feet away, hidden from the road, between two of the largest trees. A dark summer mackintosh, a headscarf, trousers, a seemingly black shirt; the paler oval of her face. In spite of what I first said, I knew at once: there was something about the way she waited, with her hands in her mackintosh pockets.

'Julie?'

'It's me. June. Thank God you've come.'

I went close to her. 'Where's Julie?'

She looked at me a long moment, then let her head sink.

'I thought you'd realized.'

'Realized what?'

'What's going on.' She met my eyes. 'Between her and Maurice.' I left a silence, and she looked down again.

'What the hell do you all take me for?' She said nothing. 'You seem to have forgotten I've been through the rich man's mistress farce already.'

She shook her head. 'I didn't mean that. Just that she'll ... do whatever he asks. In other ways.'

Her head remained down, and I had my choice then. I should have turned straight on my heel and walked back to the school, my room, my desk, my examination-marking; because I knew I had returned to the beginning as regards the masque. In terms of hard fact I knew no more of this girl than when I had first set eyes on her naked figure running in the night below the terrace at Bourani. Yet I also knew that I could no more turn on my heel than a dropped stone can fly back into the hand.

'And what exactly are *you* doing here?'

'I don't think it's fair any more.'

'What isn't fair?'

She glanced up at me. 'It was all planned. Her being snatched away from you like that. She knew all along it would happen.'

'And this isn't planned?'

She stared resignedly beyond me, into the night.

'I don't blame you for supposing it is.'

'You haven't told me where Julie is.'

'In Athens. With Maurice.'

'From where you've just come?' She nodded. 'Why this extraordinary hour?'

'I didn't get here till dusk.'

I searched her expression. It contrived, with her stance, an air of hurt innocence, of reproach at my suspicion. She was transparently playing a part.

'Why didn't you wait at the gate?'

'I panicked. He was gone such a long time.'

Lightning flickered again. There was a waft of air, the smell of coming rain, and an almost continuous and increasingly ominous rumble from the east.

'What's there to panic about?'

'I've run away, Nicholas. They must have guessed where.'

'Why didn't you go to the police – the embassy?'

'It's not a criminal offence. Making someone fall in love with you under false pretences. And she is my sister.' She added, 'It's not what Maurice is doing. But what Julie is.'

There were telltale little pauses between the sentences, as if she had to have each one swallowed by me before she could go on. I did not leave her with my eyes. In the darkness she looked hallucinatorily like her sister.

She said, 'I've only come to warn you. That's all.'

'And console me?'

She was saved from answering by the sound of a low voice from the road. We both looked round the cypress. Three dim shapes, men, were pacing slowly down it towards the bridge, talking in Greek.

People, villagers, masters, often strolled to the end of the road and back in the evening, for the coolness. June gave me what was meant to be a frightened look. That also did not convince me.

'You came on the noon boat?'

But she avoided that trap. 'I found a way by land. By Kranidi.'

Occasionally thalassophobic parents used that route – it meant changing at Corinth, and taking a taxi from Kranidi and then hiring a boat to bring one across from the mainland; a full day's journey; and difficult if you didn't speak reasonable Greek.

'Why?'

'Because Maurice has spies everywhere here. In the village.'

'I'll believe that part of it.'

I looked down again towards the road. The three men were strolling calmly on past the avenue of trees, their backs to us; the greyish strip of road, the black scrub beyond, the dark sea. They were plainly exactly what they seemed.

I said, 'Look, I'm getting bloody tired of this. Games, okay. But not with people's emotions.'

'Perhaps I feel exactly the same.'

'Once too often. Sorry. It won't wash.'

She said in a low voice, 'She really has fooled you, hasn't she?'

'A good deal more convincingly than you have – and we've also been through this conversation before. So come on. Where is she?'

'At this moment? Probably in bed with her real lover.'

I drew a breath. 'Maurice?'

'The man you know as Joe.'

I laughed, it was too much. She said, 'All right. You don't have to believe me.'

'And you'll have to do a damn sight better than this. Or I'm going back to my room.' She was silent. 'I suppose that's why he stands and watches us making love together.'

'You can do that if you're really making love to someone every night. If you know the other man is only being made a fool of.'

She was far too persistent, it was like trying to sell a pig in a poke twice over to the same customer.

'This is getting sick. I've had enough.'

I turned to go, but she caught my arm.

'Nicholas, please ... apart from anything else I don't know where to spend tonight. I can't go to the house in the village.'

'Try the hotel.'

She swallowed that rebuff, then tried again. 'They'll probably be here tomorrow, and if I'm going to be accused of anything, I'd like you beside me. To back me up. That's all. Honestly.'

Just for a moment there was a more authentic tone in her voice; and she had finally a little smile, a nice mixture of ruefulness and appeal for protection. I made my voice a shade gentler.

'You shouldn't have told me the story of *Three Hearts*.'

'Is it so improbable?'

'You know damn well the improbability is in your bending reality to fit it.'

'I don't see what's so unreal in our finding each other ... ' she shook her head, and avoided my eyes.

'We spend the night together. Is that the idea?'

'I'm just saying that when you discover the truth about Julie, if ... ' but again she shook her head.

'Why do we have to wait that long?'

'Because ... I know you don't believe me yet.'

'I thought there'd be some snag.'

My tone had been growing more and more sarcastic, but now she looked me in the eyes. Hers had the exaggerated dilation of a dared child.

'If that's a challenge, I accept it. If it would make you believe me.'

'The more I know you two, the more incredible you get.'

'Because we both find you rather attractive? And I happen to feel sorry for you? As well as for myself. If that matters.'

I stared at her, half tempted to put her to the test. But it was so obvious that the real test was for me.

'Did Julie tell you I'd written to your mother?'

'Yes.'

'I had an answer a couple of days ago. I'm just wondering what she'd think if I wrote back and told her what her two daughters are really up to.'

'She wouldn't think anything. Because she doesn't exist.'

'You just happen to have someone in Cerne Abbas who writes letters to you and forwards your mail?'

'I've never been in Dorset in my life. My real name isn't Holmes. Or June, for that matter.'

'I see. We're back on that one. Rose and Lily?'

'I'm usually called Rosie. But yes.'

'Balls.'

She contemplated me, then looked down. 'I can't remember the exact words, but our mythical mother's letter to you went something like this: Dear Mr Urfe, I've given your letter to Mr Vulliamy, who's head of the primary school here. Then there was something about pen-pals in France and America being old hat. And how her two daughters don't write often enough. Yes?'

Now it was I who began to fall; as so often before, stable ground had turned in a few seconds to quicksand.

She said, 'I'm sorry. But there's a thing called a universal post-marker. The letter was written here, an English stamp put on it, then ... ' she made a little post-marking gesture. 'Now will you believe me?'

I was thinking back desperately: if they opened my outgoing letters, then ...

'Do you open mail to me as well?'

'I'm afraid so.'

'Then you know about ... ?'

'About what?'

'My Australian friend.'

She made a little movement of the shoulders: of course she knew about her. But in some intuitive way I knew that she didn't, that I had her in a trap.

'Then tell me.'

'Tell you what?'

'What's happened.'

'You had an affaire with her.'

'And?' She made another vague gesture. 'You've read all my mail. So you must know.'

'Of course.'

'Then you know that in fact I did meet her in Athens at half-term?'

She was caught, she didn't know which way she was being bluffed. She hesitated, then smiled back, but said nothing. I had left her mother's letter lying about on my desk – Demetriades or anyone could have slipped in and read it. But Ann Taylor's letter and its contents I had hidden well away, in a locked suitcase.

'We really do know everything, Nicholas.'

'Then prove it. Did I or didn't I meet her in Athens?'

'You know perfectly well you didn't.'

Before she could move I gave her a slap across the cheeks. It was controlled, not hard, just enough to sting, but it shocked her. She put a slow hand to her cheek.

'Why did you do that?'

'I'll do it a fucking sight harder if you don't start telling the truth. Is *all* my mail opened?'

She hesitated, still clasping her cheek; then conceded.

'Only ... what looks as if it might concern us.'

'That's a pity. You should be more thorough.' She said nothing. 'If you had opened it, you'd have known I did meet that poor bloody girl in Athens.'

'I don't see what – '

'Because of your sister, I asked her to kindly get out of my life.' June looked more frightened now, at a loss, not knowing what this was leading to. 'A couple of weeks later, she didn't get merely out of my life, but out of her own as well. She killed herself.' I left a pause. 'Now you know the cost of your fun and fireworks at Bourani.'

She stared, for a moment I thought she had believed me; but then she looked away.

'Please don't try to play Maurice's game.'

I caught her arms and shook her. 'I'm not playing games, you moronic little fool! She *killed* herself.'

She began to believe, yet still tried not to. 'But ... why didn't you tell us?'

I let go of her arms. 'Because I felt bad about it.'

'But people don't just kill themselves because ... '

'I think some people take life more seriously than any of you begin to imagine.'

There was a silence. Then she spoke with a kind of naïve timidity.

'She ... loved you?'

I hesitated. 'I tried to play fair. Perhaps too fair. I'd have done it all by letter if you hadn't called that week-end off. Then it seemed mean not to tell her to her face that ... ' I shrugged.

'You told her about Julie?'

I detected a true alarm in her voice.

'You're safe. Ashes can't blab.'

'I didn't mean that.' She glanced down. 'She ... took it badly?'

'Not outwardly. If I'd realized ... I was just trying to be honest. Set her free from waiting for me.'

There was another silence, then she said in a low voice, 'If it's true, I can't think how you could have ... let us go on like this.'

'Because I was foolishly in love with your sister.'

'But Maurice warned you.'

'When did he ever tell me the truth?'

Again she was silent, calculating. She had changed now, I noticed the pretence that she had come over to my side was dropped. She looked me in the eyes.

'Nicholas, this is very important. You're not lying?'

'I have proof in my room. Do you want to see it?'

'Please.'

Her voice was tentative, apologetic now.

'Right. Be at the gate in two minutes. If you're not there, then forget it. You can all go to hell, as far as I'm concerned.'

I turned and strode away before she could answer, and resolutely refused to look back to see if she was following me. But as I unlocked the side-gate into the school, there was lightning again, closer, a huge forked streak, and I glimpsed her slowly coming down the road a hundred yards away.

Two minutes later, when I came back with Ann Taylor's letter and the press cuttings, I saw her at once, standing at the side of the road opposite the gates. Barba Vassili stood in his lit doorway, but I ignored him. She came to meet me, took the envelope I silently thrust at her. Her nervousness was unconcealed now, she even dropped the letter as she took it out of the envelope, and had to stoop to retrieve it. Then she turned to catch the light from the lodge and began to read. She finished Ann Taylor's covering letter, but remained staring at it a moment; then lifted the page and looked briefly at the newspaper cuttings. Suddenly her eyes closed and she bent her head, almost as if she were praying. Then she very slowly folded the papers back together, put them inside the envelope, and passed it back to me. Her head stayed bowed.

'I'm so sorry. I don't know what to say.'

'That makes a welcome change.'

'We honestly didn't know.'

'Well now you do.'

'You should have told us.'

'And have Maurice inform me it's all part of the comedy of life?'

She looked up quickly, stung. 'If you knew ... that honestly isn't fair, Nicholas.'

'*If* I knew.'

She contemplated me gravely, then looked down. 'I really don't know what to say. It must have been ... '

'Wrong tense.'

'Yes, I can ... ' then she said, 'I'm so sorry.'

'You're not the most to blame.'

She shook her head. 'That's the thing. In a way, I am.'

But she did not explain why. For a few moments we stood there like two strangers at a graveside. There was lightning again, and it seemed to force her to a decision. She gave me the ghost of a sympathetic smile, touched my sleeve.

'Just wait here a moment.'

She turned and walked through the side-gate up the path towards Barba Vassili, who had been idly watching us from his doorway.

'*Barba Vassili* ... ' then I heard her speak Greek, rapidly, far more fluently than myself. After the first words it was in too low a voice for me to follow. I saw the old man bow his head once, then twice more, accepting some instruction. Then June came back through the gate and stopped six feet from me; gave me a wry, confessing look.

'Come on.'

'Come on where?'

'To the house. Julie's there. Waiting.'

'Then why the hell – '

'It doesn't matter now.' Her eyes flicked towards the approaching rain-clouds. 'Match abandoned.'

'You seem to have learnt Greek very fast.'

'Because I've spent three summers here.'

She smiled, but gently, to appease my lost, angry face; then came abruptly and caught my arms, so that I had to look at her.

'I want you to forget every single thing I've said this evening. My name is June Holmes. She is Julie. We do have a dotty mother, though not in Cerne Abbas.' I still wouldn't surrender. She said, 'She does write like that. But we made up the letter.'

'And Joe?'

'Julie … likes him.' There was a transient dryness in her eyes. 'But I can assure you she doesn't go to bed with him.' She seemed almost impatient now, at a loss how to convince and mollify me. She raised her hands in a prayer gesture. 'Nicholas? Please, *please* trust me. Just for a few minutes, till we get there. I swear to God we didn't know about your friend. That we'd have stopped tormenting you at once if we had. You must believe that.' There was a force, a convincingness about her now; a different girl, a different nature. 'If one minute with Julie doesn't make you realize you have nothing to be jealous about, you may drown me in the nearest cistern.'

Still I refused to budge.

'What have you just told him in there?'

'We have a kind of emergency codeword. Stop the experiment.'

'Experiment?'

'Yes.'

'Is the old man here?'

'At Bourani. The message will be radioed to him.'

Behind her Barba Vassili had been locking the side-gate. I saw him set off up the path to the masters' block. June glanced round after my own look, then took my hand and pulled it.

'Come on.'

I still wavered, but a coaxing determination in her won. I was drawn into walking beside her, a hand caught in hers like a prisoner.

'What experiment?'

She pressed my hand, but said nothing for a few steps.

'Maurice will go mad.'

'Why?'

'Because what your friend did is what he's devoted most of his life to trying to prevent.'

'Who is he?'

She hesitated, then abandoned secrecy. 'Very nearly what he told you he was. At one stage.' With one last encouraging pressure, she let go of my hand. 'He's the French equivalent of an emeritus professor of psychiatry. Until a year or two ago he was a pillar of the

Sorbonne medical school.' She gave me a quick side-glance. 'And I wasn't at Cambridge. I read psychology at London University. Then I went to Paris to do postgraduate work under Maurice. So did Joe, from America. And several of the others here you haven't met yet.' She said, 'Which reminds me ... you must have got so many false impressions, but one thing – you must forgive Joe for what he did that evening. He's really a very intelligent ... and gentle person.' I looked at her: something in her face was shy, and she gave a little confirmatory shrug. 'Julie isn't the one of us he might feel masculine about.'

'I'm lost.'

'Don't worry. You'll understand very soon. There's one other thing. Julie wasn't lying when she told you it was her first summer here. It is. In a way she's even been a fellow-victim.'

'Yet knowing what was going on?'

'Yes, but ... also having to find her way through the maze. We've all been through it. In the past. Joe. Me. Everyone else. We do know what it's like. The being lost. The rejection. The anger. And we all know it's finally worth it.'

There were great skittering sheets of lightning behind us, almost continuous. Islands to the east, ten, fifteen miles away, stood palely out, then vanished. The smell of rain was heavy in the air, little scurries of precursory wind. We were walking fast through the village. Somewhere a shutter slammed, but there seemed no one about.

'An experiment in what?'

Unexpectedly she stopped; made me turn and face her.

'Nicholas, first, you've been our most interesting subject yet. Second, all your secret reactions, feelings, guesses ... all the things you haven't even told Julie ... are vitally important to us. We have hundreds of questions to ask you. But we don't want to spoil their validity by giving you all the explanations beforehand. I'm asking you to be patient for just a day or two more.'

Her eyes were very direct, so direct I looked down from them.

'I've got very short on patience.'

'I know it must seem to be asking a lot. But we would be so grateful.'

I gave no sign of acceptance, but I did not argue any more. We began walking again. She must have sensed my recalcitrance. After a few steps she threw me a sop.

'I'll give you one clue. Maurice's lifelong special field has been the nature of the delusional symptoms of insanity.' She put her hands in her pockets. 'Psychiatry is getting more and more interested in the other side of the coin – why sane people are sane, why they won't accept delusions and fantasies as real. Obviously it's very difficult to explore that if you tell your sane guinea-pig, your very sane guinea-pig in this case, that everything he's going to be told is an attempt to delude him.' I said nothing, and she went on. 'You must be thinking we're running a very delicate tightrope in medical ethics. We are ... aware of that. But our justification is that one day the sane temporary victims like you may have helped some very sick people. Perhaps far more than you can imagine.'

I let a few steps pass in silence.

'What was the delusion planned for tonight?'

'That I was your last true friend.' She added quickly, 'Which wasn't all a lie. The friend part, anyway.'

'I wasn't going to buy it.'

'You weren't really expected to.' She gave me another quick smile. 'If you can imagine playing chess, but not to win ... merely to see what moves the other person makes.'

'All that Lily and Rose nonsense.'

'The names are a kind of joke. There's a card in the Tarot pack called the magus. The magician ... conjuror. Two of his traditional symbols are the lily and the rose.'

We came past the hotel into the little square round the main harbour. The lightning made its shuttered façades spring luridly to life, like a stage set ... and what she was beginning to tell me, that too was like the lightning: flashes of seeing all, darkness of still doubting it. But as with the real lightning, illumination began to overcome night.

'Why is it Julie's first year?'

'Her emotional life's been – I gather she told you.'

'She was at Cambridge?'

'Yes. Her affaire with Andrew really was a disaster. I knew she hadn't got over it. I thought this might help her. And Maurice was attracted by the possibilities that twin sisters afforded. That was another reason.'

'I was meant to fall for her?'

She hesitated. 'Nothing in the course of our experiments is "meant" in that sense. You can force people to do many things, but not feel sexual attraction. Or the opposite.' She looked down at the cobbles. 'It's improvised, Nicholas. Not planned. If you like, the rat is given a kind of parity with the experimenter. It also can dictate the walls of the maze. As you have, perhaps without fully realizing it.' A few steps passed, then she said in a lighter voice. 'I'll tell you one other secret. Julie wasn't at all happy about Sunday. The kidnapping. In fact we weren't at all sure she would do it. Till she did.'

I thought back: and remembered Julie's marked reluctance to show me that wretched subterranean hiding-place before our picnic and what had followed it; and even then I had almost forced it on her.

'Do I have any sisterly approval – in real life?'

'You should have met her last answer to every maiden's prayer.' She added quickly, 'I'm being catty. Andrew was very clever. Sensitive. But a bisexual. They do have awful problems. She needs someone ... ' I saw her mouth curve. 'My strictly clinical opinion is that she's found him.'

We climbed an uphill alley towards the square of the execution.

'All the old man has told me about his past – is that all invention?'

'We're very anxious to hear your guesses and conclusions first.'

'But you know the truth?'

She hesitated. 'I think I know most of the truth. I know what Maurice has let us know.'

I pointed at the wall where the plaque commemorating the execution stood. 'And about that?'

'Ask anyone in the village.'

'I know he was here. But did it happen as he said?'

She was silent a moment. 'Why do you think it didn't?'

'All that vision of the pure essence of freedom was very fine. But eighty lives seems rather a high price for it. And hardly to tie in with the hatred of suicide you claim he has.'

'Then perhaps he made a terrible error of judgment?'

That set me back a moment. 'That's what I felt.'

'Did you tell him so?'

'Not in so many words.'

I saw her smile. 'Then perhaps that was your error of judgment.' She went on before I could answer. 'When I was once … what you are now, he spent an evening destroying every belief I had in my own intelligence, every pride I had in my work, all in circumstances where I had to believe him … in the end I broke down, I just kept saying, It isn't true, it isn't true, I'm not like that. Then I looked up, and he was smiling. He just said, At last.'

'I wish he didn't seem to get such genuine sadistic enjoyment out of doing it.'

'But that's precisely why one believes him. Or he would say, precisely why one doesn't stand up against the real thing.' She glanced drily at me. 'The apparently sadistic conspiracy against the individual we call evolution. Existence. History.'

'I realized that was what the meta-theatre was about.'

'He used to give a famous lecture on art as institutionalized illusion.' She grimaced. 'One secret horror we always have is that someone like you will have read it. It's one reason we could never do this to a young French intellectual.'

'He is French?'

'No. Greek. But he was born in Alexandria. Mostly brought up in France. His father was very rich. Cosmopolitan. At least I imagine. Maurice seems to have rebelled against the life he was supposed to lead. He claims he first went to England to escape from his parents. To study medicine.'

'And obviously you admire him a lot.'

She gave a little nod as she walked, then said quietly, 'I think he's the greatest teacher in the world. I don't even think. I know.'

'How did it go last year?'

'Oh God. That dreadful man. We had to find another subject. Not from the school. Someone in Athens.'

'And Leverrier?'

She had a smile, unmistakably of affectionate memory. 'John.' Then she touched my arm. 'That's a very different story. Tomorrow? Now it's your turn. Tell me a bit more about … you know.'

So I told her a little about Alison. I hadn't misled her in any way in Athens, of course. I simply hadn't realized how much she had been hiding.

'There was no previous record of suicide attempts?'

'Absolutely none. She'd always seemed someone who could take things as they came.'

'No depressive … ?'

'No.'

'It does happen. With women. Out of the blue. The tragedy is, they often don't really mean it.'

'I'm afraid she did.'

'It was probably always latent. Though there are usually signs.' She said, 'And usually there's a better reason for it than just breaking off a relationship.'

'I've tried to feel that.'

'At least it's not as if you lied to her in any way.' She pressed my hand briefly. 'You mustn't blame yourself.'

We had come to the house, and in high time, because the first sporadic but heavy drops of rain were beginning to splash down. The storm seemed to be heading straight for the island. June pushed the outer gate open and I followed her up the path. She took a key and unlocked the front door. The hall was lit, though the current kept wavering under the much greater currents of electricity being discharged in the sky. There she turned and kissed my cheek quickly, almost shyly.

'Wait here. She may be asleep. I won't be a second.'

I watched her run up the stairs and disappear. There was a tap, and she called Julie's name in a low voice. A door opened and closed. Then silence. The thunder and lightning outside, an abrupt squall of more consistent rain on the windowpanes, a gust of cool air from somewhere. Two minutes passed. Then the invisible door upstairs opened.

Julie came first, barefooted, in a black kimono over a white nightdress. She paused a moment, a distressed face, staring down at me, then she came running down the stairs.

'Oh Nicholas.'

She fell into my arms. We didn't kiss. June stayed at the top, smiling down. Julie held me away from her, searching my eyes.

'Why *didn't* you tell me?'

'I don't know.'

She sank against me again, as if she was the one who needed

comforting. I patted her back. June blew a light kiss, a benison, down at me from the top of the stairs, then disappeared.

'June's told you?'

'Yes.'

'Everything?'

'Some of it.'

She held me a little closer still. 'I'm so relieved it's all over.'

'I haven't forgiven you for Sunday.'

She looked up, with a good deal more seriousness in her face than there had been in my voice; beseeched me to believe her.

'I *hated* it. Nicholas, I nearly didn't do it. Honestly. It was so terrible, knowing it was going to happen.'

'You hid it disgustingly well.'

'Only because I knew it was all nearly over.'

'I hear it's your first year as well.'

'And my last. I couldn't do it again. Especially now ... ' again she appealed for understanding, forgiveness. 'June's always been so mysterious about it. I had to see what it was like.'

'I'm glad. Finally.'

She came close against me again.

'I haven't lied about one thing.'

'I wonder what that is.'

My hand was found, gently pinched in reproach. Her voice dropped to a whisper. 'Anyway, you can't go back to your school in this rain.' She added, 'And I hate being alone in thunder and lightning.'

'So do I. Now you mention it.'

Our next lines were not spoken; and once they were exchanged, she took my hand and led me upstairs. We came to the door of the room I had searched three days before. But there she hesitated, then gave me a faintly self-mocking yet genuinely shy look.

'What I said on Sunday?'

'You long ago made me forget every other girl I've ... '

She looked down. 'This is where my witchcraft stops.'

'I always liked us better as Ferdinand and Miranda.'

She smiled a moment, as if she had forgotten that; gave me an intense look, seemed about to say something else, changed her mind. She opened the door and we went in. There was a lamp on by the bed, the shutters were closed. The bed was as she had left it, the sheet and a folk-weave bedspread thrown aside, the pillow crumpled; some open book of poetry beneath the lamp, I could see its broken lines of print; an abalone-shell used as an ash-tray. We stood a little at a loss, as people do when they have foreseen such moments too long. Her hair was down, the white hem of her nightdress reached almost to her ankles. She glanced round the room, as if with my eyes, as if I might be contemptuous of such domestic simplicity; made a little grimace. I smiled, but her shyness was contagious – and the changed reality between us, what she had really meant by no more 'witchcraft': no more games, evasions, tantalizings. For a bizarre few seconds those seemed, in retrospect, to hold a paradoxical innocence; Adam and Eve before the Fall.

Mercifully the world outside came to our aid. There was a flash of lightning. The lamp shuddered, then went out. We were plunged into pitch darkness. Almost at once there was a tremendous peal of thunder overhead. Before it had died away she was in my arms and we were kissing hungrily. More lightning, even louder and closer thunder. She twisted against me, clinging like a child. I kissed the crown of her head, patted her back, murmured.

'Shall I undress you and put you to bed and hold you?'

'Let me sit on your lap a minute. It makes me so nervous.'

I was led in the darkness to a chair opposite the bed, against the wall. I sat, she sat across my knees, and we kissed again. Then she nestled against me; found my free hand and laced her fingers through mine.

'Tell me about your friend. What really happened.'

I told her what I had told her sister a few minutes before. 'It was a spur-of-the-moment thing. I felt so fed up with Maurice. With you. I couldn't face just hanging around here.'

'Did you tell her about me?'

'Only that I'd met someone on the island.'

'Was she upset?'

'That's the absurd thing. If only she had been. Hadn't buried it all so well.'

Her hand squeezed mine gently. 'And you didn't want her at all?'

'I felt sorry for her. But she really didn't seem too surprised.'

'Not answering my question.'

I smiled in the darkness at this not very well concealed battle between sympathy and feminine curiosity.

'I kept thinking how much rather I'd be with you.'

'Poor girl. At least I can imagine how she must have felt.'

'She wasn't like you. She never took anything seriously. Especially if it was male.'

'But she must have taken you seriously. In the end.'

I had anticipated that. 'I think I was just a kind of symbol, Julie. Of all sorts of other things that had gone wrong in her life. The last straw, I suppose.'

'What did you do in Athens?'

'A few sights. Had a meal. Sat and talked. Drank too much. It was all very civilized, really. Or seemed it.'

Her nails dug gently into the back of my hand. 'I bet you did go to bed.'

'Would you be angry if we had?'

Her head shook against mine. 'No. I deserved it. I'd understand.' She raised my hand and kissed it. 'I wish you'd tell me.'

'Why are you so curious?'

'Because there's so much I don't know about you.'

I took a breath.

'Perhaps I should have. Then at least she might still be alive.'

There was a little silence, then she kissed my cheek. 'I'm only trying to find out if I'm spending the night with a callous swine or a bruised angel.'

'There's only one way to find that out.'

'You think?'

Another light kiss, then she slipped gently free of my arm and moved away a little beside the bed. It was very dark in the room, and I could see nothing. But then lightning shivered through the shutters. For a brief flash I saw her by the cassone, peeling her nightdress over her head. Then it was sound, her feeling her way back towards me, a crack of thunder, a little shocked outbreath. I reached and found her groping hand and pulled her back naked to my lap.

Our mouths met, and I explored her body: the breasts, the smooth stomach, the little thatch of hair, the thighs. I could have used a dozen hands, not one … to have her surrendered at last, compliant, mine. She shifted, stood a moment, then straddled my lap and began to unbutton my shirt. In another flash of lightning I glimpsed the expression on her face – a kind of intent seriousness, like a child undressing a doll. She forced the shirt, and the jacket I was still wearing, back away from my body. Then she clasped her hands behind my neck, as she had in the sea at Moutsa, and sat away a little.

'You're the most beautiful thing I've ever seen.'

'You can't see me.'

'Felt.'

I bent and kissed her breasts, then pulled her against me and found her mouth again. She was wearing some strange scent, musky and faintly orange, like cowslips; and it seemed to match something both sensual and innocent in her, a growing abandon to passion that was also a willed attempt to be what she felt I must want: feverish, strained, not playful at all. In the end she tore her mouth away, as if she was exhausted. After a few moments, she whispered.

'Let's open the shutters. I love the smell of the rain.'

She slipped away and went to open them. I got quickly out of my remaining clothes, and caught her as she turned back from the window; made her turn, held her close from behind, so that we stood with the rain teeming down three feet away, the cool wall of dark air. All the lights in the village were out, the generator fuse must have blown. Lightning split the sky over towards the mainland and for a moment or two the crowded houses below us, all the walls and the roofs, even the sea below, were illuminated with an uncanny pale-violet light. But the thunder took longer to arrive; the short centre of the storm had already passed on.

Julie leant back against me, abandoning the front of her body to the night and my encircling hands. I smoothed down the little belly, ruffled the pubic hair. Her head turned against me, then she raised her right leg and rested it on a stool below the window, so that the hand could caress more easily. She took my other hand, led it to her breasts; then stood absolutely passive, letting me excite her – as if the rain was her real lover, and the outside night; as if I was now to do to her what she had done to me in the sea. Little splashes of the downpour bounced from the sill against my lower hand and her skin, but she seemed oblivious of them.

I whispered, 'I wish we could go outside.'

Her mouth twisted to kiss me in quick assent, but then her hands found mine again and pressed to keep them where they were. She preferred this now: to be gently abused, slowly coaxed … there was still lightning, but it began to seem from another world, the only real world was her body and my own … the curves of her back, the warmth there, the pods of silken skin with their aroused tips, the indulged, solicited, caress below. It was a little as I had imagined it in the beginning, the Lily Montgomery phase: this delicate, elusive creature half-swooning, succumbed to the animal part of herself; and not quite adult yet – beneath her airs and graces, something of the innocent perversity of a little girl playing at sex with little boys.

Suddenly, half a minute later, she caught my hands and made them lie on her stomach; imprisoned them.

'What's wrong?'

'You're being wicked.'

'That was the idea.'

She turned against me, her face buried.

'Tell me what you liked her doing to you best.'

I remembered an old Urfe law: that girls possess sexual tact in inverse proportion to their standard of education. But I saw some delicious instruction ahead in this case.

'Why do you want to know?'

'Because I want to do it to you.'

I held her a little closer. 'I like you as you are.'

She whispered, 'You're so big.'

Her hands stole down between us. We stood apart a little. There seemed something virginal about her; yet wanting to be corrupted, led further. She whispered again.

'Have you got a thing?'

'In my coat.'

'Shall I put it on for you?'

I went and found the contraceptive, and Julie moved beside the bed. There was a little more light now, the clouds must have thinned slightly, I could just see her silhouette. She took the sheath, made me sit on the end of the bed, knelt on the island rug, leant forward and rolled the sheath on; bent and gave it a little kiss. Then sat back on her heels, hands folded across her loins, demure. I could just see her smile.

'Liar. I don't think you're shy at all.'

'I did spend five years in a convent dormitory. Where nothing was left to the imagination.'

The rain was easing, but the freshness of it, the smell of cistern, water on stone, pervaded the room. I saw it secretly streaming down the walls of hundreds of cisterns; the excited eels at the bottom.

'All that talk of running away.'

Her smile deepened, but she said nothing. I reached for her, and she rose, let herself be drawn down on top of me. Silence then, a retreat from everything but the conversation of bodies. She pretended to possess me, mocked and consoled me with her mouth; then a silence even of movement, as if in time she would melt down into me; but that began to seem a waiting in her. I broke the spell, and she shifted, lay back on the rough bedspread, her head on the pillow. I knelt and kissed down her body to the ankles, surveyed her a moment from the bottom of the bed. She lay a little twisted to one side, an arm flung out, her head sideways. But as I moved forward, she turned fully on her back. A few moments later I was deep inside her. It was not like any other such moment of first entry I had ever gained; something well beyond the sexual, there was such a fraught, frustrated past, such a future inherent in it; such a possession. I knew I had won far more than her body. I lay suspended on my arms over her. She was staring up in the darkness.

I said, 'I adore you.'

'I want you to.'

'Always?'

'Always.'

I began to thrust slowly – but then something strange happened. Without warning, the lamp beside the bed came on again. They must have mended the generator, down in the village. I stopped my movement, for a second or two we were comically like two shocked strangers, our eyes locked in embarrassment; so much so that we had to smile. I looked down her slim body to where we were joined, then back to her face. I sensed something troubled and shy in her look, but then she closed her eyes and let her head fall sideways in profile. If I wanted it so …

I began to drive. Her arms bent back behind her head, as if she was defenceless, doubly naked, completely at my mercy; that lovely slavelike limpness in everything but the loins. There was a tiny rhythmic creaking somewhere in the bedframe. She seemed so small, fragile, asking for the brutality she had said she had felt in the chapel at Moutsa. Her hands clenched, as if I was really hurting her. I came, it was too soon, but irresistible. I thought it was much too soon for her, but just as I was dying, about to give up, she suddenly raised her arms and urged me on: a brief but convulsive little thrusting against me. Then I was pulled violently down to meet her mouth.

We lay still joined for a little time, in the profound silence of the house; then we were separate, and I moved beside her. She reached out for the lamp-switch and we were in darkness again. She turned on her stomach, her face turned away. I stroked down her back, patted the small bottom, kept caressing its curves. Already, despite the traditional nature of the moment, I felt a marvellous surge of euphoria. I hadn't expected it to be so shared, so full of promise, like the skin beneath my hand; that she could be so warm, capable of giving. I told myself I ought to have guessed, there was that feeling about June of a girl who enjoyed it, and the same need must have lain buried in the less extravert sister beside me. At last our bodies had expressed themselves; and I knew it would be much better still ... subtler, longer, infinite variations. That appled bottom, the tangled hair against my mouth. A distant, receding roll of thunder. Already, outside, there was more light, the moon must have broken partially from behind the clouds. All storms were past, and we lay in the silence of Eden regained.

It was some five minutes later. We had lain in total silence, no words were needed. But then she pushed herself up, leant over me for a moment, stooped and quickly kissed me. She leant back, her face above mine in a hanging cloud of hair, a faint smile, her eyes on mine.

'Nicholas, will you always remember something about tonight?'
I grinned. 'What?'
'That it's also how, not why.'
Still I smiled. 'How was beautiful.'
'As I wanted it to be.'
For the briefest moment she hesitated, almost as if it were some formula she expected me to repeat. Then suddenly she knelt back,

turned and was off the bed, and reaching for her kimono. I should have reacted more quickly, at least to the briskness with which she reached for the garment, if not to something in her voice and face when she was looking down at me – a seriousness that had nothing to do with the naïvety I first took it for. I leant up on an elbow.

'Where are you going?'

She didn't answer for a moment, then turned, tying the kimono sash, and looked down at me. I think there was still a trace of a smile on her face.

'To the trial.'

'The what?'

It all happened so impossibly fast. She was already moving away before I had fully registered the change in her voice, its now patent lack of innocence.

'Julie?'

She turned at the door; left the tiny pause of the actress before her exit line.

'My name isn't Julie, Nicholas. And I'm sorry we can't provide the customary flames.'

This time I sat fully up – flames, what flames – but before I could speak she had pulled the door open and stepped aside. Light flooded in.

There was a violent cascade of figures.

59

Three men, all in dark trousers and black polo-neck jumpers – they came so quickly that, paralyzed in everything but instinct, I had no time to do anything but grab the bedspread over my loins. The one in the lead was Joe, the Negro. He flung himself at me just as I was about to shout. His hand clapped brutally over my mouth and I felt the strength and weight of him throw me back. One of the others must have turned on the bedside lamp again. I saw another face I knew: the last time I had seen it had been on the ridge, when the owner had been in German uniform, playing Anton. The third face belonged to the blond-headed sailor I had seen twice at Bourani that previous Sunday. I tried as I struggled under Joe to see Julie – I still couldn't accept that this was not some nightmare, like some freak misbinding in a book, a Lawrence novel become, at the turn of a page, one by Kafka. But all I glimpsed was her back as she left the room. Someone met her there, an arm went round her shoulders as if she had just escaped from an air disaster and drew her out of sight.

I began to fight violently, but they had obviously anticipated that, had loops of rope ready. In less than half a minute I was tied up and lying on my face. I don't know if I was still shouting obscenities at them; I was certainly thinking them. Then I was gagged. Somebody threw the bedspread over me. I managed to twist my head to see the door.

Another figure appeared in it: Conchis. He was dressed like the others, in black. Flames, devils, hell. He came and stood over me, looked down at my outraged eyes absolutely without expression. I hurled all the hate I had in me at him, tried to make sounds that he could understand. My mind flashed back to that incident in the war: a room at the end of a corridor, a man lying on his back, castrated. My eyes began to fill with tears of frustrated rage and humiliation. I realized at last what Julie's final look at me had been like. It was that of a surgeon who has just performed a difficult operation success- fully; peeling off the rubber gloves, surveying the suture. Trial, flames ... they were all mad, they must be, and she the most vicious, shameless, degenerate ...

'Anton' held out a small open case to Conchis. He took out a hypodermic syringe, checked it was correctly filled, then leant over me a little and showed it.

'We shall not frighten you any more, young man. But we want you to go to sleep. It will be less painful for you. Please do not struggle.'

The absurd memory of the pile of examination papers I had still to mark went through my mind. Joe and the other man turned me on my back again and gripped my left arm like a vice. I resisted for a few moments, then gave in. A dab of wet. The needle pricked into my forearm. I felt the morphine, or whatever it was, enter. The needle was withdrawn, another dab of something wet. Conchis stood back, watched me a moment, then turned and replaced the syringe in the black medical case it had come from.

I tried to realize what I had got into: a world of people who knew no laws, no limits.

A satyr with an arrow in his heart.

Mirabelle. *La Maîtresse-Machine*, a foul engine made fouler flesh. Perhaps three minutes passed. Then June appeared in the doorway. She did not look at me. She was dressed like the men, in black shirt and trousers – and I seethed again, remembering she had worn those very clothes outside the school, even then knowing this was to happen – and all this, after I had at last told them about Alison! She moved across the room, her hair tied back now with a black chiffon scarf and coolly began to empty clothes from the corner wardrobe into a suitcase. My head began to swim. Faces and objects, the ceiling, receded from present reality; down and down a deep black mine of shock, incomprehension and flailing depths of impossible revenge.

60

I was to have no sense of time for the next five days. When I first woke up I did not know how many hours had passed. I was very thirsty, and that must have been what woke me. I remember one or two things indistinctly. A sense of surprise that I was in my own pyjamas but not in my room at school; then realizing I was in a bunk, at sea, but not in a caïque. It was the narrowing forecabin of a yacht. I was reluctant to leave my sleep, to think, to do anything but sink back into it. I was handed a glass of water by the young sailor with crewcut blond hair, who had evidently been waiting for me to wake. I was so thirsty that I had to drink the water, even though I could see it was suspiciously cloudy. Then I must have blurred into sleep again.

The same man made me go to the heads in the bows of the yacht at some later point, and I remember he had to hold me upright, as if I was drunk; and I sat on the pan and just went to sleep again. There were port-holes, but the metal shields were screwed down. I asked one or two questions, but he didn't answer; and it didn't seem to matter.

The same procedure happened again, once, twice, I don't know, in different circumstances. This time I was in a room in a proper bed. It was always night, always, if there was light, an electric light; shadowy figures and voices; then darkness.

But one morning – it seemed like morning, though it might have been midnight for all I knew, because my watch had stopped – I was woken up by the sailor-cum-nurse, made to sit on my bed, to dress, to walk up and down the room twenty or thirty times. Another man I hadn't seen before stood by the door.

I became conscious of something I had hazily thought to have dreamt: an extraordinary mural that dominated the whitewashed wall opposite the bed. It was a huge black figure, larger than lifesize, a kind of living skeleton, a Buchenwald horror, lying on its side on what might have been grass, or flames. A gaunt hand pointed down to a little mirror hanging on the wall; exhorting me, I supposed, to look at myself, to consider that I must die. The skull-face had a startled and startling intensity that made it uncomfortable to look at; and it was no comfort to think of the mind that had put it there for me. I could see it was newly painted.

There was a knock on the door. A third man appeared. He carried a tray with a jug of coffee on it. It had the most beautiful smell; of real coffee, something like Blue Mountain, not the monotonous 'Turkish' powder they use in Greece. And there were rolls, butter, and quince marmalade; a plate of ham and eggs. I was left alone. In spite of the circumstances it was one of the best breakfasts of my life. Every flavour had a Proustian, mescalin intensity. I seemed to be starving, and I ate everything on the tray, I drank every drop of coffee and I could have done it all over again. There was even a pack of American cigarettes and a box of matches.

I took stock. I was wearing one of my own pullovers and whip-cord trousers I hadn't put on since the winter. The high curved ceiling was that of a cistern under a house; the windowless walls were dry, but subterranean. There was electric light. A small suitcase, my own, stood in a corner. My jacket was by it, on a hanger hooked to a nail.

The wall against which the table stood was new-built of brick. It had a heavy wooden door in it. No handle, no spyhole, no keyhole, not even a hinge. I gave it a push, but it was bolted or barred outside. There was another triangular table in the corner – an old-fashioned wash-bowl, with a sanitary bucket underneath. I rummaged in my suitcase; a clean shirt, a change of underclothes, a pair of summer trousers. I saw my razor, and that reminded me that I had a clock of sorts on my chin. At least two days' stubble stared at me from the mirror. My face was strange to me; degraded and yet peculiarly indifferent. I looked up at the death-figure on the wall above. Death-figure, death-cell, the traditional last breakfast: a mock execution was about the only indignity I had left to undergo.

Behind and beneath everything there was the vile and unforgivable, the ultimate betrayal not just of me, but of all finer instincts, by Julie ... Lily ... whoever she was. I started to think of her as Lily again, perhaps because her first mask now seemed truer, more true because more obviously false, than the others. I tried to imagine what she really was – obviously a consummate young actress, and consummately immoral into the bargain. Only a prostitute could have behaved as she had; a pair of prostitutes, because I guessed that her sister, June, Rose, might well have been prepared to carry out that final abominable act. Probably they would have liked me to be thus doubly humiliated.

All their stories had been lies; or groundbait. The letters were plainly forgeries – they could not make it so easy for me to trace them. In a grim flash I guessed: none of my post left or came to the island unread. From that I leapt to the grim realization that they must all along have known the truth about Alison. When Conchis had advised me to go back and marry her he must have known she was dead; Lily must have known she was dead. My mind plunged sickeningly, as if I had walked off the edge of the world. I had seen forged newspaper cuttings about the sisters, therefore if it was just a case of forging cuttings ... I went to my jacket, where I had put Ann Taylor's letter after 'June' had read it outside the school gates. It was still there. I stared at it and its attachments, searched for some sign that they were all invented ... in vain. I remembered that other envelope that I had left in my room and not shown her, with its superscription in Alison's own handwriting, the pathetic little tangle of withered flowers. Only she could have given them that.

Alison.

I stared into my own eyes in the mirror. Suddenly her honesty, her untreachery – her true death – was the last anchor left. If she too, if she ... I was swept away. The whole of life became a conspiracy. I strained back through time to seize Alison, to be absolutely sure of her; to seize a quintessential Alison beyond all her powers of love or hate, beyond all their corrupting. For a while I let my mind wander into a bottomless madness. Supposing *all* my life that last year had been the very opposite of what Conchis so often said – so often, to trick me once again? – about life in general. That is, the very opposite of hazard. The flat in Russell Square ... but I had got it by answering a chance advertisement in the *New Statesman*. Meeting Alison that very first evening ... but I might so easily have not gone to the party, not have waited those few minutes ... and Margaret, Ann Taylor, all of them ... the hypothesis became top-heavy, and crashed.

I stared at myself. They were trying to drive me mad, to brain-wash me in some astounding way. But I clung to reality. I clung, too, to something in Alison, something like a tiny limpid crystal of eternal non-betrayal. Like a light in the darkest night. Like a tear-drop. An eternal inability to be so cruel. And the tears that for a brief moment formed in my own eyes were a kind of bitter guarantee that she was indeed dead.

They were not only tears for her, but also tears of rage at Conchis and Lily; at the certainty that they knew she was dead and were using this new doubt, this torturing possibility that could not be a possibility, to rack me. To perform on me, for some incomprehensible reason, a viciously cruel vivisection of the mind.

As if they only wanted to punish me; and punish me; and punish me again. With no right; and no reason.

I sat with my hands clenched against my head.

Fragments of things they had said kept on coming back, with dreadful double meanings; a constant dramatic irony. Almost every line Conchis and Lily had spoken was ironic; right up to that last, transparently double-meaning dialogue with 'June'.

That blank week-end: of course they had cancelled it to give me reasonable time to receive the 'letter of reference' from the bank; holding me back only to hurl me faster down the slope.

Again and again images of Lily, the Lily of the Julie phase, surged back; moments of passion, that last total surrender of her body – and other moments of gentleness, sincerity, spontaneous moments that could not have been rehearsed but could only have sprung out of a deep identification with the part she was playing. I even went back to that earlier theory I had had, that she was acting under hypnosis. But it wasn't conceivable.

I lit another Philip Morris. I tried to think of the present. But everything drove me back to the same anger, the same profound humiliation. Only one thing could ever give me relief. Some equal humiliation of Lily. It made me furious that I had not been more violent with her before. That was indeed the ultimate indignity: that my own small stock of decency had been used against me.

There was noise outside, and the door opened. The crewcut blond sailor came in; behind him was one of the other men, in the same black trousers, black shirt, black gymshoes. And behind him came Anton. He was in a doctor's collarless white overall. A pocket with pens. A bright German-accented voice; as if on his rounds. And he had no limp now.

'How are you feeling?'

I stared at him; controlled myself.

'Wonderful. Enjoying every minute of it.'

He looked at the breakfast tray. 'You would like more coffee?'

I nodded. He gestured to the second man, who took the tray out. Anton sat on the chair by the table, and the young sailor leaned easily against the door. Beyond appeared a long corridor, and right at the end steps leading up to daylight. It was much too big a cistern for a private house. Anton watched me. I refused to speak, and we sat there in silence for some time.

'I am a doctor. I come to examine you.' He studied me. 'You feel ... not too bad?'

I leant back against the wall; stared at him.

He waved his finger reprovingly. 'Please to answer.'

'I love being humiliated. I love having a girl I like trampling over every human decency. Every time that stupid old bugger tells me another lie I feel thrills of ecstasy run down my spine.' I shouted. 'Now where the hell am I?'

He gave me the impression that my words were meaningless; it was my manner he was watching.

He said slowly, 'Good. You have woken up.' He sat with his legs crossed, leaning back a little; a very fair imitation of a doctor in his consulting room.

'Where's that little tart?' He seemed not to understand. 'Lily. Julie. Whatever her name is.'

He smiled. '"Tart" means bad woman?'

I shut my eyes. My head was beginning to ache. I had to keep cool. The man in the door turned; the second man appeared down the distant steps with a tray and came and put it on the table. Anton poured out a cup for me and one for himself. The sailor passed me mine. Anton swallowed his quickly.

'My friend, you are wrong. She is a good girl. Very intelligent. Very brave. Oh yes.' He contradicted my sneer. 'Very brave.'

'All I have to say to you is that when I get out of here I am going to create such bloody fucking hell for all of you that you'll wish to Christ you – '

He raised his hand, calmingly, forgivingly. 'Your mind is not well. We have given you many drugs these last days.'

I took a breath.

'How many days?'

'It is Sunday.'

Three totally missing days: I remembered the wretched exam papers. The boys, the other masters … the whole school could not be in league with Conchis. It was the enormity of the abuse that bewildered me, far more than the aftermath of the drug; that they could crash through law, through my job, through respect for the dead, through everything that made the world customary and habitable and orientated. And it was not only a denial of my world; it was a denial of what I had come to understand was Conchis's world.

I stared at Anton.

'I suppose this is all good homely fun to you Germans.'

'I am Swiss. And my mother is Jewish. By the way.'

His eyebrows were very heavy, charcoal tufts, his eyes amused. I swilled the last of the coffee in my cup, then threw it in his face. It stained his white coat. He pulled out a handkerchief and wiped his face and said something to the man beside him. He did not look angry; merely shrugged, then glanced at his watch.

'The time is ten thirty- … eight. Today we have the trial and you must be awake. So good.' He touched his coat. 'I think you are awake.'

He stood up.

'Trial?'

'Very soon we shall go and you will judge us.'

'Judge you!'

'Yes. You think this is like a prison. Not at all. It is like ... how call you the room where the judge lives?'

'Chambers.'

'Ah so. Chambers. So perhaps you would like to ... ' He gestured round his chin.

'Christ!'

'There will be many people there.' I stared incredulously at him. 'It will look better.' He gave up. 'Very well. Adam' – he nodded at the blondhead, stressing the name on the second syllable – 'he will return in twenty minutes to prepare you.'

'Prepare me?'

'It is nothing. We have a small ritual. It is nothing for you. For us.'

'"Us"?'

'Very soon – you will understand all.'

I wished I had saved the coffee to throw till then.

He smiled, bowed, and went out. The other two closed the door, and a bolt was shot. I stared at the skeleton at the wall. And in his necromantic way he seemed to say the same: very soon, you will understand. All.

61

I rewound my watch; and in precisely twenty minutes the same two men as before came back into the cell. The black clothes made them look more aggressive, more fascist, than they were; there was nothing particularly brutal about their faces. The blond Adam stood in front of me; in his hand he carried an incongruous small grip.

'Please ... not fight.'

He set the grip on the table and fished inside it; came up with two pairs of handcuffs. I held out my wrists contemptuously and allowed myself to be linked to the other two beside me. Now he produced a curious black rubber mouthmask; concave, with a thick projection that one had to bite.

'Please … I put this on. No hurt.'

We both hesitated a moment. I had determined that I wouldn't fight, that it would be better to keep cool and wait until a time when I could hurt someone I really wanted to hurt. He cautiously held out the rubber gag, and I shrugged. I took its black tongue between my teeth; a taste of disinfectant. Adam expertly fastened the straps behind. Then he went back to the case for some wide black adhesive, and taped the edges of the gag against my skin. I began to wish I had shaved.

The next move took me by surprise. Adam knelt and pushed my right trouser-leg up to above the knee, and fastened it there with an elastic garter. Then I was made to stand again. With a warning gesture that I was not to be alarmed, he pulled my sweater back over my head and forced it down till it hung from my wrists behind me. Then he unbuttoned my shirt to the bottom and forced the left side back until the shoulder was bare. Next he produced two inch-wide white ribbons, each with a blood-red rosette attached, from the grip. He tied one round the top of my right calf, another under my armpit and over the bare shoulder. Next, a black circle, some two inches in diameter and cut in adhesive tape, was fixed like a huge patch on the middle of my forehead. Finally with one last domesticating gesture he put a loose-fitting black bag over my head. I was more and more inclined to struggle; but I had missed my chance. We moved off. I had a hand on each arm.

They stopped me at the end of the corridor and Adam said, 'Slow, we go upstairs.' I wondered if 'upstairs' meant 'into the house'; or was just bad English.

I toed forward and we climbed into the sun. I could feel it on my bare skin, though the bag occluded all but the thinnest glints of light. We must have walked some two or three hundred yards. I thought I could smell the sea, I wasn't sure. I half expected to feel a wall against my back, to find myself facing a firing squad. But then once again they halted me and a voice said, 'Downstairs now.' They gave me plenty of time to manoeuvre the steps; more than those leading to my cell, and the air grew cool. We went round a corner and down yet more steps and then I could hear by the resonance of the sounds we made that we had entered a large room. There was also a mysterious, ominous smell of burning wood and acrid tar. I was stopped, someone pulled the bag from my head.

I had expected to see people. But I and my two guards were alone. We were at one end of a huge underground room, the kind of enormous cistern, the size of a small church, that is found under some of the old Venetian-Turkish castles that are crumbling away in the Peloponnesus. I remembered having seen one very like it that winter at Pylos. I looked up and saw two telltale chimney-like openings; they would be the blocked-off necks at ground level.

At the far end there was a small dais and on the dais a throne. Facing the throne was a table, or rather three long tables put end to end in a flat crescent and draped in black cloth. Behind the table were twelve black chairs and an empty thirteenth place in the middle.

The walls had been whitewashed up to a height of fifteen feet or so, and over the throne was painted an eight-spoked wheel. Between table and throne, against the wall to the right, was a small tiered bank of benches, like a jury box.

There was one completely incongruous thing in this strange courtroom. The light I saw it by came from a series of brands that were burning along the side walls. But in each of the corners behind the throne was a battery of projectors trained on the crescent-shaped table. They were not on; but their cables and serried lenses added a vaguely sinister air of the interrogation room to the already alarming Ku Klux Klan ambience. It did not look like a court of justice; but a court of injustice; a Star Chamber, an inquisitorial committee.

I was made to go forward. We marched down one side of the room, past the crescent table and up towards the throne. I suddenly realized that I was to sit there. They paused for me to step up on to the dais. There were four or five steps leading to a little platform at the top, on which stood the throne. Like the roughly carpentered dais, it was not a real throne, simply a bit of stage property, painted black, with armrests, a pointed back and columns on either side. In the middle of the solid black panel was a white eye, like those that Mediterranean fishermen paint on the bows of their boats to ward off evil. A flat crimson cushion; I was made to sit.

As soon as I had done so, my guards' ends of the handcuffs were unlocked, then immediately snapped on to the armrests. I looked down. The throne was secured to the dais by strong brackets. I mumbled through the gag, but Adam shook his head. I was to watch, not to speak. The other two guards took up positions behind the throne, on the lowest step of the dais, against the wall. Adam, like some mad valet, checked the handcuffs, pulled away the shirt I had tried to shrug back on to my left shoulder, then went down the steps to the ground. There he turned, as if to the altar in a church, and made a slight bow; after which he went round the table and out through the door at the end. I was left sitting with the silent pair behind me and the faint crackle of the burning torches.

I looked round the room; forced myself to observe it dispassionately. There were other cabbalistic emblems. On the wall to my right a black cross – not the Christian cross, because the top of the upright was swollen, an inverted pearshape; to the left, facing the cross, was a deep-red rose, the only patch of colour in the black-and-white room. At the far end, over the one large door, was painted in black a huge left hand cut off at the wrist, with the forefinger and little finger pointing up and the two middle fingers holding down the thumb. The room stank of ritual; and I have always loathed rituals of any kind. I kept repeating the same phrase to myself: keep dignity, keep dignity, keep dignity. I knew I must *look* ridiculous with the black cyclops eye on my forehead and the white ribbons and the rosettes. But I somehow had to contrive not to be ridiculous.

Then my heart jolted.

A terrifying figure.

Suddenly and silently in the doorway at the far end, Herne the Hunter. A neolithic god; a spirit of darkness, of northern forest, of a time before kings, as black and chilling as the touch of iron.

A man with the head of a stag that filled the arched door; who stood silhouetted, giant, unforgettable image, against the dimly lit whitewashed wall of the corridor behind. The antlers were enormous, as black as almond branches, many-tined. And the man was in black from head to foot, with only the eyes and the nostril-ends marked in white. He imposed his presence on me, then came slowly down the room to the table; stood centrally and regally behind it for another long moment, then moved to the extreme left end. By that time I had noted the black gloves, the black shoes beneath the narrow *soutane*-like smock he wore; that he had to move slowly because the mask was slightly precarious, being so large.

The fear I felt was the same old fear; not of the appearance, but of the reason behind the appearance. It was not the mask I was afraid of, because in our century we are too inured by science fiction and too sure of science reality ever to be terrified of the supernatural again; but of what lay behind the mask. The eternal source of all fear, all horror, all real evil, man himself.

Another figure appeared, and paused, as they were all to do, in the archway.

This time it was a woman. She was dressed in traditional English witch costume; a brimmed black-peaked hat, long white hair, red apron, black cloak, and a malevolent mask; a beaked nose. She hobbled, bentbacked, to the right end of the table and set the cat she was carrying on it. It was dead, stuffed in a sitting position. The cat's glass eyes were on me. Her black-and-white eyes. And the stag-man's.

Another startling figure: a man in a crocodile head – a bizarre maned mask that projected forwards, more negroid than anything else, with ferocious white teeth and bulging eyes. He hardly paused, but came swiftly to his place beside the stag, as if the wearer was un-comfortable in costume; unused to such scenes.

A shorter male figure came next: an abnormally large head in which white cube-teeth reached in a savage grin from ear to ear. His eyes seemed buried in deep black sockets. Round the top of his head there rose a great iguana frill. This man was dressed in a black poncho, and looked Mexican; Aztec. He moved to his place beside the witch.

Another female figure appeared. I felt sure it was Lily. She was the winged vampire, an eared bat-head in black fur, two long white fangs; below her waist she wore a black skirt, black stockings, black shoes. Slim legs. She quickly went to her place beside the crocodile, the clawed wings held rigidly out, bellying a little in the air, un-canny in the torchlight; a great flickering shadow that darkened the cross and the rose.

The next figure was African, a folk-horror, a corn-doll bundle of black strips of rag that hung down to the ground in a series of skirted flounces. Even the head mask was made of these rags; with a topknot of three white feathers and two huge saucer eyes. It appeared armless and legless, and indeed sexless, some ultimate childish night-mare. It shuffled forward to its place beside the vampire; added to the chorus of outrageous stares.

Then came a squat succubus with a Bosch-like snout.

The following man was by contrast mainly white, a macabre pierrot-skeleton; echo of the figure on the wall of my cell. His mask was a skull. The outline of the pelvis had been cleverly exaggerated; and the wearer had a stiff, bony walk.

Then an even more bizarre personage. It was a woman, and I began to doubt whether, after all, the vampire was Lily. The front of her stiffened skirt had the form of a stylized fishtail, which swelled up into a heavy pregnant belly; and then that in turn, above the breasts, became an up-pointed bird's head. This figure walked forward slowly, left hand supporting the swollen eight-month's belly, right hand between the breasts. The beaked white head with its almond-shaped eyes seemed to stare up towards the ceiling. It was beautiful, this fish-woman-bird, strangely tender after the morbidity and threat of the other figures. In its upstretched throat I could see two small holes, apertures for the eyes of the real person beneath.

Four more places remained.

The next figure was almost an old friend. Anubis the jackal-head, alert and vicious. He strode lithely to his place, a Negro walk.

A man in a black cloak on which were various astrological and alchemical symbols in white. On his head he wore a hat with a peak a yard high and a wide nefarious brim; a kind of black neck-covering hung from behind it. Black gloves, and a long white staff surmounted by a circle, a snake with its tail in its mouth. Over the face there was no more than a deep mask in black. I knew who it was. I could see the gleaming eyes and the implacable mouth.

Two more places at the centre. There was a pause. The rank of figures behind the table stared up at me, unmoving, in total silence. I looked round at my guards, who stared ahead, like soldiers; and I shrugged. I wished I could have yawned, to put them all in their place; and to help me in mine.

Four men appeared in the white corridor. They were carrying a black sedan chair, so narrow that it looked almost like an upright coffin. I could see closed curtains at its sides, and in front. On the front panel was painted in white the same emblem as the one above my throne – an eight-spoked wheel. On the roof of the sedan was a kind of black tiara, each of whose teeth ended in a white meniscus, a ring of new moons.

The four porters were black-smocked. On their heads they had grotesque masks – witch-doctor faces in white and black and then rising from the crown of each head enormous vertical crosses a yard or more high. Instead of breaking off cleanly, the ends of the arms and the upright of these crosses burst out in black mops of rag or raffia, so that they seemed to be burning with black flame.

They did not come directly to the centre of the table, but as if it was some host, some purifying relic, carried their coffin-sedan round the room, up the left side, round in front of my throne, between me and the table, so that I could see the white crescent-moons, the symbols of Artemis-Diana, on the side panels, then on down the right side to the door again and then finally back to the table. The poles were slipped out of the brackets, and the box was lifted forward to the central empty place. Throughout, the other figures remained staring at me. The black porters went and stood by the brands, three of which were almost extinguished. The light was getting dim.

Then the thirteenth figure appeared.

In contrast to the others he was in a long white smock or alb that reached to the ground; whose only decoration consisted of two black bands round the end of the loose sleeves. He carried a black staff in red-gloved hands. The head was that of a pure black goat; a real goat's head, worn as a kind of cap, so that it stood high off the shoulders of the person beneath, whose real face must have lain behind the shaggy black beard. Huge backswept horns, left their natural colour; amber glass eyes; the only ornament, a fat blood-red candle that had been fixed between the horns and lit. I wished I could speak, for I badly needed to shout something debunking, something adolescent and healthy and English; a 'Doctor Crowley, I presume.' But all I could do was to cross my knees and look what I was not – unimpressed.

The goat-figure, his satanic majesty, came forward with an archi-diabolical dignity and I braced myself for the next development: a black Mass seemed likely. Perhaps the table was to be the altar. I realized that he was lampooning the traditional Christ-figure; the staff was the pastoral crook, the black beard Christ's brown one, the blood-red candle some sort of blasphemous parody of the halo. He came to his place, the long line of black-carnival puppets stared at me from the floor. I stared down the line: the stag-devil, the crocodile-devil, the vampire, the succubus, the bird-woman, the magician, the coffin-sedan, the goat-devil, the jackal-devil, the pierrot-skeleton, the corn-doll, the Aztec, the witch. I found myself swallowing, looking round again at my inscrutable guards. The gag was beginning to hurt. In the end I found it more comfortable to stare down at the foot of the dais.

Perhaps a minute passed like that. Another of the brands stopped flaming. The goat-figure raised his staff, held it up a moment, then made to lay it on the table in front of him; but he must have got it caught in something because there was a comforting little hitch in the stage business. As soon as he had managed it, he raised both hands sacerdotally, but fingers devil-horned, and pointed at the corners behind me. My two guards went to the projectors. Suddenly the room was flooded with light; and, after a moment of total stillness, flooded with movement.

Like actors suddenly off-stage, the row of figures in front of me began removing their masks and cloaks. The cross-headed men by the brands turned and took the torches and filed out towards the door. But they had to wait there, because a group of twenty or so young people appeared. They came in loosely, in ordinary clothes, without any attempt at order. Some of them had files and books. They were silent, and quickly took their places on the tiered side-benches to my right. The men with the torches disappeared. I looked at the new-comers – German or Scandinavian, intelligent faces, students' faces, one or two older people among them, and three girls, but with an average age in the early twenties. Two of the men I recognized from the incident of the ridge.

All this time the row of figures behind the table were disrobing. Adam and my two guards moved about helping them. Adam laid cardboard folders with white labels in each place. The stuffed cat was removed, and the staffs, all the paraphernalia. It was done swiftly, well rehearsed. I kept flashing looks down the line, as one person after another was revealed.

The last arrival, the goat-head, was an old man with a clipped white beard, dark grey-blue eyes; a resemblance to Smuts. Like all the others he studiously avoided looking at me, but I saw him smile at Conchis, the astrologer-magician beside him. Next to Conchis appeared, from behind the bird-head and pregnant belly, a slim middle-aged woman. She was wearing a dark-grey suit; a head-mistress or a business woman. The jackal-head, Joe, was dressed in a dark-blue suit. Anton came, surprisingly, from behind the pierrot-skeleton costume. The succubus from Bosch revealed another elderly man with a mild face and pince-nez. The corn-doll was Maria. The Aztec head was the German colonel, the pseudo-Wimmel of the ridge incident. The vampire was not Lily, but her sister; a scarless wrist. A white blouse, and the black skirt. The crocodile was a man in his late twenties. He had a thin artistic-looking beard; a Greek or an Italian. He too was wearing a suit. The stag-head was another man I did not know; a very tall Jewish-looking intellectual of about forty, deeply tanned and slightly balding.

That left the witch on the extreme right of the table. It was Lily, in a long-sleeved high-necked white woollen dress. I watched her pat her severely chignoned hair and then put on a pair of spectacles. She bent to hear something that the 'colonel' next to her whispered in her ear. She nodded, then opened the file in front of her.

Only one person was not revealed: whoever was in the coffin-sedan.

I sat facing a long table of perfectly normal-looking people, who were all sitting and consulting their files and beginning to look at me. Their faces showed interest, but no sympathy. I stared at June-Rose, but she stared back without expression, as if I were a waxwork. I waited above all for Lily to look at me, but when she did there was nothing in her eyes. She behaved like, and her position at the end of the table suggested, a minor member of a team, of a selection board.

At last the old man with the clipped white beard rose to his feet and a faint murmuring that had begun among the audience stopped. The other members of the 'board' looked towards him. I saw some, but not many, of the 'students' with open notebooks on their laps, ready to write. The old man with the white beard gazed up at me through his gold-rimmed glasses, smiled, and bowed.

'Mr Urfe, you must long ago have come to the conclusion that you have fallen into the hands of madmen. Worse than that, of sadistic madmen. And I think my first task is to introduce you to the sadistic madmen.' Some of the others gave little smiles. His English was excellent, though it retained clear traces of a German accent. 'But first we must return you, as we have returned ourselves, to normality.'

He signed quietly to my two guards, who had come back beside me. Deftly they untied the rosetted white ribbons, pulled my clothes back to their normal position, peeled off the black forehead patch, turned back my pullover, even brushed my hair back; but left the gag.

'Good. Now … if I may be allowed I shall first introduce myself. I am Doctor Friedrich Kretschmer, formerly of Stuttgart, now director of the Institute of Experimental Psychology at the University of Idaho in America. On my right you have Doctor Maurice Conchis of the Sorbonne, whom you know.' Conchis rose and bowed briefly to me. I glared at him. 'On his right, Doctor Mary Marcus, now of Edinburgh University, formerly of the William Alanson White Foundation in New York.' The professional-looking woman inclined her head. 'On her right, Professor Mario Ciardi of Milan.' He stood up and bowed, a mild little frog of a man. 'Beyond him you have our charming and very gifted young costume designer, Miss Margaret Maxwell.' 'Rose' gave me a minute brittle smile. 'On the right of Miss Maxwell you see Mr Yanni Kottopoulos. He has been our stage manager.' The man with the beard bowed; and then the tall Jew stood. 'And bowing to you now you see Arne Halberstedt of the Queen's Theatre, Stockholm, our dramatizer and director, to whom, together with Miss Maxwell and Mr Kottopoulos, we mere amateurs in the new drama all owe a great deal for the successful outcome and aesthetic beauty of our … enterprise.' First Conchis, then the other members of the 'board', then the students, began to clap. Even the guards behind me joined in.

The old man turned. 'Now – on my left – you see an empty box. But we like to think that there is a goddess inside. A virgin goddess whom none of us has ever seen, nor will ever see. We call her Ashtaroth the Unseen. Your training in literature will permit you, I am sure, to guess at her meaning. And through her at our, we humble scientists', meaning.' He cleared his throat. 'Beyond the box you have Doctor Joseph Harrison of my department at Idaho, and of whose brilliant study of characteristic urban Negro neuroses, *Black and White Minds*, you may have heard.' Joe got up and raised his hand casually. 'Anton' was next. 'Beyond him, Doctor Heinrich Mayer, at present working in Vienna. Beyond him, Madame Maurice Conchis, whom many of us know better as the gifted investigator of the effects of wartime traumata on refugeee children. I speak, of course, of Doctor Annette Kazanian of the Chicago Institute.' I refused to be surprised, which was more than could be said of some of the 'audience', who murmured and leant forward to look at 'Maria'. 'Beyond Madame Conchis, you see Privatdozent Thorvald Jorgensen of Aalborg University.' The 'colonel' stood up briskly and bowed. 'Beyond him you have Doctor Vanessa Maxwell.' Lily looked briefly up at me, bespectacled, absolutely without expression. I flicked my eyes back to the old man; he looked at his colleagues. 'I think that we all feel the success of the clinical side of our enterprise this summer is very largely due to Doctor Maxwell. Dr Marcus had already told me what to expect when her most gifted pupil came to us at Idaho. But I should like to say that never have my expectations been so completely fulfilled. I am sometimes accused of putting too much stress on the role of women in our profession. Let me say that Dr Maxwell, my charming young colleague Vanessa, confirms what I have always believed: that one day all our great practising, as opposed to our theoretical, psychiatrists will be of the sex of Eve.' There was applause. Lily stared down at the table in front of her and then, when the clapping had died down, she glanced at the old man and murmured, 'Thank you.' He turned back to me.

'The students you see are Austrian and Danish research students from Doctor Mayer's faculty and from Aalborg. I think we all speak English?' Some said, yes. He smiled benignly at them and sipped a glass of water.

'Well, so, Mr Urfe, you will have guessed our secret by now. We are an international group of psychologists, which I have the honour, by reason of seniority simply' – two or three shook their heads in disagreement – 'to lead. For various reasons the path of research in which we are all especially interested requires us to have subjects that are not volunteers, that are not even aware that they are subjects of an experiment. We are by no means united in our theories of behaviour, in our different schools, but we are united in considering the nature of the experiment is such that it is better that the subject should not, even at its conclusion, be informed of its purpose. Though I am sure that you will – when you can recollect in tranquillity – find yourself able to deduce at least part of our causes from our effects.' There were smiles all round. 'Now. We have had you, these last three days, under deep narcosis and the material we have obtained from you has proved most valuable, most valuable indeed, and we therefore wish first of all to show our appreciation of the normality you have shown in all the peculiar mazes through which we have made you run.'

The whole lot of them stood and applauded me. I could not keep control any longer. I saw Lily and Conchis clapping, and the students. I cocked my wrists round and gave them a double V-sign. It evidently bewildered the old man, because he turned and bent to ask Conchis what it meant. The clapping died down. Conchis turned to the supposed woman doctor from Edinburgh. She spoke in a strong American voice.

'The sign is a visual equivalent of some verbalization like "Bugger you" or "Up your arse".'

This seemed to interest the old man. He repeated the gesture, watching his own hand. 'But did not Mr Churchill ... '

Lily spoke, leaning forward. 'It is the upward movement that carries the signal, Doctor Kretschmer. Mr Churchill's victory-sign was with the hand reversed and static. I mentioned it in connection with my paper on "Direct Anal-Erotic Metaphor in Classical Literature".'

'Ah. Yes. I recall. *Ja, ja.*'

Conchis spoke to Lily. '*Pedicabo ego vos et irrumabo, Aureli patheci et cinaedi Furi?*'

Lily: 'Precisely.'

Wimmel-Jorgensen leant forward; a strong accent. 'Is there no doubt a connection with the cuckold gesture?' He put finger-horns on his head.

'I did suggest,' said Lily, 'that we may suppose a castration motive in the insult, a desire to degrade and humiliate the male rival which would of course be finally identifiable with the relevant stage of infantile fixation and the accompanying phobias.'

I flexed muscles, rubbed my legs together, forced myself to stay sane, to deduce what reason I could get out of all this unreason. I did not, could not believe that they were psychologists; they would never risk giving me their names.

On the other hand they must be brilliant at improvising the right jargon, since my gesture had come without warning. Or had it? I thought fast. They had needed my gesture to cue their dialogue; and it happened to be one that I hadn't used for years. But I remembered having heard that one could make people do things after hypnosis, on a pre-suggested signal. It would have been easy. When I was clapped, I felt forced to give the sign. I must be on my guard; do nothing without thinking.

The old man quietened further discussion. 'Mr Urfe, your significant gesture brings me to our purpose in all meeting you here. We are naturally aware that you are filled with deep feelings of anger and hatred towards at least some of us. Some of the repressed material we have discovered reveals a different state of affairs, but as my colleague Doctor Harrison would say, "It is what we *believe* we live with that chiefly concerns us." We have therefore gathered here today to allow you to judge us in your turn. This is why we have placed you in the judge's seat. We have silenced you because justice should be mute until the time for sentencing comes. But before we hear your judgment on us, you must permit us to give some additional evidence *against* ourselves. Our real justification is scientific, but we are all agreed, as I explained, that the requirements of good clinical practice forbid us to make such an excuse. I now call on Dr Marcus to read out that part of our report on you which deals with you not as a subject for experiment, but as an ordinary human being. Dr Marcus.'

The woman from Edinburgh got up. She was about fifty, with greying hair cut boyishly short; no lipstick, a hard, intelligent, quasi-lesbian face that looked as if it had singularly little patience with fools. She began to read in a belligerent transatlantic monotone.

'The subject of our 1953 experiment belongs to a familiar category of semi-intellectual introversion. Although excellent for our purposes his personality pattern is without subsidiary interest. The most significant feature of his life-style is negative: its lack of social content.

'The motives for this attitude springs from an only partly resolved Oedipal complex. The subject shows characteristic symptoms of mingled fear and resentment of authority, especially male authority and the usual accompanying basic syndrome: an ambivalent attitude towards women, in which they are seen both as desired objects and as objects which have betrayed him, and therefore merit his revenge and counter-betrayal.

'Time has not allowed us to investigate the subject's specific womb and breast separation traumas, but the compensatory mechanisms he had evolved are so frequent among so-called intellectuals that we may posit with certainty a troubled period of separation from the maternal breast, possibly due to the exigences of the military career of the subject's father, and a very early identification of the father, or male, as separator – a role which Doctor Conchis adopted in our experiment. The subject has then never been able to accept the initial loss of oral gratification and maternal protection and this has given him his auto-erotic approach to emotional problems and life in general The subject also conforms to the Adlerian descriptions of siblingless personality traits.

'The subject has preyed sexually and emotionally on a number of young women. His method, according to Doctor Maxwell, is to stress and exhibit his loneliness and unhappiness – in short, to play the little boy in search of the lost mother. He thereby arouses repressed maternal instincts in his victims which he then proceeds to exploit with the semi-incestuous ruthlessness of this type.

'In the usual way the subject identifies God with the father-figure, aggressively rejecting any belief in Him.

'He has careerwise continually placed himself in situations of isolation. His solution of his fundamental separation anxiety requires him to cast himself as the rebel and outsider. His unconscious intention in seeking this isolation is to find a justification for his preying on women and also for his withdrawal from any community orientated in directions hostile to his fundamental needs of self-gratification.

'The subject's family, caste, and national background have not helped in the resolution of his problems. He comes of a military family, in which there were a large number of taboos resulting from a strongly authoritarian paternal regime. His caste in his own country, that of the professional middle-class, Zwiemann's *technobourgeoisie*, is of course marked by an obsessional adherence to such regimes. In a remark to Doctor

Maxwell the subject reported that "All through my adolescence I had to lead two lives." This is a good layman's description of environment-motivated and finally consciously induced para-schizophrenia – "madness as lubricant", in Karen Horney's famous phrase.

'On leaving university the subject put himself in the one environment he would not be able to tolerate – that of an expensive private school, the social transmitter of all those paternalistic and authoritarian traits the subject hates. Predictably he then felt himself forced both out of the school and out of his country, and adopted the role of expatriate, though he insured himself against any valid adjustment by once again choosing an environment – the school on Phraxos – which was certain to provide him with the required elements of hostility. His work there is academically barely adequate and his relationship with his colleagues and students poor.

'To sum up, he is behaviourally the victim of a repetition-compulsion that he has failed to understand. In every environment he looks for those elements that allow him to feel isolated, that allow him to justify his withdrawal from meaningful social responsibilities and relationships and his consequent regression into the infantile state of frustrated self-gratification. At present this autistic regression takes the form mentioned above, of affaires with young women. Although previous attempts at an artistic resolution have apparently failed, we may predict that further such attempts will be made and that there will be the normal cultural life-pattern of the type: excessive respect for iconoclastic *avant-garde* art, contempt for tradition, paranosic sympathy with fellow-rebels and non-conformers in conflict with frequent and depressive and persecutory phases in personal and work relationships.

'As Doctor Conchis has observed in his *The Midcentury Predicament*: "The rebel with no specific gift for rebellion is destined to become the drone; and even this metaphor is inexact, since the drone has at least a small chance of fecundating the queen, whereas the human rebel-drone is deprived even of that small chance and may finally see himself as totally sterile, lacking not only the brilliant life-success of the queens but even the humble satisfactions of the workers in the human hive. Such a personality is reduced to mere wax, a mere receiver of impressions; and this condition is the very negation of the basic drive in him – to rebel. It is no wonder that in middle age many such failed rebels, rebels turned self-conscious drones, aware of their susceptibility to intellectual vogues, adopt a mask of cynicism that cannot hide their more or less paranoiac sense of having been betrayed by life."'

While she had been speaking the others at the table listened in their various ways, some looking at her, others sunk in contemplation of the table. Lily was one of the most attentive. The 'students' scribbled notes. I spent all my time staring at the woman, who read, and never once looked at me. I felt full of spleen, of hatred of all of them. There was some truth in what she was saying. But I knew nothing could justify such a public analysis, even if it were true; just as nothing could justify Lily's behaviour – because most of the 'material' this analysis was based on must have come from her. I stared at her, but she would not look up. I knew who had written the report. There were too many echoes of Conchis. I was not misled by the new mask. He was still the master of ceremonies, the man behind it all; at web-centre.

The American woman sipped water from a glass. There was silence; evidently the report was not finished. She began to read on.

'There are two appendices, or footnotes. One comes from Professor Ciardi, and is as follows:

'I dissent from the view that the subject is without significance outside the matter of our experiment. In my view one may anticipate in twenty years' time a period of considerable and today almost unimaginable prosperity in the West. I repeat my assertion that the threat of a nuclear catastrophe will have a healthy effect on Western Europe and America. It will firstly stimulate economic production; it will secondly ensure that there is peace; it will thirdly provide a constant sense of real danger behind every moment of living, which was in my opinion missing before the last war and so contributed to it. Although this threat of war may do something to counteract the otherwise dominating role that the female sex must play in a peacetime society dedicated to the pursuit of pleasure, I predict that breast-fixated men like the subject will become the norm. We are entering an amoral and permissive era in which self-gratification in the form of high wages and a wide range of consumer goods obtained and obtainable against a background of apparently imminent universal doom will be available, if not to all, then to an increasingly large majority. In such an age the characteristic personality type must inevitably become auto-erotic and, clinically, autopsychotic. Such a person will be for economic reasons isolated, as for personal ones the subject is today, from direct contact with the evils of human life, such as starvation, poverty, inadequate living conditions, and the rest. Western *homo sapiens* will become *homo solitarius*. Though I have little sympathy as a fellow human being for the subject, his predicament interests me as a social psychologist, since he has developed precisely as I would expect a man of moderate intelligence but little analytical power, and virtually no science, to develop in our age. If nothing else he proves the total in-adequacy of the confused value judgments and pseudo-statements of art to equip modern man for his evolutionary role.'

The woman laid down the paper and picked up another.

'This second note comes from Doctor Maxwell, who of course has had the closest personal contact with the subject. She says:

'In my view the subject's selfishness and social inadequacy have been determined by his past, and any report which we communicate to him should make it clear that his personality deficiencies are due to circumstances outside his command. The subject may not understand that we are making clinical descriptions, and not, at least in my own case, with any association of moral blame. If anything our attitude should be one of pity towards a personality that has to cover its defici-encies under so many conscious and unconscious lies. We must always remember that the subject has been launched into the world with no training in self-analysis and self-orientation;

and that almost all the education he has received is positively harmful to him. He was, so to speak, born short-sighted by nature and has been further blinded by his environments. It is small wonder that he cannot find his way.'

The American woman sat down. The old man in the white beard nodded, as if pleased with what had been said. He looked at me, then at Lily.

'I think, Doctor Maxwell, that it would be fair to the subject if you repeated what you said to me last night in connection with him.'

Lily bowed her head, then stood up and spoke to the others. She glanced at me briefly, as if I was a diagram on a blackboard. 'During my relationship with the subject I experienced a certain degree of counter-transference. I have analysed this with the help of Doctor Marcus and we think that this emotional attachment can be broken into two components. One originated in a physical attraction for him, artificially exaggerated by the role I had to play. The second component was empathetic in nature. The subject's self-pity is projected so strongly on his environment that one becomes contaminated by it. I thought this was of interest in view of Professor Ciardi's comment.'

The old man nodded. 'Thank you.' She sat down. He looked up at me. 'All this may seem cruel to you. But we wish to hide nothing.' He looked at Lily. 'As regards the first component of your attachment, sexual attraction, would you describe to the subject and to us your present feelings?'

'I consider that the subject would make a very inadequate husband except as a sexual partner.' Ice-cold; she looked at me, then back to the old man. I had a dreadful, lancing memory of her standing against me; the night, the rain, the slow caress.

Dr Marcus intervened. 'He has basic marriage-destructive drives?'

'Yes.'

'Specifically?'

'Infidelity. Selfishness. Inconsiderateness in everyday routines. Possibly, homosexual tendencies.'

The old man: 'Would the situation be altered if he had analysis?'

'In my opinion, no.'

The old man turned. 'Maurice?'

Conchis spoke, staring at me. 'I think we are all agreed that he has been an admirable subject for our purposes, but he has masochistic traits that will get pleasure even out of our discussion of his faults. In my opinion our further interest in him is now both harmful to him and unnecessary.'

The old man looked up at me. 'Under narcosis it was discovered that you are still strongly attached to Doctor Maxwell. Some of us have also been concerned about the effect that the loss of the young Australian girl, for which, I must also tell you, you feel deeply guilty in your unconscious, and now the second loss of the mythical figure you know as "Julie", may have on you. I refer to the possibility of suicide. Our conclusion has been this: that your attachment to self-gratification is too deep to make any other than a hysterical attempt at suicide likely. And against this we advise you to guard.'

I gave a sarcastic bow of thanks. Dignity, keep some remnant of dignity.

'Now ... does anyone wish to say anything more?' He looked both ways down the table. They all shook their heads. 'Very well. We have come to the end of our experiment.' He gestured for the 'board' to stand, which they did. The 'audience' remained sitting. He looked at me. 'We have not concealed our real opinion of you; and since this is a trial we have of course been acting as witnesses against ourselves. You are, I remind you once again, the judge, and the time has now come for you to judge us. We have, first of all, selected a *pharmakos*. A scapegoat.'

He looked to his left. Lily took off her glasses, stepped round the table and came and stood at the foot of the dais in front of me, with a bowed head; the white woollen dress, a penitential. Even then I was so stupid that I saw some fantastic new development; a mock wedding, some absurd happy ending ... and I thought grimly what I would do if they dared try that on.

'She is your prisoner, but you cannot do what you like with her, because the code of medical justice under which we exist specifies a precise type of punishment for the crime of destroying all power of forgiveness in the subject of our experiments.' He turned round to Adam, who stood near the archway. 'The apparatus.'

Adam called something. The other people behind the table stood to one side; in a compact group, facing the 'students', with the old man at their head. Four black-uniformed men came in. They quickly moved the sedan-coffin and two of the tables, so that the centre of the room was left free. The third table was lifted in front of me, beside Lily. Then two of the men left and returned carrying a heavy wooden frame, like a door frame, on bracketed legs. Six or seven feet up, at the top of the uprights, were iron rings. Lily turned and walked to where they set it, some halfway down the room. She stood in front of it and held up her arms. Adam handcuffed her wrists to the rings, so that she was crucified against it, with her back to me. Then a kind of stiffened leather helmet, with a down-projecting back piece that covered the nape of her neck, was put on her head; a protector.

It was a flogging frame.

Adam then left; returned in two seconds.

I could not see what he was holding at first, but he swung it loose as he came towards me. And I understood the incredible last trick they were playing.

It was a stiff black handle ending in a long skein of knotted lashes. Adam unravelled two or three that were tangled, then laid the foul thing on the table, handle towards me. Then he went back to Lily – everything was carefully planned to be in this sequence – and pulled down the zip in the back of her dress to her waist. He even unhooked the bra, then folded it and the dress carefully aside, so that her bare back was fully exposed. I could see the pink lines on her skin where the strap had crossed.

I was the Eumenides, the merciless Furies.

My hands began to sweat. Once again I was plunged hopelessly out of my depth. Always with Conchis one went down, and it seemed one could go no farther; but at the end another way went even lower.

The Smuts-like old man came forward again and stood in front of me.

'You see the scapegoat and you see the instrument of punishment. You are now both judge and executioner. We are all here haters of unnecessary suffering; as you must try to understand when you come to think over these events. But we are all agreed that there must be a point in our experiment when you, the subject, have absolute freedom to choose whether to inflict pain on us – and a pain abhorrent to all of us – in your turn. We have chosen Doctor Maxwell because she best symbolizes what we are to you. Now we ask you to do as the Roman emperors did and to raise or lower your right thumb. If you lower it, you will be released and free to carry out the punishment as severely and brutally as you wish, up to ten strokes. That is sufficient to ensure the most atrocious suffering, and permanent disfigurement. If you raise your thumb in the sign of mercy, you will, apart from one last short process of disintoxication, be free of us for evermore. You will equally be free if you choose to punish, which will also demonstrate the satisfactory completion of your disintoxication. Now I ask one last thing of you: that you think carefully, very carefully indeed, before you choose.'

At some unseen signal the students all rose. Everyone in the room stared at me. I was aware that I wanted to make a right choice; something that would make them all remember me, that would prove them all wrong. I knew I was judge only in name. Like all judges, I was finally the judged; to be judged by my own judgment.

I saw at once that the choice they were offering me was absurd. Everything was fixed to make it impossible for me to punish Lily. The only punishment I wanted to inflict on her was to make her cry forgiveness; not cry pain. In any case I knew that even if I put my thumb down, they would find some way of stopping me. The whole situation, with all its gratuitously sadistic undertones, was a trap; a false dilemma. Even then, through all my seething resentment and anger at being so mercilessly exposed in the village stocks, I had a feeling that was certainly not forgiveness of them, even less gratitude, but a recrudescence of that amazement I had felt so often before: that all this could be mounted just for me.

Not without hesitation, thinking, gauging whether I was free to choose, and feeling sure that this was not a pre-conditioning, I turned my thumb down.

The old man stared at me a long moment, then signed to the guards and went back to the group. My wrists were freed. I stood up and rubbed them, then tore the gag off. The tape ripped at the stubble on my chin, and for a moment all I could do was blink foolishly with pain. The guards made no move. I rubbed the skin round my mouth, and looked round the room.

Silence. They expected me to speak; so I would not speak.

I went down the wooden steps and picked up the cat. I had half expected it to be a stage property. But it was surprisingly heavy. The handle, of plaited leather over wood; a knop end. The thongs were worn, the knots as hard as bullets. The thing looked old, a genuine Royal Navy antique from the Napoleonic wars. As I handled it, I calculated. The most likely solution was that they would put the lights out; there would be a scuffle. The four men and Adam were by the door and it would be impossible to escape.

Without warning I picked up the cat and swung it down on the table. A savage hiss. The thrash of the lashes on the deal table-top sounded like a gun. It made one or two of the students jump. I saw one of them, a girl, look away. Yet no one moved nearer. I began to walk towards where Lily was. I did not expect to get to her.

But I did. Still no one moved, I was suddenly within hitting range and the nearest person was thirty feet away. I stood as if measuring my distance, with my left foot forward, turned to strike. I even gave the beastly thing a little testing reach, so that the thongs brushed the middle of her back. Her face was hidden by the head-protector. I swung the cat back over my shoulder, as if I was going to swing it down with all my force on that white back. I half expected a shout to ring out, to see or hear someone dash for me. But no one moved and I knew, as they must have known, that it would have been too late. Only a bullet could have stopped me. I looked round, half expecting to see a gun. But the eleven, the guards, the 'students', all stood immobile.

I looked back at Lily. There was a very real devil in me, an evil marquis, that wanted to strike, to see the wet red weals traverse the delicate skin; not so much to hurt her as to shock them, to bring them to a sense of the enormity of what they were doing; almost of the enormity of making her risk so much. 'Anton' had said it: *Very brave.* I knew they must be absolutely certain of my decency, my stupid English decency; in spite of all they had said, all the *bandillera* they had planted in my self-esteem, absolutely sure that not once in a hundred thousand years would I bring that cat down. I did bring it down then, but very slowly, as if making sure of my distance again, then took it back. I tried to determine whether once again I was pre-conditioned not to do it, by Conchis; but I knew I had absolute free-dom of choice. I could do it if I wanted.

Then suddenly.

I understood.

I was not holding a cat in my hand in an underground cistern, I was in a sunlit square ten years before and in my hands I held a German sub-machine-gun. And it was not Conchis who was now playing the role of Wimmel. Wimmel was inside me, in my stiffened, backthrown arm, in all my past; above all in what I had done to Alison.

The better you understand freedom, the less you possess it.

And my freedom too was in not striking, whatever the cost, whatever eighty other parts of me must die, whatever the watching eyes might think of me; even though it would seem, as they must have foreseen, that I was forgiving them, that I was indoctrinated, their dupe. I lowered the cat, and I could feel tears gathering – tears of rage, tears of frustration.

All Conchis's manoeuvrings had been to bring me to this; all the charades, the psychical, the theatrical, the sexual, the psychological; and I was standing as he had stood before the guerilla, unable to beat his brains out; discovering that there are strange times for the calling in of old debts; and even stranger prices to pay.

The group of eleven, standing by the wall; standing with the sedan half-hidden in their centre, as if they were guarding it from me. I saw June, who had the grace not to meet my look. I somehow knew that she was frightened; she for one had not been sure.

The white back.

I walked towards them, towards Conchis. I saw 'Anton', who was standing beside him, tilt forward infinitesimally. I knew he was getting on to the balls of his feet ready to spring. Joe was watching me like a hawk, too. I stood in front of Conchis and handed him the cat, handle first. He took it, but he never moved his eyes from mine. We stared at each other for a long moment; that same old stare, simianly observing.

He expected me to speak; to say the word. But I would not. Could not.

I looked round the faces of the group. I knew they were only actors and actresses, but that even the best of their profession cannot in silence act certain human qualities, like intelligence, experience, intellectual honesty; and they had their share of that. Nor could they take part in such a scene without more inducement than money; however much money Conchis offered. I sensed a moment of comprehension between all of us, a strange sort of mutual respect; on their side perhaps no more than a relief that I was as they secretly believed me to be, behind all the mysteries and the humiliations; on my side, a dim conviction of having entered some deeper, wiser esoteric society than I could without danger speak in. As I stood there, close to their eleven silences, their faces without hostility yet without concession, faces dissociated from my anger, as close-remote and oblique as the faces in a Flemish Adoration, I felt myself almost physically dwindling; as one dwindles before certain works of art, certain truths, seeing one's smallness, narrow-mindedness, insufficiency in their dimension and value.

I could see it in Conchis's eyes; something besides *eleutheria* had been proved. And I was the only person there who did not know what it was. I looked for it in his eyes; but that was like looking into the darkest night. A hundred things trembled on my lips, in my mind; and died there.

No answer; no movement.

Abruptly I went back to the 'throne'.

I watched the 'students' go out, I watched Lily being unfastened. June helped her dress, and they rejoined the others. The frame was removed. Finally only the group of twelve remained. Once again, as drilled as a Sophoclean chorus, they bowed, then turned and walked out.

The men stood aside for the women to lead the way at the arch and Lily was the first to disappear. But when the last of the men had gone, she came back for a moment in the archway, staring at me as I stared at her, her face without expression, without gratitude, leaving a dozen reasons in the air as to why she might have given me this last glimpse; or herself this last glimpse of me.

62

I was alone with the same three guards who had brought me. They waited a minute, two minutes. Adam offered me a cigarette. I smoked, racked between an anger and a relief, between a feeling that I should have made some excoriating denunciation of them and all their practices and a feeling that I had done the only thing that could leave me any dignity. The cigarette was almost finished when Adam looked at his watch, then at me.

'Now ... '

He pointed at the handcuffs that were still dangling from the supports of the armrests.

'Look. Finished. No more of this.' I stood up, but my arms were caught at once. I took a deep breath. Adam shrugged.

'*Bitte.*'

I let myself be handcuffed to the two men. Then he came with the gag. That was too much. I began to struggle, but they simply jerked me sharply back on to the throne; once again choiceless, I submitted. He slipped the gag over my head, this time without taping it. Then I was masked, and we set off. We walked through the archway, but outside we turned right, not left; we were not going back the way we came. Twenty or thirty paces, then down five steps and apparently into yet another large room or cistern.

I was forced backwards, there was a fiddling with the handcuffs. Then my left arm was abruptly raised, there was a click, and with an icy new apprehension I realized what they had done. I had been fastened to the flogging frame. I really began to struggle then. I kicked and kneed, I wrenched at the man to whose wrist I was still attached. They could have beaten me up at will. There were three of them and I couldn't see and it was ridiculous. But they must have been under orders to do things as gently as possible. Eventually they forced my other arm up and linked it to the second ring. The mask was taken off.

It was a very long narrow room, another cistern, but lower-vaulted; eighty feet long and about twenty wide. Halfway down was a white cinema screen, like the one that had been used at Bourani. Three-quarters way down, a pair of drawn black curtains stretched the width of the room. The obscure end-wall was just visible over their tops. It was an enlarged version of the chapel at Moutsa with the iconostasis. I was fixed to the frame, but frontways on, and it had been set against the wall. Just in front of me and slightly to my right was a small cinema projector with a reel of 16-mm. film. What light there was came from through the doorway I could see to my left.

My trio of blackshirts wasted no time. They went to the projector, switched it on, checked that the film was correctly fed and then set it going. It began with the black wheel on white, as if it was a film company emblem. One of the men adjusted the lens focus a little. Adam came back and stood in front of me – out of reach of any kick I might attempt – and spoke.

'The final disintoxication.'

I understood that I had been forced to 'forgive' so that I could be moved on to this ultimate humiliation; a metaphorical, if not a literal, flogging.

I had still not reached the bottom.

I was alone with the whirring projector and whatever lay beyond the curtains. The emblem faded and words appeared.

POLYMUS FILMS
PRESENT

The screen went white for a moment. Then:

THE SHAMEFUL TRUTH

The black wheel. Then:

WITH
THE FABULOUS WHORE
IO

A blank.

WHOM YOU WILL REMEMBER AS
ISIS
ASTARTE
KALI

A long blank.

AND AS THE CAPTIVATING
'LILY MONTGOMERY'

There was a brief shot of Lily kneeling behind a man. It had almost ended before I realized that the man was myself. Someone, Conchis, most have taken us with a telephoto lens, the day she recited from *The Tempest*. I remembered she had even warned me he was using exactly such a camera.

AS THE UNFORGETTABLY DESIRABLE
'JULIE HOLMES'

Another brief shot: I was standing and kissing her in bright sunlight. The same day, beside the statue of Poseidon.

AND AS THE LEARNED AND COURAGEOUS
'VANESSA MAXWELL'

This time it was a still. She was behind a desk, a laboratory desk covered with papers. A rack of test-tubes. A microscope. Little Madame Curie.

AND NOW IN HER GREATEST ROLE AS

The wheel reappeared for a moment.

HERSELF!

Blank film.

Then a fade-in shot of Joe in his jackal-mask running down the track towards the house at Bourani; a devil in sunlight; he ran right up into the camera lens, blacking it out.

CO-STARRING
THE MONSTER OF THE MISSISSIPPI

A blank.

JOE HARRISON

The wheel again.

AS HIMSELF

Then there were words in an over-ornamented frame.

> Lady Jane, a depraved
> young aristocrat, in
> her hotel room.

I was going to see a blue film.

It began: a lushly furnished, frill-laden bedroom in Edwardian style. Lily appeared in a peignoir, her hair down. The peignoir gaped absurdly over a black corset. She stopped by a chair to adjust a stocking, in a hackneyed leg-showing routine, though the close-up also allowed her to show the scarred wrist. She looked suddenly towards the door, and called something. A page entered with a letter on a tray. She took it and the page left. Shot of her opening the letter, sneering, and tossing it aside. The camera closed on the letter on the floor.

The quality of the film was bubbly and blistery, badly synchronized, like early silent film. Another flickering framed title appeared.

> ' ... now I know the abominable truth about
> your perverted lusts, all is over between us.
> I remain, but not for long, your disgusted
> husband ... Lord de Vere!'

A new shot. Lily was lying on the bed, with the camera shooting down on her. The peignoir had gone. The corset, fishnet stockings. She had managed to give her heavily rouged and mascara'd face a suitably pouting and *femme fatale* look, but the visual effect was not far removed from the verbal: like so much pornography – in this case I supposed intentionally – it was dangerously near the ridiculous.

It was all to end in a joke; a joke in bad taste, but a joke.

> Panting with desire she waits for the
> arrival of her coal-black Partner in
> unspeakable sin.

Back to the same shot. Suddenly she sat up with a leer on the French brothel brass bed. Someone else had come in.

> The entry of Black Bull,
> a vaudeville singer.

A shot of the open door. It was Joe, dressed in absurdly tight trousers and a sort of loose-sleeved white blouse. More like a black bullfighter than a black bull. He closed the door; a smouldering look.

> The only language they know.

The film veered into nastiness. There was a shot of her running to meet him. He stepped forward and gripped her by the arms and then they were kissing wildly. He forced her back to the bed and they fell across it. Then she rolled on top of him, covering his face, his neck in kisses.

> A buck nigger and a white woman.

She was standing in the black underwear, against the wall, her arms out. Joe was kneeling in front of her, bare above the waist, feeling with open hands up over her corset to her breasts. She caught his head and pressed it against her.

> For this she has sacrificed a
> loving husband, lovely children,
> friends, relations, religion, all.

Next there came a five-second fetishist interlude. He was lying on the floor. There was a close shot of a naked leg ending in a foot in a high-heeled black shoe resting on his stomach. He caressed it with his hands. I began to suspect. It could easily have been any white woman's leg; and any black man's stomach and hands.

> Passion rises.

A shot across the room of her pressing him back against the wall, kissing him. His hand slipped round her back and began to unhook the corset. A long bare back bound in black arms. The camera closed, then tracked down clumsily. A black hand moved suggestively into shot. Joe was now apparently naked, though hidden by her white body. I could see his face, but the quality of the film was so bad that I could not be sure it was Joe. And her face was invisible throughout.

> Shameless.

I began to be more suspicious than shocked. A series of very short shots. Bare white breasts, bare black thighs; two naked figures on the bed. But the camera was too far back to make identification possible. The woman's blonde hair began to seem too blonde, too shiny: wiglike.

> Decent people lead ordinary lives
> while this bestial orgy takes place.

A street shot in a city I did not recognize, though it looked American. Crowded pavements, a rush-hour. It was of better quality than the other sequences and had obviously been cut in from some other film; and it made the 'blue' sequences seem even more antiquated and claustrophobic.

Obscene caresses.

An anonymous white hand stroked an anonymous phallus in one of the most unexceptionable caresses of love. Its obscenity lay in the fact that two people could lie and be photographed doing it. But it was the wrist of the right, the unscarred hand that was in the frame; and although it made a playful flute-fingering gesture, I would now have bet that it was not Lily's.

The invitation.

There was the most brutally pornographic shot yet, down-angled, of the naked girl lying on the bed. Once again it did not reveal her face, which was twisted back almost out of sight. It showed her waiting to receive the Negro, whose blurred dark back was close to the camera.

Meanwhile.

Suddenly the quality of the film changed. It was shot, very jerkily, by a different camera in different circumstances. Two people in a crowded restaurant. With an acute shock, a flush of bitter anger, I saw who it was: Alison and myself, that first evening, in the Piraeus. There was a flash of blank film, then another shot of us, which for a moment I could not place. Alison walking down a steep village street, myself a yard or two behind her. We both looked exhausted; and though it was too far to see the facial expressions, one could tell from that gap between us, the way we walked, that we were miserable. I recognized it: our return to Arachova. The cameraman must have been hidden in a cottage, shooting from behind a shutter perhaps, because a transverse black bar obscured the end of the shot. I remembered the wartime sequence of Wimmel. I also recognized the implications; that we had been followed, watched and filmed throughout. It would not have been possible on the bare upper slopes of Parnassus, but in the trees ... I remembered the pool, the sun on my naked back and Alison beneath me. It was too horrible, too blasphemous, that that, of all moments, could have been public.

Stripped, flayed by the knowledge; and their always knowing.

Blank film again. Then another title.

The act of copulation.

But the film ran through a series of numbers and flashing white scratches: the end of the reel. There was a flipping sound from the projector. The screen stared white. Someone ran in through the door and switched the projector off. I gave a grunt of contempt; I had been waiting for that failure of nerve, of the courage of their pornography. But the man – I saw by the faint light through the door that it was Adam again – walked to the screen and lifted it aside. I was left alone once more. For thirty seconds or so the room remained in darkness. Then light came from behind the curtains.

Someone began to pull them, from behind, by cords, as they do for plays in parish halls. When they were about two-thirds open, they stopped; but long before that the parallel with parish halls had vanished. The light came from a shade hung from the ceiling. It let no light through, so that the illumination was thrown down in a soft, intimate cone on to what lay beneath.

A low couch, covered by a huge golden-tawny rug, perhaps an Afghan carpet. On it, completely naked, was Lily. I could not see the scar, but I knew it was her. The tan was not dark enough for her sister. Lying against a mound of pillows, deep gold, amber, rose, maroon, themselves piled against an ornate gilt and carved headboard, she was turned sideways towards me in a deliberate imitation of Goya's *Maja Desnuda*. Her hands behind her head, her nakedness offered. Not flaunted, but offered, stated as a divine and immemorial fact. A bare armpit, as sexual as a loin. Nipples the colour of cornelians, as if they alone in all that honeyed skin had been, or could be, bitten and bruised. The tapering curves, thighs, ankles, small bare feet. And the level, unmoving eyes staring with a kind of arrogant calm into the shadows where I hung.

Beyond her, on the rear wall, had been painted an arcade of slender black arches. I thought at first that they were meant to represent Bourani; but they were too narrow, and had slender Moorish-ogive tops. Goya ... the Alhambra? I realized the couch was not legless, but that the far end of the room was on a slightly lower level, rather like a Roman bath. The curtains had concealed further steps down.

The slender form lay in its greenish-tawny lake of light, without movement; and she stared at me as from a canvas. The tableau pose was held so long that I began to think this was the great finale; this living painting, this naked enigma, this forever unattainable.

Minutes passed. The lovely body lay in its mystery. I could just see the imperceptible swell of her breathing ... or could I? For a few moments I was looking at a magnificently lifelike wax effigy.

But then she moved.

Her head turned in profile and her right arm reached out gracefully and invitingly, in the classical gesture of Récamier, to whomever had switched on the light and drawn open the curtains. A new figure appeared.

It was Joe.

He was in a cloak of indeterminate period, pure white, lined heavily with gold. He went and stood behind the couch. Rome? An empress and her slave? He stared at me, or towards me, for a moment, and I knew he could not be meant to be a slave. He was too majestic, too darkly noble. He possessed the room, the stage, the woman. He looked down at her and she looked up, a grave affection; the swan neck. He took her outstretched hand.

Suddenly I understood who they were; and who I was; how prepared, this moment. I too had a new role. I tried then desperately to get rid of the gag, by biting, by yawning, by rubbing my head against my arms. But it was too tight.

The Negro, the Moor, knelt beside her, kissed her shoulder. A slim white arm framed and imprisoned his dark head. A long moment. Then she sank back. He surveyed her, slowly ran a hand down from her neck to her waist. As if she was silk. Sure of her surrender. Then he calmly stood up and unbroached his toga at the shoulder.

I shut my eyes.

Nothing is true; everything is permitted.

Conchis: *His part is not ended yet.*

I opened my eyes again.

There was no perversion, no attempt to suggest that I was watching anything else but two people who were in love making love; as one might watch two boxers in a gymnasium or two acrobats on a stage. Not that there was anything acrobatic or violent about them. They behaved as if to show that the reality was the very antithesis of the absurd nastiness in the film.

For long moments I shut my eyes, refusing to watch. But then always I seemed forced, a *voyeur* in hell, to raise my head and look again. My arms began to go numb, an additional torture. The two figures on the lion-coloured bed, the luminously pale and the richly dark, embraced, re-embraced, oblivious of me, of all except their enactment.

What they did was in itself without obscenity, merely private, familiar; a biological ritual that takes place a hundred million times every night the world turns. But I tried to imagine what could make them bring themselves to do it in front of me; what incredible argument Conchis used; what they used to themselves. Lily now seemed to me as far ahead of me in time as she had at first started behind; somehow she had learnt to lie with her body as other people could lie only with their tongues. Perhaps she wanted some state of complete sexual emancipation, and the demonstration of it was more necessary to her as self-proof than its exhibition was to me as my already supererogatory 'disintoxication'.

Everything I had ever thought to understand about woman receded, interwove, flowed into mystery, into distorting shadows and currents, like objects sinking away, away, down through shafted depths of water.

The black arch of his long back, his loins joined to hers. White separated knees. That terrible movement, total possession between those acquiescent knees. Something carried me back to that night incident when she played Artemis; to the strange whiteness of Apollo's skin. The dull gold crown of leaves. An athletic body, living marble. And I knew then that Apollo and Anubis had been played by the same man. That night, when she had left … the next day's innocent virgin on the beach. The chapel. The black doll swung in my mind, the skull grinned malevolently. Artemis, Astarte, eternal liar.

He silently celebrated his orgasm.

The two bodies lay absolutely still on the altar of the bed. His turned-away head was hidden by hers, and I could see her hands caressing his shoulders, his back. I tried to wrench my aching arms free of the frame, to overturn it. But it had been lashed to the wall, to special staples; and the rings were bolted through the wood.

After an unendurable pause he rose from the bed, knelt and kissed her shoulder, almost formally, and then, gathering his cloak, calmly quit the stage for the shadows. She lay for a moment as he had left her, crushed back among the cushions. But then she raised herself on her left elbow and lay posed as she had at the beginning. Her stare fixed me. Without rancour and without regret; without triumph and without evil; as Desdemona once looked back on Venice.

On the incomprehension, the baffled rage of Venice. I had taken myself to be in some way the traitor Iago punished, in an unwritten sixth act. Chained in hell. But I was also Venice; the state left behind; the thing journeyed from.

The curtains were pulled slowly to. I was left where I had started, in darkness. Even the light behind was extinguished. I had a vertiginous moment in which I doubted whether it had happened. An induced hallucination? Had the trial happened? Had anything ever happened? But the savage pain in my arms told me that everything had happened.

And then, out of that pain, the sheer physical torture, I began to understand. I was Iago; but I was also crucified. The crucified Iago. Crucified by … the metamorphoses of Lily ran wildly through my brain, like maenads, hunting some blindness, some demon in me down. I suddenly knew her real name, behind the masks. Why they had chosen the Othello situation. Why Iago. Plunging through that.

I knew her real name. I did not forgive, if anything I felt more rage.

But I knew her real name.

A figure appeared in the door. It was Conchis. He came to where I hung from the frame, and stood in front of me. I closed my eyes. The pain in my arms drowned everything else.

I made a sort of groaning-growling noise through the gag. I did not know myself what it really meant to say: whether that I was in pain or that if I ever saw him again I would tear him limb from limb.

'I come to tell you that you are now elect.'

I shook my head violently from side to side.

'You have no choice.'

I still shook my head, but more wearily.

He stared at me, with those eyes that seemed older than one man's lifetime, and a little gleam of sympathy came into his expression, as if after all he might have put too much pressure on a very thin lever.

'Learn to smile, Nicholas. Learn to smile.'

It came to me that he meant something different by 'smile' than I did; that the irony, the humourlessness, the ruthlessness I had always noticed in his smiling was a quality he deliberately inserted; that for him the smile was something essentially cruel, because freedom is cruel, because the freedom that makes us at least partly responsible for what we are is cruel. So that the smile was not so much an *attitude* to be taken to life as the *nature* of the cruelty of life, a cruelty we cannot even choose to avoid, since it is human existence. He meant something far stranger by 'Learn to smile' than a Smilesian 'Grin and bear it'. If anything, it meant 'Learn to be cruel, learn to be dry, learn to survive.'

That we have no choice of play or role. It is always *Othello*. To be is, immutably, to be Iago.

He gave the smallest of bows, one full of irony, of the contempt implicit in incongruous courtesy, then went.

As soon as he had gone, Anton came in with Adam and the other blackshirts. They undid the handcuffs and got my arms down. A long black pole two of the blackshirts were carrying was unrolled and I saw a stretcher. They forced me to lie down on it and once again my wrists were handcuffed to the sides. I could neither fight them nor beg them to stop. So I lay passively, with my eyes shut, to avoid seeing them. I smelt ether, felt very faintly the jab of a needle; and this time I willed the oblivion to come fast.

63

I was staring at a ruined wall. There were a few last patches of plaster, but most of it was of rough stones. Many had fallen and lay among crumbling mortar against the foot of the wall. Then I heard, very faintly, the sound of goat-bells. For some time I lay there, still too drugged to make the effort of finding where the light I could see the wall by came from; and the sound of the bells, of wind, and of swifts screaming. I was conditioned to be a prisoner. Finally I moved my wrists. They were free. I turned and looked.

I could see chinks of light through the roof. There was a broken doorway fifteen feet away; outside, blinding sunlight. I was lying on an air-mattress with a rough brown blanket over me. I looked behind. There stood my suitcase, with a number of things on it: a Thermos, a brown-paper packet, cigarettes and matches, a black box like a jewellery case, an envelope.

I sat up and shook my head. Then I threw the blanket aside and went unevenly over the uneven floor to the door. I was at the top of a hill. Before me stretched a vast downward slope of ruins. Hundreds of stone houses, all ruined, most of them no more than grey heaps of rubble, decayed fragments of grey wall. Here and there were slightly less dilapidated dwellings; the remnants of second floors, windows that framed sky, black doorways. But what was so extraordinary was that this whole tilted city of the dead seemed to be floating in mid-air, a thousand feet above the sea that surrounded it. I looked at my watch. It was still going; just before five. I clambered on top of a wall and looked round. In the direction in which the late-afternoon sun lay I could see a mountainous mainland stretching far to the south and north. I seemed to be on top of some gigantic promontory, absolutely alone, the last man on earth, between sea and sky in some medieval Hiroshima. And for a moment I did not know if hours had passed, or whole civilizations.

A fierce wind blew out of the north.

I returned inside the room and carried the suitcase and other things out into the sunshine. First of all I looked at the envelope. It contained my passport, about ten pounds in Greek money, and a typewritten sheet of paper. Three sentences. 'There is a boat to Phraxos at 11.30 tonight. You are in the Old City at Monemvasia. The way down is to the south-east.' No date, no signature. I opened the Thermos: coffee. I poured myself a full capful and swallowed it; then another. The packet contained sandwiches. I began to eat, with the same feeling I had had that morning, of intense pleasure in the taste of coffee, the taste of bread, of cold lamb sprinkled with origan and lemon-juice.

But added to this now was a feeling, to which the great airy landscape contributed, of release, of having survived; a resilience. Above all there was the extraordinariness of the experience; its uniqueness conferred a uniqueness on me, and I had it like a great secret, a journey to Mars, a prize no one else had. Then too I seemed to see my own behaviour, I had woken up seeing it, in a better light; the trial and the disintoxication were evil fantasies sent to test my normality, and my normality had triumphed. *They* were the ones who had been finally humiliated – and I saw that perhaps that astounding last performance had been intended to be a mutual humiliation. While it happened it had seemed like a vicious twisting of the dagger in an already more than sufficient wound; but now I saw it might also be a kind of revenge given me for *their* spying, their voyeurism, on Alison and myself.

I had this: being obscurely victorious. Being free again, but in a new freedom ... purged in some way.

As if they had miscalculated.

It grew, this feeling, it became a joy to touch the warm rock on which I sat, to hear the *meltemi* blowing, to smell the Greek air again, to be alone on this peculiar upland, this lost Gibraltar, a place I had even meant to visit one day. Analysis, revenge, recording: all that would come later, as the explanations at the school, the decision to remain or not for another year, would have to be made later. The all-important was that I had survived, I *had* come through.

Later I realized that there was something artificial, unnatural, in this joy, this glossing over all the indignities, the exploited death of

Alison, the monstrous liberties taken with my liberty; and I suppose that it had all been induced under hypnosis by Conchis again. It would have been part of the comforts; like the coffee and the sandwiches.

I opened the black box. Inside, on a bed of green baize, lay a brand-new revolver, a Smith & Wesson. I picked it up and broke it. I looked at the bases of six bullets, little rounds of brass with lead-grey eyes. The invitation was clear. I shook one out. They were not blanks. I pointed the gun out to sea, to the north, and pulled the trigger. The crack made my ears ring and the huge brown and white swifts that slit their way across the blue sky above my head jinked wildly.

Conchis's last joke.

I climbed a hundred yards or so to the top of the hill. Not far to the north was a ruined curtain-wall, the last of some Venetian or Ottoman fortification. From it I could see ten or fifteen miles of coastline to the north. A long white beach, a village twelve miles away, one or two white scattered houses or chapels, and beyond them a massively rising mountain, which I knew must be Mount Parnon, visible on clear days from Bourani. Phraxos lay about thirty miles away over the sea to the north-east. I looked down. The plateau fell away in a sheer cliff seven or eight hundred feet down to a narrow strip of shingle; a jade-green ribbon where the angry sea touched land, and then white horses, deep blue. Standing on the old bastion, I fired the remaining five bullets out to sea. I aimed at nothing. It was a *feu de joie*, a refusal to die. When the fifth crack had sounded, I took the gun by the butt and sent it whirling out into the sky. It paraboled, poised, then fell slowly, slowly, down through the abyss of air; and by lying flat at the very brink I even saw it crash among the rocks at the sea's edge.

I set off. After a while I struck a better path, which twice passed doorways that led down into large rubble-choked cisterns. At the south side of the huge rock I saw, far below, an old walled town on a skirt of land that ran steeply from the cliff-bottom down to the sea. Many ruined houses, but also a few with roofs and eight, nine, ten, a covey of churches. The path wound through the ruins and then to a doorway. A long downward tunnel led to another doorway with a hurdle across it, which explained the absence of a goat-herd. There was evidently only one way up or down, even for goats. I climbed over the hurdle and emerged into the sunlight. A path with a centuries-old paving of slabs of grey-black basalt graphed down the cliff, finally curving towards the red-ochre roofs of the walled town.

I picked my way down through alleys between whitewashed houses. An old peasant-woman stood in her doorway with a bowl of vegetable parings she had been emptying for her chickens. I must have looked very strange, carrying a suitcase, unshaven, foreign.

'*Kal' espera.*'

'*Pois eisai?*' she wanted to know. '*Pou pas?*' The old Homeric questions of the Greek peasant: Who art thou? Where goest thou?

I said I was English, a member of the company who had been making the film, *epano*.

'What film up there?'

I waved, said it didn't matter, and ignoring her indignant queries, I came at last to a forlorn little main street, not six feet wide, the houses crammed along it, mostly shuttered, or empty; but over one I saw a sign and went in. An elderly man with a moustache, the keeper of the wineshop, came out of a dim corner.

Over the blue iron mug of retsina and the olives we shared I discovered all there was to discover. First of all, I had missed a day. The trial had not been that morning, but the day before; it was Monday, not Sunday. I had been drugged again for over twenty-four hours; and I wondered what else. What probing into the deepest recesses of my mind. No film company had been in Monemvasia; no large group of tourists; no foreigners since ten days ago ... a French professor and his wife. What did the professor look like? A very fat man, he spoke no Greek ... No, he had heard of no one going up there yesterday or today. Alas, no one came to see Monemvasia. Were there large cisterns with paintings on the walls up there? No, nothing like that. It was all ruins. Later, when I walked out of the old town gate and under the cliffs I saw two or three crumbling jetties where a boat could have slipped in and unloaded three or four men with a stretcher. They need not have passed the handful of houses that were still inhabited in the village; and they would have come by night.

There were old castles all over the Peloponnesus: Korone, Methone, Pylos, Koryphasion, Passava. They all had huge cisterns; could all be reached in a day from Monemvasia.

I went over the causeway through the gusty wind to the little mainland hamlet, which was where the steamer called. I had a bad meal in a taverna there, and a shave in the kitchen – yes, I was a tourist – and questioned the cook-waiter. He knew no more than the other man.

Pitching and rolling, the little steamer, made late by the *meltemi*, came at midnight; like a deep-sea monster, festooned with glaucous strings of pearly light. I and two other passengers were rowed out to her. I sat for a couple of hours in the deserted saloon, fighting off sea-sickness and the persistent attempts to start a conversation made by an Athenian greengrocer who had been to Monemvasia to buy tomatoes. He grumbled on and on about prices. Always in Greece conversation turns to money; *not* politics, or politics only because it is connected with money. In the end the seasickness wore off and I came to like the greengrocer. He and his mound of newspaper-wrapped parcels were referable and locatable; totally of the world into which I had returned; though for days I was to stare suspicously at every stranger who crossed my path.

When we came near the island I went out on deck. The black whale loomed out of the windy darkness. I could make out the cape of Bourani, though the house was invisible, and of course there were no lights. On the foredeck, where I was standing, there were a dozen or so slumped figures, poor peasants travelling steerage. The mystery of other human lives: I wondered how much Conchis's masque had cost; fifty times more, probably, than one of these men earned in a year's hard work. So had cost their lifetime.

De Deukans. Millet. Hoeing turnips.

Beside me was a family, a husband with his back turned, his head on a sack, two small boys sandwiched for warmth between him and his wife. A thin blanket lay over them. The wife had a white scarf tied in a medieval way, tight round her chin. Joseph and Mary; one of her hands rested on the shoulder of the child in front. I fumbled in my pocket; there were still seven or eight pounds left of the money that had been given me. I looked round, then swiftly stooped and put the little wad of notes in a fold of the blanket behind the woman's head; then furtively left, as if I had done something shameful.

At a quarter to three I was silently climbing the stairs in the masters' wing. My room was tidy, all in order. The only thing that had changed was that the piles of examination papers were no longer there. In their place were several letters.

The first one I opened I chose because I couldn't think who would be writing to me from Italy.

July 14th   *Monastery of Sacro Speco,*
                                              Near Subiaco

Dear Mr Urfe,

Your letter has been forwarded to me. I at first decided not to reply to it, but on reflection I think it is fairer to you if I write to say that I am not prepared to discuss the matter that you wish me to discuss. My decision on this is final.

I should greatly appreciate it if you would not renew your request in any way.

Yours sincerely,
JOHN LEVERRIER

The writing was impeccably neat and legible, though rather crabbed into the centre of the page; I saw – if it was not a last forgery – a neat, crabbed man behind it. Presumably on some sort of retreat, one of those desiccated young Catholics that used to mince about Oxford when I was an undergraduate, twittering about Monsignor Knox and Farm Street.

The next letter was from London, from someone who purported to be a headmistress, on nicely authentic headed notepaper.

Miss Julie Holmes

Miss Holmes was with us only for one year, in which she taught the classics and also some English and Scripture to our lower forms. She promised to develop into a good teacher, was most reliable and conscientious and also popular with her pupils.

I understood that she was embarking upon a stage career, but I am very pleased to hear that she is returning to teaching.

I should add that she was a very successful producer of our annual play, and also took a leading part in our 'Young Christians' school society.

I recommend Miss Holmes warmly.

Very funny.

Next I opened another envelope from London. Inside was my own letter to the Tavistock Repertory Company. Someone had done impatiently but exactly as I requested, and scrawled the name of June and Julie Holmes's agent across the bottom of the page in blue pencil.

Then there was a letter from Australia. In it was a printed black-edged card with a blank space for the sender's name to be written in; a rather pathetically childlike hand had done so.

> R.I.P.
>
> **Mrs Mary Kelly**
>
> thanks you for your kind letter
> of condolence in her recent
> tragic bereavement.

The last letter was from Ann Taylor: inside, a postcard and photographs.

> We found these. We thought you might like copies. I've sent the negatives to Mrs Kelly. I understand what you say in your letter, we must all feel to blame in different ways. The one thing I don't think Allie would want is that we take it hard, now that it won't do any good. I still can't believe it. I had to pack all her things and you can imagine. It seemed so unnecessary then, it made me cry again. Well, I suppose we must all get over it. I am going home next week, shall see Mrs K. at the earliest possible time. Yours,   ANN

Eight bad snaps. Five of them were of me or of views; only three showed Alison. One of her kneeling over the little girl with the boil, one of her standing at the Oedipus crossroads, one of her with the muleteer on Parnassus. She was closest to the camera in the one at the crossroads, and she had that direct, half-boyish grin that somehow always best revealed her honesty ... what had she called herself? Coarse; the candour of salt. I remembered how we had got in the car, how I had talked about my father, had even then only been able to talk to her like that because of *her* honesty; because I knew she was a mirror that did not lie; whose interest in me was real; whose love was real. That had been her supreme virtue: a constant reality.

I sat at my desk and stared at that face, at the strand of hair that blew across the side of the forehead, that one moment, the hair so, the wind so, still present and for ever gone.

Sadness swept back through me. I could not sleep. I put the letters and photographs in a drawer and went out again, along the coast. Far to the north, across the water, there was a scrub fire. A broken ruby-red line ate its way across a mountain; as a line of fire ate its way through me.

What was I after all? Near enough what Conchis had had me told: nothing but the net sum of countless wrong turnings. I dismissed most of the Freudian jargon of the trial; but all my life I had tried to turn life into fiction, to hold reality away; always I had acted as if a third person was watching and listening and giving me marks for good or bad behaviour – a god like a novelist, to whom I turned, like a character with the power to please, the sensitivity to feel slighted, the ability to adapt himself to whatever he believed the novelist-god wanted. This leechlike variation of the super-ego I had created myself, fostered myself, and because of it I had always been incapable of acting freely. It was not my defence; but my despot. And now I saw it, I saw it a death too late.

I sat by the shore and waited for the dawn to rise on the grey sea. Intolerably alone.

64

Whether it was in the nature of my nature, or in that of whatever Coué-method optimism Conchis had pumped into me during my last long sleep, I got progressively more morose as the day dawned. I was well aware that I had no evidence and no witnesses to present in support of the truth; and such a firm believer in logistics as Conchis would not have left his line of retreat unorganized. He must know that his immediate risk was that I should go to the police; in which case his move was obvious. I guessed that by now he and all the 'cast' had left Greece. There would be no one to question, except people like Hermes, who was probably even more innocent than I suspected; and Patarescu, who would admit nothing.

The only real witness was Demetriades. I could never force a confession out of him, but I remembered his sweet innocence at the beginning; and that there must have been a time, before I went to Bourani, when they had relied largely on him for information. As I knew from discussing students with him, he was not without a certain shrewdness of judgment, especially when it came to separating genuine hard workers from intelligent idlers. It enraged me to think what his more detailed report must have been on me. I wanted some sort of physical revenge on someone. I also wanted the whole school to know I was angry.

I didn't go to the first lesson, reserving my spectacular re-entry into school life till breakfast. When I appeared there was the sudden silence you get when you throw a stone into a pool of croaking frogs; an abrupt hush, then the gradual resumption of noise. Some of the boys were grinning. The other masters stared at me as if I had committed the final crime. I could see Demetriades on the far side of the room. I walked straight towards him, too quickly for him to act. He half rose, then evidently saw what was coming and, like a frightened Peter Lorre, promptly sat down again. I stood over him.

'Get up, damn you.'

He made a feeble attempt at a smile; shrugged at the boy next to him. I repeated my request, loudly, in Greek, and added a Greek jibe.

'Get up – brothel-louse.'

There was a total hush again. Demetriades went red and stared down at the table.

He had in front of him a plate of pappy bread and milk sprinkled with honey, a dish he always treated himself to at breakfast. I reached forward and flipped it back in his face. It ran down his shirt and his expensive suit. He jumped up, flicking down with his hands. As he looked up in a red rage, like a child, I hit him where I wanted, plug in his right eye. It was not Lonsdale, but it landed hard.

Everyone got to their feet. The prefects shouted for order. The gym master rushed behind me and seized my arm, but I snapped at him that it was all right, it was all over. Demetriades stood like a parody of Oedipus with his hands over his eyes. Then without warning he whirled forwards at me, kicking and clawing like an old woman. The gym master, who despised him, stepped past me and easily pinned his arms.

I turned and walked out. Demetriades started to shout petulant curses I didn't understand. A steward was standing in the door and I told him to bring coffee to my room. Then I sat there and waited.

Sure enough, as soon as second school began, I was summoned to the headmaster's office. Besides the old man there was the deputy headmaster, the senior housemaster and the gym master; the latter, I presumed, in case I should cut up rough again. The senior housemaster, Androutsos, spoke French fluently and he was evidently there to be the translator at this court martial.

As soon as I sat down I was handed a letter. I saw by the heading that it was from the School Board in Athens. It was in French officialese; dated two days before.

> The Board of Governors of the Lord Byron School having considered the report submitted by the headmaster has regretfully decided that the said Board must terminate the contract with you under clause 7 of the said contract: Unsatisfactory conduct as teacher.
>
> As per the said clause your salary will be paid until the end of September and your fare home will be paid.

There was to be no trying; only sentencing. I looked up at the four faces. If they showed anything it was embarrassment, and I could even detect a hint of regret on Androutsos's; but no sign of complicity.

I said, 'I didn't know the headmaster was in Mr Conchis's pay.'

Androutsos was obviously puzzled. '*A la solde de qui?*' He translated what I angrily repeated; but the headmaster too seemed nonplussed. He was in fact far too dignified a figurehead, more like an American college president than a real headmaster, to make it likely that he would connive in an unjust dismissal. Demetriades had deserved his black eye even more than I suspected. Demetriades, Conchis, some influential third person on the Board. A secret report ...

There was a swift conversation in Greek between the headmaster and his deputy. I heard the name Conchis twice, but I couldn't follow what they said. Androutsos was told to translate.

'The headmaster does not understand your remark.'

'No?'

I grimaced menacingly at the old man, but I was already more than half persuaded that his incomprehension was genuine.

At a sign from the vice-master Androutsos raised a sheet of paper and read from it. 'The following complaints were made against you. One: you have failed to enter the life of the school, absenting yourself almost every week-end during this last term.' I began to grin. 'Two: you have twice bribed prefects to take your supervision periods.' This was true, though the bribery had been no worse than a letting them off compositions they owed me. Demetriades had suggested it; and only he could have reported it. 'Three: you failed to mark your examination papers, a most serious scholastic duty. Four: you – '

But I had had enough of the farce. I stood up. The headmaster spoke; a pursed mouth in a grave old face.

'The headmaster also says,' translated Androutsos, 'that your insane assault on a colleague at breakfast this morning has done irreparable harm to the respect he has always entertained for the land of Byron and Shakespeare.'

'Jesus.' I laughed out loud, then I wagged my finger at Androutsos. The gym master got ready to spring at me. 'Now listen. Tell him this. I am going to Athens. I am going to the British Embassy, I am going to the Ministry of Education, I am going to the newspapers, I am going to make such trouble that ... '

I didn't finish. I raked them with a broadside of contempt, and walked out.

I was not allowed to get very far with my packing, back in my room. Not five minutes afterwards there was a knock on the door. I smiled grimly, and opened it violently. But the member of the tribunal I had least expected was standing there: the deputy headmaster.

His name was Mavromichalis. He ran the school administratively, and was the disciplinary dean also; a kind of camp adjutant, a lean, tense, balding man in his late forties, withdrawn even with other Greeks. I had had very little to do with him. The senior teacher of demotic, he was, in the historical tradition of his kind, a fanatical lover of his own country. He had run a famous underground news-sheet in Athens during the Occupation; and the classical pseudonym he had used then, *o Bouplix*, the oxgoad, had stuck. Though he always deferred to the headmaster in public, in many ways it was his spirit that most informed the school; he hated the Byzantine accidie that lingers in the Greek soul far more intensely than any foreigner could.

He stood there, closely watching me, and I stood in the door, sur-prised out of my anger by something in his eyes. He managed to suggest that if matters had allowed he might have been smiling. He spoke quietly.

'*Je veux vous parler, Monsieur Urfe.*'

I had another surprise then, because he had never spoken to me before in anything but Greek; I had always assumed that he knew no other language. I let him come in. He glanced quickly down at the suitcases open on my bed, then invited me to sit behind the desk. He took a seat himself by the window and folded his arms: shrewd, in-cisive eyes. He very deliberately let the silence speak for him. I knew then. For the headmaster, I was simply a bad teacher; for this man, something else besides.

I said coldly, '*Eh bien?*'

'I regret these circumstances.'

'You didn't come here to tell me that.'

He stared at me. 'Do you think our school is a good school?'

'My dear Mr Mavromichalis, if you imagine – '

He raised his hands sharply but pacifyingly. 'I am here simply as a colleague. My question is serious.'

His French was ponderous, rusty, but far from elementary.

'Colleague … or emissary?'

He lanced a look at me. The boys had a joke about him: how even the cicadas stopped talking when he passed.

'Please to answer my question. Is our school good?'

I shrugged impatiently. 'Academically. Yes. Obviously.'

He watched me a moment more, then came to the point. 'For our school's sake, I do not want scandals.'

I noted the implications of that first person singular.

'You should have thought of that before.'

Another silence. He said, 'We have in Greece an old folksong that says, He who steals for bread is innocent, He who steals for gold is guilty.' His eyes watched to see if I understood. 'If you wish to resign … I can assure you that *Monsieur le Directeur* will accept. The other letter will be forgotten.'

'Which *Monsieur le Directeur*?'

He smiled very faintly, but said nothing; and would, I knew, never say anything. In an odd way, perhaps because I was behind the desk, I felt like the tyrannical interrogator. He was the brave patriot. Finally, he looked out of the window and said, as if irrelevantly, 'We have an excellent science laboratory.'

I knew that; I knew the equipment in it had been given by an anonymous donor when the school was re-opened after the war and I knew the staff-room 'legend' was that the money had been wrung out of some rich collaborationist.

I said, 'I see.'

'I have come to invite you to resign.'

'As my predecessors did?'

He didn't answer. I shook my head.

He tacked nearer the truth. 'I do not know what has happened to you. I do not ask you to forgive that. I ask you to forgive this.' He gestured : the school.

'I hear you think I'm a bad teacher anyway.'

He said, 'We will give you a good *recommandation*.'

'That's not an answer.'

He shrugged. 'If you insist … '

'Am I so bad as that?'

'We have no place here for any but the best.'

Under his oxgoad eyes, I looked down. The suitcases waited on the bed. I wanted to get away, to Athens, anywhere, to non-identity and non-involvement. I knew I wasn't a good teacher. But I was too flayed, too stripped elsewhere, to admit it.

'You're asking too much.' He waited in silence, implacably. 'I'll keep quiet in Athens on one condition. That he meets me there.'

'*Pas possible.*'

Silence. I wondered how his monomaniacal sense of duty towards the school lived with whatever allegiance he owed Conchis. A hornet hovered threateningly in the window, then caroomed away;

as my anger retreated before my desire to have it all over and done with.

I said. 'Why you?'

He smiled then, a thin, small smile. '*Avant la guerre.*'

I knew he had not been teaching at the school; it must have been at Bourani. I looked down at the desk. 'I want to leave at once. Today.'

'That is understood. But no more scandals?' He meant, after that at breakfast.

'I'll see. If ... ' I gestured in my turn. 'Only because of this.'

'*Bien.*' He said it almost warmly, and came round the desk to take my hand; and even shook my shoulder, as Conchis had sometimes done, as if to assure me that he took my word.

Then, briskly and sparsely, he went.

And so I was expelled. As soon as he had gone, I felt angry again, angry that once again I had not used the cat. I did not mind leaving the school; to have dragged through another year, pretending Bourani did not exist, brewing sourly in the past ... it was unthinkable. But leaving the island, the light, the sea. I stared out over the olive-groves. It was suddenly a loss like that of a limb. It was not the meanness of making a scandal, it was the futility. Whatever happened, I was banned from ever living again on Phraxos.

After a while I forced myself to go on packing. The bursar sent a clerk up with my pay cheque and the address of the travel agency I should go to in Athens about my journey home. Just after noon I walked out of the school gate for the last time.

I went straight to Patarescu's house. A peasant-woman came to the door; the doctor had gone to Rhodes for a month. Then I went to the house on the hill. I knocked on the gate. No one answered; it was locked. Then I went back down through the village to the old harbour, to the taverna where I had met old Barba Dimitraki. Georgiou, as I hoped, knew of a room for me in a cottage near by. I sent a boy back to the school with a fish-trolley to get my bags; then ate some bread and olives.

At two, in the fierce afternoon sun, I started to toil up between the hedges of prickly pear towards the central ridge. I was carrying a hurricane lamp, a crowbar and a hacksaw. No scandal was one thing; but no investigation was another.

65

I came to Bourani about half past three. The gap beside and the top of the gate had been wired, while a new notice covered the *Salle d'attente* sign. It said in Greek, *Private property, entrance strictly forbidden*. It was still easy enough to climb over. But I had no sooner got inside than I heard a voice coming up through the trees from Moutsa. Hiding the tools and lamp behind a bush, I climbed back.

I went cautiously down the path, tense as a stalking cat, until I could see the beach. A caïque was moored at the far end. There were five or six people – not islanders, people in gay swimming-costumes. As I watched, two of the men picked up a girl, who screamed, and carried her down the shingle and dumped her into the sea. There was the blare of a battery wireless. I walked a few yards inside the fringe of trees, half expecting at any moment to recognize them. But the girl was small and dark, very Greek; two plump women; a man of thirty and two older men. I had never seen any of them before.

There was a sound behind me. A barefooted fisherman in ragged grey trousers, the owner of the caïque, came from the chapel. I asked him who the people were. They were from Athens, a Mr Sotiriades and his family, they came every summer to the island.

Did many Athenian people come to the bay in August? Many, very many, he said. He pointed along the beach: In two weeks, ten, fifteen caïques, more people than sea.

Bourani was pregnable: and I had my final reason to leave the island.

The house was shuttered and closed, just as I had last seen it. I made my way round over the gulley to the Earth. I admired once again the cunning way its trapdoor was concealed, then raised it. The dark shaft stared up. I climbed down with the lamp and lit it; climbed back and got the tools. I had to saw halfway through the hasp of the padlock on the first side-room; then, under pressure from the crow-bar, it snapped. I picked up the lamp, shot back the bolt, pulled open the massive door, and went in.

I found myself in the north-west corner of a rectangular chamber. Facing me I could see two embrasures that had evidently been filled in, though little ventilator grilles showed they had some access to the air. Along the north wall opposite, a long built-in wardrobe. By the east wall, two beds, a double and a single. Tables and chairs. Three armchairs. The floor had some kind of rough folkweave carpeting on top of felt, and three of the walls had been whitewashed, so that the place, though windowless, was less gloomy than the central room. On the west wall, above the bed, was a huge mural of Tyrolean peasants dancing; *Lederhosen* and a girl whose flying skirt showed her legs above her flower-clocked stockings. The colours were still good; or re-touched.

There were a dozen or so changes of costume for Lily in the ward-robe, and at least eight of them were duplicated for her sister; several I had not seen. In a set of drawers there were period gloves, hand-bags, stockings, hats; even an antiquated linen swimming-costume with a lunatic ribboned Tam o'Shanter cap to match.

Blankets were piled on each mattress. I smelt one of the pillows, but couldn't detect Lily's characteristic scent. Over a table between the old gunslits, there was a bookshelf. I pulled down one of the books. *The Perfect Hostess. A Little Symposium on the Principles and Laws of Etiquette as Observed and Practised in the Best Society. London. 1901.* There were a dozen or so Edwardian novels. Someone had pencilled notes on the flyleaves. *Good dialogue,* or *Useful clichés at 98 and 164. See scene at 203,* said one. *'Are you asking me to commit oscula-tion?' laughed the ever-playful Fanny.*

A chest, but it was empty. In fact the whole room was disappoint-ingly empty of anything personal. I went back and sawed through the other padlock. The room behind was similarly furnished; another mural, this time of snow-covered mountains. In a wardrobe there I found the horn that the 'Apollo' figure had called with; the Robert Foulkes costume; a chef's white overall and drum hat; a Lapp smock; and the entire uniform of a First World War captain with Rifle Brigade badges.

At last I returned to the shelf of books. In irritation I pulled down the whole lot and out of one of the books, an old bound copy of *Punch 1914* (in which various pictures had been ticked in red crayon), spilled a little folded pile of what I thought at first were letters. But they were not. They were pieces of roneographed paper. They had apparently conveyed some kind of orders. None was dated.

1. *The Drowned Italian Airman*
   We have decided to omit this episode.

2. *Norway*
   We have decided to omit the visits with this episode.

3. *Hirondelle*
   Treat with caution. Still tender.

4. *If subject discovers Earth*
   Please be sure you know the new procedure for this even-tuality by next week-end. Lily considers the subject likely to force such a situation on us.

I noted that 'Lily'.

5. *Hirondelle*
   Avoid all mention with the subject from now on.

6. *Final Phase*
   Termination by end of July for all except nucleus.

7. *State of subject*
   Maurice considers that the subject has now reached the malleable stage. Remember that for the subject any play is now better than no play. Change modes, intensify with-drawals.

The eighth sheet was a typewritten copy of the *Tempest* passage Lily had recited to me. Finally, on different paper, a scrawled message:

Tell Bo not to forget the unmentionables and the books. Oh and tissues, please.

Each of these pieces of paper had writing on the back, obviously (or obviously intended to look like) Lily's rough drafts. There were crossings-out, revisions. They all seemed to be in her hand.

1. What is it?
    If you were told its name
    You would not understand.
    Why is it?
    If you were told its reasons
    You would not understand.
    Is it?
    You are not even sure of that,
    Poor footsteps in an empty room.

2. Love is the course of the experiment.
    Is to the limit of imagination.
    Love is your manhood in my orchards.
    Love is your dark face reading this.
    Your dark, your gentle face and hands.
    Did Desdemona

This was evidently unfinished.

3. *The Choice*
    Spare him till he dies.
    Torment him till he lives.

4. ominus dominus
    Nicholas
    homullus est
    ridiculus

    igitur meus
    parvus pediculus
    multo vult dare
    sine morari

    in culus illius
    ridiculus
    Nicholas
    colossicus ciculus

5. Baron von Masoch sat on a pin;
    Then sat again, to push it in.

'How exquisite,' cried Plato,
'The idea of a baked potato.'
But exquisiter to some
Is potato in the tum.

'My dear, you must often be frightened,'
Said a friend to Madame de Sade.
'Oh not exactly frightened,
But just a little bit scarred.'

Give me my cardigan,
Let me think hardigan.

That must have been some game between the sisters; alternate different handwritings.

6. Mystery enough at noon.
The blinding unfrequented paths
Above the too frequented sea
Hold labyrinth and mask enough.
No need to twist beneath the moon.
Here on the rising secret cliff
In this white fury of the light
Is mystery enough at noon.

The last three sheets had a fairy story on them.

THE PRINCE AND THE MAGICIAN

Once upon a time there was a young prince, who believed in all things but three. He did not believe in princesses, he did not believe in islands, he did not believe in God. His father, the king, told him that such things did not exist. As there were no princesses or islands in his father's domaines, and no sign of God, the young prince believed his father.

But then, one day, the prince ran away from his palace. He came to the next land. There, to his astonishment, from every coast he saw islands, and on these islands, strange and troubling creatures whom he dared not name. As he was searching for a boat, a man in full evening dress approached him along the shore.

'Are those real islands?' asked the young prince.

'Of course they are real islands,' said the man in evening dress.

'And those strange and troubling creatures?'

'They are all genuine and authentic princesses.'

'Then God also must exist!' cried the prince.

'I am God,' replied the man in full evening dress, with a bow.

The young prince returned home as quickly as he could.

'So you are back,' said his father, the king.

'I have seen islands, I have seen princesses, I have seen God,' said the prince reproachfully.

The king was unmoved.

'Neither real islands, nor real princesses, nor a real God, exist.'

'I saw them!'

'Tell me how God was dressed.'

'God was in full evening dress.'

'Were the sleeves of his coat rolled back?'

The prince remembered that they had been. The king smiled.

'That is the uniform of a magician. You have been deceived.'

At this, the prince returned to the next land, and went to the same shore, where once again he came upon the man in full evening dress.

'My father the king has told me who you are,' said the young prince indignantly. 'You deceived me last time, but not again. Now I know that those are not real islands and real princesses, because you are a magician.'

The man on the shore smiled.

'It is you who are deceived, my boy. In your father's kingdom there are many islands and many princesses. But you are under your father's spell, so you cannot see them.'

The prince returned pensively home. When he saw his father, he looked him in the eyes.

'Father, is it true that you are not a real king, but only a magician?'

The king smiled, and rolled back his sleeves.

'Yes, my son, I am only a magician.'

'Then the man on the shore was God.'

'The man on the shore was another magician.'

'I must know the real truth, the truth beyond magic.'

'There is no truth beyond magic,' said the king.

The prince was full of sadness.

He said, 'I will kill myself.'

The king by magic caused death to appear. Death stood in the door and beckoned to the prince. The prince shuddered. He remembered the beautiful but unreal islands and the unreal but beautiful princesses.

'Very well,' he said. 'I can bear it.'

'You see, my son,' said the king, 'you too now begin to be a magician.'

The 'orders' looked suspiciously as if they had all been typed out at the same time, just as the poems were all scribbled in the same pencil with the same pressure, as if they had been written *ad hoc* in one sitting. Nor did I believe such 'orders' could ever have been sent. I puzzled over Hirondelle ... *still tender*; must not be mentioned to me; some surprise, some episode I was never shown. The poems and the little epistemological fable were easier to understand; had clear applications. Obviously they could not have been sure that I would break into the Earth. Perhaps there were such clues littered all over the place, it being accepted on their side that I would find only a very small proportion of them. But what I did find would come to me in a different way from the blatantly planted clue – with more conviction; and yet might be as misleading as all the other clues I had been given.

I was wasting my time at Bourani; all I might appear to find there would only confuse confusion.

That was the meaning of the fable. By searching so fanatically I was making a detective story out of the summer's events, and to view life as a detective story, as something that could be deduced, hunted, and arrested, was no more realistic (let alone poetic) than to view the detective story as the most important literary genre, instead of what it really was, one of the least.

On Moutsa, at that first sight of the party, I had felt, in spite of everything, a shock of excitement; and an equally revealing disappointment when I realized they were nothing: mere tourists. Perhaps that was my deepest resentment of all against Conchis. *Not that he had done what he did, but that he had stopped doing it.*

I had intended to break into the house as well, to wreak some kind of revenge there. But suddenly that seemed petty and mean; and insufficient; because it was not that I still did not intend to have my revenge. Only now I saw quite clearly how I would have it. The school could dismiss me. But nothing could prevent my coming to the island the following summer. And then we would see who had the last laugh.

I got up and left the Earth, and went to the house; walked one last time under the colonnade. The chairs were gone, even the bell. In the vegetable-garden the cucumber plants lay yellowed and dying; the Priapus had been removed.

I was full of a multiple sadness, for the past, for the present, for the future. Even then I was not waiting only to say, to feel, goodbye, but fractionally in the hope that a figure might appear. I did not know what I would have done if one had, any more than I knew what I was going to do when I got to Athens. If I wanted to live in England; what I wanted to do. I was in the same state as when I came down from Oxford. I only knew what I didn't want to do; and all I had gained, in the matter of choosing a career, was a violent determination never again to be a teacher of any sort. I'd empty dustbins rather than that.

An emotional desert lay in front of me, an inability ever to fall in love again that was compounded of the virtual death of Lily and the actual death of Alison. I was disintoxicated of Lily; but my disappointment at failing to match her had become in part a disappointment at my own character; an unwanted yet inevitable feeling that she would vitiate or haunt any relationship I might form with another woman; stand as a ghost behind every lack of taste, every stupidity. Only Alison could have exorcized her. I remembered those moments of relief at Monemvasia and on the ship coming back to Phraxos, moments when the most ordinary things seemed beautiful and lovable – possessors of a magnificent quotidianeity. I could have found that in Alison. Her special genius, or uniqueness, was her normality, her reality, her predictability; her crystal core of non-betrayal; her attachment to all that Lily was not.

I was marooned; wingless and leaden, as if I had been momentarily surrounded, then abandoned, by a flock of strange winged creatures; emancipated, mysterious, departing, as singing birds pass on overhead; leaving a silence spent with voices.

Only too ordinary voices, screams, came faintly up from the bay. More horseplay. The present eroded the past. The sun slanted through the pines, and I walked one last time to the statue.

Poseidon, perfect majesty because perfect control, perfect health, perfect adjustment, stood flexed to his divine sea; Greece the eternal, the never-fathomed, the bravest because the clearest, the mystery-at-noon land. Perhaps this statue was the centre of Bourani, its *omphalos* – not the house or the Earth or Conchis or Lily, but this still figure, benign, all-powerful, yet unable to intervene or speak; able simply to be and to constitute.

66

The first thing I did when I arrived at the Grande Bretagne in Athens was to telephone the airport. I was put through to the right desk. A man answered.

He didn't know the name. I spelt it. Then he wanted to know mine. He said, 'Please wait a minute.'

He seemed to have meant it literally; but finally I heard a female voice, a Greek-American accent. It sounded like the girl who had been on duty when I met Alison there.

'Who is that speaking, please?'

'Just a friend of hers.'

'You live here?'

'Yes.'

A moment's silence. I knew then. For hours I had nursed the feverish tiny hope. I stared down at the tired green carpet.

'Didn't you know?'

'Know what?'

'She's dead.'

'Dead?'

My voice must have sounded strangely unsurprised.

'A month ago. In London. I thought everyone knew. She took an overd –'

I put the receiver down. I lay back on the bed and stared at the ceiling. It was a long time before I found the will to go down and start drinking.

The next morning I went to the British Council. I told the man who looked after me that I had resigned for 'personal reasons', but I managed to suggest, without breaking my half-promise to Mavro-michalis, that the Council had no business sending people to such isolated posts. He jumped quickly towards the wrong conclusions.

I said, 'I didn't chase the boys. That's not it.'

'My dear fellow, heaven forbid, I didn't mean that.' He offered me a cigarette in dismay.

We talked vaguely about isolation, and the Aegean, and the ab-solute hell of having to teach the Embassy that the Council was not just another Chancellery annexe. I asked him casually at the end if he had heard of someone called Conchis. He hadn't.

'Who is he?'

'Oh just a man I met on the island. Seemed to have it in for the English.'

'It's becoming the new national hobby. Playing us off against the Yanks.' He closed the file smartly. 'Well, thanks awfully, Urfe. Most useful chat. Only sorry it's turned out like this. But don't worry. We'll bear everything you've said very much in mind.'

On the way to the door he must have felt even sorrier for me, because he invited me to dinner that evening.

But I was no sooner crossing the Kolonaki square outside the Council than I wondered why I had said yes. The stiflingly English atmosphere of the place had never seemed more alien; and yet to my horror I had detected myself trying to fit in acceptably, to conform, to get their approval. What had they said in the trial? *He seeks situa-tions in which he knows he will be forced to rebel.* I refused to be the vic-tim of a repetition compulsion; but if I refused that, I had to find courage to refuse all my social past, all my background. I had not only to be ready to empty dustbins rather than teach, but to empty them rather than ever have to live and work with the middle-class English again.

The people in the Council were the total foreigners; and the anonymous Greeks around me in the streets the familiar compatriots.

I had, when I checked in at the Grande Bretagne, asked whether there had been two English twins, fair-haired, early twenties ... recently staying at the hotel. But the reception clerk was sure there had not; I hadn't expected there to be, and I didn't insist.

When I left the British Council, I went to the Ministry of the Interior. On the pretext that I was writing a travel-book I got to the department where the war crimes records were filed; and within fifteen minutes I had in my hands a copy in English of the report the real Anton had written. I sat down and read it; it was all, in every but very minor detail, as Conchis had said.

I asked the official who had helped me if Conchis was still alive. He flicked through the file from which he had taken the report. There was nothing there except the address on Phraxos. He did not know. He had never heard of Conchis, he was new in this department.

I made a third call then, this time on the French embassy. The girl who dealt with me managed finally to lure the cultural attaché down from his office. I explained who I was, that I was very anxious to read this distinguished French psychologist on art as institutionalized illusion ... the idea of that seemed to amuse him, but I was in trouble as soon as I mentioned the Sorbonne. He peremptorily regretted that there must be some mistake: there was no medical faculty at the Sorbonne. However, he led me to a shelf of reference books in the embassy library. A number of things were very soon established. Conchis had never been in any capacity at the Sorbonne (or at any other French university, for that matter), he was not registered as a doctor in France, he had never published anything in French. There was a Professor Maurice Henri de Conches-Vironvay of Toulouse, who had written a series of learned treatises on the diseases of the vine, but I refused to take him as a substitute. In the end I escaped feeling that I had at least done my bit for Anglo-

French understanding – not in any way impaired the happy Gallic belief that most English are both ignorant and mad.

I went back in the sweltering midday heat to the hotel. The reception clerk turned to give me my key; and with it came a letter. It had my name only, and was marked *Urgent*. I tore upon the envelope. Inside was a sheet of paper with a number and a name. *184 Syngrou*.

'Who brought this?'

'A boy. A messenger.'

'Where from?'

He opened his hands. He did not know.

I knew where Syngrou was: a wide boulevard that ran from Athens down to the Piraeus. I went straight out and jumped into a taxi. We swung past the three columns of the temple of Olympic Zeus and down towards the Piraeus, and in a minute the taxi drew up outside a house standing back in a fair-sized garden. The chipped enamel figures announced that it was number 184.

The garden was thoroughly disreputable, the windows boarded up. A lottery-ticket seller sitting on a chair under a pepper tree near by asked what I wanted, but I took no notice of him. I walked to the front door, then round the back. The house was a shell. There had been a fire, evidently some years before, and the flat roof had fallen in. I looked into a garden at the rear. It was as dry and unkempt and deserted as the front. The back door gaped open. There were signs, among the fallen rafters and charred walls, that tramps or Vlach gypsies had lived there; the trace of a more recent fire on an old hearth. I waited for a minute, but I somehow sensed that there was nothing to find. It was a false trail.

I returned to the waiting yellow taxi. The dust from the dry earth rose in little swirls in the day-breeze and powdered the already drab leaves of the thin oleanders. Traffic ran up and down Syngrou, the leaves of a palm tree by the gate rustled. The ticket-seller was talking to my driver. He turned as I came out.

'*Zitas kanenan?*' Looking for someone?

'Whose house is that?'

He was an unshaven man in a worn grey suit, a dirty white shirt without a tie; his rosary of amber patience-beads in his hands. He raised them, disclaiming knowledge.

'Now. I do not know. Nobody's.'

I looked at him from behind my dark glasses. Then said one word. 'Conchis?'

Immediately his face cleared, as if he understood all. 'Ah. I understand. You are looking for *o kyrios* Conchis?'

'Yeah.'

He flung open his hands. 'He is dead.'

'When?'

'Four, five years.' He held up four fingers; then cut his throat and said '*Kaput.*' I looked past him to where his long stick of tickets, propped up against the chair, flapped in the wind.

I smiled acidly at him, speaking in English. 'Where do you come from? The National Theatre?' But he shook his head, as if he didn't understand.

'A very rich man.' He looked down at the driver, as if he would understand, even if I didn't. 'He is buried in St George's. A fine cemetery.' And there was something so perfect in his typical Greek idler's smile, in the way he extended such unnecessary information, that I began almost to believe that he was what he seemed.

'Is that all?' I asked.

'*Ne, ne.* Go and see his grave. A beautiful grave.'

I got into the taxi. He rushed for his stick of tickets, and brandished them through the window.

'You will be lucky. The English are always lucky.' He picked one off, held it to me. And suddenly he knew English. 'Eh. Just one little ticket.'

I spoke sharply to the driver. He did a U-turn, but after fifty yards I stopped him outside a café. I beckoned to a waiter.

The house back there, did he know who it belonged to?

Yes. To a widow called Ralli, who lived in Corfu.

I looked through the rear window. The ticket-seller was walking quickly, much too quickly, in the opposite direction; and as I watched, he turned down a side-alley out of sight.

At four o'clock that afternoon, when it was cooler, I caught a bus out to the cemetery. It lay some miles outside Athens, on a wooded slope of Mount Aegaleos. When I asked the old man at the gate I half expected a blank look. But he went painfully inside his lodge, fingered through a large register, and told me I must go up the main alley; then fifth left. I walked past lines of toy Ionic temples and columned busts and fancy steles, a forest of Hellenic bad taste; but pleasantly green and shady.

Fifth left. And there, between two cypresses, shaded by a mournful aspidistra-like plant, lay a simple Pentelic marble slab with, underneath a cross, the words:

ΜΩΡΙΣ ΚΟΓΧΙΣ
1896–1949

Four years dead.

At the foot of the slab was a small green pot in which sat, rising from a cushion of inconspicuous white flowers, a white arum lily and a red rose. I knelt and took them out. The stems were recently cut, probably from only that morning; the water was clear and fresh. I understood; it was his way of telling me what I had already guessed, that detective work would lead me nowhere – to a false grave, to yet another joke, a smile fading into thin air.

I replaced the flowers. One of the humbler background sprigs fell and I picked it up and smelt it; a sweet, honey fragrance. Since there was a rose and a lily, perhaps it had some significance. I put it in my buttonhole, and forgot about it.

At the gate I asked the old man if he knew of any relatives of the deceased Maurice Conchis. He looked in his book again for me, but there was nothing. Did he know who had brought the flowers? No, many people brought flowers. The breeze raised the wispy hairs over his wrinkled forehead. He was an old, tired man.

The sky was very blue. A plane droned down to the airport on the other side of the Attic plain. Other visitors came, and the old man limped away.

The dinner that evening was dreadful, the epitome of English vacuity. Before I went, I had some idea that I might tell them a little about Bourani; I saw a spellbound dinner-table. But the idea did not survive the first five minutes of conversation. There were eight of us, five from the Council, an Embassy secretary, and a little middle-aged queer, a critic, who had come to do some lectures. There was a good deal of literary chit-chat. The queer waited like a small vulture for names to be produced.

'Has anyone read Henry Green's latest?' asked the Embassy man.
'Couldn't stand it.'
'Oh I rather enjoyed it.'
The queer touched his bow-tie. 'Of course you know what dear Henry said when he ... '

I looked round the other faces, after he had done this for the tenth time, hoping to see a flicker of fellow-feeling, someone else who wanted to shout at him that writing was about books, not the trivia of private lives. But they were all the same, each mind set in the same weird armour, like an archosaur's ruff, like a fringe of icicles. All I heard the whole evening was the tinkle of broken ice-needles as people tried timidly and vainly to reach through the stale fence of words, tinkle, tinkle, and then withdrew.

Nobody said what they really wanted, what they really thought. Nobody behaved with breadth, with warmth, with naturalness; and finally it became pathetic. I could see that my host and his wife had a genuine love of Greece, but it lay choked in their throats. The critic made a perceptive little disquisition on Leavis, and then ruined it by a cheap squirt of malice. We were all the same; I said hardly anything, but that made me no more innocent – or less conditioned. The solemn figures of the Old Country, the Queen, the Public School, Oxbridge, the Right Accent, People Like Us, stood around the table like secret police, ready to crush down in an instant on any attempt at an intelligent European humanity.

It was symptomatic that the ubiquitous person of speech was 'one' – it was one's view, one's friends, one's servants, one's favourite writer, one's travelling in Greece, until the terrible faceless Avenging God of the Bourgeois British, One, was standing like a soot-blackened obelisk over the whole evening.

I walked back to the hotel with the critic, thinking, in a kind of agonized panic, of the light-filled solitudes of Phraxos; of the losses I had suffered.

'Dreadful bores, these Council people,' he said. 'But one has to live.' He didn't come in. He said he would stroll up to the Acropolis. But he strolled towards Zappeion, a park where the more desperate of the starving village boys who flock to Athens sell their thin bodies for the price of a meal.

I went to Zonar's in Panepistemiou and sat at the bar and had a large brandy. I felt upset, profoundly unable to face the return to England. I was in exile, and for ever, whether I lived there or not. The fact of exile I could stand; but the loneliness of exile was intolerable.

It was about half past twelve when I got back to my room. There was the usual hot airlessness of nocturnal Athens in summer. I had just stripped off my clothes and turned on the shower when the telephone rang by the bed. I went naked to it. I had a grim idea that it would be the critic, unsuccessful at Zappeion and now looking for a target for his endless Christian names.

'Hallo.'

'Meester Ouf.' It was the night porter. 'There is telephone for you.'

There was a clicketing.

'Hallo?'

'Oh. Is that Mr Urfe?' It was a man's voice I didn't recognize. Greek, but with a good accent.

'Speaking. Who are you?'

'Would you look out of your window, please?'

Click. Silence. I rattled the hook down, with no result. The man had hung up. I snatched my dressing-gown off the bed, switched out the light, and raced to the window.

My third-floor room looked out on a side street.

There was a yellow taxi parked on the opposite side with its back to me, a little down the hill. That was normal. Taxis for the hotel waited there. A man in a white shirt appeared and walked quickly up the far side of the street, past the taxi. He crossed the road just below me. There was nothing strange about him. Deserted pavements, street lights, closed shops, and darkened offices, the one taxi. The man disappeared. Only then was there a movement.

Directly opposite and beneath my window was a street-light fixed on the wall over the entrance to an arcade of shops. Because of the angle I could not see to the back of the arcade.

A girl came out.

The taxi-engine broke into life.

She knew where I was. She came out to the edge of the pavement, small, unchanged yet changed, and stared straight up at my window. The light shone down on her brown arms, but her face was in shadow. A black dress, black shoes, a small black evening handbag in her left hand. She came forward from the shadows as a prostitute might have done; as Robert Foulkes had done. No expression, simply the stare up and across at me. No duration. It was all over in fifteen seconds. The taxi suddenly reversed up the road to in front of her. Someone opened a door, and she got quickly in. The taxi jerked off very fast. Its wheels squealed scaldingly at the end of the street.

A crystal lay shattered.

And all betrayed.

67

At the last moment I had angrily cried her name. I thought at first that they had found some fantastic double; but no one could have imitated that walk. The way of standing.

I leapt back to the phone and got the night porter.

'That call – can you trace it?' He didn't understand 'trace'. 'Do you know where it came from?'

No, he didn't know.

Had anyone strange been in the hotel lobby during the last hour? Anyone waiting for some time?

No, Meester Ouf, nobody.

I turned off the shower, tore back into my clothes and went out into Constitution Square. I went round all the cafés, peered into all the taxis, went back to Zonar's, to Tom's, to Zaporiti's, to all the fashionable places in the area; unable to think, unable to do anything but say her name and crush it savagely between my teeth.

Alison. Alison. Alison.

I understood, how I understood. Once I had accepted, and I had to accept, the first incredible fact: that she must have agreed to join them. But how could she? And why? Again and again: why.

I went back to the hotel.

Conchis would have discovered about the quarrel, perhaps even overheard it; if he used cameras, he could use microphones and tape-recorders. Approached her during the night, or early the next morning ... those messages in the Earth: *Hirondelle*. The people in the Piraeus hotel, who had watched me try to persuade her to let me back into the room. As soon I mentioned her name, Conchis must have pricked up his ears; as soon as he knew she was coming to Athens, envisaged new complications in his plans. He would have had us followed from the moment we met; then persuaded her, all his charm, perhaps half deceiving her to begin with ... I had a strange moment of non-sexual jealousy, a vision of his telling her the truth: I wish to give this selfish young man of yours a lesson he will never forget. I remembered old spats with Alison over something not entirely unconnected: various contemporary writers and painters. Pointing out their faults had always pleased me more than hearing her fall for their virtues; even there I had used to feel slighted personally ... as she had been shrewd enough to tell me, often enough.

Or had she always been working for him? Hadn't he almost forced me to meet her by cancelling that half-term week-end? Even offered me the village house, if I wanted to bring her to the island? But I remembered something 'June' had said on that last night – how they improvized, how the 'rat' was granted parity with the experimenter in constructing the maze. I could believe that: so they must somehow, after her screaming at the Piraeus hotel, have found a way to buy Alison with their sick logic, their madness, their lies, their money ... perhaps told her the great secret I was not allowed to know: why they had chosen me in the first place. I also remembered all the lies I had told them about Alison, over matters on which they must have had full knowledge. I growled out loud at the recall.

Then too, on reflection, it had always been odd how little use had been made of 'June'. There were all her costumes in the Earth. A much fuller role must have been planned for her before Alison's unexpected 'entry'. That very first face-to-face – mouth-to-mouth – meeting with her, with its implicit sneer at my inconstancy, that repeated nonsense about the *Three Hearts* story – they showed how things might have gone. Then the Sunday, on the beach, that flaunting of her bare body ... perhaps Conchis had not been sure of Alison so soon after the first approach, other contingencies had to be allowed for. Then Alison must have been won, and 'June' withdrew from the action. That was also why Lily's character and part had changed and why she had to take on – and so rapidly – the Circe role.

The sedan-coffin. It had not been empty; they would have wanted her to witness the success of their method. I writhed mentally under the mercilessness of it, the endless exposure. The trial: my 'preying on young women' – she must also have put them up to that. And the suicidal mood she had been in before I left London. All their knowledge of my past.

I was mad with anger. I thought of that genuine and atrocious wave of sadness I had felt when the news about Alison came. All the time she would have been in Athens; perhaps in the house in the village; or over at Bourani. Watching me, even. Playing an invisible Maria to Lily's Olivia and my Malvolio – always these echoes of Shakespearean situations.

I walked up and down my room, imagining scenes where I had Alison at my mercy. Beating her black and blue, making her weep with remorse.

And then again, it all went back to Conchis, to the mystery of his power, his ability to mould and wield girls as intelligent as Lily; as independent as Alison. As if he had some secret that he revealed to them, that put them under his orders; and once again I was the man in the dark, the excluded, the eternal butt.

Not a Hamlet mourning Ophelia. But Malvolio.

I couldn't sleep, and I felt rather like going down to Ellenikon and wringing the neck of the girl at the airline counter. Both the man who had first answered and the girl herself had, I saw now, been a little too anxious to establish who I was; they must have been persuaded, perhaps by Alison herself, to co-operate. But I knew I would get nowhere there. Very probably they would produce the same forged cuttings.

Meanwhile, I had to do something. I went down to the hotel foyer and found the night porter.

'I want a line to London. This number.' I wrote it down. A few minutes later he pointed to a box.

I stood listening to the phone burr-burr in my old flat in Russell Square. It went on a long time. At last it was picked up.

'For goodness' sake ... who's that?'

The operator said. 'I have a long-distance call for you from Athens.'

'From where!'

I said, 'Okay, operator. Hallo?'

'Who *is* that?'

She sounded a nice girl, but she was half asleep. Though the call cost me four pounds, it was worth it. I discovered that Ann Taylor *had* gone back to Australia, but six weeks before. No one had killed herself. A girl the girl on the other end didn't know, but 'I think she's a friend of Ann's', had taken over the flat; she hadn't seen her 'for weeks'. Yes, she had blonde hair; actually she had only seen her twice; yes, she thought she *was* Australian. But who on earth ...

Back in my room I remembered the flower in the buttonhole of the coat I had worn that afternoon. It was very wilted, but I took it out and stuck it in a glass of water.

I woke up late, having finally slept sounder than I expected. I lay in bed for a while, listening to the street-noises down below, thinking about Alison. I tried to recall exactly what her expression had been, whether there was any humour, any sympathy, an indication of anything, good or bad, in her small standing there. I could understand the timing of her resurrection. As soon as I got back to London I should have found out; so it had to be in Athens.

And now I was to hunt for her.

I wanted to see her, I knew I wanted to see her desperately, to dig or beat the truth out of her, to let her know how vile her betrayal was. To let her know that even if she crawled round the equator on her knees I could never forgive her. That I was finished with her. Disgusted by her. As disintoxicated of her as I was of Lily. I thought, Christ, if I could only lay my hands on her. But the one thing I would not do was hunt for her.

I only had to wait. They would bring her to me now. And this time I would use the cat.

I went down to a noon breakfast; and the first thing I discovered was that I did not have to wait. For there was another letter by hand for me. This time it contained just one word: *London*. I remembered that order in the Earth: *Termination by July for all except nucleus*. Nucleus, Ashtaroth the Unseen, was Alison.

I went to the travel agency and got a seat on the evening plane; and seeing a map of Italy on the wall, as I stood waiting for the ticket to be made out, I discovered where Subiaco was; and decided to take a gamble. The marionette would make the manipulators of strings wait a day, for a change.

When I came out I went into the biggest bookshop in Athens, on the corner of Stadiou, and asked for a book on the identification of flowers. My belated attempt at resuscitation had not been successful, and I had had to throw the buttonhole away. The assistant had nothing in English, but there was a good French flora, she said, which gave the names in several languages. I pretended to be impressed by the pictures, then turned to the index; to Alyssum, p.69.

And there it was, facing page 69: thin green leaves, small white flowers, *Alysson maritime ... parfum de miel ...* from the Greek *a* (without), *lyssa* (madness). Called this in Italian, this in German.

In English: *Sweet Alison*.

3

*Le triomphe de la philosophie serait de jeter du
jour sur l'obscurité des voies dont la providence se
sert pour parvenir aux fins qu'elle se propose sur
l'homme, et de tracer d'après cela quelque plan de
conduite qui pût faire connaître à ce malheureux
individu bipède, perpétuellement ballotté par les
caprices de cet être qui dit-on le dirige aussi
despotiquement, la manière dont il faut qu'il
interprète les décrets de cette providence sur lui.*

De Sade, *Les Infortunes de la Vertu*

68

Rome.

In my mind Greece lay weeks, not the real hours, behind. The sun shone as certainly, the people were far more elegant, the architecture and the art much richer, but it was as if the Italians, like their Roman ancestors, wore a great mask of luxury, a cosmetic of the over-indulged senses, between the light, the truth, and their real selves. I couldn't stand the loss of the beautiful nakedness, the humanity of Greece, and so I couldn't stand the sight of the opulent, animal Romans; as one sometimes cannot stand one's own face in a mirror.

Early the morning after my arrival I caught a local train out towards Tivoli and the Alban hills. After a long bus-ride I had lunch at Subiaco and then walked up a road above a green chasm. A lane branched off into a deserted glen. I could hear the sound of running water far below, the singing of birds. The road came to an end, and a path led up through a cool grove of ilex, and then tapered out into a narrow flight of steps that twisted up round a wall of rock. The monastery came into sight, clinging like an Orthodox Greek monas-tery, like a martin's nest, to the cliff. A Gothic loggia looked out prettily over the green ravine, over a little apron of cultivated terraces falling below. Fine frescoes on the inner wall: coolness, silence.

There was an old monk in a black habit sitting behind the door through to an inner gallery. I asked if I could see John Leverrier. I said, an Englishman, on a retreat. Luckily I had his letter ready to show. The old man carefully deciphered the signature, then – to my surprise, I had decided I was on a wild-goose chase – nodded and silently disappeared down into some lower level of the monastery. I went on into a hall. A series of macabre murals; death pricking a young falconer with his longsword; a medieval strip-cartoon of a girl, first titivating herself in front of a glass, then fresh in her coffin, then with the bones beginning to erupt through the skin; then as a skeleton. There was the sound of someone laughing, an old monk with an amused face scolding a younger one in French as they passed through the hall behind me. '*Oh, si tu penses que le football est un digne sujet de méditation* ... '

Then another monk appeared; and I knew, with shock, that this was Leverrier.

He was tall, very close-cut hair, with a thin-cheeked brown face, and glasses with 'standard' National Health frames; unmistakably English. He made a little gesture, asking if it was me who had asked for him.

'I'm Nicholas Urfe. From Phraxos.'

He managed to look amazed, shy, and annoyed, all at the same time. After a long moment's hesitation, he held out his hand. It seemed dry and cold; mine was stickily hot from the walk. He was a good four inches taller than I am, and as many years older, and spoke with a trace of the incisiveness that young dons sometimes affect.

'You've come all this way?'

'It was easy to stop off at Rome.'

'I thought I'd made it clear that – '

'Yes, you did, but ... '

We both smiled bleakly at the broken-ended sentences. He looked me in the eyes, affirming decision.

'I'm afraid your visit must still be considered in vain.'

'I honestly had no idea that you were ... ' I waved vaguely at his habit. 'I thought you signed your letters ... '

'Yours in Christ?' He smiled thinly. 'I am afraid that even here we are susceptible to the forces of anti-pretension.'

He looked down, and we stood awkwardly. He came, as if impatient with our awkwardness, to a kinder decision; some mollification.

'Well. Now you are here – let me show you round.'

I wanted to say that I hadn't come as a tourist, but he was already leading the way through to an inner courtyard. I was shown the traditional ravens and crows, the Holy Bramble, which put forth roses when Saint Benedict rolled on it – as always on such occasions the holiness of self-mortification paled in my too literal mind beside the vision of a naked man pounding over the hard earth and taking a long jump into a blackberry bush ... and I found the Peruginos easier to feel reverence for.

I discovered absolutely nothing about the summer of 1951, though

I discovered a little more about Leverrier. He was at Sacro Speco for only a few weeks, having just finished his novitiate at some monastery in Switzerland. He had been to Cambridge and read history, he spoke fluent Italian, he was 'rather unjustifiably believed to be' an authority on the pre-Reformation monastic orders in England, which was why he was at Sacro Speco – to consult sources in the famous library; and he had not been back to Greece since he left it. He remained very much an English intellectual, rather self-conscious, aware that he must look as if he were playing at being a monk, dressing up, and even a little, complicatedly, vain about it.

Finally he took me down some steps and out into the open air below the monastery. I perfunctorily admired the vegetable and vineyard terraces. He led the way to a wooden seat under a fig tree a little farther on. We sat. He did not look at me.

'This is very unsatisfactory for you. But I warned you.'

'It's a relief to meet a fellow-victim. Even if he is mute.'

He stared out across a box-bordered parterre into the blue heat of the sun-baked ravine. I could hear water rushing down in the depths.

'A fellow. Not a victim.'

'I simply wanted to compare notes.'

He paused, then said, 'The essence of ... his ... system is surely that you learn not to "compare notes".' He made the phrase sound cheap. His wanting me to go was all but spoken. I stole a look at him.

'Would you be here now if ... '

'A lift on the road one had already long been travelling explains when. Not why.'

'Our experiences must have varied very widely.'

'Why should they be similar? Are you a Catholic?' I shook my head. 'A Christian even?' I shook my head again. He shrugged. He had dark shadows under his eyes, as if he was tired.

'But I do believe in ... charity?'

'My dear man, you don't want charity from me. You want confessions I am not prepared to make. In my view I am being charitable in not making them. In my position you would understand.' He added, 'And at my remove I trust you will understand.'

His voice was set cold; there was a silence.

He said, 'I'm sorry. You force me to be more brusque than I wish.'

'I'd better go.'

He seized his chance, and stood up.

'I intend nothing personal.'

'Of course.'

'Let me see you to the gate.'

We walked back; into the whitewashed door carved through the rock, up past doors that were like prison cells, and out into the hall with the death murals, the grim mirror of eternity.

He said, 'I meant to ask you about the school. There was a boy called Aphendakis, very promising. I coached him.'

We lingered a little in the loggia, beside the Peruginos, exchanging sentences about the school. I could see that he was not really interested, was merely making an effort to be pleasant; to humiliate his pride. But even in that he was self-conscious.

We shook hands.

He said, 'This is a great European shrine. And we are told that our visitors – whatever their beliefs – should leave it feeling ... I think the words are "refreshed and consoled".' He paused as if I might want to object, to sneer, but I said nothing. 'I must ask you once again to believe that I am silent for your sake as well as mine.'

'I'll try to believe it.'

He gave a formal sort of bow, more Italian than English; and I went down the rock staircase to the path through the ilexes.

I had to wait till evening in Subaico for a bus back to the station. It ran through long green valleys, under hilltop villages, past aspens already yellowing into autumn. The sky turned through the softest blues to a vesperal amber-pink. Old peasants sat at their doorways; some of them had Greek faces, inscrutable, noble, at peace. I felt, perhaps because I had drunk a bottle of Verdicchio while I waited, that I belonged, and would for ever belong, to an older world than Leverrier's. I didn't like him, or his religion. And this not liking him, this half-drunken love of the ancient, unchanging Greco-Latin world seemed to merge. I was a pagan, at best a stoic, at worst a voluptuary, and would remain for ever so.

Waiting for the train, I got more drunk. A man at the station bar managed to make me understand that an indigo hilltop under the lemon-green sky to the west was where the poet Horace had had his farm. I drank to the Sabine hill; better one Horace than ten Saint

Benedicts; better one poem than ten thousand sermons. Much later I realized that perhaps Leverrier, in this case, would have agreed; because he too had chosen exile; because there are times when silence is a poem.

69

If Rome, a city of the vulgar living, had been depressing after Greece, London, a city of the drab dead, was fifty times worse. I had forgotten the innumerability of the place, its ugliness, its termite density after the sparsities of the Aegean. It was like mud after diamonds, dank undergrowth after sunlit marble; and as the airline bus crawled on its way through that endless suburb that lies between Northolt and Kensington I wondered why anyone should, or could, ever return of his own free will to such a landscape, such a society, such a climate. Flatulent white clouds drifted listlessly in a grey-blue sky; and I could hear people saying 'Lovely day, isn't it?' But all those tired greens, greys, browns ... they seemed to compress the movements of the Londoners we passed into a ubiquitous uniformity. It was something I had become too familiar with to notice in the Greeks – how each face there springs unique and sharp from its background. No Greek is like any other Greek; and every English face seemed, that day, like every other English face.

I got into a hotel near the air terminal about four o'clock and tried to decide what to do. Within ten minutes I picked up the phone and dialled Ann Taylor's number. There was no answer. Half an hour later I tried again, and again there was no answer. I forced myself to read a magazine for an hour; then I failed a third time to get an answer. I found a taxi and drove round to Russell Square. I was intensely excited. Alison would be waiting for me, or if not there would be some clue. Something would happen. Without knowing why I went into a pub, had a Scotch, and waited another quarter of an hour.

At last I was walking up to the house. The street door was on the latch, as it always had been. There was no card against the third-floor bell. I climbed the stairs; stood outside the door and waited, listened, heard nothing, then knocked. No answer. I knocked again, and then again. Music, but it came from above. I tried Ann Taylor's flat one last time, then went on up the stairs. I remembered that evening I had climbed them with Alison, taking her to have her bath. How many worlds had died since then? And yet Alison was somehow still there, so close. I decided she really was close; in the flat above. I did not know what would happen. Emotions exploded decisions.

I shut my eyes, counted ten, and knocked.

Footsteps.

A girl of nineteen or so opened the door; spectacles, rather fat, too much lipstick. I could see through another door into the sitting-room beyond her. There was a young man there and another girl, arrested in the act of demonstrating some dance; jazz, the room full of evening sunlight; three interrupted figures, still for an instant, like a contemporary Vermeer. I was unable to hide my disappointment. The girl at the door gave an encouraging smile.

I backed.

'Sorry. Wrong flat.' I began to go down the stairs. She called after me, who did I want, but I said, 'It's all right. Second floor.' I was out of sight before she could put two and two together; my tan, my retreat, peculiar telephone calls from Athens.

I walked back to the pub, and later that evening I went to an Italian restaurant we had once been fond of; Alison had been fond of. It was still the same, popular with the poorer academic and artistic population of Bloomsbury: research graduates, out-of-work actors, publishers' staff, mostly young, and my own kind. The clientele had not changed, but I had. I listened to the chatter around me; and was offput, and then alienated, by its insularity, its suddenly seen innocence. I looked round, to try to find someone I might hypothetically want to know better, become friendly with; and there was no one. It was the unneeded confirmation of my loss of Englishness; and it occurred to me that I must be feeling as Alison had so often felt: a mixture, before the English, of irritation and bafflement, of having this same language, same past, so many same things, and yet not belonging to them any more. Being worse than rootless ... speciesless.

I went and had one more look at the flat in Russell Square, but there was no light on the third floor. So I returned to the hotel, defeated. An old, old man.

The next morning I went round to the estate agents who looked after the house. They had a shabby string of green-painted rooms above a shop in Southampton Row. I recognized the adenoidal clerk who came to the counter to look after me as the one I had dealt with the previous year; he remembered me, and I soon extracted from him what little information he had to give. The flat had been assigned to Alison at the beginning of July – ten days or a fortnight after Parnassus. He had no idea whether Alison had been living there or not. He looked at a copy of the new lease. The assignee's address was the same as the assigner's.

'Must have been sharing,' said the clerk.

And that was that.

And what did I care? Why should I go on searching for her?

But I waited in all the evening after my visit to the estate agent, hoping for another message. The next day I moved to the Russell Hotel, so that I had only to stroll out of the entrance and look across the square to see the house, to wait for the windows on that black third floor to light. Four days passed, and no lights; no letters, no phone-calls, not the smallest sign.

I grew impatient and frustrated, hamstrung by this inexplicable lapse in the action. I thought perhaps they had lost me, they did not know where I was, and that worried me; and then it angered me that I was worried.

The need to see Alison drowned everything else. To see her. To twist the secret out of her; and other things I could not name. A week passed, a week wasted in cinemas, theatres, in lying on my hotel bed and staring at the ceiling, waiting for that implacably silent telephone beside me to ring. I nearly sent a cable to Bourani with my address; but pride stopped that.

At last I gave in. I could stand the hotel and Russell Square, that eternally empty flat, no longer. I saw a place advertised on a tobacconist's board. It was a scruffy attic 'flat' over two floors of sewing-rooms at the north end of Charlotte Street, on the other side of the Tottenham Court Road. It was expensive, but there was a telephone and, though the landlady lived in the basement, she was an unmistakable Charlotte Street bohemian of the 'thirties vintage: sluttish, battered, chain-smoking. She managed to let me know within the first five minutes I was in the house that Dylan Thomas had once been 'a close friend' – 'God, the times I've put him to bed, poor sod.' I didn't believe her; 'Dylan slept (or slept it off) here' is to Charlotte Street rather what the similar claim about Queen Elizabeth used to be to the country inns of England. But I liked her – 'My name's Joan, everyone calls me Kemp.' Her intellect, like her pottery and paintings, was a mess; but her heart was in the right place.

'Okay,' she said at the door, after I'd agreed to take the rooms. 'As long as I have your money. Bring in who you want when you want. The last boy was a ponce. An absolute sweetie. The bloody fascists got him last week.'

'Good Lord.'

She nodded. 'Them.' I looked round, and saw two young policemen standing on the corner.

I also bought an old M.G. The body was bad and the roof leaked, but the engine seemed to have a year or two of life left. I took Kemp out to Jack Straw's Castle on a grand inaugural run. She drank like a trooper and talked like one, but in every other way she was what I wanted and what I needed: a warm heart and a compulsive gossip about herself, who accepted without suspicion my explanation of my joblessness; partly reconciled me, in her bitter-warm way, to London and being English; and – at least to begin with – stopped me from being, whenever I felt it, too morbidly abandoned and alone.

70

A long August passed, and I had fits of acute depression, fits of torpid indifference. I was like a fish in stale water, stifled by the greyness of England. Just as I looked back, Adam after the fall, to the luminous landscapes, the salt and thyme of Phraxos, I looked back to the events of Bourani, which could not have happened, but which had happened, and found myself, at the end of some tired London afternoon, as unable to wish that they had not happened as I was to forgive Conchis for having given me the part he did. Slowly I came to realize that my dilemma was in fact a sort of *de facto* forgiveness, a condonation of what had been done to me; even though, still too sore to accept that something active had taken place, I thought of 'done' in a passive sense.

I thought in the same way of Lily. One day I nearly crashed, braking hard at the glimpse of a slim girl with long blonde hair walking down a side street. I swerved the car into the kerb and raced after her. Even before I saw the face I knew it was not Lily. But if I had rushed after the girl in the side street it was because I wanted to face Lily, to question her, to try to understand the ununderstandable; not because I longed for her. I could have longed for certain aspects of her, for certain phases – but it was that very phasality that made her impossible to love. So I could almost think of her, the light-phase her, as one thinks tenderly but historically of the moments of poetry in one's life; and yet still hate her for her real, her black present being.

But I had to do something while I waited, while I absorbed the experience osmotically into my life. So throughout the latter half of August I pursued the trail of Conchis and Lily in England; and through them, of Alison.

It kept me, however tenuously and vicariously, in the masque; and it dulled my agonizing longing to see Alison. Agonizing because a new feeling had seeded and was growing inside me, a feeling I wanted to eradicate and couldn't, not least because I knew the seed of it had been planted by Conchis and was germinating in this deliberate silence and absence he had surrounded me with; a feeling that haunted me day and night, that I despised, disproved, dismissed, and still it grew, as the embryo grows in the reluctant mother's womb, sweeping her with rage, then in green moments melting her with ... but I couldn't say the word.

And for a time it lay buried under inquiries, conjectures, letters. I decided to ignore everything I had been told by Conchis and the girls as to what was false and what was true. In many things I merely wanted to discover some trace, some fingerprint: just to catch them out at their own skill at deception.

The newspaper cutting about Alison. Different type from that of the *Holborn Gazette*, where the inquest report would have appeared.

Foulkes pamphlet. Is in the British Museum Catalogue. Conchis's are not.

Military history. Letter from Major Arthur Lee-Jones.

Dear Mr Urfe,

I'm afraid your letter does ask, as you say yourself, for the impossible. The units engaged in the Neuve Chapelle set-piece were mostly regular ones. I think it most unlikely that any Princess Louise's Kensington Regiment volunteers would have seen that engagement, even under the circumstances you suggest. But of course we have poor detailed records of that chaotic time, and I can't hazard more than an opinion.

I can find no trace in the records of a captain called Montague. Usually one is on safer ground with officers. But perhaps he was seconded from one of the county regiments.

De Deukans. No family of this name in the Almanach de Gotha or any other likely source I looked at. Givray-le-Duc was absent from even the largest French gazetteers. The spider *Theridion deukansii* doesn't exist, though there is a genus *Theridion*.

Seidevarre. Letter from Johan Fredriksen.

Dear Sir,

The mayor of Kirkenes has passed to me, who is the schoolmaster, your letter to answer. There is in Pasvikdal a place of the name Seidevarre and there was in that place many years from now a family of the name Nygaard. I am very sorry we do not know what is become with this family.

I am very pleased to help you.

I was even more pleased to have been helped. Conchis had once been there, something had happened there. It was not all fiction.

Lily's mother. I drove down to Cerne Abbas, not expecting to find Ansty Cottage – or anything else. I did not. I told the manageress at the little hotel where I had lunch that I'd once known two girls from Cerne Abbas – twins, very pretty, but I'd forgotten their surname. It left her deeply worried – she knew everyone in the village and couldn't think who it could have been. The 'headmaster' at the primary school: in reality a headmistress. Obviously the letters had been invented on Phraxos.

Charles-Victor Bruneau. Not in Grove. A man I spoke to at the Royal Academy of Music had never heard of him; or, needless to say, of Conchis.

Conchis's costume at the 'trial'. On my way back from Cerne Abbas I stopped for dinner in Hungerford, and passed an antique shop on my way to the hotel. Propped up in the window were five old Tarot cards. On one of them was a man dressed exactly as Conchis had been; even to the same emblems on his cloak. Underneath were the words *LE SORCIER* – the sorcerer. The shop was shut, but I took its address and later they sold me the card by post; 'a nice eighteenth-century card'.

It gave me a sharp shock when I first saw it – I looked round, as if it had been planted there for me to notice; as if I were being watched.

The 'psychologists' at the trial. I tried the Tavistock Clinic and the American Embassy. All the names totally unknown, though some of the institutes exist. Further research turned up nothing on Conchis.

Nevinson. This was the pre-war master whose Oxford college was in a book in the school library. The Bursar's Office at Balliol sent me an address in Japan. I wrote him a letter. Two weeks later I had a reply.

Faculty of English,
Osaka University

Dear Mr Urfe,

Thank you for your letter. It came, as it were, from the distant past, and gave me quite a surprise! But I was delighted to hear that the school has survived the war, and I trust you have enjoyed your stay there as much as I did.

I had forgotten about Bourani. I remember the place now, however, and (very vaguely!) the owner. Did I have a violent argument with him once about Racine and predestination? I have an intuition, no more, that I did. But so much has flowed under the bridges since those days.

Other 'victims' before the war – alas, I can't help you. The man before me I never met. I did know Geoffrey Sugden, who was there for three years after me. I never heard him refer especially to Bourani.

If you are ever in this part of the world, I should be delighted to talk over old times with you, and to offer you, if not an ouzo, at least a saké *pou na pinete*.

Yours sincerely,
DOUGLAS NEVINSON

Wimmel. In late August, a piece of luck. One of my teeth began to hurt and Kemp sent me to her dentist to have it seen to. While I was in the waiting-room I picked up an old film magazine of the previous January. Halfway through I came on a picture of the false Wimmel. He was even dressed in Nazi uniform. Underneath there was a caption paragraph.

Ignaz Pruszynski, who plays the fiendish German Town Commandant in Poland's much-praised film of the resistance, *Black Ordeal*, in real life played a very different role. He led a Polish underground group all through the Occupation, and was awarded the Polish equivalent of our own Victoria Cross.

Hypnotism. I read a couple of books on this. Conchis had evidently learnt the technique professionally. Post-hypnotic suggestion, implanting commands that are carried out on a given signal after the subject has been woken from the trance state and is in all other ways returned to normal, was 'perfectly feasible and frequently demonstrated'. But I thought back. At no point could I see that I had been unconsciously forced to behave any differently than I would have done consciously – than I had in fact behaved. No doubt I had been 'pumped' under hypnosis. But my own free will must have made further manipulation, except in very minor things, unnecessary.

Raising both arms above the head. Conchis got this from ancient Egypt. It was the Ka sign, used by initiates 'to gain possession of the cosmic forces of mystery'. In many tomb-paintings. It meant: '*I am master of the spells. Strength is mine. I impart strength.*' Another Egyptian symbol was the ring-topped cross on the walls of the trial room. It was their 'key of life'.

The wheel symbol. 'The mandala, or wheel is a universal symbol of existence.'

The ribbon on my leg, the bare shoulder. From masonic ritual, but believed to descend from the Eleusinian mysteries. Associated with initiation.

'*Maria.*' Probably really was a peasant, though an intelligent one. She spoke only two or three words of French to me; sat silent all through the trial, rather conspicuously out-of-place. Unlike the others, *she* may have been what she first seemed.

Lily's bank. I wrote another letter, and got back a reply from the manager of the real Barclay's branch. His name was not P. J. Fearn; and the headed paper he wrote on was not like that I had received.

Her school. Julie Holmes – unknown.

Mitford. I wrote a card to the address in Northumberland I had had the year before and received a letter back from his mother. She said Alexander was now a courier, working in Spain. I got in touch with the travel firm he was working for, but they said he wouldn't be back till September. I left a letter for him.

The paintings at Bourani. I started with the Bonnards. The first book of reproductions of his work I opened had the picture of the girl drying by the window. I turned to the attributions list at the back. It was in the Los Angeles County Museum. The book had been printed in 1950. Later I 'found' the other Bonnard; at the Boston Museum of Fine Arts. Both had been copies. The Modigliani I never traced; but I suspect, remembering those curiously Conchis-like eyes, that it was not even a copy.

'Evening Standard' of January 8th, 1952. No sign of a photo of Lily and Rose, in any edition.

L'Astrée. Did Conchis remember that I believed myself remotely connected with d'Urfé? The story of *L'Astrée* is: The shepherdess Astrée, hearing evil reports of the shepherd Celadon, banishes him from her presence. A war breaks out, and Astrée is taken prisoner. Celadon manages to rescue her, but she will not forgive him. He does not gain her hand until he has turned the lion and unicorns who devour unfaithful lovers into statues of stone.

Chaliapin. Was at Covent Garden in June 1914, and in *Prince Igor*.

'You may be elect.' When he said that, at our first strange meeting, he meant simply, 'I've decided to use you.' That was also the only sense in which, at the end, I could be elect. He meant, 'We *have* used you.'

Lily and Rose. Two twin sisters, both very pretty, gifted (though I came to doubt Lily's classical education), must, if they had been at Oxford or Cambridge, have been the double Zuleika Dobsons of their years. I could not believe they had been at Oxford – since our years must have overlapped – so I tried the 'other' place. I searched through student magazines, tracked down stills from various college and university theatre productions, even braved one or two of the women's college bursaries ... and all in vain. Girton, her supposed college, had not a single likely candidate. London University proved a similar blank.

I also tried a few London theatrical agencies. Three times I was shown photographs of twin sisters; and was three times disappointed. I had no more luck at Berman's and one or two other theatrical costumiers I went to. The Tavistock Repertory had not put on any production of *Lysistrata*. RADA could not help. Indeed all I derived from the whole exercise – since my inquiries involved the concocting of various reasons for them – was a grudging retrospective admiration for the two girls' own skill in improvising lies.

Of course there was one extra cunning in the 'Julie Holmes' invention. We always tend to believe people who have had the same experiences as ourselves. Her Cambridge equalled my Oxford, and so on.

Othello, Act I, Scene III.

> She is abus'd, stol'n from me, and corrupted
> By spells and medicines bought of mountebanks;
> For nature so preposterously to err,
> Being not deficient, blind, or lame of sense,
> Sans witchcraft could not.

And:

> A maiden never bold;
> Of spirit so still and quiet, that her motion
> Blush'd at herself; and she – in spite of nature,
> Of years, of country, credit, everything –
> To fall in love with what she fear'd to look on!

The fabulous whore Io. Lemprière: *In the ancient Gothic Io and Gio signified 'earth', as Isi or Isa signified 'ice' or water in its primordial state; and both were equally titles of the goddess, who represented the productive and nutritive power of the earth.* Indian Kali, Syrian Astarte (Ashtaroth), Egyptian Isis and Greek Io were considered one and the same goddess. She had three colours (on the walls in the trial): white, red, and black, the phases of the moon, and also the phases of woman: virgin, mother, and crone. Lily was evidently the goddess in her white, virgin phase; and perhaps in the black, as well. Rose would have stood for the red phase; but then Alison was given that role.

Polymus Films. I didn't see the obvious, that one misplaced letter, until painfully late.

Tartarus. The more I read, the more I began to re-identify the whole situation at Bourani – or at any rate the final situation – with Tartarus. Tartarus was ruled by a king, Hades (or Conchis); a queen, Persephone, bringer of destruction (Lily) – who remained 'six months with Hades in the infernal regions and spent the rest of the year with her mother Demeter on earth'. There was also a supreme judge in Tartarus – Minos (the presiding 'doctor' with a beard?); and of course there was Anubis-Cerberus, the black dog with three heads (three roles?). And Tartarus was where Eurydice went when Orpheus lost her.

I was aware that in all this I was acting the role I had decided not to act: that of detective, of hunter, and several times I abandoned the chase. But then one, and one of the apparently least promising, of my bits of research bore spectacular results.

71

It began, one Monday, with a very long shot, the assumption that Conchis *had* lived in London as a boy and that there had indeed been an original Lily Montgomery in St John's Wood. I went to Marylebone Central Library and asked to look at the street directories for 1912 to 1914. Of course the name Conchis would not appear; I looked for Montgomery. Acacia Road, Prince Albert Road, Henstridge Place, Queen's Grove ... with an A to Z of London by my side I worked through all the likely streets on the east of Wellington Road. Suddenly, with a shock of excitement, my eyes jumped a page. *Montgomery, Fredk, 20 Allitsen Road.*

The neighbours' names were given as Smith and Manningham,

although by 1914 the latter had moved and the name Huckstepp appeared. I wrote down the address, and then went on searching. Almost at once, on the other side of the main artery, I came across another Montgomery; this time in Elm Tree Road. But I no sooner caught sight of it than I was disappointed, because the full name was given as Sir Charles Penn Montgomery; an eminent surgeon, by the look of the trail of initials after his name; and obviously not the man Conchis described. The neighbours' names there were Hamilton-Dukes and Charlesworth. There was another title among the Elm Tree Road residents; a 'desirable' address.

I searched on, double-checking everything, but without finding any other Montgomery.

I then followed up in later directories the two I had found. The Allitsen Road Montgomery disappeared in 1922. Annoyingly the Elm Tree Road Montgomery went on much longer, though Sir Charles must have died in 1922; after that the owner's name appeared as Lady Florence Montgomery, and continued so right up to 1938.

After lunch I drove up to Allitsen Road. As I swung into it, I knew it was no good. The houses were small terrace houses, nothing like the 'mansions' Conchis had described.

Five minutes later I was in Elm Tree Road. At least it looked more the part: a pretty circumflex of mixed largish houses and early Victorian mews and cottages. It also looked encouragingly unaltered. Number 46 turned out to be one of the largest houses in the road. I parked my car and walked up a drive between banks of hydrangeas to an imposing front door; rang a bell.

But it sounded in an empty house, and sounded so all through August. Whoever lived there was on holiday. I found out his name in that year's directory – a Mr Simon Marks. I also found out from an old *Who's Who* that the illustrious Sir Charles Penn Montgomery had had three daughters. I could probably have found out their names, but I had by then become anxious to drag my investigations out, as a child his last few sweets. It was almost a disappointment when, one day early in September, I saw a car parked in the driveway, and knew that another faint hope was about to be extinguished.

The bell was answered by an Italian in a white housecoat.

'I wonder if I could speak to the owner? Or his wife?'

'You have appointment?'

'No.'

'You sell something?'

I was rescued by a sharp voice.

'Who is it, Ercole?'

She appeared, a woman of sixty, Jewish, expensively dressed, intelligent-looking.

'Oh, I'm engaged on some research and I'm trying to trace a family called Montgomery.'

'Sir Charles Penn? The surgeon?'

'I believe he lived here.'

'Yes, he lived here.' The houseboy waited, and she waved him away in a *grande-dame* manner; part of the wave came my way.

'In fact ... this is rather difficult to explain ... I'm really looking for a Miss Lily Montgomery.'

'Yes. I know her.' She was evidently not amused by the astounded smile that broke over my face. 'You wish to see her?'

'I'm writing a monograph on a famous Greek writer – famous in Greece, that is, and I believe Miss Montgomery knew him well many years ago when he lived in England.'

'What is his name?'

'Maurice Conchis.' She had clearly never heard of him.

The lure of the search overcame a little of her distrust, and she said, 'I will find you the address. Come in.'

I waited in the splendid hall. As ostentation of marble and ormolu; pier-glasses; what looked like a Fragonard. Petrified opulence, tense excitement. In a minute she reappeared with a card. On it I read: *Mrs Lily de Seitas, Dinsford House, Much Hadham, Herts.*

'I haven't seen her for several years,' said the lady.

'Thank you very much.' I began backing towards the door.

'Would you like tea? A drink?'

There was something glistening, obscurely rapacious, about her eyes, as if while she had been away she'd decided that there might be a pleasure to suck from me. A mantis-woman; starved in her luxury. I was glad to escape.

Before I drove off I looked once more at the substantial houses on either side of number 46. In one of them Conchis had perhaps spent his youth. Behind number 46 was what looked like a factory, though I had discovered from the A to Z that it was the back of the stands of

Lord's cricket ground. The gardens were hidden because of the high walls, but the 'little orchard' must now be dwarfed by the stands overhead. Very probably they had not been built before the First War.

The next morning at eleven I was in Much Hadham. It was a very fine day, cloudless September blue; a day to compare with a Greek day. Dinsford House lay some way out of the village, and although it was not quite so grand as it sounded, it was no hovel; a five-bay period house, posed graciously and gracefully, brick-red and white, in an acre or so of well-kept grounds. This time the door was opened by a Scandinavian *au pair* girl. Yes, Mrs de Seitas was in – she was down at the stables, if I'd go round the side.

I walked over the gravel and under a brick arch. There were two garages, and a little farther down I could see and smell stables. A small boy appeared from a door holding a bucket. He saw me and called, 'Mummy! There's a man.' A slim woman in jodhpurs, a red headscarf, and a red tartan shirt came out of the same door. She seemed to be in her early forties; a still pretty, erect woman with an open-air complexion.

'Can I help you?'

'I'm actually looking for Mrs de Seitas.'

'I am Mrs de Seitas.'

I had it so fixed in my mind that she would be grey-haired, Conchis's age. Closer to her, I could see crowsfeet and a slight but telltale flabbiness round the neck; the rich brown hair was probably dyed. She might be nearer fifty than forty; but that made her still ten years too young.

'Mrs Lily de Seitas?'

'Yes.'

'I've got your address from Mrs Simon Marks.' A minute change in her expression told me that I had not recommended myself. 'I've come to ask you if you would help in a matter of literary research.'

'Me!'

'If you were once Miss Lily Montgomery.'

'But my father – '

'It's not about your father.' A pony whinnied inside the stable. The little boy stared suspiciously at me; his mother urged him away, to go and fill his bucket. I put on all my Oxford charm. 'If it's terribly inconvenient, of course I'll come back another time.'

'We're only mucking out.' She leant the besom she was carrying against the wall. 'But who?'

'I'm writing a study of – Maurice Conchis?'

I watched her like a hawk; but I was over a bare field.

'Maurice who?'

'Conchis.' I spelt it. 'He's a famous Greek writer. He lived in this country when he was young.'

She brushed back a strand of hair rather gauchely with her gloved hand; she was, I could see, one of those country Englishwomen who are abysmally innocent about everything except horses, homes, and children. 'Honestly, I'm awfully sorry, but there must be some mistake.'

'You may have known him under the name of ... Charlesworth? Or Hamilton-Dukes? A long time ago. The First World War.'

'But my dear man – I'm sorry, not my dear man ... oh dear – ' she broke off rather charmingly. I saw a lifetime of dropped bricks behind her; but her tanned skin and her clear bluish eyes, and the body that had conspicuously not run to seed, made her forgivable. She said, 'What is your name?'

I told her.

'Mr Urfe, do you know how old I was in 1914?'

'Obviously very young indeed.' She smiled, but as if compliments were rather continental and embarrassing.

'I was ten.' She looked to where her son was filling the bucket. 'Benjie's age.'

'Those other names – they mean nothing?'

'Good Lord yes, but ... this Maurice – what did you call him? – he stayed with them?'

I shook my head. Once again Conchis had tricked me into a ridiculous situation. He had probably picked the name with a pin in an old directory; all he would have had to find was the name of one of the daughters. I plunged insecurely on.

'He was the son. An only son? Very musical.'

'I'm afraid there must be a mistake. The Charlesworths were childless, and there was a Hamilton-Dukes boy but – ' I saw her hesitate as something snagged her memory – 'he died in the war.'

'I think you've just remembered something else.'

'No – I mean, yes. I don't know. It was when you said musical.' She looked incredulous. 'You couldn't mean Mr Rat?' She laughed, and put her thumbs in the pockets of her jodhpurs. '*The Wind in the Willows*. He was an Italian who came and tried to teach us the piano. My sister and me.'

'Young?'

She shrugged. 'Quite.'

'Could you tell me more about him?'

She looked down. 'Gambellino, Gambardello … something like that. Gambardello?' She said the name as if it was still a joke.

'His first name?'

She couldn't possibly remember.

'Why Mr Rat?'

'Because he had such staring brown eyes. We used to tease him terribly.' She pulled an ashamed face at her son, who had come back, and now pushed her, as if he was the one being teased. She missed the sudden leap of excitement in my own eyes; the certainty that Conchis had used more than a pin.

'Was he shortish? Shorter than me?'

She clasped her headscarf, trying to remember; then looking up, puzzled. 'Do you know … but this can't be … ?'

'Would you be very kind indeed and let me question you for ten minutes or so?'

She hesitated. I was politely adamant; just ten minutes. She turned to her son. 'Benjie, run and ask Gunhild to make us some coffee. And bring it out in the garden.'

He looked at the stable. 'But Lazy.'

'We'll do for Lazy in a minute.'

Benjie ran up the gravel and I followed Mrs de Seitas, as she peeled off her gloves, flicked off her headscarf, a willowy walk, down beside a brick wall and through a doorway into a fine old garden; a lake of autumn flowers; on the far side of the house a lawn and a cedar. She led the way round to a sun-loggia. There was a canopied swing seat, some elegant cast-iron seats painted white. I deduced that Sir Charles Penn Montgomery had had a golden scalpel. She sat in the swing seat and indicated a chair for me. I murmured something about the garden.

'It is rather jolly, isn't it? My husband does almost all this by himself and now, poor man, he hardly ever sees it.' She smiled. 'He's an economist. Stuck in Strasbourg.' She swung her feet up; she was a little too girlish, too aware of her good figure; reacting from a rural boredom. 'But come on. Tell me about your famous writer I've never heard of. You've met him?'

'He died in the Occupation.'

'Poor man. What of?'

'Cancer.' I hurried on. 'He was, well, very secretive about his past, so one has to deduce things from his work. We know that he was Greek, but he may have pretended to be Italian.' I jumped up and gave her a light for her cigarette.

'I can't believe it was Mr Rat. He was such a funny little man.'

'Can you remember one thing – his playing the harpsichord as well as the piano?'

'The harpsichord is the plonkety-plonk one?' I nodded, but she shook her head. 'You did say a writer?'

'He turned from music to literature. You see, there are countless references in his early poems – and in, well, a novel he wrote – to an unhappy but very significant love affair he had when he was still in England. Of course we just don't know – or didn't – to what extent he was recalling reality and to what extent embroidering on it.'

'But – am I mentioned?'

'There are all sorts of clues that suggest the girl's name was a flower name. And that he lived near her. And that the common bond was music ... '

She sat up, fascinated.

'How on *earth* did you trace this to us?'

'Oh – various clues. From literary references. I knew it was very near Lord's cricket ground. In one ... passage he talks of this girl with her ancient British family name. Oh, and her famous doctor father. Then I started looking at street directories.'

'How absolutely extraordinary.'

'It's just one of those things. You meet hundreds of dead ends. But one day you really hit a way through.'

Smiling, she glanced towards the house. 'Here's Gunhild.' For two or three minutes we had to go through the business of getting coffee poured; polite exchanges about Norway – Gunhild had never been farther north than Trondheim, I discovered. Benjie was ordered to disappear; and the *ur*-Lily and I were left alone again.

For effect, I produced a notebook.

'If I could just ask you a few questions ... '

'I say – glory at last.' She laughed rather stupidly; horsily; she was enjoying herself.

'I believed he lived next to you. He didn't. Where did he live?'

'Oh, I haven't the faintest idea. You know. At that age.'

'You knew nothing about his parents?' She shook her head. 'Would your sisters perhaps know more?'

Her face gravened.

'My eldest sister lives in Chile. She was ten years older than me. And my sister Rose – '

'Rose!'

She smiled. 'Rose.'

'God, this is extraordinary. It clinches it. There's a sort of ... well, a sort of mystery poem that belongs to the group about you. It's very obscure, but now we know you have a sister ... '

'Had a sister. Rose died just about that time. In 1916.'

'Of typhoid?'

I said it so eagerly that she was taken aback; then smiled. 'No. Of some terribly rare complication following jaundice.' She stared out over the garden for a moment. 'It was the great tragedy of my childhood.'

'Did you feel that he had any special affection for you – or for your sisters?'

She smiled again, remembering. 'We always thought he secretly admired May – my eldest sister – she was engaged, of course, but she used to come and sit with us. And yes ... oh goodness, it's strange, it does come back, I remember he always used to show off, what we called showing off, if she was in the room. Play frightfully difficult bits. And she was fond of that Beethoven thing – "For Elise"? We used to hum it when we wanted to annoy him.'

'Your sister Rose was older than you?'

'Two years older.'

'So the picture is really of two little girls teasing a foreign music-teacher?'

She began to swing on the seat. 'Do you know, it's frightful, but I can't remember. I mean, yes, we teased him, I'm jolly sure we were perfect little pests. But then the war started and he disappeared.'

'Where?'

'Oh. I couldn't tell you. No idea. But I remember we had a dreadful old battleaxe in his place. And we *hated* her. I'm sure we missed him. I suppose we were frightful little snobs. One was in those days.'

'How long did he teach you?'

'Two years?' She was almost asking me.

'Can you remember any sign at all of strong personal liking – for you – on his side?'

She thought for a long moment, then shook her head. 'You don't mean ... something nasty?'

'No, no. But were you, say, ever alone with him?'

She put on an expression of mock shock. '*Never*. There was always our governess, or my sister. My mother.'

'You couldn't describe his character at all?'

'I'm sure if I could meet him now, I'd think, a sweet little man. You know.'

'You or your sister never played the flute or the recorder?'

'Goodness no.' She grinned at the absurdity.

'A very personal question. Would you say you were a strikingly pretty little girl ... I'm sure you were – but were you conscious that there was something rather special about you?'

She looked down at her cigarette. 'In the interests, oh dear, how shall I say it, in the interests of your research, and speaking as a poor raddled mother, the answer is ... yes, I believe there was. Actually I was painted. It became quite famous. All the rage of the 1913 Academy. It's in the house – I'll show you in a minute.'

I consulted my notebook. 'And you just really can't remember what happened to him when the war came?'

She pressed her fine hands against her eyes. 'Heavens, doesn't this make you realize – I think he was interned ... but honestly for the life of me I ... '

'Would your sister in Chile remember better? Might I write to her?'

'Of course. Would you like her address?' She gave it to me and I wrote it down.

Benjie came and stood about twenty yards away, by an astrolabe on a stone column, looking plainer than words that his patience was exhausted. She beckoned to him; caressed back his forelock.

'Your poor old mum's just had a shock, darling. She's discovered she's a muse.' She turned to me. 'Is that the word?'

'What's a muse?'

'A lady who makes a gentleman write poems.'

'Does *he* write poems?'

She laughed and turned back to me. 'And he's really quite famous?'

'I think he will be one day.'

'Can I read him?'

'He's not been translated. But he will be.'

'By you?'

'Well … ' I let her think I had hopes.

She said, 'I honestly don't think I can tell you any more.' Benjie whispered something. She laughed and stood up in the sunlight and took his hand. 'We're just going to show Mr Orfe a picture, then it's back to work.'

'It's Urfe, actually.'

She put her hand to her face, in shame. 'Oh dear. There I go again.' The boy jerked her other hand; he too was ashamed of her silliness.

We all walked up to the house, through a drawing-room into a wide hall and then into a room at the side. I saw a long dining-table, silver candlesticks. On the panelling between two windows was a painting. Benjie ran and switched on a picture-light above it. It showed a little Alice-like girl with long hair, in a sailor-dress, looking round a door, as if she was hiding and could see whoever was looking for her searching in vain. Her face was very alive, tense, excited, yet still innocent. In gilt on a small black plaque beneath I read: *Mischief, by Sir William Blunt*, R.A.

'Charming.'

Benjie made his mother bend down and whispered something.

'He wants to tell you what the family calls it.'

She nodded at him and he shouted, ' "How Soppy Can You Get." ' She pulled his hair as he grinned.

Another charming picture.

She apologized for not being able to invite me to lunch, but she had 'a Women's Institute do' in Hertford; and I promised that as soon as a translation of the Conchis poems was ready I would send a copy.

Listening to her, I had realized I was still the old man's victim; had till then still half believed that last version of his rich cosmopolitan past he had foisted on me and then confirmed through 'June'. Now I remembered the repeated echo in his stories of some vital change of life, or fortune, in the 1920s. I began to erect a new hypothesis. He would have been the gifted son of some poor Greek immigrant family, perhaps from Corfu or the Ionian Islands, ashamed of his Greek name, taking an Italian one; trying to rise in the alien Edwardian world of London, to shake off his past and background, already living a kind of double life ... all of us who had been through the 'system' at Bourani must have been scapegoats for all the humiliations and unhappiness he had suffered in the Montgomery household, and no doubt others like it, during those distant years. I smiled as I drove, half at the thought of this very human rancour lying behind the intellectual theorizing, half at the prospect of this promising new lead to follow.

I came out into the main street of Much Hadham. It was half past twelve and I decided to get a bite to eat before I did the drive back to London. So I stopped at a small half-timbered pub. I had the lounge bar all to myself.

'Passing through?' asked the landlord, as he drew me a pint.

'No. Been to see someone. Dinsford House.'

'Nice place she's got there.'

'You know them?'

He wore a bow-tie; had a queasy inbetween accent.

'Know *of* them. I'll take the sandwiches separate.' He rang up the till. 'Used to see the children round the village.'

'I've just been out there on business.'

'Oh yes.'

A peroxided woman's head appeared round the door. She held out a plate of sandwiches. As he handed me back my change, he said, 'Singer in opera, wasn't she?'

'I don't think so.'

'That's what they say round here.'

I waited for him to go on, but he evidently wasn't very interested. I finished half a sandwich. Thought.

'What's her husband do?'

'Isn't a husband.' He caught my quick look. 'Well, we been here two years now and I never heard of one. There're ... gentlemen friends, I'm told.' He gave me a minute wink.

'Ah. I see.'

'Course they're like me. London people.' There was a silence. He picked up a glass. 'Good-looking woman. Never seen her daughters?' I shook my head. He polished the glass. 'Real corkers.' Silence.

'How old are they?'

'Don't ask me. I can't tell twenty from thirty these days. The eldest are twins, you know.' If he hadn't been so busy polishing the glass in the old buy-me-a-drink ploy he would have seen my face freeze into stone. 'What they call identicals. Some are normals. And others are identicals.' He held the glass up high to the light. 'They say the only way their own mother can tell 'em apart one's got a scar or something on her ...'

I was out of the bar so fast that he didn't even have time to shout.

72

I didn't feel angry at first; I drove very fast, and nearly killed a man on a bicycle, but I was grinning most of the way. This time I didn't park my car discreetly by the gate. I skidded it on the gravel in front of the black door; and I gave the lion's-head knocker the hardest using it can have had in its two centuries of existence.

Mrs de Seitas herself answered the door; she had changed, but only from her jodhpurs into a pair of trousers. She looked past me at my car, as if that might explain why I had returned. I smiled.

'I see you're not going out for lunch after all.'

'Yes, I made a stupid mistake over the day.' She gathered her shirt collar together. 'Did you forget something?'

'Yes.'

'Oh.' I said nothing and she went on brightly, but a fraction too late, 'What?'

'Your twin daughters.'

Her expression changed; she didn't appear in the least guilty, but she gave me a look of concession and then the faintest smile. I wondered how I had not seen the similarity; the eyes, the long mouth. I had let that spurious snapshot Lily had shown me linger in my mind. A silly woman with fluffed-up hair. She stepped back for me to enter.

'Yes. You did.'

Benjie appeared at a door at the end of the hall. She spoke calmly to him as she closed the door behind me.

'It's all right. Go and have your lunch.'

I went quickly and bent a little in front of him. 'Benjie, could you tell me something? The names of your twin sisters?'

He stared at me, still suspicious, but now I detected a trace of fear as well, a child caught hiding. He looked at his mother. She must have nodded.

'Lil' and Rose.'

'Thank you.'

He gave me one last doubtful look, and disappeared. I turned to Lily de Seitas.

She said, as she moved self-possessedly towards the drawing-room, 'We called them that to placate my mother. She was a hungry goddess.' Her manner had changed with her clothes; and a vague former disparity between her vocabulary and her looks was accounted for. It was suddenly credible that she was fifty; and incredible that I had thought her rather unintelligent. I followed her into the room.

'I'm interrupting your lunch.'

She have me a dry backwards look. 'I've been expecting an interruption for several weeks now.'

She sat in an armchair and gestured for me to sit on the huge sofa in the centre of the room, but I shook my head. She was not nervous; even smiled.

'Well?'

'We start from the fact that you have two enterprising daughters. Let me hear you re-invent from there.'

'I'm afraid my invention's at an end. I can only fall back on the truth now.' But she was still smiling as she said it; smiling at my not smiling. 'Maurice is the twins' godfather.'

'You do know who I am?' It was her calmness; I could not believe she knew what they had done at Bourani.

'Yes, Mr Urfe. I know *exactly* who you are.' Her eyes warned me; and annoyed me. 'And what happened?'

She looked down at her hands, then back at me. 'My husband was killed in 1943. In the Far East. He never saw Benjie.' She saw the impatience on my face and checked it. 'He was also the first English master at the Lord Byron School.'

'Oh no he wasn't. I've looked up all the old prospectuses.'

'Then you remember the name Hughes.'

'Yes.'

She crossed her legs. She sat in an old wing chair covered in pale-gold brocade; very erectly. All her 'county' horsiness had disappeared.

'I wish you'd sit down.'

'No.'

She accepted my bleakness with a little shrug, and looked me in the eyes; a shrewd, unabashed and even haughty stare. Then she began to speak.

'My father died when I was eighteen. Mainly to escape from home I made a disastrous – a very stupid – marriage. Then in 1928 I met my second husband. My first husband divorced me a year later. We married. We wanted to be out of England for a time and we hadn't much money. He applied for a teaching post in Greece. He was a classical scholar ... loved Greece. We met Maurice. Lily and Rose were conceived on Phraxos. In a house that Maurice lent us to live in.'

'I don't believe a word. But go on.'

'I funked having twins in Greece and we had to come back to England.' She took a cigarette from a silver box on the tripod table beside her. I refused her offer of one; and let her light her cigarette herself. She was very calm; in her own house; 'My mother's maiden name was de Seitas. You can confirm that at Somerset House. She had a bachelor brother, my uncle, who was very well off and who treated me – especially after my father's death – as much as a daughter as my mother would allow him to. She was a very domineering woman.'

I remembered that date Conchis had given me for the finding of Bourani: April, 1928.

'You're saying now that you never met ... Maurice before 1929?'

She smiled. 'Of course not. But I supplied him with all the details of that part of his story to you.'

'And a sister called Rose?'

'Go to Somerset House.'

'I shall.'

She contemplated the tip of her cigarette; made me wait a moment.

'The twins arrived. A year later my uncle died. We found he had left me nearly all his money on condition that Bill changed his name by deed poll to de Seitas. Not even de Seitas-Hughes. My mother was mainly responsible for that meanness.' She looked at the group of miniatures that hung beside her, beside the mantelpiece. 'My uncle was the last male of the de Seitas family. My husband changed his name to mine. In the Japanese style. You can confirm that as well.' She added, 'That is all.'

'It's very far from all. My God.'

'May I, as I know so much about you, call you Nicholas?'

'No.'

She looked down, once again with that infuriating small smile that haunted all their faces – her daughters', Conchis's, even Anton's and Maria's in their different ways, as if they had all been trained to give the same superior, enigmatic smiles; as perhaps they had. And I suspected that if anyone had done the training, it would be this woman.

'You mustn't think that you are the first young man who has stood before me bitter and angry with Maurice. With all of us who help him. Though you are the first to reject the offer of friendship I made just now.'

'I have some ugly questions to ask.'

'Ask.'

'Some others first. Why are you known in the village as an opera-singer?'

'I've sung once or twice in local concerts. I was trained.'

'"The harpsichord is the plonkety-plonk one"?'

'It is rather, isn't it?'

I turned my back on her; on her gentleness; her weaponed lady-hood.

'My dear Mrs de Seitas, no amount of charm, no amount of

intelligence, no amount of playing with words can get you out of this one.'

She left a long pause.

'It is you who make our situation. You must have been told that. You come here telling me lies. You come here for all the wrong reasons. I tell you lies back. I give you wrong reasons back.'

'Are your daughers here?'

'No.'

I turned to face her.

'Alison?'

'Alison and I are good friends.'

'Where is she?'

She shook her head; no answer.

'I demand to know where she is.'

'In my house no one ever demands.' Her face was bland, but as intent on mine as a chess player on the game.

'Very well. We'll see what the police think about that.'

'I can tell you now. They will think you very foolish.'

I turned away again, to try to get her to say more. But she sat in the chair and I felt her eyes on my back. I knew she was sitting there, in her corn-gold chair, and that she was like Demeter, Ceres, a goddess on her throne; not simply a clever woman of nearly fifty, in 1953, in a room with a tractor droning somewhere near by in the fields; but playing a role so deep-rooted in fidelity to concepts I did not understand, to people I could not forgive, that it had almost ceased to be a role.

She stood up and went to a bureau in the corner and came back with some photos, which she laid out on a table behind the sofa. Then she went back to her chair; invited me to look at them. There was one of her sitting on the swing seat in front of the loggia. At the other end sat Conchis; between them was Benjie. Another photo showed Lily and Rose. Lily was smiling into the camera, and Rose in profile, as if passing behind her, was laughing. Once again I could see the loggia in the background. The next photo was an old one. I recognized Bourani. There were five people standing on the steps in front of the house. Conchis was in the middle, a pretty woman beside him was obviously Lily de Seitas. Beside her, his arm round her, was a tall man. I looked on the back; *Bourani, 1935.*

'Who are the other two?'

'One was a friend. And the other was a predecessor of yours.'

'Geoffrey Sugden?' She nodded, but with a touch of surprise. I put the photo down; decided to have a small revenge. 'I traced one pre-war master at the school. He told me quite a lot.'

'Oh?' A shadow of doubt in her calm voice.

'So do let's stick to the truth.'

There was an awkward moment's silence. Her eyes probed mine. 'What did he say?'

'Enough.'

We stared at each other. Then she stood up again and went to the desk. She took a letter out and detached a bottom sheet; checked it, then came and handed it to me. It was a carbon copy of Nevinson's letter to me. On the top he had scrawled: *'Hope this dust does not cause any permanent harm to the recipient's eyes!'* She had turned away and was looking along some bookshelves beside the desk, but now she came back and silently handed me three books in exchange for the letter. I swallowed a sarcasm and looked at the one on top – a school textbook, clothbound in blue. *An Intermediate Greek Anthology for Schools, compiled and annotated by William Hughes, M.A. (Cantab.), 1932.*

'He did that as hackwork. The other two he did for love.'

The second one was a limited edition of a translation of Longus, dated 1936.

'1936. Still Hughes?'

'An author can use whatever name he likes.'

Holmes, Hughes: I remembered a detail from her daughter's story.

'Did he teach at Winchester?'

She smiled. 'Briefly. Before we married.'

The other book was an edition of translations from the poems of Palamas, Solomos, and other modern Greek poets; even some by Seferis.

'Maurice Conchis, the famous poet.' I looked sourly up. 'Brilliant choice on my part.'

She took the books and put them on the table. 'I thought you did it very intelligently.'

'Even though I'm a very foolish young man.'

'Silliness and intelligence are not incompatible. Especially in your sex and at your age.'

She went and sat in her wing chair again, and smiled again at my unsmiling face; an insidiously warm, friendly smile from an intelligent, balanced woman. But how could she be balanced? I went to the window. Sunlight touched my hands. I could see Benjie and the Norwegian girl playing catch down by the loggia. Every so often their cries reached back to us.

'Supposing I'd believed your story about Mr Rat?'

'I should have remembered something very interesting about him.'

'And?'

'You would have come out again to hear it?'

'Supposing I'd never traced you in the first place?'

'A Mrs Hughes would in due course have asked you to lunch.'

'Just like that?'

'Of course not. She would have written a letter.' She sat back, closed her eyes. '"My dear Mr Urfe, I must explain that I have obtained your name from the British Council. My husband, who was the first English master at the Lord Byron School, died recently and among his private papers we have come across an account, hitherto unknown to me, of a remarkable experience that ... "' She opened her eyes and raised her eyebrows interrogatively.

'And when would this call have come? How much longer?'

'I'm afraid I can't tell you that.'

'Won't tell me.'

'No. It is not for me to decide.'

'Look, there's just one person who has to do the deciding. If she –'

'Precisely.'

She reached up to the mantelpiece beside her and took a photo out from behind an ornament there.

'It's not very good. Benjie took it with his Brownie.'

It was of three women on horseback. One was Lily de Seitas. The second was Gunhild. The third, in the middle, was Alison. She looked insecure, and was laughing down into the camera.

'Has she met ... your daughters?'

Her blue-grey eyes stared up at me. 'Please keep it if you wish.'

I flung my will against hers.

'Where is she?'

'You may search the house.'

She watched me, chin on hand, in the yellow chair; unnettled; in possession. Of what, I didn't know; but in possession. I felt like a green young dog in pursuit of a cunning old hare; every time I leapt, I bit brown air. I looked at the photo of Alison, then tore it in four and threw it into an ashtray on a console table by the window. Silence, which eventually she broke.

'My poor resentful young man, let me tell you something. Love may really be more a capacity for love in oneself than anything very lovable in the other person. I believe Alison has a very rare capacity for attachment and devotion. Far more than I have ever had. I think it is very precious. And all I have done is to persuade her that she must not underestimate, as I believe she has all her life till now, what she has to give.'

'How kind.'

She sighed. 'Sarcasm again.'

'Well, what do you expect? Tears of remorse?'

'Sarcasm is so ugly. And so revealing.'

There was silence. After a time, she went on.

'You are really the luckiest and the blindest young man. Lucky because you are born with some charm for women, even though you seem determined not to show it to me. Blind because you have had a little piece of pure womankind in your hands. Do you not realize that Alison possessed the one great quality our sex has to contribute to life? Beside which things like education, class, background, are nothing? And you've let it slip.'

'Helped by your charming daughters.'

'My daughters were nothing but a personification of your own selfishness.'

A dull, deep rage was brewing in me.

'I happened – stupidly, I grant you – to fall in love with one of them.'

'As an unscrupulous collector falls in love with a painting he wants. And will do anything to get.'

'Except that this wasn't a painting. It was a girl with as much morality as a worn-out whore from the Place Pigalle.'

She let a little silence pass, the elegant drawing-room reprove, then said quietly, 'Strong words.'

I turned on her. 'I begin to wonder how much you know. First of all, your not so virgin daugher – '

' I know precisely what she did.' She sat calmly facing me; but a little more erect. 'And I know precisely the reasons behind what she did. But if I told you them, I would tell you everything.'

'Shall I call those two down there? Tell your son how his sister performs – I think that's the euphemism – one week with me, the next with a Negro?'

She let silence pass again, as if to isolate what I said; as people leave a question unanswered in order to snub the questioner.

'Does a Negro make it so much worse?'

'It doesn't make it any better.'

'He is a very intelligent and charming man. They have been sleeping together for some time.'

'And you approve?'

'My approval is unasked for and unnecessary. Lily is of age.'

I grinned sourly at her, then looked out at the garden. 'Now I understand why you grow so many flowers.' She shifted her head, not understanding. I said, 'To cover the stink of sulphur.'

She got up and stood with one hand on the mantelpiece, watching me as I walked about the room; still calm, alert, playing me like a kite. I might plunge and flare; but she held the string.

'Are you prepared to listen without interrupting?'

I looked at her; then shrugged assent.

'Very well. Now let us get this business of what is and what is not sexually proper out of the way.' Her voice was even, as matter-of-fact as one of those woman doctors determined to ban gender from the surgery. 'Because I live in a Queen Anne house do not think I live, like most of the rest of our country, by a Queen Anne morality.'

'Nothing was further from my mind.'

'Will you listen?' I went and stood by the window, my back to her. I felt that at last I ought to have her in a corner; I must have her in a corner. 'How shall I explain to you? If Maurice were here he would tell you that sex is perhaps a greater, but in no way a different, pleasure from any other. He would tell you that it is only one part – and not the essential part – in the relationship we call love. He would tell you that the essential part is truth, the trust two people build between their minds. Their souls. What you will. That the real infidelity is the one that hides the sexual infidelity. Because the one thing that must never come between two people who have offered each other love is a lie.'

I stared out over the lawn. I knew it was prepared, all she was saying; perhaps learnt by heart, a key speech.

'Are you daring to preach to me, Mrs de Seitas?'

'Are you daring to pretend that you do not need the sermon?'

'Look – '

'Please listen to me.' If her voice had held the least sharpness or arrogance, I should not have done so. But it was unexpectedly gentle; almost beseeching. 'I am trying to explain what we are. Maurice convinced us – over twenty years ago – that we should banish the normal taboos of sexual behaviour from our lives. Not because we were more immoral than other people. But because we were more moral. We attempted to do that in our own lives. I have attempted to do it in the way I have brought up our children. And I must make you understand that sex is for us, for all of us who help Maurice, not an important thing. Or not the thing it is in most people's lives. We have more important things to do.'

I would not turn and look at her.

'Before the war I twice played roles somewhat similar to Lily's with you. She is prepared to do things that I was not. I had far more inhibitions to shed. I also had a husband whom I loved sexually as well as in the other more important ways. But since we have penetrated so deep into your life, I owe it to you to say that even when my husband was living I sometimes gave myself, with his full knowledge and consent, to Maurice. And in the war he in his turn had an Indian mistress, with my full knowledge and consent. Yet I believe ours was a very complete marriage, a very happy one, because we kept to two essential rules. We never told each other lies. And the other one ... I will not tell you until I know you better.'

I looked round then, contemptuously. I found her calmness uncomfortable; the madness seething underneath. She sat down again.

'Of course, if you wish to live in the world of received ideas and received manners, what we did, what my daughter did, is disgusting. Very well. But remember that there is another possible explanation. She may have been being very brave. Neither I nor my children pretend to be ordinary people. They were not brought up to be ordinary. We are rich and we are intelligent and we mean to live rich, intelligent lives.'

'Lucky you.'

'Of course. Lucky us. And we accept the responsibility that our good luck in the lottery of existence puts upon us.'

'Responsibility!' I wheeled round on her again.

'Do you really think we do this just for you? Do you really believe we are not ... charting the voyage?' She went on in a milder voice. 'All that we did was to us a necessity.' She meant, not self-indulgence.

'With all the necessity of gratuitous obscenity.'

'With all the necessity of a very complex experiment.'

'I like my experiments simple.'

'The days of simple experiments are over.'

A silence fell between us. I was still full of spleen; and in some obscure way frightened to think of Alison in this woman's hands, as one hears of a countryside one has loved being sold to building developers. And I also felt left behind, abandoned again. I did not belong to this other-planet world.

'I know young men who would envy you.'

'Not if I ever tell the story.'

'Then they will pity you your narrowmindedness.'

She came behind me and put her hand on my shoulder and made me turn.

'Do I look an evil woman? Did my daughters?'

'Actions. Not looks.' My voice sounded raw; I wanted to slap her arm down, to get out.

'Are you absolutely sure our actions have been nothing but evil?'

I looked down. I wouldn't answer. She took her hand away, but stayed close in front of me.

'Will you trust me a little – just for a little while?' I said nothing and she went on. 'You can always telephone me. If you want to watch the house, then do. But I warn you that you will see no one you want to see. Only Benjie and Gunhild and my two middle children when they come home from France next week. Only one person is making you wait at the moment.'

'She should tell me so herself.'

She looked out of the window, then sideways at me. 'I should so like to help you.'

'I want Alison. Not help.'

'May I call you Nicholas now?' I turned from her; went to the sofa-table, stared down at the photos there. 'Very well. I will not ask again.'

'I could go to a newspaper and sell them the story. I could ruin your whole blasted … '

'Just as you could have brought that cat down across my daughter's back.'

I looked sharply back at her. 'It was you? In the sedan?'

'No.'

'Alison?'

'You were told. It was empty.' She met my disbelieving eyes. 'I give you my word. It was not Alison. Or myself.' She smiled at my still suspicious look. 'Well. Perhaps there was someone there.'

'Who?'

'Someone … quite famous in the world. Whose face you might have recognized. That is all.'

Tendrils of her sympathy began to sneak their way through my anger. With a curt look, I wheeled and walked towards the door. She came after me, snatching up a sheet of paper from the top of the desk.

'Please take this.'

I saw a list of names; dates of birth; *Hughes to de Seitas, February 22nd, 1933*; the telephone number.

'It doesn't prove anything.'

'Yes, it does. Go to Somerset House.'

I shrugged, pushed the list carelessly in my pocket and went on without looking at her. I jerked open the front door and went down the steps. She came behind me, but stopped at the top of them. I stood by the driving-door of my car and stared balefully across at her.

'I'll see Alison in hell before I come to you again.'

She opened her mouth as if to answer, but changed her mind. Her face showed a kind of reproach; and a patience, as towards a wayward child. I found the first expression unwarranted and the second, exasperating. I got in the car and switched on. As I went out of the

605

gate I glimpsed her figure in the mirror, beneath the Tuscan porch. She was still standing there, ridiculously as if she were sorry to see me go.

73

Yet even then I knew I was pretending to be angrier than I really was; that just as she was trying to break down my hostility by calm, I was trying to break down her calm by hostility. I didn't in the least regret being ungracious, rebuffing her overtures; and I more than half meant, at the time, what I said about Alison.

Because this was now the active mystery: that I was not allowed to meet Alison. Something was expected of me, some Orphean performance that would gain me access to the underworld where she was hidden ... or hiding herself. I was on probation. But no one gave me any real indication of what I was meant to be proving. I had apparently found the entrance to Tartarus. But that brought me no nearer Eurydice.

Just as the things Lily de Seitas had told me brought me no nearer the permanent mystery: what voyage, what charts?

My anger carried me through the next day; but the day after that I went to Somerset House and found that every fact Lily de Seitas had given me to check was true, and somehow this turned my anger into a depression. That evening I rang up her number in Much Hadham. The Norwegian girl answered the phone.

'Dinsford House. Please, who is it?' I said nothing. Someone must have called, because I heard the girl say, 'There is no one to answer.'

Then there came another voice.

'Hallo. Hallo.'

I put down the receiver. She was still there. But nothing would make me speak to her.

The next day, the third after the visit, I spent in getting drunk and in composing a bitter letter to Alison in Australia. I had decided that that was where she was. It said everything I had to say to her; I must have read it twenty times, as if by reading it enough I could turn it into the definitive truth about my innocence and her complicity.

But I kept on putting off posting it, and in the end it spent the night on the mantelpiece.

I had got into the habit of going down and having breakfast with Kemp most mornings, though not those last three, when I had carried with me a scowl against the whole human condition. Kemp had no time at all for the kitchen, but she could make a good cup of coffee; and on the fourth morning, I badly needed it.

When I came in she put the *Daily Worker* down – she read the *Worker* 'for the truth' and a certain other paper 'for the fucking lies' – and sat there smoking. Her mouth without a cigarette was like a yacht without a mast; one presumed disaster. We exchanged a couple of sentences. She fell silent. But during the next few minutes I became aware that I was undergoing a prolonged scrutiny through the smoke she wore like a merciful veil in front of her Gorgonlike morning face. I pretended to read, but that didn't deceive her.

'What's up with you, Nick?'

'Up with me?'

'No friends. No girls. Nothing.'

'Not at this time of the morning. Please.'

She sat there dumpily, in an old red dressing-gown, her hair uncombed, as old as time.

'You're not looking for a job. That's all my fanny.'

'If you say so.'

'I'm trying to help you.'

'I know you are, Kemp.'

I looked up at her face. It was pasty, bloated, with the eyes permanently narrowed against tobacco smoke; somehow like a mask in a *Noh* play, which in an odd way suited the Cockney resonances that loitered in her voice and the hard anti-sentimentality she affected. But now, in what was for her an extraordinary gesture of affection, she reached across the table and patted my hand. She was, I knew, five years younger than Lily de Seitas; and yet she looked ten years older. She was by ordinary standards foul-mouthed; a blatant member of what had been my father's most hated regiment, one he used to consign far lower even than the Damned Socialists and the Blasted Whitehall Airy-fairies – the Longhaired Brigade. I had a moment's vision of his standing, his aggressive blue eyes, his bushy colonel's moustache, in the door of the studio; the unmade divan, the stinking old rusty oil-stove, the mess on the table, the garish sexual-foetal abstract oils that littered the walls; a tat of old pottery, old clothes, old newspapers. But in that short gesture of hers, and the look that accompanied it, I knew there was more real humanity than I had ever known in my own home. Yet still that home, those years, governed me; I had to repress the natural response. Our eyes met across a gap I could not bridge; her offer of a rough temporary motherhood, my flight to what I had to be, the lonely son. She withdrew her hand.

I said, 'It's too complicated.'

'I've got all day.'

Her face peered at me through the blue smoke, and suddenly it seemed as blank, as menacing, as an interrogator's. I liked her, I liked her, yet I felt her curiosity like a net drawn round me. I was like some freakish parasitic species that could establish itself only in one rare kind of situation, by one precarious symbiosis. They had been wrong, at the trial. It was not that I preyed on girls; but the fact that my only access to normal humanity, to social decency, to any openness of heart, lay through girls, preyed on me. It was in that that I was the real victim.

There was only one person I wanted to talk with. Till then I could not move, advance, plan, progress, become a better human being, anything; and till then, I carried my mystery, my secret, round with me like a defence; as my only companion.

'One day, Kemp. Not now.'

She shrugged; gave me a stonily sibylline look, auguring the worst.

The old woman who cleaned the stairs once a fortnight bawled through the door. My telephone was ringing. I raced up the stairs, lifting the receiver on what seemed the dying ring.

'Hallo. Nicholas Urfe.'

'Oh, good morning, Urfe. It's me. Sandy Mitford.'

'You're back!'

'What's left of me, old man. What's left of me.' He cleared his throat. 'Got your note. Wondered if you were free for a spot of lunchington.'

608

A minute later, a time and place fixed, I was reading once more my letter to Alison. The injured Malvolio stalked through every line. In another minute there was no letter; but, as with every other relationship in my life, an eschar of ashes. The word is rare, but exact.

Mitford hadn't changed at all, in fact I could have sworn that he was wearing the same clothes, the same dark-blue blazer, dark-grey flannels, club tie. They looked a little shabbier, like their wearer; he was far less jaunty than I remembered, though after a few gins he got back some of his old guerilla cockiness. He had spent the summer 'carting bands of Americans' round Spain; no, he'd received no letter from Phraxos from me. They must have destroyed it. There was something they hadn't wanted him to tell.

Over sandwiches we had a talk about the school. Bourani wasn't mentioned. He kept on saying that he'd warned me, and I said, yes, he'd warned me. I waited for a chance to broach the only subject that interested me. Eventually, as I'd been hoping, he made the opening himself.

'Ever get over to the waiting-room?'

I knew at once that the question was not as casual as he tried to make it sound; that he was both afraid and curious; that in fact we both had the same reason for meeting.

'Oh God now, I meant to ask you about that. Do you remember, just as we said goodbye ... '

'Yes.' He gave me a tightly cautious look. 'Never went to a bay called Moutsa? Rather jolly, over on the south side?'

'Of course. I know it.'

'Ever notice the villa on the cape to the east?'

'Yes. It was always shut up. I was told.'

'Ah. Interesting. Very interesting.' He looked reminiscently across the lounge; left me in suspense. I watched him lift, an infuriating upward arc, his cigarette to his lips; the gentleman connoisseur of fine Virginia; then fume smoke through his nostrils. 'Well that was it, old boy. Nothing really.'

'But why beware?'

'Oh it's nothing. No-thing at all.'

'Then you can tell me.'

'I did, actually.'

'You did!'

'Row with collaborationist. Remember?'

'Yes.'

'Same man who has the villa.'

'Oh but ... ' I flicked my fingers ... 'wait a moment. What was his name?'

'Conchis.' He had an amused smile on his face, as if he knew what I was going to say. He touched his moustache; always preening his moustache.

'But I thought he did something rather fine during the resistance.'

'Not on your nelly. Actually he did a deal with the Germans. Personally organized the shooting of eighty villagers. Then got his kraut chums to line him up with them. See. As if he was all brave and innocent.'

'But wasn't he badly wounded, or something?'

He blew out smoke, despising my innocence. 'You don't survive a German execution, old boy. No, the bugger pulled a very fast one. Acted like a traitor and got treated like a bloody hero. Even forged a phoney German report on the incident. One of the neatest little cover-up jobs of the war.'

I looked sharply at him. A dreadful new suspicion crossed my mind. New corridors in the labyrinth.

'But hasn't anyone ... ?'

Mitford made the Greek corruption gesture; thumb and forefinger.

I said, 'You still haven't explained the waiting-room business.'

'His name for the villa. Waiting for death or something. Had it nailed up on a tree in Frog.' His finger traced a line. '*Salle d'attente.*'

'What happened between you?'

'Nothing, old boy. Absolutely nothing.'

'Come on.' I smiled ingenuously. 'Now I know the place.'

I remembered as a very small boy lying on the bough of a willow over a Hampshire stream; I was watching my father casting for a trout. It was his one delicacy, casting a dry fly, posing it on the water as soft as thistledown. I could see the trout he was trying to coax into a rise. And I remembered that moment when the fish floated slowly up and hovered beneath the fly, a moment endlessly prolonged in a heart-stopping excitement; then the sudden swift kick of the tail and the lightning switch of my father's strike; the ratcheting of the reel.

'It's nothing, old boy. Really.'

'Of for God's sake. What's it matter?'

'All damned absurd.' The fish took the fly. 'Actually I was out walking one day. May or June, can't remember. Bit browned off at the school. Went over to Moutsa to swim and well, I came down, you know the place, through the trees and what did I see – not just a couple of girls. But a couple of girls in next to nothing. Quick recce. Niftiest beeline I knew how towards them, said something in Greek, and damn me they answered in English. They *were* English. Gorgeous creatures. Twins.'

'Good Lord. Let me get you another gin.'

I stood at the bar waiting for the drinks and watched myself in the mirror; gave myself the smallest wink.

'*Sygeia*. Well, you can imagine, I moved in *poly* fast. Consolidated position. Found out who they were. Old boy's godchildren up at the villa. Bang out of the top drawer, finished in Switzerland, All that. Said they were there for the summer and that the old boy would very much like to meet me, why didn't I come up for tea. Nuff said. Off we trotted. Meet the old boy. Tea.'

He had the same old habit of stretching his neck up, as if his collar was too tight; to make himself look a man of the world.

'This what's-his-name spoke English?'

'Perfect. Moved round Europe all his life, best society and all that. Well, actually I found one of the twins a shade off. Not my type. Rather marked the other for my area of ops. Okay, the old man and the not-on twin faded away after tea and this girl, June, that was her name, took me round the property.'

'Nice work.'

'Didn't actually get round to unarmed combat at that point, but I sort of felt she was ready and willing. You know how it was on the island. Full magazine on and nothing to shoot at.'

'Rather.'

He flexed his arm, caressed the back of his hair. 'Right. I trotted off back to the school. Tender farewell. Invitation to dinner the next week-end. Week passes, I present myself over there in my number ones. Other necessary equipment. Drinks, girls looking smashing. But then.' He gave me a taut, suspenseful look. 'Well, as a matter of fact the other girl, not June, got stinkers.'

'Christ.'

'I'd got her number the week before. One of these bloody intellectual girls. Pretend to be as tough as nuts, but a couple of gins put 'em out stone cold. Well, it got pretty bloody dicey during dinner. Damned embarrassing. This Julie girl took against me. Didn't take much notice at first. I thought, well, the girl's a bit squiffy. Time of the month or something. But ... actually she began, well she began to make fun of me in a damn silly sort of way.'

'How?'

'Oh ... you know, copied my voice. Way I say things. I suppose she was quite good at it. Damned offensive all the same.'

'But what was she saying?'

'Oh a load of stupid cock about pacifism and the bomb. You know the type. And I just wasn't having any.'

'Didn't the others join in?'

'Hardly said a word. Too damn embarrassed. Well anyway suddenly wham this Julie girl shouted a whole string of really bloody nasty insults. Lost her temper completely. And then all hell broke loose. This other June girl got up and went for her. The old man flapped his hands like a wounded crow. Then the Julie one rushed away. Then her sister. I was left sitting there with the old man. He started talking about them being orphans. Load of guff. Sort of apology.'

'What were these insults she shouted?'

'Old boy, I can't remember now. The girl was pissed.' He dredged his memory. 'Called me a Nazi, actually.'

'A Nazi!'

'One of the things we were rowing about was Mosley.'

'You're not a – '

'Of course not, old boy. Good God.' He laughed, then flicked a look at me. 'But let's face it, not all Mosley says is rot. If you ask me this country *has* got bloody sloppy.' He stretched his neck. 'Bit more discipline. National pride ... '

'Maybe, but Mosley?'

'Old man, don't get me wrong. Who the hell do you think I was fighting against in the war? It's just that ... well, take your Spain. Look what Franco's done for Spain.'

'I thought all he'd done was build a lot of dungeons in Barcelona.'

'Ever been to Spain, old man?'

'No, I haven't, as a matter of fact.'

'Well, till you have I'd keep quiet about what Franco has and hasn't done.'

I silently counted five.

'Sorry. Forget it. Do go on.'

'As it happens I've read some of Mosley's stuff, and a lot of it makes sense.' He articulated the words with curt clarity. 'Quite a lot of sense.'

'I'm sure.'

He metaphorically preened his ruffled feathers and went on.

'My twin came back, the old bloke left us for a few minutes and actually she was, seemed, damn sweet. Course I played up the hurt line and sort of indicated that a little stroll in the moonlight later would help me get back to normal. And then, she said wham – Stroll? How about a swim? And believe me, old boy, you only had to hear her say it to see swimming might lead to very interesting other activities. Midnight on the dot, at the gate. Okay, we go to bed at eleven, I sit round waiting for zero-hour. Slip out of the house. No problems. Get to the gate. Five minutes later, along she comes. And old man, I can tell you, I've been in some clinches in my time, but that girl lit up like a bomb. Began to think Operation Midnight Swim was going to be cancelled for a more important exercise. But she said she wanted to cool off for a while.'

'I'm glad you didn't tell me all this before I went. The disappointment would have killed me.'

He smiled condescendingly. 'We got down to the beach. She says, I haven't got a costume, do you mind going in first. I think, well maybe she's shy, maybe she wants to do the necessary. Fine. Operation undress. She retires into the trees. Charley does exactly what he's told, swims out fifty yards, treads water, waits two minuutes, three, four, actually in the end about ten, begins to feel damn cold. Still no girl.'

'And your clothes gone.'

'You've got it, old boy. Stark naked. Standing on that bloody beach hissing the damn girl's name.' I laughed, but his smile was very thin. 'So. Big joke. Message received. You can imagine how damned angry I was by then. I gave her half an hour to come back. Searched round. No go. Marched off to the house. Didn't do my feet much good. Tore a bit of pine-branch off to cover the old privates if necessary.'

'Fantastic.'

I was beginning to find it difficult not to grin all over my face; but I was clearly meant to share the outrage.

'Through the gate, up the drive thing, towards the house. Go round the front. What do you think I see there?' I shook my head. 'A man hanging.'

'You're joking.'

'No, old boy. They were doing the joking. Actually it was a dummy. Like one of those things you use in bayonet practice, yes? Filled with straw. Strung up with a rope round its neck. And my clothes on. Head painted to look like Hitler.'

'Good God. What did you do?'

'What could I do? Pulled the damn thing down and got my clothes off it.'

'And then?'

'Nix. They'd gone. Hooked it.'

'Gone?'

'Caïque. Heard it down at Moutsa. Thought it was a fisherman. Left my bag out for me. Nothing pinched. Just that bloody four-mile walk back to the school.'

'You must have been furious.'

'*Was* slightly chokka. Yes.'

'But you didn't let them get away with it.'

He smiled to himself.

'Right. Quite simple. I composed a little report. First about the thing during the war. Then a few little facts about where our friend Mr Conchis's present political sympathies lay. Sent it to the appropriate quarters.'

'Communist?' Since the end of the civil war in 1950, Communists had been hounded relentlessly in Greece.

'Knew some in Crete. Just said I'd seen a couple on Phraxos and followed them to his house. That's enough, that's all they want. A little bit goes a long way. Now you know why you never had the pleasure.'

I fingered the stem of my glass, thinking that, on the contrary, this absurd man beside me was probably why I had had 'the pleasure'. Somewhere that previous year, as 'June' had admitted, they must have made a bad miscalculation, and given up: such an absence of cunning in the fox must have made them call off the hunt almost as soon as it started. What had Conchis said about my own initial participation being a matter of hazard? At least I had given them a run for their money. I smiled at Mitford.

'And so you had the last laugh.'

'Habit of mine, old boy. Suits my complexion.'

'Why on earth did they do it in the first place? I mean, all right, they didn't like you … but they could have given you the brush-off from the beginning.'

'All that stuff about their being the old boy's godchildren. All my eye. Course they weren't. They were a pair of high-class tarts. Language the Julie one used gave the game away. Damn funny way of looking at you … suggestive.' He glanced at me. 'It was the sort of set-up you run across in the Mediterranean – especially your Eastern Mediterranean. I've met it before.'

'You mean … '

'I mean, quite crudely, old boy, that the rich Mr Conchis wasn't quite up to the job, but he … shall we say … still got pleasure from seeing the job performed?'

Again I surreptitiously eyed him; knew myself lost in the interminable maze of echoes. Was he, or wasn't he?

'But they didn't actually suggest anything?'

'There were hints. I worked them out afterwards. There were hints.'

He went away and got two more gins.

'You might have warned me.'

'I did, old boy.'

'Not very clearly.'

'You know what Xan – Xan Fielding – used to do to any new chaps who were 'chuted in when we were up in the Levka Ore?

Sent 'em wham straight out on a job. No warnings, no sermons. Just – "Watch it." Okay?'

I disliked Mitford because he was crass and mean, but even more because he was a caricature, an extension, of certain qualities in myself; he had on his skin, visible, the carcinoma I nursed inside me. I had to suspect the old paranoia, that he might be another 'plant' – a test for me, a lesson; but yet there was something so ineffably impervious about the man that I could not believe he was so consummate an actor. I thought of Lily de Seitas; how to her I must seem as Mitford did to myself. A barbarian.

We moved out of the Mandrake on to the pavement.

'I'm off to Greece next month,' he said.

'Oh.'

'Firm's going to start tours there next summer.'

'Oh God. No.'

'Do the place good. Shake their ideas up.'

I looked down the crowded Soho street. 'I hope Zeus strikes you with lightning the moment you get there.'

He took it as a joke.

'Age of the common man, old boy. Age of the common man.'

He held out his hand. I would have dearly loved to have known how to twist it and send him wham straight over my shoulder. The last I saw of him was of a dark-blue back marching towards Shaftesbury Avenue; eternally the victor in a war where the losers win.

Years later I discovered that he *had* been acting that day, though not in the way that I feared. His name caught my eye in a newspaper. He had been arrested in Torquay on charges of issuing cheques under false pretences. He'd been doing it all over England, using the persona of Captain Alexander Mitford, D.S.O., M.C.

'In fact,' said prosecuting counsel, 'although the accused went to Greece in the occupying forces after the German collapse, he played no part whatever in the Resistance.' Later there was another bit: 'Some time after demobilization Mitford returned to Greece, where he obtained a teaching post by forging false references. He was subsequently dismissed from this post.'

Late that afternoon I dialled the Much Hadham number. It rang a long time but then someone answered. I heard Lily de Seitas's voice. She was out of breath.

'Dinsford House.'

'It's me. Nicholas Urfe.'

'Oh, hallo.' She said it with a bright indifference. 'Sorry. I was in the garden.'

'I'd like to see you again.'

There was a small pause. 'I have no news.'

'I'd still like to see you.'

I knew she was smiling, in the silence that followed.

She said, 'When?'

74

I was out the next morning. When I got back, about two, I found Kemp had slipped a note under my door: 'A Yank called. Says it's urgent. Will come again four.' I went down to see her. She was splaying great worms of viridian green with her thumb across murky black and umber explosions of Ripolin. She did not like to be interrupted when she was 'making a painting'.

'This man.'

'Said he must see you.'

'What about?'

'Going to Greece.' She stood stockily back, fag in mouth, contemplating her mess. 'Your old job or something.'

'But how did he find where I live?'

'Don't ask me.'

I stood staring at the note. 'What sort of man was he?'

'Christ, can't you wait a couple of hours?' She turned. 'Buzz.'

He came at five to four, a tallish man with a lean body and the unmistakable cropped head of an American. He wore glasses, was a year or two younger than me; pleasant face, pleasant smile, pleasant everything; as wholesome, and as green, as a lettuce. He thrust out a hand.

'John Briggs.'

'Hallo.'

'You're Nicholas Urfe? Is that how I pronounce it? The lady … '

I made him come in. 'Not much of a place, I'm afraid.'

'It's nice.' He looked round for a better word. 'Atmosphere.' We clambered up the stairs.

'I wasn't expecting an American.'

'No. Well. I guess it's the Cyprus situation.'

'Ah.'

'I've been over here this last year at London University. All along I've been trying to figure how I could get myself a year in Greece before I return home. You don't know how excited I am.' We came to a landing. He saw some of the sewing-girls at work through an open door. Two or three of them whistled. He waved to them. 'Isn't that nice? Reminds me of Thomas Hood.'

'Where did you hear about the job?'

'In *The Times Educational Supplement*.' He gave even the most familiar English institutions an interrogative intonation, as if I might not have heard of them.

We came to my flat. I closed the door.

'I thought the British Council had stopped doing the recruiting.'

'Is that so? I suppose the school committee decided that as Mr Conchis was over here he might as well do the interviewing.' He had gone into the sitting-room and was looking at the view down grimy old Charlotte Street. 'This is great. You know, I *love* this city.' I indicated the least greasy of the armchairs.

'And … Mr Conchis gave you my address?'

'Sure. Was that wrong?'

'No. Not at all.' I sat on the window-seat. 'Did he tell you anything about me?'

He raised his hand, as if I might need quietening down. 'Well yes, he – I do know, I mean … he warned me how dangerous these college intrigues can get. As I understand you had the misfortune … ' he gave up. 'You still feel sore about it?'

I shrugged. 'Greece is Greece.'

'I bet they're rubbing their hands already at the thought of a real live American.'

'They probably are.' He shook his head, as if the thought that anyone could involve a real live American in a Levantine academic intrigue was almost past belief. I said, 'When did you see Mr Conchis?'

'When he was here three weeks ago. I'd have gotten in contact earlier, but he lost your address. He just sent it me from Greece. Only this morning.'

'Only this morning?'

'Yep. A cable.' He grinned. 'Surprised me too. I thought he'd forgotten about it. You ... you know him pretty well?'

'Oh I ... met him a few times. I was actually never terribly clear about his position on the school committee.'

'What he told me, no official position. Just helping out. Jesus, his English is marvellous though.'

'Isn't it?'

We sized each other up. He had a relaxed way about him that seemed inculcated by education, by reading some book on How To Be At Ease With Strangers, rather than by any intuitive gift. Nothing, one felt, had ever gone wrong in his life; but he had a sort of freshness, an enthusiasm, an energy that couldn't be totally cancelled by envy.

I analysed the situation. The natural coincidence of his appearing and my call to Much Hadham was so improbable that it was almost an argument in favour of his innocence. On the other hand Mrs de Seitas must have deduced from my telephone call that I was undergoing a change of heart; and this was nicely timed to test its genuineness. Yet telling me about the cable made him sound truly innocent; and though I had understood that the 'subject' had to be a matter of hazard, perhaps there was some reason, some unknown result of that summer, that had made Conchis decide to choose his next guinea-pig. Faced with the guileless, earnest Briggs I felt a little of what Mitford must have felt with me: a malicious amusement, bedevilled in my case by a European delight in seeing brash America being taken for a ride; and beyond that a kinder wish, which I would never have admitted to Conchis or Lily de Seitas, not to spoil his experience.

Of course they must have known (if Briggs was innocent) that I might tell him everything; but they also knew I knew the cost of it, if I did. It could only mean, to them, that I accepted nothing; and could be given nothing further in return. I was torn before the risks they took: tempted to punish, forced to admire. But finally, once again, I was left standing with the cat in my hand, unable to bring it down.

Briggs had pulled out a pad from the briefcase he had with him.

'May I ask questions? I've got quite a list.'

And again: the coincidence. He was doing exactly what I had done only a few days before, at Dinsford House. His eager, deceitless face smiled up at me. I smiled back.

'Shoot.'

He was terrifyingly methodical. Teaching methods, textbooks, clothes, climate, sports facilities, medicines to take, food, the size of the library, what to see in Greece, character sketches of the other masters – he wanted information about every conceivable aspect of life on Phraxos. Finally he looked up from his pad and the notes he had copiously pencilled and took up the beer I had poured him.

'Thanks a million. This is wonderful. Covers everything.'

'Except the actual business of living there.'

He nodded. 'Mr Conchis warned me.'

'You speak Greek?'

'Little Latin, less Greek.'

'You'll pick it up.'

'I'm taking lessons already.'

'And no women.'

He nodded. 'Tough. But I'm engaged, so anyway.' He produced a wallet and handed me a photo. A black-haired girl smiled rather intensely out at me. She had too small a mouth; I detected the ghostly beginnings of the mask of the bitch-goddess Ambition.

I handed it back. 'Looks English.'

'She is. Well, Welsh, actually. She's studying drama right here in London.'

'Really.'

'I thought maybe she could come out to Phraxos next summer. If I haven't I got the sack by then.'

'Did you … mention it to Mr Conchis?'

'I did. And he was really nice about it. Even said she might be able to stay in his house.'

'I wonder which one. He has two, you know.'

'I think he said in the village.' He grinned. 'Matter of fact he said he'd make me pay for her room.'

'Oh?'

'Wants me to help him on this ... ' he made a kind of you-know gesture.

'On this?'

'Didn't you ... ' but he obviously saw from my face that whatever it was, I didn't. 'Well, maybe ... '

'Oh good lord, you can tell me.'

He hesitated, then smiled. 'It's just that he does want it kept secret. I thought you might have heard, but if you didn't meet him much ... this remarkable find on his estate?'

'Find?'

'You know the house? It's some place on the other side of the island.'

'I know where it is.'

'Well, it seems part of a cliff fell away this summer and they've discovered what he believes to be the foundations of a Mycenean palace.'

'He'll never keep that quiet.'

'I'd guess not. But he thinks he can for a while. Apparently he's covered it up with loose dirt. Then next spring he's going to dig. But naturally right now he doesn't want everyone visiting all over.'

'Of course.'

'So I hope I shan't be too bored.'

I saw Lily dressed as the snake-goddess of Knossos; as Electra; as Clytemnestra; Doctor Vanessa Maxwell, the brilliant young archaeologist.

'Doesn't sound as if you will.'

He finished his beer, and looked at his watch.

'Jesus, I must run. I'm meeting Amanda at six.' He shook my hand. 'You don't know how much this has meant to me. And believe me, I'll write and let you know how it goes.'

'Do that. I'd very much like to know.'

I followed him down the stairs and watched his crewcut head. I began to understand why Conchis had picked him. If one had taken a million young college-educated Americans and distilled them down into one quintessential exemplar one would have arrived at something like Briggs. I did not like to think of the omnipenetrating Americans reaching to so private a European core. But I remembered his name; much more English than my own. And there was already Joe; the prosecuting Doctor Marcus.

We came out on the front step.

'No last words of wisdom?'

'I don't think so. Just my very good wishes.'

'Well ...'

We shook hands again.

'You'll be all right.'

'You really think so?'

'Of course you'll find some of the experiences distinctly strange.'

'Oh sure. Don't think I'm not going with a wide open mind. And prepared for everything. Thanks to you.'

I gave him a long smile; I wanted him to remember that it was a smile that had said more than the occasion warranted. He raised his hand and set off. After a few paces he looked at his watch, and began to run; and in my heart I lit a candle to Leverrier.

75

She was ten minutes late; came quickly, a polite small torment of apology on her face, and straight to where I had been standing next to the postcard counter.

'I'm so sorry. The taxi crawled.'

I shook her outstretched hand. For a woman half a century old she was impressively good-looking; and she was dressed with an easy flair that made most of the dull afternoon visitors to the Victoria and Albert around us look even drabber than they really were; defiantly bareheaded, and in a grey-white Chanel suit that set off her tan and her clear eyes.

'It's such a mad place to meet. Do you mind?'

'Not in the least.'

'I bought an eighteenth-century plate the other day. They're so good at identifying here. It won't take a moment.'

She evidently knew the museum well and led the way to the lifts. We had to wait. She smiled at me; the family smile; soliciting, I suspected, what I was still not prepared to give. Determined to tread delicately between her approval and my own dignity, I had a dozen things ready to say, but her breathless arrival, the sudden feeling I had that I was being fitted, inconveniently, into a busy day, made them all seem wrong.

I said, 'I saw John Briggs on Tuesday.'

'How interesting. I haven't met him.' We might have been talking about the new curate. The lift came, and we stepped inside.

'I told him everything I knew. All about Bourani and what to expect.'

'We thought you would. That's why we sent him to you.'

We were both smiling, faintly; a cramped silence.

'But I might have.'

'Yes.' The lift stopped. We emerged into a gallery of furniture. 'Yes. You might.'

'Perhaps he was just a test.'

'A test wasn't necessary.'

'You're very sure.'

She gave me that same wide-eyed look she had had when she handed me the copy of Nevinson's letter. At the end of the gallery we came to a door: *Department of Ceramics*. She pressed the bell beside it.

I said, 'I think we've got off on the wrong foot.'

She looked down.

'Well, yes. Shall we try again in a minute? If you wouldn't mind waiting?'

The door opened and she was let inside. It was all too rushed, too broken, she gave me no chance, though her last quick look back before the door closed seemed apologetic; almost as if she was afraid I might run away.

Two minutes later she came back.

'Any luck?'

'Yes, it's what I hoped it was. Bow.'

'You don't trust your intuition in everything, then.'

She gave me an amused look. 'If there was a Department of Young Men ... '

'And then keep me labelled on a shelf?'

She smiled again, and glanced at the hall behind me. 'I don't really like museums. And especially those of past attitudes.' She moved. 'They say there's a similar plate on display. Just through here.'

We went into a long deserted gallery of china. I began to suspect she had rehearsed this scene, since she went straight to one of the wall-cases. She took the plate out of her basket and held it up, walking slowly along until behind a group of cups and jugs, an almost identical blue-and-white plate appeared. I went beside her.

'That's it.'

She compared them; wrapped her own loosely in its tissue paper again, and then, taking me completely by surprise, presented it.

'For you.'

'But –'

'Please.' She challenged my almost offended face. 'I bought it with Alison.' She corrected herself. 'Alison was with me when I bought it.'

It was pushed gently into my hands. At a loss, I unwrapped it, and stared down at a naïvely drawn Chinaman and his wife, their two children between them, eternal ceramic fossils, in the centre. For some reason I thought of peasants travelling steerage, the swell, the night wind.

'I think you should get used to handling fragile objects. And ones much more valuable than that.'

I still stared down at the inky-blue figures.

'That's really why I asked to meet you.'

Our eyes met; and for the first time I had a sense of not just being assessed.

'Shall we go and have our tea?'

'Well,' she said, 'why you really asked to meet me.'

We had found a table in the corner, and been served.

'Alison.'

'I did tell you.' She picked up the tea-pot. 'It depends on her.'

'And on you.'

'No. Not in the least on me.'

'Is she in London?'

'I have promised her not to tell you where she is.'

'Look, Mrs de Seitas, I think – ' but I swallowed what I was going to say. I watched her pouring the tea; not otherwise helping me. 'What the hell does she want? What am I supposed to do now?'

'Is that too strong?' I shook my head impatiently at the cup she held out. She poured some milk into her own cup, passed me the jug. She had a small smile. 'I never take anger at face value.'

I wanted to shake that off as I had wanted to shake off her hand the week before; but I knew that behind the implicit condescension it was a valid statement of the difference between our two experiences of life. There was something discreetly maternal in it, a reminder to me that if I rebelled against her judgment, I rebelled against my own immaturity – if against her urbanity, against my own lack of it. I looked down.

'It's simply that I'm not prepared to wait much longer.'

'Then she will be well rid of you.'

I drank some of the tea. She began calmly to spread honey over her toast.

I said, 'My name is Nicholas.' Her hands were momentarily arrested, then she went on spreading the honey ... in more senses than one, perhaps. 'Is that the right votive offering?'

'If it is made sincerely.'

'As sincerely as your offer of help the other day.'

'Did you go to Somerset House?'

'Yes.'

She put down her knife, faced me.

'Wait as long as Alison makes you wait. I do not think it will be very long. But I can't do anything to bring her to you. Now it is simply between you and her. I hope she will forgive you. But you must not be certain that she will. You still have to gain her back.'

'There's gaining back to be done on both sides.'

'Perhaps. That is for the two of you to settle.' She surveyed the sliver of toast in her hand a moment, then smiled up. 'The godgame is over.'

'The what?'

'The godgame.' For a moment there was something both faintly mischievous and sardonic in her eyes. 'Because there is no God, and it is not a game.'

She began to eat her toast, and I glanced past her at the busy, banal tea-room. The discreet chink of cutlery on china, the murmur of middle-class voices; sounds as commonplace as sparrows' chirruping.

'That's what you call it?'

'A kind of nickname we use.'

'If I had any self-respect left, I'd get up and walk out.'

'I'm counting on you to help find me a taxi in a minute. We've been doing Benjie's school shopping today.'

'Demeter in a department store?'

'No? I think she would have liked them. Even the gaberdine mackintoshes and gym shoes.'

'And does she like questions?'

'That depends on the questions.'

'Am I ever going to be told what you really think you're doing?'

'You have been told.'

'Lie upon lie.'

'Perhaps that's our way of telling the truth.' But then, as if she knew she had smiled once too often, she looked down and added quickly. 'Maurice once said to me – when I had just asked him a question rather like yours – he said, "An answer is always a form of death".'

There was something else in her face then. It was not implacable; but in some way impermeable.

'I think questions are a form of life.' She said nothing, though I waited. 'All right. I treated Alison very badly. I'm a born cad, a swine, whatever you want. But why the colossal performance just to tell one miserable moral bankrupt what he is?'

'Have you never wondered why evolution should have bothered to split itself up into so many different shapes and sizes? Doesn't that also seem an unnecessary performance?'

'Maurice gave me that line. I know what you're saying in some vague metaphysical way, but –'

'I should like to be sure. Tell me.'

'That there must be some purpose in our not all being perfect – not all the same.'

'And what is the purpose?'

I shrugged. 'That it allows the duds like me freedom to become a little less imperfect?'

'Did you have any sense of that before this summer?'

'I didn't need to be told I was far from perfect.'

'Had you done anything about it?'

'Not very much, no.'

'Why not?'

'Because it ... ' I took a breath and looked down. 'I'm not defending what I was.'

'And still not accepting what you might become?'

'It's not the lesson. The manner of it.'

She hesitated, and once more I was being assessed, but she spoke much less peremptorily.

'I know they said some terrible things to you at that mock trial, Nicholas. But you were the judge. And if the terrible things had been all that was to be said about you, you would not have given the verdict that you did. Everyone there knew that. Not least my daughters.'

'Why did she let me make love to her?'

'I understand it was her wish. Her decision.'

'That doesn't answer my question.'

'Then I imagine to teach you that physical pleasure and moral responsibility are two very different things.' I recalled Lily's last words to me on that bed; and decided I had one small secret to myself. That night had been more complex, or less certain, than a planned lesson; or at least it had been a lesson that went both ways. Her mother went on. 'Nicholas, if one is trying to reproduce, however partially, something of the mysterious purposes that govern existence, then one also has to go beyond some of the conventions man has invented to keep those purposes at bay. That doesn't mean that in our ordinary lives we think such conventions should be swept away. Far from it. They are necessary fictions. But in the godgame we start from the premise that in reality all is fiction, yet no single fiction is necessary.' She smiled. 'And I'm being lured into deeper waters than I meant to enter.'

I gave her a little smile back. 'But I notice not into what began this – why in practical terms you picked on me.'

'The basic principle of life is hazard. Maurice tells me that this is no longer even a matter of debate. If one goes deep enough in atomic physics one ends with a situation of pure chance. Of course we all share the illusion that this can't be so.'

'But next year you are fixing the odds a little?'

'Hardly. Who knows how he will react?'

'What would have happened if I'd brought Alison to the island? It was suggested at one point.'

'I can assure you of one thing. Maurice would have recognized at once that she was not a person whose emotional honesty needed to be put to the test.'

I looked down. 'Does she know about … ?'

'She understands what we are about. The details … no.'

'Did she agree at once?'

'I know she agreed finally, at least to the pretence of suicide, only in the certainty that you would soon discover it was a pretence.'

I left a pause.

'Have you told her I want to see her?'

'She knows my views on that.'

'I'm not worth a further second's thought.'

'Only when you say such things.'

I traced patterns with the cake-fork on the table-cloth; determined to seem guarded, unconvinced.

'What happened to you that very first year?'

'The desire to help Maurice through following years.' She was silent a moment, then went on. 'I will tell you that it all began one week-end, not even that, one long night of talking that began in a guilt. When my uncle died, Bill and I suddenly found ourselves comparatively rich. It had been something of what people nowadays call a traumatic experience for us. We were discussing it with Maurice. Certain … leaps were taken. Certain gaps bridged. I imagine – don't you? – all new discoveries happen like that. Very abruptly. But totally. And from then on you are obliged to explore them to their limits.'

'And their victims'?'

'Nicholas, our success is never certain. You have entered our secret. Now you are like a radio-active substance. We hope to keep you stable. But we are not sure.' She glanced down. 'Someone … rather in your position … once told me that I was like a pool. He wanted to throw a stone into me. I am not so calm in these situations as I may appear.'

'I think you handle them very intelligently.'

'*Touchée.*' She bowed her head. Then she said, 'Next week I'm going away – as I do every autumn when the children are off my hands. I shan't be hiding, but just doing what I do every September.'

'You'll be with ... him?'

'Yes.'

Something curiously like an apology lingered in the air; as if she knew the twinge of strange jealousy I felt and could not deny that it was justified; that whatever richness of relationship and shared experience I suspected, existed.

She looked at her watch. 'Oh dear. I'm so sorry. But Gunhild and and Benjie will be waiting for me at King's Cross. Those lovely cakes ... '

They lay in their repulsive polychrome splendour, untouched.

'I think one pays for the pleasure of not eating them.'

She grimaced agreement, and I beckoned to the waitress for the bill. While were were waiting she said, 'One thing I wanted to tell you is that in the last three years Maurice has had two quite serious heart attacks. So there may not even be ... a next year.'

'Yes. He told me.'

'And you did not believe him?'

'No.'

'Do you believe me?'

I answered obliquely. 'Nothing you said could make me believe that if he died there would not be another year.'

She took off her gloves. 'Why do you say that?'

I smiled at her; her own smile.

She nearly spoke, then chose silence. I remembered that phrase I had had to use of Lily: out of role. Her mother's eyes, and Lily's through them; the labyrinth; privileges bestowed and privileges rejected. A truce.

A minute later we were going down the corridor towards the entrance. Two men came down it towards us. They were about to pass when the one on the left gave a kind of gasp. Lily de Seitas stopped; she too was caught completely by surprise. He was in a dark-blue suit with a bow tie, a mane of prematurely white hair, a voluble, fleshy mouth in a florid face. She turned quickly.

'Nicholas – would you excuse me – and get me that taxi?'

He had the face of a man, a distinguished man, suddenly become a boy again, rather comically melted by this evidently unexpected meeting into a green remembering. I made a convenient show of excessive politeness to some other people heading for the tea-room, which allowed me to hang back a moment. He was holding both her hands, drawing her aside, and she was smiling, that strange smile of hers, like Ceres returned to the barren land. I had to go on, but I turned again at the end of the corridor. The man he was with had walked on and was waiting by the tea-room door. The two of them stood there. I could see the tender creases round his eyes; and still she smiled, accepting homage.

There were no taxis about and I waited by the kerb. I wondered if it had been the 'someone quite famous' in the sedan; but I didn't recognize him. I recognized only the fascination. His eyes had been for her only, as if the business he had been on shrivelled into nothing-ness at the sight of that face.

She came out hurriedly a minute or two later.

'Can I give you a lift?'

She was not going to make any explanation, and something about her hermetic expression made it, yet once again, infuriatingly, seem vulgar to be curious. She was not good-mannered, but expert with good manners; used them like an engineer, to shift the coarse bulk of me where she wanted.

'No thanks. I'm going to Chelsea.' 1 wasn't; but I wanted to be free of her.

I watched her covertly for a moment, then I said, 'I used to think of a story with your daughter, and I think of it even more with you.' She smiled, a little uncertainly. 'It's probably not true, but it's about Marie Antoinette and a butcher. The butcher led a mob into the palace at Versailles. He had a cleaver in his hand and he was shouting that he was going to cut Marie Antoinette's throat. The mob killed the guards and the butcher forced the door of the royal apartments. At last he rushed into her bedroom. She was alone. Standing by a window. There was no one else there. The butcher with a cleaver in his hand and the queen.'

'What happened?'

I caught sight of a taxi going in the wrong direction and waved to the driver to turn.

'He fell on his knees and burst into tears.'

She was silent for a moment.

'Poor butcher.'

'I believe that's exactly what Marie Antoinette said.'

She watched the taxi turn.

'Doesn't everything depend on who the butcher was crying for?'

I looked away from her eyes. 'No, I don't think so.'

The taxi drew up beside the kerb, and I opened the door. She watched me for a moment, then gave up, or remembered.

'Your plate.' She handed it to me from her basket.

'I'll try not to break it.'

'It carries my good wishes.' She held out a hand. 'But Alison isn't a present. She has to be paid for.'

'She's had her revenge.'

She had been about to release my hand, but now she retained it. 'Nicholas, I never told you the other commandment my husband and I kept with each other.'

She said it, and the accompanying look was without a smile. Her eyes held mine a long moment, then she turned into the taxi. I gazed after it until it disappeared out of sight past Brompton Oratory; without tears, but just, I imagined, as that poor devil of a butcher must have stared down at the Aubusson carpet.

76

And so I waited.

It seemed sadistic, this last wasteland of days. It was as if Conchis, with Alison's connivance, proceeded by some outmoded Victorian dietetic morality – one couldn't have more jam, the sweetness of events, until one ate a lot more bread, the dry stodge of time. But I was long past philosophizing. The next weeks consisted of a long struggle between my growing – not diminishing – impatience and the manner of life I took up to dull it. Almost every night I contrived to pass through Russell Square, rather in the way, I suppose, that the sailors' wives and black-eyed Susans would, more out of boredom than hope, haunt the quays in sailing days. But my ship never showed a light. Two or three times I went out to Much Hadham, at night, but the darkness of Dinsford House was as complete as the darkness in Russell Square.

For the rest, I spent hours in cinemas, hours reading books, mainly rubbish, because all I required of a book during that period was that it kept my mind drugged. I used to drive all through the night to places I did not want to go to – to Oxford, to Brighton, to Bath. These long drives calmed me, as though I was doing something constructive by racing hard through the night; scorching through sleeping towns, always turning back in the small hours and driving exhausted into London in the dawn; then sleeping till four or five in the afternoon.

It was not only my boredom that needed calming; well before my meetings with Lily de Seitas I had had another problem.

I spent many of my waking hours in Soho or Chelsea; and they are not the areas where the chaste fiancé goes – unless he is burning to test his chastity. There were dragons enough in the forest, from the farded old bags in the doorways of Greek Street to the equally pick-up-able but more appetizing 'models' and demi-debs of the King's Road. Every so often I would see a girl who would excite me sexually. I began by repressing the very idea; then frankly admitted it. If I resolutely backed out of, or looked away from, promising situations, it was for a variety of reasons; and reasons generally more selfish than noble. I wanted to show *them* – if they had eyes present to be shown, and I could never be sure that they hadn't – that I could live without affaires; and less consciously I wanted to show myself the same thing. I also wanted to be able to face Alison with the knowledge as a weapon, an added lash to the cat – if the cat had to be used.

The truth was that the recurrent new feeling I had for Alison had nothing to do with sex. Perhaps it had something to do with my alienation from England and the English, my specieslessness, my sense of exile; but it seemed to me that I could have slept with a different girl every night, and still have gone on wanting to see Alison just as much. I wanted something else from her now – and what it was only she could give me. That was the distinction. Anyone could give me sex. But only she could give me ... I couldn't call it love, because I saw it as something experimental, depending, even before the experiment proper began, on factors like the degree of her contrition, the fullness of her confession, the extent to which she could could convince me that *she* still loved me; that her love had caused her betrayal. And then I felt towards the godgame some of the mixed fascination and repulsion one feels for an intelligent religion; I knew there 'must be something' in it, but I as surely knew that I was not the religious type. Besides, the logical conclusion of this more clearly seen distinction between love and sex was certainly not an invitation to enter a world of fidelity. In one sense Mrs de Seitas had been preaching to the converted in all that she had said about a clean surgical abscission of what went on in the loins from what went on in the heart.

Yet something very deep in me revolted. I could swallow her story, but it lay queasily on my stomach. It flouted something deeper than convention and received ideas. It flouted an innate sense that I ought to find all I needed in Alison and that if I failed to do so, then something more than morality or sensuality was involved; something I couldn't define, but which was both biological and metaphysical; to do with imagination and with death. Perhaps Lily de Seitas looked forward to a sexual morality for the twenty-first century; but something was missing, some vital safeguard; and I suspected I saw to the twenty-second.

Easy to think such things; but harder to live them, in the meanwhile-still-twentieth century. Our instincts emerge so much more nakedly, our emotions and wills veer so much more quickly, than ever before. A young Victorian of my age would have thought nothing of waiting fifty months, let along fifty days, for his beloved; and of never permitting a single unchaste thought to sully his mind, let alone an act his body. I could get up in a young-Victorian mood; but by midday, with a pretty girl standing beside me in a bookshop, I might easily find myself praying to the God I did not believe in that she wouldn't turn and smile at me.

Then one evening in Bayswater a girl did smile; she didn't have to turn. It was in an espresso bar, and I had spent most of my meal watching her talking opposite with a friend; her bare arms, her promising breasts. She looked Italian; black-haired, doe-eyed. Her friend went off, and the girl sat back and gave me a very direct, though perfectly nice, smile with her eyes. She wasn't a tart; she was just saying, if you want to start talking, come on.

I got clumsily to my feet, and spent an embarrassing minute waiting at the entrance for the waitress to come and take my money. My shameful retreat was partly inspired by paranoia. The girl and her friend had come in after me, and had sat at a table where I couldn't help watching them. It was absurd. I began to feel that every girl who crossed my path was hired to torment and test me; I started checking through the window before I went in to coffee-bars and restaurants, to see if I could get a corner free of sight and sound of the dreadful creatures. My behaviour became increasingly clownish; and I grew angrier and angrier with the circumstances that made it so. Then Jojo came.

It was during the last week of September, a fortnight after my last meeting with Lily de Seitas. Bored to death with myself, I went late one afternoon to see an old René Clair. I sat without thinking next to a humped-up shape and watched the film – the immortal *Italian Straw Hat*. By various hoarse snuffling noises I deduced that the Beckett-like thing next to me was female. After half an hour she turned to me for a light. I saw a round-cheeked face, no make-up, a fringe of brown hair pigtailed at the back, thick eyebrows, very dirty fingernails holding a fag-end. When the lights went on and we waited for the next feature she tried, with a really pitiable amateurishness, to pick me up. She was dressed in jeans, a grubby grey polo-necked sweater, a very ancient man's duffel coat; but she had three queer asexual charms – a face-splitting grin, a hoarse Scots accent, and an air of such solitary sloppiness that I saw in her at once both a kindred spirit and someone worthy of a modern Mayhew. Somehow the grin didn't seem quite real, but the result of pulling strings. She sat puppy-slumped like a dejected fat boy, and tried very unsuccessfully to dig out of me what I did, where I lived; and then, perhaps because of the froglike grin, perhaps because it was a lapse so patently unlikely to lead to danger, so patently not a test, I asked her if she wanted a coffee.

So we went to a coffee-bar. I was hungry, I said I was going to have some spaghetti. At first she wouldn't have any; then she admitted she had spent the last of her money on getting into the cinema; then she ate like a wolf. I grew full of kindness to dumb animals.

We went on to a pub. She had come from Glasgow, it seemed, two months before, to be an art student. In Glasgow she had belonged to some bizarre Celtic-Bohemian fringe; and now she lived in coffee-bars and cinemas, 'with a wee bitta help from ma friends'. She had packed art in; the eternal provincial tramp.

I felt increasingly sure of my chastity with her; and perhaps that was why I liked her so much so fast. She amused me, she had character, with her husky voice and her grotesque lack of normal femininity. She also had a total absence of pity about herself; and therefore all the attraction of an opposite. I drove her to her door, a rooming-house in Notting Hill, and she evidently thought I would be expecting to 'kip' with her. I quickly disillusioned her.

'Then we'll no see each other again.'

'We could.' I looked at her dumpy figure beside me. 'How old are you?'

'Twenty-one.'

'Rubbish.'

'Twenty.'

'Eighteen?'

'Ge' away wi' you. I'm all of twenty.'

'I've got a proposition to make.' She sniffed. 'Sorry. A proposal. Actually, I'm waiting around for someone … a girl … to come back from Australia. And what I'd very much like for two or three weeks is a companion.' Her grin split her face from ear to ear. 'I'm offering you a job. There are agencies in London that do this sort of thing. Provide escorts and partners.'

She still grinned. 'I'd awfla like you just to come up.'

'No – I meant exactly what I offered. You're temporarily drifting. So am I. So let's drift together … and I'll take care of the finances. No sex. Just companionship.'

She rubbed the insides of her wrists together; grinned again and shrugged, as if one madness more was immaterial.

So I took up with her. If they had their eyes on me, it would be up to them to make a move. I thought it might even help to precipitate matters.

Jojo was a strange creature, as douce as rain – London rain, because she was seldom very clean – and utterly without ambition or meanness. She slipped perfectly into the role I cast her for. We slopped round the cinemas, slopped round the pubs, slopped round exhibitions. Sometimes we slopped round all day up in my flat. But always, at some point in the night, I sent her slopping back to her cubbyhole. Often we sat for hours at the same table reading magazines and newspapers and never exchanging a word. After seven days I felt I had known her for seven years. I gave her four pounds a week and offered to buy her some clothes and pay her tiny rent. She accepted a dark-blue jersey from Marks and Spencers, but nothing else. She fulfilled her function very well; she put off every other girl who looked at us and on my side I cultivated a sort of lunatic transferred fidelity towards her.

She was always equable, grateful for the smallest bone, like an old mongrel; patient, unoffended, casual. I refused to talk about Alison, and probably Jojo ceased to believe in her; accepted, in her accept-all way, that I was just 'a wee bit cracked'.

Then one October evening I knew I wouldn't sleep and I offered to drive her anywhere she wanted within a night's range. She thought for a moment and said, goodness knows why, Stonehenge. So we drove down to Stonehenge and walked around the looming menhirs at three o'clock with a cold wind blowing and the sound of peewits in the moon-drenched wrack above our heads. Later we sat in the car and ate chocolate. I could just see her face; the dark smudges of her eyes and the innocent puppy-grin.

'Why are you grinning, Jojo?'

''Cause I'm happy.'

'Aren't you tired?'

'No.'

I leant forward and kissed the side of her head. It was the first time I'd ever kissed her, and I started the engine immediately. After a while she went to sleep and slowly slumped against my shoulder. When she slept she looked very young, fifteen or sixteen. I got occasional whiffs of her hair, which she hardly ever washed. I felt for her almost exactly what I felt for Kemp; great affection, and not the least desire.

One night soon after that we went to the cinema. Kemp, who thought I was mad to be sleeping with such an ugly layabout – I didn't attempt to explain the true situation – but was glad I was showing at least one sign of normality, came with us, and afterwards we all went back to her 'studio' and sat boozing cocoa and the remains of a bottle of rum. About one Kemp kicked us out; she wanted to go to sleep, as indeed I did myself. I went with Jojo and stood by the front door. It was the first really cold night of the autumn, and raining hard into the bargain. We stood at the door and looked out.

'I'll sleep upstairs in your chair, Nick.'

'No. It'll be all right. Stay here. I'll get the car.' I used to park it up a side street. I got in, coaxed the engine into life, moved forward; but not far. The front wheel was flat as a pancake. I got out in the rain and looked, cursed, and went to the boot for the pump. It was not there. I hadn't used it for a week or more, so I didn't know when it had been pinched. I slammed the lid down and ran back to the door.

'I've got a bloody flat.'

'Gude.'

'Thank you.'

'Don't be such a loon. I'll sleep in your auld armchair.'

I considered waking Kemp, but the thought of all the obscenities she would hurl round the studio soon killed that idea. We climbed up the stairs past the silent sewing-rooms and into the flat.

'Look, you kip in the bed. I'll sleep here.'

She wiped her nose on the back of her hand and nodded; went to the bathroom, then marched into the bedroom, lay on the bed and pulled her wretched old duffel coat over her. I was secretly angry with her, I was tired, but I pulled two chairs together and stretched out. Five minutes passed. Then she was in the door between the rooms.

'Nick?'

'M'm.'

'Come on.'

'Come on where?'

'You know.'

'No.'

She stood there in the door for a silent moment. She liked to mull over her gambits.

'I want you to.' It struck me that I'd never heard her use the verb 'to want' in the first person before.

'Jojo, we're chums. We're not going to bed together.'

'It's only kipping together.'

'No.'

'Just once.'

'No.'

She stood plumply in the door, in her blue jumper and jeans, a dark stain of silent accusation. Light from outside distorted the shadows round her figure, isolated her face, so that she looked like a Munch lithograph. Jealousy; or Envy; or Innocence.

'I'm so cold.'

'Get under the blankets then.'

She gave it a minute more and then I heard her creep back to bed. Five minutes passed. I felt my neck get stiff.

'I'm in the bed. Nick, you could easy sleep on top.' I took a deep breath. 'Can you hear?'

'Yes.'

Silence.

'I thought you were asleep.'

Rain poured down, dripped in the gutters; wet London night air pervaded the room. Solitude. Winter.

'Could I come in a wee sec and put the fire on?'

'Oh God.'

'I won't wake you at all.'

'Thanks.'

She slopped into the room and I heard her strike a match. The gas phutted and began to hiss. A pinkish glow filled the room. She was very quiet, but after a while I gave in and began to sit up.

'Don't look. I havna any clothes on.'

I looked. She was standing by the fire pulling down an outsize man's singlet. I saw, with an unpleasant little shock, that she was

638

almost pretty, or at least clearly female, by gaslight. I turned my back and reached for a cigarette.

'Now look, Jojo, I'm just not going to have this. I will *not* have sex with you.'

'I didna fancy to get into your clean bed with all m' clothes on.'

'Get warm. Then hop straight back.'

I got halfway through my cigarette.

'It's only 'cause you been so awfla nice to me.' I refused to answer. 'I only want to be nice back.'

'If it's only that, don't worry. You owe me nothing.'

I slid a look round. She was sitting on the floor with her plump little back to me, hugging her knees and staring into the fire. More silence.

She said, 'It isn't only that.'

'Go and put your clothes on. Or get into bed. And then we'll talk.'

The gas hissed away. I lit another cigarette from the end of the last.

'I know why.'

'Tell me.'

'You think I took one of your nasty London diseases.'

'Jojo.'

'I mebbe have. You don't have to be ill at all. You can still carry all the microbes round with you.'

'Stop it.'

'I'm only sayin' what you're thinkin'.'

'I've *never* thought that.'

'I don't blame you. I don't blame you at all.'

'Jojo, shut up. Just shut up.'

Silence.

'You just want to keep your beautiful Sassenach coddies clean.'

Then her bare feet padded across the floor and the bedroom door was slammed – and sprung open again. After a moment I heard her sobbing. I cursed my stupidity; I cursed myself for not having paid more attention to various signs during the evening – washed hair done into a ponytail, one or two looks. I had a dreadful vision of a stern knock on the door, of Alison standing there. I was also shocked. Jojo never swore and used as many euphemisms as a girl of fifty times her respectability. Her last line had cut.

I lay a minute, then went into the bedroom. The gasfire cast warm light through. I pulled the bedclothes up round her shoulders.

'Oh Jojo. You clown.'

I stroked her head, keeping a firm grip on the bedclothes with the other hand, in case she made a spring for me. She began to snuffle. I passed her a handkerchief.

'Can I tell you somethin'?'

'Of course.'

'I've never done it. I've never been to bed with a man.'

'Jesus.'

'I'm clean as the day I was born.'

'Thank God for that.'

She turned on her back and stared up at me.

'Do you not want me now?'

That sentence somewhat tarnished the two before. I touched her cheek and shook my head.

'I love you, Nick.'

'Jojo, you don't. You can't.'

She began to cry again; my exasperation.

'Look, did you plan this? That flat tyre?' I remembered she had slipped out, allegedly to go upstairs, while Kemp was making the cocoa.

'I couldna help it. That night we went to Stonehenge. I didna sleep a wink all the wa' back. I juist sat there pretendin'.'

'Jojo. Can I tell you a long story I've never told anyone else? Can I?'

I dabbed her eyes with the handkerchief and then I began to talk, sitting with my back to her on the edge of the bed. I told her everything about Alison, about the way I had left her, and I spared myself nothing. I told her about Greece. I told her, if not the real incidents of my relationship with Lily, the emotional truth of it. I told her about Parnassus, all my guilt. I brought it right up to date, to Jojo herself and why I had cultivated her. She was the strangest priest to confess before; but not the worst. For she absolved me.

If only I had told her at the beginning; she would not have been so stupid then.

'I've been blind. I'm sorry.'

'I couldna help it.'

'I'm sorry. I'm so sorry.'

'Och. I'm only a teenage moron from Glasgow.' She looked at me solemnly. 'I'm only seventeen, Nick. It was all a fib.'

'If I gave you your fare, would you – '

But she was shaking her head at once.

There were minutes of silence then and in them I thought about the only truth that mattered, the only morality that mattered, the only sin, the only crime. When Lily de Seitas had told me her version of it at the end of our meeting at the museum I had taken it as a retrospective thing, a comment on my past and on my anecdote about the butcher. But I saw now it had been about my future.

History has superseded the ten commandments of the Bible; for me they had never had any real meaning, that is, any other than a conformitant influence. But sitting in that bedroom, staring at the glow of the fire on the jamb of the door through to the sitting-room, I knew that at last I began to feel the force of this super-commandment, summary of them all; somewhere I knew I had to choose it, and every day afresh, even though I went on failing to keep it. Conchis had talked of points of fulcrum, moments when one met one's future. I also knew it was all bound up with Alison, with choosing Alison, and having to go on choosing her every day. Adulthood was like a mountain, and I stood at the foot of this cliff of ice, this impossible and unclimbable: *Thou shalt not inflict unnecessary pain.*

'Could I have a fag, Nick?'

I went and got her a cigarette. She lay puffing it; intermittently red-apple cheeked, watching me. I held her hand.

'What are you thinking, Jojo?'

'Sposin' she ... '

'Doesn't come?'

'Yes.'

'I'll marry you.'

'That's a fib.'

'Give you lots of fat babies with fat cheeks and grins like monkeys.'

'Och you cruel monster.'

She stared at me; silence; darkness; frustrated tenderness. I remembered having sat the same way with Alison, in the room off Baker Street, the October before. And the memory told me, in the simplest and most revealing way, how much I had changed.

'Someone much nicer than I am will one day.'

'Is she like me at all?'

'Yes.'

'Oh aye. I'll bet. Puir girl.'

'Because you're both … not like everybody else.'

'There's only one of everyone.'

I went out and put a shilling in the meter; then stood in the door-way between the two rooms. 'You ought to live in the suburbs, Jojo. Or work in a factory. Or go to a public school. Or have dinner in an embassy.'

A train screamed to the north, from Euston way. She turned and stubbed the cigarette out.

'I wish I was real pretty.'

She pulled the bedclothes up round her neck, as if to hide her ugliness.

'Being pretty is just something that's thrown in. Like the paper round the present. Not the present.'

A long silence. Pious lies. But what breaks the fall?

'You'll forget me.'

'No, I won't. I'll remember you. Always.'

'Not always. Mebbe a wee once in a while.' She yawned. 'I'll remember you.' Then she said, minutes later, as if the present was no longer quite real, a childhood dream, 'In stinkin' auld England.'

77

It was six o'clock before I got to sleep, and even then I woke up several times. At last, at eleven, I decided to face the day. I went to the bedroom door. Jojo had gone. I looked in the kitchen that was also a bathroom. There, scrawled on the mirror with a bit of soap were three X's, a 'Goodbye', and her name. As casually as she had slipped into my life, she had slipped out of it. On the kitchen table lay my car pump.

The sewing-machines hummed dimly up from the floor below; women's voices, the sound of stale music from a radio. I was the solitary man upstairs.

Waiting. Always waiting.

I leant against the old wooden draining-board drinking Nescafé and eating damp biscuits. As usual, I had forgotten to buy any bread. I stared at the side of an empty cereal packet. On it a nauseatingly happy 'average' family were shown round a breakfast table; breezy tanned father, attractive girlish mother, small boy, small girl; dreamland. Metaphorically I spat. Yet there must be some reality behind it all, some craving for order, harmony, beyond all the shabby cowardice of wanting to be like everyone else, the selfish need to have one's laundry looked after, buttons sewn on, ruts served, name propagated, meals decently cooked.

I made another cup of coffee, and cursed Alison, the bloody bitch. Why should I wait for her? Why of all places in London, a city with more eager girls per acre than any other in Europe, prettier girls, droves of restless girls who came to London to be stolen, stripped, to wake up one morning in a stranger's bed ...

Then Jojo, the last person in the world I had wanted to hurt. It was as if I had kicked a starving mongrel in its poor, thin ribs.

A violent reaction set on me, born of self-disgust and resentment. All my life I had been a sturdy contrasuggestible. Now I was soft; remoter from freedom than I had ever been. I thought with a leap of excitement of life without Alison, of setting out into the blue again ... alone, but free. Even noble, since I was condemned to inflict pain, whatever I did. To America, perhaps; to South America.

Freedom was making some abrupt choice and acting on it; was as it had been at Oxford, allowing one's instinct-cum-will to fling one off at a tangent, solitary into a new situation. I had to have hazard. I had to break out of this waiting-room I was in.

I walked through the uninspiring rooms. The Bow *chinoiserie* plate hung over the mantelpiece. The family again; order and involvement. Imprisonment. Outside, rain; a grey scudding sky. I stared down Charlotte Street and decided to leave Kemp's, at once, that day. To prove to myself that I could move, I could cope, I was free.

I went down to see Kemp. She took my announcement coldly. I wondered if she knew about Jojo, because I could see a stony glint of contempt in her eyes as she shrugged off my excuse – that I had decided to rent a cottage in the country, I was going to write.

643

'You taking Jojo, are you?'

'No. We're bringing it to an end.'

'*You're* bringing it to an end.'

She knew about Jojo.

'All right, *I'm* bringing it to an end.'

'Tired of slumming. Thought you would be.'

'Think again.'

'You pick up a poor little scob like that, God only knows wny, then when you're sure she's head over fucking heels in love with you, you act like a real gentleman. You kick her out.'

'Look – '

'Don't kid *me*, laddie.' She sat square and inexorable. 'Go on. Run back home.'

'I haven't got a bloody home, for Christ's sake.'

'Oh yes you have. They call it the bourgeoisie.'

'Spare me that.'

'Seen it a thousand times. You discover we're human beings. Makes you shit with fright.' With an insufferable dismissiveness she added, 'It's not your fault. You're a victim of the dialectical process.'

'And you're the most impossible old – '

'Dah!' She turned away as if she didn't care a damn, anyway; as if life was like her studio, full of failures, full of mess and disorder, and it took her all her energy to survive in it herself. A Mother Courage gone sour, she went to her paints table and started fiddling.

I went out. But I had hardly got to the top of the stairs to the ground floor when she came out and bawled up at me.

'Let me tell you something, you smug bastard.' I turned. 'You know what will happen to that poor damn kid? She'll go on the game. And you know who'll have put her there?' Her outstretched finger seared its accusation at me. 'Mister Saint Nicholas Urfe. Esquire.' That last word seemed the worst obscenity I had ever heard pass her lips. Her eyes scalded me, then she went back and slammed the studio door. So there I was, between the Scylla of Lily de Seitas and the Charybdis of Kemp; bound to be sucked down.

I packed in a cold rage; and lost in a fantasy row with Kemp, in which I scored all the points, I lifted the Bow plate carelessly off its nail. It slipped; struck the edge of the gasfire; and a moment later I was staring down at it in the hearth, broken in two across the middle.

I knelt. I was so near tears that I had to bite my lips savagely hard. I knelt there holding the two pieces. Not even trying to fit them together. Not even moving when I heard Kemp's footsteps on the stairs. She came in and I was kneeling there. I don't know what she had come up to say, but when she saw my face she did not say it.

I raised the two pieces a little to show her what had happened. My life, my past, my future. Not all the king's horses, and all the king's men.

She was silent for a long moment, taking it in, the half-packed case, the mess of books and papers on the table; the smug bastard, the broken butcher, on his knees by the hearth.

She said, 'Jesus Christ. At your age.'

So I stayed with Kemp.

78

The smallest hope, a bare continuing to exist, is enough for the anti-hero's future; leave him, says our age, leave him where mankind is in its history, at a crossroads, in a dilemma, with all to lose and only more of the same to win; let him survive, but give him no direction, no reward; because we too are waiting, in our solitary rooms where the telephone never rings, waiting for this girl, this truth, this crystal of humanity, this reality lost through imagination, to return; and to say she returns is a lie.

But the maze has no centre. An ending is no more than a point in sequence, a snip of the cutting shears. Benedick kissed Beatrice at last; but ten years later? And Elsinore, that following spring?

So ten more days. But what happened in the following years shall be silence; another mystery.

Ten more days, in which the telephone never rang.

Instead, on the last day of October, All Hallows Eve, Kemp took me for a Saturday afternoon walk. I should have suspected such an uncharacteristic procedure; but it happened that it was a magnificent day, with a sky from another world's spring, as blue as a delphinium petal, the trees russet and amber and yellow, the air as still as in a dream.

Besides, Kemp had taken to mothering me. It was a process that needed so much compensatory bad language and general gruffness that our relationship was sergeant-majored into something outwardly the very reverse of its true self. Yet it would have been spoilt if we had declared it, if we had stopped pretending that it did not exist; and in a strange way this pretending seemed an integral part of the affection. Not declaring we liked each other showed a sort of mutual delicacy that proved we did. Perhaps it was Kemp who made me feel happier during those ten days; perhaps it was an aftermath of Jojo, least angelic of angels, but sent by hazard from a better world into mine; perhaps it was simply a feeling that I could wait longer than I had till then imagined. Whatever it was, something in me changed. I was still the butt, yet in another sense; Conchis's truths, especially the truth he had embodied in Lily, matured in me. Slowly I was learning to smile, and in the special sense that Conchis intended. Though one can accept, and still not forgive; and one can decide, and still not enact the decision.

We walked north, across the Euston Road and along the Outer Circle into Regent's Park. Kemp wore black slacks and a filthy old cardigan and an extinguished Woodbine, the last as a sort of warning to the fresh air that it got through to her lungs only on a very temporary sufferance. The park was full of green distances, of countless scattered groups of people, lovers, families, solitaries with dogs, the colours softened by the imperceptible mist of autumn, as simple and pleasing in its way as a Boudin beachscape.

We strolled, watched the ducks with affection, the hockey-players with contempt.

'Nick boy,' said Kemp, 'I need a cup of the bloody national beverage.'

And that too should have warned me; her *manes* all drank coffee.

So we went to the tea pavilion, stood in a queue, then found half a table. Kemp left me to go to the ladies'. I pulled out a paperback I had in my pocket. The couple on the other side of the table moved away. The noise, the mess, the cheap food, the queue to the counter. I guessed Kemp was having to queue also. And I became lost in the book.

In the outer seat opposite, diagonally from me.

So quietly, so simply.

She was looking down at the table, not at me. I jerked round, searching for Kemp. But I knew Kemp was walking home.

She said nothing. Waited.

All the time I had expected some spectacular re-entry, some mysterious call, a metaphorical, perhaps even literal, descent into a modern Tartarus. And yet, as I stared at her, unable to speak, at her refusal to return my look, I understood that this was the only possible way of return; her rising into this most banal of scenes, this most banal of London, this reality as plain and dull as wheat. Since she was cast as Reality, she had come in her own, yet in some way heightened, stranger, still with the aura of another world; from, but not of, the crowd behind her.

She was wearing a delicate-patterned tweed suit, autumn flecked with winter; a dark green scarf, tied peasant-fashion, round her head. She sat with her hands primly in her lap, as if she had done her duty: she was here. Every other move was mine. But now the moment had come I could do nothing, say nothing, think nothing. I had imagined too many ways of our meeting again, and yet none like this. In the end I even stared down at my book, as if I wanted no more to do with her – then angrily up past her at a moronically curious family, scene-sniffing faces across the gangway. She did at last give me a little, lancing look; of only a fraction of a moment, but it caught the face I had really meant for the ones opposite.

Without warning she stood and walked away. I watched her move between the tables: her smallness, that slightly sullen smallness and slimness that was a natural part of her sexuality. I saw another man's eyes follow her through the door.

I let a few stunned, torn seconds pass. Then I gave chase, pushing roughly past the people in my way. She was walking slowly across the grass, towards the east. I came beside her, and she gave the bottom of my legs the smallest token glance. Still we said nothing. I felt so caught unawares – it was even in our clothes. I had lost all interest in what I wore, how I looked ... had taken on the cryptic colouring of

Kemp's and Jojo's worlds. Now I felt uncouth beside her, and resented it; she had no right to re-appear like some clothes-conscious and self-possessed young middle-class wife. It was almost as if she wanted to flaunt the reversal in our roles and fortunes. I looked round. There were so many people, so many too far to distinguish. And Regent's Park. That other meeting, of the young deserter and his love; the scent of lilac, and bottomless darkness.

'Where are they?'

She gave a little shrug. 'I'm alone.'

'Like hell.'

We walked more silent paces. She indicated with her head an empty bench beside a tree-lined path. She seemed as strange to me as if she had indeed come from Tartarus; so cold, so calm.

I followed her to the seat. She sat at one end and I sat halfway along, turned towards her, staring at her. It infuriated me that she would not look at me, had made not the slightest sign of apology; would not say anything.

I said, 'I'm waiting. As I've been waiting these last three and a half months.'

She untied her scarf and shook her hair free. It had grown again, as when I first knew her, and she had a warm tan. From my very first glimpse of her I realized, and it seemed to aggravate my irritation, that the image, idealized by memory, of a Lily always at her best had distorted Alison into what she was only at her worst. She was wearing a pale-brown shirt beneath the suit. It was a very good suit; Conchis must have given her money. She was pretty and desirable; even without ... I remembered Parnassus, her other selves. She stared down at the tip of her flat-heeled shoes.

I looked out over the grass. 'I want to make one thing clear from the start.' She said nothing. 'I forgive you that foul bloody trick you played this summer. I forgive you whatever miserable petty female vindictiveness made you decide to keep me waiting all this time.'

She shrugged. A silence. Then she said, 'But?'

'But I want to know what the hell went on that day in Athens. What the hell's been going on since. And what the hell's going on now.'

'And then?'

'We'll see.'

She took a cigarette out of her handbag and lit it; and then without friendliness offered me the packet. I said, 'No thanks.'

She stared into the distance, towards the aristocratic wall of houses that make up Cumberland Terrace and overlook the park. Cream stucco, a row of white statues along the cornices, the muted blues of the sky.

A poodle ran up to us. I waved it away with my foot, but she patted it on the head. A woman called, 'Tina! Darling! Come here.' In the old days we would have exchanged grimaces of disgust. She went back to staring at the houses. I looked round. There were other seats a few yards away. Other sitters and watchers. Suddenly the peopled park seemed a stage, the whole landscape a landscape of masquers, spies. I lit one of my own cigarettes; willed her to look at me, but she wouldn't.

'Alison.'

She glanced at me briefly, but then down again. She sat, holding the cigarette. As if nothing would make her speak. A plane leaf lolloped down, touched her skirt. She bent and picked it up, smoothed its yellow teeth against the tweed. An Indian came and sat on the far end of the bench. A threadbare black overcoat, a white scarf; a thin face. He looked small and unhappy, timidly alien; a waiter perhaps, the slave of some cheap curry-house kitchen. I moved a little closer to her, lowered my voice, and forced it to sound as cold as hers.

'What about Kemp?'

'Nicko, please don't interrogate me. Please don't.'

My name; a tiny shift. But she was still set hard and silent.

'Are they watching? Are they here somewhere?'

An impatient sigh.

'Are they?'

'No.' But at once she qualified it. 'I don't know.'

'Meaning you do.'

Still she wouldn't look at me. She spoke in a small, almost a bored, voice.

'It's nothing to do with them now.'

There was a long pause.

I said, 'You can't lie to me. Face to face.'

She touched her hair; the hair, her wrist, a way she had of raising her face a little as she made the gesture. A glimpse of the lobe of an ear. I had a sense of outrage, as if I was being barred from my own property.

'You're the only person I've ever felt could never lie to me. Can you imagine what it was like in the summer? When I got that letter, those flowers ... '

She said, 'If we start talking about the past.'

All my overtures were in some way irrelevant; she had something else on her mind. My fingers touched a smooth dry roundness in my coat pocket: a chestnut, a talisman. Jojo had passed it to me wrapped in a toffee-paper, her pawky joke, one evening in a cinema. I thought of Jojo, somewhere only a mile or two away through the brick and the traffic, sitting with some new pick-up, drifting into her womanhood; of holding her pudgy hand in the darkness. And suddenly I had to fight not to take Alison's.

I said her name again.

But coming to a decision, determined to be untouched, she threw the yellow leaf away. 'I've returned to London to sell the flat. I'm going back to Australia.'

'Long journey for such a small matter.'

'And to see you.'

'Like this?'

'To see if I ... ' but she cut her sentence short.

'If you?'

'I didn't want to come.'

'Then why are you here?' She shrugged. 'If it's against your will?'

But she would not answer. She was mysterious, almost a new woman; one had to go back several steps, and start again; *and know the place for the first time.* As if what had once been free in her, as accessible as a pot of salt on the table, was now held in a phial, sacrosanct. But I knew Alison. I knew how she took on the colour and character of the people she loved or liked, however independent she remained underneath. And I knew where that smooth impermeability came from. I was sitting with a priestess from the temple of Demeter.

I tried to be matter-of-fact. 'Where have you been since Athens? At home?'

'Perhaps.'

650

I took a breath. 'Have you thought about me at all?'

'Sometimes.'

'Is there someone else?'

She hesitated, then said, 'No.'

'You don't sound very certain.'

'There's always someone else – if you're looking for it.'

'Have you been looking for it?'

She said, 'There's no one.'

'And I'm included in that "no one"?'

'You've been included in it ever since that … day.'

The sullen profile, that perverse stare into the distance. She was aware of my look, and her eyes followed someone who was passing, as if she found him more interesting than me.

'What am I meant to do? Take you in my arms? Fall on my knees? What do they want?'

'I don't know what you're talking about.'

'Oh yes, you damn well do.'

Her eyes flicked sideways at me, and she looked down. She said, 'I saw through you that day. That's all. For ever.'

'I made love to you that day. Also … in a sense … for ever.'

I watched her breathe in, as if on a pent-up scorn; waited for her to say something, anything, even the scorn; quelled my own growing anger with her, tried to sound calm.

'There was a moment on that mountain when I loved you. I don't think you know, I know you know. I saw it. I know you too well not to be sure you saw it too. And remember it.' I added, 'And I'm not talking about bodies.'

Again she waited to answer.

'Why should I remember it? Why shouldn't I do everything I can to forget it?'

'You know the answer to that, too.'

'Do I?'

I said, 'Alison … '

'Don't come closer. Please don't come closer.'

She would not look at me. But it was in her voice. I had a feeling of trembling too deep to show; as if the brain cells trembled. She spoke with her head turned away. 'All right, I know what it means.' Her face still averted, she took out another cigarette and lit it. 'Or it meant. When I loved you. It meant everything you said or did to me had meaning. Emotional meaning. It moved me, excited me. It depressed me, it made me … ' she took a deep breath. 'Like the way after all that's happened you can sit there in that tea place and look at me as if I'm a prostitute or something and – '

'It was a shock. For God's sake.'

I touched her then, my hand on her shoulder, but she shook it off. I had to move closer, to hear what she said.

'Whenever I'm with you it's like going to someone and saying, "Torture me, abuse me. Give me hell. Because – "'

'Alison.'

'Oh you're nice now. You're nice now. So bloody nice. For a week, for a month. And then we'd start again.'

She was not crying, I leant forward and looked. In some way I knew she was acting, and yet not acting. Perhaps she had rehearsed the saying this; but still meant it.

'As you're going back to Australia anyway … '

I spoke lightly, without sarcasm, but she twisted a glance at me, as if my crassness was monstrous. I made the mistake of beginning to smile, of calling her hand. Suddenly she was on her feet. Crossing the path, she walked out under the trees on to the open grass. After a few steps there she stopped.

If it was plausible as a reaction, it was far less so as a movement, and especially the stopping. Something about the way she stood, the direction she faced … and then in a flash I knew for certain. Beyond her stretched the grass, a quarter-mile of turf to the edge of the park. Beyond that rose the Regency façade, bestatued, many and elegantly windowed, of Cumberland Terrace.

A wall of windows, a row of statues of classical gods. They surveyed the park as if from a dress circle. And Alison's complicity – she had led me out of the tea pavilion, she had chosen the seat we sat on, now she stood in full view waiting for me to join her. But once too often: I got up and went and stood in front of her, my back to the distant buildings. She lowered her eyes. It was not a difficult part to play: that bruised face, very near tears, but not in tears.

'Now listen, Alison. I know who is watching us, I know where he's watching, I know why we are here. So first. I'm nearly broke. I haven't got a job, and I'm never going to have a job that means anything. Therefore you're standing with the worst prospect in London. Now second. If Lily walked down that path behind us and beckoned to me ... I don't know. The fact that I don't know and probably never shall is what I want you to remember. And while you're about it, remember she isn't one girl, but a type of encounter.' I paused a moment. 'Third. As you kindly told me in Athens, I'm not much good in bed.'

'I didn't say that.'

I stared at the top of her head, and knew behind my own the blank upper windows of Cumberland Terrace; those white stone divinities. 'Fourth. He said something to me one day. About males and females. How we judge things as objects, and you judge them by their relationships. All right. You've always been able to see this ... whatever it is ... between us. Joining us. I haven't. That's all I can offer you. The possibility that I'm beginning to see it.'

'Can I speak?'

'No. You now have a choice. And you'd better make it very fast. It's me or them. But either way, for good.'

'You have no right – '

'I have as much right as you did in that hotel room in Greece. Which is every right.' I added, 'And for exactly the same reason as you had then.'

'It's not the same thing.'

'Oh yes it is. You have my part now.' I gestured back towards Cumberland Terrace. 'They have everything to offer. But I'm like you. I have only one. I can't even blame you if you made my mistake – think their everything is a much better choice than any future we might have. The only thing is you've got to bet. In their sight. And now.'

She glanced up at the houses, and I too turned a moment. The afternoon sun made them gleam with light, that Olympian elixir of serene, remote, benign light one sometimes sees in summer clouds.

She said, as if she rejected both them and me, 'I'm going back to Australia.'

I had a sense of an abyss between us that was immeasurably deep, yet also absurdly narrow, as narrow as our real distance apart, crossable in one small step. I stared at her psychologically contused face, her obstinacy, her unmanoeuvrability. There was the smell of a bonfire. A hundred yards away a blind man was walking, freely, not like a blind man. Only the white stick showed he had no eyes.

I began to walk towards the path that led to the south gate home. Two steps, four, six. Then ten.

'Nicko!'

It sounded strangely peremptory, harsh; not in the least conciliatory. I checked momentarily and half looked round, then forced myself to move on. I heard her running, but did not turn until she was almost up to me. She stopped five or six feet away, breathing a little hard. She wasn't pretending, she was going back to Australia – or at least to some Australia of the mind, of the emotions, to live the rest of her life without me. Yet she wouldn't let me go like this. Her eyes were wounded, outraged. I was more than ever impossible. I took two steps back towards her, raised an angry finger.

'You still haven't learnt. You're still playing to their script.'

She held my eyes, returning every degree of my bile.

'I came back because I thought you'd changed.'

I do not know why I did what happened next. It was neither intended nor instinctive, it was neither in cold blood nor in hot; but yet it seemed, once committed, a necessary act; no breaking of the commandment. My arm flicked out and slapped her left cheek as hard as it could. The blow caught her completely by surprise, nearly knocked her off balance, and her eyes blinked with the shock; then very slowly she put her left hand to the cheek. We stared wildly at each other for a long moment, in a kind of terror: the world had disappeared and we were falling through space. The abyss might be narrow, but it was bottomless. Behind Alison I could see people stopped on the path. A man stood up from his seat. The Indian sat and watched. Her hand stayed over the side of her face and her eyes were growing wet, certainly with the pain and perhaps partly also with a sort of incredulity.

The final truth came to me, as we stood there, trembling, searching, between all our past and all our future; at a moment when the difference between fission and fusion lay in a nothing, a tiniest movement, betrayal, further misunderstanding.

There were no watching eyes. The windows were as blank as they looked. The theatre was empty. It was not a theatre. They had perhaps told her it was a theatre, and she had believed them, and I had believed her. Perhaps it had all been to bring me to this, to give me my last lesson and final ordeal ... the task, as in *L'Astrée*, of turning lions and unicorns and magi and other mythical monsters into stone statues. I looked away from Alison and at those distant windows, the façade, the pompous white pedimental figures that crowned it. It was logical, the perfect climax to the godgame. They had absconded, we were alone. I was so sure, and yet ... after so much, how could I be perfectly sure? How could they be so cold, so inhuman – so incurious? So load the dice and yet leave the game?

I looked back towards the path. The far more natural watchers there were strolling on, as if this trivial little bit of masculine brutality, the promised scene, had lost their interest also. Alison hadn't moved, she still held a hand to her cheek, but now her head was bowed. There was a little shuddered outbreath as she tried to stifle the tears; then her voice, broken, hardly audible, in despair, almost self-amazed.

'I hate you. I *hate* you.'

I said nothing, made no move to touch her. After a moment she looked up and everything in her expression was as it had been in her voice and words: hatred, pain, every female resentment since time began. But I clung to something, the something I had never seen, or always feared to see, in those intense grey eyes, the quintessential something behind all the hating, the hurtness, the tears. A small step poised, a shattered crystal waiting to be reborn. She spoke again, as if to kill what I was looking at.

'I *do*.'

'Then why wouldn't you let me walk away?'

She shook her abruptly lowered head, as if the question was unfair.

'You know why.'

'No.'

'I knew within two seconds of seeing you.' I went closer. Her other hand went to her face, as if I might hit her again. 'I understand that word now, Alison. Your word.' Still she waited, face hidden in her hands, like someone being told of a tragic loss. 'You can't hate someone who's really on his knees. Who'll never be more than half a human being without you.'

The bowed head, the buried face.

She is silent, she will never speak, never forgive, never reach a hand, never leave this frozen present tense. All waits, suspended. Suspend the autumn trees, the autumn sky, anonymous people. A blackbird, poor fool, sings out of season from the willows by the lake. A flight of pigeons over the houses; fragments of freedom, hazard, an anagram made flesh. And somewhere the stinging smell of burning leaves.

"I AM VERY RICH" AS IF RICH WELL A NATION

cras amet qui numquam amavit
quique amavit cras amet

MONKEY GLANDER
AVUNCULAR.

A tale of a champion
of the disadvantaged and
hard done by - for another

Happy birthday
Steven

THE FLOCKMASTERS

Alastair MacRory of Gleneidart came home to his native glens to find that, while the Highland regiments fought on the battlefields of Europe, the clansfolk and the crofters were being dispossessed of their lands. Shrewd men in positions of authority were sending unwilling settlers to Canada to make room for thousands of sheep upon the hills of Wester Ross.

A

THE FLOCKMASTERS

by

NIGEL TRANTER

London

HODDER AND STOUGHTON

The characters in this book are entirely imaginary and have no relation to any living person

Printed in Great Britain for
HODDER AND STOUGHTON LTD., by
T. AND A. CONSTABLE LTD., Printers,
Edinburgh

Chapter One

LIEUTENANT ALASTAIR MACRORY of the Seventieth Foot, the Clanrory Highlanders, backed away from the royal presence, bowed at the great double doors—though not nearly so low as did the two resplendent gentlemen who flanked him—and so got himself out of the audience of stuffy and eccentric Majesty. He was not much of a bower to anybody, was Black Alastair MacRory, especially to a monarch who was little better than a half-wit, like His Gracious and Britannic Majesty George the Third, and no Stewart into the bargain.

With a sigh of relief the young man straightened up before ever he was out into the lofty corridor; certainly before either of his companions. And since these were respectively the Colonel-Commandant of the Seventieth, the Lord Viscount Clanrory himself, and His Majesty's Adjutant-General, Sir Charlecote Styles, this eagerness for the perpendicular might have seemed a little unsuitable. Though, of course, the only half-healed sabre wound in his left shoulder might be accepted as excuse.

"Thank the good Lord that is over!" Lieutenant MacRory said, with warm piety—and before ever the powdered flunkeys had time to close those doors behind them—to the alarm of his distinguished supporters, whose downbent glances darted hastily back into the presence chamber.

"Tut, man—hush!" General Styles spluttered as the doors closed, resuming an upright stance. "Have a care how you speak, sirrah!" He thumped on the marble floor with the staff of the tattered and stained ensign that he held in his hand, for emphasis.

Clanrory, who was getting on in years, straightened his back more cautiously. "The lad's no courtier, I doubt," he said. "Better on a battlefield than in a palace! But never heed that, now." He mopped his brow, for King George kept his palace like a hot-house. "I'm proud of you, Alastair Dubh. The Seventieth's proud of you. The Army's proud of you—eh,

General? Aye, and here's proof that His Majesty's proud, too!" And he tapped the bright-shining silver medal pinned askew on MacRory's scarlet-coated chest.

"Him! Proud of me! *Dia*, I shouldn't think that he was hearing a word that was said!" the younger man exclaimed. "More interested he was in choosing which sweetmeats to gobble next!"

"Young man, such talk is unseemly!" the Adjutant-General reproved stiffly. "I'll thank you to hold your tongue. This way, if you please."

Down the long marble-tiled corridor of the palace the three men paced. MacRory and Lord Clanrory were in the full fig of Highland officers' splendour—black ostrich-feather bonnet with white vulture hackle, scarlet doublet with gold lace and epaulets and green facings, gilt breastplate, MacRory tartan shoulder plaid, sporran of white goat's hair with eight golden tassels, red morocco dirk-belt and green shoulder-belt supporting the great claymore or broadsword, with red-and-white tartan hose and buckled brogues; they were alike save that where the young man wore the kilt, the other's spindly legs were encased in tartan trews with fringes. General Styles was a much less eye-catching figure, in blue double-breasted frock-coat with epaulets, white Cashmere pantaloons and short Hessian boots, even though he had the crimson ribbon of the Bath across his breast. He walked in front, using the tattered ensign on its staff like an over-long walking-stick—the same ensign that Alastair MacRory had wrested single-handed on the bloody field of Vimeiro from a colour-party of Soult's French sharpshooters who had been holding up the British left, and which MacRory's company of the Seventieth had been ordered to charge point-blank. The sole survivor of that charge had remained, the only man of either side on his feet, on that reeking Portuguese hillside, holding himself up by means of the captured ensign. Hence His Majesty's mumbled words, a specially-struck medal, and this escort of his betters, some six weeks later.

Past innumerable guards, ushers, and lackeys they marched, down a vast marble staircase, and so to the great pillared and gilded vestibule of the palace, where Sir Charlecote Styles halted, and turned.

"Well, young man, that will be all," he said. "I shall attend to the disposal of this, er, relic." He gave the ragged flag a jerk. "You will be rejoining your regiment at the earliest, no doubt? General Moore has need of every man, in the present dangerous situation in the Peninsula."

MacRory, letting his less than deferential dark eyes rove over the host of gilded militarists who lounged about everywhere, lifted his undamaged shoulder in the faintest shrug beneath the tartan folds of his plaid. "No doubt, sir," he agreed, dryly.

The General's fine brow clouded for a moment. Then he inclined his head briefly, stiffly, sketched a bow to Clanrory, and said, "Y'servant, m'lord," and turning, stalked away, spurs jingling, ensign staff tap-tapping.

"Damned cavalryman!" Clanrory muttered. "Resents any honours going to anyone but the Hussars! Come along, Alastair."

The sharp air of late October was welcome after the overheated palace, as the two men stepped out into the huge courtyard. The elder, chief of the MacRorys, the great Clan Ruari, settled his magnificent feather-bonnet on his head and made for his waiting carriage.

"Can I set you down anywhere in the town?" he asked.

"My thanks, but I'd rather walk, sir. Stretching my legs, if you please," the young man said, taking great breaths of the fresh air into his lungs. "I feel . . . cramped. Besides, my humble quarters in Saint Edda's are near at hand."

"As you will." They paused at the heraldically-decorated carriage door, which a powdered postillion held open. "It has been a great occasion, has it not?" Lord Clanrory held out his hand. "Though, egad, you could have made your account of the engagement a trifle more dramatic for His Majesty, Alastair! But never heed. This is a day that you will remember all your life with pride, I doubt not. As shall all Clan Ruari."

The tall, dark, hatchet-faced young man, who towered over him, raised expressive black brows. "I doubt it, sir," he answered briefly.

"Eh?" Clanrory looked surprised. "What d'you mean, man?"

"I mean, sir, that what I fear I shall remember all my days

7

are the ninety-three good MacRorys and MacBrides and MacIvers who died around me on that Vimeiro hill, and will never again see Strathdonan and Glen Eidart."

"Ummm. Ah . . . h'rr'mmm," the older man said. "Quite. Ah, er, understandable, of course. But . . . well, they died a glorious death. Worthy of their fathers. Of the clan."

"Aye," Alastair MacRory said heavily. "But for what? Yonder torn scrap of French silk? This little disc of silver?" He tapped the medal on his breast. "Or the honour of the regiment, just?"

Clanrory looked askance at the tone of voice used. "Come, come, Alastair Dubh," he protested. "That is no way to be speaking, 'fore God! They died a soldier's death. They died for their country—to defeat Boney. All of us must be ready to do that." He cleared his throat loudly. "They died obeying orders, to wipe out that nest of sharpshooters, so that our left might advance to victory. As it did. Glorious victory. And you led them, under orders . . ."

"Aye, God forgive me, I led them—on the orders of a mad, Irish aide to an English general! And all the time, close at our backs, was a full battery of artillery that could have blown those Frenchmen out of their redoubt with a couple of salvoes, without a casualty—but did not fire a single shot. Under the same orders."

His Colonel-Commandant and chief grunted, frowning, and turned away to mount into his carriage. One foot on the step, however, he looked back. "Lieutenant," he said, "it is no part of a junior officer's duty to criticise orders from above. You do not know all the circumstances. No doubt there was good reason for the artillery to remain silent. Such talk does not become you, sir."

"Those men were my clansmen—and yours, sir!"

The two men's eyes met—and it was Clanrory's that looked away.

"Aye," he said, heavily. "That is the price we pay in our Highland regiments. Perhaps we know each other too well." His voice lightened. "But enough of this talk. You are still suffering from the effects of your wound. Such things affect the judgement, we all know. Take your time, see that you make a full recovery before you return to the regiment. When you

8

do, I shall make it my business to see that your are gazetted Captain. You have earned it, lad. But no more unconsidered talk, see you. Call on me, before you sail, and I shall give you a message for Lieutenant-Colonel Macleod."

"Aye, *Mac Ruaraidh Mor*—but would you not wish first to give me a message that I may take to the widows and mothers of those ninety-three that died, up in Strathdonan?"

"Eh . . .? What's that?" The older man looked almost startled. "Strathdonan, did you say?"

"Strathdonan, yes. I am minded to return home for a short visit, while my wound is knitting, see you. It is four long years since I smelt the heather. I weary for it, for the scent and the sight of it. And I have a duty to the men that I led to their deaths—to see their womenfolk, and tell them. No pleasant duty, but . . ."

"Lord, man, you cannot do that!" Clanrory interrupted. "You cannot be serious? To journey all that way up there! And at this time of the year. For what? Some womanish notion . . ."

"A last service to the men I brought out of Glen Eidart, sir. It is the least that I can do. It is my home, too—and I also have a mother!"

"But, the time it will take! You are an officer in my regiment. You have your duties to me. And to your King."

Black Alastair drew himself up. "I am also MacRory of Gleneidart, with other duties, sir, that *Mac Ruaraidh Mor* should be the first to acknowledge!"

At the fire in the younger man's dark eyes, Clanrory seemed almost to crumble. He shook his grey head under the enormous bonnet, climbed into the coach, and sat down heavily on the richly-upholstered seat, hands clasped over the silver basket-hilt of his broadsword. His handsome but sagging features just then but ill-matched his martial finery.

"Besides," Alastair MacRory went on, "it need not take so long. And my time is as well spent travelling as in sitting in the wine shops of this London town. The surgeon gives my shoulder a month to heal fully. And you yourself, sir, said to take my time so as to make a full recovery. I can be in Strathdonan in ten days, by the Leith packet, post to Glasgow, and passage on one of the island cattle-schooners. A week there

9

will serve, and I shall be back here before my leave of absence is over, never fear."

Lord Clanrory stroked his chin. "Is that not but curious treatment for healing a wound, young man? I would prefer that you remained in the south, here. It might be that your presence could be valuable. For consultations. About the regiment. See you—I have a pleasant property down in Surrey. A fine house, and good company. My sister lives there. With three handsome daughters. You would do very nicely there, I think, Alastair Dubh . . ."

"I thank you, sir, but I am resolved to go north. My mind is quite made up."

The other sank back on his seat. "You are headstrong, boy —but I cannot stop you." That was true. The officers in the clan regiments at this period were in a very different category from those of the army in general, and bore a special relationship to their colonels-in-chief. They were all Highland gentlemen of the same or allied clans, who looked upon their superior officers in terms of cousinship rather than rank, who were apt to bring their own quota of men with them into the unit, and who consequently were infinitely and sometimes awkwardly more independent of authority than other officers of the service. Persuasion, mutual confidence and sentiment went much further with most of them than did flat orders and rigid commands—a circumstance which southern commanders were notoriously slow and reluctant to credit. As a result, there were conflicting views held as to the value of these Highland regiments—though such doubts tended to be forgotten when there was fierce fighting and long odds to be faced, for none could question the Highlanders' gallantry and military abilities.

"You have no message, then sir?"

"Ah . . . my sympathy, of course. And pride. Concern," the other jerked, shortly. "And, er, confidence that the sacrifice will not be in vain. Napoleon will be defeated, and our country freed from the shadow of, ah, tyranny."

"I see," MacRory said evenly.

Tight-lipped, Clanrory nodded. He waved to the postillion, who shut the carriage door and shouted to the coachman.

MacRory saluted. "I shall do myself the honour of calling upon you when I return, sir," he said.

"Just so." Suddenly the older man sat forward again. "Alastair Dubh," he began, almost urgently—and then paused.

"Sir . . .?"

Indecision flickered across those once hawklike features—a tamed and dispirited hawk now, perhaps, He sank back once more, shaking his head.

The heavy coach lurched into creaking rumbling motion.

After only a few yards, however, Lord Clanrory's head was thrust out of the window. "If you were to bring back with you some more volunteers—replacements," he called, "I could commend your journey as profitable. And circumstances . . . may be propitious, I think."

Black Alastair gazed after that handsome equipage until it swept past the sentries at the palace gates, one of his buckled brogues tap-tapping on the flagstones.

As thereafter he sought to ignore as best he might the sniggers, cat-calls and even thrown stones that bare Highland knees ever tended to produce in London streets, the returned hero was thoughtful indeed.

Chapter Two

"How much longer, Shipmaster?" Alastair MacRory demanded, shading his eyes against the murky blood-red Hebridean sunset. "It is hazy, but that looks like the mountains of Rhum to larboard. Will you make Strathdonan tonight? Or Camusewan, at the least?"

The skipper of the schooner *Sarah Bell*, a stocky Clydesider, shrugged wide shoulders. "I was hoping that way, sir," he answered in the sing-song voice of Glasgow. "But, och, it depends on yon stour, there." He pointed ahead, north by east. "If it gets ower thick, we'll no' can thread the narrows o' the Sound o' Sleat. We'll need to anchor off Inverdruin, an' wait for daylight. Or a change in the wind."

"Stour? You mean that mist, in front?" Ahead of them was only a vagueness out of which, dimly discernible, half-left, loomed a darker mass that could only be the Point of Sleat, the thrusting southernmost tip of Skye. It looked as though the Misty Isle was living up to its name.

"Mist!" the shipman retorted. "Yon's no mist. Yon's smoke!"

"Eh? Smoke?" Alastair repeated, puzzled. "What do you mean—smoke? All that cannot be smoke." His wave embraced not only the denser opacity in front but all the wide seascape around, blurred in all directions that November afternoon by the film of haze.

"Smoke it is, jist the same," the other asserted. "D'you no' catch the stink o' it, yet?"

The Highlander sniffed. There was just the taint of something sharp, acrid, on the chilly salt-laden air; but having lived in the strong, oily odour of sheep ever since leaving Dumbarton three days before, the man had not noticed it. Some hundreds of North Country English sheep, Swaledales, packed the schooner's holds, bound for an estate in the north of Skye—an unlikely cargo, Alastair had thought, for this cattleship that plied between the Hebrides and Glasgow, normally sailing north merely in ballast and returning south with the shaggy black cattle of the Highlands and Islands. It had been explained to the passenger, however, that such two-way traffic in livestock was no longer unusual. Northern landowners were becoming more and more intent on improving their properties, and turning sheep-minded, spurred on by the soaring prices of mutton and wool caused by Napoleon's blockade. The *Sarah Bell*'s passengers had not been allowed to overlook the fact. Apart from the smell, the woeful baa-ing had scarcely ceased since leaving the Clyde.

"I think that I do catch the hint of it," Black Alastair admitted. "But what could cause so much smoke as that? It is not the season for moorburn—for burning down the old heather. That is done in the spring . . ."

The seaman eyed his questioner curiously, sidelong. "You'll no' tell me, sir, that you havena heard tell o' the Improvements that are going on in the Hielands these days? Och, I wouldna hae thought any man could hae missed the word o' it."

"I have been furth of Scotland for four years," MacRory

explained. "With the Clanrorys, in India and Egypt and latterly in the Peninsula. I have heard some rumour of certain new English owners of land up here seeking to improve their properties, yes. And these sheep that are being tried out in some quarters. But what has that to do with all this smoke?"

"Plenty!" the other said grimly. "Improvements and smoke seem to go together, as you might say. Or fire. Och, aye, you'll no' get the one without the other, it seems. Mind you, sir, I'm no' complaining. It's all right good for the carrying trade. Shipping's never been sae brisk. What with the sheep coming, an' the cattle—aye, an' better cargo than that, jist—going, fast as we can turn around, it's no' for the likes o' me to grumble!"

"But I do not take the point of all this heather burning, just now. At this season . . .?"

"Who said it was heather? There's mair than heather will burn, given a bit spark!" the skipper pointed out. "Roofing an' straw will blaze up nicely—thatch. Though wi' a deal o' smoke."

"Thatch? *Dia*, you are not telling me that those are *houses* burning? That all this smoke comes from a few roofs . . .?"

"I didna say a *few* roofs, did I? When a glen is cleared, it's no' a few roofs that hae to be burned. It could be a hundred. Plenty smoke then. Aye, an' if the wind should happen frae the east, as it is the now, it's a right hazard to navigation. I mind when . . ."

"Cleared, did you say?" Alastair interrupted. "What do you mean by glens being cleared? What is this?"

"Jist what I tell't you, sir—Improvements. Och, the first step in Improving, it seems, is to clear all the folk out o' the glens. To make room for the sheep, see you. They do say that these folk here, these crofters, jist waste the land. Wi' their scraggy cattle an' scratches o' oats. But sheep are the thing, these days. There's money in sheep, that's clear. You canna hae both sheep an' crofters, they tell me—sae the folk are cleared, and the glens turned into great muckle sheep-runs. The trouble is, the crofters are gey hard, usually, to get oot o' their turf cabins an' hovels. The puir foolish critturs winna leave them, maist times. Sae there's naething for it but to light the thatches. It's the quickest way to clear a glen, in the end . . ."

"Good God, man—are you out of your wits!" the younger man interrupted hotly. "Are you talking about people, human beings? And their homes. Or about brute beasts? Cattle to be shipped and slaughtered! Damn you, man—tell me!"

At the sudden fury, almost ferocity, of his tall and martial passenger, the shipmaster took an involuntary step away, edging closer to his helmsman. "Hey, dinna blame *me* for it!" he cried. "It's nae work o' mine. I'm jist telling you. About the sheep, an' the Improvements—telling you what I've heard. . . ."

"Telling me fables and folly, I swear! Old wives' tales . . ."

"Goad—was it auld wives' tales that on my very last voyage up here I ran this vessel on to a sandbank off the Isle o' Muck in braid daylight, an' near wrecked her? Me that's been sailing these waters all my days! Because o' the thickness o' the smoke frae Glen Monar in Ardnamurchan, ten miles away, that was being cleared. Yon was nae fable, I warrant you! It was dark as night. Aye, an' on the way back, we fell in wi' the brig *Harrietta*, John Maxwell master that I've kennt all my days, outward bound for the Canadas wi' two hundred o' the same cleared folk frae Glen Monar under his hatches. Yon was nae fable either, my young friend."

Alastair stared at the man. "The Canadas?" he repeated. "Two hundred people, from Glen Monar? Leaving Scotland, leaving their homes? Emigrants?"

"Aye, you could call them that, I reckon."

"Monar is Clanranald MacDonald country . . ."

"*Was* Clanranald country," the other amended. "Since Clanranald was forfeit after the 'Forty-five Rising, it's been York Buildings Company's property. An' now it's sold to a Mr. Calthwaite. And he is a gentleman strong for the Improvements."

"But . . . Lord, it was the clan's land! Not Clanranald's own. No Englishman—no man soever—can come up here and turn two hundred MacDonalds off MacDonald land!"

"He has done it, sir. An' mair than Mr. Calthwaite! Plenty mair."

"But, the law? What of the law?"

The seaman shrugged. "The law, I reckon, says that a laird can dae what he will wi' his ain!"

14

"How can it be his own, when it is the clan's land? Tell me that, man!"

"Me, I canna tell you that. I'm nae lawyer, nor yet a Hielandman mysel'. All I ken is what's been done, an' is being done yet. Being done ower yonder this day, it seems!" He gestured north by east into the ever-thickening pall of smoke. "I ken that the folk are gone, an' the sheep are come. That's what I've seen, sir."

"Aye—and *I've* seen a whole company of MacDonalds from that same Ardnamurchan wiped out in the Battle of Assaye in India, standing fast against ten times their number of Mahrattas, fighting for King George! And others dying like flies at the Cape, fighting fever and the Dutchmen both! And more, cut down by French grapeshot by the hundred at Aboukir and Vimeiro! While this went on in their glens at home!"

The skipper cleared his throat, and found nothing to say.

Fists clenched, the tall Highlander glared down at his stocky companion. "I have been away from Scotland over long, I think!" he said thickly, as with difficulty. "Aye, and so has the Highland Brigade—and that is God's truth!" Not trusting himself with further words, he turned abruptly away and strode forward alone into the schooner's bows, there to stare unseeing into the gloom ahead.

*   *   *

As the *Sarah Bell* moved on into the mouth of the Sound of Sleat from the Sea of the Hebrides, between the mountains of Skye on the one hand and those of Knoydart on the other, her master grew more and more uneasy. He was sailing close enough into the wind as it was, and the ever-narrowing funnel of the Sound offered little scope for tacking. Moreover, the making tide surged up the long strait as through a race. These conditions were normal enough, of course, though the wind was usually south-west, not east-north-east as now. It was the densely billowing smoke, allied to the onset of night, that really worried him, blinding him as badly as the thickest fog. He knew the Sound as well as he knew his own features; but that meant that he knew its dangers equally well. Sail reduced to a minimum to keep way on the ship against the thrust of the tide, and with leadsmen chanting the depths monotonously on both hands, above the baa-ing of the sheep, the schooner crept onwards. They could not see the looming land-masses to right and left—but they could sense them all too potently. The master cursed all smoke-making Improvers with a fervour that should have commended him to his military passenger.

That young man himself was beyond cursing. Still standing alone in the bows, his bitter thoughts had progressed from general indignation to a more particular alarm and apprehension. Plain geography was responsible for this. He was drawing near to his home country, Strathdonan of the MacRorys, and this smoke, rolling down out of the north-east, was ever thickening as they progressed. Each mile made it seem more likely that it emanated from somewhere in upper Strathdonan than in Knoydart, as he had assumed. The notion was scarcely tenable, of course, for unlike the less-fortunate MacDonald lands of Knoydart and Ardnamurchan, Strathdonan was still all held by Clanrory, as far as Alastair was aware. Had not Clanrory redeemed his father's forfeiture and exile, for his share in the 'Forty-five, by making Hanoverian George a present of a whole regiment?

The pungent smell of burning now permeated and dominated everything, quite obliterating the stench of sheep and the tarry odour of the vessel.

As the advancing night and the ramparts of the Skye hills to the west between them blotted out the last of the sunset, it became pitchy dark in the gut of the Sound, with an intensity that not even the darkest night could have produced. Men's eyes streaming from the acrid sting of the smoke did nothing to improve the situation. The master was now up in the bows beside MacRory, peering, muttering, and shouting instructions larded with expletives back to his helmsman. At length he turned to his passenger.

"Sink me, I'm haeing nae mair o' this!" he cried. "It's as black as the Earl o' Hell's waistcoat! I'm no' going to pile up the ship. We'll hae to anchor for the night."

"Can you do that?" Alastair wondered. "Here, in mid-Sound? With this tide running?"

"Na, na—no' here. But the shore to the east shelves fast. We'll be right enough jist, close in at the mouth o' the Druin River. She'll no' drag there."

"You do know where you are, then? I took it that you could not tell your position in this damnable smoke."

"Och, fine I ken where I am. What d'you take me for, man? But wi' the currents an' reefs an' shoals o' this Sound, you need mair than jist kenning where you are to take a ship through. We'd never make the narrows o' Sandaig Island in this. You'll no' get to Strathdonan this night, Mr. MacRory."

His decision made, the skipper shouted new orders and went to take the wheel himself. Soon the motion of the vessel changed, as the drag of the tide eased. The breeze fell away too, indicating that high ground close on the east was sheltering them. Commands for dousing sails and for the anchor to be run out followed, and presently the schooner came to rest, swinging gently to her cable.

"We've crossed the mouth o' Loch Hourn," Alastair was told. "We're in a shelving bay I ken of, jist a mile or so south o' Inverdruin. Unless the wind changes, I'll no' can put you into Camusewan o' Strathdonan till near noon the morn."

"Inverdruin?" MacRory repeated. "Only a mile or so? Then . . . could you not be putting me ashore in a small boat, Shipmaster, and I can be finishing my journey by land? I have but little time before I must return south. Even half a day will count. From Inverdruin I can get a horse to take me up Glen Druin and over the pass of Mam Dearg into the head of Strathdonan."

"In the dark, sir? In this?"

"Why not? I know this country as well as, it seems, you do these waters. There is a track all the way. It would save you putting into Camusewan tomorrow," Alastair pointed out.

That point carried weight with the shipman, saving him a beat up a long arm of the sea, and assuring him of hours saved the next day. So it was agreed. MacRory would end his voyage here and now.

It was a strange homecoming to the Highlandman's native soil. A boat lowered, the skipper himself descended into it with his passenger, and with unerring skill and accuracy steered through the mirk. After about a quarter of an hour of the rowers' efforts, he ran the prow lightly ashore on a shelving pebbly beach.

"Yonder's Inverdruin," he said, pointing into the black obscurity, wherein neither form showed nor light gleamed. "Will you be right enough, think you, man?" He sounded a little doubtful about leaving his passenger thus.

"Surely," MacRory declared. "It is six years since I was in Glen Druin, but I know the place fine." He took up his comparatively modest bundle of belongings, rolled in a plaid, and leapt lightly shore.

"I hae been here since then," the other mentioned. "I landed two cargoes o' sheep at Inverdruin, last year."

"Sheep, you say? Here?"

"Aye."

"I see. Well—my thanks, friend. I shall look for you at Camusewan, on your return voyage, on Wednesday or Thursday of next week, all being well."

"Aye—Goad willing, I'll be there. An' . . . guid fortune to you, Mr. MacRory. I'm thinking maybe . . . och well, never heed. Guidnight to you."

"Goodnight."

Visibility seemed to be better on land than on water, though that might only have been because there were more details to be picked out close at hand. Ahead, the darkness was unrelieved still. Crunching up over the stones of the beach, Alastair peered this way and that. He had expected some lights of the township to be showing, even through the screen of smoke, for it was early evening yet, and houses were scattered all round Inverdruin Bay. None such showed. Presently he was walking on close-cropped grass.

Then the black bulk of a house loomed up, completely dark. The man called out, but there was no response. He walked round it, stumbling over litter and tumbled stones. The place was empty and the doorway boarded up. He moved on.

It was only a short distance to the next house, a small farmery, with outbuildings as well as cot-house. This too was dark—but the darkness was not sufficient to hide the fact that there was no roof to this cottage. The outbuildings, however, still were roofed and in fair order. Opening a door in one, Alastair found it to be full of hay, fresh and sweet-smelling, a pleasant scent to counter the prevailing tang of burning. The next shed unfortunately emitted a less pleasing odour, the oily smell of fleeces. It was packed to the roof with large sacks stuffed with wool. Set-faced, the man stalked on.

He was brought up soon thereafter by what he took to be a gate, where no gate had ever been before, but which on inspection proved to be only part of a series of such, hurdles of wood and willow-wands, staked up to form a long fence. Working round this, the newcomer perceived it to be some sort of huge sheep-pen or fold, though there appeared to be no beasts in it at present. The township of Inverdruin most evidently had suffered a change of character.

Alastair decided to make for the Manse, which surely would have withstood the flood of the sheep. Along with the church, it lay within a little wood. On penetrating the belt of the trees the man was thankful to see light at last, the yellow gleam of brightly-lit windows. He went forward to rap on the door.

At the sound of his knocking a pandemonium of barking broke out, from within and without. Two black-and-white shaggy dogs, of a type that Alastair had never seen in the Highlands previously, came rushing round the side of the larger, two-storeyed house, snarling and snapping straight at the caller's long kilted legs. Alastair kicked out at them in vigorous and prompt self-defence. The brutes were not lightly discouraged, and he was still battling with them when the door was flung open. Along with a beam of light, still another dog of the same sort flew out at him. Alastair hurled his bundle at this one, and had managed to place a shrewd kick to the ribs of another, when an angry bellow from the doorway altered the situation. The dogs slunk back a little way, though with lips still curled up from white teeth and with rumblings in their throats, and Alastair turned to face the newcomer, panting.

The bellowing, if at first it had been directed at the collies, was so no longer. "Keep your dirty feet off my dogs, damn you, you Highland scum!" the man in the doorway shouted.

MacRory stared. A heavily built, paunchy man of middle years stood there, dressed in hodden breeches and house slippers, a long waistcoat unbuttoned, and stock loosened and awry. In one hand he held a flickering lamp and in the other a cocked pistol.

"*Dia*, here's an unlikely greeting to receive at the Manse of

19

Glendruin!" Alastair cried. "You can call off your brutes, sirrah, and put away that pistol. I am not used to being welcomed so!"

"Are you not, b'God?" The other looked closer, nevertheless, no doubt struck by the visitor's tone of voice and manner of speaking, in which accustomed authority was not to be disguised. If he knew anything of costume, he must have perceived that he was talking to a soldier, even though Alastair did not travel in the fullest of his regimental finery; only a soldier could be wearing the kilt and plaid, the tartan, of course being proscribed and forbidden under the savage Acts for punishing and disarming the Jacobite Highlands, still unrepealed. "Who in hell are you that speaks to me like that?" The man's voice held the broad vowels of the North of England.

"I am Alastair Dubh MacRory of Gleneidart, Lieutenant, Seventieth Foot, the Clanrory Highlanders—seeking the Reverend Farquhar MacDonald."

"D'you say that! Then you should have more sense, man, than to go banging on honest men's doors after dark in this country!" the other returned harshly. "The land's full o' masterless men and thieving wastrels. Wise men keep indoors o' nights—and keep their throats unslit!"

"Indeed! And who does the throat-slitting, may I ask, sir?"

"I told you—wastrels, vagabonds, good-for-nothing Highland riff-raff."

"Could it be that you refer to the people of this glen, sir? Its former occupants, perhaps? If so, I do not think that I like your choice of words!"

"And I don't like your tone o' voice, young feller! You're not talking to your bare-shanked army scum now, I'd remind you! You are not, Name o' God!"

"Aye, that Name does remind me. It is not such as you that I wish speech with at all," Alastair returned, holding in his hot temper. "It is with the Reverend Mr. MacDonald, minister of this parish. Is he here?"

"No."

"Then where is he, may I ask? This is his Manse."

"It is not. This is my house, now. As for the parson

MacDonald, I neither know where that black, croaking, old crow may be—nor care!"

"But . . . this is the parish church, here. How can this be? Who is the minister here, then . . .?"

"Nobody is the minister here, Mister—but I am *master* here! I am George Cousins, manager and flockmaster o' this estate and its sheep-walks. Do I make myself clear?"

"You do indeed! The flock, it seems, has changed—and so has the style of its master! I regret having disturbed you." Alastair stopped to pick up his bundle. The dogs growled again. "I bid you goodnight, Master Cousins. I hope that you are master of these dogs, as well as of all else!"

Curtly the other ordered the animals to heel. He raised his voice. "Hey, what are you about, anyway?" he demanded. "Where have you come from?"

"I am about my own business, sir—and wager that it has little in common with yours! Goodnight." The younger man turned on his heel, and strode away without a backward glance.

The flockmaster's voice followed him. "I advise you, Mister, if you know what's good for you, to watch your step! B'God I do! And watch your words too, damn you! In fact, you'd be wise to get back to your soldiering, where you belong." The door slammed resoundingly.

Black Alastair's expression was at its blackest as he stalked off.

Inverdruin had boasted an inn, a little way north of the church. The man headed in this direction now, encouraged by the glimmer of more lights. As he drew near, however, he perceived that more than light emanated from the group of buildings. The sound of singing reached him, and while any such indication of cheer and good-fellowship should have been welcome in the circumstances, the MacRory's frown but deepened. For the singing sounded hoarse and liquor-inspired, its shanty-like rhythm being beaten out by what might be heavy boots and tankards; moreover, clearly neither words nor tune were of Highland origin.

Even as Alastair hesitated, a great barking of more dogs broke out from the vicinity of the inn—many dogs, obviously. Sighing, the traveller turned away. There would be no welcome for such as himself there either, he judged. No doubt the place had been turned into some sort of barracks or bothy for the man Cousins' south-country shepherds. There seemed to be no other customers for a hostelry left in Inverdruin.

This apparently was what the word Improvement, spelt with a capital letter, meant in the Scottish Highlands this year of Our Lord eighteen hundred and eight.

Shrugging his uninjured shoulder, Alastair MacRory made for the riverside and its track that struck off in a north-easterly direction inland, up the glen. He would walk up Glen Druin until he found a farm or a croft that would hire him a garron, one of the sturdy ponies of that country, to finish his journey of some eighteen miles to his own glen of Eidart off Strath-donan. And meanwhile he would find himself a stout stick, which seemed to be a pre-requisite of travel in the modern Highlands

Chapter Three

GLEN DRUIN runs for some seven miles from the swift tides of the Sound of Sleat towards the great mountains that crowd in around the head of green Strathdonan, and Alastair MacRory had to walk all of those miles on his own feet that night, for the simple reason that nowhere on the way did he find anywhere to hire a mount. Nor did he even see a horse throughout. Yet this fair valley had been known as one of the most fertile and populous in all the north-west, with crofts and farms and cot-houses scattered over the length of it. But not now. No single light was visible in all its extent. After turning off to approach the first three or four houses near the track, and finding them all mere deserted rickles of stones, he held to the path which followed the riverside. He did find the house of Veolary intact, the large farm of a tacksman, or tenant-in-chief, but it was shut up, devoid of man or animal. MacDonald of Veolary was a serving officer in the Seventy-eighth Highlanders, the Seaforths, Alastair knew—but where was his family?

It was a lonely walk for the homing soldier, and the sheep

which flounced away from him all the way up the glen did little to comfort him.

The blanket of smoke still covered the land, though now the man had the impression that it had thinned considerably. He could see further, at any rate; though that might be merely his sight adjusting itself, smart as his eyes still did. The improvement, however, brought no easement of MacRory's mind; the reverse indeed, for now, ahead of him, a distinct and increasing tinge of red was beginning to permeate and infuse the gloom, a sombre and ominous flush in the night sky. However obvious it had been from the first that all this smoke must in fact represent a corresponding amount of flame, that grim refulgence affected the man quite powerfully. His sense of foreboding grew apace. The glow ahead was ever more clearly emanating from a wide area north of east, further north than he had hitherto allowed his mind to contemplate. Towards its head this Glen Druin bent away to the south-east, barred by a tall black ridge of hill. At the other side of that ridge lay upper Strathdonan, end of the traveller's long road from London. And it was behind that same black ridge that the ruddy stain of reflected fire waxed ever brighter.

The track that Alastair was following forked after about five miles, the right arm continuing to accompany the river along the floor of the southward-turning glen, the left to climb in a long zig-zag ascent towards the summit of the ridge and the lofty pass of Mam Dearg. The man took this latter.

He climbed at a steady stride. Walking was no hardship to him, as became a Highlander and an infantryman; only his shoulder pained him a little, and made his bundle seem the heavier. Long legged as he was, he would have covered the ground only slightly more speedily on a garron. As the rough track rose, the smoke thinned and the baleful brightness in front grew stronger. Presently the smoke was almost gone, and the sore-eyed traveller walked in a crimson glow, which made the heather around him seem to live again in wine-red bloom, and turned the puddles of the track into pools of blood.

Alastair was impatient, and at the same time almost reluctant, to reach the head of the high pass. Mam Dearg was one of the finest viewpoints in a land of unsurpassable vistas, with far below the head of the great sea-loch of Donan at the hub of three noble glens, and as background the soaring jagged peaks and pinnacles of some of the most majestic mountains in Scotland. At night, of course, no panorama was to be looked for; but at least there was nothing other than lack of light to obstruct the view.

Despite all apprehensive anticipation, Alastair was quite unprepared for what he saw when at length he reached the final summit. Appalled, he halted, gazing. Though below him the smoke-clouds obscured much detail, the general impact was overwhelming. The whole of Strathdonan seemed to be ablaze, from the close-knit lochside townships to the scattered crofts and shielings far up the mountainsides, not in broad sheets of flame but in innumerable individual fires and beacons. The multitude and pattern of them, so farflung and extensive, was perhaps more devastating in its effect on the eye than any mere unbroken conflagration. As far as smoke and topography permitted vision down long Loch Donan-side, the fires reached, some flaring brightly still, but more now merely the glowing, smoking crimson of embers; over all the fertile bottom lands and meadows about the head of the loch they spread, and up into each of the three glens that opened off therefrom. It was the comprehensiveness of the holocaust that most struck the observer.

After the first shock of it, Alastair's gaze lifted inevitably over and beyond the far ridge of hill that rose at the other side of Loch Donan, to the north. The parallel and smaller, narrower glen of the Eidart lay there. Thitherwards at least all seemed to be dark, no glow of fires silhouetting the intervening barrier of mountains.

The man, after some unspecified time of staring, found that he was counting those fires. It was a major task, however profitless. He reached two hundred and fifteen before he gave it up—and undoubtedly many had died out ere this, or were hidden by smoke and natural features. A due recognition of what all that implied, whether in terms of human misery, loss, betrayal, or in sheer planning and destructive effort, just was not to be grasped as yet. Two hundred odd homes no longer homes, two hundred families dispersed. This very day. And all those of Clanrory's people on Clan Ruari land; Strathdonan, unlike Glendruin and Knoydart and Ardnamurchan and so many others, was no forfeited estate, bought over from the Government in London by some new English owner. Strathdonan was still the hereditary and ages-old home of the MacRorys and MacBrides and MacIvers, still under the care of their powerful and traditional chief. The thing was not to be comprehended.

His head throbbing with more than the effect of smoke in his eyes, Alastair Dubh went heavy-footed down into it all.

*   *   *

The descent to the head of the loch was much less steep than on the southern side, and very quickly the heather gave place to rough pasture. Quite soon Alastair was into the smoke again. On the hill-top it had been blown clear.

Perhaps half-way down he came to the first house. It had been a small croft, consisting of a single range of low, rough, stone building, cottage at one end, byre and hay-shed at the other, the latter seeming to dig itself into the very side of the hill. Both were now roofless and soot-blackened, their interiors a glowing bed of ashes still emitting much heat and murky, choking smoke. There had been another smaller fire outside. Possibly this had been a henhouse or other outbuilding, made of timber, for here were no stones. Closer inspection revealed, however, that some of the smouldering ends of wood were the remains of pieces of rough furniture, worn and polished with use. The peaty turf was burning around this fire, producing especially dark and acrid smoke. Angrily, if pointlessly, the man stamped it out, muttering to himself. The small patch of garden ground near by was trampled flat, and everywhere feathers clung and blew in the breeze. Alastair found a child's toy horse smashed over a large stone, and a wooden bowl split as by an axe-blow. That was all. Small haystacks still stood amongst the little areas of tilth scratched on the hillside, but there were no animals, no signs of life.

The man stood amidst it all for a moment or two, and the burning in his dark eyes was not wholly a reflection of the glowing embers around him. Then, set-faced, he moved on, downhill.

He passed another and another of these burnt-out home-steads, differing only in minor detail from the first. At one a dog howled mournfully to the sky, and growled as he approached, but would not leave the former threshold. Its movement therein, however, painfully made, revealed a dragged hind leg, obviously broken. The man sought in his bundle for pistol, powder and ball, loaded and primed the weapon, and then put the brute out of its misery. The bang of the shot sounded shatteringly loud on the night.

After that the newcomer did not turn aside to examine each croft that he passed. There were many of them scattered over the skirts of the hillside, small-holdings carved by generations out of the rock-ribbed wilderness, stones laboriously cleared and collected, burns channelled and boggy patches drained, multi-shaped plots that were mere pocket-handkerchiefs of cultivation, tilled wherever the rugged rocky slopes permitted. All now, without exception, smoked and glowed.

Just before he reached the levels at the head of the loch, however, Alastair did turn aside, a little off his way. He followed a side-track that ran up the edge of a noisy, prattling burn and through an area of birch-wood where the smoke had caught in the trees and lingered thickly. Beyond this, faintly above the uncaring song of the stream, another sound came to him, an unchancy and unpleasing sound that lifted the hairs at the back of the man's neck. As he moved away from the burn-side, the noise became clearer—the high, thin, sobbing notes of a woman keening. He thought that the sound came from higher up the hill, some way off, though it was hard to tell, so much did it seem part of the moaning of the night wind and the sibilant sigh of falling waters. Alastair spent some time trying to locate that woeful plaint, stumbling up over rough ground in the darkness, casting about over the wide brackeny and birch-covered slopes. He shouted once or twice, and only his echo returned to him hollowly—and the keening was maintained. At length, unable to tell whether it came from above him or below, he turned back. After all, what could he do for, or say to, the soul that was thus calling its anguish to the smoke-filled, heedless night? What easement could he offer, here and now? Alastair moved down again towards the house that he had been making for.

This was the little mill of Moulin Riach, where Murdo the Mill ground the oats for most of the Kinlochdonan area. Murdo's only son was Corporal Callum MacIver, of Alastair's own Company. The last time that he had seen him, Callum had been lying in the straw of a Portuguese barn, with both legs shot away below the knee by French grapeshot. Alastair had a message from Callum to his wife, his father and his mother, though whether the sender might still be alive he did not know.

Because the mill and its house were situated in a fairly deep hollow that the burn had excavated for itself, where a small pond had been dammed up, Alastair, seeing no reflection of flame immediately ahead, foolishly allowed himself to hope. Arrival at the top of the slope above the place, however, revealed his folly. Moulin Riach was like all the others, only slightly more so in that there was here rather more to burn. Down at the reeking ruins the man peered into the red desolation, his lips moving soundlessly. As he drew back from leaning against the doorpost, he found his hand to be sticky. He stooped to wipe it on the trampled, grain-littered grass, assuming it to be resin melted from the wood by the heat. A licking spurt of flame, however, amongst the embers, revealed it to be blood. Blood on a doorpost that had not burned. MacRory turned away, and went heavily whence he had come. He had seen enough for one night, surely.

Though a soldier, and inured to the sights and sounds of the battlefield, he was glad of the noisy splash and tinkle of the tumbling burn that took him back to the lochside, to drown the sound, or the memory of the sound, of that woman's keening. It had had a mad and eerie note to it. The thought that it might have been Callum's wife would not leave his mind.

Down at the wide saltings and water-meadows at the head of the loch, a new sound reached the man. It came apparently from across the flame-reddened water, over the mile-wide loch. He thought that he recognised it as the lowing of cattle, of very many cattle, that rose and fell but never died away entirely, carried on the night breeze. Alastair wondered whether to move round in that direction. It was on his way, but he had thought to visit first the Manse of Kinlochdonan and his cousin therein. He was in two minds over the matter when he glimpsed, through the drifting smoke banks, the first light other than that of fire that he had seen since leaving Inverdruin. It was down this southern side of the loch, a little way. That yellow ray almost certainly would come from his cousin's Manse—if indeed the Reverend Angus was still Minister of Kinlochdonan. Late as it was, Alastair decided to make for its warm and beckoning gleam.

At least no sheep-dogs came barking at the nocturnal visitor as he knocked at this Manse door. Indeed all seemed to be entirely unexceptional about the place. An old woman opened to him, cautiously, and when the visitor asked for the Minister, brought him doubtfully within, locked the door behind him and, leaving the lamp with him, knocked at an inner door. After a brief interval she signed to the caller to enter.

The man who rose from the fireside chair, with the open book and the glass of steaming toddy, was not the Reverend MacRory, He was a younger man, good-looking in a delicate, small-boned way, dressed in decent, grey broadcloth and tolerably fresh linen. In that comfortable book-lined room, well-furnished and carpeted and with heavy curtains shutting out the night, he looked so entirely at ease, so utterly normal, so completely divorced from the conditions that prevailed outside, that the newcomer was for the moment thrown somewhat off balance, bereft of words. Even the all-pervading smell of smoke did not seem to have penetrated into this snug and pleasant apartment.

"Good evening, sir," the man by the hearth said, civilly "What can I do for you?" He spoke with the level and comparatively harsh and throaty intonation of southern Scotland, so different from the musical light Highland voice—though there was nothing harsh about his manner.

"Your pardon, sir, at this intrusion. At this late hour. I regret to trouble you," Alastair jerked, seeking to adapt himself, his mood and frame of mind, to this sudden and to him extraordinary change of atmosphere. "I was looking to see Angus, my cousin. The reverend MacRory. The minister of this parish. I am Gleneidart. I have just returned to this country. Landed at Inverdruin."

"Ah, I see. Mr. MacRory, I regret, is no longer here, sir. I

28

succeeded him as parish minister just a year ago. My name is Dunlop—Amos Dunlop. At your service, if there is anything that I can do to assist you?"

"Thank you. I came, in the first instance, to borrow a garron. A horse. To take me on my way to Glen Eidart," Alastair said. "But . . . where is Angus Crubach? The Reverend MacRory? He is not dead . . .?"

"No, no, sir. Mr. MacRory is not dead. Dear me, no! He is merely no longer parish minister."

"You mean that he has transferred to another parish? After twenty-five years?"

"Not to another parish, no. He does not have a parish now. He is, as you might say, retired." The other sounded as though he was choosing his words with care.

"Retired? Angus Crubach? At fifty-five? Is he sick? Ill?"

"No. Not in body, at any rate. In the mind, perhaps, a little. He has acted foolishly, perhaps. But it is not for me to judge. You will understand that though I have replaced him in this charge, the decision to do so was none of my making."

"Replaced, is it? How was he replaced? By whom?"

"By the proper authorities, of course, sir. The same authorities who appointed me to his place. My lord of Clanrory, the heritor of this parish, in consultation with the Presbytery of Glenelg, Synod of Ross."

"I see," Alastair said levelly. "Replaced by the proper authorities. Because he acted a little foolishly. Because he was perhaps a little sick in his mind." The visitor drew a deep breath. "*Dia*, it would seem that not a few people are sick in their minds in these parts, today! Mr. Dunlop, could it be, I wonder, that the Reverend Farquhar MacDonald of Glendruin suffered from a similar malady?"

"H'mmm. Mr. MacDonald was before my time," the other answered slowly. "He, er, vacated his parish, I understand, almost two years ago."

"Vacated? Not replaced?"

"No. The situation there was rather different, as I understand it. Mr. MacDonald chose to emigrate. To Upper Canada. With most of his parishioners."

"Chose to emigrate?" The Highlander strove hard to keep

his voice even. "You are telling me, sir, that Farquhar Mac-
Donald and the whole people of Glen Druin *chose* to leave
their homes and glens, the homes of their fathers, and go
thousands of miles away to the wildernesses of Upper Canada?
Can it be that you are using the right word, Mr. Dunlop?"

The clergyman raised expressive hands. "They went, at any
rate, sir. And Mr. MacDonald elected to accompany them.
As I say, it was before my time in this neighbourhood." He
shrugged. "But come, won't you be seated? Accept some small
refreshment? Have a glass of toddy with me, and a morsel to
eat?"

"I thank you, no." That was short.

"Dear me, sir, the wayfarer must not turn from my door
lacking a little hospitality. It is the kindly custom."

"Your door, I noticed, sir, was locked! And it is locked
again, behind me. It could be that, this night, there are other
wayfarers more in need of your aid and sustenance than am I!"

"Then let them come knocking, my friend, and I shall see
what my poor resources can offer them, as befits a minister of
the gospel. Meanwhile, sit in. It is my habit—not too in-
temperate a one, I hope?—to indulge in a little toddy, a
bannock, and a Chapter of The Word, last thing at night. I
find that it promotes sleep and tranquillity of mind." He
smiled cordially.

"God of Mercy!" Abruptly Alastair MacRory could contain
himself no longer, as he stared at this pleasantly spoken, unruffled man, at the comfortable room with the drawn curtains
and air of secure and settled ease and peace. "Tranquillity,
you talk about! Lord—are you crazy-mad, or am I? Out there,
man, outside this door of yours, a whole country burns. A
whole people is dispossessed. *Your* people, *your* parishioners!
Evicted. Ravished from their homes. Gone God knows where!
And you sit here, undisturbed, with your curtains drawn, and
talk of tranquillity, of kindly hospitality, of sleep! Is it all
nothing to you, man? Nothing?"

The other raised his brows. "You speak a little wildly, sir,
surely? I am concerned for these people's welfare, naturally—
their material welfare as well as their spiritual welfare, which
is my prime mission. They are going through an unsettling
period, admittedly, but they are on their way to better things.

That is a cause for satisfaction. The road towards betterment, in things material as in spiritual, is not always the wide and easy one. That road, Scripture tells us, leadeth to destruction. It is the strait and narrow gate that leadeth to eternal life, I would remind you, sir . . ."

"Damnation, man, do you know what you are saying?" Alastair interrupted him hotly. "Are you out of your wits completely? I counted over two hundred roof-trees blazing from up there on Mam Dearg. Tonight two hundred families of this parish are homeless, wherever they are. Why? For what crime? On whose authority? Is that the way to spiritual betterment, the narrow gate to salvation? Tell me."

"It is not for us to question God's way and purposes," the minister said sternly. "Those whom He loveth, He chasteneth . . ."

"*God's* purposes! Mercy on us—you are not blaming those burning homes on God, are you? It is not God who lit the thatches, is it? Has God taken up land improvement and sheep-raising . . .?"

"Young man, you will not blaspheme the Almighty in this house!" Dunlop cried, "You forget yourself! Impious words I will not permit . . ."

"But you *will* permit eviction, extortion, savagery, and the turning of a fair country into a blackened wilderness!"

"You know not what you say, sir. You are ignorant. Of your own admission, you say that you have just returned to this country. This estate has just embarked on a great and worthy project of Improvement. It entails moving many people to new quarters, because up until now they have been wastefully devouring the land in unproductive idleness and squalor. But this is for their own betterment and ultimate welfare. As well as for the well-being and advantage of the entire country and nation. Some immediate discomfort and inconvenience there will be, inevitably, but that is a small price to pay for the great benefit that will follow. Moreover, the people here have only themselves to blame for such temporary discomfort. Apart from their idleness, their Popish leanings and wicked superstition, their general recalcitrance—which in themselves merit the dire judgement of Almighty God—they have almost wholly and wilfully ignored the warnings given them to be ready to

vacate their holdings this November term-day. They have had
ample warning from the estate. And from my own pulpit I
have informed them repeatedly of the fruits of obstinacy and
disobedience. So far as I have heard, no single household was
prepared and ready to move when the factor's men resumed
possession of the holdings these last two days, in the name of
Lord Clanrory. If they now suffer some discomfort and
tribulation, they have none to blame but themselves."

His visitor gazed at him, almost unbelievingly. "I heard
aright, did I?" he demanded. "You *are* parish minister here?
The pastor and spiritual shepherd of this flock? Not some sort
of agent of the estate? The factor's principal assistant, perhaps?"

"Sir!" Dunlop exclaimed indignantly. "I would urge that
you watch your words! Your remarks are both insolent and
unjust. Their only excuse is that presumably they are born out
of ignorance. Unless you adopt a more respectful and suitable
manner, I must ask you to leave my house."

"That I shall do, Mr. Dunlop, never fear. I think that I
prefer even the choking atmosphere out there to that of this
comfortable room! But before I go, perhaps you will conde-
scend to disperse just a little of the ignorance which I display?
I would ask who is responsible for this policy of eviction?"

"The Lord Viscount Clanrory, as I told you. The proprietor of this estate. Who else?"

"Clanrory is not the proprietor of this estate. Clanrory is
chief of Clan Ruari, yes, but Strathdonan is the clan's land,
not Clanrory's own."

The other shook his head. "I fear that is a romantic and
outdated notion that has no basis in law, sir. Lord Clanrory
is the legal owner of this property, and can do with it as he
will. The barbaric and archaic clan system is dead, sir—and
well so!"

"Indeed!" Alastair's grip upon himself now had to be so
fierce that his knuckles gleamed white. "I could dispute those
statements. All of them," he said, tight-voiced. "But I shall
not, now. Lord Clanrory is in London. I had speech with him
only a few days ago. He said nothing of all this. But he is still
the chief and leader of this people. As such I am convinced
that he would never consent to what is being done here today.

No chief could behave so to his own clansmen. It is unthinkable, whatever the legalities—and whatever the Kirk of Scotland may say! Someone else is doing it, in his name. Who is that man?"

"The policy is Lord Clanrory's, young man. The carrying out of the programme of improvement is in the hands of his lordship's factor, Mr. Rory MacRory. Son of MacRory of Camusewan. An able and conscientious man . . ."

"Rory Mor! Son of the Chamberlain!" Alastair exclaimed. "I do not believe it!"

"Whether you believe it or not, sir, that is the fact. Mr. Rory MacRory Younger of Camusewan, Lord Clanrory's factor, is carrying out this large-scale and enlightened project at the behest of the proprietor, and with due authority and in legal fashion."

This time the minister had his visitor silenced. That Big Rory, Rory Mor MacRory, son of the old Chamberlain of Strathdonan, should be responsible for this outrage against his own people, was almost beyond conception. No Lowlander, no incomer this, no Englishman, but a Highlander of the Highlanders, a MacRory of long and resounding lineage, a leader of the clan, indeed at some removes a relative of Alastair's own. Here was word that left the enquirer speechless, floundering.

The minister, seeing his advantage, went on: "You will perceive, my young friend, that a little knowledge and understanding puts a very different complexion upon the matter. Hot-headed accusations and unfounded charges aid no one. I would remind you . . ."

Alastair cut him short with a peremptory gesture of the hand. "Where are these people now?" he demanded. "The dispossessed?"

The other sighed. "Down at the sea coast, I believe. The factor has provided alternative land for them there. At Ardglass . . ."

"Ardglass! That barren strip! Lord, how many has he jettisoned on that stony beach?"

"I do not know. That is no concern of mine, sir. I am a minister of the gospel, not a land-agent. As you yourself indicated."

"No concern of yours? Yet you advised them to go. Not to resist. You warned them, from your pulpit. Your flock!"

"I preached to them obedience to due and lawful authority, as was my duty. I urged repentance of their grievous sins, and a humble submission to God's will, with faith in His divine purpose towards them."

"Aye." That was heavily said. "And having so done, you were satisfied?"

The clergyman tapped long fingers on the table. "I can conceive of no reason why I should put up with this inquisition from you, sir."

"No. Perhaps not. So . . . no one of your parishioners has come knocking at their minister's door this night?"

"No, sir. None."

"I see. Why would they, indeed! I bid you goodnight then, Mr. Dunlop. May your sleep be undisturbed, tranquil indeed! Your conscience easy!" The MacRory swung on his heel and strode to the door. Reaching for the handle, he paused, and turned. "Sir—do you speak the language?" he asked suddenly. "The Gaelic?"

"No, sir. I have not that facility, as yet. Why, pray?"

Alastair said something short but vehement under his breath, and flung out of that house into the smoke-filled night, slamming the door behind him.

Chapter Four

THE man stalked round the head of Loch Donan, his weariness forgotten in his wrath and bitterness. The Kirk, Clanrory himself—and now Rory Mor . . .! Scarcely able to take it in, he strode on. Crossing the Bridge of Donan, where the main river entered the loch, after a mile or so, he recollected that he had intended to borrow a horse at the Manse. He tossed the thought aside angrily; better to walk than to accept anything from that man.

He passed many more burnt-out cottages around the lochhead. These were all only dully glowing now. Being readily accessible, they would have been amongst the first to be fired. They could still smoke, however.

As he walked, the sound of the complaining cattle was always before him. The nearer that he drew to the source of the noise, however, the more distinctly he perceived another sound that seemed to come through and above it, to rise and fall and sometimes fade away entirely, but always to return, a thinner higher sound than that of lowing cattle. At first he thought that it might be sheep, penned somewhere near by and baa-ing, as they had done in the schooner. Presently, however, he knew that it was not sheep, and the recognition gave him no comfort.

When the loch-shore began to slant away westwards once more. Alastair should have walked straight on into the last of the valleys that radiated from that great, green amphitheatre like the spokes of a wheel, and which would bring him eventually over the hill and into his own place of Glen Eidart. The noise in his ears, however, little as he relished it, drew him off to the left, down the track which followed the northern shore of the loch. He could not just walk away from that sound unheeding.

It was not long before the sources of noise separated and established themselves. On the right of the track, on the higher ground, a great concourse of cattle was gathered, the small, shaggy, black beasts of the north-west, made restless and uneasy by being close herded and by the smell of fire. Judging by the uproar, there were hundreds upon hundreds of them penned within a natural enclosure that the hillsides here formed, requiring fencing and hurdles and the like only at this side nearest the track. As Alastair came up, two figures materialised out of the gloom and ordered him curtly, roughly, to keep away from the beasts, to be gone. They spoke in English, threateningly. Alastair might have questioned their authority and their manners, in practical fashion, but he was not really very interested in cattle just then. It was the sound on the other side that beckoned him, and that sound emanated from nearer the water. He knew now from whence it came. Out there, across the reedy water-meadows, a grassy mound thrust into the loch, a small promontory on which the ruined gables

35

of an ancient church still stood, surrounded by the moss-grown, reeling gravestones of its God's acre. Down towards this he turned, without answering his challengers, to take the broken causeway that crossed the marshy levels.

It was a grievous, dolorous sound that drew him on, forlorn and hopeless, now lifting, now fading, but ever persisting, so much more affecting than the outcry of the frightened cattle. He had listened askance to the cry of that lone and unknown woman above the mill of Moulin Riach; this was the keening, sobbing plaint of many women, a multitude, interspersed and pierced by the thinner wailing of children, and all as it were led up and unified by the high, wild notes of bagpipes playing a lament, to distil sorrow upon the night with all the extremity and fervour of grief of which the Celtic nature is capable.

The man stood at the broken-down wall of the churchyard, biting his lip. The place was full of people, crowded amongst the gravestones, crouching, sitting, lying. At first glance it seemed as though not a foot of the turf was unoccupied. Goods and chattels were piled everywhere, tied poultry flapped and protested. There was very little movement apparent, nor indeed room for such. Most people sat hunched, wrapped in their plaids, leaning against tombstones or each other, and as far as Alastair could see, the great majority were women, many with their plaids thrown right over their bowed heads. And from the melancholy assemblage as a whole, as it seemed, rather than from individuals, the wailing arose like a dirge, a chant.

Hesitantly, pitifully, Alastair spoke to the nearest woman. The child within her arm and plaid looked up at him great-eyed, unspeaking, but the woman did not so much as raise her head. He turned to an old man, who crouched near by, a trembling hand clutching an empty cooking-pot. At first he did not seem to hear. Then he shook his head; no other re-action could the young man obtain from him. As he moved further over, a child cringed back at his words and from his outstretched hand, as though from a blow.

Alastair sighed, and turned away.

Up at the summit of the mound, where the red-tinged sky silhouetted the black fangs of broken masonry that had once been the pre-Reformation church of Strathdonan, he sensed the stir of movement. It was from up there that the piper played his heart-wringing lament. Alastair, picking his way amongst the crouching, motionless figures, climbed up thereto.

He saw that in and around the ruined masonry, a man was moving from one recumbent figure to another, pausing, stooping, kneeling. Towards him Alastair worked his way.

As he drew close, something in the other man's gait, the fact that he walked with a limp, struck the newcomer as familiar. Snatches of words, caught between the piper's notes, confirmed the matter.

"Angus!" he cried, stepping forward. "Angus Crubach! *Dia*, it is you!"

The other straightened up, peering from tired, smoke-sore eyes. "Yes, my son. Angus of the Limp it is. And you? I cannot see you clearly. It is not . . . it is not . . .? By the mercy of God, it is not Alastair Dubh? Black Alastair of Gleneidart!"

"None other, Angus. Alastair of Gleneidart it is. And the better man for seeing yourself, Cousin."

The two men clasped each other, the frail, stooping pastor and the tall soldier. Always they had been friends, these two, though more in the relationship of uncle and nephew than the full cousins that they were. Alastair had been the son of his father's old age, born after the latter's eventual return to his native glen from exile for his share in the Rising of 'forty-five. The Reverend Angus had christened him, tutored him, guided him. Now, they considered each other over the twitching body of an old woman who lay beside a broken tombstone, whimpering and moaning.

"I thank the good Lord for the sight of you, Alastair *a graidh*," the minister said. "Where are you from? How come you here? Can it be . . . can it be that Almighty God has indeed heard my prayers and brought the lads home? Home, to their people's dire need? Is it so indeed, Alastair?"

"No." The younger man's tone was harsher than he knew, in his pain at dashing the sudden surge of hope in the other's voice. "No, Angus—I am alone. To my sorrow. Would that I were not. I have come here from London. I landed at Inverdruin but this evening. On a short leave of absence, only. I came to see my mother. Knowing nothing . . . of all this. We had no word . . ."

"Your mother, boy?" the older man said, uncertainly. "You . . . you had no word? My letter . . .?"

"I cannot hear you," Alastair cried. The high, wild wailing of the pipes and the enduring keening of the women required almost that they shouted.

Angus of the Limp looked around him slowly, before, almost reluctantly, his weary eyes came back to his cousin. "Here is but a woeful welcome home to you, lad," he said. "And your mother . . . at least she did not live to see this day. She died six months back, Alastair. God rest her soul."

Alastair stood very still. For moments on end he looked straight before him, unseeing, while his cousin reached out to grip and press the arm that held his bundle. He did not speak.

"I wrote you a letter," the other went on. "It did not reach you? I am sorry, boy. It will be a sore, sore blow to you. She went peaceably. I was with her at the end. Her last words were of you . . ."

The moaning of the old woman at their feet was suddenly interrupted by a hard, choking paroxysm of coughing that racked and convulsed her meagre frame. As the pastor knelt down to her, Alastair was almost glad to do likewise.

"Who is she? What ails her? Can I help?" he asked, jerkily.

"I fear not. She is old Seana Daloran. She has not left her bed these many weeks. I fear that the shock . . . and this cold air . . . too much for her." Angus Crubach smoothed the old woman's brow and murmured softly, soothingly, close to her ear.

Alastair stood up, consumed with a great helplessness, a great pity, and a great wrath. An active, vigorous man, never had he known such frustration, such inability to affect a situation that shouted aloud for action, for aid, for rescue.

"Where are the men?" he demanded of the other, as Angus of the Limp rose again. "These are all women and children and dotards. I know where the *young* men are, God forgive me! But where are the others?"

"They have gone on ahead. Down to Ardglass, at the coast. Where Rory Mor is giving them some land."

"But that is folly. There is no good land at Ardglass. It is only beach and rock and peat-bog. There is not enough there to support ten families, much less two hundred. Has Rory Mor lost his wits?"

"Not his wits, I think. His soul, perhaps—but not his wits, no! He does not intend Ardglass to support these people. It is merely a halting place, a place where they may wait until the ship arrives, see you."

"Ship? What ship?"

"*Mac Ruaraidh Mor's* ship. Clanrory's ship, that is to be taking them to Canada."

"*Diabhol!* Canada! It is true, then? This is Clanrory's work?"

"Clanrory's, and his Chamberlain's. And Rory Mor's. Yes. May God in His mercy forgive them."

"But . . . I can scarcely credit it!" Alastair cried. "Our own chief, condemning his people to transportation! That is all that it is. Stealing their land and transporting them."

"Clanrory says that the land is his, now—the clan's no longer. The clan is a thing of the past, Alastair; its day is done, over. Now there is only landlord and tenant. And the tenants have no rights, no claims to the land, even to their own houses that they and their fathers built, it seems. Clanrory has the law to say that that is true, and the Sheriff to enforce his eviction orders. There is no *Mac Ruaraidh Mor* any longer, no clan chief—only the Lord Viscount Clanrory in London, and his factor here."

"This is beyond all belief!" the younger man protested. "Clanrory should be the last to say that the clan is no more, means nothing to him. He uses the clan to man his regiment, does he not? And with his regiment he buys power and position and royal favour. The loyal and patriotic subject of King George! The Clanrory Highlanders win battles—aye, and medals, Heaven help us! And Clanrory garners the glory and honours. Clanrory, I tell you, without his clan, would be nothing! An old, done man; weak and impotent."

"Yet they say, Alastair, that it is because of that very regiment that all this is being done. That the cost of maintaining and equipping the regiment in the field is so great that Clanrory must have more money. So he must turn all these lands into a great sheep-run, to be farmed by Rory Mor and his father. The sheep are to pay for the soldiers, see you!"

Alastair all but added his groan to the others. "That is the most hellish infamy of all!" he cried. "To purchase favour with the lives of men! While the men are gone, to dispossess their families! Then to claim that the profit is needed to equip more lives to sacrifice! Here is shame unequalled!"

"Aye, lad. So I see it. Betrayal. As do these poor folk. But not the State. Not the law."

"Nor the Kirk, either, it seems!"

Angus Crubach sighed. "So you have heard of that?"

"I have been knocking at the doors of two Manses this night," the younger man said grimly. "At Inverdruin, and at your own house. In each I found strange shepherds of the flock! One, a bullying oaf, with a drawn pistol and dogs—but at least no hypocrite. The other a, a whited sepulchre! A well-filled and contented wolf in sheep's clothing! Your supplanter."

"Och, he is not all that bad, the man," the Reverend Angus protested, but sadly. "He just does not understand, at all. He is a Lowlander, and ignorant of our Highland ways. He cannot speak to the people in their own tongue. He hears only Clanrory's side of the matter. And Clanrory is the sole heritor of this parish. The living is as good as in his gift. Amos Dunlop, to keep his charge, must not work against the man who had him appointed. Or against his factor."

"And the Kirk itself? The Presbytery? The Synod? They threw *you* out, after all these years, and appointed this time-server. This lickspittle! So the Kirk is on Clanrory's side, also?"

"Do not be too hard on the Kirk, man Alastair," the older man urged. "You saw what has happened at Inverdruin, where church and parish are lost altogether. All the heritors, the new landlords, are for this policy. Improvement, they call it! They say that the glens are over-populated. That the New World needs the people. The Kirk has no material weapons to fight them with . . ."

"So it changes to their side, against the people!" Alastair finished for him. "Faugh—it makes me spew, the whole of it! Kirk and chief and law—aye, and the folk here, too! For bowing down to it all, for accepting eviction like a flock of sheep themselves! For not fighting. The clansmen were warriors once . . ."

"What can they do, lad? Their leaders and their young men gone, to fight Napoleon. The law enforced against them, in a language that they do not understand. Their own chief ordering them to quit. Most of them accepting it as the will of God . . . which perchance it may be. Who am I to say otherwise . . .?"

"But you *did* say otherwise, Angus?"

"Aye. That is why this old ruin is all the church I have now, Alastair."

"Of course. Forgive me, Angus *a graidh*." The younger man drew a hand across his brow. His head and eyes ached; the smoke, no doubt, and physical weariness, allied to the nagging pain of his wounded shoulder, would account for that. And the everlasting keening that rose and fell around them. "Can this wailing not be stopped?" he asked, irritably. "It is no help."

"That is where you are wrong, lad. It does help them, I think. The women. It is a sort of release. Better than bottling up their sorrow and loss. Let them be, Alastair. Anything that aids them to pass this night . . ."

"Yes. I am sorry. It is this standing here, doing nothing. In their great need. So easy to talk. Less easy to act, to effect anything. What can I do to help, old friend?"

"Little enough, I fear. Perhaps if you will speak to some of them, just. Tell them of how their husbands and sons fare, in the regiment. It may serve to take their minds off themselves, for a little."

Alastair frowned. "That is not so easy either," he said. And quickly, to change the subject, he gestured around him. "This place. It is not suitable for the sick and aged to pass a November night. Can we not seek to move a few of them somewhere under cover, at the least?"

The pastor shook his head. "That is not possible, I am afraid. There is nowhere for them to go, No one who has a roof left over his head may take in any of the evicted, on pain of being evicted himself. That is Rory Mor's order. Not even into a byre or a stable. Few there are left unburned, anyway. Only some tacksmen's farms."

"But why, in the name of Heaven? Why this savagery? How will that benefit Clanrory, or anybody else?"

"It is a punishment, just. To show who is master; as a

warning to other glens that are yet to be cleared. Rory Mor is angry. You see, Alastair, all were warned that they would have to leave at this Martinmas term, warned six months ago. That Clanrory would resume possession of their holdings, was the way that it was put. On this eleventh day of November. Few understood it, and none really believed it, I think. Then at the next quarter-day, at Lammas, eviction notices were served on all tenants, requiring them to have vacated their crofts and farms before the following term-day. That is, two days ago. The notices, of course, were in English, and none could read them. They were told what they meant, but . . . well, few could think it possible. I fear that I may have misled them. I wrote letters to Clanrory, twice, hoping that he might relent. I think that I encouraged the people with false hopes. In that I am to blame. For Clanrory has not so much as answered my letters."

"Blame!" Alastair exclaimed. "*You* take blame to yourself?"

"Aye. For I had other examples of this Improvement before me, in Glen Druin, and Ardnamurchan, and Sutherland. But it could not happen here, I thought. I prayed, not in the great Clan Ruari's land by Clan Ruari's chief *Mac Ruaraidh Mor*. But I was wrong. Two days ago, the legal term was reached—and none of the people had moved out of their crofts and down to Ardglass. Thus, by law, it seems that the folk could be held to be in illegal possession. So, as elsewhere, sheriff-officers and their hirelings were brought in, and fire was used to drive the cottars out—and to make sure that they did not return to the shelter of their homes again, afterwards. Every roof was lit. Their cattle are impounded, lest they consume what is now the estate's pasture. And none may succour the evicted, without the same treatment resulting. I brought them here, since there is nowhere else that they may go." Angus MacRory looked around him, shaking his head. "It is but poor sanctuary, I admit. But at least it is holy ground. And God be thanked that it is not raining."

Alastair's breath was released in a long sigh, as he moved after the minister, who went to soothe a child who had awakened screaming. "I cannot think that God is to be thanked for anything in unhappy Strathdonan, this night!" he commented, caustically.

"Say not so, lad, never say it," the other reproved. He was

occupied with the child for a little, before turning back to his cousin. "God's purposes may be hid from our eyes, but His mercy endureth for ever," he said. "If the Almighty's hand is heavy upon us, it is without doubt for our own grievous fault, for our many sins. We must believe that good will come of it."

"*You* say that, now! Lord, an hour or so ago I was listening to the same from the man Dunlop! Man's cruelties are God's will, to be accepted humbly as just deserts! That may be the Kirk's way of it, but I swear it is not mine! This, to my mind, is the Devil's work, not God's. And as such, to be fought, battled with, not humbly accepted."

"Bold words, Alastair *a graidh*. I do not blame you for them, mind. You are a soldier. But how would you do battle? With what? The ill is done, lad. The homes are no more. What would you do?"

Black Alastair MacRory straightened up. "I do not know," he admitted. "I do not know—yet. But, 'fore God, I must do something, if I am not to run mad!"

The two men's eyes met, the priest's and the soldier's, met and held.

Chapter Five

THE need for action, any sort of positive action, rather than further talk or mere passive waiting and resignation, soon grew too strong for Alastair MacRory. He was not a patient or a long-suffering man, at all. There seemed to be nothing that he could do here, and this crowded churchyard with its wailing, unhappy women was no place for such as himself—even when the elderly piper had blown himself to blessed silence, and the keening, denied this spur and encouragement, was steadily diminishing from exhaustion. Weary as he was, Alastair could not contemplate sleep; the restless urgency that possessed him had to find an outlet. Just to continue his journey over the hill to his own Glen Eidart now seemed to be quite unimportant, inadequate for the occasion.

43

That could wait. His mother, God rest her soul, would not fret for him, now.

He said as much, presently, to Angus of the Limp. "I must be doing, old friend," he declared. "I have not your forbearance, your restraint. I am no help to you here, and if I stay much longer I think I shall go crazy."

The other nodded. "I understand, lad. Will you be for over the hill, then? To your own place?"

"No. Not now. I will get me down the loch, I think. To the sea."

"To Ardglass? And the men?"

"Aye. But I come to Camusewan before I reach Ardglass!" That was grimly said.

"Camusewan . . .!" The pastor looked at him, searchingly. "In the night? What could you achieve there? At such time?"

"That remains to be seen, But . . . let us say that this night should not be one for tranquil sleep for any man in Strathdonan!"

"I fear, Alastair . . ." His cousin shook his head, and then sighed. "You will do what you must. But it is a long road. To walk. You will be weary . . ."

"I shall get there, never fear. I have been cooped up on shipboard too long, anyway. Some small activity will not hurt me—of varied sorts!"

"God go with you then, boy."

The younger man opened his mouth to answer that—and then had second thoughts. "And with you," he muttered, gripping the other's hand. "With you all. I shall see you again, before long." And turning away, still with his bundle under his good arm, he picked his way down through the sad throng.

Across the causeway through the meadows he stalked, over the track beyond, and on towards that other source of the night's complaint, the mass of penned and impounded cattle. He came to the fence of hurdles before the dark, seething mass of animals and was peering along it, when a couple of dozing guards at the gate rose up to challenge him, cudgels in hand.

"Hey, off wi' you!" one of them cried. "Keep away from these beasts, if you don't want your head broke!"

"Silence!" Alastair barked, in English. "Mind how you speak to one of the King's officers, oaf! I want a garron. A horse. From amongst these. Where are the horses?"

Clearly impressed by the authoritative manner, the challenger hesitated. "Eh? Hosses?" he said. "What do'you want a hoss for?"

"To ride on, man. What else? Where are they?"

The guard glanced at his companion, and rubbed his chin. "See, Mister," he said, "our orders are no beasts to be taken out o' this, see."

"I don't care what your orders are, fellow. *I'm* giving you an order, now! I am one of Lord Clanrory's officers. I have walked from Inverdruin, and that is far enough, sink me! All the horses are impounded here, I am told. I want one. On Lord Clanrory's business."

This high-handed attitude seemed to have some effect on the man; not on his colleague, however. This individual, a short stocky man, by his voice a Lowland Scot, spoke dourly.

"We tak oor orders frae the sheriff-officer," he said. "Naebody else. He said, nae beasts oot o' this—sae nae beasts it is!"

"Fool! No sheriff-officer, or anybody else, has the right to deny me the use of one of these animals," Alastair declared haughtily. "They are the property of these dispossessed tenants. The only excuse for impounding them is to keep them from eating Lord Clanrory's pasture. I want one to ride, to Camusewan—and I am going to have it."

"Y'are, are you!" The second man swung his cudgel significantly. "We'll see aboot that!" To his companion he jerked, "He's jist anither o' thae damned Hielantmen! I ken them."

"We'll see, indeed!" the MacRory agreed, and thrusting a hand within the tartan folds of his bundle, he whipped out the long-barrelled cavalry pistol that he had used on the injured dog. The click of the snapped-back hammer sounded clearly. There was enough of the red glow in the sky still to reflect evilly on the polished steel.

The two guards' breath caught in their throats as they stared at the pointing weapon.

"We'll drop those uncouth clubs, for a start," Alastair suggested. "Drop them, I say!" The pistol jabbed menacingly.

The two cudgels dropped to the ground, one more promptly than the other.

"Now—where have you the horses penned?"

"They're just in amongst the cattle, sir," the man with the English voice told him. "They ain't separate."

Alastair frowned. He had not anticipated this. Anyone caring anything for the stock would have kept them apart. Here was a complication. If he ordered one or both of these men to go in and fetch him out a garron, they could most easily hide themselves amongst the mass of the cattle, safe from the threat of his pistol. If he went in himself, they could keep the gate closed on him, and so prevent him getting a horse out. If he went in with them, leaving the gate open, one of them might dodge away amongst the beasts, and get back to shut it again. It was difficult. He made up his mind.

"Open that gate," he ordered. "And pick it up. The gate. Carry it. Quickly!" The gate was just one of a series of roughly-made hurdles of willow-wands and frames, staked into the ground and tied with grass-rope to form a fence. It was tied at only the one end, so as to swing open at the other. "You," he jerked the pistol at the man with the Scots voice, whom he conceived to be the more dangerous, "take this open end. And no tricks, see you." The other he instructed to untie the fastened end. "Now, up with it. Straight in amongst the beasts. I am right at your backs, with this pistol, and I am accounted an excellent shot. Move."

So the little procession moved in amongst the restive cattle, the Englishman leading, with one end of the gate, the Lowlander following at the other end, and the tall Highlander close behind. If they looked ridiculous, at least it kept both guards in front of the visitor, and meant that the gap in the fence could not be closed behind them.

It took a little time before the higher-held heads of a couple of horses became apparent over the serried backs of the cattle; there were many times more cattle than there were garrons, of course. Alastair shouted directions to the foremost man, while his pistol-muzzle poked into the back of the other. Undoubtedly the former, had he acted boldly, could have

46

ducked down, dropping the gate, and darted under the bellies of the nearest cattle, with little danger of being hit by a pistol-ball—even if the pistol had been primed and loaded, which it was not. But these men were only hirelings, and not desperate enough to take risks. No such attempt was made.

Pushing and jostling through the press of beasts, and all but choked by the smell of them, they came to the nearest shaggy, long-tailed pony. Alastair, however, shouted to move on to the other one—a ruse only, to keep the men occupied during the dangerous moments when he was mounting. As they edged onwards, further, Alastair thrust the pistol into his belt, reached a hand up to take a firm grip of the beast's plentiful mane, and bracing himself to withstand the certain pain in his shoulder, part vaulted, part scrambled on to the broad back. Fortunately the Highland garron is a short-legged creature. With the noise going on around them, neither of the guards heard anything of this as they pushed on.

Alastair troubled himself no further with them. Dragging the horse's head round, he kicked heels into its flanks, urging it through the press. It was difficult to know now just where the open gateway lay. He could only head in a general direction.

Suddenly shouts broke out behind him. The guards had perceived the new situation. Their cries sounded as though they were summoning help. Presumably there were other minions of authority near by.

The shouting further alarmed the already excited cattle. The beasts began to mill and eddy, hither and thither. But in the general stir, Alastair recognised one coherent drift, and going roughly in the direction that he was himself. He realised what it meant; some of the cattle had found the open gateway, and were streaming out, others drifting after them. Nothing could have been more convenient. Adding a shout or two of his own, as encouragement, Alastair rode with the tide. In only a few moments he swept out through the gap, in loud-lowing, steaming company. As soon as he might thereafter, he turned his garron's head westwards along the track. Behind him the stream of animals converging on the gateway grew ever denser.

Once clear of the cattle, Alastair kicked his mount into a trot, with a shout of laughter. It was of brief duration and only wryly mirthful—but it was the first laughter that the man had produced for days.

*　　　*　　　*

As he rode down long Loch Donan-side, now at the water's edge, now in dizzy heights above it, Alastair recognised that what he had done was rash, perhaps foolish, and might well lead to further complications. Nevertheless, he felt very considerably the better therefore, much more like himself—which surely was worth while. It had been necessary, for his own sake, to make some gesture, some positive indication of non-acceptance in what was being done here. Until he had made it, he was a man adrift.

On his seven-mile ride he passed innumerable burnt-out holdings. About none of them did there appear any sign of life, though he did not investigate any of them closely. All their people could not be back in the old graveyard with Angus Crubach, obviously. He wondered where they were. He noted that the larger houses, Inveroran and Suilaig and Baradale, that were the homes of tacksmen such as himself, gentlemen of the clan and tenants-in-chief, had not been given over to the flames apparently. From none of them did any light shine, but then the hour of night could account for that. Suilaig, a major, had died in Egypt, and Baradale was still with the regiment.

Down near its meeting with the tortured and isle-strewn Hebridean Sea, Loch Donan narrowed in suddenly, where a green, thrusting promontory reached out to within only a few hundred yards of the southern shore. In the very throat of the tide-race thus formed, rose a steep pinnacle of naked rock. And towering dramatically sheer with the sides of the rock rose the tall, broken walls of Castle Rory. No MacRory dwelt within that shattered shell today, for two English frigates had battered it into ruin at point-blank range nearly a hundred years before, after the fatal Battle of Glenshiel in 1719, and it had never been rebuilt. Near by, however, pleasantly situated on the grassy promontory itself, between the jagged fang of the castle and the scattered township of Camusewan that faced the sea, stood a large farmhouse and many outbuildings, the whitewashed walls glowing palely through the gloom—for there was no smoke here, the north-east wind blowing it all well to the south. This has been Alastair's projected landing-point, from the *Sarah Bell*. There would still be a MacRory to be found in that white house, he was satisfied. He turned his mount's head and rode down thereto.

The traveller noted that much new building had been going on since last he was here: barns, stables, storehouses and a row of cottages. No lights shone meantime; it was nearly three hours past midnight. Alastair rode directly to the front of the long, two-storeyed, slate-roofed farmhouse, and, dismounting, beat loudly on the heavy door. When his open hand seemed to make insufficient noise, he used the butt of his pistol. He kept it up, too, lest there be any doubt in sleep-bemused minds as to the need for response.

At first only a great outcry of dogs resulted, not the high-pitched barking of sheep-collies but the deep baying of hounds. Then, after some muffled shouting, a voice from behind the door demanded in the name of God who made such a to-do at this time of night.

"One gentleman of the MacRorys, to see another," Alastair answered, vigorously. "Gleneidart to see Young Camusewan. Open!"

There was a muttering beyond, and a drawing of bolts, and a shouting to hounds to be quiet. Then the door was opened, not widely, and two men peered out, one elderly, wrapped in a plaid and carrying a lantern, the other holding up hastily-donned breeches with one hand, a thick stick in the other.

Alastair strode inside, pushing past these two without ceremony. "My compliments to Rory Mor," he announced. "I would have a word with him. Tell him that Gleneidart is here."

The elderly house-servant was gabbling anxious incoherencies, and his younger companion gaping, when another voice broke in angrily:

"Who the devil comes making this uproar? What spawn of Satan dares come clamouring at *my* door at this hour?" It was a rich voice, deep and vibrant.

"I do, Rory Mor!" Alastair returned strongly. "Gleneidart. And I would expect you to be in close accord with any spawn of Satan, this night!"

At the head of the stairway, looking down into the wide

D   49

lobby of the house, stood a big man, a huge man, with a wild shock of red hair, wrapped round like his servant in a plaid in lieu of dressing-gown, a candle-stick held high. At his side two graceful deerhounds stood. He was staring, great head thrust forward, small eyes all but lost in the florid folds of his features.

"Alastair!" this apparition gasped. "Black Alastair, on my soul!"

"None other," the visitor agreed grimly. "On your soul— if you yet have one!"

The other hesitated, drawing a long breath, as though to gather his wits. Then, raising mighty voice to sudden, hearty laughter, he came all but tripping down the stairs, extraordinarily lightly for so vast a man, not troubling to hold the plaid close enough to hide his enormous hairy nakedness. Right up to his untimely caller he strode, to clasp him to him, enveloping him in a bear-like embrace, bundle and all, his plaid enwrapping the pair of them. Alastair stood stiff, frowning, and winced as much at the animal smell of the man as at the hurt of the powerful clutch on his ill-used wound. The candle-stick fell with a crash to the floor behind them, unheeded.

"*Dia!*" he protested. "I think . . . we may spare ourselves . . . this foolery!" That inevitably came out in gasps.

The other did not appear to hear it. "Man, Alastair—here is joy!" he cried, grasping the visitor's arms now, and holding him away from him, as though for inspection. "The black lad himself, back from the wars! Happy the day! But och man, man, you are thin! Worn, just—not the strapping hero that you were. What has Boney been doing to you at all, *a graidh*?"

"Little enough. Nothing—nothing to what *you* seem to have been doing back here, Rory Mor . . ."

"Nothing, is it, and you but a shadow of yourself! Dear God—but am I happy to see you, even if only half of yourself, man!" The big man roared with mirth, so that all of him quivered like jelly. He slapped his great belly. "And look at me! You half yourself, lad, and me twice *my*self! Here's proof that I chose the better part, hey? For swack Alastair, the glory and the clash of arms! And for poor simple Rory, the dull round, the daily toil, and the fireside of an evening! Aye, aye."

Out of the laughter, and quick as rapier strokes, came the questions. "How came you, now? Are you alone, man? The regiment, it is not all returned?"

"The pity of it—no! Else I would not have given a penny for your life this night! I am alone, unhappily. Would I were not!"

"To be sure, yes. But, Lord—no croaking about that now, boy! No spoiling this moment! Come you, in here." Rory Mor MacRory practically propelled his guest from the lobby into one of the front rooms, gustily roaring for lights, logs for the fire, food and drink.

Alastair sought to stem the flood of noise and joviality, of goodfellowship and hospitality. "Damnation—I am not here for pleasure and chatter, man!" he protested. "Keep your cheer and your welcome. I have had a sufficiency of welcome back to Strathdonan this night! I . . ."

"Ha, I do not believe it! You have the look of a starveling. When last did you eat? Better, when last did you sup our own excellent whisky? You are grey as a ghost. That is your need. I'll wager that you tasted nothing so good in the Indies or Africa or whatever barbarous land you've come from!"

"That is true. True also that I have not seen such barbarities in those lands as I have seen tonight in Clan Ruari's land of Strathdonan . . ."

"Tush, Cousin—you have the illusions, the vapours. They say that an empty belly makes a sore head. Away with this gloom. Here's a homecoming that calls for celebration . . ."

"Lord, man, will you listen to me? Have done with this play-acting, for sweet mercy's sake. I did not come to your door at this hour for food or drink or because I could not wait for a sight of you! Of God's truth, I did not! I came because I found the fires of hell ablaze out there! Our whole land afire, and lit by you, it seems! I would not have believed it, had I not seen it with my own eyes. And you—you slept sound in your bed!"

"Man, man Alastair, what has come over you? Here's a great to-do over nothing. You have it all wrong, I swear. We are in the midst of a great work of improvement, a noble work by which the whole land will benefit. Och, a national duty it is, man, by which . . ."

"A national duty to burn your own clansmen and women

51

out of their homes by the hundred, harrying your own people, like any bloodthirsty tyrant?"

"Hey! Bloodthirsty? Me? Tyrant! Rory Mor?" The other lifted his voice to positively hoot his merriment. "*Diabhol*, that is rich! Rory Mor burning and harrying! Blind me, Alastair—you were a jester, ever! I am helping the folk, can you not see? Bettering their state . . ."

"By shipping them off to Canada!"

"Such of them as elect to go, yes. Why not, Stair boy? Is it not the Land of Promise? Plenty of room there for all. Land unlimited for the taking."

"A wilderness to be cleared. And wrested first from painted savages. Snow and ice half of the year . . ."

"Ha, this proves it! You are out of sorts, lad, seeing no good in anything. Your stomach it is, I vow! Not another word out of you until you have eaten and drunk and can speak sense. Sit, Cousin, and a truce to morbid fears and fancies." On the word, the big man flung out a hand to grasp his visitor's shoulder, to push him bodily back into a chair.

Somehow Alastair managed to resist the powerful thrust, and staggeringly avoided the chair—but he could not stifle the involuntary exclamation of pain nor prevent the spasm from showing on his face.

Rory Mor perceived it, and instantly was a changed man. "Stair—you are hurt! Injured!" he cried. Swiftly he reached out to open and draw aside the other's doublet, firmly, gently. "Your shoulder? Wounded? God punish me, I should have guessed it! Let me see it, man—we must have this dealt with. At once." The man's plaid had slipped unheeded to the floor and he stood there in all his monstrous nakedness, brows furrowed anxiously, small mouth puckered, strangely delicate fingers feeling soothingly, efficiently at the other's shirt and less than fresh bandaging below, gentle as any woman.

Angrily the wounded man dashed those fingers away from him. "Keep your hands off me!" he commanded. "I want nothing of you, this night—save your orders to your minions to undo some little of the hurt and harm you have done to those poor damned people!" Alastair was actually backing, retreating round that untidy room before the other. It was an extraordinary scene, the two men equally tall but otherwise

52

so startlingly different, the one dark, hatchet-faced, frowning blackly, dressed in the gallantry of a Highland officer, retiring before the red-furred grossness of the unclothed colossus, whose lumpish, fleshy features were creased and moulded in lines of grotesque sympathy and pleading and reproach. Such was the situation when the servants returned with a tray loaded with food and drink, more light, and logs for the fire.

Rory Mor ignored them. "Alastair, my heart, let me attend *your* hurt," he urged. "The others will do finely, never fear. Here is folly. You should be abed, being cared for. You *shall* be, too! My own bed is warm, and ready—into it you shall go. None shall say that Black Alastair of Gleneidart came home to his own place in the night, wounded from the wars, and found none to cherish him. No, no!"

At the warm, coaxing, almost caressing note in that rich and expressive voice, the other shook his head helplessly. "Are you crazy, man?" he demanded. And even as he said it, the thought crossed Alastair's mind that this might be no figure of speech. The man perhaps was deranged, near to madness. Could that account for what was going on in Strathdonan? "Have you taken leave of your senses? There is but one thing that you can do for me—send men up the loch-side to Kinloch-donan countermanding the devilish orders that none may offer shelter to these wretched women and children whom you have made homeless on a November night! Do that for a start. Now. And let them have their garrons, to carry the sick and aged. The rest can wait till morning."

"Yes, yes," the naked man said soothingly. "It shall be done as you say. Now, let me see that shoulder, *a graidh*."

"Give your orders first. About the shelter. And the garrons."

Patiently Rory Mor spread out his hands. "You are head-strong, Stair. The garrons are but held conveniently, so that they do not stray, during the shift to new quarters. And as for shelter, the folk have had six months to provide shelter, down at the new township. If they have not gone to it . . ."

"At Ardglass? That barren waste! What shelter is there there?"

"You have not been to see? You have not been there?" That was swift. "Och, lad, how can you say, if you have not seen

53

it? There is shelter in plenty there, if the folk will but use it. As doubtless most of them *are* doing. Belatedly. Och, och, one has to be patient with them, the foolish ones. Like children they are, just. I must chide them for their fecklessness, but I bear with them, too."

Alastair stared at the man. "Do you know what your are saying?" he exclaimed. "Do words mean anything to you? *You* bearing with them. *You* being patient!"

"Why not? Do you think otherwise, Cousin? You know Rory Mor. But what can you know of conditions here? You have been gone years—and back but a few hours. In the darkness. You have seen a few thatches burning, on hovels that have been resigned to the estate and are no longer required. Yet you talk wildly of tyranny and the like!" The big man's voice all but broke, and his astonishingly mobile, if indeterminate, features took on an expression of deepest hurt—to be succeeded swiftly, however, by a warm forgiveness and sheerest understanding and affection. "But you are a sick man, Stair. Forgive me for such talk. Come, let me tend your wound."

Suddenly Alastair MacRory knew that he must get out of that house, if he was not to lose his reason. Already he felt dizzy, light-headed. More of Rory Mor, and he would not remain responsible for his actions. Swiftly he darted to the still open door.

Framed therein, Alastair turned. The other, curiously, seemed abruptly to become concerned over his nudity. He went to pick up his plaid, and wrap himself carefully in it, shaking his head.

"Will you do as I say? Send men to tell the people that they can move into shelter? Tonight?" the dark man demanded. "They are up at the ruined church. Angus Crubach is with them."

"Do you doubt it, man, do you doubt it? But, I tell you, there is shelter in plenty at Ardglass."

"That I shall go and see. That is where I am going now," Alastair said.

"Now? In the darkness. At this hour?"

"Yes. Why not? There will be shelter there for me too, will there not?"

"I think that you would be better here, man, nevertheless. By God I do!"

"I doubt it. I think that I shall feel . . . more at home . . . with these others."

"You fool! You insufferable, purblind, crazy fool!" That was flashed out like a rapier stroke.

Alastair met the other's eyes directly for a long moment. Then he stepped back, slammed the door shut, and turned blindly to stride down the lobby and through the outer door. Behind him he heard a curious choking noise, which rose and developed into laughter, braying and continuous.

He shivered as he faced the night air, but not on account of the clean salt-laden chill of it.

*　　*　　*

If Alastair MacRory had imagined that at Camusewan he had plumbed the full bitterness and degradation of this unhappy night, he knew better less than two hours later. He stared at the ring of faces around him, and not even the shades of night and the wan glimmer from the dying fire could hide the fact that on none of them was there any hint of enthusiasm, any faintest reflection of his own fervour, any gleam of fight or revolt. On those faces, set, haggard, lined and weary, he read only despondency, disillusion, resignation. They were middle-aged to elderly to old, those faces, of course, and none looking the younger for that day's events; nevertheless, these men were the fathers and uncles and cousins of the same gallant fighters whom he had seen purchase victory on a score of the world's fiercest battlefields with matchless *élan*, whatever the cost. It seemed hardly credible that no spark of the same proud spirit could he now strike from these, their own flesh and blood.

It was not for want of trying. He had sought them out, roused them from torpor and sleep—such as he could—sought to rouse them to action, to resistance, to rebellion. He had besought them, urged them, challenged them, upbraided them, argued, striven and pleaded with them. But he had not been eloquent enough, it appeared. Perhaps he was too tired, himself. Perhaps there had been something wrong, unsuitable, in his approach. Perhaps his own personal position, so different from theirs, militated against him. Perhaps in the morning, with daylight, when all were more rested . . .?

They sat or crouched around him now, at the very tip of the peninsula of Ardglass, the Grey Point, a promontory notably different from the fair green one of Camusewan, and some three miles north of it along the open windswept seaboard of the Sound, with only the swift-running tide between them and the savage mountains of Skye. There were many men who had listened to him—but only a small proportion of the numbers who lay, wrapped in their plaids, asleep or at least motionless, amongst the rocks and boulders and reeds of that grim foreland. There, he had hoped, might be the leaders, those with sufficient spirit at least to come and hear him.

It had been many years since Alastair had been at Ardglass, but his memories of the place, of bare rock and foam, of little cliffs and stony strands, of rough bent-grasses and salt-stunted alder scrub, with in its centre a boggy, reedy waste, had not retreated before any better impression now. The darkness admittedly had hidden full details, but the general effect was wholly of barrenness, of a hostile place. Rory Mor had said that there was shelter in plenty here, but he had omitted to mention that apart from a single fisherman's bothy out here at the point, and a few small caves and crannies near by, the shelter consisted only of the amplitude of stones available for building into walls. There was no timber for roofing, other than the thin alder wands, and of course the roof-trees of the evicted, a precious heritage in a land short of wood, had been burned within the thatches. No provision had been made here for anything in the way of shelter.

The promontory, from a base perhaps half a mile in width, thrust out into the Sound for the best part of a mile. Alastair had come out to this furthermost point, picking his way amongst the recumbent who littered the place, whether they were sunk in sleep, exhausted stupor, or drunkenness—for not a few obviously had turned to the potent, home-distilled spirit of the country, traditional friend of the distressed and the hopeless, for forgetfulness and oblivion. Out here, he had been informed, at the largest of the caves, there had been a sort of conference of elders. He had hoped that this might have provided a nucleus of men who would head up some kind of organised opposition to the estate's policy. He had been mistaken.

All had not been inactivity and inertia, however, since the dispossessed reached this desolate haven, he gathered. There had been considerable prospecting for cover and materials, gathering of stones, collection of firewood and driftwood, cutting of alders. Even some attempt temporarily to divide up and apportion the ground into areas for each evicted community, pitifully meagre and inadequate as anything of the sort had to be. But the fact that it was nearly dark before the first of the men had got here, weary, burdened with gear, and dispirited, and that there was a continuous arrival of ever more and more of the ejected, had made all such efforts abortive. Resignation and apathy had won the day—and fatalism, that lurking weakness in the Celtic character. God's will be done!

That phrase, indeed, was the one which Alastair was brought up against, again and again—that, and others like it. God's will be done. The hand of the Almighty was heavy, but no doubt it was for their sins. Who could tell, out of chastisement might come eventual blessing? They must not' kick against the pricks. The Kirk had taught its lesson well. One man in especial seemed to head up and emphasise this attitude —Duncan Ceistear, Duncan the Catechist. He was a fine man, too, a noble old man, a white-bearded, serene-featured patriarch, whom Alastair had found within the cave mouth, singing psalms to the night, head unbowed to personal discomfort and misery, but bowed most determinedly to what he accepted as God's will. His influence on the others was undoubted. Against the rock of his conviction, and the shifting sands of the others' submission, Alastair could avail nothing.

Now, beaten, he stood up. "You talk of the anger of God!" he said, sighing. "If only I could arouse some anger in yourselves!" He looked at the white-headed old patriarch as he said it.

"The anger of men will not work the works of God, friend," Duncan the Catechist answered, gently but firmly.

"But it might at least confound the works of the Devil!" Alastair gave back, but heavily, wearily. Indeed, he swayed on his feet as he said it.

There was nothing wrong with the other's old eyes—or his heart, for that matter. "You are tired, Gleneidart. A done man. You have driven yourself too hard. Sleep you need—and faith in God. You have talked enough. Lie down, man."

"Sleep will solve nothing . . ." Even as he said it, every inch of the younger man's body cried out that that was false, pleaded to have done, to be at rest. He shook his head.

"Then pray, friend, pray. Pray for yourself and for us all, who need it. Pray for the man Rory Mor. Aye, and pray for Clanrory himself, and him needing it most, I'm thinking. Pray!"

"First, eat," somebody said. "Eat this." A hand was holding out an oaten bannock. "It is ill sleeping on an empty stomach —aye, and praying, too!"

"Yes, then. Take this."

"And this meat. Och, take it, man."

"A small sup of whisky, Gleneidart, will be doing you no hurt."

Shaking his head again, Alastair found himself to be blinking weak tears from his eyes. It was a long time since he had had need to do that. "I cannot eat your food. Your own small store . . ." he said thickly.

"Eat, man. We are sharing alike. All of us."

"Aye, and the Lord will provide."

"A little, then, only a little . . ." There are all kinds of weaknesses in man.

Later, and only a very short while later, Black Alastair MacRory sank into sleep in the mouth of that cave, in his ears, above the draw and sigh of the tide, the thin, high singing of a psalm, quavering but persistent. Awaiting the dawn, Duncan the Catechist sang:

"*. . . man therefore is but vanity.*
Hear my prayer, O Lord, and with thine ears consider my call;
Hold not thy peace at my tears.
For I am a stranger with thee:
And a sojourner as all my fathers were.
O spare me a little, that I may recover my strength:
Before I go hence, and be no more seen . . ."

Chapter Six

IT was late when Alastair awakened next morning, with the thin, November sunshine already breaking wanly through the white mists that wreathed the mountainsides. He had slept like a log for five hours and more. Many others seemed to have done the same, around him.

Though he was stiff and cold and his shoulder ached, he felt a different man. An old campaigner, his body was attuned to such conditions. Nevertheless, neither this personal invigoration nor the morning light effected any improvement on the situation, as he saw it, at Ardglass. The evicted showed themselves to be in no more defiant, inflammatory or even animated state. Activity of sorts was going on, but haphazard and scattered and lacking in vigour; stone and driftwood collection mainly, wall-building, tent-erecting, and searching the shore for shell-fish. But more men were wandering aimlessly about than were doing anything constructive, and more still were sitting hunched and staring.

And indeed Alastair could scarcely find it in himself to blame them, as he gazed around the scene by the light of day. Instead of the sun bringing guidance and renewed energy and encouragement, visibility revealed only and starkly the utter hopelessness of the entire situation, the wretched worthlessness of this hitherto derelict corner of land. Here, on this rock-bound headland, there was not the means of subsistence for half a dozen crofts—no detailed inspection was required to reveal that. There might be two hundred or so miserable acres, all told, but the best of it was rough bent-grass, reeds, bog-myrtle and moss, and much more was naked outcropping stone and rock. The thin alder scrub had already been largely cut down, and there were no other trees. Already the place was shockingly overcrowded, before ever the women and children arrived. Not even a token proportion of the crofter's cattle and stock could be brought here. And the land stretching away on either side of the peninsula's base was no better, mere bare, rocky coast and swiftly-rising hillside. Clearly no attempt at land settlement here was worth a moment's consideration.

Alastair spoke to two or three men round about him, with little response beyond an abstracted away-looking politeness that was almost worse than hostility would have been. He could not but feel himself to look conspicuous, in broad daylight, in that drab and depressed company—a man in the colourful panoply of kilt and plaid, of tartan and scarlet, and martial accoutrement. He caught men's lack-lustre glance upon him, askance, though hastily averted when observed, and for the first time in his life felt himself to be almost ashamed of the gallant display of Highland dress. For of course none of these fellow-clansmen of his might wear the tartan. The Disarming Act of 1746, after the last Jacobite Rising, had proscribed the wearing of the tartan and the carrying of weapons in the Highlands—a lethal blow at the clan-system. All such was illegal, north of the Highland Line, and in fact Alastair was committing an offence to be dressed as he was, here in his own land. The permission to wear the kilt and tartan had been one of the most effective recruiting measures for the new Highland regiments that were so badly needed to deal with Napoleon; but the men were required by law to doff such dangerous finery before, if ever, they returned to their native glens. It was likely indeed that many of the MacRory's and MacBrides and MacIvers who now eyed him had never before seen a man wearing such a costume.

Alastair had a word with Duncan the Catechist, whom he found helping to dam up a burn to form a pool for drinking-water. Refusing the courteous offer of more of the precious food, he recognised the hopelessness of further attempts at kindling the flame of rebellion just now, and contented himself with an embarrassed declaration of sympathy, and his impression of Ardglass, seen by light of day.

"It is useless, a worthless wilderness!" he said. "There is nothing here, for a tenth of you. Rory Mor must be mad to think that even a score could settle here."

The other shook his white head. "Rory Mor does not wish that *any* should settle here. He wishes us all gone, across the sea. That is why he has brought us here, so that none shall think to stay when the ship comes."

"And you will go, all of you? To Canada? As at the cracking of a whip? You will let yourselves be driven out?" He had not meant to say that, again, but it was forced out of him.

"What else, Gleneidart? Where else can we go?"

Alastair swept his good arm impulsively around, landwards, in a great sweep. "You are Clan Ruari," he exclaimed. "All that, as far as eye can see, and ten times farther, is Clan Ruari's land—and you ask where you can go?"

"On none of that, friend, may we so much as set a foot, today. Those days are over. The man of law, the Sheriff from Dingwall, he told us. Every glen of Strathdonan is closed to us."

"That is where you are wrong—sheriff or none! One glen at least is not. My glen. Glen Eidart. It is small and high and remote, yes—but it is not closed to you, to anyone in Clan Ruari, so long as I am Gleneidart. With my own people, it will not hold you all, I fear. But some at least may go there, for the time being."

The old man shook his head again. "You mean it kindly, Gleneidart, but I think you do not know what you say. You have been gone too long. It is too late. There would be no kindness in that now, well as you mean."

"I am not talking of kindness, man. This is life or death— for a whole people! It is not too late. It is in your own hands, *our* own hands . . ."

"Nothing is in our own hands, young man! We are in the hands of Almighty God. If He has plucked us up by the roots, and burned our land behind us, it will not be to set us down again in the next glen . . ."

"God again! Spare me more of that . . ."

"Do not scoff, Gleneidart! Have a watch on your words, or you will be humbled. As we have been humbled. God's purposes are beyond our understanding. But He is very merciful. Perhaps . . . aye, perhaps it is that these flames of fire and pillars of smoke are to be guiding us also to a fair land and a goodly, a land flowing with milk and honey . . .!"

"Lord—that, now! Spare me that, at least!" Alastair Mac-Rory exclaimed. Then he drew a long, quivering sigh. "I am sorry. But . . . oh, damnation!" he cried slapping his bonnet hard down on his black head. Turning about, he went striding off.

He made for where the garron was to be seen, the only beast there, hopefully seeking pasture amongst the bog-myrtle. Vaulting on to its back, in a flurry of tartan and long legs bronzed by fiercer suns than this, he set the beast at a lumbering trot back up the overcrowded peninsula.

*   *   *

Riding south, whence he had come during the night, after a couple of miles he passed the tall, grey House of Camusewan itself, a little way north of the township, home of the hereditary Chamberlains of Strathdonan, where Rory Mor's elderly and shrunken father presumably still dwelt. Almost he turned in thereat, but on second thoughts pressed on along the weed-hung shore. Past the township, that was the anchorage and haven for Strathdonan, he rode, and bitterly pleasant it was to see a community all unburned and unimproved. Past the in-fields of the green promontory, where he noted the many tups, big-horned breeding rams, he made straight for the whitewashed farmhouse that he had awakened so cavalierly eight hours before. The front door stood ajar now, and, dismounting, he pushed it open and went inside, shouting for Rory Mor.

The same elderly servitor, unattended by the man with the stick this time, came to tell him quaveringly that the factor was gone. Where, he could not say. Perhaps if Gleneidart would go over to the estate office, across the yard, they would tell him there.

Alastair crossed a cobbled yard to what had been a range of byres and stabling. An estate office was something new for Strathdonan—as was this title of factor, which very evidently meant something much other than chamberlain. He found a long, low room of desks and tables and papers, overheated by a large log fire, with a clerkly-looking man, prim-faced and no Highlander, working a pen, who stared up at the newcomer in wonder.

"I am seeking Rory Mor. Where is he?"

"Mr. MacRory is out. He has been gone these two hours," the fellow said. And added, "Sir", as an afterthought. "They are all gone."

"Who are all gone? And where?" It was the first time that

Alastair had heard anyone referred to as Mister MacRory in Strathdonan.

"The Sheriff, and his officers. And Mr. Cousins. With Mr. MacRory. They are clearing Glen Udalain today, sir."

"What!" That was barked out.

The clerk backed in his chair, apprehensively.

"Clearing, did you say?" Alastair demanded. "More of it? More devil's work! More savagery—destroying, burning, evicting! Glen Udalain?"

The other had got to his feet, and was retreating towards a far corner of the room. "Y'yes. No, no, I mean . . . that is . . ."

Alastair halted, fists clenched. "Two hours," he said. "Udalain. Where? It is a long glen. The foot, or the head of it?"

The clerk seemed to misunderstand, but he was anxious to be accounted helpful. "It is here, sir, Glen Udalain lies here." He hurried across to point at a great map that hung on a wall. He indicated a narrow, twisting valley that stretched north by a little west from Strathdonan, for some five miles, until it almost reached the southern flank of Glen Eidart.

"I know where Udalain is, man," Alastair jerked. "Which way have they gone? Along the lochside and up the Udalain River, or over the Beallach, the pass, to its head?"

"Here, sir. This way. Over the hills. It is the wind, you see. It has changed. Yesterday it was from the north-east. Today it is back into the south-west. The smoke, you will understand. So they are starting at the far end of the glen, the north end. The wind will thus be blowing the smoke away from them as they work southwards. It is most unpleasant, I understand, working in all that black smoke, sir. So they have gone this way." The man began to trace a route on the map directly into the hills north of Camusewan.

"Damn you—unpleasant, is it!" the visitor cried. "Unpleasant for whom? So the smoke they make offends their nice noses!"

"It . . . it is but sensible, sir. The smoke becomes very thick. It becomes impossible to see what is being done. Look, here is the track they were to take . . ."

"I know the track, like my own hand. Quiet, you." Alastair's angry eyes lingered nevertheless on that large-scale map. It covered the entire area of Strathdonan and its neighbouring district. Superimposed on it was much hatching, shading-in by pencil lines, some slanting one way, some another, some criss-crossed. Practically all of the map, indeed, was shaded over in one fashion or another. "What are these lines?" he demanded.

"They represent the progress of the Improvements, sir. The areas that have already been cleared, those to be cleared from this term-day, and so on."

"I see." That was very softly said, for Alastair MacRory "And what do lines straight up and down stand for?"

"Vertical lines mean areas to be cleared after next quarter-day, sir. Candlemas, that is, to use the Scotch phrase."

The area of Glen Eidart was shaded in with vertical lines.

"I see," Alastair said again. He turned and looked at the clerk thoughtfully for a moment. Then, without another word, he swung on his heel and walked out of the office.

He went straight back into the factor's house. "I want food and drink," he told the waiting servant briefly. "Anything that I can carry with me." He had changed his mind about the ethics of accepting Rory Mor's hospitality. "Quickly."

While he waited in the front room, he helped himself to the viands and whisky still on a tray, which he had rejected the previous night. He realised that he was ravenously hungry. The old man brought him a satchel containing bannocks and cheese and a leathern bottle of whisky.

"Gleneidart," he said hesitantly, "you will be careful? My father . . . he came from Altgarve. At the head of your glen. You will be patient, a little?"

"My God, that I will not!" the young man cried. "There has been too much of patience in this place, too much of care. Give me another plaid, man, for the garron."

Alastair rode as fast now as the stocky pony would take him, due northwards and uphill, by a zig-zagging, narrow track that worked its way up the steep braeside above the loch. There were ample and recent tracks of men and horses to be seen thereon.

Quickly the loch, with its ruined castle and the compact township of Camusewan, sank away below him, and all the far-flung loveliness of the endless blue mountains, already streaked with the first white of winter snows, of the rich browns and ochres of heather and deer-hair grass and faded bracken, of the infinity of sounds and channels and islands and skerries of the Sea of the Hebrides, opened ever wider before him. Even in his present frame of mind, the man could not remain untouched by the haunting beauty of it all—had not the longing to see it all again been a pain in him for years? There was a new pain now, to go with that fair scene.

No preoccupation with either sorrow or beauty, however, did he permit to delay his going. Once the long summit ridge was surmounted, with the track snaking and dipping and climbing its way through the heathery uplands round the black, peat-stained lochans and over the thrusting shoulders of the mountains, he kept his mount to its tireless if unspectacular trot, his long legs trailing the heather on either flank. This was the airy country of the shielings, the high pastures where the cottars' cattle were brought to be herded during the long halcyon days and brief glowing nights of summer, when it had been very good to be alive and young and of the north. There were no cattle here now, nor herders, nor laughing lasses—nor would be again, perhaps.

Away to the east there was a faint film of blue to be seen, that was all that was left of the smoke of yesterday, drifting back on the changed wind. But before Alastair was half-way across the lonely emptiness of these uplands, he perceived new clouds of smoke billowing up before him beyond the farther ridge, dark and thick, rolling away to the north-east. The work of Improvement evidently was resumed.

When at length the man looked down from that final ridge into the westernmost of the two high corries that formed the heads of Glen Udalain, it was as into a trough already filled with smoke, like a cauldron, that boiled up from three fires—or, rather, from three centres of conflagration, for there was more than one fire to each place. As he recollected it, only the three families had dwelt in this upper valley; there were more in the other. All three houses, as was to be expected, were grouped down near the mouth of it, where there were areas of more level ground for their patches of tilth. A great shouting, and barking of dogs, was going on down there, though it was difficult to see what was happening for the smoke.

Alastair moved on around the rim of the corrie, to avoid the blanket of it. Before he eventually plunged down into it, he saw that the noise came from three or four men and a number of dogs seeking to round up frightened cattle on the hillsides.

Riding in the eddying clouds that assailed his nostrils and eyes with the same ominous, acrid tang of the night before, Alastair came to the first cot-house. At the source of the smoke he could see rather better. The roof of thatch was blazing furiously, but had already fallen in at one end. An outbuilding blazed likewise. A small heap of assorted household goods, some of them clearly broken, was piled out on the grass, and on them a woman sat, unmoving, as though a statue, her apron thrown over her head. A foolish, crazed hen, most of its feathers burned off, ran round and round her in circles, squawking loudly. At first this seemed to the newcomer all the life that remained to this place—until he noticed over against a tumbled stack of peats, two other figures. A man lay there, and over him crouched a young woman. At Alastair's approach the girl looked up, and shrank back. She also covered her bare breasts with an arm, for her clothing had been ripped downwards from the neck, and long, red scratches showed on the white skin. But she did not move away, for the man's head was pillowed on her lap, a grizzled head, streaked with blood. The man was breathing snoringly, his mouth open.

Alastair dismounted, uttering disjointed reassurances, and stooped to run an experienced eye and hand over the injured man's head. The wound was not serious, though the scalp was lacerated. Obviously he had been struck down with some sort of club. He would not die of that. Alastair said as much to the girl, gently. Though she did not take her eyes off him, she did not answer, gave no sign of hearing him. He reached into the satchel that hung from his good shoulder, and drew out the bottle of whisky. Raising the man's head, firmly against the young woman's resistance, he tipped a little of the fiery spirit between the open lips. The injured man choked, gasped, stirred, and his eyelids fluttered. He looked up, expressionless.

"He will do. Clean the wound with this." Alastair held

out the bottle to the girl. "Then tie it up. He will be right enough, soon. Yourself, *mo charaidh*—are you . . . are you . . .?"

She did not reply. She did not take the bottle. Her eyes were as expressionless as those of the man.

Sighing. Alastair left the bottle beside her, Rory Mor's bottle, and stood up. He went back to the garron. The woman sitting on the plenishings had not moved. He did not go to her. He did not look for anything more to see. He mounted, and rode way.

The other two blazing crofts were across the burn, the nearest a couple of hundred yards back from it. The man did not go over to them, but kept straight on down the water-side.

There was no smoke ahead of him now, and he could see clearly. About half a mile in front of him, in the very mouth of the corrie, where it opened into the main glen, a knot of men and beasts was evident. They seemed to be stationary, as though held up somehow. Three or four men were driving a mixed herd of cattle and garrons down to them, off the hill.

As he drew nearer to the party, Alastair could hear much outcry and shouting. That did not surprise him, but what did was that a considerable proportion of the noise most clearly came from women's voices, shouting, not wailing or screaming.

The corrie, a sort of hanging valley, dropped into Glen Udalain proper through a quite narrow, V-shaped gap, cut by ice and water through solid rock. It was within this restricted, stone-jawed ravine that the party ahead was halted. It was like a bottleneck, stoppered.

Alastair could hear, intermittently, Rory Mor's rich voice calling out—and being drowned in women's shrill cries.

As the newcomer rode up, within the ever-steepening walls of the place, no one turned to consider him. All were too much taken up with what went on in front. And in shouting. The general hubbub was remarkable, magnified and thrown back by the rock walls. As Alastair pressed forward amongst the throng of men, a stone whizzing past his ear drew his attention to the fact that he was the loftiest man there, the only man mounted. Another stone, finding a mark near by

67

and drawing a cry of pain, brought the matter home to him. Alastair dismounted, but continued to push forward. The men around him were Lowlanders to a man, and strangers.

*   *   *

If Alastair MacRory was unprepared for the situation that he found in the throat of Glen Udalain that November morning, so most patently had been Rory Mor MacRory and his colleagues and supporters. The latter were, in fact, ambushed in the gut of the ravine, held, around a sharp bend in it, by a barricade of fallen rock rolled down from above to block the narrow passage beside the foaming burn in its deep-scored channel. Nor were they merely halted, checked in their progress; they were actually being opposed, assaulted, attacked not only by word of mouth but by thrown stones. The worm had turned at last, it seemed. The busy torches had finally kindled a spark of another sort. And to crown all, for shame and affront and outrage, it was women who were responsible.

That aspect of the matter was the one to occupy Alastair's attention almost wholly at first, as he pushed round the bend in the gully into a position where he could see what went on. Beyond the barrier of rocks indeed, he could see none other than women and girls. A knot of them occupied the track in the foot of the V, some thirty yards or so away, facing belligerently towards the factor's party, but many more were perched and disposed on vantage-points on the steep sides of the cleft, armed with sticks and poles for levering rocks loose, clearly prepared to roll down further quantities of this almost unlimited ammunition on anyone seeking to force a passage below. These were the stone-throwers also, and women used to herding cattle in a stony country were apt to be no mean performers with such missiles. From girls in their teens to women almost old enough to be their grandmothers, they effectively blocked that corrie-mouth, and kept up as well a running fire of shrill threat and abuse.

Alastair's first instinctive and masculine reaction, to be appalled that women should so behave, decent modest Highland women who should know their place and their manners and behave to men with proper respect, was quite swiftly superseded and submerged in a rising tide, a flood, of approval, appreciation and delight—approval that at last the flag of resistance was flying in Strathdonan; appreciation, as a soldier, of the clever and thoroughly effective use of terrain and the benefit of surprise in this ambush; and delight in the even temporary confounding and embarrassment of the Improvers.

For that the evictors were at a loss was only too evident. Hiding in undignified fashion behind a sort of buttress from the thrown stones, the leadership of the estate party were huddled, Rory Mor, by his very height and bulk, having to crouch the lowest. With him were four or five men of the better-dressed sort, in long-tailed coats, knee-breeches and high Hessian boots. One, indeed, was notable in the scarlet coat and frogging of a captain of militia. Another was the man Cousins, self-proclaimed master of Glen Druin. All looked unhappy. Clearly they had been taken completely by surprise, and now could not press forward without serious danger from rolling boulders, not to mention the indignities of flying stones, could not storm the positions of their obstructors from below, and no doubt were loath indeed to admit temporary defeat at the hands of a bunch of skirling women by retiring, even to advance again by some other approach. The militiaman appeared to be no more at ease than his companions in this military predicament.

In the circumstances, it said a deal for Rory Mor's wits and judgement that, on the arrival of Alastair of Gleneidart at this inauspicious moment, he was able to seize the occasion as a welcome and time-passing diversion rather than to scowl in humiliation as did most of his colleagues. Though perhaps that could also be attributed to some form of mental un-balance. At any rate, he let out a roar of seemingly merry greeting only a few seconds after catching sight of the con-spicuously clad newcomer, and retiring further into the cover of the buttress of rock where he might stand up to full height shielded from the stone-throwers, waved a huge, beckoning hand. He was dressed this morning in Lowland clothes, but wore a shoulder plaid of plain checks and a Highland bonnet.

"Ha—Alastair *a graidh*!" he cried in the English. "The top of the morning to you! But, come you—over here. Quickly, boy, or these confounded women will do for you what old

Boney couldn't do!" And he roared with laughter. Nobody else so much as quirked a smile.

"I'll risk the stones, I think, for I am particular in the company I keep!" Alastair gave back, which was a rash thing to say, for the words were scarcely out before a jagged stone flew immediately under his garron's nose, causing even that placid animal to rear and plunge in alarm, requiring to be soothed down and held fast.

Rory Mor positively hooted his mirth. "Sink me, Stair, don't be such a damned bear! Is that you still with the sore head you had last night, man? Watch you, or one of these termagants' stones will make it the sorer!"

"My head at least need not be sunk in shame . . ." the dark man began, when such lofty pronouncement was curtailed by a stone actually striking the arm upreached to grip the pony's long mane. Fortunately it was a glancing blow from a missile already spent, but it served to underline the realities of the situation, as well as the distressing fact that some of the women of Glen Udalain, at least, saw in himself only another and outstanding target. Without actually descending to unseemly haste, Alastair left the garron to its own devices and made for cover. Inevitably it had to be more or less alongside Rory Mor and his friends.

"Sink your head in here, then, *a graidh*—before worse happens to it!" the big man chuckled, grimly. "You see what we are up against here, in our efforts to move out of the barbarous past, to start looking forwards instead of backwards in the Highlands: hostility, ignorance, prejudice . . . and stones, damn it!"

"Was the old man back there, with the broken head, being nursed by his savaged daughter—was that your moving out of the age of barbarism? Are burning homes the bright, new symbol of enlightenment, and empty glens all the future means to you, man? You, a MacRory? Is it your hope, one day, to be Chamberlain of a desert?"

"Tush, Stair, dramatics and belly-wind! Words, great swelling words! If an old fool interferes with the Sheriff's constables in the lawful execution of their duties, he cannot grumble if he gets knocked aside. If an hysterical girl will not come out of a burning hovel, she should not grumble if her clothing

70

becomes a little disarranged in saving her, b'God! But . . .
what's come over you, lad? This never used to be the way of
you. Black Alastair, of all men! Do not say that you should
have been a parson—not a soldier!"

"Like Angus Crubach, our own cousin, whom you got rid
of! Perhaps I should, Rory. At least I would then have been
here, at home, to fight against this savagery, not at the other
ends of the earth, fighting to save the skins of such as I see
here!" The dark man's lowering glance swept that crouching
company contemptuously.

"Damn you . . .!"

"Have a care for your words, sir!"

"Blast you, you'll not speak o' George Cousins that way!"

"No, no, gentlemen—not so hot, not so hasty!" Rory Mor
intervened, jovial yet. "I'll not have it. This is my dear cousin
and good friend, Black Alastair of Gleneidart, a loyal officer of
King George—if a trifle sore in the head! *Dia*, and hasn't he
the reason, too, and him new back from the wars with a
wounded shoulder unhealed! A damaged hero, no less! Och,
of course, whether our Alastair came by his wound on the
field of battle, or in an epic fight over the wenches of some
London taproom, is no concern of ours, gentleman! Ha!"

The man Cousins refused to laugh with the others. "That's
all very fine, MacRory," he declared. "But this bare-shanked
bog-walloper ain't going to misname me that way . . ."

"Hush, George, you are too touchy by half! I'll hear nothing
against my good Gleneidart . . ."

"Have done, man!" Alastair broke in angrily. "Have done
with this foolery!" He knew himself to be unwise in allowing
his wrath its head in dealing with Rory Mor, putting himself
at a disadvantage with that nimble-tongued giant. But for the
life of him he could not dissemble his disgust, he could not,
must not, even seem to dally with hypocrisy. "These women
here have the rights of it, and you know it! You it is that is at
fault. They have the right and decency and justice on their
side . . ."

"Damme—are you mad, sir?" a spare, grey-haired, middle-
aged man exclaimed, in a thin stilted voice. "Do you dare to
talk about justice, in front of His Majesty's principal justiciary
in this county! Have a care, sir, have a care!"

"Mr. Halcrow Walker, Stair—Sheriff-substitute, from Dingwall," Rory Mor introduced, with a twinkling smile.

"The more shame on you, then, if you countenance what is being done here to these defenceless people . . . whom I'd have thought it your duty to protect . . ."

"Silence, sirrah! I am here to see that the King's peace is kept! You, by your rash and shameless talk, could be helping to endanger that peace. I warn you, sir, for your own good . . ."

"There, there, Sheriff, be patient a little, will you?" the big man soothed. "He means well enough, I do believe. It is but ignorance, and him away for so long. Stair, lad, you can be over-bold in your words, see you . . ."

"He is a bold man in more than his words, I think!" That was a new speaker, the militia captain. "To appear here, in this country, dressed in that . . . that fashion, is an offence against the law. Wearing kilt and tartan. And a dirk, too! Is it not, Sheriff? A blatant challenge to the law?"

"H'mmm. Perhaps, yes. Er, undoubtedly. Yes, yes," the little justiciary agreed, almost reluctantly it seemed.

"Damn you!" Alastair turned on the militiaman in a fury of scorn. "You, that masquerade as a soldier, *you* say that! You, standing on Clan Ruari's heather, bleat against Clanrory tartan! You, in some back-door fencible's coat, decry the uniform of the Seventieth Foot, that made Hyder Ali blench, and sent Soult running for his life! *Diabhol*, what are you? Are you a Scot, at all? A man, even! Or some snivelling hireling . . .?"

"Captain Henderson, of the Ross-shire Fencibles, Alastair," Rory Mor put in, grinning wickedly.

"And . . . and your senior officer, sir!" the other declared loudly. "You are but a lieutenant, I see. This is a scandal! An insult!" He had recoiled physically against the rock wall at Alastair's attack, but now gained confidence at the sound of his own voice. "My God, I'll see that you pay for those words!"

The dark man turned his shoulder on him disdainfully, to address himself to the other Highlander. "Enough of this," he said shortly. "I did not come after you for idle talk. These evictions must be stopped. Those already evicted must be given back their land. As far as may be, the damage done must be undone. And spare us the laughter, Rory Mor, that will help nothing."

"Heigh-ho, Alastair *a graidh*! I am a patient man, but . . ."

"And I am not! Do you call a halt to this savagery, now—or . . .?"

"Aye, lad—or . . .? Or, what, at all?"

"Or do I return to the regiment, and tell the sons and brothers and husbands of these same women what you are doing to them and to their homes in their absence? Aye, and counsel them to demand an immediate recall, so that they may come home and deal worthily with those who have betrayed them? And God help you in that day, Rory, God help all who have so much as taken a step with you on your road, when I bring the Seventieth home to Strathdonan!" The same God forgive himself for implying that so many of the men of Strathdonan were not already dead in foreign graves.

Even Rory Mor forgot to smile, for a moment. A few seconds went by when only the shrill taunting of some excited woman was all that was to be heard, above the rush of the burn. Then the big man recovered himself.

"Och now, Stair, here's more foolish talk. Unworthy of you, I think. Unworthy of your intelligence, if naught else." He paused significantly. "What we are doing here is on Lord Clanrory's behalf. For the Improvement of Lord Clanrory's estate, on his express orders. You do not think that Clanrory would permit his own regiment to be brought home unnecessarily? He is its Colonel-Commandant, is he not? He will undoubtedly arrange for it to go where it is, h'mm, most needed . . . in the national welfare! When His Majesty can spare its services in the present theatre of war. To Canada, for instance. Which, in the circumstances, would be most suitable, would it not?"

Alastair drew a long breath. "I do not believe that Clanrory knows the half of what you are doing here in his name," he said. "I was speaking with him but a few days ago. But . . . even if Clanrory proves to be as big a rogue as you are, do you think that his word, his will, would prevail over the wills of a whole regiment of angry men?"

"You are not suggesting that they might *disobey* their

73

Colonel-Commandant, Alastair? You are not, by any least chance, suggesting . . . mutiny? You, a soldier?"

The two MacRorys' glances might have been locked together. "You know that I am not," the dark man grated. "But I would remind you of something that you may have forgot. The Highland regiments are not as the rest. Every man is a volunteer, fighting of his own free will. If an entire regiment, officers as well as men, demand recall, think you that the word of the Colonel-Commandant would be sufficient to deny them it?"

"If, Stair . . . if! I think you do the officers, at least, an injury if you suggest that they do not know their duty. Better than you do, it seems! They will obey their order, I have no doubt."

"No doubts? No fears, Rory? Glenudalain, for instance? Donald of Glenudalain, whose glen you are harrying this day? Think you that he will be uncaring when he hears of this? What, think you, will he consider as his prime duty? And Baradale? And Suilaig? And Lochdoul, and the rest . . .?"

"Glenudalain is dead, Stair—did you not know? Perhaps you have not been with the regiment for some time? Sad, it was. His hell-cat of a daughter is out there, beyond, now. She it is that's responsible for this folly here. I fear that she is missing her father's hand! I must needs supply the chastening in his stead, it seems! Suilaig is dead, too. Did you not know that, either? That was months ago. Is it so long since you were with the others? And I heard that Lochdoul is a sick man, more's the pity . . ."

Alastair bit his lip. So that bluff was called, likewise. Rory Mor was better informed than he had expected. That could only be Clanrory's doing. The cards were well and truly marked and dealt. "There are plenty who are not dead," he asserted, a little wearily. "Enough. Enough to make Strathdonan's voice heard, when I return. Enough to ensure retribution . . ."

"When you return, Stair, yes. Just when do you return to the regiment, man?" That was gently asked. "*If* you return . . .!"

"What do you mean—*if* I return?"

The other spread deprecating hands, and smiled.

"He means that you look damned like a deserter, man, that's

74

what he means!" George Cousins declared strongly. "That's the way you look to me, too!"

"No, no, George—no, no. Dear me, you go too fast. My innocent question was meant quite otherwise, I swear."

One other interpretation of the innocent question, at least, did not escape Alastair. He ignored Cousins. "I shall return to the regiment . . . in due course, never fear. Before I go, I intend to see these evictions halted. Whatever I have to do! You understand?"

"Aye, too well we understand!" That was still Cousins. "We understand that you are a knave. And a traitor, belike. I say the Sheriff here should take you in charge, here and now, b'God! Before you can do more harm."

"I agree," the militiaman chimed in. "You have every reason, Sheriff. The man is a danger to the peace. And he is flagrantly breaking the Disarming Act . . ."

"You all take him too seriously, my friends," Rory Mor told them, easily. "You do not know Black Alastair as I do. Always he was headstrong, but his heart is in the right place. He will learn in time that what we are doing here is the best thing for all. Including himself."

"And my glen? Glen Eidart?"

"Ah, that is your own affair, Stair. I leave Glen Eidart to you."

"Liar!" Alastair said softly.

The big man frowned.

"Have you forgotten Candlemas? The next term-day? And the map in your fine new office?"

Rory Mor opened his mouth—and then shut it again. It seemed thereafter tighter, smaller altogether.

Alastair looked from him to the others. None of them spoke.

"There you have it," he said, almost sighed. "The foolery and the play-acting done with. What is it to be, then? Do I go back with you, now, to Camusewan? And back to Ardglass, to see what may be done for those people you have marooned there? Or do I cross these rocks here, and join the women who have halted you? Since halt you I will! The choice is yours, Rory."

"Damn it, MacRory, d'you hear that, man?"

"Sheriff, arrest the fellow! What more d'you need?"

"Mr. MacRory, I must say, this has gone far enough . . ."

"So you would join the women, Stair *a graidh*?" the big man said slowly, and his great voice, though unraised, overbore all others.

"If I must, yes. Though I would rather that you left Glen Udalain, and me with you."

"I shall leave Glen Udalain when my duty here is done, lad, and not before."

"Very well . . ."

"MacRory, the fellow is a Jacobin, a danger to the peace!"

"We must hold him! Sheriff, you have the authority. Seize him! Arrest him!"

"Gentlemen," Rory Mor said, "if Gleneidart wishes to join these foolish women, let him go. On this land he shall do as he pleases. Let him go, I say." There was no doubt, whatever the authority of the Sheriff-substitute, whose authority ruled here. "Go on, Stair *a graidh*, go to them. If you wish it so."

Alastair knew a moment of doubt, that was no doubt but a recognition of fate, of inevitability, of taking a step that would permit of no turning back. It was a step that he had to take, nevertheless. He nodded curtly, and turned away. Leaving them there, leaving the garron also, he strode out from behind the cover of the buttress, straight towards the barricade of rocks.

There were shouts from in front and behind him. It was not them that he listened for. He heard it, presently, the laughter beginning, one man's laughter.

The first stone flew past him as he climbed up over the rock-falls. He waved a hand to the women congregated there on the track in front, thirty yards away. There was a young one, with hair black as his own, standing a little way in front of the others. She was gesturing towards the women up on the cliffside.

More stones came at him. One struck his bare knee. The shouting rose, in pitch and volume, but still did not drown the laughter. Alastair began to run.

He was half-way to the women when the first loosened boulder came bounding down at him. He dodged it, but there was another crashing down in front. He had to halt to allow it to go past. Waving urgently to the women up above to stop, shouting that he was with them, not against them, aware of a confusion of cries ahead and a gale of mirth behind, he suddenly, instinctively, threw up his arm. It did not serve to protect him. He saw a blinding light, as a well-aimed stone struck him just above the ear. He staggered, as the world grew red around him, then black, all black. He pitched forward, knowing nothing more.

Chapter Seven

ALASTAIR MACRORY came to himself on a grassy bank close beside the chuckling burn—indeed close enough for repeated if small quantities of the burn itself to be applied on a cloth to his throbbing head. A young woman was doing this, leaning over him now, with every appearance of concern—the same dark young woman whom he had noticed before. Other women stood around.

The man stared up at them, as the faces swam into focus. For a few seconds he was uncertain in his mind, confusing his situation with that of the old man up at the croft, who also had come out of unconsciousness, with a young woman bending over him. This young woman's breast was not bare, however, and her hair was blue-black, not reddish-brown. Alastair sought to stir, made the first movements towards sitting up, and sank back with a stifled groan, as his head seemed to open and shut in consequence.

The dark girl's cool hand pushed him gently but firmly back. It was not her fault that it was on his wounded shoulder that she pressed. "Quiet, now. Hush you," she said, as though he had been a child instead of a battle-scarred veteran. "Lie still, now. You will be fine, just fine. Lie still, will you."

It came to the man that he had been saying much the same thing to that other unfortunate just a short time ago. Moistening his lips, he found halting words.

"It will be . . . just a graze? A cut. Nothing. I fell . . ." He felt distinctly embarrassed, lying there, a grown man knocked unconscious by a small stone thrown by some silly woman; but sorry for himself, too. "You are . . . devilish free with your stones!"

"Yes. I am sorry. I tried to stop them, but they did not understand. You . . . you were in bad company, Gleneidart."

"So, you know me, then?"

"Of course I know you, Black Alastair." She shook a lovely dark head a trifle ruefully. "I take it that you cannot say as much for me!"

He frowned. "Here, you must be Glenudalain's daughter? Rory Mor said something . . . But I do not remember her so dark. Nor so . . . so handsome!"

"*Co'ar sinn*—you are improving! That would be my sister, Martha. She is married now, and gone. I am Marsala."

"M'mmm. I am sorry. It is so many years. Six or seven . . ." Alastair vaguely recollected that Donald of Glenudalain had had a second daughter, a child only. Now, this! "You cannot be very old," he said foolishly.

"I shall be twenty before the year is out. Old enough to fight Rory Mor for this glen!"

"Aye." Again Alastair sought to sit up. "What is he at, now? Is he still there. What is happening?"

"They are turning back. All of them. At last. I think . . . well, they saw what happened to you!" She smiled, faintly. "They have had enough, it seems. They are bold at burning thatches, and fighting with one woman at a time, or two! But face them with more than that, face them with women who will strike back, and they have second thoughts. Rory Mor is going home, I think."

"No! You are wrong. He is not." Despite hands pressing him back, the man managed to achieve a sitting position, even if he swayed therein. "Never think it. If he is going back now, it will be only a little, to come round on you some other way. He will need more beating than this, will Rory Mor. He told me. He said that he would not leave Glen Udalain until he had done his duty. Lord, his duty! Done what he came to do, that is. You must not underestimate Rory Mor. You must take heed, watch him . . ." That came out in something of a gabble.

The girl was eyeing him curiously. "You *are* against him,

then? You are not like the other men? You are for fighting Rory Mor?"

"Of course I am! Could you think otherwise? What he is doing here is shame and betrayal."

"Not God's will for us?" It was not good to hear so young a voice so bitter.

"If this is God's will, then nothing that I hold holy and true is so!"

"Good it is to hear you say so," the dark girl told him. "No one else will say so, against the Kirk's teaching, save my own self. And . . . and I am young, as you have said! As all men say. Young, and headstrong, and shameless!"

He began to shake his head, but swiftly desisted. "You—*you* did all this? Yourself? You got these women together? You set this trap, chose this place?"

"With these others, yes. Why not? I am Glenudalain's daughter. The women required little coaxing."

"And the men? The men of Glen Udalain? Where are they?"

"Those that are left to us are down in the main glen, there, waiting. They are against this. They say that it is the will of God . . . and of Clanrory, the chief! They say that no good will come of resistance, only worse hurt. They say that the law is against us, as well as the Kirk. And the chief."

"Aye! So they wait, down in the glen! *Dia*, I could weep! But, see you, this will not do. Rory Mor will be working round behind you, somehow . . ."

"Do not fret yourself. I have girls up there, watching." She pointed up the steep walls of the ravine. "They will tell me what he does . . ."

"More than *knowing* what he does is needed! What do you intend? What plans have you, to follow this ambush?"

"Plans . . .?" Marsala MacRory faltered.

"Yes. When you are outflanked. What other positions are you going to take up, to halt their next move?"

"But . . . I am afraid that, that . . ."

"You are not telling me that you have *no* other plans?" The man spoke sharply, impatiently—before he recollected that he was speaking to a mere girl, a young woman who had neither call nor reason to think along military lines, to be a strategist as well as a tactician. "I am sorry," he said, running a hand over his aching brow. "Forgive me. You have done marvels in halting them here, as it is. In getting your women together, and in making such good use of the terrain. But it is not enough, see you; Rory Mor will retire up the corrie, climb on to the summit of the ridge, and move back along it to outflank you here, to the first place where he can get down into the glen. Yours is a steep glen, I know, but there are bound to be many places where determined men can get down into it, other than by this track."

"But will he do that? Now that he has seen that we will resist him? He knows now that Glen Udalain will not be like the other glens that he has cleared. Will he not leave us alone, now, at least for a time?"

"He cannot. He dare not! Don't you understand? If he leaves you now—admits defeat here—all Strathdonan will know it before nightfall. All those unhappy people will know that he can be beaten if they will only unite against him. There are hundreds of them, and only a few to support him. His whole policy could collapse if the others were to follow your example. He cannot allow that to happen, cannot allow you to seem to defeat him even for a day. He is no fool, is Rory Mor, whatever else he is."

The girl bit her lip. "I thought . . . if we showed fight . . . held him up here . . ." She stopped, squaring her slim shoulders. "What do we do now, then?" she asked simply.

"Get me on to my feet, for a start." Alastair raised a hand to grasp hers, slender but firm, and pulled himself up. He staggered a little, and for a moment the rocks seemed to reel around him. He found her good to lean on. She was tall, long-legged, with nothing frail about her, though far from lacking in womanliness. "You . . . you have no whisky, here? It might help." He had the Highland male's pathetic faith in the curative properties of his native spirit.

"Not here, no. Are you well enough? Can you walk? You were only stunned, I think—thank God! Your bonnet saved you. There is a great lump, but the skin is not broken. Will you be all right, do you think?"

"I shall tell you that . . . at the top of this cliff!" the man returned, grimly.

"Up there? But . . . can you do that? As you are?"

"Yes—perhaps with a mite of help . . ."

Leaning more heavily on the young woman than he would have wished, and choosing the easiest route available, he did surmount that steep and stony west bank of the ravine; it took him longer than his masculine pride cared to contemplate, however, and three or four times he had to halt, leaning against the bank, for dizziness. The girl Marsala gave him stalwart aid—and was rather growled at for her pains, especially when once she sought to hoist him higher by lifting his left arm. Alastair's barked curse startled her.

"I beg . . . your pardon," he gasped. "Not your fault. Got a poor shoulder. An old sore. Not your work—Bonaparte's!"

She was all solicitude, and for inspecting the trouble then and there on the cliffside; Alastair brusquely repulsed her, however, implying that getting himself to the top of the hill was enough of an ordeal without having women fiddling about with his person. He was not in his most genial frame of mind. Some sort of retort seemed about to spring from his companion's lips—for clearly she was nowise lacking in spirit—but she bit it back.

Up on the heather above the ravine at last, the man sank down suddenly on an outcrop, a red mist before his eyes. When it cleared, it was to find himself surrounded by women, the girl Marsala explaining his position and attitude. He ignored them all and, seeking to focus his unsteady vision, peered at the land around him.

He could see the factor's party plainly from up here, or as plainly as he could see anything. They were climbing now, almost straight uphill out of the corrie and above the smoke, twenty or thirty of them, with their garrons and gear. He had little doubt that once they had surmounted the long ridge enclosing the valley and were safely out of sight, they would double back in order to seek to enter the glen again further down, as he himself would have done in the circumstances. Some few others were driving the mixed flock of the crofters' cattle and ponies up the floor of the corrie, and just disappearing into the smoke from the burning houses.

Alastair's regard switched to the massive rampart of towering hillside that was Glen Udalain's western wall. For most

F

of its length it was crowned with crags above steep screes of loose stone and gravel. There were gaps, however. He picked them out. Some were nullified by more crags and precipices lower down, but he counted at least three places where a descent would be feasible, and another where it might just be practicable for determined men. He turned to Marsala MacRory, pointing.

"There, there and there, they could get down. Perhaps not the Sheriff, who looked less than nimble, but the others."

She followed his pointed line, frowning. "Well . . . perhaps. How can we stop them?"

He did not answer.

"We could block one route, perhaps. But not them all . . ."

"Stone-rolling parties, again, above each gap, would be effective, I think. Rory Mor's people would not dare to descend any of those gullies if they thought that rocks would be coming down on top of them. Only . . ."

"Only we should be seen, first. Up on the ridge. They would drive us off. Catch us, perhaps. Or leave men on guard at the top."

"Aye." He paused. "If they saw you."

"But they would, surely! They must. It is bare up there—open grass and heather."

He pointed again, but in the opposite direction this time, back up the corrie. "There's your answer. Smoke. They have used fire against you—now use it against them. Lighting the heather and deer-grass above, and the bracken below. To the west of the gullies. Right along. There is a brisk south-westerly breeze. The smoke will blanket everything, as it is doing up there. Your rock-rollers will have all the cover that they need."

"Ye-e-es. But so will Rory Mor."

"Rory Mor, seeing the smoke, will not take the risk. Having learned what you can do with rocks already, he will never risk a descent of those gullies with any of your women left above him in the smoke."

"You think not?"

"I am sure of it. I told you, he is not a fool."

"Very well . . ."

"He is after saying to burn our pasture," a strong-featured, middle-aged woman objected. "We all know how a heather-fire can spread. And it is dry, dry. We shall be destroying our pasture."

"That is true, Morag . . ."

"How much use is your pasture going to be to you in Canada, woman?" Alastair demanded.

"Aye, aye."

"He is right, Morag," the dark girl said. "Let Rory Mor into Glen Udalain, and the pasture is his thereafter. To feed his wretched sheep! You would not save it for that?"

"But we do not even know that they will do this thing. Turn back again. Likely they have had enough. Only Glen-eidart says that they will. You would not have us destroy our pasture for nothing?"

"No. But . . ."

"Send somebody up, on to the top. Just up here. To watch them," Alastair directed, impatiently. "To keep hidden, and signal back. The others climb up, further along. Westwards. Most on top, but some on the lower slopes. No need to light the fires until you get the signal. Better not, indeed. But be ready. Do you have flint and steel? Enough to light the fires?"

One or two of the older women had flints in the pockets of their skirts, but most had not. Alastair handed over his own, and said that the others should light themselves lumps of dead peat moss which would smoulder away and could be blown into flame when required. He pointed out the gullies that constituted a danger, and mentioned that the fire-makers must be prepared to keep moving back farther westwards, should Rory Mor seek to move ahead of the smoke. He himself would stay at this spot, which could be seen from anywhere along the ridge, and would relay the signal from the look-out. He still had his pistol. He would fire a shot, which could be heard over a long distance, when and if the fires were to be lit. They had all taken part in the annual moorburn for improving the next season's pastures, so he need not tell them how to light the heather. Off with them, then, for they would require all the time that there was.

Somewhat doubtfully most of the women looked from the

man to Marsala. The young woman nodded, and added her own instructions, appointing certain of the company to take charge of groups. She selected two strapping girls to climb the hill directly above, to spy on the factor's party when they were beyond the ridge; they were to remain hidden, and signal by waving their plaids to and fro if the men turned back behind the skyline, westwards.

In only a few moments, all the women were gone, bare-footed, skirts kilted high, chattering like starlings. Only Marsala MacRory remained.

"And you?" Alastair asked, a hand to his splitting head.

"I am as well here, where I can see on both sides," she said. "In case we have to make a sudden change. Rory Mor might always come back here, if he thought that we were all gone. Meantime, I am going to look at that shoulder of yours." That was determinedly said.

The man groaned.

*   *   *

So, at last, the impatient convalescent's wound was inspected, shaken head over, bathed—which entailed a descent to the burn by the young woman, where some minor disrobing presumably took place, to provide the white linen dressing that materialised thereafter—and rebandaged, the noxious former dressing being deplored and elaborately disposed of with typical feminine fuss and to-do. All this brought the two participators into fairly close and intimate contact, putting quite a severe strain on the maintenance of the man's suitably gruff, superior and military demeanour—for he was by no means as unimpressionable where the other sex were concerned as he would have liked to be thought.

And undoubtedly this young woman was not one to be disregarded or underestimated, from any point of view. That she was striking of appearance had been as apparent from the first as that she was of strong and independent character—not always a combination to commend itself to men of discernment. Proximity and time, however, revealed her as more dangerous, in that she clearly had soft ways to cover the threat of her, dancing lights in her dark eyes to belie her firm chin, and a warm flush and creamy texture of skin instead of the cold alabaster pallor that ought to go with raven-black hair. Moreover, she had a figure curved and ample enough to be disconcerting at close quarters, in her short and full-skirted gown of fine crimson homespun, wide-necked bodice of white linen, and loosely-knotted saffron silk kerchief. Altogether a young woman of whom to be wary, Alastair recognised.

Between strictures on the neglect of wounds and elementary precautions, she asked about her father, a captain in another company of the regiment, with whom Alastair had never been on very good terms. She had not seen him for six years, and but little before that, so that she seemed to have accepted his death without excessive grief. With her elder sister married away from the strath, with no close male relative, and her mother more or less an invalid, she appeared to be all that Udalain now had as tacksman. It looked as though the glen might well have had worse.

The man did not tell her how her father had died, raving mad from drink on top of fever and wounds, in the troopship bringing the Clanrorys from India to Egypt, contenting himself with the suggestion that he had died like a Highland gentleman. She gave him a very keen look, at that, and mentioned that Rory Mor always made a point of keeping everyone well informed as to family casualties in the regiment.

Alastair was digesting that when high on the skyline directly above them two small figures appeared, waving plaids vigorously to and fro over their heads.

"You were right, then," Marsala exclaimed. "Rory Mor has not learned his lesson, yet!"

"That may be one way of putting it!" the man acceded briefly. He drew his pistol and adjusted the priming. Raising it, he fired upwards into the air. The bang of the report echoed back and forth from a score of hillsides. It could hardly fail to be heard by even the farthest away of the incendiaries.

The girl had started to her feet. "Now what?" she demanded. "What do we do now?"

"Sit still, and wait," he told her.

"But . . . surely there must be something that we can do? That *I* can, anyway. To help . . ."

"A commander, once he has made his dispositions and given his orders, has little else to do but sit and wait, and be ready with a change of plan, if necessary. I grant you it is not the easiest part of his task—at least I have never found it so!" He mustered a smile for her, faint but the first. "Probably I will never make a general. I am too impatient. But, this time, your markswoman with the stone has aided me!" He pointed to his head. "Anyway, I do not think that we shall have long to wait."

He was right in that, at any rate. In only a minute or two the first wisps of yellow-brown smoke began to appear above the long serrated ridge of hill. There were three or four of them, widely interspersed. Quickly they grew in volume and density, and were added to by others, the smoke pouring away north-eastwards on the breeze, parallel with the glen itself. The fires on the lower slopes seemed to be slower of starting, but presently they too were adding their quota, though the fumes were paler and thinner. Soon, above, there was only the one solid bank of billowing brown reek, first staining and then blotting out the thin blue of the sky. Then that itself was lost to view behind the lesser but still masking clouds emanating from the lower fires, which came rolling over the two watchers to mingle with the smoke from the three burning crofts. All the north side of Glen Udalain was being blotted out.

"It will serve, I think," Alastair said, coughing in the acrid stink of it, after a little while. "Rory Mor will never risk the gullies in that. Or any descent, against opposition. He would be blinded."

"Will he go home, then? What else could he do?"

"Two things only. Turn again, and work round the head of these corries, and try to descend into the glen from the south side. Or head back to Loch Donan, and seek to enter the glen by the river, from its mouth. I think that he will do neither. For the first, he knows that you could cross the glen and set that side afire likewise, before he could get round. The second would take him a long time. It is well past noon now. Also, he would be working in his own smoke all the while, again against opposition. No, I think that Rory will have to leave Glen Udalain for another day!"

"Another day . . .!" the girl repeated.

"Unless we can persuade others to follow your example," he said.

86

After a while, one of the young women who had done the signalling came down to them through the smoke, to announce that the factor's party had indeed given up, and were on their way back across the hills by the track that led to Camusewan, the way that they had come. Her sister was trailing them, keeping out of sight.

Alastair supposed that he should have felt at least moderately elated.

*　　*　　*

Though the man would have liked to have proceeded on to his own glen of the Eidart, only a few miles further now to the north-east, he allowed himself to be dissuaded. Marsala was insistent that he should go home with her to Glenudalain House, for food and rest and proper attention to his hurts. Also she wanted him to speak to the men of the glen, to try to rouse them to back her. And it was still not certain that Rory Mor would not make another attempt up the riverside from the mouth of the valley. Alastair, on his feet, and finding himself to be less than in fettle for further climbing and travelling, acquiesced. He had to recognise that he might just possibly have more responsibility towards Glen Udalain than to Glen Eidart, at the moment. Indeed, this question of responsibility for what he was initiating was beginning to nag at the back of his mind more than a little.

So, sending their signaller to recall the fire-raisers, he suffered himself to be led down into the main valley, even accepting the support of a firm, honey-coloured arm on occasions when his sense of balance seemed to fail him.

He found the men of the glen gathered in a disconsolate and ill-humoured group down where the burns from the two corries met, at odds with each other, with their womenfolk and with fate, frowning and shaking their heads over all the smoke and what it implied, and revealing neither elation nor relief at the sight of Alastair of Gleneidart. He spoke to them, explained, challenged and upbraided them, but though many looked distinctly shamefaced and uncomfortable at his words, he achieved nothing with them. Their attitude, though incoherently expressed and less than unanimous on all points, was approximately the same as that held by Duncan the

Catechist and the men at Ardglass. They could not and should not rebel against all the authority that they knew: their chief, the Kirk, and the law. Glenudalain was dead, many of their sons and brothers were dead likewise, it seemed, the Highlands themselves were dying, the clans were no more . . . and God's will be done. The women had acted shamelessly and disobediently, and only worse trouble would result.

In vain Alastair argued with them and railed at them, abetted by Marsala. Some youngsters, mere boys, he swayed perhaps, but not sufficiently to turn them against their elders. He was not at his best or most eloquent, of course. Indeed, he hardly knew what he was saying most of the time. A great weariness was upon him.

Marsala saw it; she could not do otherwise. Presently she took his right arm firmly, shaking her dark head. "It is no use," she said. "Not now. Later, perhaps. You are tired, ill. Come, you."

The man did not take a lot of persuading.

At the first croft they came to, Marsala borrowed a couple of garrons, and they rode the mile or so further down the glen to the long, low, whitewashed House of Glenudalain beside its tiny loch.

It was not his intention to remain for any time in that house, but even wilful, obstinate and impatient men have their breaking-points, and Alastair MacRory had almost reached his. A warm room, a beaker of whisky, and the feckless, inconsequential bletherings of Marsala's mother, completed the business—or it may have been rather that they just saved him from reaching that breaking-point. At any rate, at the table, in the middle of a substantial meal and of Lady Glenudalain's breathless monologue, he achieved sudden and blissful oblivion. Whether he merely fell asleep, or swooned away, or something of both, he was never in a position to know; but peace and painlessness and silence descended upon him, and in the moment of transition he knew overwhelming thankfulness.

Chapter Eight

THOUGH dimly aware of ministrations, times when he came somewhere near to the surface of consciousness, and a vague but comprehensive sense of tranquillity and well-being, Alastair was quite unaware of the passage of time thereafter until, opening his eyes and staring at a lighted, three-branch, silver candlestick, he perceived that it was dark outside, and that he was lying on a couch in the same room where he had been eating, with plaids and blankets thrown over him. His doublet, kilt and shirt lay over a chair beside the couch. The grandfather-clock said nearly eight o'clock. He was blaming himself for having slept so long, with so much to be done, when something about his shirt attracted his inspection. It was much whiter than usual, smoothly ironed, and neatly stitched and patched where it could do with this—but his own old shirt, indubitably. His perplexity over how all this should have been achieved in the time was resolved by the quiet entry of Marsala MacRory, who amongst authoritative instructions about lying still and doing this and not doing that, informed him that he had in fact lain on that couch for thirty hours.

In the wordy turmoil of exclamation and alarm, reproach and pleading, that ensued, it was the man who promptly took over the mantle of authority, and in fact eventually drove the young woman from the room by the simple process of throwing the blankets from him in favour of donning the more material mantle of his clothing. The question of how his nakedness had been achieved under these coverings, though it exercised him momentarily as he dressed, was quickly overlaid by larger anxieties. But at least he felt more like himself, quite astonishingly better. Quite phenomenally hungry, too.

While satisfying this latter need thereafter, he urgently sought information as to what had transpired in the interim, and was assured by the girl that nothing had happened, nothing at all as far as Glen Udalain was concerned. Rory Mor had not attempted any assault the previous afternoon from the opening of the glen, and made no gesture towards them today either. The heather fire was still smouldering in one area, but elsewhere the men of the glen had managed to extinguish it. Some of the said men were even a little impressed at the success of the demonstration. It looked to Marsala as though Rory Mor might be having second thoughts about the Improvement policy.

Alastair was notably less sanguine. Rory Mor was not the man to be so readily turned aside. He emphasised that this display of opposition in Glen Udalain could only be successful, in the long run, if it aroused others to do likewise and touched off a more general revolt. Otherwise, the estate had only to bide its time, and sooner or later the factor would get his way. Time was vital. The area of resistance must be spread, and before Rory could take steps to counter it. That was why his own prolonged sleeping here was so unfortunate, such a wicked waste of time and opportunity. He should have been down to Ardglass twenty-four hours ago, to seek to rouse the men congregated there with the news that Rory Mor had been forced back from Glen Udalain. Moreover, his own time here was short indeed; there were only six more days before he must rejoin the *Sarah Bell* on her southwards voyage, on his way to the regiment.

The word that Alastair was to be in Strathdonan for so short a period quite obviously came as a shock to the young woman. Once again, a pang of responsibility struck at the man.

When he announced that he must be off forthwith, down to the Ardglass peninsula, dismissing her protests about his health, the hour and the darkness, Marsala countered by declaring that she would go with him. She was quite decided about it. Though he attempted to dissuade her, he did so less than forcibly, for he recognised that her presence there might indeed be valuable. It was just possible that she might help to shame the men there into a more militant attitude, and moreover the evicted womenfolk had probably reached there by now, and she might well have a rousing effect on them. Somewhat feebly he asked her if her mother would not object to her going off in the darkness with himself—to be assured spiritedly that she was no child, that she was quite capable of looking after herself, and that her mother knew better than to make any such foolish suggestions. Alastair was left in no doubts as to who ruled in Glen Udalain.

His trouble with this young woman, of course, was that because she was the daughter of a fellow-officer of his own, and he had last seen her as a mere child, he tended to think of her as a child still, or at least as very much of a youngster—despite the evidence of his eyes and senses; a misleading, not to say dangerous, notion in the circumstances. It behoved him to remind himself that she was, in fact, no more than seven years younger than himself.

Mounted on ponies, they set out together for the coast. They did not risk the low route, by Loch Donan-side and Camus-ewan, but went climbing by hill-tracks and cattle- and deer-paths, through high gaps in the intervening ridges. The girl it was who led the way, the man, not unaware of long legs gleaming palely before him on either side of the broad-backed garron. The darkness laid its own hush upon them; they did not talk much, but went perhaps the more companionably therefore.

They came down upon Ardglass steeply, zig-zagging down the hillside, with a few red glimmers of camp-fires beckoning them on. At the foot of the hill, and base of the peninsula, they were suddenly challenged by someone with a Lowland voice and scant manners, from behind an alder bush. Him Black Alastair ordered peremptorily to stand aside and not impede his betters—and was obeyed, even if uncertainly. Marsala was herself impressed at the tone of authority barked into the night. Admittedly the fellow shouted to unseen colleagues thereafter, but the two riders pressed on without halting, the man now in the lead. It seemed that the evicted were now under guard as well as homeless.

It was soon evident that the women and children had indeed arrived to join their menfolk in this barren refuge. If the peninsula had been crowded before, it was choked and over-flowing now; no daylight was required to establish that. Alastair and Marsala had to dismount, to lead their garrons through the press and gear. Families and groups and individuals were lying everywhere, however uncomfortably and shelterless. Not all were asleep by any means, obviously, but there was little of stir or movement. The air of dejection and misery hung over the place like a cloud, even though there was no keening now. Some sobbing there was, punctuated by the wails of cross children.

Enquiry elicited the fact that the Reverend Angus was here, with the others, but further out, near the point somewhere.

Alastair's heart sank as they pushed on. Despite his own warnings to Marsala, the Udalain action had encouraged him more perhaps than he had realised. Without consciously telling himself so, he had anticipated some improvement here, some accession of spirit and temper. But nothing of the sort came to him now. Almost, the air of despair and resignation seemed worse, the gloom deeper. Somehow, he was ashamed even to speak to Marsala throughout.

He made for the area of the caves, out at the ness, and there found old Duncan the Catechist, and Angus of the Limp with him, sitting over a dull and smoky fire of dried seaweed and bog-myrtle stems.

They were greeted kindly by the minister, courteously by the patriarch. Alastair sensed reserve, nevertheless.

"I am happy to see you, Angus *a graidh*," he said. "I had hoped that I would. I would have come before, but . . . well, I fear that I overslept!"

"He was ill. Hurt. Worn out," the girl declared quickly. "He had only slept for four or five hours out of fifty. And done so much. An injured man."

"Och, now . . ."

"Better, perhaps, had Gleneidart slept more and done less," Duncan the Catechist said quietly. "Better for us all."

"Eh? What do you mean by that?"

"Just that we had enough of trouble, Gleneidart, without you bringing us more. You and this misguided young woman!"

"Misguided! *Dia—you* sit there and call her that?"

"Duncan means, Alastair, that a hot head, even over a warm heart, can work ill as well as good," the pastor intervened sadly. "He means that what you have done in Glen Udalain, and what you have encouraged Marsala here to do, may have seemed to you bold and even successful, but it has brought but added hurt upon the rest of us—that we can ill bear."

"You know then, what has been done in Glen Udalain? But what . . .?"

"It was not Gleneidart who encouraged me to resist Rory Mor!" the young woman interrupted strongly. "I, with the women of my glen, held him up before ever I knew that Gleneidart was back in Scotland . . ."

Alastair overbore her. "What do you mean by 'added hurt to the rest', Angus? What is this?"

"Just that Rory Mor has been here this day, on account of what you have done, Alastair, and these poor people are the worse off in consequence. He said that a state of rebellion and insurrection against properly instituted authority has broken out, that the law had been flouted and officers of the law assaulted. He called upon the Sheriff to read some Act, the Riot Act I think he named it, whereby such small legal rights as we still possessed, it seems, are banished, and we are all without the law. At the mercy of all who care to pillage and persecute us!"

"But, damnation, you had no hand in the business! *You* were not rioting here, even if we were! Lord, you were not! Would that you were . . .!"

"That is ill-judged and impious talk, young man!" Duncan reproved sorrowfully. "Angry words will heal nothing. The thing is done."

"You mean that you have accepted, swallowed what was done . . .!"

"Duncan is right, Alastair lad," Angus Crubach said. "The thing is done. Whether rightly or wrongly, this Riot Act was read by the Sheriff. No words of yours or mine will unread it. And it means, Rory Mor says, that what little protection these poor folk had under the law, is gone. Those who would despoil them, even assault them, may now do so, it appears, with impunity. Rory made many threats, in his soft way, and coming from him they are not likely to be idle ones. We are likely to pay dear for your resistance, I fear."

"But this is ridiculous! A travesty of justice and law! The Riot Act, surely, if it applies here at all, may only be read in the face of serious threat to the peace . . ."

"The paper *was* read, Gleneidart. In front of us all," the patriarch insisted. "There is no way of talking round it. To our cost. Our cattle and beasts before were but impounded, so that they should not eat Clanrory's pasture. Now they are confiscate, Rory Mor says. Before, the people here could be going along the shore on either side, to be gathering bits of wood and shell-fish. Now confined we are to this Ardglass only, like pounded beasts our own selves. You would see the guards . . .?"

"Aye, like pounded beasts!" Alastair exclaimed. "You have said the word, man! And like pounded beasts you allow it! Rory's own sheep could not be more obedient! Instead of rising in your wrath at this wickedness, you bow the head still lower! And say, God's will be done! Not Rory Mor's will, och, never that! God's will, only. It is easier to bow to it, that way!"

"Gleneidart, will you add blasphemy to your other sins!" the old man cried, voice quavering.

"Me? No, yours is the blasphemy, I think! Imputing to a merciful Father the evil deeds of wicked, grasping men. I cannot think that God is flattered!" He turned hotly on the lame pastor. "Angus, if this is what your Kirk has done to Strathdonan, then I will have none of it! If this is the result of your preaching, of the years of your ministry, I do not congratulate you!" He felt a hand on his arm, Marsala's hand seeking to restrain him, but he shook it off impatiently. "If you have taught men to bow their heads before evil and call it God's will, then I cannot conceive that you are greatly better than that whited sepulchre Amos Dunlop who sits snug in your Manse this night!"

The minister, whose head had been sunk on his breast throughout the younger man's tirade, raised it slowly, to shake it sadly. "I am sorry, Alastair my friend," he said. "Sorry indeed. Sorry that you esteem me so. Sorry that this should be the way it appears to you. Would to God that I had your fine certainty. You may be right. I may be wrong. Who am I to say that it is not so? I have sought to do my duty, as I saw it, and it has cost me somewhat dear. So long as there was hope, I sought to counter this policy of eviction. Perhaps for too long. When there was no hope, indeed, I still encouraged these my people to hope. I take the blame for that. But now that the deed is done, Alastair, now that the roofs are burned, the homes destroyed, I cannot find it to be God's will to bring these folk to still greater suffering by urging them to resist and rebel. Not when it is hopeless, and the deed done . . ."

"And the other glens, still to be cleared?" Alastair demanded. "Where the deed is not yet done? These too are to be handed over, abandoned? *Dia*, I came here to tell of what a few women could do in one such small glen. Marsala of Glenudalain turned Rory Mor back, and her glen is yet unravished. I hoped that we could stir others to do likewise, to take up the torch of resistance that these women have lit. Faced with hundreds against him, with widespread revolt, Rory must draw back. He cannot fight a whole people, even with the law in his pocket. But now, you counsel only more submission! More shameful surrender! You, Angus—you mean well, I doubt not. And Duncan Ceistear here. But you have led the people wrongly, given them ill advice. They are following weak, tired men . . ."

"And, think you, Gleneidart, that they will follow *you*, a deserter!" Duncan asked, enunciating that last word slowly, deliberately.

"My God!" Alastair swung towering over the old man, fists clenched. For a moment he could find no other words. "You . . . *you* say that?" he gasped, at length. "You dare to call me that? If you were a younger man . . .!"

"It is not what I say, Gleneidart. It is what Rory Mor and the Sheriff and the soldier-man said. They said that you are a deserter from the regiment. That you have run away from the wars. That you will be arrested and tried for it . . ."

"And you believed them?"

"Why are you here thus, then, Gleneidart? Alone. Where are your men, that you took with you to the wars? How comes it that none of the others returned with you?"

"I came back to London . . . for a special reason. On leave of absence. On Clanrory's orders. I was wounded. I came home here, for a few days, to see my mother."

"God rest her. But others get wounded, do they not, Gleneidart—more sorely than you, it would seem? Yet we do not see them here."

"I came at my own charges. If you must know, I was brought to London to receive an award, a medal. Not for anything that I did myself, but for my company. They . . . they . . . well, let that be. Clanrory knows that I am here."

"Yet you work and speak against Clanrory, in this."

"*Dia*, would you have me support it, man?"

"I would not. But it seems strange, just, what you are doing, if your are still one of Clanrory's officers. You cannot wonder, Gleneidart, if we do not understand it. If we . . ."

"If you believe Rory Mor rather than myself, you mean!" Alastair turned to the minister. "You, Angus, do you believe that I am a deserter?"

For a moment or two the other did not answer; a significant moment. Then he sighed, "I pray to God that you are not, *a graidh*," he said. "I think that you may have been headstrong, foolish. But not . . . never deliberately . . . that!"

"So-o-o!" That came out on a long exhalation of breath. He looked round him at the four or five elderly men who had moved up to listen, at the sound of heightened voices. Dark as it was, he could not but perceive how no single glance met his own as he stared from one to the other. "There we have it, then," he said, and all the fire and urgency had drained out of his tone. "You all believe it. Black Alastair of Gleneidart is a deserter—because Rory Mor, the man who stayed at home, the man who is eating you up, would have it so! It is of no use appealing to you here, I see, as I intended. No use calling the men together. The spark is gone out of you. Your fire is out, God pity you!"

There was silence then, into which it was Marsala who spoke. She had not raised her voice throughout.

"The women . . .?" she said. "Perhaps the women, if I spoke to them, might think differently."

"The women will do as they are told, child!" the patriarch said, sternly. "Anyway, you shall not speak to them."

"Think you that you can say me nay, Duncan Ceistear? You cannot stop me!"

"But I can *ask* you not to, my dear," Angus of the Limp put in, unhappily. "I do so ask you, Marsala, you whom I christened and brought to the Table of the Lord. You have heard me—I ask you not to do this thing. Have these folk around us not suffered enough? Is there to be no end to their misery? To seek to turn the women now against their men, to divide families, and sow discord amongst those who have only each other left . . .! You will not do it, my dear?"

"I . . . I . . ." Marsala turned to Alastair, questioningly.

That man's answer was short, bitter, "Come, you," he said. "There is nothing for us here. Leave them to their misery . . . and their God! Come; if you can stomach the company of a deserter!" And, swinging on his heel, he strode from there without a backward glance, to his garron.

After only a second or two, the young woman followed him.

*   *   *

Alastair did not wait for her, nor speak to her, all the way back across that crowded promontory. At its base he mounted, and turning, signed to her to do likewise, waving her forward. The hand that made the gesture, she saw with a start, held a pistol.

"What . . . what do you intend?" she faltered.

"That neither fools nor knaves shall cross me further this night!" he threw back at her, harshly. "Keep close."

He rode on. Quite soon the expected challenge was forthcoming, a trifle thickly, sleepily, two figures making for them this time, from the shadowy bushes at the foot of the steep slope.

"Out of my way, oafs, dolts!" Alastair cried back at them. "Do you not know one of His Majesty's officers when you see one? We rode in here an hour ago, and now we ride out. Back, I say!"

"It's 'im, Tom, it's the perishin' orficer! 'Im wi' the kilts . . ." That sounded extraordinarily like the individual that Alastair had had occasion to reason with at the cattle-pound two nights before.

"It is Gleneidart, of the Seventieth Foot, with his pistol pointing at your thick head, numbskull! Out of our way, and let this lady past!"

The guard, who seemed to be armed only with his thick cudgel, retreated circumspectly. Once again, however, his discretion was not shared by his colleague. From the other side, the same dour, Lowland Scots voice whose owner had refused to be intimidated at the other encounter, grated out.

"No' sae fast, my mannie! No' sae fast! I've got a gun, tae—an' I've the wumman covered. Stand still, or I shoot."

Quick as thought, Alastair acted. Jerking his beast's head round, and kicking its barrel ribs, he urged the garron across

G   97

diagonally in front of Marsala, ignoring the man who had spoken first. The second guard, as was to be expected, thought better of shooting at the girl, and swung the musket that he held to bear on this urgent threat. Alastair's hand rose as soon as he saw the man clearly, and with all his strength he hurled the heavy, cavalry pistol at the guard. It was unprimed, anyway. Spinning, it took the fellow on the side of the head and on the left shoulder. His yelp of pain was drowned in the loud report of his musket, as it went off harmlessly into the air, and the clatter of both weapons falling to the ground.

"Quick, up the hill!" Alastair shouted to the girl.

Marsala required no second bidding. To an outburst of shouting, she drove forward her pony. Alastair pulled round after her. The first guard's flung cudgel came flying at him, to strike his garron on its broad rump. It but made the beast run the faster. Up the steep slope the two horses pounded, sending turf and gravel flying from scrabbling hooves. The shouting and commotion swiftly fell away below and behind.

A fair way up the hillside, the girl reined up, to wait for him. "They will not follow us?" she panted.

"Not them. On the hill, in the dark, they would be lost. Those ones are more at home firing roofs!"

"Yes. You . . . lost your pistol?"

He nodded. "Better that way, perhaps," he said briefly, and pushed on in front once more.

They rode back in silence through the night-bound hills. Thoughtfully the young woman considered her companion's dark back. She did not know how to reach him, in his black mood. Something about his whole aspect and attitude repelled any approach.

It was not until they were topping the final ridge above Glen Udalain that he turned to look back at her, over his shoulder, without halting his mount. "Do *you* think I am a deserter?" he demanded abruptly.

"Not if you say that you are not," she answered, without hesitation, "But what of it? I should not greatly care if you were. I fear that I have not such great respect for soldiering, and this regiment that has been the plague of us, as have others. As men seem to have. To have left it, I think, might be nothing to be ashamed of—the act of a brave man and a true son of Clan Ruari. That regiment has been the death of Strathdonan!"

Alastair frowned. Words rose to his lips—and died there. "M'mmm," he said, and rode on.

They were almost at the foot of the long, slantwise track that brought them to the floor of the glen, when the man suddenly pulled up, raising a hand. "Ssshh!" he hissed back at her, as the girl behind him began to speak.

They waited, listening. Only the rush and chuckle of the river below sounded, and up in the heather above somewhere a curlew calling, calling in sorrow.

"Heard something. Metal on stone. I think. Down there, downstream," Alastair whispered. "What might that be, at this hour of night?"

"Cattle? A stone rolling? It might be anything."

"There is no house near here, is there?"

"Not near enough for a sound to carry . . ."

"Listen! There it is again."

Through and above the noise of the river they distinctly heard a metallic sound, carried up the glen on the south-westerly breeze, a thin clatter repeated, that suggested consistent movement. The girl would have ridden on, but her companion was suspicious, legacy of many night operations in hostile territory. He remained stationary, blocking the track.

Presently he spoke, quietly. "Somebody coming up the glen. More than one, I think. Horses. Would it be any of your people?"

"Not that I would expect, no. Not at this time. It must be near midnight."

He gave a single brief nod, and dismounted. "Stay here, still, with the beasts," he directed. "I will have a look." Without waiting for any agreement, he moved off downwards on foot, swiftly, silently.

Udalain, as has been indicated, was a narrow, steep glen in most places, though it broadened out here and there. In this sector, the constricted floor of it was wide enough only to hold the river, a road of sorts, and quite a slender belt of turf littered with rock-falls and alder and hazel bushes. The man reached the shadowy cover of these, and crouched down.

99

He had not long to wait. He could hear the scruffle and clink of hooves on the sand and stones of the track before ever the first figures materialised out of the gloom. It did not take long, either, to establish the identity of one of the leading riders thereafter; Rory Mor MacRory's massive proportions had their disadvantages at times.

It seemed to be quite a long cavalcade that came pacing quietly but deliberately up the glen road beside the river. Alastair counted fully thirty riders pass him, in pairs. They were obviously going as silently as they might, talking only in undertones. Even at that the listener caught snatches of subdued converse as they passed. He recognised the Sheriff again, and the man Cousins. He also perceived muskets slung across the backs of many.

When all were past, Alastair turned and hurried back uphill to the young woman.

"Rory Mor, paying a night visit," he panted. "Many men. The Sheriff and the rest. Being quiet about it."

Marsala did not speak, though he heard her sudden intake of breath.

"It is a mile still, to your home? To the House?"

"Yes. More. He . . . he has got thus far? I arranged for women to be on watch, day and night. At the mouth of the glen. And up at the head of it . . ."

"He could have come partly over the hill, as we have done. You cannot guard all the glensides."

"I suppose not. Is he going to . . . to start evictions, by night? In the darkness?"

"I should not think so. He has not done so yet, anyway, and he has passed many crofts lower down the glen. No sign of fires. No, it is your house that he is making for, I have no doubt. He intends to trap us there."

"You mean . . . take us? Take *me* . . . out of my own house? Can he do that?"

"With the Sheriff dancing attendance he can do almost anything, it seems! If he can have the Riot Act read . . ."

"What could he do? Do *with* us, I mean? Where would he take us?"

"I suppose the Sheriff could send us to Dingwall, to the County gaol. Me, as an accused deserter, you on some civil charge of rioting or assault. Anything to get us away from here, out of this country. So that Rory Mor can get on with his evictions unhindered."

"Then . . . then what are we to do?" There was just a tremor in her voice, there.

"Follow quietly on behind them for a start, I think," the man said slowly. "Find out just what they are up to. And then . . ."

"Yes, and then?"

He shrugged one shoulder. "That can wait," he said. "Come on."

They rode on cautiously, down to the road, and up it in the wake of the factor's cavalcade.

As they neared the vicinity of Glenudalain House, the glen broadened out. There was cultivation, scattered cot-houses, and many trees. Leaving the horses, they crept forward on foot. No lights showed anywhere in the valley. Nothing disturbed the hush of the night.

It was low-set voices ahead that warned them. Moving round, silently, making use of the trees and bushes as cover, they discovered that a circle of men surrounded the House at perhaps a hundred yards, each a few yards apart.

Abruptly the quiet of the night was rudely broken. A muffled barking of hounds from within the House was followed by a loud banging, obviously on the front door. Rory Mor's great voice was uplifted to shout a demand to open in the name of King George. Again and again the order was repeated, amidst an increasing tumult. Behind the screen of armed, waiting, and now vocal, men, the hidden pair crouched, listening.

With apparently only the baying dogs answering his summons, Rory Mor's shouting grew the louder and more specific. "Open, I say, in the King's name, or I break down this door on you! The house is surrounded. The Sheriff is here. He has warrant for the arrest of the man Alastair, formerly of Gleneidart, and the woman Marsala of Glenudalain. Any resistance will be broken with the utmost severity, see you. The Sheriff's officers are armed. Open, I say, and quickly!"

Behind their bush the man and the girl exchanged glances.

"Rory Mor flies his true colours, at last!" Alastair whispered.

His companion shook her head. "It is horrible. Here, in our own glen! Poor Mother! She . . . she is not very brave. Nor very clear in her mind. She will be in terror. There is only one old man, Colin, in the house. What can we do . . .?"

"Nothing I fear, not now. Not tonight. They will not hurt or take your mother, however much they may affright her. Us it is that they seek. And once they find that we are not within . . .!"

"What will they do?"

"They will start looking for us, I imagine!"

"Then . . . then . . .?"

Their eyes met.

"It would be better that we were not here!" the man said briefly, nodding. "I think . . ."

Three crashes interrupted his whispering, the last accompanied by the noise of splintering wood. Immediately the barking of the deerhounds sounded much louder, and the general uproar swelled. Clearly Rory had not waited. The door was battered in.

Alastair took the girl's arm. "In only a minute or so now they will discover that we are gone," he said tensely. "They will question your mother. She will not be able to gainsay them. She will be forced to tell them where we went. Then they will come looking for us. They are not going to find *me*! I have work to do, yet, by God! And you?"

For precious seconds she stared at him, or through him. Then she shook her head decisively. "No," she breathed. "Nor me, either!"

"Good! Then we go—quickly. Together, or separately, Marsala?"

"Together, of course."

"Think well, but swiftly, girl! What this means. Your . . . your good name, and . . ."

"Will my good name be safer in Dingwall gaol? Or in Rory Mor's clutch? It is my own, and I shall look after it!"

"Very well, so. Come you, then."

"Yes. But where?"

"To somewhere Rory Mor will not find us, with all his Sheriffs and constables. Where I am master yet! Quickly, now —and quietly!"

Crouching, dodging from cover to cover, they doubled back to the waiting garrons.

Chapter Nine

AND SO, out of much arduous riding and climbing, by cattle-tracks and deer-tracks and no tracks at all, over high passes, by forded torrents and quaking bogs and round the long skirts of the sleeping hills, Alastair MacRory came home at last to Glen Eidart. Over the watershed, the hard way, he came, like a thief in the night, to his own place, and at his heels rode the silent daughter of a man whom he had disliked and mistrusted. Their escape had not been observed, and they had not been followed; from the first they had made sure of that. They had carefully avoided all the remote haunts of men, even where a warm if humble welcome would have greeted them. That is the sort of homecoming it was.

Even in Glen Eidart itself the man kept far from the settled areas, not approaching within a couple of miles of his own house. Well up above the wide, enclosed valley he led the girl, the well-remembered lie and trend of the land speaking to him, even in the darkness, as though he had left it but yesterday. Out of the head of it, where it shallowed and faded into the billowing, green breasts of a vast, uptilted land-mass, they climbed, up and up, over endless, shelving grass slopes that lifted in slow, rolling undulations to the ultimate extremity of a long hogs'-back ridge, black against the deep blue of the northern sky. That slow and interminable final ascent had a timeless unreal quality about it, as the tired beasts plodded doggedly on, their riders sunk away into their own abstracted worlds beyond thought and words.

At long last, within a hundred feet or so of that withdrawn skyline, Alastair pulled up before a barrier of rock, an extensive escarpment of cliff crowning the lengthy crest of the hill. Here, in this lofty playground of the winds, riven and fissured by the storms and frosts of centuries, were many seams and crevices and caves in the wall of stone. Amongst the massive rock-falls at the cliff-base, the man pointed upwards, and spoke out of long silence.

"Up there," he said. "Up there, Rory Mor shall not reach us. No man shall reach us, unwelcome. Here was my castle as a boy, where I defied and challenged all the clans of the north and the chiefs thereof, where I was a greater hero than Fionn or Cuchulain! Here is a dry cave for shelter, all the world for vista, dug bog-pine for warmth, heather for couch, springs to drink from, and rock-falls to hide the garrons. What more could we ask for?"

Marsla looked about her, slow to come to words out of the deep trough of silence. "Only perhaps a back door?" she suggested, at length.

He laughed—and Black Alastair's laughter had been scarce of late. "Well said, woman of the MacRorys!" he commended. "You have the makings of a soldier in you. But we have better than a back door, see you. There is a narrow route up this cliff face to the top, from my cave. And though the south face of this hill, Braemore, is a slope as open as it is long, the north face behind us is a breakneck precipice. Fifteen hundred feet of it. Just at our backs. We shall not be surprised from behind. But . . . leave the beasts here. There is grass for them amongst the rocks. And come, you."

He led her up, on foot, by a series of ledges, this way and that. Where one of these negotiated a crevice, a tiny stream tinkled down musically over the rock. Grasses and heather and even small rowan-trees grew on shelves and crannies wherever they could find a foothold. And some forty feet up, from a wider ledge, opened Alastair's cave. It did not yawn blackly at them; indeed it seemed to be no more than just one other crevice in the cliff, at first. But bending back, at right angles, within the narrow slit of an entrance, it widened into a sizable cavern, lofty and dry. The man's flint and tinder lit it up for a moment, inadequately, a strange, flickering hall of shadows. Then it was dark again.

"I have thought of this place many a time, in many a strange land, but I little thought that it would be here that I would come for refuge on my return to Glen Eidart," Alastair mentioned. He did not sound resentful or sorry for himself, nevertheless. The cave echoed his words hollowly. "It must be a dozen years since I last was here, and I doubt if any man will have set foot in it meantime."

"It is very dark," she said. "And quiet."

"Your are not afraid of the dark, lass? Or . . . or anything else?"

"No. I am not afraid. I think that I like it here." She looked at him thoughtfully, though they could scarcely distinguish each other's outlines. "This place must mean much to you, somehow, I think? You have sounded differently, since you reached here. Different from what you have been up till now."

"H'mmm," the man said. "I . . . ah . . . perhaps. See you, I shall go down to the garrons. Get the plaids from them, to sleep in. I shall bring you water. Here is flint and tinder. Find you a place where you may lie comfortably. There are shelves. I shall sleep in the mouth, here. Tomorrow, we shall gather heather. You . . . you will be all right, Marsala."

"I do not doubt it," she said.

When Alastair came back with the plaids, it was to present the young woman with water in a curling cattle-horn. When she exclaimed at this, he told her that he had found it where he had left it all those years before, in a cavity beside the tinkling burn. For a hero, no ordinary cup or beaker would have served, he pointed out.

"There was no Deirdre nor Maeve to share your cup with you, then?" she said, sipping.

"No," he agreed. "The world was . . . was less complicated in those days!"

"Easier for heroes?"

"I am not saying so."

"I am an encumbrance to you, Alastair, a weight upon you. I am sorry for that."

"Have I said that, either, girl? Or hinted it?"

"Perhaps not. But I feel it. Or feel that *you* feel it. You must not let me be that. In any way."

He did not answer.

"I have my own pride," she went on, levelly.

"Do I not know it! Like the rest of you, it shall not suffer, from me! Now, will you take these plaids and yourself within, there, and let a man sleep!"

"You are tired? Your shoulder? It hurts? Does it need dressing . . .?"

"My shoulder is well enough, woman, and can await the daylight like all else."

She took one of the plaids only, that had been used as saddles for the garrons. "You have named me woman, at least —and not girl! For that I must be thankful!" she said. "Good-night, Alastair Dubh."

He looked after her, brows furrowed, as she disappeared into the deeper darkness.

Despite his declared desire for sleep, the man sat long in the mouth of the cave, gazing blankly out into the night.

*   *   *

Alastair awakened to find the young woman sitting near by, staring out in the same direction, but over a strange and very different scene. The sun was already risen, and its yellow rays were slanting levelly between a gap in the hills to the east, to make a golden glory of the rolling table-land of fleecy cloud that stretched beneath them. Perhaps one hundred feet below, the cloud lay, solid seeming, motionless, reaching as far as eye could see, unbroken save by the floating summits of mountains as high as their own, thrusting above it like basking leviathans in a sea of gold. He yawned.

"Late," he muttered. "Sun up."

"It is strange. Beautiful. But a little frightening," Marsala said, as though there had been no interruption of the conversation. "We might be in another world! Is that what you meant when you said that we should have a world for vista?"

"Did I say that?" the man wondered, shortly, "I do not usually talk such nonsense. I must have been light-headed!"

"And you are not, now? You are . . . yourself again? Glen-eidart, Lieutenant of Foot—not . . . not Cuchulain of this Braemore?" That was unevenly said.

He looked at her, now, instead of the view. She looked to him most confoundedly fresh, even spick and span, for the place and the hour, with colour in new-washed cheeks, black hair smoothed and gleaming, clothing neat and tidy. How she achieved this he could not guess. Rasping a hand over his own blue, unshaven chin, and grievously aware of all his unsavoury dishevelment, the man scowled at her, living up to his name.

"No hero was ever a hero before his breakfast!" he declared, sourly. "Excuse me." He rose stiffly, and went stalking off to the burn and his toilet with as much dignity as his tousled and crumpled finery would permit.

Returning presently, with as much water inside him to help fill his empty belly as he had used for washing, and feeling only little the better therefor, Alastair found his companion sitting as before, unmoving, her expression sombre in the face of all that yellow radiance.

"What do we do now?" she asked him, with no lift to her normally lively voice. "What *can* we do? Last night, to come away, to come here, seemed to be the right course, the only thing to do. But, now . . .?"

"But now you have an empty stomach, and life is grey, grey." He looked down at her, and mustered a smile. "There is much that we can do—or, at least, attempt. Just as much as there was last night. More. But first, we must find food, or we shall discuss nothing with profit. Any hero will tell you that!"

"We shall find no food on a mountain top! We must go down into the glen before we may eat. We could have stayed down there last night, and come on here this morning, fed and supplied."

"And risked all men seeing us come? Until I know how things are in Glen Eidart, I could not risk that. More is at stake than just our safety." He shook his head. "But we do not need to go down into the glen for food. Not the main glen, at any rate. There is a house not two miles from this cave, though difficult miles. Behind us. In Corrie Liath, below the precipices of Braemore. A man of mine, one Hector MacBride, lives there. A drover. He will give me food, and what is necessary. I can be there in less than an hour. Can you wait two hours for your breakfast, lassie?"

"Not if I can go with you . . ."

"Better that you stay here, I think. I shall be going down the cliff."

"I can climb well enough. With no injured shoulder to trouble me! And if you are for bringing back supplies, two carriers are better than one."

"As you will," he allowed. "At least you will eat the sooner."

They delayed only long enough for Marsala to dress the man's shoulder with a clean, damp pad, and to proclaim that it looked better. Then they set off, climbing up the escarpment above their cave, and leaving the garrons to forage amongst the rocks at the foot of it. The ascent was easier than it looked from below, taken zig-zag, and they reached the summit without difficulty. Alastair noted, thankfully, that his companion seemed to have a good head for heights. What lay ahead was less simple.

The gravelly top of Braemore, so smooth and flat and bare above the sea of cloud, suddenly dropped sheer away at their feet, with stomach-catching abruptness. How far it dropped thus they could not see, for on this side too, the cloud table spread. It was debatable whether this curtailment decreased or increased the dizzy impression of height.

Looking from the yawning void to the young woman, Alastair asked, "You will be all right? Or would you rather stay here?"

Marsala shook her head.

"Follow me closely, then. And perhaps it would be best that you try not to look downwards. Save only at your feet. The first step over the edge is the worst."

"I hope that you have a good memory," was all that she said in answer.

He had no doubts as to where to commence the descent. It all came back to him clearly. At far from the most hopeful-seeming point, he stepped over on to a foot-wide grassy shelf that slanted away to the left, turning to face the cliff as he did so. Marsala was only a pace behind him. Together they moved along, and wide was the void at their backs. Where the shelf changed into grass steps, progress was more complicated, but not difficult if the emptiness behind could be forgotten. A shelf again, but narrower, brought them a sort of chimney that plunged steeply downwards—steeply, but not perpendicularly; indeed little or nothing of the entire precipice was perpendicular, whatever its general appearance. The chimney, a watercourse in melting snows, no doubt, was in fact graded off sufficiently to retain a lining of scree and gravel. Down into this Alastair descended, backwards. The flanking rock was sound, and full of knobbly handholds. The young woman did not follow him immediately; when she did, she had her wide skirts kilted up and fastened somehow between her thighs—as well she might. The man waved approval and encouragement, making faces at the gravel she sent down on him.

The chimney took them right down into the cloud, before it petered out into slab rock. More transverse movement along shelves and steps took them further over for quite some way, but, maddeningly, slanting upwards again all the time, before another chimney opened, wider and better than the first.

"Two hundred feet of this, no more, and we are down on to open scree," Alastair informed. "Easy, is it not, when you know the way?"

"It is not the only way to get into Corrie Liath?" his companion questioned, breathing a shade noticeably.

"It is not. But any other route would be taking three hours and more. Would you be waiting that long for your breakfast?"

They emerged from the mists just where the second chimney tailed away into a long slope of scree and fallen stone, steep but walkable. Now all the corrie was open to them, though glooming grey under the pall of cloud. A mile down its centre, below its grassy moraines and by the side of a white foaming burn, a single cottage crouched, oppressed, only the plume of blue peat-smoke above it proclaiming it different from the great rocks and outcrops that surrounded it.

"Hector MacBride lives a lonely life," Alastair said, "I fear that my coming is going to make it lonelier still."

Approaching the cottage, before they were within a hundred yards of it a man came hurrying to meet them. He was elderly, grey-haired, and stooping a little, but lean and muscularly built—and no laggard afoot, obviously.

"Gleneidart! Gleneidart!" his cry came before him. "Alastair Dubh, praise be to God! Yourself, in the flesh, after all the years! And the image of your own father, looking, and him young!"

"Aye, Hector, old friend, myself it is. And feeling not all that young! Good it is to see you."

109

The two men clasped each other in their arms, and quietly, unspeaking, the young woman stepped forward and loosed the older man's clasp from Alastair's left shoulder, gently.

Hector MacBride stared, and Alastair turned, one arm still about the other. "This is Marsala *nic* Donald of Glenudalain, Hector," he introduced, "looking for her breakfast!"

"And welcome. I have heard only good of Glenudalain's daughter. My poor house is yours, *mo baintighearn*."

"You are kind," the girl said.

"So you have come back to your own place, at last, Gleneidart? It has been long, long. You come alone?"

"Aye," Alastair cleared his throat. "To my sorrow, I do. And for but a short while. I wish . . . I fear . . . would God it was otherwise, old friend. But I bring you ill tidings . . ."

"About Hughie, that will be? Och, well—Hughie will be fine where he is, I'm thinking. Just fine. There are worse things than dying in battle, Alastair Dubh."

"You knew, then?"

"Rory Mor sent to tell me, nearly a month back. He is thoughtful, the man Rory of Camusewan, in this matter. None does he fail to tell, when the blow falls. In the name of Clanrory. Even to so far and humble a place as Corrie Liath, he sent the word. Aye, and at the same time as the paper telling me to quit this house by next Candlemas term!"

"*Dia!* You, too! He did that to you, Hector? The man is a devil! Here, too—in *my* glens!"

"Aye. Here, too. Can he do it, Gleneidart? Is it possible? Here?"

"Anything is possible, it seems, if he has Clanrory, and the law, and the Kirk behind him. Clanrory is claiming that all Strathdonan is his, his own, not the clan's land, to do as he will with. Eidart and Udalain and the rest, likewise. That is why I am here, at this hour, and Marsala of Glenudalain with me. Rory Mor raided her house last night. We are as good as put to the horn, outlawed. Any who shelter us will suffer. I took her to my cave, on Braemore. We shall fight him from there, if we may. But . . . food we need . . ."

"God in His heaven, sorrow the day that this should be the homecoming of Alastair of Gleneidart! But . . . but, come you.

No man can fight on an empty stomach." The older man turned to Marsala. "So he brought you down the great cliff? A hard road for a woman."

"Hector it was who showed me that road," Alastair explained. "As a boy. Proud I was. Few know it."

"Three only," the other said. His blue eyes clouded for a moment. "*Two*, I should say. But now—three again. And well so." He smiled at her.

Alastair bit his lip. "Hughie died in my arms," he said abruptly. "And near a hundred others around us. From these glens. He did not suffer, I think. He was smiling, too . . ."

They went into the cottage.

*   *   *

Hunger assuaged by an adequate meal of porridge, cold venison, oatcakes and honey, with milk, they sat at widower Hector MacBride's simple board under the soot-blackened thatch, and sought to plan some course of action. Hector included himself into any such action, from the start. A drover, whose occupation, apart from managing his own remote croft, was to drive the harvest of shaggy black cattle from these western glens to the east-coast markets of Dingwall and Inverness, he was a man of wide experience and independent character. He suggested that his visitors take up their abode in his cottage meantime, but Alastair would have none of it. Any house that sheltered them would be the target of the factor's wrath, undoubtedly—and this cottage was too useful to lose, if only that. Moreover, Corrie Liath could be a death-trap, if they were cornered here; safer far up in the cave on Braemore, where they could watch all approaches, far and near. That was accepted.

Their own safety, however, was not the principal pre-occupation. How to seek to counter the estate's policy of eviction was the problem. It was clear that little could be hoped for in the way of rousing to action those already evicted; but it might still be possible to save some of the outlying glens. They might be able to give a lead. The fact that any real success must depend upon the spirit of the people themselves constituted the major difficulty, it was recognised.

Hector MacBride shook his grey head over the likelihood of

any widespread revolt, even by the men of Glen Eidart itself. The same subtle forces of disintegration were at work there, interplaying one upon another. The clan system, which had constituted the fabric of their society, was in ruins. The regiment had drained them white of vigour and leadership and hope for the future. The authorities were all-powerful, alien, and had set their face against the Jacobite Highlands. Resistance was useless, and there was talk of transportation for the obdurate. Better, men said, to be shipped to the New World in families and groups, to new holdings, than as convicts to forced labour. It was the end of an age, the break-up of an entire way of life, and the dramatic Celtic character, that knew no half-measures, saw its fate writ large and, calling it the will of God, would lift no hand to change it. The old drover used no such words as these, but that was the sorrowful sum of his comment. A few bolder spirits they might find, he thought, but no large numbers. The bolder spirits were no longer in Strathdonan.

Marsala was indignant. That might serve for the men, she declared. But the women were different. The women had never taken chiefs and authorities, the law and the Kirk, so seriously, nor yet fate! Given a lead they would fight, as they had fought in Glen Udalain. Not all, perhaps, but many. If somehow they could use the women . . .

Alastair rubbed his chin, slowly, The women, yes. The women might conceivably prove more of a problem to Rory Mor and the authorities than would their menfolk. From his own war experience he knew that it was difficult, demoralising, to deal effectively with angry women. If they could only reach and stir them, they might gain time, and arouse not only the men but the conscience of the country outside these ravaged glens.

Hector MacBride said nothing. The young woman nodded encouragement.

"What is needed," Alastair went on, "is something of a gesture. A few gestures. Sorties, as soldiers would name them. Small assaults. Dirk play, as it were. To harrass the enemy, and encourage the faint-hearted. To let the people know that we are fighting back. To show them the way. To carry the war into the enemy's camp, see you."

"What have you in mind, Gleneidart?" the other man asked, keenly now.

"Nothing sure and settled—yet. Reprisals, just. Such as raiding Rory Mor's farm, for a change, and driving off *his* stock! His devil-damned sheep! Doing some fire-raiding on our own, maybe—his estate office roof, for instance. Releasing the pounded cattle. Suchlike. For these no large numbers are required."

"By the Powers, that is Gleneidart talking, now!"

Marsala's eyes had lit up—but the light in them sank again. "Large numbers may not be required, Alastair," she said quietly. "But *time* is required. And you go south again in four or five days, do you not?"

The younger man remained very still for a moment or two. Then he looked away through the open door to where the first rays of thin sunshine were piercing the cloud curtain. "We shall have time and enough," he said, slowly. "I am not going."

"But . . . but . . . the regiment?"

"I shall resign my commission. To Clanrory. And buy my release. I have the money." Alastair's voice rose. "They have named me deserter. I am not that, but they shall pay for that word as though I was! I am done with Clanrory's regiment! Would that I had never joined it, and emptied my glen to fill it! If I had stayed here, where I belonged, the evictions would never have got thus far without a fight. It seems that I should have been fighting Clanrory, not Clanrory's enemies! Last night, in the cave, I made my decision." He paused, for he was at heart an honest man. "Or, maybe, had it made for me."

The young woman's eyes were gleaming again. "I am glad," she said, simply.

Hector got up, and paced to the door and back, brows furrowed. "Man, Alastair, this is a big thing," he said. "A thing to stir the heart. One of the old chief's speaking, it could be. The decision does you credit, yes. But . . . have you thought well? And long enough, lad? Is it not perhaps too late? Too late for you to pay so great a price? Too late, not only for Strathdonan, but for all the north? Other straths have been cleared, other glens emptied. For the sheep. More will be yet. I have no doubt. The tide has turned against us, I fear. The

Highlands no longer belong to the Highlanders, it seems. Small battles you may win, lad, but can you win a war?"

"That does not sound like the Hector MacBride that once was! Who taught me the way of the heroes."

"Perhaps not, *a graidh*, but I would not see you sacrifice so much, your future indeed, for a lost cause."

"The cause is not lost yet, Hector old friend. And since when was such the test of a man's conduct? Aye, and what of the price that the rest of you are paying, each and all?" He rose from his seat also. "No, my mind is made up. When I go south again, one task only will I have—to see Clanrory. And then return. But before that, there is work to do!"

The drover nodded. "Aye, then, if that is to be the way of it." He held out his hand. "I am with you on your road, Alastair Dubh. To the end of it, whatever."

The young woman indulged in no such masculine dramatics. "Where do we start?" she asked, quietly. "And when?"

Chapter Ten

THEY made no delay. Living so isolated a life, Hector MacBride had in Corrie Liath most of the essential supplies that they needed: oatmeal, dried meat, cooking utensils, an old fowling-piece, powder and shot, plaids, and even the product of his own whisky still. He also had two garrons amongst his cattle. They would carry the gear to the cave on Braemore, but not up the face of its daunting precipice. To get the ponies up there, they must go the long road east-about, down to the mouth of the corrie and up its lofty eastern flank to cross the col between Braemore and its next neighbour; or else west-about, round another mountain and over a ridge into Glen Eidart itself, and then up the long, long ascent that they had made during the night. Alastair was anxious to visit Glen Eidart, naturally, to sound out opinion there, to see his own house again, and to lay hands on certain of his belongings —a change out of his spectacular regimentals, for instance,

was overdue, scarlet being a somewhat conspicuous garb for
what they envisaged—but he did not wish to give away the
secret of their hiding-place at this stage, and inevitably after
their appearance in the glen their progress to its head and on
up the wide skirts of Braemore would not pass unremarked.
Rory Mor would guess that they were in the Eidart district
somewhere, but it was inadvisable that he should learn details.

So they went eastwards, climbing into high unoccupied
country, discussing possibilities and projects as they went.
Everywhere the clouds were lifting and breaking up now.
Rory Mor was having the Devil's luck, with a dry late autumn,
for all his burning.

That thought was emphasised and underlined presently,
when around noon the little party reached the high *bealach*
between Carn Ban and Braemore, and the view to the south-
west suddenly opened wide before them. Dark smoke was
rising over a long but narrow front ahead of them, and at no
very great distance. That it marked the line of Glen Udalain
demanded little debate. Rory Mor, quite evidently, was not
one for delay either. Once in the glen, it seemed, he had
remained there.

Marsala was thrown into a fever of agitation. Strategic
planning and coherent tactics were promptly forgotten in the
clamant call to do something for her people in their dire need
—and right away. Alastair, on whom the sight of the smoke
now worked like a corrosive, was not the man to deny her—
though he did point out, less than vigorously, that they must
take the long view, must fight the estate's superior numbers
and resources with craft, not in open conflict where all was
against them, must use guile, surprise, terrain and darkness as
their allies, rather than mere righteous wrath. All of which
Hector supported. Nevertheless, they agreed that they should
make for Glen Udalain at once, after depositing their supplies
at the cave.

The gear disposed of, and the other two garrons collected,
they set off in a south-westerly direction at their ponies' best
speed, keeping to the high ground. They had five miles at least
to cover before they reached the other glen. They were not
more than half-way there before the sun was blotted out for
them beyond the towering pall of smoke.

"The newer smoke is rising from further away," Alastair pointed out. "That means that they started burning at the top end of the glen, again. Working against the wind, as before."

"We can approach them under cover of the smoke, then?" the girl suggested.

"Aye, but to what purpose? Rory has thirty or forty men, armed. We have one old fowling-piece between three! Better, I think if we work down to the foot of the glen, and try to arouse resistance in those not yet burned out."

That was agreed.

Bearing well to the south, they made a curving approach to Udalain's ravished valley, intending to slip down into it some-where near its mouth. The smoke was arising already from almost half-way down the glen's length, though of course there were more crofts in the lower half than in the upper. But they had underestimated Rory Mor. As they drew near to the rim of the glen, Hector spotted a mounted figure on a hillock at the very lip of the declivity. Even as they paused, this sentinel fired a shot into the air, and began to wave, presumably to others below.

"*Dia*, they have set a watch! They are not going to be caught a second time!" Alastair said. "This is bad."

"If there is the one watcher, likely there will be more," Hector pointed out.

"Yes. And now they will be looking for us."

"If they are trying to repel us, or catch us, at least they will burn the fewer crofts," Marsala declared.

The men looked doubtful at that.

They moved on, parallel with the glen and perhaps a mile from it. And along the edge of it, the sentinel moved with them. Presently they saw that he had been joined by another.

"There is no profit in this," Alastair said, at length. "They can keep us in sight, and we cannot get down into the glen without a fight—a fight which we could not hope to win."

"If we were to divide? To separate, and each try alone . . .?" the girl suggested.

"And only one with a gun!" The man shook his head. "We must do better than that." His eyes searched the land around them. The ground slanted slowly down, through rolling, heather moorland broken by peat-hags and burn-channels, to the east, the other side from Glen Udalain. He nodded in that direction. "If we were to ride away, over there, and out of sight, they might think that we had gone. Given up. Then we could creep back, on foot, using the burns and peat-bogs to hide us, and slip down into the glen unseen."

"That would take time, a long time," the young woman objected. "Meanwhile, my people's houses are burning."

"Can you think of anything else that we may do? More swiftly?"

Biting her lip, she shook her head. "Not unless we just ride straight for the glen. Before they can gather more to stop us. There are many places where we can get down from this side. We . . . we might get through."

"They would be waiting for us at the bottom, as well as at the top," Hector reminded. "Many of them, I've no doubt."

"And if we did not get through—as I fear we should not—that is the end of resistance in Strathdonan!" Alastair pointed out. "No, that would be folly."

They turned their garrons' heads and rode away openly, eastwards across the shelving moor.

Though every pace of their solid mounts was as salt in a wound, they kept on, not only until they were out of sight of sentinels on the rim of the glen, but further still, to cross another small rise beyond, where watchers might expect to see them reappear. Also they did not hurry their beasts noticeably, so that the impression of defeat should be maintained. It was a silent ride. Only their eyes were busy.

At last they could halt, hidden. Alastair pointed.

"That burn over there. I have been watching it. In its channel we could get most of the way back. I think that there is only one place where it shallows away over bare rock, near the top . . ."

It was the best part of an hour later, however, before they were at that shallowing place, after an exhausting, clambering, leaping progress up the course of a splashing stream, frequently, for want of other foothold, in the bed of the stream itself. There was no room for ponies here, so they had left them tethered in a hollow. They had not dawdled, either. Alastair had set a swift unflagging pace, which he did not find it necessary to slacken on account of either of his companions

—after twice offering a hand to the girl and finding it unwanted; nevertheless, because of the innumerable times that
they had to cross the burn, and the difficult slippery nature
of the footwork, their progress was less than rapid, and the
way back seemed long, long. At least, thus far, they had not
had to stoop much to remain hidden.

Just before the burn shallowed to an apron over bare rock,
they made use of a billowing heather wave to leave it and work
along into an area of broken peat-hags and hummocks, black
and water-logged. Now it became a matter of darting and
crouching, dodging and crawling, from hollow to heather-
clump, from hummock to peat cornice, a doubled-up, breathless, mud-splattering business that undoubtedly Marsala found
even more exhausting and objectionable than did the men,
made the way she was. Still she voiced no complaint, however
red in the face she became.

They were now back to within a quarter of a mile of the edge
of the glen. They could see no sign of watchers, but that was
not to say that such were not lying up somewhere, waiting.
Only the ordinary irregularities of the open hillside lay before
them. The smoke rose billowing ahead, but because of a brisk
south-westerly breeze, it streamed up the trough of the valley
itself and did not blanket the flanking ground. They could
have done with some of its obscurity now.

"Nothing for it but to creep our way as best we may,"
Alastair said. "What about the glen? Can we get down here-
abouts somewhere?"

"Almost anywhere here," Marsala panted. "Steep. Too
steep for garrons. But possible on foot."

That last stretch was the worst, entailing much tacking this
way and that to gain advantage of even the faintest folds and
hollows of the ground, much hands-and-knees crawling—and
all the time the fear that they might be under observation, and
by men with guns. Hector MacBride still carried or dragged
his old fowling-piece, and less than a help he found it.

At length, however, all three were at the broken lip of the
glen. And no alarm had sounded. Below them the smoke
poured and eddied. For only a short distance downhill would
there be any danger of their being spotted; thereafter the pall
would hide them. Alastair frowned.

"Better if we had just entered the glen at the head of it, at the beginning," he said, "and worked down it under cover of this smoke. We would have saved a deal of time."

"We could not know that they would have watchers posted up here," the girl pointed out.

"I should have thought of it. I blame myself."

They hurried on and down, amongst rock buttresses and crags and boulders, which provided good cover, if dangerous going. It was with relief that they entered the smoke belt, however unhappy its significance.

Safe under the streaming shroud, they changed direction, to move diagonally along the glen-side, down-river. The factor's men were working fast, most evidently, and their burnings had progressed substantially. It was necessary to get in front of them, and it would be best done well above the scene of their activities.

Presently the smoke began to thin ahead of them, as they drew level with the advance of the evictors. This corresponded with the central widening of the valley, wherein was a larger scattering of crofts and cot-houses grouped around the House of Udalain. Already the factor's men were at work on some of these crofts, with ragged groups standing forlornly around or streaming away from them. Rory Mor's minions seemed to work in teams of four or five, with reserve parties to deal with difficulties, and others to round up the livestock. It was a scene of great and efficient activity on the one hand, achieved out of much practice, and of complete disorder and helplessness on the other, born out of misery and despair. Savagely Alastair remarked on this, as they stared. Hector MacBride began to curse, with a slow and solemn deliberation.

Strangely, the girl was silent. When Alastair turned to her, it was to find her glance concentrated elsewhere. She was looking further ahead, in fact, where the incendiaries had not yet reached. And there, beyond the faded gold of the birches and the dark of the pines, rose the gables of her own home. Whitewashed those gables had been, previously, but now they were blacker than the pines. There was no roof to the house, any more, no glass to the windows, no sign of life or movement about it—save only for the thin, curling wisps of blue-black smoke that still rose from the charred interior.

"My God!" Alastair exclaimed. "This . . . this too! I . . . I . . . Marsala, I am sorry, lass. Desperately sorry."

"Lord in His heaven, they are burning tacksmen's houses now!" Hector cried. "*Dia*, I did not think that Rory Mor would do that!"

"It is as a punishment, rather than an eviction, I should think," the younger man said. "A punishment, and a warning." He looked at the girl. "I fear, Marsala, that this is aimed at *me*. That I have brought it on you. Your home . . ."

She had to moisten her lips before she spoke. "If . . . if it is the price of resistance, I brought it on myself. Before ever I knew that you were here." She spoke levelly.

"Yes. But I think that he might not have gone so far. You sheltered me there . . ."

She interrupted him suddenly fierce. "And why should *I* complain? So far, you say! He has gone no farther than he has gone with the others, with my people! Why should I escape? But . . . but Mother . . .!"

"She will be safe, I am sure," Alastair declared. "It would serve Rory Mor nothing to cause her injury. She is a cousin of Clanrory's own, is she not?"

"He burned her roof over her! This was done before the others. See, there is scarcely smoke now. Last night, no doubt. A sick woman, in the night! I should not have left her . . ."

The men said nothing.

Their companion drew herself up. "It is too late for regrets," she said. "Too late. Shall we go on?"

Without the smoke to hide them they had to go warily again, working along the steep hillside. Fortunately there were many rock-falls and spines of granite and dry washes to hide them. Moreover, the folk below were much preoccupied in their own activities, and it was unlikely that any sentinels above would look for trouble down here.

Well past the area of the House and its amphitheatre, they slanted down to the floor of the glen. They could walk about openly here meantime, Alastair's kilt being the only item that might distinguish them, at a distance, from other folk.

A straggling party was coming trudging down the track by the riverside, the same track on which Alastair had spied the raiders the previous night. It represented the families from two crofts higher up the glen, a sad company of two elderly men, three women, one of them young, and five children, laden with sundry belongings, bedding, clothing, foodstuffs, cooking utensils, trussed poultry, and the like. The oldest woman was weeping, one of the men helping her along, and the younger woman carried a bawling baby.

Any thought of urging this pathetic group to halt, turn back, and engage in some sort of resistance to the ruthless forces behind, died in the breasts of the newcomers. It just was not to be considered, even though the younger woman had been one of Marsala's band of two days before. Something of the Reverend Angus' point of view was borne in on them, watching. These folk were in trouble enough. They were in no state to initiate a rebellion.

Marsala did speak to them, pitifully, and drew little reaction, barely recognition. She asked about her mother, but these, from the upper glen, knew of nothing save their own tragedy. They passed on. They were making for Ardglass, they said.

There was a croft just a little further downstream. Alastair made for this. Three people, a man, wife, and daughter, were busy here, pulling plenishings out from the house, bundling up possessions and victuals, and tying gear on to a garron, while near by an ancient, toothless dame cackled in lunatic merriment at it all. Once again Alastair's courage failed him. These people, striving desperately to rescue some few humble fragments of a shattered life, could not be asked to desist, to leave all and start a hopeless struggle against their armed oppressors. Marsala talked with them, but haltingly, without conviction. In their agitation obviously they barely knew what she said. She did learn from the man, however, that the Lady Glenudalain had been carried off in the night to Rory Mor's own house of Camusewan.

They were still discussing the import of this information when they came to a small farmery where two strapping sisters of early middle age were actively preparing for evacuation. They had been prominent supporters of Marsala's intransigence before, so that they were approached more hopefully. But though they were loud in their wrath and bitterness

against Clanrory and his factor, and agreed that this wickedness must be fought and resisted still, they did not see that
there was anything that they could do about it. Not now, at
any rate. They had other things to do, just now—to save what
could be saved from the wreck. They intended to be away
from their holding before the devil-damned despoilers arrived,
with as much of their chattels as they could load on to two
garrons. And two cows, as well. They would fire their own
roof, since they themselves had thatched it. That was plenty
for them to be doing, just now.

Reluctantly the others bowed to the inevitable. It was not
in them to say that the sisters were wrong. Helping them to
empty their cot-house and tie their goods on to the ponies,
Alastair conceded that possibly this was not the moment
either to foster successful revolt or to help materially the
unhappy clansfolk. All that they could do, it seemed, would be
to move amongst them, assuring them of sympathy and a
determination that Rory Mor and his like should not go un-
punished, and by their presence reveal that not all of the clan's
natural leaders had betrayed them. The others did not con-
tradict him.

So these things they did as the short November afternoon
drew towards dusk, and shadow filled all the trough of that
unhappy valley, and the shadows themselves, like the advancing smoke-clouds, became tinged with red. They spoke with
many, gave what little aid they could, sought to encourage if
not cheer, and always to sow the seeds of reprisal and opposition. And finally, down at the mouth of the glen, they did
rather more than that.

Where the Udalain River flowed into Loch Donan, a narrow
hump-backed stone bridge carried the roadway across. Over
this all the refugees must go. And in the centre of it, a picket
of four of the factor's men, armed with muskets and clubs,
held up all at gun-point, and impounded all garrons or other
livestock that had been brought thus far—and taking whatever
else might seize their fancy, including the inevitable liberties
with the women. It was a masterly final touch, typical of
Rory Mor.

Alastair's party, moving down with others, and with the
sisters Anna and Morag MacIver not far behind, paused. Only

a glance was required, on rounding the last bend of the glen, to reveal the situation.

"Ha, it only required this!" Alastair grated, through clenched teeth. Eyes busy, he scanned the terrain. "I think," he said, "I think that I shall have occasion to feel better, hereafter!" He turned to Marsala. "Come. Quickly. Back to those two sisters with you. Tell them to delay approaching the bridge. To hold back, but in sight. Others too. I want a few minutes when there is no one on the bridge, save these. You understand? You stay with them. Put a plaid over your head and shoulders, to hide you. You have it?"

She nodded, unspeaking.

He jerked his head at the older man. "Down to the river with us, Hector. And your gun with you."

After the first few yards, their scramble down into the rocky gorge that the Udalain River had cut for itself was out of sight of the bridge. The peat-brown, foaming water here formed a series of pools and cascades, and though it averaged some twenty feet in width it was not difficult for agile men to splash across, leaping from ledged shallows to boulders. Beyond, the steep bank was wooded with birch and hazel. Into the cover of this they clambered, Hector as spry as the younger man.

They hurried along through the trees. Soon they were near the bridge. A bold bluff projected here, narrowing the gorge considerably—the cause of the bridge's site. Round the back of this the men worked their way, to climb up and creep to the wooded summit.

They were some thirty feet above the bridge-end, and perhaps three times that in distance. The four guards were amusedly busy, detaching a led calf and some leg-tied poultry from their protesting owners, less than gently. Beyond that there were no other refugees near, until the sizable party that included the MacIver sisters and Marsala, clearly holding back.

"How fast can you reload this piece of yours?" Alastair panted, in the other man's ear.

"Fast enough, if I have all ready beside me."

"Good. Then here is the way of it. Give me time to get down to yonder big rock. I can throw a dirk from there, and can make sure that they do not hide behind the parapet of the bridge. When I am there, and the bridge is clear, fire you a shot above their heads. Then reload fast, whatever they do. I shall do the talking."

"Aye, then. And the second shot?"

"It may not be needed. You will decide for yourself whether to shoot—and where!"

Slipping back over the crest of the bluff, Alastair climbed down and round. There was no difficulty in it, the trees and the rocks hiding him. He gained the large boulder that he had indicated, a few yards on the Camusewan side of the bridge-end just as the bereft family came by. Crouching behind it he let them pass.

Looking upwards, he could just distinguish Hector's head, grey amongst the russet of fading bracken. He raised one finger.

Almost immediately the crash of the discharge blasted out.

In the stunned silence thereafter, Alastair leapt out into the roadway, right hand raised, his gleaming *sgian dubh* gripped therein, facing the men on the bridge.

"Drop those muskets!" he barked, in the English. "At once! And the stick. Quickly, now!" And to reinforce his command, the little dagger went spinning evilly through the air, to bite deeply into the wood of a hurdle that was being used to close the bridge. It quivered there, between two of the men. In almost the same movement, the thrower reached down to whip out the dirk from his belt; the other had been only the smaller weapon from his hose-top.

The four men facing him were too shocked by surprise to act swiftly, either obediently or otherwise. All had crouched down instinctively at the explosion and the whistle of shot above their heads. Now they could only stare from the kilted apparition at the bridge-end to the shivering *sgian dubh*, and back again, helplessly. Two wearing arm-bands, and presumably constables or Sheriff-officers, carried muskets, though one had been in process of propping his against the bridge parapet. The two others had only cudgels, but one of these had laid his aside and was dragging away the calf and an armful of poultry at the other side of the bridge.

"I said drop them!" Alastair shouted, advancing, dirk

shaking threateningly. "Or do you prefer a salvo, and fired low this time?"

One musket and the club clattered to the roadway. The calf-leader halted, dropping his tied fowl. But the fourth man flung himself forward and down, to get himself below the stone parapet of the bridge, where he would be safe from shot fired from that side.

Quick as thought Alastair threw, aiming his dirk at the stonework just a foot in front of the fellow's face. Sparks flew as the steel hit the masonry of the parapet. The crouching man leapt backwards and up, saving himself only by an instant. And immediately thereafter Hector's gun crashed out a second time. All the men on the bridge threw themselves flat, and the disputed musket was hurled urgently beyond its owner's reach.

"Very well, so!" Alastair commented, striding forward to pick up the weapon. "Wise men. Stay you where you are, all of you." Turning to the bluff, he raised his voice, still speaking in the English. "Come down, Hector. Just your own self. The rest wait where they are, keeping the bridge covered." Then he waved forward the waiting crofters from along the road.

That was all there was to it. With lengths of grass-rope from the abandoned garrons and their loads, they bound those four men hand and foot, and tied them to their own gate and then to the side of the bridge, where they would be objects of interest to all who passed that way. They gagged them too, so that better folk's ears should not be deeved with them. Then, telling the MacIver sisters, and the others, to drive the impounded beasts along before them, for their owners eventually to reclaim, and assuring all that this was but a start on the business, they took the picket's own garrons, their muskets, ball, and all else that might be useful, and set off to ride eastwards again. They were well aware that the sound of those shots might produce investigation.

Undoubtedly some of those crofters watched them go with a new light in their eyes.

They had not gone far when, above the clop-clop of their mounts' hooves, they heard a voice behind them, shouting. It was a boy, a youth of about sixteen, running after them. He had one of the guard's cudgels in his hand.

"I have come to be with you, Gleneidart," he panted. "I am for fighting. You have another garron there. Let me come with you."

"Ian Beg, Altdurie," Marsala told them. "A good lad. Does your father know that you have come after us, Iannie?"

"Och, yes. He was telling me that I could come. He said that he would have come his own self, if he had not had the old ones to see to."

The young woman looked at Alastair, questioningly.

That man looked the lad over, sternly. "I think that I know your brother, Ian Beg," he said. "Tell me, can you walk thirty heather miles, and then ten more? Can you live without food for days together? Can you see in the dark, and shoot with a musket, Ian Beg?"

"Och, yes," the boy answered stoutly.

Alastair smiled. "Very well—and so you shall, too! Come, you."

Chapter Eleven

SOME six hours later, four riders drew their eight horses to a halt on the dark hillside high above Camusewan. Below them the land crouched black, but the loch held some wan luminosity of its own, and against this the jagged fang that was the ruined Castle Rory stood out as though etched. A single light gleamed yellow down there.

"Rory Mor sits late," Alastair commented. "Too much to hope that his conscience does not let him sleep! Nor yet that he worries overmuch at *our* activities."

"That may be my mother's light," Marsala faltered. "Perhaps it is who cannot sleep, in that house. Why has he taken her there?"

"He will have his reasons, that one. Perhaps to try to use her as a hostage for your good behaviour, to worry you. Or perhaps only because she is Clanrory's full cousin. Either way, he will not harm her, you may be sure!"

They waited for nearly an hour for that light to be extinguished, Alastair going over his plan of action and the lay-out of the factor's establishment below. The stakes were too high to risk blunders here.

Leaving the garrons tethered in a hollow, they headed down-hill. Presently they could make out the pale glimmer of the whitewashed buildings before them.

They scented the cattle smell before ever they were down to the level ground. Soon, with it, they could hear the stir of restless beasts. That almost certainly meant that the im-pounded Udalain stock was penned here, at Camusewan. So much the better, except that cattle pounds were apt to mean armed guards.

Alastair left the others, to make a quick reconnaissance. One of the infields was being used as pound. He remembered its position well enough to make a circuit of it. He discovered that its gate was at the side nearest to the house, and that there two men crouched, dozing—or at least motionless and silent. He could see no others.

Back with his companions, he told them to follow him. Skirting the cattle, they approached the vicinity of the farm-house, its cottages and appendages.

Hounds were their prime anxiety—or worse, sheep-dogs; though, with so many strangers around the place, Sheriff's men, constables and Cousins' people from Inverdruin, it was likely that little attention would be paid to barking dogs. They kept as far from the cottages as they might, however.

At the corner of the yard of the house itself, they crouched down. They had brought torches made of resinous bog-pine, and ample tinder in the shape of chips and splinters of the same. They had for targets the two wool stores, the grain shed, and the estate office. Alastair was reserving the last for himself.

There was little need to repeat instructions. All knew their tasks. One point only remained to be stressed. "We all must act together. At the one time," Alastair reminded. "The moment that the first flame leaps high enough to be seen by the cattle-guards, we must be ready to be off. I doubt not that it will bring them running. So that one fire must not start before the others. When I whistle twice, as the curlew whistles, light your fires. Not before. Small fires, close together. Then blow them into the one. I told you where to put them. Then, when you hear my whistle again, three calls, leave you at once and come back here. You remember, bring the torches back. Douse them, but bring them." He paused. "You are not afraid, Ian Beg?"

"No, Gleneidart."

"*I* am," Marsala said. "A little."

"How much? Enough to prevent you from lighting your fires, girl?"

"No," she said.

They separated then, each slipping away alone into the shadows. Alastair made straight across the cobbled yard to the converted stabling that now housed the estate office. The door was locked, but that he had anticipated. The point of his dirk around a window-frame soon enabled him to lift out a pane of glass. Getting himself inside, through the gap, was uncomfortable, with his damaged shoulder. Within, he strode over to the fireplace and pulled down the large map from the wall above, folding it up and stuffing it inside his doublet. Then he made one or two heaps of paper and ledgers from the desks, in strategic positions; there was little need for tinder in here, or torches either.

Back at the window he peered out. Nothing seemed to have been disturbed about the establishment. The others ought to have had long enough to prepare their fires, for it was unlikely that their outbuildings would be locked up. Facing inwards and downwards, to muffle somewhat the noise, he whistled the long yittering trill of the curlew, twice—and hoped that to any wakeful person it would not sound as though emanating from business premises.

He returned to his heaps of paper, with flint and steel. The office was lined with pitch-pine boarding, most suitably inflammable. Only a few seconds sufficed to get the fires going, and to see that the woodwork was catching. There was no need to blow or otherwise cherish the flames in here.

Struggling out through the window again, he gazed around him. A dog was barking now somewhere, indoors. One other source of fire was already apparent—Marsala's wool store at the end of the same range of outbuildings. The other wool store and the grain shed lay behind, in former barns. Hastening to the corner of the yard where he could see round, he perceived a flickering light coming from the former, but nothing to be seen from the latter. Hector, with the grain, probably had the most difficult task.

Alastair looked back at the farmhouse itself. Already the flames from within the office were beginning to reflect redly on the windows opposite. The place was blazing up almost too promptly. He could not risk waiting longer. Anyone sleeping at this side of the house surely would not be long in waking, for, apart from the light, the pine-boarding was beginning to make cracking noises. Also the unpleasant smell of burning, oily fleeces was growing very evident. He whistled again, three times, not muffling it this time, on account of extraneous sounds.

Marsala came running lightly, almost immediately, a smouldering torch still in her hand. Taking this from her, the man ground out the glowing embers lest any least glimmer in the darkness should reveal their presence. He sensed the girl's tenseness as she stood panting beside him, and gripped her arm for a moment.

Then Ian Beg came thudding round the corner of the building. "Och, my goodness, easy it was, just!" he gasped. "No trouble . . ."

"Quiet, you!" Alastair snapped. "Listen!"

There was shouting arising from the direction of the cattle pound.

"They have seen the glare of it. They will be here any moment, now," the man jerked. "*Dia*, where is Hector?"

A faint wavering light was showing from the grain shed now, outshone by the growing brightness around it.

They waited there, and the moments seemed to drag themselves out endlessly. Alastair thought he heard running feet above the shouting, and from the same direction. He bit his lip.

"Perhaps somebody has found him, caught him?" Marsala exclaimed.

"Shall I go for him?" the boy suggested.

"No. Wait. Keep close in, under this building. In the shadow. Look, there are lights going on in the house! If the hounds get out, they could scent us, find us. Here the guards come, from the cattle . . .!"

The pounding of boots came close. Both guards clearly had left the gateway of the infield, as it had been hoped that they would. Drawing close back against the wall, where the flames did not light them up, the three of them watched the men run by. They clattered on over the cobbles, voices upraised hoarsely.

Then suddenly Hector MacBride was beside the watchers. "Och, that was ill stuff to burn," he said, breathing deeply. "To get started. And I was after leaving the old gun behind. I had to go back for it . . ."

"Come. And quickly," Alastair interrupted him, and began to run back towards the cattle by a circuitous route, avoiding the vicinity of the cottages.

Reaching the infield, they hurried round its far flank until they came to the corner most distant from the buildings and nearest to the roadway up the strath. An ordinary dry-stone dyke enclosed the field. On the corner of this they set to work, pulling down the stones.

They did not worry overmuch about the noise that they made now. There was a sufficient and ever-increasing uproar coming from the purlieus of the factor's house to cover them, what with men shouting, dogs barking, and woodwork crackling. Flames were leaping high now from two of the fires, casting a lurid and eerie light on the oily, unpleasant smoke billowing from the burning wool. The cattle too were milling about, out of their instinctive fear of fire, and beginning to low loudly in alarm.

Soon a sufficient gap was torn in the wall for their purpose. Alastair and Marsala ran to one side, Hector and the boy to the other. Quite some distance they hurried back, round the field, towards the conflagration. Roughly half-way round they halted and clambered over the wall, Alastair aiding the girl. Down behind it they crouched, to strike flint to steel and light their bog-pine torches. Swiftly these flared up, the melting resin spitting and sparkling. Then, waving them around them and above their heads, they ran towards the dark mass of the huddled frightened cattle.

It did not take long to stampede that herd, already agitated and restless. Fire suddenly appearing so close at hand sent them off in plunging rearing panic. The torch-bearers sought

to converge so that there was a semicircle of flame driving the
herd towards the gap in the wall, and already the creatures had
tended to move as far away from the area of burning as they
might. It was obvious that the foremost animals had quickly
found the break in the stonework and were streaming out,
from the way in which the surging tide of beasts steadied its
direction at the same time as increasing its impetus. Packed
tight, jostling, over-riding each other, steaming, bellowing
their fright, the cattle rushed to get way from the fire, to get
out of that dire confinement, out into the open hills that were
their home. There might have been two hundred or more of
them, looted from the stricken crofts of Glen Udalain; they
were all out of Rory Mor's field and pounding up the roadway
towards their own glen in almost as brief a time as it takes to
tell. Swiftly, at any rate, they outdistanced their new herders,
and disappeared in thunderous, horn-clashing, loud-voiced
freedom into the night.

Hurriedly extinguishing their torches, the breathless incendiaries looked back. Though two of the fires were still the
most prominent, the central one—the estate office—most
vigorous of all, the other two now clearly could be seen. All
were growing, quite evidently, fanned by the night breeze
from the Atlantic.

"You managed then, Hector. Your fire burned," Alastair
panted. "Once started, the grain will not easily be put out."

"It seems wrong, wicked somehow, to have set light to all
that corn. Winter feed," Marsala faltered. "And good wool..."

"To destroy your enemy's strength is never wrong," the
soldier answered. And, more understandingly, "If it helps to
save more crofters' roofs from burning, that grain and wool
is well burnt, *mo charaidh*."

"Aye, then," Hector agreed. "But . . . we should not be
lingering here, see you. If those hound-dogs were to be after
us, before we get to the garrons . . ."

"I doubt if any men will follow," Alastair said. "All Rory's
people will have enough to do, for some time to come!" He
looked eastwards up the lochside, after the cattle. "Those
beasts . . .? Perhaps some of us should keep on after them, to
keep them moving, while the others go up the hill for the
horses and then follow on? We do not want the cattle to stop,

131

to slow down and remain where Rory can catch them again readily."

"Those ones will not stop until they are back in their own pastures in Udalain," the older man asserted. "On foot we should not see them again this night. But if we get back to the garrons now, and ride over the hills and into the glen part-way up, och, we can be picking up the beasts again and driving them right up to the head of the glen and out on to the high ground beyond. On our way home, just. Where Rory Mor will have to be a clever man to be collecting them again."

Alastair nodded. He was content to follow the drover's expert advice where cattle were concerned. Uphill the four of them climbed, then back to where they had left their ponies, their way made light for them by the beacons blazing below on that green promontory. They hoped that the reflection of those fires might lighten more than these dark hillsides.

Chapter Twelve

FROM the first paling of the dawn sky, when they arrived wearily back at their lofty refuge after dispersing those tired and bewildered cattle over the high watershed of heather plateau and peat-bog that encircled all the glens of Strathdonan, Alastair's party slept the sleep of the exhausted in the cave on Braemore until well past noon. This was longer than was intended, needless to say, at least as far as Alastair was concerned. He was possessed of a great urgency, the need for haste ever with him. He saw their campaign as a race against time, almost as much as a fight against evil and long odds. Ultimately the law and the state could bring forces to bear upon them, even in this remote country, which must preponderate and prevail—the man was well aware of this; their hope lay in forcing Rory Mor to hold his hand, to bargain, before his personal loss was too great, his credit hopelessly spent, and while the crofters might still conceive that there was hope. In this, time would work against them. But over and above that, the winter was drawing perilously close, when any sort of active campaigning, even any prolonged hiding-out in caves and mountains, was impracticable; though this western seaboard was on the whole a mild one, with snow and ice in the main confined to the high tops, nevertheless it was no country for living outdoors into December. That applied as much to the dispossessed down at Ardglass as to themselves. The issue would be settled, one way or another, before the real winter closed in. Concerning which, the thought of tightly-packed emigrant ships in even early winter crossings to the Canadas scarcely bore contemplation.

As though to emphasise this very matter of season and weather, they awoke to grey mists and driving thin rain, to chill and incipient despondency. But Alastair would have no resting, no sitting round a warm, bog-pine fire. He proclaimed the gospel of urgency and declared that the mists and rain would serve them nicely, shrouding their activities and keeping shepherds and others at their own firesides. For they themselves were going shepherding.

Rory Mor's flocks were for the time being deployed mainly over his father's lands of Camusewan and Letterblair, though presently, it seemed, they were to spread over the entire extent of Strathdonan. Camusewan territory reached inland and northwards from the township of that name for some five thousand acres, and still further to the north the even larger but less fertile tack of Letterblair extended towards the wild Mackenzie country. Camusewan itself must be the prime target meanwhile, then.

Wrapping plaids around them against the rain and chill, hunched on the broad swaying backs of their garrons, the four of them rode back again, south by west, keeping as ever to the high ground, the excited chatter of last night, behind the freed herds, replaced by monosyllabic gloom. No soul did they see, throughout that depressing ride. At least the rain had damped down the smoke of burned Glen Udalain on their left.

None of them, even Hector, had any real experience of herding sheep *en masse*, as distinct from cattle. They hoped, however, that the principle of the thing would be approximately similar, and perhaps even easier because of the acceptedly less independent character of the sheep. Though the idea of sheep-dogs was anathema to all of them, a symbol of all that they hated and feared, they recognised that they could well have done with the services of two or three of the creatures this day.

It was decided to work in pairs, and the terrain, well-known to them all, was plotted and worked out with great care, so that, as far as was possible, each trend and fold and burn-channel of the land would contribute to the gathering together and coalescing into one great herd of the sheep scattered wide-spread over many hillsides, mosses and hollows.

At the furthest point of their penetration, on the crest of the ridge above Camusewan farm-place itself, they turned, to split up. Below them mist and rain shrouded the green promontory, perhaps aided by still smouldering wool and grain.

Alastair and Marsala took the southernmost flank of the high pasture area, closest to the Udalain march. Keeping within hailing distance of each other, they began to comb the shelving braesides methodically, in a shuttling back-and-forward lateral movement, always working from high ground to low, their patient ponies picking their way unhurriedly, sure-footedly. Though no great numbers of sheep appeared at first sight to be occupying that hill, it was remarkable how quickly a sizable flock began to form. Out of all the depressions and crevices, the indentations and scars, from amongst the heather hummocks and the peat-hags of that slanting land-mass, the flouncing, baa-ing sheep emerged, to stream away downhill. Cattle were never so obliging.

Probably they by no means cleared every sheep from the hill, but that was not important. Certainly they moved the vast majority.

When the pair of them were finished, and they came down into the floor of that immediate valley, a damp place of reeds and mosses, it was to find a seething mass of sheep, with Hector and Ian Beg already there, and seeking, by riding round and round the protesting concourse, to keep it from dispersing. They had been equally successful at clearing their area to the north, it appeared.

"Och, I am beginning to see something in these brutes,

Alastair man," the drover admitted. "Mind you, they foul the ground and stink to heaven—but, my goodness, they are amenable, just! They go where they're told."

"Like the folk they are replacing!" the younger man said, grimly. "Clanrory's new clansmen!"

The water from this valley flowed down to the sea-coast not far from the Ardglass area, which was opposite to the direction that they wished to take. Alastair and the girl, therefore, now started to herd the combined flock *up* the valley while the other two set off over the ground that they had lately cleared, to surmount the far summit and so work the next dip to the north of that great ridge-and-valley system, driving the results up eventually to meet the others on the watershed.

That process was carried out, and repeated once more. The herd grew hearteningly. By nightfall all three main sections of the terrain had been cleared, and that was most of Camusewan. How many sheep they had collected was not clear, the guesses varying from three to five hundred. It was no mean flock, at all events, Cheviots and Swaledales, and becoming something of a handful to control.

To collect more obviously would serve no useful purpose. The success of their plans, problematical enough in all conscience already, would only be the more gravely hazarded. Anyway, the gloomy dark of a wet November dusk was less than helpful for the gathering. It was enough.

They turned to face the north-east again, all four of them— towards Glen Eidart. But that was not their destination, yet awhile. Indeed, Alastair and the young woman did not even continue long in that direction, only for long enough to see the other two out of dangerous territory with their loud-voiced charges, over into the head of an east-going glen that would eventually bring them down to the main cross-Scotland drove road, from Skye and the West to the markets of Dingwall. Somewhere along that drove road, sooner or later, they would come across an encampment of broken men, of tinkers-cum-drovers-cum-whisky smugglers, relics of the small clans that had died at Culloden and afterwards—all of whom were apt to be friends and sometimes assistants of Hector MacBride. To these the sheep would be passed on, with instructions that they should be looked after, in some inaccessible no-man's-land, until further notice, when no finicky and highly-exact count of numbers would be insisted upon. Hector and Ian would then return to the cave on Braemore.

Meanwhile the other two had their own tasks to attempt.

They parted at the dim head of Glen Array, and Alastair and Marsala turned back, whence they had just come, with the thin rain once more in their faces. It was surprising how quickly the baa-ing complaint of sheep faded into the night.

*   *   *

They had ridden, heads down and in silence, for quite some time through the damp and dismal dark, and the man had drawn more than one quick breath, glanced sidelong at his companion, and held his peace, before at last he spoke abruptly—and more militarily than he knew, in consequence of the delay.

"Marsala," he jerked, "there is a matter which demands our attention. A matter of importance. It is time that we spoke of it. I am referring to your reputation and good name."

Swiftly she looked at him. "Well?" she said, after a moment. "What of it?"

He gazed firmly ahead. "It is—it must be—in danger. In the circumstances."

"In danger of what? You mean, because of my actions? My opposition to the estate and the law?" She knew very well that he did not mean that.

"No. Because of me. Of your association with my own self. Bad enough it would be, before—after you took me to your house, But now . . . now that we are fighting back, drawing the attention of all to our position, it will be worse. Much worse."

"My association . . . with a proclaimed deserter, is it? With an enemy of the authorities? Unsuitable in a woman? Is that it?"

He frowned. He had not thought that she would be so stupid. She was young, of course—innocent and inexperienced. "Not that. It is just . . . that I am a man. That you are keeping the company of a man, alone. Day and night. In lonely places. It will not go unmentioned, you may be sure. Tongues will be busy with our names. We wish to make them so, in the one

136

way; they will be in the other. And I would not have yours to suffer."

"If talk will do that, then we cannot alter it, I fear—since we cannot bridle people's tongues."

"I think that we can," he said.

She waited.

He drew one of his quick breaths. "We could marry," he said. "Still the tongues that way."

It was the young woman's turn to draw swift breath, to gasp indeed. In the mirk she peered at him. "*Marry*, you said? You . . . you are not serious?"

"I am, yes." Alastair cleared his throat. "But never fear. Not . . . not *real* marriage."

Now he had her confounded indeed. Almost she choked. "This . . . this is . . . I did not think . . . are you beside yourself?" she demanded.

"I do not think so. Far from it, at all. A handfast marriage would solve our problem, see you. That problem, at the least."

"Handfast!" she repeated, in a different tone. "You mean . . .?"

"I mean the old handfast marriage of our people. Marriage for a year and a day. It was a common enough custom, once. Do not think that I would ever seek to impose myself on you, Marsala—a comparative stranger, a man so much older, and with little to offer you. I am not a fool—or, I hope, a knave. I have been thinking of this a great deal this last day or so. It is the best thing for you, I believe."

"Indeed." That was curiously intoned.

"Yes. It will be a formality, just. You will be free entirely, as you are now. You know the terms of a handfast marriage, of course?" He wrapped a lock of his garron's long mane round and round his finger. "If no child is conceived within a year and a day, the marriage is null, unmade, as though it had never been. And . . . and since such could not happen in a marriage of name only, a year and a day later you would be as free in name as in fact."

"I see," she said.

He looked at her now, wondering. He had been prepared for various reactions, but hardly for this level, impersonal quiet, almost disinterest. "You . . . you understand, Marsala?" he asked.

"Oh, yes. Certainly."

"We could ask Angus Crubach to do it for us, I thought. He would understand."

"You mean . . . soon?" That was slightly less even.

"Why not? The sooner the better, surely? That all may know. That is all the point of it. For your name's sake."

"My name has become powerfully important, of a sudden, has it not?" she asked. "I had not known that it meant so much!"

"To me, at the least, it does," the man declared, with simple gallantry.

She actually laughed, then, though it was short and not very mirthful. She pulled in her mount a little, also, so that it was no longer side by side with the other. The man looked round at her, brows furrowed. He hesitated, and then pressed his own beast onward again. A woman was entitled to her privacy on such an occasion, he recognised.

In silence they rode on and downwards, towards the sea.

They took their way through the same valley on Camusewan, eventually, in which they had gathered the first flock of sheep. It brought them, in due course, to the coast about a mile south of the Ardglass peninsula. The cot-houses of two or three salmon fishermen clustered here, facing the Sound.

They left the horses tethered amongst hazels at the mouth of the valley, and slipped down to the shore, circling well clear of the houses. No lights showed. Passing the nets, festooned on posts, and the piles of lobster-pots, they came to a rough jetty beside which four boats were drawn up on the shingle, above high-water mark. The smallest of these they proceeded to push down to the water's edge, finding it a heavy task, for the tide was barely half in. The oars were lying inboard. No sound nor move came from the cottages.

Alastair was only able to pull one oar, on account of his injured shoulder, but the girl had previously insisted that she was quite capable of wielding the other. After their former experiences with the guards around Ardglass, clearly any landward approach was almost bound to be perceived and contested, and in the circumstances secrecy was very advisable.

Little more than a mile's rowing should not tax them too greatly.

With the south-westerly breeze in their favour, and after only a little initial awkwardness, they pulled together fairly effectively, the man using one hand, Marsala two—and even if their progress was slightly crabwise, that was of no matter. The sea was jabbly, without being rough, the motion of the small coble-shaped boat lively.

Even in the darkness no navigational feats were required of them, for the sound of the seething tide and its white lacework around the rocky border of the peninsula drew them on, the latter glowing dimly.

The jetty-breakwater at the point itself was readily found, and though its stones were gapped and broken, mooring thereto presented no problem.

It was hardly to be expected that they should have found the situation at Ardglass to be improved; the influx of the Glen Udalain refugees must only have added to the chaos. Their hope had been, however, that their campaign against Rory Mor at least would have raised the general spirits of the dispossessed and imbued them with some hope, some urge to strike a blow or two of their own. At first sight this did not appear to be the case—though admittedly it was difficult to be sure, with practically everyone huddled within their plaids or lying beneath contrived shelters, asleep or at least endeavouring to keep out the rain and cold as best they might. In the circumstances, appearances might have been deceptive.

Angus of the Limp and Duncan the Catechist they found, as before, in the largest of the caves, now crowded to capacity. They heard the patriarch's psalm-singing before ever they reached the place. He had a notably true and clear tenor voice, if thin, and sang with a feeling and pathos that was entirely moving, losing nothing from the faint quaver of age.

The Reverend Angus greeted them courteously, but with restraint. Very obviously he was still not in accord with what they were doing. Nor was the Catechist, even more certainly.

"All they that take the sword shall perish with the sword!" he declared, pointing an accusing finger at Alastair. "So said our Saviour." That was his greeting to them.

The younger man frowned, and then shrugged his one

shoulder. "I shall be content if it is *my* sword on which Rory Mor perishes, since he it was first drew it!" he answered.

"Scoffer! Man of blood, why did you return to plague us? In our time of need and heaviness of heart?"

"*Me* plague you? *Dia*, I think that you have your plagues something mixed, my friend! My efforts have been to plague your enemy—and my own—not you. And with some little success, perhaps."

"Spare us your successes, then, Gleneidart, for they bear but the more heavily on us!"

Alastair began to speak, hotly, but the minister interrupted him. "Rory Mor has been here again, Alastair," he said. "This burning at Camusewan, he blames it upon us all here. Your work it is, but these poor people are to pay for it. Pay dearly. Under Riot Act conditions and with the Sheriff's backing, he can do anything, it seems. Some of our men, six of them, have been arrested already. They are to be taken to Dingwall tomorrow. To prison. Charged with this thing. With complicity, the Sheriff called it—complicity in your crime, Alastair. Our protests availed nothing, like our pleas. They are gone."

Alastair looked from the older men to Marsala. "So that is how Rory fights his battles! With hostages—innocent folk! *Dia*, I might have guessed it!"

"You might indeed! Would that you had, Cousin. But that is not all. Such property as remains to us is to be confiscated, to pay for the damage of your burnings. Not only the cattle and garrons. He is without pity or mercy. We can do nothing against such ruthlessness."

Alastair began to speak, but Marsala's voice overbore his. Eagerly she spoke. "But we can! Indeed already we have done so. Done something. We have something to bargain for your property, now. Sheep. We have four hundred of Rory's Mor's precious sheep, taken off the hill, and on their way to safe pastures this moment! He shall not have them back until he restores what he may take from our people!"

"Sheep! Four hundred sheep!" Angus Crubach repeated, incredulously. "You have just . . . just taken them?"

"Yes. Today. They are in Glen Array now, on their way . . ."

"But, just to *take* them . . .!"

"To *steal* them!" the patriarch corrected him sternly. "To take others' property, even sheep, without the owner's knowledge, is theft, just. Stealing."

"Call it stealing if you like, Duncan Ceistear," the girl returned, spiritedly. "I care not. But Rory Mor has sold his soul for sheep, and now we have them! He will do a lot for sheep, it seems. He can have them back, then—at a price!"

"This is sin!" the old man cried. "The Devil's work. Evil for evil. You will not win our salvation that way, in this world or the next. I could have expected the like from Gleneidart, a man of violence. But you—are you without shame, woman? First to lead your women into unseemly disobedience against their husbands. Then to go off in open, wanton scandal with this man, alone, in flagrant immodesty. And now, this!"

"Old man, I do not like your words!" Alastair intervened, quietly but tensely. "They do not become you, as a man of God. You will take them back, if you please!"

"I shall not, then! The truth shall not be muzzled, for you Gleneidart, or for any man. Or woman. Sin shall be proclaimed as sin . . ."

"But lies shall not be proclaimed as truth! And you lie about Marsala of Glenudalain, old man. What you impute to me, I care not, but of her you shall speak only the truth."

"But he is right, Alastair. Duncan is right," Angus declared sadly. "Two blacks do not make white. Sin is sin, whatever the object. Marsala has been foolish, I think, and headstrong; but it is not herself that is to blame so much as you. You have led her astray, I fear—you, a man of the world. You have taken advantage of her inexperience . . ."

"That he has *not* done," the girl put in, evenly. "What I have done, I have done out of my own will. And would do the same again."

"Shameless, as I said!" the Catechist deplored.

"That is not the issue, my dear. Whether you went willingly or not, he *took* you. Which he should not have done, at all. A man of honour would not have allowed . . ."

"You talk of honour, in this!" she interrupted the minister, more warmly. "Honour, truth, sin, seemliness, these you talk of and debate, while Strathdonan burns! What is wrong with you, all of you, that you can only talk and sigh and shake your heads, when action is needed? Why cannot you act like men, as Alastair has acted? The only man left amongst the Mac-Rory's, I think!"

"Rash headstrong action that has resulted in more suffering and pain! No, in such times as these, Marsala, it is more important to cling to the verities, to the essential truths and virtues, than in any other . . ."

"What did the verities, the essential truths, do for me when my home was burned and evil men would have laid hands on me?" she demanded. "Where should I have turned then but to a man who would *do* something, act, find me shelter and safety if naught else?"

"You could have come here, *mo charaidh*, with the others."

"Here! To keen and weep and . . . and pray! You little know me then, though you christened and taught me, Angus Crubach!"

"Sorry I am, Marsala, if that is so," the other sighed. "For there is little that I would not do for you, child, in your need. Or at any time."

"There is something that you can do for her, now," Alastair said, almost harshly. "For me, also. You can marry us, Angus *a graidh*."

*   *   *

Intently the minister peered at his cousin in that suddenly hushed cave. "Did I hear you aright, man?" he wondered, at last. "You did say 'marry', Alastair?"

"That is what I said, yes. Will you marry us? Now."

"But . . . but are you sure? This is no jest, no whim?"

"No whim," Alastair agreed. "Something that requires to be done, it is."

"Indeed! That is . . . that sounds . . ." The minister hesitated. "I counsel thought, for all that, Alastair. This is a serious matter. A marriage, that will last a lifetime, is scarcely a thing to be hurried into, thus."

"This marriage will not last a lifetime. Only twelve months and a day! It is a handfast marriage that we want."

"Handfast! Alastair, you are never serious? This is folly. Handfast unions are no longer, no longer . . ."

142

"They are an ancient and accepted custom of our race. You do not deny that?"

"Ancient, may be. But . . ."

"Not so ancient, only. My grandmother—and yours, *a graidh*—was handfasted to our grandfather, I have heard."

"Aye, but the times were different. It was in the Jacobite wars."

"And are these times so much happier? More settled? But a truce to this talk, Cousin. Us it is that would be married, thus, not you! Will you marry us, as a minister of the Gospel?"

"No. No—that I cannot do, Alastair. The Kirk does not sanction such a union . . ."

"The Kirk has done so in the past, many times. As does the law of Scotland. Both have acknowledged it."

"Acknowledged, yes, perhaps. Not sanctioned, not performed and sanctified it." The older man turned to the girl. "Marsala, do not be misled, cozened, even tricked maybe!" he exclaimed. "This is not for you, my dear. This is no honourable proposal, holy wedlock. I fear that this man, who was my friend, would still further injure you . . ."

"He has not injured me yet," she said, calmly. "Nor has he misled or tricked me. Nor will do, I think."

"But . . . you do not understand. You are little more than a child, Marsala. And this is no right thing, no honest fulfilment for any woman."

"I am no child. And what do you know of a woman's fulfilment? I make my own judgement . . ."

That was enough for Alastair. Stepping close to her, he reached out and took her hand in his, raising them both, clasped together. "See, then," he cried, "all of you. Here, in the presence of you all, and of these representatives of the Kirk of Scotland, I, Alastair MacRory of Gleneidart declare this woman, Marsala MacRory of Glenudalain, to be my wife, by this declaration before witnesses and by the tradition and custom of handfasting, for twelve months and a day from this night, both being free and unmarried. All according to the law of Scotland. And let none say otherwise."

He felt the hand within his own stir, shiver, but it did not withdraw from his clasp.

There was a long silence in that place. Alastair lowered the girl's hand gently, and released it. He did not look at her.

As none spoke, abruptly Marsala turned and hurried out from the cave into the night.

"That was not well done, I think, Alastair," the minister said at length, flatly. "You are an impatient and obdurate man."

"So I have been told," the other admitted briefly. "Rory Mor will continue to find me so, I promise you!"

"But . . . it is no use, man, Your fighting Rory Mor and Clanrory. No use. It is too late."

"It is not too late. Far from it. Rory can yet be defeated if we will but unite."

"Rory will not be defeated, because he has already won, Alastair."

"What do you mean—won?"

"Today, we agreed. Agreed to go."

"Go where, man? Agreed to what, in the name of God?"

"To go to the territory of New Ross. In Upper Canada."

"You *what*? Lord—you *agreed* to go! To Canada! Who did? Who agreed?"

"I did. And Duncan, here. And others, elders of the people. In the name of all these unhappy souls . . ."

"Damn you, then—false leaders of a broken, spineless people! Damn you, for throwing away what was not yours to give! These folk's right to their own land . . ."

"Alastair, peace for a moment! Hold your great righteous wrath, and heed." The minister spoke quietly but with unusual authority. "Forget that you are a soldier, and remember that others are not. Fighting for fighting's sake is without virtue or value. Its only worth is that it should gain something —something that may only be gained by force. And what can it gain these people now? Look at them this night; wet, cold, with food already failing. Without shelter, without privacy. What state is this for the old and the sick? As a community we cannot exist thus for much longer, man. And the winter is almost upon us. The folk cannot survive a winter here, as Rory Mor well knows. But there is land waiting and ready in Canada, good land in abundance for the taking. Scotland, it seems, neither needs us nor wants us. Is it so foolish or so wrong to leave a land that is no longer ours, save in its history, and go to one that will be ours in truth? Is it? I cannot see it."

"I shall let your own heart answer that, Angus," Alastair said harshly.

"The people are more important to me than the land, *a graidh.* A full life in a new land is more to be valued, surely, than an empty one in an old, however dear? But these folk must *reach* the new land, Alastair, and as fit and able as may be. If we sail now, soon, we can get there before the worst of the winter storms. If we delay, then we face grave dangers—or else do not sail until the spring. And, as I have said, we cannot survive a winter here at Ardglass."

"I did not suggest that you should."

"It is all that Rory Mor will allow us. But Clanrory has chartered us a ship. It is on its way here now, Rory says. Another will follow. We shall sail in them—and, God willing, start on a new and happier life beyond the seas."

"Amen!" intoned the Catechist.

"How many?" the younger man demanded. "How many have said that they will go?"

"I hope that we shall all go. As the MacDonalds of Glen Druin did. We shall go together and keep together, a community in Canada as we have been a community here."

"Not if I can help it!" Alastair said then, simply, shortly. "Even yet." And he left them, and strode outside.

*   *   *

He found Marsala sitting on a rock near the jetty, and staring out at the restless sea.

"They have said they will go!" he told her urgently. "They have given in. Given their word. To Canada."

At first she did not seem to understand. Perhaps she was not listening, her mind on other matters.

"They have given in to Rory Mor. Agreed to emigrate," he repeated.

"Who have? Angus Crubach and the old men? Not all of them, surely? Not *my* people, from Glen Udalain?"

"That is what I do not know, what we have to find out. Angus said that he spoke for all. But there must be some who did not agree. Let us go and find those sisters. The MacIvers."

The young woman seemed as though she would speak, offer some alternative suggestion perhaps, but she held her peace.

They moved together down the crowded peninsula, asking whoever seemed to be awake and stirring where the Udalain people were encamped. The name did not seem to arouse any enthusiasm, but they did discover the approximate where-abouts of Marsala's folk—though inevitably they were much scattered, there being no unoccupied area of land available for latecomers.

Anna and Morag MacIver they ran to earth eventually under a stony bank that they had burrowed out with their hands to form a semblance of shelter. These welcomed the newcomers warmly, offering food and drink, despite the hour and the fact that they had both been asleep. They told them that the people were in great confusion of mind. They had been inspirited, yes, by the burnings at Camusewan, but almost as gravely cast down by the arrests and the certainty of further reprisals. Not all were for the emigration, but even those who were against it felt that it would likely come to that in the end. And the Kirk's voice spoke loud.

But what of her own folk? Marsala demanded. The Udalain folk? The women?

They were in somewhat better heart than the others, the sisters agreed. The affair of the bridge had encouraged them, as well as the attack on Camusewan. But there were mixed feelings here also, and two of their men were amongst the six taken. In the main the women still were more in favour of some sort of resistance than were the men. None wanted to go to Canada, but all feared that they would be forced to go. And there was a certain feeling against the Udalain people, here at Ardglass. Rory Mor's reprisals, in some measure, were blamed on them. Then again, thanks to Gleneidart, many of them had managed to bring in livestock and goods considerably in excess of the others. The Sheriff's men had come for the beasts, that day, at the gun-point—but most, like themselves, had foreseen this and killed the animals for meat. This had been shared round, and hidden. But amongst the Udalain folk only. There was not enough for all. There was some ill-feeling . . .

Alastair brushed all this aside. Now that they had seen that the fight was on, that Rory Mor could be struck back at, would not some of them be prepared to come and join in the fight, actively? Join Marsala and himself in the hills, to carry on the struggle? The women, possibly, if not the men?

The sisters shook their heads. They were sorry, but the thing just was not possible, was not to be expected. It had been different before, in their own glen, when there was still the hope of saving their homes. It was too late for that now. They had done what they could, at the time, with Marsala—and it had profited them nothing. Now, what could they do? The women were bitter, yes, and against this agreement to emigrate. But that was not the same thing as to be asking them to take to the hills like caterans, outlaws. It was not to be thought of. There would just be more reprisals from Rory Mor, more folk arrested, more hurt done. Besides, the men would never permit it. Already the men-women complication was strong, since Marsala's revolt. The men did not like the women doing these things at all. It was unnatural, they said, and unsuitable. If the men thought that there was any likelihood of the women seeking to break out, or slip out, and take an active part in fighting, they would try to stop it, for sure. They would seek to exert their authority, say that this was men's business, as they had done already. Crowded together as they were here, and with no privacy, they could not slip away unseen. You could not ask the women to go against their men, in this extremity. And were there not armed guards fencing them in?

Alastair was all angry opposition, but Marsala quietly held the others probably to be right. He would not change the age-old Celtic attitude to women overnight. Nor was it practicable, in their great trouble, to try to turn the women against their menfolk, to further add to the sorrows of this place. Angus Crubach was right in that. And rebels had to be whole-hearted and single-minded, surely? If they were not that, then they would be but a source of weakness.

But the man was adamant. Let them put the matter to the test, at least. Let them gather together the Udalain folk, men and women, here and now, and he would speak to them, seek to convince them of the folly of weakness, the need for unity of action, the hope of victory.

The MacIvers, though reluctant, and pointing out the

difficulty of assembling in the darkness and in a crowded area folk, many of whom would be already asleep, did not refuse to try, at Alastair's urgency.

And so, slowly, inconveniently, uncomfortably, the Udalain folk were roused and besought and assembled—not all of them, inevitably, and as inevitably with others amongst them. And to them, eventually, Alastair spoke, to the dark mass of plaid-shrouded silent people, only a few of whom he could actually see, however many might be able to see him. He spoke with energy and eloquence, with patience and persuasion. And they listened courteously, with only a wailing child or two, or a coughing ancient, to interrupt him. But before long, even in the darkness, and long before he finally gave up, he knew that he was not reaching them, not moving them, knew that his words were like the waves that beat against the shore near by, beating against an impregnable wall of weariness and hope-lessness and apathy. When at last his hoarse voice faltered and sank away, no other single voice was raised to support, to question, even to counter his own. Only an uncomfortable stirring, whispering, murmuring echoed his call to arms.

The man's head sank, as he savoured the bitter taste of failure.

He felt his arm gripped tightly, and then heard Marsala's clear young voice uplifted. "If you will not heed Gleneidart, you will not heed me!" she cried. "But I tell you that he is right, nevertheless. Right, right—do you hear? You men of Clan Ruari, are you dead? Did Rory Mor burn your manhood and your wills, as well as your houses? Did he?" The hand that gripped Alastair's arm was trembling now. "Was Ian Beg, Altdurie, a boy of sixteen, the only man left in my glen? I . . . I . . ." She all but choked. "I cannot speak to you . . . I cannot find words for you, now. But, know this—that *I* at least know a man when I see one! Well enough to follow him, to support him, and . . . and to wed him! I . . ." She gulped, and abruptly turned to bury her head on the man's chest, sobbing.

"Och, Marsala, wheesht, lassie, wheesht!" he said, stroking the dark damp hair. "Och, my dear, never heed! My goodness me, no. There now, there."

Decently, quietly, without a word spoken, the crowd moved away, dispersed and faded into the night, leaving them alone.

Even the MacIver sisters, though they pressed the girl's hand, had nothing to say.

Presently the man and the woman made their way back to the boat, back across the heaving waters to their garrons, back into the valley beyond and the enclosing hills, and a silent and preoccupied journey they made of it, with a new constraint between them like a wall. Almost the first exchange, beyond a brief word or two here and there, was when, a little way up that valley, the man reined up.

"You could find your way back to Braemore, to the cave, alone, could you?" he asked her. "In the dark?"

She was surprised. "I could, yes. But why? Why should I?"

"*I* have elsewhere to go," he told her. "I shall spend what is left of this night on the hillside above Camusewan. Those six men, the hostages, are to be taken to Dingwall tomorrow—or today, it is now. I must know when they set out, and by what route."

"You mean . . .?"

"That I cannot allow these others to pay the price of my actions. I must rescue them if I can. That goes without saying. And I shall not do that in our fine cave, lassie."

"No. Then I shall come with you."

"It is a poor night for sitting out on an open hillside. Wet and chill."

"No wetter for me than for you. And that cave, alone, is no abode of the blessed! A . . . a shade lonely, for my wedding-night!" That last was all but strangled at birth.

Quickly the man glanced at her. "H'rr'mmm," he said, and led the way uphill and to the right, without further debate.

Up and up to the crest of the ridge they rode, and over and down beyond, to approximately the spot where they had waited only the night before, previous to the attack on Camusewan. It seemed inconceivable that but twenty-four hours should have passed since then. This was a bare hillside of short heather and tussocks, with little of cover and shelter about it. Alastair found a hollow, however, that at least offered some protection from the south-west breeze blowing off the sea—and where, in daylight, the garrons would not be seen from the strath below. Here he set about pulling armfuls of heather to heap it up in an additional bank and shelter, utilising also the folded plaids that served as saddles on the horses, to form a sort of tented nest.

"You will lie snug enough in there," he declared presently. "As warm as the cave, likely."

"And you?"

"I shall sit over yonder. On that hummock. Where I can see downhill."

"You will not see downhill in this darkness."

"I should see lights, if they were to move before daybreak. In this hollow I should see nothing, for I should sleep too sound."

"But sleep you must, Alastair. You cannot go lacking sleep, night and day!"

"I shall sleep, never fear—with one eye open. An old campaigner's trick. Do not worry about me, lassie, I am used to this sort of life."

"They will not move before daylight, surely? I think . . . I think that you would be better here, sleeping in comfort. Soundly. Till dawn, at least."

"You it is that needs the sound sleep. And they may well start early, for it is fifty rough miles to Dingwall, a long day's riding. Off with you now, girl. To sleep. It has been a long hard day for you, Marsala. Long, long—and trying. But you have borne up to it well. As well as any man."

"Thank you."

"You will be very tired. Not every woman could have done what you have done, this day."

"Perhaps not. Not every woman is proposed marriage to, wed, and . . . and given notice of divorcement that same day!" she answered, tight-voiced.

He hesitated. Her head was turned away and he could not see her expression. "No. No, I suppose not. But . . . it is not a true marriage, at all. Do not distress yourself, Marsala. It means nothing."

"Nothing," she repeated, though whether as agreement, question, or statement, it would be hard to say.

"Nothing. Merely a formality, never fear." He reached out a hand to pat her shoulder, he hoped reassuringly. "Sleep well, lassie, for you have earned it." And he moved off, towards his hummock.

He heard her draw a stifled breath behind him.

Later that night, much later, she came to him, quietly, where he crouched hunched up on his heather hummock. He was asleep, head sunk on chest, his plaid slipped from one shoulder—and whether with one eye open or not, he did not stir nor give any sign of awareness of her approach.

She stood for a moment over him, before she stooped and gently replaced his slipped plaid. Then she sat herself down beside him, and with great care draped her own plaid so that it enfolded them both. Thus, silent and still she sat, and stared out into the windy void where lay the Sea of the Hebrides.

The rain had stopped.

Chapter Thirteen

IT was sunrise when the man awoke, cramped and stiff, blinking in surprise at the dazzlement. But it was not the level yellow rays, which came flooding through the narrow gap between the eastern hill-tops and the heavy, leaden cloud base, that penetrated his deep slumber, nevertheless; it was Marsala's hand shaking him, and then pointing downwards.

"Eh? I . . . I . . . damnation!" he swore. "Me for a sentry! Lord—I have seen men shot for less! I've slept . . . for hours!"

"They are on their way, then," she mentioned. "Up the strath. By Kinlochdonan." She was standing, not too close, holding her folded plaid over her arm, and the golden light making a glory about her.

Alastair looked owlishly from her to the riders down in the valley below, and back again. "Yes. Yes, I . . . you . . . so I see. I am sorry. As well that you did better." He stood up, yawning. "Yes, by Kinlochdonan. The easiest road, though not the quickest. A pity." The alternative, north first and then east, was four or five miles shorter, but entailed a climb up and over the high pass of the Lairig na Bo. But clearly the route chosen was that eastwards up the loch-side and over the watershed into Glen Array, and so down to join the other about half-way across the desolate mountains that formed the spine of Scotland. The same route that Hector MacBride had taken with the sheep.

It was of Hector and Ian Beg that Alastair was thinking. What stage had they reached in their mission? Would they have got rid of the sheep yet? Could they be on their way back, in time to assist in this enterprise? It did not seem very likely. All would depend on where and when they found the tinkers; these might be anywhere along that drove road, over a score of difficult miles. And sheep, amenable as they might be, would not travel so fast as well-driven cattle. It would not do for this Dingwall party to come up with the sheep, and them still being herded.

"Better had they gone by the Lairig na Bo," he said. "This way, they might run into Hector."

"Of course, yes. That would be bad."

"Yes."

"I count twelve of them, I think. It is a little difficult, from this height, riding close as they are. But I think a dozen. That means six guards. They will be armed. Six to overcome . . .!"

"I have known worse odds. So much depends on their quality. I have not been impressed by most of the people working for the estate, up till now." Alastair frowned. "We must give them a few minutes more, unfortunately, lest any of them should look up and back, before we can risk the garrons."

There was no mist this morning, and the little cavalcade of horsemen riding along the loch-shore far below were only a little more visible than they themselves would be were they to move away from their present position.

Though it was a patience-taxing business, wait they did, until the riders were sufficiently distant. And there was always the risk that someone down at the farmery itself might be looking uphill, even thus early in the morning.

"I should have thought of this," Alastair blamed himself. "We could have done without this waste of time. We have got to get in front of them, somehow. We have got to make sure that they do not run into Hector's back, as well as try to ambush them."

"Will they not be far enough on, with the sheep, by now?"

"I fear not. It is not twelve hours since we left them. They would not drive all night, for there was no great haste. I do not know a great deal about sheep, but they are short-legged creatures and may tire quickly. Over rough territory, and with so many, and only two drovers, I doubt if they will make much more than a mile in the hour. They may not be ten miles on their way, from where we left them, yet. And these horsemen will cover that in two or three hours."

When at last they dared to make a move, there was no more talking. Up and over the skyline they urged their garrons, and along, parallel with the strath though hidden from it. But hasten as they would, heel and slap their stolid mounts, they knew that everything, at this stage, was against them. The others had a start, fresher horses, and a fair drove road to follow, whereas they must go up hill and down dale, heather-hopping and bog-trotting, circling and twisting. It was galling to consider. At least they knew the country, almost as well as they knew their own features, and could take advantage of every least opportunity that it might offer, and avoid the pit-falls and morasses with which it was so liberally endowed.

So they rode, hard, and the girl was seldom more than a length behind the man. Sometimes they were far from the line of the road, at others they were daringly close to it. Soon their garrons were steaming and frothing, at the unaccustomed pace.

Crossing the watershed beyond the head of the strath, here at least they believed that they might have made up some of the leeway. Since they could not risk being anywhere near the road anyway, up on these high open spaces, they strung the bow of it, as it were, by cutting right across at a tangent, caring nothing for the emerald bogs, the black peat-hags and the seas of tussock-grass. Somewhere out of sight the drove road coiled and veered circumspectly.

A couple of hours after their start, flushed and mud-spattered, they approached the steep lip of Glen Array perhaps half-way down its barren and empty length. Peering cautiously over, they gave thanks. Almost a mile further up, the group of horsemen were just rounding a bend of the glen, and not apparently in any notable hurry.

This was a considerable relief; but for ambushing purposes a much greater lead than that was necessary, to give time to prospect a suitable spot and to make preparations. And with only the two of them to work it, the spot would require to be very suitable indeed.

Keeping well back out of sight, they hurried on. As far as Alastair recollected, there was nowhere remotely apt for their purpose in Glen Array itself nor on the stretch of open drove road beyond. But after that, three or four miles further, there was a broken area of innumerable small rocky hills, through which the track had to thrust its difficult winding way. Somewhere thereabouts should be the place for them.

They could have done with yesterday's rain and mist now, but this was a fine morning, autumnal and golden, with visibility excellent. They would have to be very careful crossing the intervening area of open moorland.

At last they won into the cover of the multitude of bluffs and hillocks—they believed unobserved, and at least two miles ahead of the Dingwall party. At once they came down to the track, seeking a rocky gorge or defile where they might set their doubtful trap. Marsala was somewhat breathlessly demanding how it was proposed that the two of them should attempt this, when Alastair suddenly held up his hand.

"Listen!" he commanded.

Clear above the rushing noise of the river below them sounded a thin plaintive bleating of weary sheep.

"*Dia!*" Alastair exclaimed. "You hear that? Sheep! And near at hand."

"Must they be *our* sheep? Or, at least, Rory Mor's? Might they not be some others . . .?"

"On this road, at this time! The Highlands are not so full of the brutes, yet, that there is one chance in ten of that."

They pounded on, along the road for the first time. The droppings only too evidently showed which way the sheep had come, and that it was a large flock. The people coming on behind could not fail to read the same signs—even though it was unlikely that they would know, yet, about the theft of the Camusewan beasts.

The track twisted and turned interminably through and amongst the jumble of small, rock-ribbed, barren hills and craggy knolls, following a foaming river in a deep bed, a narrow place with no range of visibility save upwards. The beat of their garrons' broad hooves echoed hollowly from the enclosing banks and bluffs as they rode, and all the time the bleating of the sheep ahead grew louder. The noise seemed to come from all around them, thrown back and distorted by the steep and erratically-facing slopes.

In the event, they came upon the flock abruptly. They rounded a tight bend, beyond a thrusting rocky shoulder, and there the steaming rearguard of the sheep were, not thirty yards away, the long packed column of them stretching ahead, filling the narrow floor of the defile, its head out of sight around the next bend. And not only its head out of sight; of herders there was no sign.

Even as the riders pulled up their hard-pressed mounts, Hector MacBride and his young assistant stepped out from behind rock-falls at the track-side, where they had hidden, with their garrons, at the sound of hoof-beats behind in pursuit. Loud were their shouts of relief and greeting, above the everlasting baa-ing.

Alastair cut such short without ceremony. "There is an armed party only a mile behind, taking hostages to Dingwall. From Strathdonan," he declared. "Six guards. They may not know that these are Rory Mor's sheep, but they will likely recognise the blue brand-mark on their rumps. We were trying to find a place to hold them up, to ambush them, trying to rescue the prisoners. But, now, these damned sheep . . .!"

"There is nowhere to hide them here, nowhere!" Marsala cried.

They stared around them. The place was a trap, with the river close on the right, and the steep scree-lined boulder-strewn braeside rising immediately on the left. The sheep, and all else, had to go either forward or back.

"Ahead?" Alastair jerked. "Round the next bend? Will it be any better? Do you know it, Hector?"

"Och, no, likely not," the older man said. "This place is all this way, just. There is a deal of it ahead, yet. If they are only a mile behind, and on garrons, we will not be getting these brutes out of the way, or any distance on, at all. Slow, they are, slow."

"We will just have to leave them, then," the girl said. "Leave the sheep here. Try to make our ambush further on, somewhere. There is nothing else for it."

"What will they do, at all?" Hector wondered. "With the sheep? Will they turn back with them? Some of them, maybe? If there are six of them, they might be splitting up, see you . . ."

"We have no time for discussing it all, like this!" Marsala objected. "They will be on us soon. And we have to push our way through all these sheep, to get away. That will take time, itself . . ."

"Push through the sheep! Of course!" Alastair took her up. "That is it—why did I not see it? Here is our answer—here is our ambush, ready and waiting for us! The sheep are a godsend, not a pest! Don't you see! These people behind will have to push through all this long press of sheep, too. There is not room for them to do otherwise. Whatever they decide to do, if even to turn back with the sheep, they will have to get through them first, to the far end—the brutes will not just turn and follow them. And to get through they will have to disperse, string out in single file. They will be slow—and helpless, if we are up above them, with muskets!"

"Man Alastair, of course! Nothing could be nicer," Hector agreed. "Och, but they might take fright, see you, if they were to see nobody herding the creatures?"

"*I* could do that. Wait with the sheep," Marsala volunteered.

"No, you would look strange. A woman. And they will know you, these men, perhaps. No, but Ian Beg could do it. Three of us hidden, with muskets. The garrons out of sight. Iannie down here, herding them alone . . ."

"Then they would stop to question him. Here, at this end. Especially if they were recognising the blue marks. They might hold back, here," Hector objected. "We would not get them strung out, amongst the sheep, and held up the way that we want . . ."

"Oh, quickly!" the young woman urged. "We have not time for all this . . ."

"We must know what we are doing. See, if Ian Beg was to go forward, amongst the sheep, himself? Yes, that is it," Alastair decided. "He will go on, push on on foot, into the middle of the flock. Then, to question him, Rory's men will have to ride in after him. He will not be able to hear them, for

the baa-ing. You have it, Iannie? Get you well forward, but
not out of sight. They must see you, and try to reach you.
Once they are entangled amongst the sheep, we shall act. You
all have it?"

"Och, that is best, yes."

"Yes, yes, but quickly!"

"Where can we hide the horses . . ."

The spot where the herders had previously hidden, with
their mounts, was no longer suitable, since the flock had moved
on. This process had to be allowed for, and not knowing just
how long the others would take to catch up, it was difficult to
decide how far ahead they should go to be safe. Better if the
sheep could have been halted where they were, but there was
no means of effecting that; the creatures would drift on in their
slow, erratic fashion, unless stopped away at the front. The
same problem would apply, to some extent to the ambushers,
though it might be possible for them to change their position
a little, perhaps with difficulty, as the sheep moved on. It was
resolved to hide all four garrons down in the gut of a burn-
channel between the track and the river, just before the next
bend in the defile, perhaps a hundred and fifty yards ahead,
a rocky hole where, however, some alder and hazel scrub clung,
to offer cover. It was to be hoped that the sheep would not
have moved past there by the time that the enemy had
arrived. Hector would take them, and remain in that position
himself, available for any close-range challenge.

Alastair and the girl detached the captured muskets from
their garrons, and went clambering as swiftly as they might
up the steep slope on the left, moving half-right, diagonally.
The surface was treacherous scree and bare red earth, but
there were numerous outcropping rocks and fallen boulders
to hide behind. The problem was to know how far along to go,
again; they wanted to be in a good position, well forward of the
tail-end of the flock, by the time of action—but not too far
forward. Though not to go far enough would entail having to
change position, possibly in full view from below if the riders
delayed or the sheep moved on faster than calculated. It was
an awkward and complicated issue.

Alastair decided on a rock about thirty yards short of the
burn-channel where Hector would be, and some hundred feet

above it for Marsala, he himself moving on for another fifty yards or so. He jerked a few words of instruction at the girl as he hurried on; she knew how to load and fire the musket, but what her aim might be like remained to be seen. Thankfully he sank down behind his own chosen boulder, with still no enemy in sight.

Though their climbing scramble up the slippery screes had seemed dilatory enough to them, down below the progress of Hector and Ian Beg was infinitely more so, especially that of the former, delayed by the string of led horses. Pushing their way forward, through the tightly packed sheep, was obviously a desperately slow and snail-like process. This was heartening enough in one way, but most exasperating both to achieve and to watch, with anxiety about the opposition making an appearance round the bend behind nagging at the minds of all concerned. Moreover, all this pushing and activity at the rear was having the effect of urging the wretched sheep onward at a slightly faster pace, the very last thing that was wanted.

At length, however, Hector reached his burn, and cautiously guided his garrons down into it. That took an unconscionable time also, for the descent was very rough and steep, and each beast had to be led down individually. Ian aided him with the task, with one eye on the track behind, and up above the watchers fretted with apprehension. Even when it was done, the horses were not completely hidden from aloft—but presumably they would be from road level. Ian Beg moved on a little further through the steaming, seething flock, and then halted, seeking not very successfully to delay the drift forward.

And now, of course, impatience and anxiety was concentrated on the non-appearance of the Dingwall party. Strain their ears as they would, the pair above could hear no cautionary clatter of hooves. What could be delaying them? It would be galling, maddening, if they had chosen this moment to halt for a midday break. It was still a little short of noon. They should have reached here by this time, surely? Minutes were dragging out. And all the time those sheep were moving forward, forward. If the last of them should come level with that burn-channel, with Hector's hiding-place . . .

They were spared that, at least. Without any sort of warning, by some trick of the sound waves of that place, the first two riders suddenly were there, rounding the westernmost bend at a jog-trot, muskets slung across their backs. Behind them came the prisoners, two by two, hands tied, their garrons linked together by ropes so that none might try to make an individual dash for freedom. Then the remaining four guards. These did not carry their muskets at the ready, either.

At sight of the sheep the leading file reined up, but not in any aspect of alarm. There was some pointing and talk. Then voices were upraised, directed at Ian Beg, marooned amongst the flock. He had turned, to look back.

A deal of shouting and vociferation followed. with Ian pretending either that he could not hear, above the baa-ing, or could not understand. The latter was more than a mere pretence, for only one of the guards shouted in the Gaelic. At length the youth shrugged elaborately and, turning, proceeded to move onward with the sluggish current of his charges.

There was not a great deal of distance left between the last of the sheep and the spot where Hector and the garrons were hidden.

With nothing for it but to move on after him through the press of animals, the leaders of the cavalcade urged their mounts into the sheep, kicking and laying about them with ropes or sticks or anything that was available. For all the hullabaloo, they were no more speedy and successful than Hector had been. The only speed about the entire proceedings was the rate at which they became separated from each other, strung out and islanded in that steaming sea of wool. The prisoners especially, linked together in pairs, became all but immobilised, their horses in fact proceeding no faster than the sheep themselves. Two of the guards from the rear sought to force their way forward to try to clear the way somewhat—a hopeless task. Great was the outcry and cursing.

Grimly Alastair watched from above. It was all even more effective than he had visualised. The only trouble was the delay in time, which meant that the entire throng below was tending to move further eastwards than was convenient for his own position or for Hector's. He could not risk waiting longer.

Turning, he raised a hand to Marsala behind her rock.

THE FLOCKMASTERS

Aiming her musket low, but not low enough to hit man or beast, she pulled the trigger.

The crash of the report, reverberating vastly in that narrow place, had an even more compelling effect than had the similar tactics at the bridge over the Udalain River two days before, for here the victims of the attack were still more vulnerable, better targets, devoid of cover, scattered, and unable to move into any defensive positions. As soon as the girl fired, Alastair was on his feet, his own musket at his shoulder pointing down at the second rider—leaving the first for Hector.

"Not a move from any of you!" he shouted, in English, into the echoes of the shot. "Not a hand lifted—if you would save your skins. We have you all covered. One move from any of you, and you will not move again!"

"That is right, yes!" Hector's voice came loudly, from lower down, as he clambered up on to the road, old fowling-piece in hand. "Stand, you!"

No word, no movement, came from any of the horsemen, save for the darting of their glances. But the sheep went on baa-ing, and moving slowly forward, and perforce so moved the garrons also, and therefore their riders. It all looked rather ridiculous.

"Ian," Alastair called, in the Gaelic this time. "Their muskets. Get them. Cut them off their backs. Use your dirk." He translated that into English for the benefit of the ambushed, repeating the warning about the least hint of unco-operative movement.

So Ian Beg worked his way back through those sheep, knife in hand, with Hector carefully covering each guard in turn that the boy reached. Only one of the muskets was provided with a leather sling; all the others were merely tied across their owners' backs with cord, the cutting of which presented no difficulties. There was no attempt at resistance, which was hardly to be wondered at. Ian tossed the captured weapons aside, one after the other, save the last, which he retained, to point threateningly at all concerned, exceedingly pleased with himself. He had some cheerful things to say to the erstwhile captives, too—one of whom turned out to be his own Uncle Rob.

And that is practically all there is to relate about the rescue of the Ardglass hostages. In the end, like so many well-conceived military exercises, it took on the nature of an anti-climax. The ropes were removed from the former prisoners, and transferred to their escort. The muskets likewise changed hands, though only five of these were available for the crofters, for Ian Beg was not to be parted from the best of them. Not that the late hostages showed any anxiety to take over the weapons. As much bewildered as relieved, and just slightly doubtful at finding themselves pitched into the role of armed outlaws, they as yet did not react in any very positive way to their deliverance, as who would blame them, perhaps?

The Dingwall party had been well provided with food, and since Alastair and Marsala at least had had no breakfast, a hearty and hasty meal was consumed then and there. Then, since prisoners would only have been an embarrassment to Alastair, and it would have been a pity to let them go back to Rory Mor, Hector was given charge of the captives, with instructions to hand them over, with the sheep, to the clan of tinkers and drovers, where no doubt they could be kept out of the way for some time. Three of the rescued crofters were also allocated to Hector, to aid him in his herding, and Ian Beg, to his delight, restored to the main body.

So the company divided once more, Hector, his three assistants, the six prisoners and the sheep to continue eastwards looking for the tinkers' camp, and Marsala, Ian, and the three remaining crofters to accompany Alastair westwards whence they had come, heading for Braemore of Glen Eidart. Ian Beg, at least, carolled like any lark.

Chapter Fourteen

WHEN Alastair emerged from the cave-mouth next morning, it took only moments for his eyes to fasten on the smoke. Not on this occasion the widespread, rolling pall that they had become so unhappily used to in Strathdonan, but the lesser if still voluminous column arising from a single source. It was quite clear, unmistakable, where the smoke originated, even though the actual spot, far below him in the floor of the glen, was embowered in trees—as clear as that no other houses or crofts were burning in company. It was his own home, Gleneidart House, that was the latest victim of this mania of fire and destruction which had overtaken their country.

Since the others were stirring in the cave behind him, Alastair moved away some little distance, amongst the ledges and buttresses of the cliff-face, to a spot where he could be alone with his contemplation of that burning and its implications. Sitting on a rock, he considered it, his face set in hard, graven lines.

And yet, somewhere within him, he knew surprise. Not surprise at the sight itself—surprise at himself. Something was not responding to the scene as he might have expected it to do. The sight itself could hardly have surprised him. When so many houses blazed, why should his own escape? The wonder was that Rory Mor should have held his hand for so long. Presumably that had been policy—policy which no longer applied. What startled him as he sat there was his recognition of the fact that the thing did not harry him desperately. He was angry, yes—sorry, concerned. But that was all. For some reason that he could not have explained, something of the significance and enchantment of Gleneidart House, for him, had disappeared, evaporated. It was not merely his mother's death; there was more to it than that. He had been dimly aware of this before, putting the thought from him—though perhaps the fact that he had always found himself too busy with other activities to visit it yet, since his return, might have enlightened him. But now, watching, he knew it and wondered. With almost more concern, indeed, he scanned as much of the rest of the glen as he could see, lest other fires should indicate that this was the beginning of more wholesale eviction and not just Rory Mor's spleen against himself. But, no, the smoke rose only and obviously from the trees that enclosed his own boyhood home, the home of generations of his line. And it did not look like new smoke; he was becoming something of an expert on smoke and its significance, and this was not the pouring black clouds of a house fire in its prime but a blue-brown, residual reek. That meant that it had been lit during the night, which again implied that Rory had not dared to do it in day-light, presumably for fear of interference and opposition. This was, then a venomous counter-blow at himself, and not part of a planned programme. Glen Eidart as a whole, it seemed, was still to have its legal period of notice between announce-ment and eviction.

The man was still sitting there, thoughtful-eyed, when Marsala found her way to him, flushed and lovely from a long and much-needed sleep. She came to stand at his back, gazing downhill.

"I am sorry, Alastair," she grieved. "So very sorry. Your house. *Your* home, now. It is so cruel, so savage. The man is a monster!"

"He is no crueller to me—or to you, for that matter—than he is to others." he answered her. "Less so, surely? All these others have done nothing to hurt or counter him. We have. Against us he has some reason for savagery. If roofs must burn, mine no doubt burns with most reason, most excuse!"

She looked at him searchingly, but held her peace.

"That he has waited so long before doing it it is probably the greatest matter for surprise," he went on. "For some reason, Rory must have wished not to do so, I think. I wonder why? He has made a point of not damaging the tacksmen's houses, of course—save your own. And that was a special case, as warning and example, to try to bring you to heel, undoubt-edly. He has not wished seriously to offend the tacksmen, the gentry of the clan; he went to some lengths to placate me personally. Myself, you might have thought that I was his dearest friend, his long-lost brother. And yet he is utterly ruthless about the crofters and clansfolk. He is afraid of some-thing, I think. It may be Clanrory himself. It may be that he is going beyond Clanrory's wishes in all this, and fears that the tacksmen may have access to Clanrory's ear, where the crofters have not. I wonder . . .?"

"Perhaps. But . . . it is good that you can be so . . . so philosophical, while your home burns, Alastair!" That was said with some wonder.

He looked up at her. "I am a little surprised my own self," he admitted. "For years, half-way across the world, I have

163

thought of Glen Eidart with longing, wondered why I had ever left it. Now, something seems to have changed, see you. I love this place still—more, perhaps, than ever, since it is threatened with what amounts to death. But that house down there, somehow, is not the important thing any more—even my tack of the glen. Something else . . . seems to have come first, come between." He did not say what that was, but rose to his feet and took the few paces away from her that the ledge permitted.

She watched him steady-eyed, unspeaking.

He turned back, frowning at her. "But this is no time for such small-talk, such chatter," he said, almost harshly. "It is action that is required of us, not soul-searching. Prompt action, for the time is short. This emigrant ship may be here any day, they said. It is on its way."

She sighed a little. "I suppose so. More action? But . . . what can we do? That is effective? That can alter the situation of these people? Yesterday's rescue was good, successful. But will it make the least difference to whether or not our folk stay in Strathdonan or sail for Canada?"

"That is the point, yes. Look, Marsala, I have been thinking. Thinking quite a lot. Not only about the house down there. About all this that we are trying to do, this whole fight that we are making. I have come to a number of conclusions. The most important is that, despite these small successes that we have had, we are not going to win it. Not this way, I mean—not the way that I had hoped and planned."

"You . . . you think that too?" she asked.

His brows rose. "I see that you have been thinking, also!"

"Yes, Alastair. I . . . I am sorry."

He smiled, then. "Well, do not wear so long a face, lassie— the campaign is not lost. Far from it. Only the strategy will have to be changed, I think. This is how I see it. The folk down at Ardglass, the mass of the clansfolk, are not going to rise whatever we do, whatever we achieve. I fear that we must accept that. The scales are weighted too heavily against them. And yet, that was what we set out to do all this for, not just to hit back at Rory Mor but to try to rouse the people to resistance. But that is not happening. I was wrong, it seems, in thinking that it could. There is too much arrayed against them. I am not blaming them so much as once I did, either. They are caught in a trap. And whatever we do, Rory and the powers that he represents can always take it out on the evicted by reprisals."

"That is true. I see that."

"We must change out methods, then. The objective is the same: to try to keep our people here in their own land. But instead of seeking to do this by getting the people themselves to revolt against Rory Mor, we must do the thing more directly. Rory himself is the key to it all, therefore it is Rory Mor himself that we must go for."

"What do you mean—go for?"

"Just that—go for him. Indeed, I think that I will go for Rory this very night!"

The man laughed at her expression, laughed cheerfully, naturally. The shadow of that smoke down in the valley seemed to have disappeared from his face.

*　　*　　*

Not far to the west of Rory Mor's house at Camusewan, in a very carefully selected spot indeed, Alastair considered their preparations, and nodded, satisfied.

"That will do, I think," he said. "Give me twenty minutes. Then light up, and make all the noise that you can. Fire the muskets. But do not linger for long afterwards, for Heaven's sake! Either of you. Straight back and up the hillside with you, and do not pause until you are well clear of any possible pursuit. There must be no hanging back. You understand?"

"And you?" Marsala asked.

"Wait for me at the white stone beyond the ridge. Wait for perhaps an hour. No more, certainly. If I have not come, go back to the cave. I will join you as soon as I may."

"And what if . . . if you do not? What if you are caught, Alastair?"

"Then you have four hundred sheep to bargain with, not to mention six prisoners. Enough surely to release one man!"

The girl shook her head. "I doubt if Rory Mor would consider it a fair exchange—for you!"

He shrugged. "You honour me above my deserts, lass. But I shall not be caught, never fear."

They stood at a point not far from where they had commenced their activities at Camusewan three nights before, near the corner of the now empty infield, beside a wooden shack for the storage of hay-sleds, equidistant from both the row of cottages and the farmhouse. Piled against the shack were dead pine branches and other inflammable material that they had brought on the spare garron.

"Be careful, Alastair," Marsala urged, as he took his own horse and the led beast, and moved off quietly around the wall of the field.

The man made a wide circuit of the farm to the east. At that side there were no cottages, no buildings of any sort, only a garden within a wall. Alastair tethered the two garrons to a tree beside this wall, as near to the house itself as he dared, and moved on alone through the gloom. It was between two and three in the morning.

He knew that house and its courtyard fairly well by now. The smell of charred wood and materials still lingered unpleasantly about the place, and the gaunt gables that were all that remained of the south range of buildings could just be distinguished against the night sky. The small porch at the main door in the centre of the long front of the house was his objective. Cautiously, close to the wall, he edged along to it. In the corner that it made, he tucked himself as into a well of deeper shadow, and waited. No hint of sound or movement came to him from the sleeping house.

He did not have to wait for long. The reflected glow of flame, from the west, began to show, flickering at first but growing ever brighter. Shouting sounded, thinly at that distance, and notably high-pitched. Then the crack of musket-shots, and more shouting. The latter, Alastair had to admit, was not very impressive—but surely the shooting would penetrate, wake the establishment?

The second couple of shots had just rung out, when, with relief, Alastair heard sounds of commotion in the house behind him. There was the brief baying of a hound, quickly silenced, then muffled shouting, of a very different calibre from that in the distance, and the thud of hurrying feet on wooden floors.

Other masculine shouts, too, began to echo from the direction of the cottages. Alastair slipped off his plaid, to hold it
open and ready, and drew his dirk.

The cries from within grew louder, closer, and there came
the noise of the heavy bolt being shot back. Then the door was
flung open, and two men rushed out. Alastair pressed back
into his corner.

The pair stopped, to stare westwards towards the fire and
the hubbub, pulling up their breeches over their shirts, a bare
five paces from the hiding man. He did not find them familiar
figures.

Another man came stamping out, clutching a gun. They
shouted to each other, in English, pointing and gesticulating,
and, as with one accord, set off hot-foot towards the source of
the disturbance.

The old manservant appeared next, to stand just outside the
porch, shaking his head and plucking at his chin. Then he was
galvanised by a great bull-like roar from within the house.

"What is it, man? In the name of God, what is it?"

The other turned. "It is a fire, I think, Rory Mor," he
answered.

"Damn you to hell, fool, I know that it is a fire! What is
burning? Where? What was that shooting? Is it that devil
Gleneidart again?"

"I do not know, at all. The others—they have gone running.
To see what it is . . ."

"Then, after them, man. Off with you, and bring me word,
quickly. Do not stand there gaping, dolt—get me word."

"Yes, then. I will, yes, Rory Mor . . ."

Alastair grinned to himself, and as the old man hurried off
unsteadily, he began to edge round the rustic pillars of the
porch, to slip inside the door. Only women's skirls were
issuing from within the house, now.

But at the very moment of turning the corner into the doorway, he froze. More by instinct than hearing he suddenly
realised that somebody was silently approaching the door,
from within—Rory Mor, no doubt. Alastair stepped back,
swiftly. The movement had been only a few feet from him.

It was indeed Rory Mor. He came padding outside, to stand
staring westwards, like the others, his back therefore to the

hiding man. Why he had been so silent was now evident. He was barefooted; indeed, save for the plaid wrapped round his bulky person, as before, he appeared to be naked from his bed. He had not glimpsed or sensed the other's movement in the shadows, clearly.

Alastair rejoiced. He had anticipated having to go inside for Rory Mor; this was so much more simple. Only the thought of hounds held him back momentarily. But no sign or sound of such materialised. Drawing a long quiet breath, and flicking his plaid into better position over his left arm, he leapt.

All save the drawback of his damaged shoulder was in favour of the attacker—surprise, a lean and sinewy strength, and best of all the fact that the other was huddled within the folds of his own plaid, restricting movement, especially of his arms, from the first. Alastair's bound flung him on to Rory Mor's wide back, and his right arm, that clasped the dirk, whipped round the other across the chest in a fierce grip, pinioning him tightly, and a bare knee drove viciously behind the victim's thighs, to throw him backwards off balance. At the same time, Alsatair's left hand hurled the folds of his own plaid over the factor's head, and, pained shoulder or none, pressed some of the thick tartan hard over the mouth. A strangled, choking cry did escape before full pressure was brought to bear, but with the shouting going on outside and the women's voices up-raised within, this was unlikely to attract attention. As the big man reeled backwards, gasping, his assailant exerted all his strength to jerk the heavy body over the obstacle of his bent knee. Rory's bare feet went from under him, and he toppled helplessly.

In that moment of unbalance, Alastair sought to steer the other's tottering fall back behind the upright pillars of the porch, as far as possible, so that the attention of anyone else emerging from the house might not be attracted. But Rory Mor, even staggering, was a heavy load to influence, and he fell not just where the other would have directed—indeed he all but brought down his attacker with him, entangled in the folds of heavy cloth.

Alastair's words were jerked out of him. "Struggle, Rory . . . and you will taste . . . cold steel!" he panted. "My dirk . . . at your fat belly!"

From the other issued gasping, grunting protest.

"Silence! Or you will pay . . for burning Gleneidart House . . . here and now!"

Rory Mor twisted convulsively, baring all his gross lower parts in the process. Quick as thought Alastair's dirk flickered, and a dark line was scored across one large white buttock. The sufferer emitted a muffled yelp, and stiffened into immediate immobility.

"Another sound . . . another struggle . . . and it will be your vitals!" the other declared. "And my pleasure!"

The big man lay still. Undoubtedly naked steel on naked flesh makes a potent persuasion.

"Up with you!" Alastair ordered. "And have a care, Rory, have a care!" The dagger-tip just tentatively pricked the other buttock.

Urgently, if less than nimbly, the martyred man turned over and scrambled to his feet, his own plaid slipping from him though that of his assailant still hung over his head and shoulders. Alastair grabbed at the former, and thrust some portion of it into Rory's trembling hands, curtly commanding him to wrap it round himself. As the other fumblingly did so, Alastair whipped out the length of rope tucked within his shoulder-belt, and opening the prepared noose in it, swiftly slipped this over Rory's enwrapped head and shoulders, down over the barrel of his chest where he pulled it tight, effectively pinioning the arms and fastening both plaids approximately in position. Round and round he rolled the remainder of the rope about his victim's unhappy person, till the factor looked like nothing so much as a trussed and hooded fowl, the lower half suitably plucked.

It was at this stage that a woman, a servant of some sort, emerged from the house doorway. Her gaze was directed to the other side, of course, but turning to call something back to a colleague within, she glimpsed the peculiar sight to eastward. What she thought of it, what she even fully perceived in the gloom, is not to be known. But it was enough to send her shrieking indoors again, hands as well as voice upraised. The eloquent gesture that a dirk made towards her, its gleaming blade redly reflecting the glow of fire, may have had something to do with it, of course.

Alastair delayed no longer, for fear of possible repercussions. Grasping his captive by the shoulder, he jerked him round and pushed him forward, along the side of the house towards the garden and the waiting garrons. "Move, Rory, move quickly." he ordered. "I will steer you—with my dirk-point! Do nothing foolish, for you own comfort's sake. I have this rope entirely secure." He jerked it roughly, in demonstration. Also, he kicked the other's bare shins, as indication of the tone and tenor of the forthcoming journey.

Walking gingerly on bare feet, with a gait curiously compounded of the hesitancy of a man blind, the reluctance of the condemned, and the urgency of one pursued by devils, Rory Mor went whither he was guided. No pursuit seemed to develop. They reached the horses without incident other than a certain amount of understandable stumbling and bumping on the part of the prisoner.

"You may prefer riding," Alastair observed sardonically. "I shall have secure hold of both your garron and yourself, so you need anticipate no parting of company! Up with you, man."

Without the use of his hands, the other made but a doubtful business of mounting, but suitably encouraged at the rear by both muscle and metal, he eventually achieved it. Retaining the captive's rope and that of the led garron, Alastair vaulted on to his own beast, and, close alongside, left that place at a sedate walking pace. It would have been a pity if the beat of hooves should have disturbed anyone, or if Rory Mor should have fallen off.

The latter, despite the folds of material over his mouth, could have made himself heard; he chose, however, throughout that ride, to hold his tongue if not his peace. His companion found no fault with that.

They reached the white quartz boulder high up beyond the flanking ridge to the north not so very long after Marsala and Ian Beg arrived there themselves. As the girl's relieved greetings faded at sight of the distinctly peculiar figure that the factor made, sitting bare shanked on his mount, top-heavily swathed as to the upper parts, Alastair apologised.

"You must forgive Rory," he said. "He is scarcely dressed for meeting ladies. He came away in something of a hurry."

Ian Beg gasped, and then sniggered.

"Boy," Alastair said sternly. "Instead of laughing heartlessly, it would be more civil if you were to be lending the son of the Chamberlain of Strathdonan your own plaid, decently to be covering the bare legs of him!"

"It went well? Are you all right?" Marsala asked. "You are not hurt?"

"Myself. no, Rory here is hurt deep, though—but only in his pride. Where, of course, it hurts a Highland gentleman most! I fear that he will survive, however. And you? You were not followed?"

"I think not. At the top of the hill we waited for a while, watching and listening. But there was nothing."

"Good. If young Camusewan is ready, then, let us go."

Chapter Fifteen

AT the mouth of the cave on Braemore, next morning, Rory Mor MacRory sat, amongst voluminous plaiding, and laughed. He laughed with heartiness and every appearance of amusement, a man of the world, of forbearance and acceptance, without rancour, acknowledging the swings of fate's pendulum with entire good humour, and a man grossly misunderstood, but forgiving. He had not been quite like that last night, admittedly, when at last he had arrived at this place, sore and cold and humiliated. But this was another day. Rest and food and daylight seemed to have worked a transformation, and Rory was now Rory again. Even the plaid that was wrapped around his great middle like a kilt, and the other, draped and swathed about his torso, shawl-fashion, moved him to mirth. He would have to be watching his step, he pointed out to Alastair and Marsala, or the old Sheriff would be charging him with contravention of the Disarming Act and wearing the banned and offensive tartan!

Alastair, a-lean against the rock wall of the cave, eyed him curiously. Just how sane was this man, he wondered? Quite crazed, a little unbalanced; or merely very clever?

171

"It may be that you will not be seeing your friend the Sheriff again for some time," he said.

"With the affairs of men ever so unpredictable, who can tell?" the other agreed easily. "I should not weep too sorely over that."

"No? Yet you make a . . . an effective partnership, do you not? The law and the criminal, and the Kirk thrown in for good measure! I wonder how they will fare without you down there? How urgent about your business? It will be interesting to watch."

"To watch?" the other repeated, looking up. "A strange way of putting it, Stair. It sounds, shall we say, prolonged!"

Alastair nodded. "Prolonged is a good word, Rory, an excellent word. Let it stand."

The other screwed up his somewhat cherubic features. "Dear God, prolonged, is it? Dear Alastair, how you love mysteries! See you, is it asking too much to seek the reason for this pleasant little gathering? You are my very good and old friend, admittedly, and Marsala here has always been a favourite of mine, But still, the urgency of the summons is a little beyond me!"

"It is very simple, Rory, nevertheless. Since you, undoubtedly, are the leader and motive force behind this wickedness in Strathdonan, and you will not pay heed to my other pleas to stop it, there only remains to remove you from the scene. It is as simple as that."

For moments the big man stared at him. Then he lifted his voice, to laugh again, loudly. "Good Lord, Alastair, you do not really believe such nonsense, do you?" he demanded genially. "Any of it? For instance, that this policy of Improvement is *my* idea? That removing me would have any effect at all? If so, you do me too much honour, Cousin. This is something that is going to go on, all over the Highlands. It is the *nation's* policy, not mine. If you disapprove of what is being done in Strathdonan, for one reason or another, then Clanrory is the man that you should see—not me, his humble factor."

"Clanrory is solely responsible, then? Not you?"

"Exactly. Surely you realised that?"

"Did Clanrory order the burning of Glenudalain House,

then? And of my own home?" That was snapped out like a whip cracking.

Rory only hesitated for a brief moment. "Well, no. Not directly. That is different, as you will understand. A warning, just—a gesture. You made it unavoidable, I am afraid, both of you. A pity. We could not allow such blatant flouting of the law to go unchallenged, naturally. The Sheriff was very strong on that. You left us no option. You burned down estate property, stole cattle and arms, assaulted officers of the law . . ."

"So you burned our homes . . ."

"And took my mother a prisoner," Marsala put in, from across the cave. "You abducted her, in the middle of the night, setting her roof ablaze above her!"

"Your mother is well and comfortable under *my* roof, *a graidh*," the big man assured her. "Not as any prisoner, but as my honoured guest. She suffered neither hurt nor indignity." Earnestly he turned to Alastair. "I did not burn your house because I wanted to, Stair, believe me. My hand was forced. Indeed *I* did not burn it, at all. Say that I had to accede to its burning. For this is not just a matter between you and me, see you, or between you and Clanrory, even. The law is involved now, the nation, the State . . ."

"Rory," Alastair interrupted him, a shade wearily, "save your breath. You may talk until Loch Donan runs dry, but it will avail you nothing. We know you for what you are, having had overmuch experience of your actions. We did not bring you here to listen to your excuses . . ."

"Yes, then, why *did* you bring me here, Stair? Since apparently it was not out of your love for me, and my good company."

"I have, in part, told you. If you are here, with us, you cannot be down there working your evil will on these defenceless people, and it may be that your lieutenants and lackeys will be less active without you. And also, we can perhaps persuade you, while you are here, to mend your ways a little, to change this notable policy of yours in some degree. While there is still time."

The other frowned his perplexity. "I cannot see it, Stair, I am sorry. Forgive me if I am stupid. But how can you persuade

me against my plain duty? To Clanrory? For that is all that I
am concerned with."

"Liar!" Alastair observed, but without passion. "Whose
sheep are those with the blue markings?"

"They are mine, of course, and my father's."

"Not Clanrory's? And it will be your sheep, and not Clanrory's, that spread in due course all over the lands taken from
the crofters? The wool and the mutton that the London
Government is crying for, they will be sold by you, not
Clanrory?"

"I shall be paying large rents for those lands, to Clanrory.
Three times and more the sums paid under the old wasteful
tack system . . ."

"More rent for Clanrory, and you paying it. Rory Mor,
tenant of all Strathdonan! An ambitious project . . ."

"No, no, not all Strathdonan, Stair. Only the cottars' land.
You tacksmen will be left in possession of suitable holdings . . ."

"You are kind, thoughtful, But it is the cottars, as you name
them, the clansfolk, that we are concerned for. I fear that
Lord Clanrory is going to be, shall we say, disappointed if,
having lost the rents of all these small crofters, *you* cannot
afford to pay him this great new rent, after all!"

"Do not distress yourself unnecessarily for his lordship,
Alastair. It shall be paid, never fear."

"I wonder? In the first year, at least? It will cost you a deal
of money, will it not, to replace the four hundred sheep you
have already lost?"

"Lost? Four hundred . . .? What are you talking about,
Alastair?"

"*Dia*, can it be that you do not know? That you have not yet
heard that you are four hundred sheep the poorer, Rory? This
is extraordinary. Do your shepherds never count your flock?
Never set foot on the hill?"

"Stop talking riddles, man. What is this?" Rory Mor's
confident good humour was wearing just a little thin.

"It is a matter that I would have expected you to know, you
the great flockmaster to be! Namely, that two days ago we
gathered some four hundred sheep from your hill grazing of
Camusewan, and took them . . . well, elsewhere. Where they

will be safe, shall we say. Certainly where you and yours will not lay hands on them."

The other man was on his feet now, jaws working, lips seeking words that would not come. He made a strange and rather frightening picture as he stood there in huge and quivering impotence. Marsala, at least, involuntarily drew back a pace or two into the cave.

"Other sheep you have too, I understand, Rory," Alastair went on evenly, inexorably. "On Letterblair, for instance. Very vulnerable."

"My God—this is robbery, pillage!" the other got out. "Sheer wicked knavery, naked theft!"

"Say, rather, another gesture, another warning," Alastair amended. "Like our burned roofs. Only, with this difference: that you may win your sheep back. If you will change your attitude to our unhappy clansfolk."

"Damn you, you brigand, you thieving cateran . . .!"

"Softly, Rory, softly! Where is now all the laughter and benevolence? Here is a change, surely? So much heat! Can it be that these poor, silly sheep mean so much to you? If so, then I have just told you how to win them back. All that you have to do is to recognise that human beings have their value, too. Halt these evictions. Call off your Sheriff and his minions . . ."

"I cannot, you fool—I cannot!" the big man cried. "I tell you, it is Clanrory's policy, not mine."

"Then you are a very energetic disciple, I think. You can influence your master."

"How can I—a man like Clanrory? A lord, with the ear of the King and the Government! How can I influence such a man?"

"Very easily, I think. If for no worthier reason than just that you may not be able to pay this magnificent new rent that he is apparently selling his soul for. With your sheep gone, will you be able to pay, Rory, and restock with more sheep at the same time? A costly business, I would say, at the price of sheep today."

"Are you crazy, a lunatic?" the prisoner demanded. "Do you think that you can steal hundreds of sheep, and keep them? That I will not get them back again . . .?"

"I do not think it, I know it. And in the state of Highland Scotland today, you know it too. Those sheep are lost to you, Rory—unless you come to terms with me. We can take others, as we took those. And how will Clanrory get his rent then?"

"Fool, thrice-damned fool, you little know what you set yourself up against!" the other burst out. "Do you imagine that I am alone in this venture? That it is only myself you have to fight? Do you conceive that I and my father could stock all Strathdonan with sheep, all its hundred thousand acres? I have friends, associates—rich and influential men, I tell you—who will pay Clanrory's rent twice over and scarce notice it."

"A-a-ah!" Alastair's head nodded slowly. "So now we have it! The secret is out. I had suspected something of the sort. Friends, eh? Associates. Rich and influential men. Here is where the notion came from, the damnable plot to make a baa-ing desert out of this smiling strath. Here is why the man Cousins dances so close attendance on you, Rory. He is in it, for a certainty, and his precious master, the army contractor Calthwaite, eh? And no doubt the good Sheriff himself? A . . . a syndicate? That is the word for it, is it not?"

Rory Mor had suddenly changed expression. His small mouth had pursed up, and his glance became darting, wary. Undoubtedly he realised that he had said too much, had been stung into committing an indiscretion. He drew the plaiding closer around his shoulders, and shrugged. "Call it what you like. The result is the same. You are doomed to failure. As well that you should realise it." The rich voice was flat now, the anger subdued in calculation.

Alastair was calculating too. "Yet it is Clanrory's policy, you insist?" he said. "Despite your precious associates, your syndicate?"

"Yes. Clanrory needs the money. For his regiment. His name and prestige demands it. Also, honours are being granted, I understand, for the colonising of the Canadas. The Government is grateful to those who can produce large numbers of settlers. It is prepared to help . . . with shipping."

"I see. So each variety of roguery has its reward! The patriot, and the speculator . . . and the Judas!"

"I would watch your words, Alastair," the other answered, evenly still. "You may need my good offices, I think—need them direly. I would remind you that sheep-stealing is a capital offence, in law. It can carry a sentence of death. Especially, I should think, for a deserter from the army. If you have the flock returned to me at once, however, and intact, I might be prepared to put in a word for you. For old times' sake. Transportation might be made to serve—it might be arranged, even to Canada!"

Alastair smiled over towards the girl. "Rory is generous, is he not? Magnanimous. But I think that we are not quite ready to accept his good offices, yet. We shall wait a little while—with Rory as our guest here, of course—and see how much they miss him down there. Their loss, of course, being our gain!"

"I fear that you cannot afford the luxury of delay," the big man declared. "We are expecting the *Dolphin*, of Bristol, off Camusewan today or tomorrow. To embark the emigrants for Canada."

"So soon?" Marsala cried. "To ship them off, like cattle!"

"Haste is necessary. Winter is almost upon us. The sooner the ships are gone, the easier, the safer, will be the voyage."

"Perhaps if you are not there, Rory, to hasten this unhappy exodus, lacking your . . . your zeal and authority, there may be less haste? Folk may have second thoughts," Alastair suggested, "when they hear what has happened to you. Two can play at hostages, you see."

"There will be no lack of authority and zeal—even if I am not there—I assure you, my friend." Rory Mor achieved a brief laugh once more. "Clanrory will see that they embark, never fear."

"Clanrory! You mean . . .?"

"Clanrory in person. He is sailing up in the *Dolphin*. He probably will be sleeping in my father's house tonight."

Alastair was silent, as he tried to grapple with the implications and complications that this news represented.

Rory went on. "I think that you had better send me back to Camusewan forthwith, don't you, Alastair? You have sadly mistimed your banditry, I am afraid. If I am to plead with Clanrory for you, to save you from a hanging, it would be as well that I should be there, in person, to do it! And as his factor, it is important that I be present to greet his lordship."

"I think that he will survive if you are not."

"Perhaps. But will you? See you, the first thing that Sheriff Walker intends to do is to ask Lord Clanrory, as His Majesty's Lieutenant for this County, to authorise the bringing in of the military, to maintain the King's peace. And once the military are in Strathdonan, my good Alastair, I fear that even *my* good offices will not save you!"

"The military! My God, you would not bring in the military? Against your own people?"

"Not me, Stair, not me—Clanrory, on the advice of the chief law officer of this County. And, er, of Captain Henderson of the Ross-shire Fencibles, who is the expert on such matters! To deal with rebellion, theft, arson, flagrant violation of Riot Act provisions, sheep-stealing, and a general threat to the peace of this realm. Led by a notorious deserter from the King's forces! I think, Stair, that you would be wise to let me plead your very doubtful case before Clanrory at the very earliest opportunity!"

"Rory," Alastair said quietly, as he stepped forward until he was very close to the big man, "I do not like that word deserter. Any more than I like your own self. Like you, it is false, anyway. I had a month's special leave of absence from the regiment, on account of wounds. The month is not yet fully passed. Clanrory knows that, if you did not. But you know it now. You will not mention that word in my presence or out of it again, or by all that I hold sacred I shall ram it down your fat throat, with your false and deceitful tongue, and choke you with it! Aye, and rejoice to do it? You understand!"

For moments they stood eye to eye, tall men both, and each commanding in his own way. Then Rory Mor shrugged found a smile, and moved sidelong, only a fraction of a pace, but enough.

"Very well, Alastair," he said. "What is a word . . . between cousins. I shall not forget. That, and other things."

"Do not, no. You will have time enough to think of it. For I do not intend that you should plead my case, to anyone. Certainly not to my Colonel-Commandant. I shall see Clanrory myself. You will remain here. And do not seek to escape, Rory. I shall leave very clear instructions. A naked man roaming these hills, as well as being very cold, would look quite ridiculous. Especially a man the shape of yourself. The least move out of you, and those plaids will be taken away from you." He turned to the girl. "Come, Marsala, the air outside this cave will be the sweeter, I swear."

"God damn, blast and blister you, Alastair Dubh! Break, scourge and burn you everlastingly! Curse and afflict you . . .!"

"Surely, surely, Rory. That is better. You sound almost like an honest man, at last! A good day to you."

They went out, to where Ian Beg and the three crofters waited decently.

Chapter Sixteen

THE man and the girl arrived at the hill crest above Camusewan again soon after noon. No ship lay at anchor below. Though it was a breezy day of sun and showers, and visibility was good, no vessel of any sort showed anywhere in what they could see of the Sound of Sleat or on the wider isle-strewn waters to the north.

Choosing a good vantage point, but well hidden, they waited there all of that blowy afternoon, Marsala assured that it was all a lie, that no ship was expected that day, no Clanrory, that it had just been a trick of Rory's to seek to gain his release. Alastair admitted, as time went on, that she might well be right.

But, as the sun was beginning to sink behind the jagged peaks of Skye, the white top-sails of a large, full-rigged ship began to emerge out of the narrows of the Sound, to the south. Soon she was in full view, and heading in towards them.

"For once, we owe Rory Mor an apology, it seems," Alastair said. "Though whether Clanrory is in fact aboard is another matter."

They watched as the vessel edged slowly into the wide but shallow bay between Camusewan and Ardglass, and dropped anchor well off-shore, with much too deep a draught to draw in close to any of the little jetties.

Not much more than a mile from them she lay, but too far to see signs of activity aboard. No boat was lowered, however; that much they could see. Activity, indeed, seemed to be concentrated on the shore. Clearly the ship's arrival had aroused much excitement around Camusewan, whatever its effect at Ardglass. There was a great deal of coming and going around the farmhouse, as well as at the larger building to the north that was the house of the old Chamberlain. It was surprising to see how many people the area could produce in only a few minutes. Undoubtedly most of Rory's minions, and the Sheriff's constables and officers would be concentrated thereabouts.

When a boat was launched, it was not from the ship but from Camusewan jetty, to be rowed out to the vessel.

"The reception committee," Alastair commented. "Big with news. But sorely missing Rory Mor, I wager. Six in the boat, just, one in scarlet. The military adviser, the warrior Henderson!"

Still they waited, after the boat had reached the ship, waited until the light was nearly gone. Then dimly they could distinguish the boat coming back, presumably the same one. It was only when it had reached its jetty, almost directly below them, and its folk were disembarking again, that the peering watchers were able to establish that there had been still only six people in it.

"None of the ship's company has come ashore, then," Alastair said. "I wonder what that means? That they are staying aboard tonight? Clanrory also, if he is there?"

"They might be coming later."

"They might, yes. If so, how much later? It would be a deal easier for us to get out to the ship, see you, and talk to Clanrory there, than to try to see him in the Chamberlain's house, or anywhere else on land. The shipmen will not know us, but here every man's hand is against us."

"Borrow that boat?" Marsala suggested. "Or better still, the smaller one that we took last time, along at the fishermen's cottages. Easier to handle."

"Yes. And less dangerous to approach. We shall do that, and

take the chance that Clanrory does not come ashore in the meantime. It will be dark by the time that we reach the cottages."

They moved back to their garrons, and rode downwards and northwards behind the hill.

Acquiring the boat, the same small one that they had borrowed previously, proved to be of little trouble. Alastair had been prepared to dispute the matter, if necessary, with the fishers—for these of course would be tenants of Rory's father; moreover they could not be expected to be in bed at this time in the evening. Presumably, however, they were from home, for neither light nor sound issued from the cottages, and two of the larger boats were missing from the strand. The main difficulty, again, was pushing the craft down over the pebbly beach to less than half-water.

The sea was choppy, rougher than three nights before. Marsala found the rowing heavy work, and their progress was distinctly crabwise, wet and slow. Moreover the tide had just turned, and, coming flooding up the narrow funnel of the Sound of Sleat, offered quite a formidable hindrance, since they had to pull directly south-west into both it and the wind. Fortunately the distance to row was not great, and the ship's position clearly shown by her lights.

Under the lee of the *Dolphin* it was easier, and they drew close, hailing for a line. Once Alastair had made himself heard, there was no difficulty about the boarding, a seaman throwing them a rope to tie up to, and then lowering a rope-ladder. No doubt the fellow was surprised to find a young woman climbing nimbly up this, and at the aspect of the kilted and authoritative if somewhat bedraggled soldier who followed her. He took them to one of the ship's officers without comment, however.

"One of Lord Clanrory's officers to see his lordship," Alastair announced, taking a chance. "He is aboard, I understand?"

"Yes, sir," the mate answered. "He is in his cabin. Follow me. A bit rough in a small boat for a lady, ma'am?"

"Perhaps," said Marsala.

They were led aft to a large cabin at deck-level in the stern, at the door of which the mate knocked, and waited. At a call from within, he opened, and announced an officer and lady to see his lordship, ushering them in.

Lord Clanrory sat alone in a spacious stateroom, beside an iron stove that glowed redly. Bottles, glasses and dishes littered the table near by. He was dressed not in Highland regimentals this time, but in coat and breeches of a sober richness, and long, flowered waistcoat; and looked the less impressive therefor, an elderly man, thin, and of insignificant physique, sagging-featured—however haughty the nose and brow—and seemingly feeling the chill.

"Good evening, *Mac Ruaraidh Mor*," Alastair greeted. "I hope that I see you well? May I present Marsala of Glenudalain—your cousin, of course."

Clanrory was staring, as though at an apparition—and certainly his visitors' appearance was somewhat wild and unkempt, Alastair especially being a very different figure from the resplendent officer of the royal audience, when last they had foregathered.

"Gleneidart!" the older man gasped. "What . . . how the devil . . . damme, what is the meaning of this?"

"A call to welcome you to Strathdonan, sir, on behalf of, shall we say, the large proportion of your clan and people who cannot feel themselves to be adequately represented by factors, sheriffs, constables and hired bullies!"

"My God!" Clanrory exclaimed, half-rising. "This is beyond all! I wonder that you have the effrontery to face me, man! To come openly, brazenly, and to bring this . . . this young woman with you . . ."

"Why not, sir? Why should we not come openly, here in Strathdonan, before our chief, the head of our name—and my Colonel-Commandant? Is it so strange?"

"Deuce take it, boy; do not seek to fox me with words! I know what you have been up to, since you returned to Strathdonan, the trouble that you have stirred up, the folly and wickedness of your pride and arrogance. That any officer of mine could have acted in such shameless fashion is almost beyond belief . . ."

"That is not true!" Marsala interrupted spiritedly. "You cannot say that, sir. The shame lies wholly elsewhere . . ."

"Be quiet, girl! Hold your foolish tongue!" the Viscount

snapped. "You of all people, to mention the word shame! You, who have elected to live with this misguided young man in boldest shame and disgrace. Soiling your name and . . ."

"Sir," Alastair intervened crisply. "I would inform you that your are speaking of my wife."

"Your wife!" Clanrory repeated, moistening thin lips. He sank back in his chair. "Your wife?"

"Yes. We were handfasted three days ago. So that the unpleasant things that you, sir, seemed about to say, should not be said."

"I . . . er . . . I had not heard this," the other man admitted, disconcerted.

"There may be other things, *Mac Ruaraidh Mor*, that you have not heard. Many such. Despite Rory Mor's remarkable abilities as an informant."

"I know enough, young man, to realise that you seem to have taken leave of your senses, and have been acting up here contrary to sanity, and also contrary to *my* interests."

"Your interests, sir, or Rory Mor's? I cannot believe that they are the same!"

"Mine," the other said decidedly, briefly. "And where *is* Rory Mor, Gleneidart? Why was he not here to greet me?"

"Rory was unable to be present, sir, for the good reason that I have him in safe-keeping in the hills, in the hope that he may perhaps do less harm there than when running loose like a mad dog!"

"Good God, man! Have you the utter presumption to stand there and tell me—*me!*—that you have laid violent hands on my factor and taken him prisoner, so that he cannot meet me, cannot carry out my orders? As Heaven's my witness, I was right in judging that your wits were gone, that you were crazed, wholly mad!"

"I think not, sir. Though there may be more than one sort of madness—madness for power, madness for wealth, for glory. If I am mad, then I think that I am mad out of pity— pity for your clansfolk, *Mac Ruaraidh Mor*, the people who look to you as chief and protector, and who are now huddled in misery and despair waiting for this very ship to take them away to transportation and exile. That is what your factor has achieved in your name, sir. On whom lies the madness?"

"On you, man, if you cannot see beyond your nose! These

people were overcrowded, enforcedly idle, and therefore lazy. They existed here, and little more. In Canada a wonderful new land awaits them, a new, wider, happier life. A certain amount of discomfort there must be, about any move. It is inevitable But a year or so from now, these feckless folk will be thanking me. I have gone to considerable trouble and expense making the arrangements, getting a Charter from the King for these new lands, hiring this ship . . ."

Alastair stared at the man. It might have been Rory Mor speaking. "You believe this?" he demanded harshly. "You even suggest that you are doing all this for the people's sake, not for your own? Did Rory Mor speak truth, after all, when he said that it was all *your* policy, not his?"

"Of course that is so," the other returned, coldly. "Do you imagine that such as I would permit any agent, any servant of mine, to decide what should be done with my lands and my tenantry?"

"Tenantry!" the younger man repeated. "That is all that they are to you, then—tenantry? I fear that I have been misjudging Rory Mor somewhat!"

"You have misjudged everything, young man, apparently. Including my patience."

"I must trespass upon it a little longer, nevertheless, I fear. Tell me this, Clanrory, about the sheep," Alastair said softly. "You claim that all this eviction is for the ultimate benefit of the people. What of the sheep, sir? What of the wool and the mutton? And the doubled and trebled rents?"

"I do not forget the sheep, the wool and the mutton, naturally. The Government, the country, is desperate for meat and wool, with this blockade. It is the duty of every landowner, every patriotic owner of property, in this emergency, to use his land in the national interest. I shall put ten thousand sheep on these hillsides of mine, Gleneidart, and the country will benefit accordingly. What I am doing is best for the people and the country both."

"And for Rory Mor!"

"Tut, man, have you Rory Mor on the brain? What has Rory Mor to do with it, beyond being my agent in working the initial stages of this improvement?"

"*You* gain increased rents, yes, but Rory and his friends

184

gain the golden harvest of the wool and mutton. Out of the people's sorrow."

"Lord knows what you mean, man. More misjudgements, I must assume," the other said testily. "I am not interested in rents. And what harvest will Rory Mor reap—in Canada?"

"What?" The word was ejaculated like a bark.

"Do not yap at me, Gleneidart." The older man pinched a long and pointed chin. "You sound surprised."

"You . . . you did say Canada? And Rory?"

"I did, yes."

"*Dia!*" Alastair turned to the girl, and their eyes met.

"I think that . . . Rory Mor has found . . . his equal! At last!" Marsala said, chokingly.

"You are right!" Grimly Alastair turned back to Clanrory. "So you are not going to rent Rory and his associates most of Strathdonan as a sheep-run?"

"Indeed I am not! Do not tell me that he also is having delusions? That he imagines something of the sort?"

"He does, yes. As do others."

"How foolish. How mistaken!" The Viscount sounded almost old-maidish in pained regret. "When they have omitted even to have anything from me in writing on the subject!"

"I see!" For moments Alastair stared at his Colonel-Commandant. "I see," he said, at length. "So you have used Rory Mor to do this thing for you, to soil *his* hands and take the opprobrium for evicting your people, allowing him to believe that he should win great riches as a result. And all the time, he is to be transported to Canada, like the others! He is not even to manage your sheep-run for you?"

"Of course not. A project on the scale that I have planned would be quite beyond any capabilities of Rory's. He knows nothing of large-scale sheep-rearing. I have engaged an experienced manager from one of the great sheep-runs of Cumberland. He is in fact on board this ship."

Alastair had difficulty in finding words. He shook his head. "I . . . I . . . this is almost beyond belief! I did not fully realise, sir, the sort of man that you are!"

"I am not a fool, Gleneidart, if that is what you mean."

It was Marsala who spoke. "Rory Mor will not go," she said. "He will not go to Canada. He will never agree to that."

Clanrory shrugged. "I think that he will," he said, indifferently almost. "There will be nothing for him here. And I shall need an agent, a factor, in Canada also. The King has granted me the charter of a large tract of land in New Ross to develop, half as large as all Scotland. Rory will have ample scope for his, er, especial abilities."

The girl shook her dark head. "Rory will not go," she said. "He is no settler, no pioneer. He is soft of body, whatever the mind of him . . ."

"She is right," Alastair agreed. "He will not go. He still has his father's tack of Camusewan. He will stay . . ."

"Not so." Calnrory put his long fingers together and considered them from heavy-lidded eyes. "I told you, there will be nothing for him here. No tack of Camusewan, or anywhere else. I am, ah, resuming possession of all tacks on this estate as from the next term-day, Whitsunday. *All* tacks, you understand!"

It was out, at last. The long silence in that cabin was broken only by the slap-slap of waves against the ship's hull, and the uneasy creak of timbers.

Clanrory himself it was who broke the hush, "For the other tacksmen," he said, "I am prepared to arrange suitable holdings in Canada, if they wish them. You two, however, have forfeited all claim upon my generosity by your actions here. I might have overlooked Marsala's part, as the folly of a headstrong, ignorant girl, as my cousin's daughter, and for the sake of her father's loyal service in my regiment. But since she has married *you*, Gleneidart, to do so would be as good as overlooking your offences also. And that I should have to consider very carefully indeed."

"I think that you need not trouble, sir," Alastair returned levelly. "Though we are only handfasted, and Marsala will be a free woman in a year. But I cannot believe that either of us would desire your generosity, or your holdings in Canada. You cannot force us to Canada, I personally shall stay here in Scotland. My line has held Glen Eidart for five hundred years. I . . ."

"Under your chief, and without written lease or legal binding," the other put in sharply.

"Without written lease or legal binding," the younger man

nodded. "For five hundred years the word and honour of Clan Ruari's chief was sufficient surety!"

Clanrory licked his bluish lips. "Times have changed, and the old barbarous days are dead. And the old clans with them. This is the nineteenth century . . ."

"*You* say the clan is dead! You, Clanrory?"

"I do."

"And the regiment?"

"The regiment is not the clan."

"Yet its men are your clansmen, and its officers all either tacksmen or of the families of tacksmen. How think you that they will accept this taking of their tacks in their absence?"

"They will be loyal to their chief and King. Unlike you, it appears. When Bonaparte is disposed of, the regiment will be taken to Canada for disbandment. The men will rejoin their families, the former tacksmen will obtain their new holdings. All will be looked after."

Alastair drew a long breath. "So-o-o! All will be looked after." He shook his head slowly. "We came here tonight hoping to show you the truth, hoping to convince you that you were being duped by clever rogues. I find that you are much the cleverest rogue of all!" He held up a fiercely commanding hand as Clanrory half-rose angrily. "Wait, you! We came hoping that we could make your love and pride in your clan prevail, to halt this wicked eviction and transportation; but I see that is useless. For you the clan is dead, and money and power alone have any voice. I came still esteeming you an honourable man, if misled, still honouring you as chief and Colonel. I can do so no longer. If the clan is dead, so is its chief—and the sorrow that he died in shame! I accept no allegiance to you as chief a moment longer! Wait you, I say! And as for being my Colonel—voluntarily I joined your regiment, fool that I was. Voluntarily I leave it, a wiser man. My commission I resign to you, here and now. From this on, I owe you nothing. Nothing but supreme contempt!"

Lord Clanrory, nibbling his underlip, reached out a somewhat shaky hand for bottle and glass. He made but a poor job of pouring his liquor. But when he spoke, at length, his voice at least was steady, cold, dry. "Are you finished, young man?" he asked.

"I am, yes."

"Good. I feared that there was going to be no end to your folly and insolence. I perceive that you are a fool, Alastair, amongst other things. An ingenuous fool. Did you really think that I would accept your resignation? That would be folly indeed. If you are to resign, you will do so in the proper and orderly fashion—through your battalion commander and my Lieutenant-Colonel. In Portugal. You are still a serving officer in the Seventieth Foot, Gleneidart, and under my orders. I could call the captain of this vessel and have you put in irons, for a variety of offences, either as your Colonel or as Lord Lieutenant of this County. I understand that the Sheriff desires your apprehension on a number of charges, also. But I prefer, for the honour of the regiment, to deal with you myself. Your gazetting as Captain is already countermanded. You will return to your unit forthwith, Lieutenant. Your leave-of-absence is hereby terminated. You will report at the earliest possible moment to Lieutenant-Colonel Macleod, and await my further instructions. And this young woman will return at once to her mother, whom I understand is now in my Chamberlain's house. You understand—both of you?"

The young people exchanged glances.

"We hear you, sir, at any rate," Alastair said stiffly. "What Marsala does is her own affair. For myself I must point out that if you are so concerned with all being done in correct military fashion, then so am I. My leave-of-absence was granted to me by Lieutenant-Colonel Macleod on the advice of the Regimental Surgeon. Its time is not yet expired. Any previous termination should come from the same source, should it not? I suggest, sir, that you transmit your orders through the approved channels!"

"Damme, this is insubordination as well as insolence! Do you wish to force me to clap you in irons, fool?"

"That, I think, would demand more, shall we say, agility, than I think you possess, sir! I do not think that you will insist upon it!"

"You . . . you would resist?"

"I do not intend to be here to resist. I shall merely take myself off."

"And I with him," Marsala added.

"What do you mean to do?" That sounded distinctly less confident and authoritative.

"Say that I have things to attend to. Urgent matters to clear up, before I could possibly return to the regiment."

"But you *will* return?"

"Have you not ordained it, sir?"

The other frowned. "See here, Alastair," he said, in a different tone, "the honour of the regiment is at stake. It means much to both of us, I think, whatever our differences. Many men have died for that honour, friends and comrades-in-arms of your own. You would not wish it smirched?"

"I have not smirched it yet, sir, nor intend to."

"That is a matter of some doubt."

"You did not think that in London!"

"It is what you have done since London that endangers its honour." The other shrugged. "But leaving that aside, our endeavour now should be to ensure than there is no further ill done to it. That demands that you return to it, to the Peninsula, forthwith, quietly and without disorder. Of your own accord. And promptly. If you do so, Alastair, I think that I may promise you that my attitude towards you, my right and proper indignation, may be, h'r'mm, somewhat modified. Quite considerably modified. You understand?"

The two men gazed at each other. Then the younger nodded. "I understand," he said shortly. "And I bid you goodnight."

"Yes. And you, Marsala, if you have any influence with this young man, see that he does as I say. For his sake, for everyone's sake. Do you hear?"

"I hear," she answered expressionlessly, and turned to the door that Alastair held open for her.

Chapter Seventeen

As they pushed the plunging boat away from the rope-ladder and the towering sides of the *Dolphin*, Alastair's pent-up eloquence and emotion overflowed.

"Curse the man for as big a scoundrel, as sheer a rascal, as

I have ever known!" he exclaimed. "Curse him and all his works! A miserable trickster! A wretched two-faced Shylock! He is worse than Rory Mor, by far. The high-born chief of Clan Ruari! *Dia*, he makes me spew!"

"He is an evil man, yes," the girl panted. They were struggling with their oars to bring the boat's prow round towards the shore. Already the wind and the now strongly flowing tide had drawn them quite a distance away from the ship. The waves were noticeably larger than when they had come out, and the pulling correspondingly more difficult. Marsala's oar waved erratically, amidst much splashing.

"He is a dastard! Selling his own people! Selling anybody and anything . . ." Alastair dug in his oar savagely.

"What . . . will we do . . . now?"

"Lord knows! Nothing that we can do or say will affect him, that is clear. He is out of reach of us, safe in his power and position. And utterly determined."

"Yes. But he is afraid of something, too. He is not so sure of himself as all that, Alastair. At the end, there, you could feel it. He did not want to have you arrested. I am sure of that. He does not want trouble with you. Why, who knows? Unless he really *is* concerned with the honour of his precious regiment?"

"Honour!" The man snorted, and heaved viciously on his oar. It was just unfortunate that this indignant thrust coincided with and magnified a heave of the boat to the same side, as a wave struck them. In consequence the young woman's side lifted high, her oar missed the water altogether, slewed abruptly forward, and, as the little craft rocked, jerked right out of her grasp. Though she grabbed desperately after the shaft, it was too late. The oar was swept over the side and away.

It was a moment or two before Alastair perceived what had happened, and another two or three before the full gravity of the situation struck them.

They stared at each other, appalled. There was no spare oar in the boat. A single oar was of no use for propulsion in a coble-style craft; any kind of sculling was impossible. They were at the mercy of wind and tide.

Marsala began to gasp her remorse and self-reproach, but

the man cut her short. It was his fault as much as hers—more so. He should have kept his wits about him, his mind on what they were doing. In his anger against Clanrory, he had been careless, thoughtless . . .

The foaming crest of a comber spilling inboard put an end to this mutual and unprofitable self-recrimination. They were drifting round, beam-on to the seas, and wallowing unpleasantly. Lifting their remaining oar out of the wooden pins that formed its rowlock, Alastair lurched to the stern, there to thrust the oar into the water, as a sort of rudder, all but falling in the process. He sat down heavily, grunting at the hurt to his shoulder, but clinging on to the oar, difficult as it was to hold it in place on the smooth timbering.

The oar used thus did check their swing, and to some extent even brought them back stern-on to the tide. The fact that it did so, bore eloquent testimony to the strength of the current and the wind. But this last was gusty, and not entirely consistent in direction, tending to slew them this way and that. They had not really got steerage-way.

As they rolled and yawed and plunged, Alastair had the girl come and sit beside him in the stern-sheets. so that the jerking oar-shaft should be wedged between their bodies, thus preventing it from slipping and slithering.

"This . . . this will not bring us back to the shore," Marsala said. That was a statement rather than a question.

"No. But it could save us from being swamped."

"The rocks," she mentioned. "The skerries, at the Point of Ardglass."

"Yes, I know. That ship was lying closer in than the horns of the bay. We may be drifting right towards Ardglass— almost bound to be. Only, this tide-race, this current—it will tend to swing round the peninsula. It has to. It may just take us with it."

"The skerries and reefs stretch out quite a distance beyond the Point. Half a mile, perhaps."

He shrugged. "We must just hope . . ." Frowning, he groped on the floor boards. "Look—this boat-hook. If we could hoist my plaid up on that, as a kind of sail? With this wind, it might just give us enough thrust to steer by."

Leaving the oar to his companion meantime, Alastair strove

to rig up something like a sail. It was not a very successful attempt, for the problem of keeping the boat-hook upright all but defeated him. He tied it, at length, to the front thwart with the anchor-rope, very much aslant, hooking the edge of his plaid to the tip of it, and pinning the outstretched folds of the tartan to either gunwale with dirk and *sgian dubh*. The result looked more like a collapsing tent than a sail, but undoubtedly it did serve to catch the wind, and made steering easier and slightly more effective. It was all that they could do.

Back in the stern-sheets they sat, waiting. They had no means of knowing how fast they were moving; so much depended upon the speed of the current. But they could hear the roar of breaking water ahead through the wind, which must mean that they were already approaching Ardglass. It was not a pleasant sound. They thought that they could discern a paleness on their starboard bow also, which would represent white water, either breakers on the shore of the peninsula, or else on skerries. How far out they were they could not tell, either, though now Alastair was deliberately seeking to steer seawards, deciding that the current would be taking them out of the bay anyway, and that at all costs they must avoid being smashed up on the reefs reaching out from Ardglass.

At least they were not shipping water now, their devices being effective enough to keep the craft stern-on to the seas.

Presently, peering shorewards, Marsala pointed. "Is that not a light? Two lights?" she asked. "Red. Like fires. And, look—there is another. To the left."

"Yes. I believe you are right. Fires. Three of them. That can only be Ardglass. Cooking fires. There is white water in between, too. That means . . . that means that we are away to the west of the Point already, that we are being carried well to seaward of it. The current, it must be, strong and taking a wide sweep out of the bay. Taking us far further out than I thought, thank the Lord! That is a relief."

"Is it?" The girl sounded less sure. "Where is it taking us? We may be swept out to sea!"

"Better that than smashed up on skerries or a rocky coast," Alastair pointed out. "Anyway, Skye lies between us and the main ocean."

"Skye has a savage coast, too. Could we not be smashed up as surely on that as on our own?"

"That will not happen, I think. Not on Skye, anyway. We are being swept north, see you, not west. The incoming tide drives up the Sound of Sleat from the south-west, in a race. Then on through the narrows of the Kyle, and up here, through the Inner Sound. It will take us with it, I think, straight up—especially with this wind behind us. At least until the tide turns."

"When will that be? And where?"

"Full tide will not be for three hours yet, at least, I would say. How far it will have taken us by then, I do not know. It depends, I suppose, on how fast the tide runs. As well as on the strength of the wind."

"But it will be a long way, whatever?"

"Well . . . yes. A dozen miles, perhaps. Or even more. Though, as the Inner Sound broadens out, the tide will run less fiercely. It soon grows very wide, you know—fifteen miles, perhaps, from Applecross over to Skye. Though there is the Isle of Raasay between . . ."

"Yes. The Isle of Raasay. And others! All with their rocks and skerries and reefs. In between!" Her voice was tense. "And . . . what will happen when the tide turns?"

"There will be almost an hour of slack water. Then will be our chance, perhaps." Hastily Alastair changed the subject. "But never fear, lass; we will manage. Fine we will manage. Better the tide and the wind to deal with, than men like Clanrory and Rory Mor!"

She did not answer that. But Marsala could change a subject also. "You hurt your shoulder, when you stumbled that time?" she put to him. "With the oar. Is it bad? Painful?"

"No. It was nothing. A mere jerk."

"But you are huddled, as though in pain?"

"No, no. Nothing of the sort. It is just a little chilly, perhaps. Without my plaid . . ."

"At least there is no need for that," she said. "No need for you to be cold." She loosed the plaid that was about her own shoulders and, moving closer, wrapped it around him also, drawing it tight.

"My thanks," he said simply, seemed as though he would

say more, then changed his mind, and slipped the arm that held the oar within her own.

For a long time they sat thus, wordless, close, swaying together to the heave of the boat, warming each other, arms linked over the oar. Past them the combers hissed in unnumbered succession, with snarling crests and veined with white, and sometimes the sobbing wind sent spindrift across their faces, like a chill warning, so that presently the girl drew the plaiding higher, to cover their heads also, and they were closer still. But still they did not speak. Not with their lips, at any rate.

It was the skerry that did it, an isolated reef that seemed to rise before them out of the waves without warning. One moment the sea was empty, the next this crouching, foaming thing was lifting directly in their path, a low table of weed-hung rock off which the water streamed in boiling, frothing cascades. Desperately Alastair dragged the oar behind them to port, digging it deep. It seemed to make no impression. Forcing it over with all his strength, the man leaned far out from their cockleshell's stern, over the black water. But the ledge of stone seemed positively to extend itself before them, as though utterly to bar their way, roaring its venom.

They were only three or four yards from the rock when the surging back-wash of a sea struck them, flinging their bows round violently, so that they wallowed broadside on to the menace. Alastair cursed, as the new danger of being rolled right over was added to that of striking.

Marsala cried out as still another threat bore down on them from behind: a wave higher than the others, spilling over its crest as though in drooling anticipation as it came. Furiously the man wrenched the oar the other way, to strive to meet this at least stern-on. But there was no time. The monster took them beam-on, poured some of its chill, foaming frienze inboard, lifted them higher and higher, canting them over so that their port gunwale was all but submerged, and then flung them forward, carrying them irresistibly on its rearing head.

They felt a long grinding below them as their flat bottom scraped across weed-grown stone, and the oar kicked viciously between them. But that was all. Crazily they surged onwards. It came to some detached portion of Alastair's mind that he had been too soon in cursing both that backwash and the larger wave; the one had fended them off the skerry those seconds long enough for the other to catch them up and hurl them over the top of it, just as another such great wave had hidden it from them in the first place.

Plunging on, the man was endeavouring frantically to gain some sort of control of the craft again, when another rock loomed up before them, no table or ledge this time but a jagged tooth thrusting high, black but white-rimmed. Again Alastair hurled his weight on the oar, all but sobbing at the inadequacy of anything that they could do. This fang should have been simpler to avoid than the flat and more extensive table behind them, but their wave seemed as though it was actually aiming them at the stack's spouting base. All that could be done was to dig in that almost useless oar—and pray.

Which of these activities actually saved them was not to be known, for the man found his efforts at both more than a little distracted by the fact that Marsala was clinging to him tightly, convulsively, head buried against his chest. But whatever the cause, they swept past that soaring pinnacle with only inches to spare, indeed their port side rasped against an out-thrusting shoulder, spinning them round alarmingly. Then they were past, and though Alastair stared ahead over Marsala's dark hair, he could see no further signs of reefs or white water. For the moment, it seemed, they were safe.

He told his companion so. He found that she was shuddering violently within his arms, drawing great gulping sobs. He stroked her damp hair.

"Hush you, hush you," he soothed. "It is all right now, lassie. All past. See, my dear, we are past them. None ahead. Och now, it is all right."

Slowly, almost reluctantly, she raised her head, to peer, not in front of them, but at his face, unspeaking.

He nodded reassurance. "It is over—for the moment, anyway. There was just the two of them."

She turned her head. "There will be others," she said.

"Not necessarily. I think that we are in deep water again, now."

"And the boat? It is all right? We struck that rock . . ."

"Only scraped over it. These flat-bottomed cobles are good. And stout."

"Yes. Yes, of course. Alastair, I am sorry! Sorry to be like this, to have failed you . . ."

"Now, now, here is nonsense."

"It is true. I am sorry."

"See you, this water in the boat. We must bale it out. There is an old pot, I saw, under this seat. I do not think that it is the bottom leaking, only what came in from that big wave. But we must get it out before we can be sure."

"Yes."

Holding on to the oar, Alastair deliberately let the young woman do most of the baling, to keep her occupied. When she had most of the water out, it seemed fairly clear that if more was leaking in, it was doing so only very slowly, Marsala came back and sat beside him again. It was the man's turn to wrap the plaid, somewhat damp now, around them both. She felt cold, but her shuddering had stopped. He slipped his arm through hers, and began to talk.

He spoke of many things, but nothing of their plight in drifting helplessly through the windy dark up the Inner Sound of the Hebridean Sea, nothing of the collapse of their hopes for the evicted, nor of what the future might hold; nothing indeed tasting of the bitterness of failure and defeat. He was, in fact, far away on the dusty sun-scorched plains of India, when, without warning or apology, the girl interrupted him.

"Alastair," she said, urgently, "you must understand. I hate to be like this, to be a burden to you. No—wait! I think that I have not been so, up till now. But this . . . this is different, you see. Always I have had a great fear, a great horror of drowning. I do not know why. I dream of it, at nights. It is foolish, I know, but the thought of it unnerves me quite. I am sorry . . ."

"My dear, say no more of it. Though I am sorry too . . ."

"But I must speak. For nothing that you can say, Alastair, can alter the fact that we are in grave danger of drowning. This sea is full of islands and reefs and skerries. At any moment we may be upon one. It would be foolish to pretend that it is not so. And we may not always be so fortunate. You must see that. And so, Alastair, I would have you make me a promise, if you will? Because of . . . because of my weakness in this thing. Promise me that if we do come to that, come to . . . to drowning, that you will keep hold of me! Tight hold of me, Alastair, whatever happens. So that I . . . I am not alone. Will you do that, please?"

"But Marsala, Marsala *a graidh*, you must not talk like that, you must not distress yourself . . ."

"No, but tell me. Will you do it? It is very important to me, Alastair."

"Of course I will do it, lass. I promise it. But I do not think . . ."

"Thank you, thank you," she whispered. "And thank God, too! I shall be better now, I promise *you*. I know that I am foolish, but I think that I can face it now. And we . . . we can at least die as husband and wife—even if we cannot live that way!"

Alastair caught his breath. He turned, to peer into her eyes. "Marsala!" he exclaimed. "Marsala, what are you saying? Do you know what you said? Do you mean . . .? Can it be that you *want* to be married to me? Properly? To be my wife, in truth . . .?"

"Of course," she said simply. "I have wanted only that, I think, since the first day that I saw you!"

"Dear God!" he cried. "And I . . . I have been thinking . . . I have been holding myself back. Feeling that perhaps I had done you a great wrong, a hurt. Had forced you into a false position . . ."

"Hurt, yes! Always you kept saying that ours was no proper marriage. That it meant nothing—nothing at all. A mere formality. That I would be a free woman—and therefore you a free man—in a year. Just a device, this handfasting, to still people's tongues. How often you have said it! And every time a stab at my heart!"

"But, Lord, did I not owe that to you, at least? Me, years older than you. With nothing to offer you—save a disgraced name. And you scarcely knowing me . . ."

"Seven years older—what is that? And I know you as well as you know me, if not better! You are very foolish, Alastair."

"Am I? Yes, it may be so. But so are you, I think. Why did you not tell me, Marsala?"

"Tell you! If you had eyes to see, and ears to hear, you should have known. Surely you would . . ."

She got no further. Black Alastair MacRory's senses and

faculties may have failed him previously, but now, circumstances notwithstanding, they came into full play—and the more vigorously for the delay, perhaps. The girl offered a muffled and purely symbolical protest, ostensibly for the care of a wounded shoulder, and then wisely submitted. Coherent words were dispensed with, save only for one fervent prayer.

"This oar be damned!" the man said hotly.

The sobbing wind, the racing tide, the snarling combers and all the foaming skerries of the Hebrides were as if they had never been. Even the fear of drowning. A more potent force even than these had come into its own.

Chapter Eighteen

TIME was not a calculable commodity for Alastair and Marsala that night, but sometime in the early hours of the morning they did become aware that the sea was more calm. The waves had eased off quite suddenly, and the wind seemed to have dropped. They were uncertain as to just when the tide was due to turn, and at first assumed that this was what had happened and that they were in the slack water period before the ebb. But the apparent dropping of the wind, allied to the fact that they still seemed to be moving forward as steadily as ever, induced second thoughts. In these narrow waters, more than the change of tide and wind can affect sailing conditions greatly. They might well have come into the lee of an island, one large and high enough to act as breakwater and to deflect the wind away above them.

Even with only half their minds on the matter, what to do now was something of a problem. Once the tide did turn, slack water would not last long, they knew, and the ebb tide could flow just as strongly as the flood, carrying them away in the opposite direction. Overfalls, indeed, could be worse on the ebb, and the wind against the tide could produce all sorts of dangers for a small craft not in proper control. If there was a fair-sized island close at hand, it might be better to make for it, while the tide was still taking them onwards and giving them steerage, than to risk the reverse; though approaching rocky islands in the darkness was a fool's game. Whether indeed they could manœuvre their boat towards it remained to be seen, since, if island there was, it lay to windward, which meant trying to work their coble half into the wind.

Alastair rearranged their poor impromptu sail, and sought to steer with the oar as close to windward as he might.

It was not long before they heard the sustained roar of breaking waters, a disagreeable sound, even though it proclaimed the presence of land. Any significant wind now was only reaching them in gusts, probably indicating a line of hills with gaps between. Either they had drifted right over to the Skye shore, or else they were close in to a sizable island.

Almost at the same moment, peering, they were able to distinguish the jet black silhouette of land, fairly high against the dark night sky, and also the long line of white that represented breakers, seemingly unbroken, stretching away to north and south. How far off this might be, had to be only a guess—perhaps half a mile. It seemed an ominous mark to steer for.

The approach to land had to be very gradual, half into the wind. The thought that the tide might slacken off at any moment was never far from their minds.

For a considerable time it seemed as though they were getting no closer. Then, quite suddenly, it became evident that this was not so, that they were indeed quite near to the shore. And at the same time the man came to a conclusion that had been growing on him.

"That line of breakers," he said. "It is not rocks. It is a sandy beach, or perhaps shingle or pebbles. A long beach. The line has remained unbroken, regular, all the time. It would never be that with rocks or cliffs. It is a long, smooth, shelving beach."

"We can go in there, then? Safely?"

"Yes. Even in this surf our flat bottom will take us in."

The tide, however near it may have been to full, carried them in. Soon they were heaving and tossing wildly in the combers and surf, but their broad-beamed, sturdy coble took that in its stride. Alastair touched sand with his oar.

After that it was only brief minutes until the man could take the painter, step over the side into the swirling shallows, lift the girl up in his arms, and stride ashore, drawing the boat behind them.

Thankfully they dragged the coble well above the tideline, on a strand of glimmering white, cockle-shell sand. Then hand in hand they moved up the beach into soft, dry sand between rocks, and sank down there, exhaustion suddenly flooding over them.

For long they were content to lie thus, hands still joined, unspeaking, listening to the surge of the waves. Then Marsala uttered a long sigh.

"Where are we?" she asked. "How shall we get away from here? What can we do? What is there left for us? What is to happen to our poor people? What hope is left, for any of us?" She spoke slowly, calmly, almost impersonally.

"Many questions," Alastair said. "Large questions. We will answer them in the morning, if we can."

"Will we, Alastair? Will we ever answer them? Are we not lost? Ourselves and our people and all we have fought for? Everything?" Still there was no despair in that, only a kind of level acceptance.

"Lost? Lost is an ill word, *mo charaidh*, a poor wretched word that is beat before it starts. And how can we be lost when we have just found each other? We cannot be lost, this night of all nights!"

She turned to him. "Oh, Alastair, my dear!" she said, arms wide.

*   *   *

The sun in its morning splendour wakened them, high enough to be topping the tall mountains of Applecross eastwards beyond the Inner Sound. There was even the hint of warmth in it, enough to give promise of one of those golden late autumn days stolen from the greedy clutch of winter.

They stared about them, wondering, bewildered, at a scene of quiet and placid loveliness. The sea, blue already reflecting the pale wash of the sky, tinted with green and purple in the shallows where weed and rock and sand showed through, broke in smooth, lazy rollers on a mile-long strand of dazzling white, whereon the oyster-catchers ran piping and the eiders sunned and preened. Around them the land rose in gentle grassy braes, rolling and open, scored with watercourses that gleamed in the sunlight, and patched with thickets of hazel and birch and rowan. Out of these pleasant braes lifted a steeper, stone-ribbed spine of small hills, golden with turning bracken, and culminating, at its northern extremity, in a great thrusting snout of rock rising to a lofty flat platform fully five hundred feet above the sea. Obviously they were on an island, long and seemingly narrow, and never the coast of Skye.

Alastair pointed to that soaring snout of granite. "Askeray!" he declared. "With that stack there, it cannot be anywhere else. To think that we have come as far north as that! We must have drifted for over twenty miles."

"Askeray," Marsala repeated. "I have never been here."

"Nor have I, my own self, though I have sailed past it. Always past it. I remember asking my father to land, but he would not."

"No. It was here that the massacre was? The Mackinnons?"

"Yes. That was why he would not land, I suppose, why nobody ever lands on Askeray."

"Yet it is a lovely place. A gentle-seeming, kindly island. I cannot think that it is evil, haunted, Alastair?"

The man snorted. "Evil is in man, not in places. I have seen enough fair places drenched in blood. Half the earth would be haunted, evil, if man's savagery could make it so. There is nothing wrong with Askeray—only the unquiet memory of guilt in our people."

There was indeed nothing wrong with Askeray, that could be seen. As the man and woman walked about it, that sunny morning, and, seeking by action to counteract the pangs of hunger, eventually climbed high up one of the hills of the central spine, they saw and exclaimed and acknowledged it. Just to the south of Raasay it lay, an isle five miles long, perhaps, by two broad, all grassy green with sandy machairs and level links, sheltered by its hills, well watered, and with the high barrier of Skye to protect it from the Atlantic storms.

All this was clear to be seen, but there was something else

that actually preoccupied the visitors more consistently. Everywhere that they looked about the island were the stocky walls of houses, their turf roofs fallen in and overgrown. Everywhere, too, were crumbling lines of dykes, heaps of cleared stones, and the long green scores of former drainage ditches. Wherever they looked were the works of man, and neither man nor beast to be seen in all the length of it.

"Aye," Alastair said heavily. "There, perhaps, is one of the sins that the MacRories are paying for now! Who knows? Even if Angus Crubach never mentioned it!"

"It was a terrible shameful thing."

Just over one hundred years before, the *Mac Ruaraidh Mor* of the day had laid violent hands on this fair and populous place. Claiming some sort of overlordship over the Mac-kinnons thereof, that was not accepted or admitted, he had descended upon Askeray in force, and in a fit of fury had driven every man, woman and child on the island into a cave, piled up brushwood against the mouth of it, and set it on fire. None had escaped flames or smoke. Over three hundred Mackinnons were said to have died then. It was not a unique happening, perhaps, in the long, bloody history of the clan feuds, though one of the last of such. Though protests there had been thereafter, declamations in faraway Edinburgh, and threats of retribution from Raasay MacLeods and Skye MacDonalds, none had ever been strong enough to try to wrest Askeray from the MacRories. But never again, for all that, had the island been a habitation of men. It was shunned by all. Not even beasts were sent to summer pasture here.

"I had no idea that it was so fertile," Alastair said. "I have counted seventy crofts and holdings, already . . ."

"Alastair," the girl interrupted. "This will be Clanrory's land now? He will claim it, along with the rest?"

"As much his, I suppose, as Strathdonan is his. No more. But, in the eyes of the Lowland law, yes." He turned to her as he perceived what lay behind her question. "*Dia*, you mean . . .?"

"I mean that if this island could support three hundred people before, it could so do again. If Clanrory would give it to us."

"Lord, if he would . . .!"

"Why should he not? If we paid him rent for it? He is doing nothing with it now."

"Aye. I should think that he scarcely knows that it exists. With all the rest of what he calls his estates, this detached and faraway island may hardly be worth his notice. But . . . hating us as he will, now, he will never give us it. Even for the money. He would have us away, far further away than this, I swear. Not still on his doorstep."

"But is there nothing that we could do? Nothing that would change his mind? No pressure that we might bring, Alastair? Nothing to do with the regiment, perhaps? It could be his weakness, as well as his strength."

"M'mmm," the man said, biting his lip.

"Think of it—if we could come here, instead of going to Canada! Bringing life back to this good island, instead of going into exile thousands of miles away."

"I know, I know! But even if we could prevail on Clanrory, how many people would come? To Askeray? To this place of ill fame?"

"Not all of them, no. Many would not. But then, they could not all come here anyway. There will be room only for three or four hundred, I suppose? Even if only our own folk would come, or most of them, from Udalain and Eidart. How much better, how much happier, still in our own land . . ."

"You do not have to convince me, my dear. Nothing would please me more, at all. But there is so much in the way . . ."

"Much, yes. But think you how much we have overcome already. How much that has been in the way."

"Stout heart! But Clanrory is a hard nut to crack. He is armoured against almost everything that we could do. The regiment might be his weakness, yes. But how to exploit it, so far away? I had thought of threatening him with going to the regiment and urging it to mutiny, telling them what is being done to their folk at home. But that would only result in bloodshed, for the Army puts down mutiny ruthlessly, as I have seen. And before that, I would probably be arrested and shot. The only thing that I have thought of that might just possibly be used against him, is the medal. My medal from the King . . ."

"You actually have a medal? You did win a medal, then? From the King? I did not know, Alastair . . ."

"It was not my own self that won it, but the company. They died to win it, scores of them. I was only the man that the King handed it to. I have it here." He reached into his sporran, groped therein, and then handed the shining trinket to the young woman. "If I was to be giving that *back* to the King now, throwing it back at him in front of all his popinjays, in the name of the regiment . . .! That possibly might hurt Clanrory. Hurt his reputation. Bring his pride down."

"But . . . would you do that, Alastair? *Could* you do such a thing?"

"I would do more than that to win this battle. If I was able. And if it would serve, if it would make Clanrory come to terms. The threat of it."

"Surely he could not let that happen," the girl agreed. "He could not let you do it. He would be the talk of London."

"That is what I would hope. I must think more of this, Marsala . . ."

A major part of Askeray surveyed, they returned to their strand and the boat, with the problem of getting off the island now to the fore in their minds. There was wood in plenty which, with Alastair's dirk, could be cut to make a mast and improvised booms, to turn the plaiding into a more effective sail. But what was really required was another oar, and that was a much less simple proposition. The shaft might not be difficult, but how to fashion and attach the blade constituted a major problem.

It was some time later, while the man was working away at the rowan poles, with less success than he would have wished, that Marsala spied the fishing-boats. There were two of them, heading northwards up the Sound, under dark sails, perhaps half a mile out.

Alastair shouted; they both shouted. They waved the plaids back and forth above their heads. They ran up on to higher ground, and waved and shouted again. But to no effect. The boats maintained their steady course, and soon disappeared around the high headland to the north.

"They did not see us, or hear us," Marsala cried. "Or if they did, perhaps they thought that we were ghosts! Mackinnons! What can we do? You will never make an oar with these things, Alastair—not one that will serve."

"If we had had a fire lit. Smoke. They would have seen that. We had better make one now. Keep it burning. In case we get another chance. There is plenty of dry wood."

"Should we not just try the boat? Our own boat. Try to launch out without the second oar? With the better sail? We might manage it . . ."

"Not until the ebb tide, at any rate. It has turned again now. It will not change until mid-afternoon. An incoming tide would only sweep us off further into the north. We must just wait, and I have not given up hope for my oar."

They lit their fire, and piled a heap of dry seaweed near by, to make smoke. No more craft appeared in the offing, however. Alastair completed, after much frustration, something which only major optimism could describe as an oar, and the efficiency of which was of exceeding doubt, even to its creator.

Thereafter they could only wait for the tide to turn. By now they were both ravenously hungry, but despite the apparent fertility of Askeray there seemed to be nothing thereon that they might use for food. They both tried wading in the shallows for flounders, but were quick enough only to catch one smallish specimen, which Alastair stabbed with his dirk, and which they roasted over their fire and devoured in two relishful mouthfuls. Perhaps neither of them realised it, but they laughed a great deal in this entire process, despite the hunger, and indeed found much else to smile over throughout. Askeray, far from wearing any aspect of gloom and foreboding, was that sort of island. The weight of care that the two young people had borne for so long slipped unnoticed from their shoulders, temporarily at least.

They were, in fact, almost reluctantly assessing the tide as suitably turned in their favour for a southward passage, when, round the headland from the north, appeared two fishing-boats—almost certainly the same pair as in the morning. Piling weed on to their fire, the castaways soon produced adequate clouds of dark smoke, which were not long in attracting the attention of the fishermen. The waving of plaids, and shouting, had the desired effect. Both craft turned their prows shorewards. The improvised oar looked as though it would not have to be put to the test, after all.

The newcomers proved to be Mathesons from Lochalsh, and full of sympathy for the plight of anyone unfortunate enough to be marooned on such a place of ill-repute as Askeray. Indeed, good Catholics, they crossed themselves in shocked alarm when they heard that the pair had actually undergone the terrors of some hours of darkness on the unhallowed isle. They were only too glad to give the couple passage down to Strathdonan, towing the coble behind one of their craft. They even provided oatcakes and honey to stay the pangs of hunger, washed down with whisky. More could not have been asked for.

It was well after dark before the fishermen were able to drop their passengers and the coble just off Ardglass, which best suited them. Rewarding the crews as suitably as they might, rescued took grateful leave of rescuers, and pulled quietly towards the shore, Alastair's oar proving less than an entire success.

"Now what?" Marsala wondered, as the fishing-boats disappeared into the gloom. "The garrons? Will they have wandered far, do you think, or have been captured? To get back to the cave."

"We shall leave the cave yet awhile, I think. And the garrons, too. They will wait. Clanrory it is that we must see, and the sooner the better. The question is: will he be on the ship still, or ashore?"

"He will surely not stay on the ship all the time? He said that he had my mother removed to the Chamberlain's house— I was to go there. It is the best house in Strathdonan. Likely he will be there."

"I do not think so. He seemed very comfortable there in the captain's stateroom. I do not think that he would be so much at ease in the Chamberlain's house, when you consider what he plans to do to the Chamberlain's son! My guess is that he will sleep on board, at any rate. We should try there first, I think."

Rowing laboriously and with much splashing, they waddled round the Point of Ardglass and into the bay beyond, the lights of the *Dolphin* drawing them on.

They reached the vessel without attracting any evident

attention and found two sets of rope-ladders hanging over the side. The climb aboard was easy and, without announcing their presence, they made their way aft to the Viscount's state-room. Considerable noise and merriment was emanating from the crew's quarters forward, possibly in tribute to Highland malted liquor.

At the cabin door, Alastair paused, frowning. The murmur of voices came from within. There could be no hanging back now, however. Knocking briefly, he opened the door and strode inside, Marsala following.

The Sheriff sat there, at wine with Lord Clanrory. No pleasure registered on either of the older men's faces as they stared at the newcomers.

Chapter Nineteen

"WHAT is the meaning of this . . . this intrusion?" Clanrory demanded. "How dare you come thrusting your way in here, Gleneidart? What are you doing here at all, man? I had hoped that you were on your way back to your regiment, obeying my orders . . ."

"I think, sir, that you should be glad that I am not!" Alastair intervened but not aggressively. He was determined, if at all possible, to hold his temper and to watch his words throughout this interview that could mean so much—however difficult that might be for such as himself.

"Call the captain, my lord!" the Sheriff cried, in his squeaking voice. "Have this man arrested at once. The woman, too. He is a common felon, a thief, an incendiarist! They have delivered themselves into our hands . . ."

"Hush, you!" Alastair said shortly. "We are here to speak with Clanrory. Privately."

"Sheriff Walker is my guest, and will remain so," the Viscount said.

"Nevertheless, sir, I believe that you would prefer to hear what I have to say privately."

"I do not wish to hear anything that you may have to say, young man. I have heard more than sufficient, I assure you. As the Sheriff suggests, I shall call the captain, and have you put in irons."

"I think that you will not," Alastair declared quietly. "And for better reasons than that I shall not permit it, whatever!"

"You are not threatening me, man!"

"No. I am only taking the liberty of advising you, sir. You may thank me, yet."

"This is insufferable!" the Sheriff burst out, his thin voice breaking. "I must insist that the man is arrested, my lord!"

"Oh, be quiet!" Marsala interjected urgently. "Listen to what he has to say. It is important, so very important! You must pay heed."

"It is, yes. For many people. For the regiment. But most of all for yourself, Clanrory."

"I doubt it . . ."

"Nevertheless, hear it. I will tell you what I intend to do It is unfortunate that the Sheriff must hear it too."

"Go on."

"Very well. I intend, sir, to crave audience of the King, through Sir Charlecote Styles, the Adjutant-General, in the name of my colleagues in the Seventieth Foot. And then I shall hand back to His Majesty the medal which you may recollect he bestowed upon me—hand it back, again in the name of the regiment, in front of all his flunkeys . . ."

"My God, you would not dare!"

"I would dare more than that. I would tell the King and his Ministers that you were shattering the morale of the troops in the Peninsula by your oppressions upon their folk at home. That mutiny was near, and that it would spread like wildfire amongst the other Highland regiments."

"Damn you, do you think that I would allow it? Do you imagine that I would ever let you reach London, fool?"

"You cannot stop me. With all respect, I think that I can travel faster than you, Clanrory. And I have many men, in the hills, to see that I am not molested on the way. You are not imagining that I would allow you to hold me, here?"

"You . . . you would never gain the King's presence."

"Would I not? The hero of Vimeiro! With Sir Charlecote's

help? Sir Charlecote, I believe, does not love your lordship greatly. I think that I would not fail to see His Majesty."

"Then you would be arrested. For sedition. Imprisoned. I would have you charged as a deserter. And shot!"

"Perhaps. But that would be afterwards! After the damage was done. When every finger at Court, in London, was pointing at you. The Highland chief whose regiment disowned him, who was causing disaffection and mutiny in the Army, who was selling his people for gold . . ."

"None would believe your lies."

"Would they not? Heroes do not usually throw back their medals at their King! Nor threaten mutiny . . ."

Clanrory licked his lips. "I cannot believe that you would attempt this, Gleneidart. It is not to be thought of. An officer, a gentleman of mine . . ."

"How can I convince you?"

"Why tell me, then? Why tell me first?"

"To give you the opportunity to save yourself. And to save others, too."

"What do you want? What sordid bargain is this? And you need not ask me to give up my Improvements here, if that is your notion. Nothing on earth will make me do that."

"I did not think it. No, I want Askeray."

"You want what?"

"Askeray. The Isle of Askeray."

"Askeray, Askeray? You mean, dammit, you mean that wretched little island somewhere to the north? Near Raasay, is it not? The one that they say is haunted?"

"Yes."

"But . . . in God's name, why?"

"We want to lease it from you. We will pay a fair rent. We must have security of tenure, of course."

"For yourselves?"

"For ourselves and as many of our people from the cleared glens as will come there with us, instead of to Canada."

"Lord, man—are you crazy? None will go with you to that barren, useless spot, ill-named as it is."

"That is a chance that we will take."

"You will be asking to get away from it in a year! Less."

"Then make the lease a long one. Twenty years. Fifty. And we will hold to it! Give me that, legally drawn up, accept my commission back here and now—and you may have your medal back, to give to whom you will, and be quit of me!"

There was silence in that cabin for long moments.

"Is it agreed, then?" Alastair demanded.

Clanrory met the younger man's eye for an instant, and shrugged. "It is of no moment to me," he said, affectedly casual. "If it will prevent you from making a fool of yourself, and causing affront and injury to His Majesty and disgrace to the regiment, then I am prepared to be infinitely more generous than you deserve. I shall let you have your island—at a suitable rent."

Alastair swallowed his sigh of relief. He allowed the other to put as good a face on it as he could. "Very well. But since you have had no money at all from Askeray hitherto, any rent is increase and profit to you. Consequently *I* claim the right to fix the rent. I will give you £70 a year for Askeray, on a long lease. Is it agreed?"

Clanrory blinked rapidly, probably as much in surprise at the generosity of the figure as at the unorthodox nature of the arrangement. The Sheriff's narrow face was a study.

"I . . . ah . . . h'mmm. Very well," the former managed to enunciate.

"You, Sheriff, being a man of the law, can no doubt make us out a suitable document to embody our bargain, to include a lease," Alastair went on easily, now. "I would suggest that you go to work on it right away, for my promise about the medal and so on will not come into force until I have that paper signed and in my hands. You will not take my caution amiss, Clanrory, I am sure!"

"But . . . but . . .!" the Sheriff spluttered.

"There is another point," the younger man added. "A small one only, sir. We shall require something in the nature of a safe-conduct, from both you gentlemen, so that I may make my arrangements, and put matters suitably and fairly before our people. We cannot do that with sheriffs-officers and Rory Mor's minions for ever on our tails."

"What . . . what confounded impertinence!" the Sheriff cried. "I have issued warrants for your arrest on numerous charges. Do you think that you can treat the law of the land like some base, bargaining counter . . .?"

"I have noticed, Sheriff, that the law of the land can be extremely, er, adaptable, in the right hands. I am sure, likewise, that no hands are more expert than your own!"

"My lord, this is a scandal! I have never been so insulted . . .!"

"Tush, Walker, do not take on so," Clanrory exclaimed irritably. "He is a crude and headstrong fellow. We know that. But let us not lose our judgement over him. First things first. National interests, His Majesty's interests, are involved in this. The letter of the law is not for such occasions."

"But, my lord, the due processes of the law must be carried out. I cannot . . ."

"Fiddlesticks, man! But if you are so squeamish, as His Majesty's Lieutenant of the County and Sheriffdom, *I* will take the responsibility. His Majesty's wider interests demand it. You may consider the charges to be dropped, Gleneidart."

"I commend your judgement, sir. His Majesty is to be congratulated on his Lieutenant! I shall come for the necessary documents in the morning then, and speak to the people thereafter."

"As you please." The other yawned elaborately.

"That is all, I think, then."

"For that I am grateful."

"Save for this," Marsala put in—only her second interjection in the entire exchange, "I would have you know, sir, that Alastair and myself are to be properly married, the handfast having served its turn. I wish to inform my mother of this. I wish her to be free to come to Askeray with us, if she will . . ."

"What of it? What makes you think, young woman, that this is a matter of any interest to me?" Clanrory said coldly. "Or that I should seek to burden myself with your mother or her affairs?"

"Oh!"

"With your amiable cousin's permission, then, we shall retire, my dear," Alastair said tautly.

"With my permission you may go to hell, both of you!" Colonel the Lord Viscount Clanrory told them explicitly.

Nevertheless, as they went out of that cabin, closing the door behind them, they found it opened again, and Clanrory himself beside them. He closed the door at his back.

"One more point to our, er, compact," he said quietly. "Rory Mor and his sheep!"

Sharply Alastair eyed him in the gloom. "Those sheep are a matter between Rory Mor and myself," he said.

"The sheep I will concede," the other shrugged. "Do as you will with them. But Rory is a different matter. He is my agent and representative. Where he is concerned, I insist on your, h'm, compliance."

"Insist, sir?" That was softly said.

"Yes. You will keep Rory Mor, wherever you have him incarcerated, until you hear from me to the contrary, until this ship is loaded and ready to sail. Is that understood?"

Alastair's swallow was loud enough almost to prevent him from hearing Marsala's gasp.

"You will see to it, then?"

"Why, yes. If you . . . yes, indeed."

"Very good," Clanrory said. "Your papers will be ready for you before noon tomorrow. Bring the medal with you."

"Not here. To Ardglass."

"As you will. To Ardglass."

Without another word, Clanrory turned and left them, and the stateroom door closed on them again.

"*Mac Ruaraidh Mor*, son of a hundred chiefs!" Alastair murmured.

The girl could find no words.

Chapter Twenty

AT noontide three days later, the new-made jetty just to the south of the headland of Argdlass was a scene of great activity. Most of the people who had laboriously built that jetty out of the plentiful stones with which alone that peninsula was endowed, were out on board the *Dolphin*, now anchored as close inshore as she dared, less than two cables' length away. The sound of the ritual keening of women and the excited cries of children, along with the shouting of the crew and the creak of winches as gear was hoisted aboard and stowed away somewhere on that overcrowded vessel, was loud across the water—but scarcely loud enough to prevail against the sounds from closer at hand. The fleet of small boats, fishing-craft gathered from a wide area around, that had ferried the emigrants and their belongings out to the ship, were now clustered at all points around the jetty, filled with other folk, bawling animals and protesting poultry. Though of lesser numbers than those aboard the *Dolphin*, there was no keening or sobbing from these people. On the uneven stones of the jetty itself it was difficult to move, even yet, for men and livestock and goods and chattels. Near the base of it alone there was space, where Lord Clanrory stood in splendid isolation, one foot tap-tapping irritably. Behind him, at a suitable distance, sealing off the entire embarkation area as it were with a red cordon, were the scarlet-clad ranks of the newly-arrived half-company of the Ross-shire Fencibles, Lowlanders recruited in the east. Along their somewhat yokel-ish files Captain Henderson paced with conscious importance. Of the Sheriff and George Cousins there was no sign.

Alastair and Marsala had been very busy superintending the embarkation of their own people for Askeray. Now they had something of a breathing-space. Alastair glanced over his shoulder inland, as he had done not a few times during the past hour, however busy.

"You are not forgetting, Alastair?" Marsala asked him quietly.

"Do you think that I would, *mo charaidh*?" He smiled. "First things last, on this occasion!"

"Hector is taking a long time."

"Yes. Clanrory is growing impatient. But there is time yet."

Near by, the Reverend Angus straightened up wearily, after helping to push off one of the last boats to the ship, assuring a tearful woman that he would be out with them shortly. Alastair stepped over to tap his bowed shoulder.

"Angus," he said. "You will have a moment or two now, I think. I have a favour to ask of you."

"Yes." The other sighed. "Anything, *a graidh*, with as much

pleasure as is in me this sad day. But the ship will be sailing . . ."

"It will not sail yet awhile. There is an important passenger
still to come."

"But Clanrory said . . .?"

"Clanrory will wait, I promise you. We would like you to
marry us, Angus. Properly."

"Alastair! You mean . . . true marriage? For all time?"

"For all time. The handfast . . . it was a mistake, just."

"I said that it was, Alastair. A poor thing. I am glad that
you have found it out. Even so late in the day."

"Yes. Will you do it for us then, before you sail away to
Canada? The last thing that you do here. Marry us truly, and
give us your blessing?"

"Here? Now?"

"Where better? When better? If you have no church—well,
you have had no church for long enough. At least you have a
congregation. And time. It will not be taking you long, at all."

The older man looked around him, and nodded. "Very
well, Cousin. If it will give you both satisfaction that it is I
that does this thing for you. And if you ask it in the fear of
God?"

"That we do, yes."

And so, there on the open jetty, under the grey November
sky, Alastair and Marsala MacRory knelt while Angus of the
Limp made them man and wife, in the sight of God and of all
men. The ceremony was short and simple, reduced to its
barest essentials, but none the worse for that. People gathered
round—indeed the difficulty was to clear sufficient space for
the principals—men doffed bonnets, all watched from the
boats; from the Fencibles came some jeers and catcalls, and
Lord Clanrory pointedly turned away. Ring there was none,
but of solemnity there was no lack. And when Angus Crubach
blessed them at the end, and all the assembled company without favour or discrimination, he added a final and unlooked-for
benediction.

". . . and of Thy great mercy, Almighty God, bless the Isle
of Askeray to which these Thy servants now travel. Cherish
and befriend it, and if there be any evil or unquiet spirit there,
on account of the past sins of men, banish and expel it. May

Thy peace be upon it, and all who go to dwell and labour there. May it bring forth abundantly and flourish exceedingly, to be a blessed garden of the Lord after these many years. In the Name of the Father and the Son and the Holy Ghost. Amen."

When Alastair rose from his knees, it was first to kiss his bride, and whisper a word to her. Then he grasped the minister's hand.

"Our thanks to you, Angus, our true thanks. That was nobly done. Bless you for it, and for the thought of that last. Many will sleep the more happily for it, in the nights to come."

"That I know, *a graidh*, for I shall, my own self."

Alastair had no answer to that.

The sisters MacIver were embracing Marsala, who curiously had produced a couple of tears. The bride's mother, near by, was weeping copiously. It was, in fact, an extraordinary scene. People were laughing and crying. In the laden boats many of the Askeray settlers were waving and cheering. From out on the *Dolphin* wailing still arose—and would do until the wide Atlantic intervened. The soldiers, not understanding the Gaelic, presumably made neither head nor tail of it all, and joked roughly, hooting their derision, unchecked by their commander. Lord Clanrory paced to and fro, frowning, apparently oblivious to the entire proceedings.

As if all this was not enough, an additional bedlam arose. The line of Fencibles was convulsed from the rear, amidst considerable shouting and to-do. Then, on Henderson's command, a way was opened and a little cavalcade of men on garrons came riding through, down on to the jetty. Young Ian Beg proudly led the way, his captured musket still strapped across his back; then, in a cluster, came the six former hostages who had been destined for Dingwall gaol, and in their midst, but towering above all, Rory Mor; Hector MacBride brought up the rear, wary-eyed, old fowling-piece across his knees.

Rory Mor's wrists were tied and he was still clad only in the improvised kilt and plaiding, belted at the waist. He should have looked ridiculous being led in thus, a huge, gross gorilla of a man, half-naked, red hair and beard tangled, jolting sack-like on too small a horse. But no one laughed, nor so much as smiled—not even the soldiery. The man's head held high, he swept the assembled company, all of it, with a glance of utter scorn.

In silence the party rode forward. They came to Lord Clanrory first. But they did not halt there. Ian Beg, no doubt, did not even know who the lone man might be. As for Rory Mor, he let his pale eyes consider his employer unhurriedly and without expression for a long moment, and then as unhurriedly lifted his glance and looked away as they passed on. Clanrory, who had stepped forward, drew back, flushed and biting his lip. The crowd pressed back, to allow the riders passage.

They pulled up in front of Alastair and Marsala, Iannie with a flourish. Rory Mor actually smiled slightly.

"Well, Stair," he said.

It was to Hector that Alastair spoke, however. "We had thought to see you before this, Hector. Clanrory was growing anxious, I think."

"Well might he, Gleneidart. Our friend here thought to be leaving us. Early this morning. For the north, whatever. I think, maybe, he was not anxious to be catching this ship, at all!"

"I see. I do not blame him overmuch for that." Alastair gestured at Rory. "Untie him, Hector. The need for that is past. He is in his master's hands, now!"

"You are thoughtful, Stair," the big man said sarcastically.

When Rory was unbound and dismounted, he still stood beside his late captors, not turning back towards Clanrory. "My things?" he asked. "My clothes?"

Alastair pointed. "All out there on the ship, awaiting you, I understand."

"So-o-o! He is very sure that I shall sail!"

"He is, yes. See, I think that he is fretting a little. Waiting for you. If you do not wish to emigrate, Rory, perhaps you may convince him otherwise. As I did."

Their eyes met. "But you do not think so, eh?"

"I do not." The dark man shrugged. "But he is your master, not mine."

Clanrory's impatience was evident now, for all to see. He had not a strong voice, to compete with the hubbub of cattle and men, but he beckoned peremptorily.

Rory Mor looked, frowned, hitched his plaids around him, and went slowly, with what dignity he could. The people on the jetty, the watching throng in the boat, the soldiers, might not have existed.

What Clanrory and his factor said to each other, there apart, is not to be known. Many would have wished to have heard it. All that can be said is that they stood there for some considerable time, during which Clanrory seemed to do most of the talking. Indeed, throughout, Rory Mor, despite his garb and the circumstances, appeared as the more self-controlled, assured, serene of the two. Much of the time he did not even look at the other.

At length the younger man bowed stiffly, and turning, came stalking back down the jetty, glancing neither to left nor right. Beside Alastair, however, he paused.

"You were right," he said briefly, grimly. "My congratulations, Stair. You assessed his lordship more accurately than I did, it seems!"

"Perhaps. You are for Canada then, Rory?"

"If I may reach there alive—which I suspect is doubtful!"

"You mean . . .?"

"I mean that there are a great many people on that ship who will rejoice to see me overboard any dark night!"

"Your own people, Rory! Blood of your blood. Your clansfolk."

"You have a pleasing sense of humour, Stair."

"Yet you sail?"

"Clanrory is . . . devilish persuasive! And it is clear that there is nothing left for me here—worse than nothing. So I will take a chance. I have always had a weakness for taking chances, Stair. And if I reach Canada alive, then I think that I may just survive. I shall have our friend's authority there, and some blessed thousands of miles to separate me from his accursed and thrice-damned presence! I may just survive!"

"I hope, then, if you do so, that it will be with more mercy to these others. Some fellow-feeling, since all have felt Clanrory's hand." That was the young woman.

"Dear Marsala! Ever the tender heart, and the headstrong spitting wildcat! How I love you, both of you. You know that, of course—I have never hidden it!" Rory held out his hand.

"One last matter," Alastair said. "Between ourselves. Your sheep, Rory. What shall I do with them?"

"The sheep? Damn the sheep! You should have thought of what to do with them before you took them, Stair! I cannot see them as of much use to me, now."

"I could have them sold, and the money sent to you . . ."

"Nonsense, man. If I cannot do better than that in Canada, I am better overboard! Keep them. Do as you will with them, so long as you do not let Clanrory get his claws on them! A wedding present—there your are! From your loving Rory. What could be fairer? Four hundred sheep, in exchange for your two burned roofs, and George Cousins and Sheriff Walker paying for the half of them! Accept them, with my affection. Goodbye to you both!" The big man laughed, threw the end of his plaiding over his bare red-furred shoulder, and strode off, down to the boat that waited to take him to the *Dolphin*, hundreds of eyes watching with varying expressions.

Nothing became Rory MacRory, factor of Strathdonan, so well as his departure therefrom.

*   *   *

Lord Clanrory had no reason for further patience. All now fell to be disposed of and completed as expeditiously as possible. He had made his chiefly and paternal speech of goodwill and *bon voyage*, briefly, to the assembled company, earlier. He was done with the *Dolphin* now, needless to say, and would return to the South at once, via Dingwall with the Fencibles, leaving his new sheep-run manager, adequately reinforced, as master of Strathdonan. All was in order, at last. He gestured curtly to the *Dolphin*'s mate, standing by the last of the ship's boats.

That man blew his whistle and shouted his orders. Final goodbyes were said, as the last rearguard of the Canada contingent hurried to embark.

The Reverend Angus kissed Marsala and wrung Alastair's hand. "Farewell, then, my friends," he said, huskily. "We have chosen different courses, and must run them with the grace God gives us. We shall not meet again in this life, I think—but in the next, who knows?"

"I wish, Angus, that you were coming with us to Askeray. There is work for you there. And love, too."

"I know it, Alastair, and could wish it myself. But there is more work, more need for me, where these others are going. In this case, I fear, my place is with the ninety and nine."

Even though that was not the exact proportions of the matter, there was truth in the minister's allegory. Of the eight hundred souls cleared from Strathdonan, a bare hundred and fifty had elected to accompany Alastair and Marsala to Askeray, though up to another hundred might come from Glen Eidart itself in the spring, when that valley was scheduled to be cleared.

"May you find peace and happiness where you are going," Marsala said. "To make up for all the sorrow that you have known here."

"If God wills. And you also, my dear. Peace and happiness, yes."

"We have the happiness now," she declared, shining-eyed. "But whether we shall ever have peace, with this Alastair of mine—who knows!"

And so he left them, smiling, and limped down to his boat, the last to leave.

All done, and his own people and their animals and gear filling the fishing-boats—save for the small party with the laden garrons and the driven cattle which Hector was going to lead north by the long, round-about, overland route to Applecross and the shorter sea crossing—Alastair turned and walked back to the man who was responsible for it all.

"Well, *Mac Ruaraidh Mor*," he said, giving him his Gaelic title for the last time. "Are you satisfied? You have your desert, now—all Strathdonan. You are rid of your encumbrance, your people, the clan that called you father and chief—there they go. Are you satisfied?"

"When I have seen the last of you, Gleneidart, yes."

"I wonder? I wonder whether you will ever have seen the last of any of us? Do you dream of a night, Clanrory? What of the dark watches? Will you not see us all, then? Will we not be always with you? My grandfather was namely for having the second sight, you will recollect. Perhaps some glimpse of it has descended to my own self. I see you, Clanrory, I see you

219

lonely always; but never do I see you alone of a night. Always you will have company—around your pillow. Your clan, Clanrory, the clan that you thought to be rid of, those you sent to die on the battlefield, and those you drove to far exile. Always they will be with you—and even the clink of gold and the baa-ing of a hundred thousand sheep will not drown the sound of them!"

The older man licked his lips. "Fool! Fool! Fool!" he cried.

"Maybe. But live you with my folly, then!"

It was Clanrory who turned away hurriedly, to stumble over the uneven stones, back towards the watching soldiery. And as he did so, the thin, high ululation of the bagpipes came shrilling and sobbing across the water from the *Dolphin*. On the crowded deck, there a piper put all the pain and sorrow and heartache of parting into his instrument, distilling in one of the profoundly moving laments of his race the poignant emotions of broken lives, severed friendships, uptorn roots and the looming mystery of the unknown future. And as the sails rose flapping on the ship, and the anchor-chain clanked and rattled inboard, hundreds of voices rose in unison and rhythm with the pipes, proclaiming their long farewell.

"There is it, then—the voice that you will hear for the rest of your days, Clanrory!" Alastair shouted to the other man's back. "Forget it if you can!"

He returned, to board the boat where Marsala and her mother were already embarked.

The two companies sailed from Strathdonan of the Mac-Rories at the same time, the tall ship swinging round southwards to tack into the freshening breeze, the fleet of fishing-boats to scud before it northwards up the Inner Sound of the Hebrides. If eyes held tears in both contingents, those in the small boats dried much the faster, as their owners turned from gazing after the *Dolphin* to face the isle-strewn, mountain-rimmed loveliness ahead. Marsala gripped Alastair's arm.

"Thank you, Alastair," she breathed. "Thank you. In the name of all these folk. For making this possible, at all. It is not victory, perhaps, but it is not defeat either. Something that you have saved from the wreck, something fine and strong and worth while. So well worth the struggle."

"I hope so," he answered. "Though the real struggle is only

beginning, my love. On Askeray. But that is a fight after my own heart. That is the warfare for which I was born, I think, with yourself by my side. I have been beating the air until now."

"Poor Askeray, it does not know what is coming to it!" She smiled. "And your medal, Alastair? You gave it back to him?"

"Yes. He has it now. Much good may it do him."

"The medal so sorely earned! Never mind. You can be a hero without a medal. *My* hero! Fionn and Cuchulain were no finer. I am happy, Alastair, very happy. Is that wrong? Should I be sad? We have won much. We stay in our own land. And it is my wedding-day, after all!"

"And mine!" he said. "Remind me of that, will you—later!" He shook his dark head. "The sadness is past, lass, and the happiness well paid for. Ours it is, for none to question—with the Kirk's blessing, too!"

"Yes," she said. "We shall call our son Angus, I think."